SHAMAN

SHAMAN

Robert Shea

BALLANTINE BOOKS
New York

Library of Congress Catalog Card Number: 90-93215

ISBN: 0-345-36048-6

Text design by Debby Jay
Map by Patrick O'Brien
Cover design by William Geller
Cover painting by Joe Burleson

Manufactured in the United States of America

First Edition: March 1991

10 9 8 7 6 5 4 3 2 1

FOR AL ZUCKERMAN
Friend, Mentor, Agent, Shaman of Letters

Acknowledgments

I'm most grateful for the help given me by Paul Brickman, Julie Garriott, David Hickey, the Illinois Historical Society, Jim and Paula Pettorini, George Weinard, Timothy J. Wheeler, and the Wisconsin Historical Society. And a special word of thanks to my bonnie wife, Yvonne Shea, who, having a sharp eye for a fine old book, brought Thomas Ford's *History of Illinois* into our home.

"Rock River was beautiful country. I loved my towns, my cornfields and the home of my people. I fought for them."
—BLACK HAWK

THE LAND THAT BLACK HAWK LOST

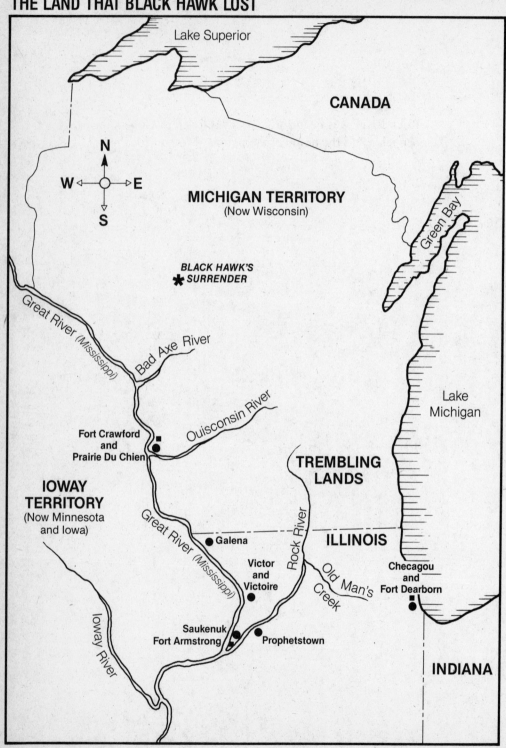

BOOK 1

1825

Moon of Ice

January

1

The Lodge of the Turtle

The black bearskin, softened by countless wearings, clasped Gray Cloud's arms and shoulders, protecting his body from the cold that cut like knives into his cheeks and forehead. The upper half of the bear's skull covered his head and weighed heavily on it, as heavily as the awful fear of the vision quest weighed on his spirit.

His moccasins whispered over the fallen brown grass that covered the trail. He had walked a long way, and his toes were numb in spite of the leaves stuffed into the moccasins.

Abruptly the path stopped, and he was facing sky. He stood at the edge of the bluff looking eastward over the frozen Great River. He gripped the deerhorn handle of his hunting knife.

For the feeling of strength it gave him, he slid the knife out of the sheath of hardened leather tied to his waist. The steel blade glistened, colorless as the sky above him, in the fading light.

The knife my father left for me, he thought. *Where are you tonight, my father?*

The clouds seemed close enough to touch. They rippled like snowdrifts painted with light and shadow. Upriver the sky was darkened almost to black, and Gray Cloud smelled snow in the air.

He saw the silhouette of a hawk, wing-tip feathers spread, circling over the Illinois country across the river, hunting in the last moments before nightfall.

Hawk spirit, help me to live through this testing. Help me to see a great vision and grow to be a mighty shaman.

3

The tiny spot of black dwindled in the sky, till he could no longer see it.

Perhaps it flies over the winter silence of Saukenuk village.

He sheathed the knife. Turning his back on sky and river, he looked westward over the way he had come. A prairie of waving tan grass almost as high as his head stretched as far as he could see. Killed by the cold, the grass yet stood, held up by the stiffness in its dead stalks. Like a fur cloak, the brown covered the hills that rolled away to the west.

He could not see his people's winter hunting camp from here; it nestled back among those hills, sheltered in a forest that grew along the Ioway River. Looking in its direction, he saw Redbird in his mind. Her eyes, black as obsidian arrowheads, shone at him. He felt a powerful yearning just to see her, to speak to her and hear her voice, to touch her cheek with his fingertips. The thought that he might never see her again, never go back to his people, chilled him more than the winter cold.

O Earthmaker, grant that I live to return to Redbird.

He knelt and peered over the edge of the bluff, the bearskin cloak bunching around him. Gray limestone, wrinkled and pitted like the face of an old man, swept down to dark masses of leafless shrubbery at the river's edge. His eyes searched out and then found an especially black shadow in the bluff wall. If he had come any later on this day, he might not have been able to find the cave mouth in the dark.

Then he might have had to wait till morning. Or, trying to climb down to it, he might have missed the way and fallen to his death. A cold hollow swelled in his belly. It would be so easy to slip.

Enough of what might have been. It was what would be that frightened him now. He might die, not of falling, but of what he found in the cave.

Or what found him.

Forcing that thought, too, out of his mind, he lowered his body over the edge of the bluff, dug his toes into footholds and carefully climbed sideways and downward. In places, the path along the bluff face widened out and was almost as easy to walk on as a forest trail. But then the crumbling stone would slant steeply, so that he had to grip hard with his buckskin-shod feet, feeling as if he were clinging to nothing at all.

A wide ledge spread before the entrance to the sacred cave. He let out a breath of deep relief as his feet stepped firmly on the flat stone.

From outside he could see nothing of the cave. But when he entered, he felt a sudden warmth, as if he were walking into a well-sealed lodge with a bright fire going. He could smell old fires—and something else. An animal smell that sent a ripple of cold through his bones. But not a fresh smell. He thanked Earthmaker for that, because he was sure it was the smell of bear.

But Owl Carver had been using this cave for his vision quests for winters beyond counting. And he had never spoken of a bear.

Gray Cloud stood uncertain in the entryway, letting his eyes adjust to the darkness. He saw round, gleaming shapes clustered against the back wall, and a motionless figure about as high as a man's waist, with a sharply curved beak and spreading wings.

Again, seeing these things, he felt the coldness of fear. Now he saw that the round objects on the floor were skulls, and he knew them for the skulls of ancestors, great men and women of the tribe. Green and white stones that had long ago been necklaces glittered around the jaws of the great dead ones. And the winged figure standing over them was the Owl spirit, who guided the footsteps of the dead along the Trail of Souls. Owl Carver had earned his name by carving this statue of the spirit and setting it here.

From a pouch tied to his belt Gray Cloud took a handful of sacred tobacco grains and sprinkled them on the cave floor as an offering.

He said, "Give me leave to enter your cave, Fathers and Mothers. You know me. I am your child."

He hesitated. Only through his mother, Sun Woman, was he the child of these ancestors who guarded the sacred cave. His father was a pale eyes, and the pale eyes had no ancestors. Would the ancestors reject him?

There was no sign or sound from the skulls on the floor, but now he could see farther into the shadows, and he saw that the cave went on around a bend, and that bend was guarded by another sacred figure. He peered at the shadowy figure for a moment and decided that it was a bear, but a bear such as he had never seen before. From head to foot this bear was white. Owl Carver had said nothing about this statue.

He sighed in his dread, feeling a trembling in his stomach.

It was good for him to be here, he tried to tell himself. He had come here to learn the shaman's secrets. This was the moment he had dreamed of ever since the first time he had seen Owl Carver, with his long white hair and his necklace of small shells of the lake-dwelling megis and his owl-crested cedar stick, step into the fire-light. That long-ago night Owl Carver had spoken, not with the voice of a man, but with the voice of a spirit, an eerily high-pitched singsong that frightened and fascinated Gray Cloud.

The shaman of the tribe was greater than the bravest brave, greater than any chief. He had the power to heal the sick and to foretell the future. Gray Cloud wanted to stand high among the Sauk and to go where the shaman went, into the spirit world. He wanted to penetrate the deepest mysteries and know the answer to every question.

After he began teaching Gray Cloud, Owl Carver had tried to discourage him—as a way of testing him, Gray Cloud was sure.

Owl Carver had said, *Many times the people do not want to listen to the shaman. The truer his words, the less they hear him.*

The warning had disturbed Gray Cloud. But he never saw the people refuse to listen to Owl Carver. And he did not lose his determination to become a shaman himself.

No one could gain such a great reward without risk. A warrior must kill an enemy at great peril to himself to gain the right to wear the eagle feather that marked him as a brave. A hunter had to kill an animal that could kill him before the tribe would consider him a man.

How, then, could one speak to these spirits of the tribe unless he, too, had faced death?

But what kind of a death? Would he freeze and starve here in this cave, his dead body remaining until Owl Carver came and found it? Or would an evil spirit come and kill him?

Whatever might come, he could only sit and wait for it in the way that Owl Carver had taught him.

He turned his back on the unknown depths of the cave and seated himself at its entrance, pulling the bearskin cloak around him for warmth. He dipped his fingers into a pouch at his belt and took out the bits of dried mushroom Owl Carver had given him from a medicine bag decorated with a beadwork owl. The sacred mushrooms grew somewhere far to the south and were traded up the Great River. One by one he put them into his mouth and slowly chewed them.

You do not need to swallow, Owl Carver had said. *Hold them in your mouth until they slide down your throat without your knowing how it happened.*

His mouth grew dry as the mushrooms turned to paste. And it was as Owl Carver had said; they were gone without his knowing when they disappeared into his body.

His stomach heaved once and he thought with terror that he might fail this first small test. But he held his breath and slowly the sick feeling died away.

The last light faded from the sky, and the far horizon across the river vanished. Blackness fell upon him like a blanket, thick, impenetrable. It pressed against his face, suffocating him.

The notches in Owl Carver's talking stick, which the shaman had taught Gray Cloud to count, said that tonight the full moon would rise. It would make no difference. Gray Cloud would not see the moon in this sky filled with clouds.

A small spot of cold struck his face, then another and another. His nose and cheeks felt wet.

Snow.

The snow would fall while he sat here, and he would freeze to death.

He must overcome his fear. He must enter the other world. There, Owl Carver had promised him, he would be safe. Without his spirit in his body, he could not be hurt by the cold. But if fear kept him tied to this world, the cold would kill him.

He heard something.

A thumping and scraping behind him in the cave.

Something heavy shuffling around that bend. He felt his heart beating hard and fast in his chest.

There *was* something in the cave. He had smelled it when he first entered. All the magic in the world could not save him now.

He heard breath being drawn through huge nostrils. Long, slow breaths of a creature whose chest took a long time to fill with air. He heard a grunting, low and determined.

The grunting changed to a rumbling growl that made the floor of the cave tremble beneath him.

Gray Cloud's breath came in gasps. He wanted to leap up and run, but Owl Carver had said it was forbidden to move once he seated himself in the cave. Only his spirit was permitted to move.

Perhaps if he did everything exactly as Owl Carver had told him, he would be safe. But Owl Carver had not told him to expect such a thing as this.

He must not look up.

The scratching of those giant claws was right behind him now. He could not breathe at all. There was a bright light all around him, and yet he could not see anything.

He felt—

A heavy hand—no, *paw!*—weighing down on his shoulder and gripping it.

He did not willingly turn his head, but his head turned. He did not mean to lift his gaze, but his eyes looked up.

He saw something like a vast white tree trunk beside his head. It was covered with white fur. Claws gleamed on his shoulder.

He looked up. And up.

Above him, golden eyes blazing, black jaws open and white teeth glistening like spearpoints, towered a Bear.

Gray Cloud was in the presence of a spirit so mighty that his whole body seemed to dissolve in dread. He wanted to shrink into himself, bury his face in his arms. But he had no power over his limbs.

The Bear's paw on his shoulder lifted him, raising him to his feet. Together they walked out of the cave.

What had happened to the clouds and the snow?

The sky was full of stars that swept down to form a bridge ending at his feet. The starlight cast a faint glow over the ice on the river, and he could see the horizon and the opposite shore. Through the dusting of tiny sparkling lights, he saw the ledge outside the mouth of the sacred cave. Two steps forward and he would fall over the edge and be killed.

The White Bear, on all fours beside him now, seemed to be waiting for him. Gray Cloud knew, somehow, what was expected of him. He must put his feet on the bridge of stars and walk out over empty air. He could not do it. Terror clawed at his stomach as he thought of standing high above the river with nothing to support him.

This, too, was a test. The bridge would be safe only if Gray

Cloud trusted it. From now on everything that happened to him would be a test. And if he did not master each one in turn, he would never be a shaman.

And what would he be, then, if he lived? Only a half-breed boy, the son of a woman with no husband, the child of a missing father. The boy they called Gray Cloud because he was neither one color nor the other, neither white nor red.

This trail was the only way for him. He must walk on this bridge, and if he fell and died, it would not matter.

He took the first step. For a terrifying moment his moccasin seemed to sink into the little sparks of light rather than rest upon them. But it was as if the bridge were made of some springy substance, and the sole of his foot did not fall through it. He took another step. Now he had both feet on the bridge. His heart was thundering, the blood roaring through his ears.

How could a bridge be made of nothing but light? How could a man stand on it?

One more step forward. His leg shook so hard he could barely put his foot down. His knees quivered. His body screamed at him to go back.

Another step, and this would be the hardest. Now he could see the abyss below him. He was out over it. He looked down, his whole body quaking. He breathed in quick bursts, and saw little clouds in front of his face in the starlight.

Another step, and another. For balance, his trembling hands went out from his sides. He looked down. The river was solid ice, and the stars reflected on its smooth black surface. If he fell he would hit that ice so hard every one of his bones would break.

He teetered dizzily. He looked to the left and the right and saw that the edges of the bridge were just on either side of him. He could topple over and nothing would stop him. Where was the White Bear?

Fear would make him fall. Even if this bridge of lights still held his weight, it was so narrow that he must surely lose his balance and die.

But if it holds me, I must be meant to live. And if I am meant to live, I will not be allowed to fall.

It was only his fear that was making the bridge feel so precarious. He knew that the more he believed, the safer it would be for him.

Never turn your back on fear, he remembered Owl Carver saying. *Never try to drive it away. Fear is your friend. It warns you of danger.*

But what about when I must face the danger and not be warned from it? he asked.

As long as you listen to its warning, fear will not stop you from doing what you have to do. But if you try to pretend you do not hear it, fear will trip you and bind you with rawhide cords.

Gray Cloud, still afraid, stepped forward more boldly. Whatever spirits were making this happen to him, surely they were not showing him these wonders only then to destroy him.

He was out over the middle of the river, and he heard a deep muttering behind him.

He turned, and it was the White Bear, as big as an old bull buffalo, moving with him on its huge, clawed feet. It came up beside him, and he reached up to touch its shoulder. He knew now that it was a great spirit, and that it was his friend. He dug his fingers into the thick fur and felt the warmth and the enormous, powerful muscle underneath.

Joy flooded through him. Where he had been nearly overcome with fear, strength and excitement had entered. He ran up the rising curve of the bridge. He felt an impulse to dance, and he broke into the half trot, half shuffle of the men when they welcomed the harvest of good things to eat that the women had planted around Saukenuk village. He flapped his arms like the wild goose.

The bridge, he saw now, did not cross the river, but followed it. He looked up. The trail of stars ended at the one star in the sky that, as Owl Carver had pointed out to him, remained fixed when all the other stars danced around it. And therefore it was called the Council Fire Star.

The little lights twinkled all around him, like flocks of bright birds, and his heart was full of happiness. It was all so beautiful, he wanted to sing.

And he did sing, the only song he knew that seemed right for this moment, the Song of Creation.

> "Earthmaker, you fill the world with life.
> You put life in earth and sky and water.
> I do not know what you are, Earthmaker,
> But you are in me and everything that lives.

Always you have dwelt in life,
Always you will dwell so."

He sang and danced and the White Bear rose up on its hind legs
and strode heavily along beside him.

The light from the Council Fire Star grew brighter and seemed
to dispel the blackness of the sky around it. The star grew until it
was a sphere of cold fire that filled the sky.

He heard a roaring sound and saw that from the bottom of the
shining globe water was pouring. The water gave off a light of its
own. His eye followed its plunge. He was far, far above the earth
now. The Great River was a shiny black ribbon, barely visible,
winding over the earth. Straight as a spear the water from the Council Fire Star was falling down to the place where the Great River
began its winding course.

He exulted. Already he had learned a secret no other Sauk knew,
unless it be Owl Carver himself—the true source of the Great River.

He saw a square, dark opening in the glowing surface of the
star. The path led to it. Still walking on its hind legs, the White
Bear pressed inexorably on toward that doorway, and Gray Cloud
walked beside it.

The colors of the rainbow shimmered in the light from the star,
and it pulsed faintly like a beating heart. When he thought of what
a mighty spirit must dwell in this magnificent lodge—perhaps Earthmaker himself—Gray Cloud's heart was once again full of fear.

He trembled and his steps slowed. He could not come face to
face with such a being. It would be like staring into the sun. His
eyes would be burned out of his head. He felt himself weakening.

The star-studded surface under his feet shook a little. He took
a step and it quivered under his footfall. The White Bear was ahead
of him now, leaving him out here alone among the stars, high above
the earth on a bridge that was beginning to fall apart.

He looked back over the way he had come.

There was no bridge behind him.

Nothing but a blackness. He screamed, waved his arms, staggered.

He started to run forward after the Bear, his only protector, and
his feet were sinking *into* the bridge. The Bear and the doorway and
the Council Fire Star itself seemed farther and farther away.

He fell to his hands and knees, afraid to stand any more.

But what was the fear trying to tell him?

It was right that Gray Cloud should be afraid, meeting a spirit so much more powerful than himself. And now he must trust that the spirit would not hurt him.

With that thought, he felt the bridge growing more solid under his hands. He pushed himself back to his feet.

He was standing before the doorway. All above him and to the sides stretched the curving, shimmering, many-colored surface of the Council Fire Star.

He did not see the White Bear. It must have gone into the star. He took a deep breath, and taking his fear with him, he plunged through the doorway.

For a moment light blinded him. The air was full of a fluttering and a rustling.

His eyes grew used to the light and he saw that he stood at the edge of a pool full of fish swimming in circles.

They were not fish, he knew, but fish spirits. The spirits of trout and salmon and bass and walleye and sunfish and pike, all the fish of lakes and streams that fed his people.

Full of fear of what else he might see, Gray Cloud raised his eyes.

He saw a Turtle.

The Turtle was frightfully big. He was on the other side of the rushing pool, but still he loomed over Gray Cloud, his head high in the air. His front feet rested on a blue-white block of ice. Behind him rose a mountain of ice crystals. The wrinkles around his eyes and mouth told Gray Cloud he was immeasurably old.

"Gray Cloud," the Turtle said. "You are welcome here." His voice was deep as thunder.

Gray Cloud fell again to his hands and knees.

"Do not be afraid, Gray Cloud," said the rumbling voice.

He looked up again and saw kindness in the enormous, heavy-lidded yellow eyes. The exposed belly of the Turtle was the pale green of spring leaves. On his bone-encased chest a bright drop of water formed, like a dewdrop or a teardrop, but big as a man's head. After a moment it fell and splashed into the pool. Gray Cloud looked into the bottom of the pool and saw the blackness of a deep pit in its center. He realized that it must be from this pool that the stream of water poured down into the Great River. And the drops of water falling from the Turtle fed the pool. The true source of the Great River was the Turtle spirit's heart.

Owl Carver had told him of the Turtle. After Earthmaker he was the oldest and most powerful spirit. He had helped to create the world and to keep it alive.

Scarcely able to believe that he was actually looking upon the Turtle, Gray Cloud lifted his gaze and saw that all manner of beasts and birds occupied the ledges on the ice-crystal mountain. All creation was here. Trees—maple, ash, elm, oak, hickory, birch, pine and spruce—clustered on the mountainside, roots somehow drawing nourishment from the ice.

He said, "Father, I thank you for letting me come here."

Instead of answering him, the huge reptilian head swung to one side. He followed the gaze of the yellow eye.

A man was standing near the Turtle's head on one of the ledges. He was tall and thin. His eyes were round and blue, his face white. A pale eyes! What would a pale eyes be doing here in the lodge of the Turtle? The man had long black hair streaked with gray, tied at the back of his head. His thin figure was dressed in a blue coat, pinched at the waist by a black leather belt with a sword and a pistol hanging from it. His white trousers were tucked into shiny black boots that came up to his calves. Seeing the sword, Gray Cloud thought this man must be one of the long knives, the dreaded pale eyes warriors.

The man was looking at Gray Cloud. His face was narrow, with deep lines. All the pale eyes Gray Cloud had seen had hairy faces—thick mustaches growing under their noses, and sometimes beards that spread out over their chests—but this man's face was clean. His nose was large and hooked like a hawk's beak. Gray Cloud saw that the man was weeping. Tears were running down his creased cheeks as he stared at Gray Cloud. The look in those blue eyes, Gray Cloud realized, was not sadness, but love.

Returning the man's gaze, Gray Cloud felt a warmth in his own chest like the heat suddenly rising from a fire that has taken hold.

"I have brought you to hear a warning," said the Turtle, his voice shaking Gray Cloud's very bones. "You must carry my words back to my children, the Sauk and Fox." As the Turtle spoke, another huge drop splashed into the pool, to add itself to the Great River.

"Evil days are coming for my children."

Gray Cloud quailed, thinking that he did not want to bring that back to his people. But perhaps there was some good word he could tell them.

"How may we escape this evil, Father Turtle?" he asked.

"This evil is from the pale eyes."

At this, Gray Cloud turned to stare at the pale eyes man, who looked sad now, even sombre. Who was this man, and why was he here?

"The pale eyes and my children cannot live on the same land," said the Turtle. "Because they do not live in the same way. Most pale eyes do not wish harm to my children, but they do harm by coming into the land where my children dwell."

Gray Cloud at once grasped what the Turtle spoke of. Generations of Sauk and their allies, the Fox, had lived in towns at the joining of the Rock River and the Great River, where in summer they raised corn, beans, squash and pumpkins. Each fall they would leave their towns and fields for winter hunting camps in the West. But the pale eyes warriors, the long knives, had been telling the Sauk and Fox that they must give up all their land on the east side of the Great River, even their principal town, Saukenuk, and move forever west, into the Ioway country. And the war chief Black Hawk had defied the long knives, leading his people each spring back across the river to farm the land around Saukenuk.

Gray Cloud knew that even the kindliest pale eyes were not to be trusted. Owl Carver was suspicious of the black-robed medicine man, Père Isaac, who talked about the spirit called Jesus and who spent many afternoons with Gray Cloud, teaching him the words and signs of the American pale eyes.

The Turtle's voice broke in upon these memories. "Tell my children that a great clash is to come between them and the long knives. The people will suffer, and many of them will die."

Gray Cloud gasped as the horror of that sank in. He looked again at the pale eyes, and now where there had been love he saw lines of sorrow carved deep into the thin face.

Is this man, then, a danger to me?

"Is there no escape, Father Turtle?" he asked again.

"The people must walk their path with courage," said the Turtle. "Black Hawk will lead them. And he and his braves will show the greatest courage, such courage that the name of Black Hawk will never be forgotten in the land where he was born."

The Turtle's golden, heavy-lidded eye seemed to fix itself on Gray Cloud.

"And you will find your own path. For some of the people the path you find will be good. But many others will journey in sorrow into the setting sun. And there they will disappear forever."

Bewildered, Gray Cloud looked from the Turtle to the pale eyes near him and back to the Turtle again. These things the Turtle had said were strange, like the words Owl Carver would chant before the council fire. Must he bring his people a message of suffering and sorrow? Would they listen?

He wanted to ask more questions but he felt a gentle pressure from the great body of the Bear beside him, and he knew that his visit to the lodge of the Turtle was ended.

2

The Spirit Bear

Redbird stood at the edge of the hunting camp, beside the grove of trees where the band's horses were sheltering from the falling snow. Her tears mingled with the snowflakes melting on her face. Wherever she looked, a white curtain hid the land.

Would Gray Cloud die? The thought made her heart feel as if a giant's fist was squeezing it. Yesterday, at midday, her father had sent Gray Cloud on his vision quest, and in the most dangerous time of the year, the Moon of Ice, when the spirits harvested the living, leaving only the strongest to survive through to the spring. And just as night fell, the snow had begun. Would the spirits take Gray Cloud?

Tears burned her eyes and she felt dizzy. She had not slept all last night, and she had waited and watched through the day.

As she stood looking eastward, where Gray Cloud had gone on his spirit journey, it came to her that he might already be dead. The wind must have been blowing snow into the sacred cave all night and all day. Gray Cloud, in a trance, might already have frozen to death. She might be weeping for a dead man.

She sobbed aloud and put her hands, in squirrelskin mittens, to her face. The snow on the mittens felt barely colder than her cheeks.

A flash of light, brighter than the sun, blinded her. A tremendous roar of thunder almost knocked her to the snow-covered ground. Another bright flash made her cover her eyes in dismay, and in a moment there was another long, rolling, earth-shaking rumble.

People stood at the doorways of their dome-shaped wickiups,

murmuring to one another. Thunder with a snowstorm. This was the heaviest snowstorm of the year so far, and a snowstorm with thunder and lightning foretold some great event. Much snow lay on the rounded roofs of the wickiups, and some women took whisks of bundled twigs to brush it away so that it would not break down the framework of poles or melt through the roofs of elm bark and cattail mats and wet the people inside and their possessions. The snow was dry and powdery because the air was so cold, and it brushed away easily.

The snow was already halfway up Redbird's laced deerskin boots. She felt the bitter cold numbing her feet and legs. What must it be like for Gray Cloud?

She saw him as vividly as if he were standing before her. How very tall he was, almost as tall as her brother, Iron Knife. But Gray Cloud's frame was slender, not broad and powerful like Iron Knife's.

She saw Gray Cloud's tender mouth curving in a tentative smile, his sharp nose giving strength to his face, his large eyes glowing. His skin so much lighter than any other man's in the British Band of the Sauk and Fox.

And—she asked herself—was it not partly because of the mystery of Gray Cloud's father that she found herself drawn to him? Pale eyes fascinated her, the few she had met, Jean de Vilbiss the trader, the black-robed medicine man called Père Isaac.

Every summer, when Père Isaac visited Saukenuk village, he took Gray Cloud aside, teaching him strange words, showing him how to understand the meaning of marks on paper and how to make such marks. How she envied Gray Cloud, and wished that Père Isaac would teach her those things, too.

Redbird wondered why pale eyes were so different and why they had so much power. No Sauk craftsman could make anything like the steel swords that pale eyes warriors carried, whence they were called long knives. The steel tomahawks that the pale eyes traded for furs could shatter a stone-headed Sauk tomahawk into fragments. A pale eyes fire weapon, of course, was something every warrior of the Sauk and Fox tribes yearned for.

But what interested Redbird most were the steel sewing needles and iron cooking pots and calico dresses and wool blankets. She wondered why Earthmaker had given the knowledge of how to make such things to the pale eyes, but not to the Sauk and Fox. Her people wore the skins of animals, scraped and pushed and pulled and tanned with the animals' brains and women's urine until they were soft and pliant and could be worn comfortably next to the skin. But the clothing of the pale eyes was more comfortable, and easier to keep clean. And more colorful. Sauk and Fox shirts and leggings and skirts, unless painted or decorated with dyed quills, were usually the brown or tan of animal skins. The best deerskin garments were worked till they were white. The dresses and shawls and blankets the pale eyes traders offered were of many colors—blue and yellow, red and green, with flowers and other pictures and designs on them. Redbird often spent long moments staring at the good calico dress her father, Owl Carver, had gotten for her from the pale eyes traders, just delighting in the tiny red roses printed on its pale blue background.

For a moment, lost in thought about the pale eyes, she had forgotten Gray Cloud's danger and her own pain. Now it came back to her like a war club crushing her chest.

Soon it would be night again. Gray Cloud had been in the cave a whole night and a whole day, while the snow fell. And the snow was falling still. If someone did not rescue him, he would surely die.

She would go to her father, Owl Carver, and demand that Gray Cloud be brought back from the sacred cave.

She turned and pushed her feet through the fresh snow, hurrying past the round-roofed, snow-covered wickiups of the British Band's winter camp in Ioway country. A dog burst out of Wolf Paw's doorway and floundered through the snow, its short pointed ears flattened, barking at her. Wolf Paw's dogs were a nuisance, barking and snapping at anyone who passed near his dwelling.

The dog stopped barking, and she heard footsteps squeaking in the snow. She stopped and turned. Wolf Paw himself was standing before his wickiup beside the tall pole from whose top hung six Sioux scalps he had taken last winter.

Wolf Paw glowered at her, arms folded under a bright red blanket. Three short black stripes near one edge were the pale eyes trader's guarantee that the blanket was of highest quality. Despite the snow, Wolf Paw's head was uncovered, all shaved except for the stiff-standing crest of red-dyed deer hair in the middle. Three black and white eagle feathers were tied into it.

Redbird did not like Wolf Paw. He never let people forget that he was the son of the great war chief Black Hawk, whose wickiup lay only a short distance from his own. He never smiled, and she knew very well what he was thinking when he looked at her.

She turned without a greeting and walked on, kicking the snow as she went. But the sight of Wolf Paw had reminded her that though Owl Carver was her father, she still had only a woman's influence. The spirit journey of Gray Cloud was a matter for men.

Owl Carver loved her and was good to her, but if she tried to interfere in his holy calling, he would be furious. He would never agree to bring Gray Cloud down from the cave before he came down on his own. Such a thing was against the way of the shaman.

She was still wondering what she dared say when she came to her family's wickiup and found Owl Carver standing beside it, hands clasped behind his back, staring eastward toward the Great River.

As she shuffled through the snow toward him, he turned and held out his hands. When she reached him, he put his hands on her shoulders. She peered into his face, hard to see now that night had fallen, and tried to read it.

Owl Carver's face was flat. His long white hair was bound at his forehead with a beaded band and fell from there to his shoulders, spreading like a white shawl. His necklace of little round, striped shells of the water creatures called megis rattled in the wind.

She trembled inwardly in his presence. The shaman of the tribe could both heal and kill.

"How can he live in this blizzard?" she said, almost weeping.

"Did you not see the lightning, my daughter, and hear the thunder? Do you think that merely betokens a young man freezing to death? Hear me—once in a thousand years a man comes among us who is capable of being a Great Shaman. Of being to other shamans, like myself, what Earthmaker is to the lesser spirits of beasts and birds. But to be known, and to discover the greatness of his powers, such a man must be as greatly tested. I saw in Gray Cloud a man beyond the ordinary."

Owl Carver's willingness to talk made Redbird feel bolder. "Surely Gray Cloud has been in the sacred cave long enough, my father. Will you not go now and bring him down?"

He pushed her away, staring at her. "Earthmaker decides what is enough. A man must *suffer* to be worthy of the power his spirit guide bestows on him. When I first began to walk the shaman's path, I wandered far away into the great desert of the West and nearly died of hunger and thirst. I did not suffer as much as Gray Cloud is suffering. But that is because he can be a much greater shaman than I, if he lives. If he does not live, he is like a foal born lame in the springtime. The wolves must get him. It is Earthmaker's way."

Frightened though she was, Redbird forced herself to speak up. "There is suffering that even the strongest cannot bear."

Owl Carver took a step toward her, his eyes round with anger. "Remember what the law of the Sauk and Fox decrees for anyone who disturbs a man on a spirit journey, even to help him. They take you to the Great River. In the summer they would throw you in with rocks tied to you. In this season they chop a hole in the ice and they push you in. The current flows swiftly under the ice. It carries you away from the opening, and you drown there in the cold and dark."

Redbird shrank back. Owl Carver had felt her pain when she first came to him, but now he was angry. She sensed that behind that anger there lurked fear. Fear that she might risk her life for Gray Cloud.

"Your mother has been calling for you," he said. "Go and help her with her work."

Afraid to say any more, Redbird hurried past him and lifted the heavy buffalo skin that covered the doorway of the family's wickiup. She looked over her shoulder once and saw that her father was once again looking toward the river where Gray Cloud had gone. Owl Carver held his hands behind his back, knotting them together.

He was afraid for Gray Cloud, too. As she sensed that, her heart sank further.

Entering the wickiup she saw, silhouetted against the light of the low fire in the center, a figure rising up big as a buffalo, her half brother, Iron Knife. Redbird took his hands in greeting.

"Gray Cloud will be well," Iron Knife said in a low, gruff voice.

Iron Knife was always kind to her. She was grateful for his words, but she knew they were no more than a well-meant wish. Though Iron Knife was the son of Owl Carver by his first wife, he had not a trace of the shaman's ability to foretell events. Iron Knife could see only with his eyes, hear only with his ears. His mother had died giving birth to him, and there were those who said the spirits had chosen to give him no gifts because he had killed his mother. Redbird had even heard that while in mourning Owl Carver had predicted that Iron Knife would one day be killed by a man whose mother had also died giving birth to him. No one dared speak of these things in Iron Knife's presence.

Redbird knew she had more of the shaman in her than Iron Knife. She knew, as her father did, that right now Gray Cloud was in terrible danger.

"Where have you been?" Wind Bends Grass called out from the shadows. She and Redbird's sisters were already bedded down for the night on buffalo-robe pallets along the wall of the wickiup. Wind Bends Grass and her two little girls, Wild Grape and Robin's Nest, slept together for greater warmth.

"I was down in the woods, seeing to our horses," Redbird lied. She had been near the horses, but only to watch for Gray Cloud.

"I needed you here," Wind Bends Grass said crossly. "I was stringing beads for a new sash for your father, and your sisters are too small to help me."

Does my mother want me to string beads while Gray Cloud freezes to death?

"The snow was heavy on the horses' backs," Redbird said. "They needed someone to brush them off."

"Nonsense," said Wind Bends Grass, sitting up. "You were waiting and worrying for that pale eyes boy. And meanwhile Wolf Paw came again to speak to your father today. How can you refuse the son of the mighty Black Hawk and think of marrying that boy who has no father? His mother lay with a pale eyes and got Gray Cloud. The pale eyes lived with her only five summers and then ran away. He would have run away sooner, but our people held him prisoner because of the war."

Redbird heard muffled giggles from the bedding beside her mother. Her little sisters thought the story of Gray Cloud's parentage funny. Wind Bends Grass struck with her hand at the two shaking bundles.

"Wolf Paw already has a wife," Redbird said.

"He is a *man*," said Wind Bends Grass. "A brave. He can make two wives, three wives, *four* wives happy."

Rage at her mother for belittling Gray Cloud when he might be dying boiled up inside her and almost choked her. She bit her lip and held back the angry words. She hurt too much to want to quarrel.

She took off her fur cap, wet boots and mittens and laid them near the fire. Keeping on her buffalo-hide cloak, her doeskin dress and leggings, she lay down on her own pallet, padded with blankets and prairie grass. Curling up her legs, she wrapped the heavy cloak around herself.

The wickiup was quiet, except for the popping of burning twigs.

Redbird knew that her fear for Gray Cloud, deepening as the night deepened, would keep her awake. She decided that when they were all asleep, she would go back to the wickiup of Sun Woman and watch with her.

She lay staring at the blackened ceiling that arched over her head. Partly obscured by drifting smoke, the curved poles cast deep shadows in the flickering light. Iron Knife had laid fresh branches on the fire. Smoke stung her eyes.

Sometimes she thought she saw spirit messages above her in the patterns of the twigs interwoven with the larger poles, and in the cracks in the sheets of bark that lined the inside of the wickiup. But tonight her mind was too absorbed in Gray Cloud's fate to try to read the patterns.

Over the breathing of the others she could hear the voice of the wind humming across the roof. From time to time it would rise to a howl, and the framework of the wickiup would creak and crackle under the strain. Even though there was a fire and the wickiup was tightly sealed, Redbird felt the cold seeping up from the earth. Its icy fingers touched her body through the buffalo robe. Her dread for Gray Cloud turned to heart-pounding panic.

If I feel the cold, here in my warm wickiup, what must it be like for him?

After the snow stopped falling, the cold of this night would be the cold that killed without mercy. Such a deepening cold often seemed to follow a great snow. After a night like this, women would find rabbit and deer lying in the drifts near the camp. The animals trying to get close to warmth had overcome their fear of people, but the cold had leeched the life from their bodies. Even the strongest animals might die. Only people, to whom Earthmaker had given the knowledge of how to shelter themselves and make fire, could withstand this death-dealing cold.

Her fists clenched on the blanket. Her heart filled up with anger. Anger against the cold, against her mother, who despised Gray Cloud, against Owl Carver, who had sent him to almost certain death. Against the spirits, who had permitted this. Out of her anger blazed up a fierce resolve.

I will not let you take him from me.

If everyone else accepted Gray Cloud's death, she did not. She would go to him. She would go to Sun Woman and gather what medicines she might have, anything that would keep the cold from draining the last bit of warmth and strength out of Gray Cloud.

Have you not been told what the tribe decrees for anyone who disturbs a man on a spirit journey, even to help him?

Her anger turned to fear, and she lay there, not wanting to move, knowing that if she threw off the blankets and stood up, she would be taking the first step on a path that might be her death.

But then she thought of that terrible wind, sharp as a pale eyes' steel knife, shrieking around Gray Cloud's body. If she did something now, he might live; and if she did nothing, he was sure to die.

She had loved Gray Cloud for as long as she could remember. To be without him—she could not bear to think of it.

She had heard tales of women who died fighting beside their men. Yes, better to die with Gray Cloud, to walk the Trail of Souls into the West with him, than live a long life grieving for him.

She listened to the sounds of the sleepers, Iron Knife's rumbling snore, Wind Bends Grass's heavy breathing that sounded like her name, the rustlings and murmurings of Wild Grape and Robin's Nest.

Owl Carver still had not come in, and he might stay out there most of the night. She dared not wait any longer. She would have to face him.

Silently she pushed off her coverings and stood up. She quickly put back on her fur cap, boots and mittens.

The deepened cold bit into her cheeks like a weasel's teeth. While she had lain in the wickiup the snow, which had been falling continually for a night and a day, had stopped at last. The clouds overhead were breaking up, and she could see the full moon, round and bright as a pale eyes' silver coin. The Moon of Ice. It seemed frozen in place in the black sky. Stars glittered, little chips of ice. With her first indrawn breath the insides of her nostrils seemed to freeze, the air burned in her nose and throat. Her heart quailed for Gray Cloud.

The black figure of Owl Carver stood just where she had left him. How could he stand the cold this long?

Owl Carver turned to her. "Where are you going?"

"To Sun Woman's wickiup, to watch with her."

She hated Owl Carver. He was the one who had sent Gray Cloud on this spirit journey, and now would do nothing to save him from death.

As if sensing her agony, he said, "The spirits will watch over Gray Cloud."

She wanted to believe him, but she could not. She had begged him to help Gray Cloud, and he had commanded her to be silent. Now she had no more to say to him. She turned from Owl Carver.

He could have forbidden her to go to Sun Woman. But he would not do that. There was an understanding between Redbird and her father that she could not put into words. She knew that when he looked at her, he was torn between pride that she, the oldest of his children by Wind Bends Grass, possessed the same gifts he did, and sorrow that she was a woman, and could never be a shaman. And she knew that of all his children, he loved her best.

The snow, blown off the roofs of the wickiups, piled up in long drifts on their western sides. The east wind battered Redbird as she plodded through the winter camp toward one low, rounded black structure that rose out of the snow a bit apart from the others, on the north side of the camp.

The skinned quarters of small animals hung frozen from a rack outside Sun Woman's doorway. Redbird went up to the flap of buffalo hide and called, "It is Redbird. May I come in?"

Redbird heard Sun Woman undoing the sinew laces that held the flap down. She bent and entered.

In the firelight within Sun Woman's wickiup, Redbird saw agony in the tightness of the older woman's wide mouth and the clenching of her strong jaw. Gray Cloud's mother was built big, with broad shoulders and hips and large hands, but there was a helplessness now in the way she stood staring into the fire. Hanging from the curving bark wall behind her were her craft objects, a medicine bundle of deerskin, the carved figures of a naked man and a naked woman, clamshells to mold maple sugar, a horse's tail dyed red, a small drum and a flute.

Redbird spoke in a rush. "If he dies I do not want to live." She feared that if she tried to address Sun Woman properly, her voice would be choked by sobs before she could say what demanded to be said.

She should not even suggest to Gray Cloud's mother that he might die. And she should not even hint to his mother of her love for Gray Cloud, when neither Sun Woman nor Owl Carver had spoken to each other of plans for their children. The band would be appalled at such rudeness.

"Forgive me for speaking so to you," she said timidly.

Sun Woman smiled, but Redbird saw that there was much sadness in the smile. "You know you can."

"Yes, you are different," Redbird said.

Even though the pale eyes killed your husband, you took a pale eyes into your wickiup.

This had happened more than fifteen winters ago, and Redbird knew it only as a story that her mother and other women liked to repeat while they did their work together. Sun Woman's husband, a brave named Dark Water, had been killed in a quarrel with pale eyes settlers. In spite of that, when Gray Cloud's pale eyes father came to live with the Sauk, Sun Woman had come to love him.

"I am different, too," said Redbird. She wondered if Sun Woman knew how different she was. Most women lived from season to season, while Redbird sometimes thought about what the tribe might be doing, where they might be, ten summers from now.

Only two kinds of people thought the kind of long thoughts that came often to Redbird—chiefs and shamans. She sometimes imagined what it would be like to be a shaman. To live in accord with the gift Earthmaker gave her. She thought so often about it that it became a longing within her, even though she knew that such a thing could not be.

This, Redbird thought, was the most she could hope for—to become a medicine woman, like Gray Cloud's mother. A medicine woman had an important place in the band, but she was not listened to, as the shaman was.

Sun Woman reached out and laid her bare hand on top of Redbird's, which was still in a mitten. "That is why I would be pleased if you and my son shared a wickiup."

Redbird was startled and, amidst her fear and grief for Gray Cloud, delighted. Truly, no mother ever spoke like this before words between parents had been exchanged. And to know that Sun Woman would accept her as her son's wife—wondrous!

But Gray Cloud might already be dead. "How can we talk and smile so?" she cried. "He is up in the sacred cave, and the snow fell all last night and all day today."

Sun Woman shook her head. "When I gave the boy to Owl Carver, I gave up the right to say what was to be done with him. Like Owl Carver, Gray Cloud belongs to the spirits now."

"But the spirits—" Redbird waved her hands helplessly. "They protect as they like and they let death strike as they like."

A shadow of pain crossed Sun Woman's face. "Do you say such things to hurt me?"

Redbird was shocked. "No!"

"Do you think I feel no pain?"

Redbird felt tears filling her eyes, burning them. She wiped her face. "I know you do."

Sun Woman brought her face closer to Redbird's, took Redbird's chin in her hand, and said, "I do not show pain because I do not want to make others suffer with me. But you know what I feel."

Sun Woman opened her arms, and Redbird pressed her body against the bigger, older woman's. She felt Sun Woman's strength flow into her and she knew that she had found more comfort here than she ever would in the arms of her own mother.

In the firelit wickiup, Redbird looked around her, thinking that this was where Gray Cloud had been a baby. She looked at the bench where she knew he slept every night. Where he must sleep again.

"Do you have anything to give a person who has been very cold for a long time?" Rebird asked urgently.

"Ah." Sun Woman went to the back of the wickiup and came back with a bundle of long, dark red peppers.

"These peppers are grown far to the south, where the sacred mushroom and the bright blue stones come from. The longer you boil them, the hotter the water will get. He is to drink the water, but not swallow the peppers. If he is very cold, give him one pepper to chew on. That would bring the dead back to life. If you meet him before I do, this is how you can help him."

She thinks I mean to try to meet him when he comes back.

"I will go to him," Redbird said abruptly.

Sun Woman stared at her. "You must not. If you interrupt his spirit journey it might kill him."

"He has been in a cave for a night and a day, and this is the second night, colder than any night I can remember. My father watches for him, but he does not come. He could still be sitting in that cave. He has no fire. He has no food or water. The wind blows in from the river. The snow here at the camp is so deep that in some places the drifts are over my head. The cave could be full of snow. When he is suffering all this, how can you say that *I* am a danger to him?"

Sun Woman sat cross-legged on the rush mat floor and stared down at her hands folded in her lap. After a silence she looked up, and her grave, dark eyes held Redbird's.

"You are a good young woman, and you love my son. But you must understand that the greater danger to Gray Cloud is not from the cold. If you try to wake Gray Cloud's body when his soul is gone from it, his spirit will never come back to his empty body. It will set its feet on the Trail of Souls and walk west, to the land of the dead."

Sun Woman's eyes shone, and the shadows and firelight gave her the face of an angry spirit. Redbird drew back.

"I will not do that," she said. "I promise you." But if she saw that Gray Cloud would surely die anyway, of freezing, would it not then be best to take the risk of waking him?

And what if he did wake on his own, but was too frozen to climb out of the cave and walk back to the camp by himself? Then he would need her help.

She decided that if she got to the cave and his spirit was still out of his body, she would do everything to help him short of waking him. She would build a fire near him. She would cover him with warm cloaks, try to warm his body if she could do that without disturbing him.

She boiled the peppers in a small tin pot set on stones over Sun Woman's low fire. After she had filled a skin with the pepper water, she rolled tinder and a pale eyes fire striker into a blanket. She put her hand on Sun Woman's snowshoes, leaning against a wall of the little wickiup, and Sun Woman nodded silently.

Redbird paddled over the snow with her head down, watching the long shadow she cast under the full moon on the sparkling white surface. Ahead, the leeward sides of the wickiups were rows of snowdrifts, all the same size. When she looked over her shoulder, their windward sides were like black holes in the snow. She could see her family's wickiup, but Owl Carver was no longer standing outside watching. She lifted her round wickerwork snowshoes high with each step. Even though she could walk over the snow, she would be exhausted, she realized, long before she pushed her way to the sacred cave.

Dogs barked. Fear made the back of her neck tingle, and she stood motionless. They might be Wolf Paw's dogs. But they did not come after her.

She heard no sounds of voices, or of people moving. She felt safe enough to keep walking.

But a feeling grew on her that someone was following her. She stopped again and listened and looked around. The wickiups were silent under their glistening blue-white hummocks. Being able to sense when she was being watched was one of the gifts she, like her father, possessed. But her eyes and ears did not confirm what her inner sense told her. She decided fear was confusing her, and she walked on.

She left the camp behind. On her right was gently rolling, snow-covered prairie. On her left were the woods that grew along the Ioway River. She saw the shadows of the horses among the trees, heard them snort and stamp their feet. Beside the woods ran the long trail leading to the bluff where the sacred cave overlooked the river. This close to the trees, she hoped, the snow would not be so deep.

A shadow appeared on the snow beside her. A bolt of terror stabbed her.

A powerful hand seized her arm. She felt paralyzed, like a rabbit about to be torn apart by a wildcat. She did not try to pull away. She could feel that the grip on her arm was too strong.

She turned slowly.

The moon was behind the man who held her, shadowing his face, but she could make out the glitter of piercing eyes, a stern mouth with strong lips under his brown fur turban.

"Where are you going?" Wolf Paw's fingers hurt her arm.

No words came to her. Frantically, she tried to think of some excuse for walking out so late on a night like this. He could have her killed, she thought, and terror made her feel like sinking into the snow.

But then she remembered some of the lore Sun Woman had taught her.

"My father sent me—to look for a certain herb whose power is greatest when the moon is full."

He barked disdainfully. "Gathering herbs when the snow is up to your knees?"

"It grows under the snow."

He brought his face so close to hers that his black eyes seemed to fill the world.

"You cannot lie to me, Redbird. I see what you are doing. You are going to *him*."

"No, no, I am looking for herbs."

"What is *this*?" With his free hand he tore away the blanket roll she had tied to her back and threw it into the snow. "And *this*?" He jerked on the water skin so hard that the strap broke, and he threw that down, too.

"Do you need those things to help you find herbs?" he shouted.

Trembling from head to foot, she felt herself starting to cry. She hated herself for showing such weakness in front of Wolf Paw. If she was to die, she wanted to be strong.

To her surprise, the sense that she was being watched from a distance came back again. There was someone else out here in the frozen darkness besides herself and Wolf Paw.

"It is death to interfere with a spirit quest," Wolf Paw growled. "The shaman's daughter of all people should know better than to break a holy law."

Her fear made her feel as cold, as breathless, as if she were already plunged into black, freezing water, swept along, an enormous weight of ice between her and the air.

"I have done nothing."

"You meant to. That is as bad."

She saw the hunting knife at Wolf Paw's belt. She could make a grab for it, try to stab him.

No, he was one of the tribe's mightiest braves. He would be too quick and strong for her. And, at least, up to now she had done no harm to anyone but herself. To try to murder the son of the war leader would be a great crime.

His grip on her arm still cruelly tight, he gestured back behind him toward the snow-covered camp. "Think of your mother's weeping over what I caught you doing. Your father, his heart torn in his chest. But he, the shaman, would have to say that you must be killed."

Hopelessness crushed her. Now she would never be able to help Gray Cloud. He was going to die. And she was caught by Wolf Paw and would be dishonored before the whole tribe and then killed.

She hung her head.

"But it is true, Redbird, you have done nothing," Wolf Paw said more softly. "I am the only one who knows that you were about to break the law."

Sun Woman knows. But Wolf Paw will never learn that from me.

"I do not want you to die, Redbird," said the low voice from the figure towering over her.

She looked up at him. Was he going to be merciful?

He said, "It makes me angry that you throw your life away for that fatherless pale eyes boy. To wed the son of Black Hawk would bring you honor."

She understood now. He was going to offer to spare her life, if she would marry him and give up Gray Cloud. He did not understand that she would rather be dead twice over than spend her life mourning Gray Cloud and married to Wolf Paw.

She was about to tell him so when she heard a rumble, almost like thunder, from the trees nearer the camp. With much whinnying and cracking of shrubbery, all the band's horses burst out of the woods and ran, floundering and kicking up clouds of snow, out on the prairie.

"Be still," Wolf Paw cautioned in a low voice, "until we see what frightened them." He stood with his head high, listening.

Whatever it was, she was grateful that it had taken Wolf Paw's mind off her.

She heard a crashing in the forest, branches breaking, snow crunching. Something large was coming toward them.

She turned. Through the trees she saw a bulky, hunched figure. It seemed to be a large animal, but it was walking on its hind legs.

It came forward slowly, a step at a time. Its forelimbs swung at its sides. It was a little taller than a man.

It looked very much like a bear. A new fear, greater than the fear of what Wolf Paw might do, assailed her.

A bear in coldest winter, when all of that people withdrew to their dens and slept? Once in a while, she had heard, a very hungry bear would awaken and forage for food and then go back to sleep again. Such a bear would kill anything it met. She tensed herself to run, though she knew she could never outrun a hungry bear.

The shambling tread of the bear, or whatever it was, had brought it closer, and she saw that it was all white, glittering in the moonlight like a snowdrift.

She glanced at Wolf Paw and saw his eyes glisten as they widened. The look on his shadowed face was one she never thought to see on him—fear.

He sucked in a shuddering breath. The hand that had held her arm suddenly released her.

No wonder Wolf Paw was afraid. This was a white bear, a spirit bear. Its eyes, reflecting the moonlight, seemed to glow.

Wolf Paw uttered a terrified, inarticulate cry. She turned to see him racing over the snow. Were she not so frightened herself, she might have laughed to see how his knees flew up, first one, then the other, as white clouds sprayed from his snowshoes. Strong as he was, he could never outrun a bear. Especially not this bear.

As for herself, she was surely doomed. She thought, *May this be a better death than drowning under the ice.*

And she turned to face the spirit bear.

3

Claw Marks

The white bear was out of the forest now. Redbird had seen bears run, and she knew it could cover the distance that separated them in a few bounds.

It did not seem to be looking at her, and she wondered if it saw her. It sparkled in the moonlight. Its breath came in huge frosty clouds, obscuring its head. Did spirit bears breathe?

She looked around again to see where Wolf Paw was. He had become a small, dark spot against the white at the edge of the village. His snowshoes had carried him far quickly. She, too, would have run, if she could run like Wolf Paw.

She did not think Wolf Paw a coward. His courage was well known. Facing a being like this, the bravest man in the world would run.

It doesn't seem to see me. Maybe it is best to stand still.

She trembled from head to foot, unable to decide what to do. She felt dizzy, as if she might collapse into the snow. The bright light that seemed to come from the bear dazzled her.

But would a spirit bear attack people in the night and kill them? Devils and cannibal giants would, but she had never heard of a spirit doing any such thing.

She was learning to be a medicine woman, and a medicine woman must deal unafraid with the beings of the other world. Talk the bad spirits out of a sick person's body and call upon the good spirits to aid in healing.

She took a deep breath. Whether this be a good spirit or a devil, she would stand here holding herself proudly. Wolf Paw, if he looked back, would see the maiden he had threatened standing in the place he had run from.

The white bear took a step toward her.

In spite of her fear, she made herself look at the spirit as it came on. It walked so slowly. Perhaps, after all, she could run away from it.

Under the pointed snout she saw eyes that seemed to glow out of a shadowed face.

It was a man she was facing.

She saw that its path was taking it past her. It—he—did not seem to see her at all. But he was close enough now for her to see the face under the bear's skull. The large, round eyes, the long, thin features ending in a pointed chin, the bony beak of a nose, the down-curving, tender mouth. His face was covered with a mask of frost.

Gray Cloud.

How could she have forgotten that when he walked out of the camp yesterday he had worn a black bear's skin draped over his arms and shoulders? Snow and frost had turned the fur white. The night and her terror had tricked her into thinking she saw a white bear spirit. Wolf Paw, the seasoned warrior, had been tricked and terrified, too.

Gray Cloud was alive!

A scream tried to force its way out of her chest, but her windpipe was so tight that all she managed was a gasp.

Joy blazed up in her like a summer campfire.

But no—he could not be alive and look like that. What she was seeing must be the ghost of Gray Cloud, or his dead body walking. The cold and snow had killed him there in the sacred cave, and this shuffling, frozen husk was all that was left of him.

"Gray Cloud," she whispered, unable to speak aloud, "talk to me."

If he walked right past her without seeing her, he must be still on his spirit journey. She had always heard that the bodies of men on a spirit journey remained motionless, sitting or lying down. But she was certain that Gray Cloud was not fully awake.

She stood staring at him, her mouth open, as he shambled on past her.

She slowly turned to follow him, and now she was facing into the moonlight and seeing the shadows of the snow-covered wickiups. He was walking in that frighteningly slow, measured way toward the village. Wolf Paw was nowhere to be seen.

The feeling came to her again of other eyes upon her. Besides Wolf Paw, besides the strange creature Gray Cloud had become, someone else seemed to be out here in the snow-covered field with her. She shuddered.

She looked around to see if she could guess where the secret watcher might be hiding. Someone might be crouching behind one of the long snowdrifts that rippled across the prairie like waves on a lake. Or in the trees by the river.

She must not let herself be caught out here. She picked up the blanket roll and water skin that Wolf Paw had thrown into the snow and padded on her snowshoes after the lumbering white figure. She must hurry and try to get to a place where her presence would be unnoticed, or if noticed, not questioned.

Her legs ached. She did not have the strength to run. Gray Cloud had left a trail of two shallow furrows in the snow where he had pushed his legs through and the snow had fallen in behind him. On her snowshoes she pressed on behind him.

Even though the snowshoes helped her, her legs ached. She wanted to throw down her burdens of blanket roll and water skin, but they were too valuable for her to let them be lost out here. Merciless pain shot up from her shins through her knees to her hips. Still, the miseries felt by her body could not touch the joy of her spirit. Gray Cloud lived.

A wall of fur coated with white snow loomed up before her. As Gray Cloud lumbered along, she quickly stepped to the side and hurried around him.

She turned for a closer look at him. His steaming breath obscured his face. He stopped. He swayed, and the bear's skull fell back from his lolling head. She screamed, a sound that rang distantly in her ears.

Gray Cloud dropped to his knees, then fell forward on his face, sending up a great puff of powdery snow that glittered in the moonlit air.

The silence after his fall was as stunning as thunder. Redbird felt tears stream from her eyes—and freeze at once on her cheeks.

That he should have lived through two nights of blizzard and cold, that he should come down alive from the sacred cave, only to die within sight of the village under her very eyes, was more than she could stand.

"Oh, no!" she whispered. "He must not die."

She fell to her knees beside him.

He lay face down, half buried. She put her hands under his shoulder and pushed to raise his head. He was heavy, but her fear and her love for him made her strong enough to move him. She lifted his upper body and turned him on his side, and she saw the beloved features, frost-white. Hope made her heart beat faster as little clouds of warm air puffed from his nostrils. But his breathing was ragged and shallow. She had to get him in out of the cold. Gasping with the effort, she rolled him over on his back.

She would have to try to drag him to the village.

Sobbing with near-exhaustion, she sat by his head, shoved her hands under his shoulders and tried to stand, pulling him up with her.

All at once there was no weight on her arms. Someone else was there, lifting Gray Cloud.

She looked up, thankful, yet afraid she might see Wolf Paw returned to do them harm.

No, it was Iron Knife.

Seeing the broad face of her half brother, a cry of relief burst from her throat.

"Oh, Iron Knife! It is so good you are here."

He smiled grimly, grunting as he hauled Gray Cloud to his feet. Gray Cloud's eyes were shut, his mouth hanging open.

"Lucky for Wolf Paw that Gray Cloud came when he did," Iron Knife said. "I was getting an arrow ready for Wolf Paw." He jerked his head at the bow slung over his shoulder.

"Even the son of Black Hawk?" She vividly remembered Wolf Paw's threats, but the thought of Iron Knife murdering him horrified her.

"Do you think I'd let him drown my sister?" Iron Knife put an arm around Gray Cloud's shoulders, bent down and picked him up under the knees, bearskin cloak and all. Blowing a cloud of steam out of his mouth, he straightened, cradling Gray Cloud in his arms. Though Gray Cloud was nearly as tall as Iron Knife, he was much lighter.

It was Iron Knife, she realized, whose eyes she had felt on her after Wolf Paw ran away.

They started off for the camp. She heard the voices of men and women raised, calling to one another. Wolf Paw must have given the alarm.

"How did you know I was out here?" she asked. "You were sleeping when I left the wickiup."

"Father woke me," Iron Knife said, striding stolidly along, his calf-high outer moccasins of buffalo hide breaking through the snow. "He knew what you were going to do. He told me to go after you, to see you came to no harm."

As they plowed steadily onward, Redbird saw figures moving about in the village. They must be terribly sleepy, she thought. Dawn was still a long way off. Still, more and more people were running back and forth among the wickiups. They were crowding in this direction, coming to meet Gray Cloud and Iron Knife and Redbird. A mass of people, dark against the moonlit snow.

In the front rank walked Owl Carver himself. The sacred necklace of megis shells swung on his chest. In one hand he held his medicine stick, a cedar staff decorated with feathers and beads, topped with the carved head of an owl. His long white hair spread out over his shoulders.

She could hear a murmuring of voices, and above them, the shaman, her father, singing:

> "Let the people welcome him.
> He has walked the spirit trail.
> He comes back
> From the sky,
> From the water,
> From under the earth.
> He comes back from the seven directions.
> Let the people welcome him."

Owl Carver was dancing as he approached them, a slow, heavy shuffle alternating with sidesteps, his upper body rising and falling. His hands, one holding his medicine stick, the other a yellow and red gourd rattle, were lifted high over his head. The necklace of small black and white shells bounced on his chest.

Iron Knife, carrying Gray Cloud, came to a stop before Owl Carver. Redbird, not wanting people to know how she cared for Gray Cloud, drew away from Iron Knife and tried to melt into the crowd.

Taking a few more steps, Owl Carver placed himself facing east, with Iron Knife and Gray Cloud on his right. He danced in a sunwise circle around them, from east to south to west to north, bobbing his head and singing.

> "The Great Wise One has sent him.
> He has walked the spirit trail.
> He brings wisdom
> From the sky,
> From the water,
> From under the earth.
> He comes back from the seven directions.
> The Great Wise One has sent him."

Nine times Owl Carver danced around Gray Cloud and Iron Knife in the circle that represented the sun, the horizon and the cycles of life and the seasons.

Then in his normal voice, not breaking step, he said, "Bring him to my medicine wickiup."

He turned abruptly and danced through the crowd that had gathered. The people parted to let him through and they stared at Gray Cloud's body in Iron Knife's arms.

The people who had followed Owl Carver had stamped down a path through the village. No longer needing Sun Woman's snowshoes, Redbird bent and unstrapped them from her feet. She was suddenly so exhausted by her efforts and by the fear and sleeplessness of two days that she could hardly stumble along behind Iron Knife. She felt that at any moment she might faint.

The light of the full moon, shining down from directly overhead and reflecting on the snow, seemed to make the whole village almost as bright as day. Sighing, Redbird looked up and saw Wolf Paw staring at her from beside the path.

His black eyes pierced her like arrowheads. Under his sharp nose his mouth was tight.

She nodded her head at him, hoping he would understand that she was saying that they should keep each other's secrets.

"Redbird!" A hand seized her arm roughly, and pain shot through up to her shoulder.

Her mother, Wind Bends Grass, glared at her furiously.

"Why did you leave our wickiup?"

Redbird felt that if she stopped walking to talk she would never be able to move again. She pulled her arm free. Her sisters, clinging to either side of her mother, stared up wide-eyed at her as if she herself had returned from a spirit journey.

Her mother walked beside her, scolding her in a shrill voice, but her words meant nothing to Redbird. She only wanted to see Gray Cloud brought safely to the shaman's wickiup.

Someone else took her arm, squeezing it gently, and she looked up into Sun Woman's face. Tears streaked the strong cheekbones.

"You saved his life," Sun Woman said, so softly only Redbird could hear the words.

"I did nothing," Redbird protested. Silently, Sun Woman took the snowshoes, the water bag and the blanket roll from her.

Owl Carver stopped at the doorway of the medicine wickiup. He danced from one foot to the other, shaking his staff.

He nodded at Iron Knife, and motioned him to carry Gray Cloud into the dark interior.

Redbird followed. The owl-headed stick barred her way.

"Go with your mother," Owl Carver said softly. "You have done enough this night."

She could not tell whether he was praising or reproaching her.

Will he live? she wanted to ask. But his solemn face forbade her to speak.

She turned away from his remoteness and faced her mother's anger. Her heart was still full of terror for Gray Cloud, but she knew that the instant she lay down she would fall into an exhausted sleep.

It seemed that no time had passed when Wind Bends Grass shook her awake.

"Your father calls the people together," she said in a voice still hard with anger.

Redbird's eyelids felt as if they were made of stone. She forced herself to sit up, and then with immense effort got to her feet.

She was still fully dressed, even in her fur cloak and mittens. She had collapsed in the wickiup without removing anything. The wickiup was now empty. Her mother and her sisters had gone ahead without her.

Her heart hammered in her chest. Owl Carver might be calling the people to tell them that Gray Cloud was dead.

Outside, the air was still deathly cold, but the sun was a bright yellow disk rising above the distant gray line of trees that marked the bluffs overlooking the Great River. The light made her blink, and she turned away from it. She stumbled in the direction all the other people were going—to the medicine wickiup in the center of the camp circle.

She found that the open area before the wickiup was crowded, and she could not get close. The spaces between nearby wickiups were also filled with people, all waiting for Owl Carver to speak.

She seated herself between two women, both of whom had small children on their laps. Redbird knew one of the mothers, Water Flows Fast, a stout woman with a round, cheerful face and shrewd eyes.

Water Flows Fast said, "You are the daughter of Owl Carver. You should go up and sit close to him." Redbird sliced her hand flat across her body to say no. She knew Water Flows Fast to be a keen observer and a gossip, always looking for signs of trouble in other people's families. The less Redbird said to her, the better.

Redbird looked over her shoulder and saw that now there were many more people packed in behind her. Everyone was talking at once, and the hundreds of voices beating upon her ears made her head hurt. About five hundred people were here, everyone in this camp, which was one of four that made up the British Band of the Sauk and Fox tribes that would come together in Saukenuk after the winter snow and ice melted.

The medicine wickiup was built on a low hill in the center of the camp, and when Owl Carver appeared, everyone who was standing sat down. Redbird's eyes devoured Owl Carver's face, trying to read in it whether Gray Cloud was alive or dead.

Another man emerged from the medicine wickiup to stand beside Owl Carver. His head was bare even on this terribly cold day, and he wore his hair in the manner of a brave, his dark brown scalp shaved except for a long black scalplock that coiled down the side of his face. His eyes were shadowed and sad-looking, and there were heavy blue-black pouches under them. His cheekbones jutted out and his mouth was wide, curving down at the corners where it met deep furrows that ran from nose to chin.

Redbird's heart beat faster as she saw that to honor this moment he had attached a string of eagle feathers to his scalplock and wore strings of small white beads around the rim of each ear. He stood with his arms folded under a buffalo robe, skin side out, painted with a red hand proclaiming that he had killed and scalped his first enemy while still a boy.

His sombre gaze fell upon Redbird like a stone striking her from a great height. She felt as if the war chief of the British Band knew every one of her secrets. She ducked her head and looked down at her mittened hands in her lap.

Owl Carver raised his arms, and the people fell silent.

"I have called on Black Hawk, our war chief, to see Gray Cloud, and he has heard great prophecies from Gray Cloud's lips," the shaman cried in a high, chanting voice.

Then Gray Cloud had lived through the night!

Owl Carver blurred in Redbird's sight, and if she had not already been seated, she might have collapsed. Relief made her heart swell up in her chest, feeling as if it might burst.

The people around her murmured in surprise, pleasure and curiosity.

The shaman stretched out his hand. "Sun Woman, stand before the people."

Nothing happened for a long moment. Then Owl Carver beckoned insistently. There was another silence. Then Black Hawk's hand emerged from under his buffalo mantle, and he crooked his finger.

A tall woman wrapped in a buffalo robe rose from among the seated people. People sighed happily and called out a welcome to her.

Sun Woman turned to face the crowd. To Redbird she seemed calm and unruffled, even though she had hesitated about standing up.

"This woman brought her son to me and asked me to train him as a shaman," Owl Carver declared. "I did not want to, because he is not a pure Sauk. She said to me, only try him for a little time and see what he can be. I tried him for a little time and I saw something in him. I saw sleeping powers!"

The people murmured in wonder. Water Flows Fast and the woman with her whispered to each other, darting curious glances at Redbird, who carefully kept her face as impassive as Sun Woman's.

"I tested him and saw that his dreams could foretell the future, that he could send his spirit walking while his body lay still, that he could talk to the spirits in trees and birds. I saw that he had the power to be a shaman and more . . ."

Owl Carver paused and stared at them fiercely.

"And so I sent him up to the sacred cave, knowing that he might meet spirits so powerful that to encounter them destroys the souls of men.

"And Gray Cloud went into the sacred cave, and he met the great spirits, and he journeyed with them," Owl Carver cried. People gasped.

"He has met the White Bear. He has spoken with the Turtle, father of the Great River. He has brought back a message for Black Hawk," said Owl Carver. "The Turtle told Gray Cloud that Black Hawk might tell others as he saw fit." The rumble of voices rose at this, and then quieted as Owl Carver raised his medicine stick.

"After the Turtle created our Mother the Earth, he mated with her, and all tribes were born in her womb," Owl Carver said. "They lived there in a warm darkness, but they had to go forth and find their way out of our Mother. Then there came to our ancestors an elder spirit, the White Bear, who led them out the womb of our Mother.

"When they were in the light, they found themselves in the midst of a ring of fiery mountains. Our people are called Osaukawug, or Sauk, the People of the Place of Fire, because that fiery place is where we first walked in the world. There was nothing to eat. There was nothing around the people but stones and fire. And they were hungry and greatly afraid, and they were angry at the White Bear for leading them out of our Mother to this place.

"But the White Bear showed them a way through the fiery mountains and over many fields of snow and ice, until he brought our ancestors to this good land where there is fish and game, where the grasslands are green and the woods are full of berries and fruit. And our friends the Fox, the Yellow Earth People, came to be our allies and to unite with us. And the Turtle opened his heart and the Great River flowed forth. Our ancestors hunted and fished in the land where the Rock River flows into the Great River. On the Rock River they built our village of Saukenuk, where they wou!d dwell in the summer and their women would grow the Three Sisters, corn, beans and squash, in the fields around the village. And there at Saukenuk, as our ancestors died, they were buried.

"The White Bear told us we should spend our summers in that land east of the Great River. In the winter it should be our custom to cross to the west of the Great River and hunt here in the Ioway Country. And here by the Great River we Sauk, the People of the Place of Fire, have lived ever since."

Redbird felt warmth on her back through her buffalo robe. The sun had risen higher.

Owl Carver called out in his high voice of prophecy, "The White Bear has come again. He has led Gray Cloud on his spirit journey. Now Gray Cloud is a true shaman. He still must be trained to use his powers, but his powers no longer sleep. And in sign that he is a shaman with another self, he shall have a new name. Let him be known to all the people as White Bear!"

Redbird heard cries of assent from the people around her.

Owl Carver crossed his arms before his chest to show that he was finished speaking, and turned to Black Hawk.

"So let it be," said Black Hawk in his harsh, grating voice. "Earthmaker has willed that the British Band shall be blessed with a mighty new spirit walker. Let his name hereafter be White Bear."

If I could make a spirit journey, Redbird thought, *I too could stand before the people and advise them.*

She came to a sudden resolve. *One day I will.*

"Now you shall see our new shaman," Owl Carver declared. He stepped back and pulled aside the buffalo-fur curtain that covered the door of his wickiup.

A tall young man came out, stooping to pass through the doorway and then standing straight before the people. Redbird's heart beat faster, and she half rose to her feet.

His slender body, despite the cold, was bare to the waist. Redbird gasped as she saw what was on his chest.

Five long, deep scratches, side by side. The blood had dried and turned black. Five long black marks down the middle of his pale chest, running almost from the base of his neck to the bottom of his rib cage.

Cries of awe and wonder arose from the people. They had all seen such marks, sometimes scratched in the bark of trees, sometimes on the half-eaten bodies of animals found in the forest in summer.

The claw marks of a bear.

And now his name was White Bear. She whispered it to herself. Her eyes saw nothing but the shining slender form, and her ears heard nothing but the sound of his name.

4

Master of Victoire

Raoul threw himself into the lake, the giant Potawatomi chief Black Salmon roaring behind him. The water resisted his legs like molasses. Black Salmon seized Raoul's neck, cutting off his breath. Strangling, he was helpless as the Potawatomi dragged him back to shore.

The huge Indian's whip tore into Raoul's back. Raoul felt the skin ripping and the blood running. He was nothing but a helpless lump of bleeding flesh, paralyzed with pain.

Other Potawatomi had torn Helene's clothes off. The warriors danced around her on the beach as she cowered, white skin, shining blond hair, trying to cover herself.

The Indian bucks were naked, too, and flaunted their erect purple cocks, big as war clubs. One of them darted into the circle and bit a piece out of poor Helene's shoulder. Bright red blood flowed down her arm.

Raoul ran to save his sister. He broke away from Black Salmon and fought his way through the Potawatomi warriors around her. She lay on her back on the sand, twisting her body from side to side in pain. Hideous bite wounds all over her body lay open like red mouths silently screaming. One breast was covered with blood.

The Indians fell upon Raoul. They had their scalping knives out and they threw him down on the ground beside Helene. Black Salmon caught up with him and whipped him till every inch of his body was slashed. The redskins tore away the last few rags of Raoul's clothing.

A circle of grimacing dark faces painted with yellow and black stripes closed in on him. They bared sharp teeth like snarling dogs. They were going to eat him alive.

Raoul's father and Raoul's brother, Pierre, faces marble and calm, appeared in the midst of the Indians. They looked down at Raoul's agony. Just curious.

Raoul tried to cry out, "Papa! Pierre! Help us! They're killing us!"

No sound came out of his mouth but a useless little wheeze. He had lost his voice.

"You should not have angered them," Papa said.

One of the savages, holding high a long, thin skinning knife, seized Raoul's balls. He brought the knife down, slowly.

Raoul kept trying to scream at his father and brother. Again and again he forced air through his aching throat. Nothing came but a silly squeak. Then a groan, a little louder.

Pierre reached out a marble hand to him. Thank God!

Just as their fingers touched, Pierre jerked his hand away and disappeared.

Raoul felt the Indian's blade like cold fire slicing through the sac between his legs. At last he let out a full-throated scream.

"Raoul!"

His body cold and wet with sweat, he sat up in darkness. He felt arms clutching at him and fought them off.

"Raoul! Wake up."

Panting, he said his name in his mind. *I am Raoul François Philippe Charles de Marion.* He repeated it over and over again to himself.

He was sitting in bed in the dark, someone beside him. Not an Indian, and not his long-dead sister Helene. He gasped again and again, as if he had run a race.

He tried to pull his mind together. His heart was still pounding against the wall of his chest, his hands trembling, his skin ice cold. That terrible dream! He hadn't had it in a year or more.

"Lordy, what a nightmare you must have had! You did a right smart of hollerin'."

In the dim light seeping in through cracks in the shuttered window, Raoul saw a woman with long blond hair sitting up beside him, staring at him with pale blue eyes.

Clarissa. Clarissa Greenglove. He looked down at her. A warmth began to creep back into his body, rising first in his loins, as he remembered what they had done together the night before. Five times! No—six! Never before had he done it that many times in one night.

He was still panting in the aftermath of the horror, but the sight of her naked body was helping him get the dream out of his mind.

Never done it with such a good-looking woman.

She looked down at herself and drew up the sheet to cover her breasts.

"Don't do that," he said, and pulled the sheet down again, none too gently.

He began to rub her breast with the palm of his hand, feeling the nipple get bigger and harder. She closed her eyes and gave a little murmur of pleasure.

How she'd enjoyed it last night! She'd sighed and groaned and whimpered and screamed and licked him and bit him and twisted her body from side to side like a soul in perdition. Her frenzy had fired him up like never before. No wonder he'd been able to mount her so many times. And somewhere near the end of it all she'd sobbed into his shoulder for what seemed like an hour. He figured that was a tribute to what he had done to her. The sheets were still damp with their sweat, and the air in the little bedroom was thick with the musky odors of their secret juices.

But the redskins were still stalking in his brain, and he was still a little frightened. He didn't want to sit here in the dark.

"Light a candle, will you?" he said. "The striker's on that table."

She hesitated. "Can I get dressed first?"

"Hell no," he laughed. "What difference would that make after last night? I know you outside and in, Clarissa."

She giggled and got out of bed while he sat hugging his knees watching her.

"It's cold out here," she whined.

"Well, hurry and get that candle lit and get back in bed." The March air whistled in through chinks in the log walls and shutters, and even though the inn's chimney ran up through this room it didn't seem to help. He guessed that downstairs in the taproom someone had let the fire die.

Clarissa's pale, rounded shape as she moved through the shadows made him feel stronger by the moment. The women he'd had up to now—many of them right here in this bed—had been older and well-used, and he hadn't enjoyed the look of their bodies that much. Clarissa was just the right age, old enough to be filled out, young enough to be slender and firm. He guessed she must be sixteen or seventeen. Raoul had been bedding women since he was sixteen, for seven years now, and he'd never had a better night than this last one, with Clarissa.

Then why, after such a shining night, did he have *that* dream?

As the oil-soaked cotton ball flared up and Clarissa held a candle-wick to the flame, the nightmare came back to him, and out of the roiling images of red limbs and painted faces and blood and torn white bodies, he dragged the reason for what he had dreamed. When he remembered it, he slumped a little, his delight in waking up next to a pretty young woman wiped away.

He heard again the stunning, infuriating words that had tumbled out of Armand Perrault's bushy brown beard.

I overheard your brother, Monsieur Pierre, talking to your father this morning. He spoke of how he has always felt that he had abandoned his Sauk Indian wife and their son, when he came back here and married Madame Marie-Blanche. Now that he is a widower, he says, he wants to "do right by her and the boy."

This thing about having a Sauk woman and a son—Pierre had never said anything about that.

To call some Indian whore a *wife*!

My brother, the master of Victoire, a squaw-man! Father of a mongrel son!

Armand had remarked sourly to Raoul, "It seems Monsieur Pierre is a great one for doing *wrong* by women."

Raoul knew what he meant. He'd heard the rumor that after Marie-Blanche had died, Pierre, a little crazy in his grief, had taken Armand's wife to bed a time or two, to comfort himself.

But that was nothing compared to what Pierre was threatening now.

Indians living in our home! A squaw in the bed where Pierre slept with good Marie-Blanche!

How could Pierre do such a thing, after what the Indians had done to Helene? After Raoul had spent two years beaten and enslaved by Black Salmon? How could Papa permit it?

Clarissa turned, holding out before her a lighted white candle in a little pewter dish. She didn't seem so shy now about letting him see her naked. He let his eyes linger over her melon-shaped breasts, narrow waist, the brown puff of hair where her long legs joined her wide hips.

He'd often felt a hankering for Clarissa since he'd hired her father, Eli Greenglove, to help him run the trading post. But he'd thought it unwise to get mixed up with her. Eli was a dangerous man. Last night that hadn't seemed to matter.

After Armand had brought him the bad news, he'd turned to Kentucky whiskey—Old Kaintuck—and to Clarissa, dancing with her to Registre Bosquet's fiddle in the taproom to take his mind off this sudden insult Pierre had flung at him. Late in the evening he'd stumbled upstairs behind Clarissa to his bedroom in the inn, his hands up her skirts, feeling the satiny skin of her legs.

And then down on the bed, and—whiskey and all—six times!

But this morning his pleasure in her was spoiled by this treachery of Pierre's.

A squaw and a redskinned mongrel. Raoul wouldn't want Indians on the estate even as servants. Now Pierre was talking about these savages living in Victoire as part of the family.

He felt a sudden, stinging bite down near his rear end, under the covers. Angrily, he slapped at himself. Damned fleas and bedbugs. Levi Pope's wife made a piss-poor job of laundering the bedding for the inn.

If I had a wife I'd make sure she kept the bugs out of my sheets.

Clarissa set the candle down on the table and climbed back into bed. She ran her hand over his back.

She brought her face close to his, and he decided that, though he liked her arms and legs and hips and breasts, he didn't care for her weak chin, her washed-out blond hair and light blue eyes and the brown stain on one of her front teeth.

She said, "You've got scars all over your back. Somebody beat you. Your paw?"

"My papa?" The thought made him smile. "No, the old man's not that sort."

But he's the kind of man who might forget about me for a while. Who might let me be captured by Indians in 1812 and not manage to find me and ransom me till 1814.

The kind of man who might actually let my brother bring Indians into our home.

The scars. The scars reminded him every day of Fort Dearborn, August 1812. The memories left scars inside. Memories of being ten years old, cowering in an Indian encampment with the other white captives from Fort Dearborn while the warriors with their clubs and tomahawks approached, grinning.

It hadn't happened the way he dreamed it. The Potawatomi had pulled a man, an army private, to his feet, while he begged for his life, and dragged him over to the campfire. In an agony of terror Raoul had pressed against Helene, seated beside him on the ground. She put her arm around his shoulders and held him tight.

His sister Helene had seen her husband's throat cut and his scalp slashed away that very morning, when the Indians fell upon the retreating soldiers of Fort Dearborn and the civilians fleeing the tiny village called Checagou. But somehow Helene kept herself calm and strong after witnessing Henri's terrible death. Raoul knew it was for his sake.

Raoul had shut his eyes, and heard the clubs thud into the head and body of the soldier at the campfire, heard his screams, heard the silence of death when the screams stopped. A man's life had ended, just like that. Raoul trembled, hiding his face in Helene's side. Around him the other prisoners, men and women, sobbed and prayed.

The Indians took another soldier. They tied him to a stake and cut away bits of his flesh with the sharpened edges of clam shells. They worked at him for hours, until he bled to death.

The warriors came back for their next victim, sauntering among the prisoners, eyes aglow, painted faces like masks of monsters, stinking of the whiskey they'd been drinking all night. This time he was sure they were coming for him.

But they took Helene.

He had never forgotten her last words to him, spoken serenely as the Potawatomi seized her arms.

"I am going to join Henri. Pray to the Mother of God for me, Raoul."

The Indians dragged Helene into the woods. They took another woman as well.

The Potawatomi squaws, seated around a nearby campfire, chattered among themselves. They laughed whenever one of the women in the woods screamed. Raoul could not believe that any of those sounds were coming from his sister's throat.

The helpless white prisoners covered their faces and prayed and wept—and the men cursed.

He had hated himself for not trying to help Helene, but he was too frightened to move. Too frightened even to cry out. Brooding about it now, nearly thirteen years later, he told himself once again that if he'd tried to help Helene the Indians would have clubbed him to death. He told himself that he had been only ten years old. That did not make any difference to the shame he felt when he remembered that night. He should have gone to her. He should have fought to the death for her. He could never forgive himself.

Why didn't we all fight and die? Wouldn't it have been better to attack the Indians barehanded and be killed than to let that happen?

But neither could he forgive Papa and Pierre. His father and brother had left Raoul in Helene's care at Fort Dearborn, where her husband, Henri Vaillancourt, ran the trading post of Papa's Illinois Fur Company. When it became apparent that a second war between England and the United States was about to break out, Papa declared that land prices in Illinois were now as low as they would ever be, and he set off in search of likely land to buy for a family seat. Pierre had gone to the Sauk and Fox Indians on the Rock River to talk about trade and land purchases with them. Raoul had been happy enough to be left with Helene, who had been a mother to him as far back as he could remember. His own mother, Helene had gently explained to him, had gone to Heaven when he was born.

When Raoul heard no more screams from the woods, he knew Helene had gone to Heaven, too.

The next morning, as the Indians began the march back to their village, dragging their bound captives, Raoul had seen Helene's naked body, with stab wounds in a hundred places, lying face down, half submerged in Lake Michigan's surf. He saw a round, red patch on top of her head. Later he saw a brave who had tied to his belt a long hank of silver-blond hair, surely Helene's, a circular piece of skin dangling down.

The Indians had chosen not to kill Raoul, perhaps because at ten he was too young to be a satisfying victim, but old enough to work. And so Black Salmon had taken him for his slave. It made no difference whether he worked well or poorly; Black Salmon let not a day go by without whipping him, and fed him entrails and hominy grits. Only after Raoul had endured two years of slavery did his father, Elysée, find him and ransom him from Black Salmon.

And when Raoul was older he came to understand the full horror of what the Indians had done to Helene. They must have raped her over and over again. And he hated himself and Pierre and Elysée all the more for letting it happen.

But most of all he hated Indians.

Indians living at Victoire? He had to kill that notion of Pierre's right now. He would put on his clothes and saddle Banner and ride up to the château and set his father and brother straight.

But would they understand? Pierre, with his oh-so-tender conscience, who had lived with the damned Sauk and Fox for years and slept with one of their dirty squaws? Elysée, buried in his books? Raoul remembered their marble faces, as he had seen them in his dream.

They'd never understood him.

"Where did you get them scars?" Clarissa asked, interrupting his thoughts as she ran her fingers lightly over the hard ridges on his back.

Raoul told her about Black Salmon. "He liked whipping me even better than he liked whiskey. And when he got hold of whiskey he liked beating me even better."

"Poor Raoul! And such a little boy." Clarissa's face drew down with sympathy. "I'm powerful sorry for you." She pulled him to her.

He lowered his head to her breast and drew the nipple into his mouth, pressing it with his teeth. They lay back together, and he enjoyed the feel of the soft, feather-filled mattress and pillows billowing up around them.

By God, if he didn't feel himself getting big and hard to do it again. Proudly he threw back the sheet and let her see what he had for her. She smiled up at him, welcoming, her pale blue eyes shining in the candlelight.

He could use her to help him forget a little longer about Pierre and his redskin wife and son.

A sharp rapping at the bedroom door brought an end to his new surge of desire.

Clarissa gasped and pulled away from Raoul, dragging the bed-clothes toward her.

Raoul put his finger to his lips and called out, "Who's there?"

"It's Eli," said a voice through the door.

Raoul's heart began hammering again, as hard as when he woke from his nightmare.

"Oh, Lord, my paw," whispered Clarissa.

She sounded frightened—but only a *touch* frightened, and Raoul eyed her suspiciously. Her eyes were wide, like a child trying to deny mischief after being caught red-handed. Could Eli and his daughter have planned this?

Did Eli know that Clarissa was in here? Raoul had been too drunkenly careless to worry about who was watching when he took her upstairs last night.

Feeling a quaking in his stomach, Raoul walked over to the door. "What, Eli?" He hoped his voice sounded strong. He no longer took pleasure and pride in his nakedness.

"Thought you should know about something I heard over to the fur store, Raoul."

"Who's minding the furs now?" The place was full of bundles of pelts, beaver, badger, fox, raccoon, skunk. And valuable trade goods. Indian bucks walking in and out all the time, this time of year. Raoul had been happy to turn most of the fur trade work over to Eli. He couldn't stomach dealing with Indians.

"I left Otto Wegner there. Raoul, there's Injuns out digging in your lead mine."

At once Raoul forgot his fear of being caught with Clarissa. In its place he felt a rage so powerful his body seemed to fill up with boiling oil. Indians, more Indians! Worming their way into his family, and now stealing from his mine.

"Came looking for lead, did they?" he growled. "We'll give them lead. Round me up a couple of good marksmen and I'll meet you down in the taproom."

He heard no sound for a moment, and wondered what Eli was doing and thinking on the other side of the plank door.

Then Eli's voice came, "I'll be a-waiting for you, Raoul."

That gets him away from here for now.

But if Eli and Clarissa were planning to try to push him into a marriage, he knew he wouldn't get out of this that easy.

Pierre bringing an Indian wife and son home, Clarissa trying to trap him into a marriage—he began to feel as if he had walked into some kind of an ambush.

And Indians at the mine.

He eyed Clarissa, who sat with a pillow between her bare back and the rough-hewn log wall, sheet and blanket pulled up to her shoulders. He walked over to her to make sure he could not be heard from outside.

"I'm going to have to ride out to the mine, and I'll be taking your father with me," he said, keeping his voice soft. "Wait till you hear us ride away, then get out of here. And make sure nobody sees you."

She was still wide-eyed. "Oh, Raoul, if he was to catch me with you he'd beat me worse'n that Injun ever beat you."

Raoul leaned forward and put his hand, gently but firmly, on her throat. "If he ever finds out from you that you and I were together," he said softly, "I'll beat you even worse than that."

In the taproom on the first floor of the inn, Eli, a short, skinny man whose thinning blond hair was turning gray, gave no sign of knowing that Clarissa was in the room upstairs. Where did he think she was? Raoul wondered. Maybe he knew, but was biding his time.

"Winnebago with a bundle of beaver pelts come in this morning," Eli said. "Said that for an extra cupful of whiskey he'd tell me a thing I might like to know. I obliged, and he told me riding over here yesterday he'd seen smoke rising from the prairie. He went for a look-see and it was three Sauk bucks carrying galena out of the mine and smelting it down."

Eli had rounded up three big men to ride out with Raoul. Levi Pope, a tall, hatchet-faced Sucker, an Illinois man, carried a Kentucky rifle that almost came up to his shoulder. Otto Wegner, a veteran of the army of the King of Prussia, was six foot three with broad shoulders. He wore his brown mustache thick and let it grow back over his cheeks to join his sideburns. Hodge Hode, like Eli, was a Puke, a Missourian. Huge as a grizzly bear, he dressed in fringed buckskins. Under his coonskin cap red hair, wild and knotted, hung down to his shoulders, and his red beard hid three quarters of his face. Besides their long rifles, Eli, Levi, Hodge and Otto had pistols stuck through their belts, powder horns slung over their shoulders, hunting knives sheathed in pockets in the front of their buckskin shirts.

Raoul let them each have a glass of whiskey, his good whiskey, Old Kaintuck from a canvas-wrapped stone jug, not the terrible-tasting corn liquor he dispensed from the barrel in the taproom. Then the five of them went out to mount their horses in the courtyard of the trading post. Raoul rode his chestnut stallion, Banner.

My domain, Raoul thought proudly, as he looked around. Surrounding the trading post was a palisade twenty feet high made of logs set vertically, with a catwalk running all around it and a guard tower in each corner. From a pole atop the southwest tower flew the flag of the United States, thirteen stripes and twenty-four stars, and below it the flag of the de Marions' Illinois Fur Company, an arrow and a musket crossing behind a beaver pelt.

Dominating the buildings inside the palisade was a blockhouse, limestone at ground level, with an overhanging second story of logs and rifle slits all around. Raoul had built it to fortify the trading post against his memories of Checagou. Pierre and Papa might have thought it foolish expense and effort, but where had they been when he needed them?

Near the east side of the blockhouse was the inn they'd just left, a log house, food and drink on the ground floor and lodgings above. On the west side, the fur store. Over in the northwest corner was the magazine, a windowless cube of limestone blocks, surrounded by its own little palisade the height of a man. Here were stored the bags and barrels of gunpowder that passed through the trading post.

They rode out through the gateway, arched over by the name DE MARION, formed out of small bits of log by Raoul's brother-in-law, Frank Hopkins, carpenter and printer. Raoul glanced down at the town of Victor, built on the steep slope below the trading post. From here he could see mostly half-log roofs and clay-lined log chimneys following the road that zigzagged across the face of the bluff. The houses all faced west, with their backs to the limestone slope. North and south from the base of the bluff stretched miles of bottomland along the Mississippi River. The spring floods that left the bottom some of the richest farmland in the world also made it necessary to build almost everything on the bluff above the high-water line.

Raoul pulled Banner's head around and led his little troop at a trot along the ridge that ran east. Now Victoire came into view, the château his father and brother had built on the edge of the prairie, its first floor, like that of the blockhouse, of stone, its upper two stories of square-hewn timber. Some day, he thought, as he rode past the hill crowned by the great house, he would enter Victoire as master.

They rode on, passing big log barns and animal sheds Raoul had helped build. They followed a narrow trail through fields planted in corn and wheat, through orchards, the trees as yet only a little higher than a man but already yielding apples and peaches. Farther out still, cattle and horses grazed on grassland that rolled eastward like the waves of the ocean.

Five miles from the Mississippi they came to the boundary stone with an M carved on it that marked Victoire's easternmost extent. From there Raoul could see, a good ten miles or more away, the sign of the Indians, a long finger of gray smoke leaning northeast-ward among the fluffy white clouds. The mine entrance was at the bottom of a ravine carved in the prairie by the Peach River, and the smoke doubtless meant the Indians were smelting lead.

After a long ride they reached the little river. The five men reined up and tethered their horses downwind from the smoke; an Indian, it was said, had a sense of smell as keen as a dog's. Raoul led his men to the edge of the ravine.

They walked quietly along the ravine until they sighted Indians down at the bottom. Sauk or Fox, Raoul saw, recognizing their shaven heads with tufts of hair in the center. One of the bucks was standing at the mine entrance holding a skin sack that appeared to be full of chunks of galena, lead ore. The other two were adding logs to the smelter's fire. Their six horses—three for riding and three for carrying lead—were standing at the edge of the river about ten feet from the smelter.

The Indians' smelter was simply a square pit dug in the hillside, lined with rocks at the bottom and filled with logs and brushwood. They were melting down the galena, letting it flow through the rocks into a slanting trench that led to a square mold dug in the earth. Raoul counted five pigs of lead already formed, cooled and stacked

beside the mold. They'd probably been at this ever since the end of
winter, thinking the mine was so far from town that no white man
would notice.

Lead was selling at seventeen dollars per thousand pounds at the
pit head up north in Galena, the new boom town named for the
ore, and if these Indians had been working since the snow melted,
they might have robbed Raoul of as much as two hundred dollars.

Raoul thought he recognized the two bucks at the smelter. Last
fall they had come to him as he was bossing the crew he'd put to
work expanding the mine before he shut it down for the winter.
The Indians had claimed it was their mine. He had told them to be
off, and when they hadn't moved quickly enough, he and his men
had cocked their flintlocks. Should have killed them then.

Raoul gripped the gilded butt of the cap-and-ball pistol that hung
at his waist and slid it out of its holster.

"Get them!" he called, standing up suddenly. He stretched out
his arm, sighted along the barrel of his pistol and fired at the nearer
Indian standing by the smelter.

Four rifles went off at once. Raoul was enveloped in the bitter
smell of gunpowder and a cloud of smoke. The Indian Raoul had
aimed at jerked, fell to his knees, then collapsed face forward beside
the smelter. The other one at the smelter ran for his horse and
leaped on its back. They must have all aimed at the same one, Raoul
thought, cursing himself for not thinking of pointing out targets for
each man.

The third Indian had disappeared. The skin sack of galena lay
beside the mine entrance.

"Dammit," said Raoul. "If that redskin on the horse gets away
there'll be raiding parties coming here. Whoever digs here'll have to
have eyes in the back of his head."

"I'll put an eye in the back of *his* head," said Eli as he poured
powder from his measure down the muzzle of his rifle. He grinned
at Raoul—two upper front teeth missing and one lower. Did he
know about Clarissa? Raoul still couldn't tell.

The other men were also reloading. Raoul pushed powder and
shot down the muzzle of his pistol, then took a percussion cap out
of a pouch at his belt and pressed it onto the nipple in the breach.
By the time he was ready to fire, the Indian was galloping down the
riverbed and had disappeared around a bend.

Hodge Hode, Levi Pope and Otto Wegner ran for their horses. Eli stayed where he was, smiling down at the rifle in his hands as if he were holding a baby.

"If we all chase after the one on horseback," Eli said, "the one that's hiding will run off in the other direction."

"True enough," said Raoul. By this time Hodge, Levi and Otto had ridden off.

"Another thing," Eli said. "Our boys is on the wrong side of the ravine. When the Injun comes out, he'll come out on the south side. By the time they ride down and in, and up and out again, he'll be a mile away."

"So what do we do?" asked Raoul.

"It's all flat land hereabouts."

Before Raoul could demand an explanation of that, he saw the fleeing Indian on his mount scramble out of the ravine and ride southward, just as Eli had predicted. Raoul glanced at his men as they came to a halt, puzzlement showing in their gestures. Hodge fired at the Indian, who rode on unharmed. Though Raoul would not have known what else to do, he despised his two men for their uselessness.

Soon the Indian, riding hell-bent south, was a tiny dark silhouette against the yellow prairie. Eli raised the barrel of his Kentucky long rifle. It was an impossible shot, Raoul thought, but he said nothing. Eli seemed to be aiming slightly high, not straight at the redskin. Raoul heard the Puke suck in a deep breath through his missing front teeth.

The rifle boomed. The muzzle flash made Raoul blink, and a cloud of blue-white smoke drifted across the canyon.

A long time seemed to pass with nothing happening. But maybe it was only a heartbeat or two. Then the dark, distant figure threw up his arms and toppled sideways from his horse. The horse kept running and was gone over the horizon a moment later.

"Right through his noodle," Eli said. "I couldn't of made that shot if he hadn't been riding due south. Too hard to get a lead on him *and* arch the bullet just right."

Eli made it seem just a simple matter of skill, but Raoul felt as if he had just seen a miracle.

The faces of the other men, as they climbed down from their horses, showed as much awe as Raoul felt.

"Pretty good shooting, for a Puke," said Levi Pope.

"Better'n any Sucker could do," Eli returned genially.

Raoul said, "Otto, go get that Indian's body and bring it back here."

Otto Wegner turned at once to remount his horse. Raoul liked the way the Prussian obeyed every order instantly.

But Hodge Hode glowered at Raoul. "Waste of time. Coyotes and buzzards have a taste for Injun meat."

Annoyed at being questioned, Raoul said, "I don't want anybody to know what happened to these redskins."

As Otto rode off, Eli, pointing to the mine entrance, said, "We got one still alive. At least one."

"I'll take care of him," said Raoul.

Eli, Hodge and Levi looked at him, surprised.

Eli's fine shot had not only awed him; he felt it, uneasily, as a challenge. The law was absent in Smith County, which was the way Raoul liked it. Gave an edge to a man who could handle a rifle as well as Eli. But now, to make sure his own word remained the closest thing to law in these parts, Raoul felt he had to equal Eli's accomplishment.

He checked the load in his pistol. He gripped the hilt of the thirteen-inch knife at his belt and loosened it in its sheath. A blacksmith in St. Louis had made it for him, assuring him it was an exact replica of the knife designed a couple of years ago by the famed Arkansas frontiersman Jim Bowie.

Raoul's mouth was dry. His heart was beating so hard he thought his men must be able to see his woollen coat quivering. His hands were cold and sweaty.

"Ain't but one way out of that mine, is there?" said Eli. "If we go in four abreast he can't get past us, and it's a hell of a sight safer."

"I'll take care of him," Raoul repeated. Every word Eli said against his going into the mine alone made him even more determined to do it. He needed to keep Eli in line, especially if it should turn out that Eli knew about him and Clarissa.

"He might have a rifle," said Eli. "Might shoot you when you walk in there."

"If we all go in, one of you might get shot," said Raoul. "This is my property."

And fighting for it will make it more truly my property than any government grant could.

But that Indian in there—what was he armed with? Rifle, knife, bow, tomahawk? How strong was he, how fast, how skilled in fighting hand to hand?

I'm a fool to put myself through this.

"Could be more'n one in there," said Eli.

Raoul felt the blood run hot through his veins as he thought of Pierre's bastard son, of Black Salmon, of the Potawatomi who raped and murdered Helene. His men had killed two Indians today, but there was a third waiting in that mine, and Raoul de Marion meant to be the death of him.

Ignoring Eli's warnings, he moved toward the black square of the mine entrance.

He walked slowly, pistol at waist level. He needed his knife out, too, he decided. Even though he was right-handed, it would be better to have a second weapon ready than have his left hand empty. He drew his knife, taking heart from its well-balanced feel.

He stepped under the logs he'd set last fall to brace the entrance. Should he light a candle? No, that would make him an even better target. He tried to pierce the blackness with his eyes; it was thick as a wool curtain.

This was foolish, he thought. If they all went in together, the way Eli said, a couple of men could carry candles, and they could flush out the Indian in no time. This way, he was going to get himself killed. If the Indian had a rifle, Raoul was dead for sure. He felt an urge to back out and call the others to help him. He stood there a moment, legs trembling.

No. He had to kill his Indian by himself. He had to show Eli and the rest.

He forced his feet to slide forward as silently as he could manage. His hesitation had given his eyes a chance to get used to the dark. He tried to remember the layout of the mine. In the dim light from the entrance he made out the downward slope of the long tunnel. About twenty feet in, another tunnel branched off to his left. His eyes ached as they tried to find the enemy hiding somewhere ahead of him.

He could see nothing but black walls lined with logs to brace the ceiling, a floor littered with chunks of rock. As he moved forward, the tunnel got narrower, the ceiling lower. He could almost feel the weight of the rock and earth above him; these logs could suddenly give way and the prairie come down on him like a boot on a bug. He began to be more afraid of the mine than he was of the hidden Indian.

He came to the branch tunnel and peered into it.

With a high-pitched shriek the Indian sprang at him.

Raoul glimpsed a steel tomahawk edge coming at his head. He jerked the pistol's trigger and jabbed with the knife in his left hand to parry the axe blade.

The blast of the pistol deafened Raoul, and in the momentary blaze of light he saw the face of a young Indian, distorted with anger and fear.

It was a face he hated on sight—dark skin, narrow black eyes, flat but for a beak of a nose, shaven skull. A face like those in his nightmares. It stayed vivid in his mind's eye when the flash of light was gone.

The Indian's war whoop ended in a cry of pain.

Got the sonofabitch! Raoul exulted. He'd been holding his pistol low, must have hit the Indian in the gut.

The flash had temporarily blinded him, but reflexes honed in dozens of riverfront brawls took over. He jammed his pistol into its holster and switched the knife to his right hand. Every fiber of him hungered to kill. He lunged forward, knife straight out in front of him. He could feel his lips stretching in a grin.

The knife hit something solid, yet yielding. With a yell of triumph he drove the point in, was rewarded with a scream of agony. He was beginning to see again. The shadow facing him lifted the tomahawk. Raoul jerked the knife free and swung; it chunked into the Indian's arm like a meat cleaver. He heard the tomahawk clang on the rock floor.

Raoul threw himself on the Indian, stabbing, stabbing. His enemy's body, smaller and lighter than his, crumpled under his weight. The fingers of his left hand dug into smooth skin and hard muscle. He felt hands pushing against him, but their efforts were weak, the struggles of a dying creature. The cries and groans of pain made him eager to hurt the Indian more. It was too dark to see where his knife was going in, but he brought it down again and again. His hands felt wet. Some of his thrusts sank deep, others were stopped by bone.

A pulse pounded in his brain. It did not matter that he was fighting in the dark; fury blinded him anyway. He forgot everything but the knife in his hand and the soft, bloody body under him. He screamed with rage and triumph, drowning out the agonized shrieks of his enemy.

After a while, no more cries. The body under him did not move. Raoul lay on top of the Indian, panting.

He began to think again. Carefully he slid his hand over the Indian's chest, the buckskin shirt slippery with warm blood. No heartbeat, no lifting of lungs.

By God, I did it, I killed him! He felt as if rockets were going off in his head, and he laughed aloud. He'd fought for his mine and spilled his enemy's blood to make it his own.

No goddamned Indian is ever going to steal what belongs to me.

He climbed to his feet. His knees were shaking violently under him.

His head ached so badly he felt as if his eyes were being pushed out of his skull. He realized that in the fight he'd completely lost control of himself. He'd become a wild thing, a creature without a mind. It had happened to him several times before, in fights that had ended with his killing a man.

Thoughts of triumph that he had killed his enemy, of terror at the realization that this fight could have gone the other way, chased each other around in his brain, but he felt even more alive and happier than he had last night with Clarissa.

Sudden light dazzled him. An arrow of fear shot through him. More Indians?

"Raoul!" It was Eli Greenglove's voice.

His eyes adjusted, and he could see Eli, Hodge Hode and Levi Pope standing at the entrance to the side tunnel. They looked at the body at his feet and the bloody knife in his hand, and then up at him and their eyes were wide and their lips parted.

Those looks are worth as much to me as this whole mine.

"You really chopped him into mincemeat," Eli said. "I'll have to get me one of them Arkansas toothpicks."

"Get the other two bodies in here," Raoul said, making an effort to keep his voice steady. "We'll find some place to bury them."

"Better search the whole mine, make sure there's no more redskins," said Eli.

Raoul agreed, but he felt certain this one he'd killed was the only one in the mine. He looked down at the dead face. The Indian wasn't much more than fifteen or sixteen years old. Good, he thought. Hadn't had long enough to do much harm.

But why, Raoul wondered, had this young buck thrown his life away attacking him near the entrance to the mine? He'd have had more of a chance of escaping if he'd hidden deeper.

Maybe he'd figured there was at least a little light to see and fight by near the entrance. If he'd gotten Raoul, then somehow managed to get away, he'd probably have claimed the right to wear a brave's feather.

The thought of himself lying dead in the dark and his scalp hanging on a pole in front of a lodge down at Saukenuk made Raoul shudder.

But it was Raoul who'd won his feather. No Indian would ever kill Raoul de Marion.

And any redskin sluts, and any mongrel bastards, that showed their face around Victoire would have to deal with a man who killed Indians as easily as he killed any other sort of vermin.

Time to have it out with Pierre.

Pierre wanted to weep as he saw what was about to happen. He rushed forward and thrust out his hand to stop Raoul.

"Not the vase!" he cried. Maman had loved it so.

Raoul was too close to the mantel for Pierre to reach him in time. He got to it in two strides and, just as Pierre had expected, seized the vase that had been in the family for four generations, had stood on the mantel ever since they built this château.

"Raoul!" Papa cried. "Think what you are doing!"

Raoul turned, holding the vase high over his head. He fixed Pierre with the wide-eyed stare of a madman. His teeth flashed under his black mustache in a grimace of fury.

He dashed the vase to the flagstone floor. The white egg shape vanished with a hollow crack, and shards scattered, some hitting Raoul's boots, others flying into the huge stone hearth.

A sudden silence filled the great hall of Victoire. Pierre felt as if his heart had broken with the vase.

You killed Maman, he wanted to cry out, *now you would kill the memory of her.*

But he held his tongue and hated himself for even thinking what he had almost said. What an evil thought! How could he blame Raoul because Maman died giving birth to him?

Think what you are doing! Papa had cried. That was precisely what Raoul never did. Thought was for afterward, for escaping the consequences of his actions. Now he had worked himself into a rage, lost all governing of himself, because, somehow, he had heard about Sun Woman and Gray Cloud.

Pierre had to try to win Raoul over, to find a way to break through the anger that divided him from his younger brother. Raoul had to be persuaded that it was only right that Sun Woman and the boy be brought here to Victoire. If Raoul did not accept that, his rage would tear their family apart.

But how, in one afternoon, batter down a wall that had been building over the past dozen years?

Pierre realized that he was still standing with his hand held out to Raoul. He lowered it slowly, feeling his shoulders slump at the same time. He had been reading with Papa when Raoul came in. Now he took off his spectacles, put them in the silver case that hung from his neck by a velvet cord and dropped the case in his vest pocket.

Elysée de Marion clutched the arms of his leather wing chair with clawlike hands, half rising from it. Raoul stood staring at the two of them, panting and trembling.

Elysée said quietly, "Why did you do that, Raoul?"

"To make you listen." Raoul's voice was deep and strong, and it resounded powerfully against the beamed ceiling and stone walls of the great hall. But in its tones Pierre heard the screams of that hysterical boy whose tantrums and nightmares, after they'd finally succeeded in ransoming him from the Potawatomi, had wrenched the hearts of the whole household and renewed their grief over the loss of Helene.

But now that painfully thin, frightened child was a broad-shouldered man over six feet tall with a knife as big as a broadsword and a pistol strapped to his waist. A very dangerous man. A man who, they said, had killed half a dozen or more opponents in fights up and down the Mississippi.

"We have been listening," Elysée said.

"Pierre hasn't," Raoul said resentfully. "*You* tell him, Papa. Tell him he'd better leave his damned squaw in the woods where she belongs."

Damned squaw. The words pierced Pierre's chest like arrows.

Elysée sat back down in his wing chair and stroked his jaw. He looked like an old turkey cock, with fierce eyes, a hooked nose and a long, wrinkled neck. The leather-bound copy of Montaigne's essays that had been lying in his lap had slipped to the floor to join newspapers piled around his feet like autumn leaves, a mixture of local papers like Frank Hopkin's *Victor Visitor*, and the Galena *Miners Journal*, months-old papers from the East—the *New York Evening Post*, the *Boston Evening Transcript*, the *National Intelligencer* from Washington City, the even older copies of *Mercure de France* from Paris.

"Come here, both of you," Elysée sighed.

Hoping his father could reconcile them where he had failed so dismally, Pierre went to stand before Elysée's chair. After a moment's hesitation Raoul approached too. But Pierre saw that he was pointedly keeping more than an arm's-length distance between the two of them.

Elysée said, "That's better. I can't see you when you stand far from me. These eyes are good for very little but reading, and when I can no longer read, I will shoot myself. And if I cannot see well enough to load the pistol, one of you must do it for me."

As he often did, Elysée was attempting to use humor to put out the fire. Pierre glanced at Raoul to see if their father had drawn a smile from him. But Raoul stood with arms folded across his chest, his mouth hidden under his black mustache, his eyes narrowed. Except when he smiled—and today he was far from any smiling—the mustache made him look perpetually angry.

"Raoul," Elysée said. "Be assured that we are listening to you. Tell us what has driven you to destroy one of our family treasures."

"Just because Pierre soiled himself with a squaw," Raoul demanded, "do we have to live with what came of it?"

Pierre felt his face burn. He wanted to slap Raoul.

My life with Sun Woman was as honorable as my life with Marie-Blanche.

He forced himself to control his temper. If he became as angry as Raoul was, this day would surely be the ruin of the house of de Marion.

Pierre felt a sudden twinge of pain in his belly. He fought down an urge to rub himself there. He wanted no one to know about his illness. Worse than the pain was the fear it brought on, the chilling suspicion that he was a dying man.

Fearfully he wondered what death would be like. Though Père Isaac said such notions were foolish, he could not help seeing God the Father as an enormous white-bearded judge, seated among the clouds. And what would the Father's sentence be if Pierre de Marion turned his back on a wife and a son?

He wished he could tell Raoul that he thought he was dying. Then perhaps his brother would understand why he had to do his duty to Sun Woman and the boy. But he feared that if Raoul was aware of his weakness, he would try to take over the whole estate at once.

Praying that his brother would understand, he said, "Ever since Marie-Blanche died, I have been thinking of Sun Woman. After five years of life together, I left her and our little son. Lately I have been seeing her and my son, Gray Cloud, in dreams. I know God wants me to make amends to them."

Pierre felt sweat break out on his forehead and upper lip. Why must Raoul stir up such turmoil with his hatred? Couldn't Raoul understand that not all red people were like the ones he had encountered? Pierre saw Sun Woman in his mind, so strong and wise, holding the hand of their grave, brown-eyed boy. How beautiful they were.

Elysée said, "I do not believe that Le Bon Dieu announces his intentions in dreams, Pierre."

Always the cynic. Papa had read too much Voltaire.

Elysée turned to Raoul. "But, Raoul, it does seem simple justice, what Pierre wants to do."

"What about justice for me?" Raoul came back. "Isn't this my home as much as Pierre's?"

Stung by Raoul's bluster, Pierre said, "Raoul, you live more at your trading post than you do in this home."

To Pierre's surprise, Raoul's face reddened, making Pierre wonder what, exactly, Raoul was doing at the trading post. It had seemed natural that he would spend most of his time there, since Papa had given him the Illinois Fur Company when he divided his property between the two of them. But perhaps it was not only work that kept Raoul at the trading post night after night. A woman? Pierre found himself hoping it might be. A woman could be good for Raoul, civilize him a bit.

He had slept there last night. How, then, could he have learned about Pierre's plans for Sun Woman and Gray Cloud?

Is someone in our household spying on me?

Pierre turned to Raoul. "How did you learn about this? I was going to tell you, but you found out before I could."

Pierre took some small satisfaction in seeing Raoul's cheeks flush a deeper red, in seeing his hesitation. He had come storming in here unprepared to explain just how he knew about Pierre's plans.

Raoul said, "I overheard you and Papa talking about it."

"Absurd! We did not speak of this till this morning. You were not here."

Could Armand have heard, and told Raoul?

Armand must certainly know about Marchette, Pierre thought. But he knew Armand would never directly attack him. Armand's ancestors had come to America when this part of the country was still New France, and such people retained a feudal outlook. The poor fellow doubtless considered him far superior in birth and breeding. But he was capable of seeking some kind of revenge, such as turning Raoul against him.

Pierre opened his mouth to chide Raoul for setting one of the servants to spy on him, but he closed it again when he saw the look of self-righteous reproach in Raoul's face.

His brother felt betrayed too. He had never stopped feeling betrayed since the massacre at Checagou. Then how could Pierre expect him to be reconciled to what must be done now?

Perhaps it would be best to leave Sun Woman and Gray Cloud where they were. He could just send them gifts. Doubtless they were content. His own years with the Sauk and Fox had shown him what a good life they had, so simple, so closely attuned to Nature, so constantly aware of the things of the spirit. Those years had been the happiest of his life.

No, sending gifts from afar would not be enough. It would be as if he was hiding his Indian wife and son away, concealing his sin in the wilderness. As he had been doing all these years, to his shame. The boy, Gray Cloud, was flesh of his flesh, the only child he had in the world. He was a de Marion as much as he was a Sauk Indian.

He had a right to come here and to know what his heritage was. He had a right to know his father, in the time his father had left to him.

I cannot face God and tell Him I turned my back on my son.

And that beautiful Sauk way of life, what a fragile thing it was! Powers were massing, Pierre knew, to drive them from their homeland, to force them to choose—exile in the Great American Desert, or annihilation. Knowledge might help Gray Cloud meet that threat.

From the depths of his chair Elysée said, "Pierre, it is quite obvious what is at the bottom of this. It is distasteful to speak of wills and inheritances, but it is best to be candid. Raoul is afraid that you will marry this Indian woman and make her son your heir in place of him. Can you set his mind at rest?"

Pierre stared at Raoul. Ten years ago, on the day of Pierre's wedding to Marie-Blanche Gagner, Papa announced that he was getting on in years and was transferring ownership of the de Marion estate to Pierre, the older of his sons. This January, consumption had taken poor, frail Marie-Blanche, still childless. The place of Raoul, fourteen years younger than Pierre, in the line of inheritance was now a certainty.

Surely Raoul could not be afraid that Pierre would take a Sauk Indian boy who knew no other life but woodland and make him heir to the de Marion fortune. The notion was so bizarre that it had never even crossed Pierre's mind. Papa, sitting in his chair by the fire day after day, reading, reading, would sometimes entertain the most ridiculous fantasies.

Pierre observed that Raoul looked equally startled.

Then Pierre saw Raoul's expression change from surprise to dawning anger. Papa had inadvertently given Raoul a new reason to be angry.

Hoping to pluck out the suspicion before it took root, Pierre quickly said, "My God, Raoul, I have no intention of changing my will. The boy, who is called Gray Cloud, is my natural son, that is all. Since I have no legitimate children, you are my heir. Surely you see that."

Raoul's black mustache drew back from his teeth. "What I don't see, brother of mine, is why in hell you couldn't get a proper son in almost ten years of marriage with Marie-Blanche. That squaw use you up?"

Again Pierre felt like striking Raoul. His face grew hot.

Elysée asked, "How old would this—Gray Cloud—be?"

Pierre frowned, subtracting dates. "He was born in 1810. So he would have just turned fifteen." He turned again to Raoul. Perhaps knowing what he really did have in mind for Gray Cloud would calm his brother somewhat.

He said, "Père Isaac, the Jesuit, visits the British Band regularly. I make offerings to the Jesuit mission in Kaskaskia, and I've asked him to teach the boy a little English, some elementary letters and ciphering. Now I want to see Gray Cloud for myself. See what sort of person he has become. And I want him to know me. And, if I thought he could benefit from it, I might help him to be educated. I might send him to that secondary school in New York where our cousin Emilie's husband is headmaster."

"Educate him so he can take over here?" Raoul demanded, and Pierre's heart sank. Perhaps he should not have said anything about educating the boy. He had momentarily forgotten what a disaster Raoul's year in New York had been, what with whores, drink, money thrown away at cards, brawls with street toughs and the police. The effort to educate Raoul had ended when he beat his Latin teacher so badly the man was in New York Hospital for a month. It had cost Papa a fortune to persuade the teacher not to press charges. Of course Raoul would be insulted at the suggestions that a savage Indian boy might succeed where he had disgraced himself.

"No, Raoul." Pierre shook his head vigorously. "At the most, I might want his mother and him to have a small bequest. Not even as much as will go to Nicole. So little you would never miss it. Surely you would not let greed for wealth and property come between us."

"I came here today to protect our family honor, and you call me greedy!" Raoul's broad chest heaved.

"What I propose *is* honorable!"

"How could you consider it honorable to make Indians part of our family after what they did to us?"

It hurt Pierre to call those awful memories to mind. Yes, perhaps if he had been there and suffered as Raoul had, and had seen Helene raped and murdered, he might hate Indians as his brother did.

Pierre said, "Raoul, when I was with Sun Woman I knew nothing of what happened to Helene and you. Once the war broke out in 1812 I was in effect a prisoner and had no word from the white world. The Sauk held me for three years from the start of the war. And then, when I found out—why do you think I left Sun Woman and Gray Cloud? And never returned, only sent messages through the priest, never tried to see them? It was because after I learned about Helene—about what they did to you—I, even *I*, Raoul, could not be with Indians anymore. It has taken all these years before I could face them again."

Elysée said with a frown, "Raoul, you keep mentioning that this woman and her child whom your brother wishes to help are Indians, as if that in itself made them intolerable. Now, I could quite agree, if they were Englishmen—"

Raoul spoke in a low, steady growl. "Being Indians does make them intolerable. They're animals."

Pierre felt anger growing inside him. He was trying to understand Raoul, but Raoul's insults were becoming more provocation than he could endure.

"Animals?" said Elysée incredulously. "Come now, Raoul. Surely you do not believe that. The red people are as human as we are."

Raoul laughed bitterly. "Sure, you'd have to say they're human. Otherwise Pierre's mating with one of them would be like a half-witted farmer mounting one of his sheep."

Something exploded in Pierre's brain and he heard his own cry of anguish as if from a long way off. He felt tears running from eyes blinded with fury.

And when his eyes cleared, all he could see was Raoul's sneer. He burned to smash his fist into those so-white teeth under that black mustache, silence that filthy tongue. He lunged forward, fist drawn back.

Raoul caught his arm in an iron grip, but the force of Pierre's rush threw his brother back against the great chimney. Pierre reached to grab Raoul's neck and slam his head against the stone.

"Stop!" Elysée cried.

The old man stood up more quickly than Pierre had seen him do in years and pushed himself between them.

Suddenly afraid that his father might be hurt, Pierre forced himself to let go of Raoul. Every muscle in his body went rigid, and he trembled from head to foot.

"You must control yourselves," Elysée said. "Pierre, you raised your hand against your brother."

Pierre took a step backward, still shaking. How could this father reproach *him*, after what Raoul had just said?

The voice of Reason, Pierre thought bitterly. *He does not know there are some feelings that cannot be reasoned with.*

Pierre realized that he was still crying. Raoul, having let go of his arm, was looking at him with disgust.

"I loved Sun Woman," Pierre stammered. "For him to speak of her so—to speak so of our love—"

"Surely," Elysée said, "Raoul spoke in the heat of anger."

"I don't take back a word," Raoul said in a hard, flat voice.

But, though it was hard to read the features behind that fierce black mustache, Pierre thought he saw uncertainty in Raoul's face. As if Raoul finally understood that he had gone too far.

He drove me to try to hit him. He's never pushed me that far before.

Perhaps, Pierre thought, Raoul would now apologize. Appalled at his own words, he might seek to be reconciled.

I will make no more overtures. He meets every attempt with insults.

Pierre waited. He could see Raoul struggling within himself. Perhaps Papa's suggestion that he might lose his inheritance had made him realize what consequences a rift between them could have.

Of course, I would never disinherit Raoul. There's no one else who could manage the estate after I die. And I may be gone sooner than anyone expects.

Pierre saw Raoul's broad chest swell as he took a deep breath. Now, thought Pierre, surely Raoul was going to apologize and ask forgiveness, and they would work out some way that Sun Woman and Gray Cloud could be brought here without stirring up old hatreds.

Raoul said, "Don't bring Indians into this house, Pierre, I warn you. If any Indian tries to claim he's a member of my family, I'll make him wish he had never been born at all."

The pain that might one day kill him sank its teeth deep into his guts. Raoul's words seared him like a branding iron. He felt his shoulders sag.

Raoul turned his back on his brother and his father, and the clump of his hard leather boot heels echoed through the great hall.

"Raoul!" Elysée cried. He held his hand outstretched, as Pierre had when Raoul was about to smash the Limoges vase.

Looking down at those glistening white shards scattered over the flagstones, Pierre wondered what would happen when Raoul inherited the de Marion fortune. Would he destroy it in one of his rages as he had this beautiful object that had been part of the family treasure? Or would he use its power as he used his fists and pistol and knife, to destroy others?

The de Marion fortune . . . Once it had been a huge tract of land in northeastern France dominated by the château of the Counts de Marion, held by them so long that no one knew when or how they first obtained it. Just as the origin of the de Marions themselves was something of a mystery.

Converted into gold, the de Marion fortune had sailed, with Elysée, the last Count de Marion, his countess and his children, across the Atlantic. Elysée, in the early 1780s, had foreseen the bloody upheaval that would sweep away the king and the nobility of France. He had made a friend of the American ambassador to France, Thomas Jefferson, and had thought much about Jefferson's new nation. Their revolution was over and done with. The de Marion fortune might thrive in those United States.

And on the American prairie the de Marion fortune had purchased a vast new estate and built a new château.

Elysée sighed and took a step toward his chair. Pierre turned the chair toward the fire so that its wings would gather in the warmth of the small fire and hold it around his father's body.

"Would you consider not bringing this woman and this boy here?" Elysée said as he sat down. "To keep the peace in our family?"

Pierre hesitated. For ten years Sun Woman and Gray Cloud had lived in their world, and he in his. Why provoke so much strife now by trying to change that?

But Gray Cloud was the only son he would ever have, and if he left things as they were, he would die without knowing him.

"She is my woman—in truth, my wife—and the boy is my child," Pierre said. "Raoul has much. They have little. Raoul is wrong to cling to this hatred. To give in to him would mean abandoning these two people to whom I owe so much. As soon as the weather is a little warmer, Papa, I mean to leave for Saukenuk. And I do dread what may happen, but, yes, I still mean to come back with my wife and my son."

5

Star Arrow

White Bear. *My name is White Bear.*

The sun, shining down through branches dotted with budding leaves, warmed his back. He wore the knife his father had left him sheathed at his waist. His eyes searched among the branches of the trees. He did not know exactly what he was looking for, but Owl Carver said that he would know it when he found it. He stopped at the base of an oak tree and looked up.

He thought he heard something moving through the bushes on the upriver side of the island. He stopped peering at the branches and looked up at the sky.

The black trunks of the oaks and hickories rose above him. He felt as if he were standing in a circle of wise old men, who were there to advise and protect him. Ever since that time of sitting in the sacred cave when his soul had gone out of his body, whenever he was by himself he never felt alone. He felt the presence of spirits in all things—trees, birds, plants, rocks, rivers.

After a moment's listening he heard nothing strange and went back to his search. He had chosen this island because he had come here many times at different seasons with his mother, gathering plants for medicines. Today he was looking for one thing. Somewhere on this island grew the branch from which he would cut his medicine stick. Owl Carver had carefully instructed him.

It will call to you out of the forest. It may be of oak or maple or ash or cedar or even hickory. You will know it because it will not be like any other branch you see, and your eye will be drawn to it.

A cloud drifted over the sun, and his arms and shoulders suddenly felt cold. The coldness felt strange, and he remembered that his spirit guide, the White Bear, was said to live in a very cold place. He stood still. He felt he should wait for something to happen.

A shaft of sunlight fell on the black trunk of a tree a short distance in front of him. Where the light struck the tree, a branch was growing out, pointing right at him. He might not have noticed it if the light had not fallen in just that way.

At the end of the branch three bright bur oak leaves were growing. This was the Moon of Buds, and the limbs of most trees bore only the many round swellings that would, as the days grew warmer, open and spread into the first leaves.

But the three oak leaves at the end of this branch were fully grown, fat leaves with deep, irregular lobes.

It was as Owl Carver had said. This branch called out to him from the forest.

He went up to the tree, and as Owl Carver had taught him, he said, "Grandfather Oak, please let me have your arm, to take with me to make strong medicine for our tribe. I promise I will not hurt you, and I will leave all your other arms untouched so that you can grow strong in this place."

It was a small, new branch growing out of the tree at eye level. When trimmed and stripped it would be just the right size for a medicine stick. He would dry the leaves and keep them, too, he decided, as part of his medicine bundle.

With his knife he reverently cut the branch away from the tree trunk.

A voice behind him said, "My son."

He jumped, startled.

At once he recognized Sun Woman's voice. As always, a warmth flooded through him at the sound.

Still, he was angry with himself. How could he let someone slip up on him like that?

He turned. He looked into his mother's brown eyes, level with his. Not so long ago, he remembered, he had to look up to see into her eyes.

He saw pain tightening the muscles of her face. Her lips trembled as they parted. Only a few times had he seen her in such distress, and his heart beat harder. What was wrong?

"You must come back to Saukenuk, my son," she said.

"I have found my medicine stick, Mother. But now I must trim it here and peel the bark in the place where I found it. Owl Carver told me how it must be done."

She swept a hand across her body to say no to that. "It is Owl Carver who says you must come now. Leave the stick here. The spirits will protect it, and you can come back to it later. A man has come to our village. You must meet him."

Tears on her brown cheeks reflected the bright sun.

"What is wrong, Mother? Who is this man?"

Again the hand gesture, rejecting his question. "It is better you see for yourself."

"But you are sad, Mother. Why?"

She turned away, the fringe of her doeskin skirt swirling about her shins.

He laid the severed oak branch at the base of the tree he had cut it from, and with thanks to Grandfather Oak, turned away.

Baffled and apprehensive, he followed Sun Woman through the forest to the edge of the island, where he saw her small elm-bark canoe pulled up beside his.

Silently they paddled their canoes side by side upstream along the narrow stretch of black-green water that separated the island from the riverbank. The Rock River was in its spring flood. Paddling against the powerful current strained White Bear's muscles. He glanced over at his mother and saw with envy how easily she wielded her paddle. She seemed to know how to do everything well. But an expression of sorrow was frozen on her face.

They left the island behind, and soon White Bear saw the hundred lodges of Saukenuk through the weeping willows, hackberries, maples and oaks that grew along the riverbank.

They grounded their canoes on tree roots growing on the edge of the river. Sun Woman beckoned, turned her back on him abruptly and started walking through the woods by the riverbank. White Bear followed.

They passed two newly made graves in the shelter of the trees, mounds of earth, each marked with a willow wand with a strip of deerskin attached to it. Coming out of the woods, they walked, amidst the band's grazing horses, through the blue-grass meadow surrounding the village. Beyond the meadows, as far up and down the river as White Bear could see, stretched stockade-fenced fields where the first shoots of corn, beans, squash and sweet potatoes dotted the freshly turned black earth like pale green stars in a night sky.

White Bear followed Sun Woman into the concentric rings of long lodges with peaked roofs, built of wooden poles and walled with bark sheets, laid out in the sacred circular pattern. Here the Sauk lived all summer, three or four families to a lodge. But today the outskirts of Saukenuk seemed empty. White Bear was surprised to see no one at the riverbank or about the lodges.

Sun Woman walked past the lodges with back straight, legs stiff, her arms rigid at her sides, her head high. Never once did she look back at him.

Reaching the heart of Saukenuk, he saw that all the people were gathered in the central clearing around Owl Carver's medicine lodge. As Sun Woman approached the crowd, a child spied her and tugged its mother's skirt. The mother looked first at Sun Woman, then at White Bear, then whispered to another woman standing next to her. That woman turned, and then the whispers spread in every direction and more and more people looked. The crowd parted, making a path through which Sun Woman walked with her stiff stride. White Bear followed.

At the end of the pathway through the crowd sat Owl Carver and another man, side by side at the door of the sacred lodge. Owl Carver's long white hair spread like a snow-covered spruce tree. His chest was bare save for his necklace of megis shells, and was painted with diagonal stripes of blue and green, the colors of hope and fear.

White Bear slowed his steps, studying the man seated beside Owl Carver. His heart thumped hard when he saw who it was.

This was the man he had seen in his vision with the White Bear and the Turtle. He stood still, his mouth open.

The vision-man had black hair streaked with white, tied with a ribbon at the back. His face was dominated by a powerful beak of a nose. He must have spent much time in the sun; his skin was tan, though not as rich and dark as the skins of White Bear's people.

A beloved face caught White Bear's eye. Redbird was standing among the people, looking not at the stranger, but at White Bear. Their eyes met, and hers were wide with worry. He wanted to take Redbird's hand and run with her into the forest, away from all these people and from whatever made Redbird and his mother look so miserable.

And especially away from the thin, pale man who was now staring at him as intently as a hunter with drawn bow watches a stag.

And yet, the pale eyes stranger had been part of the vision that had given White Bear his new name and put him on the path to becoming a shaman.

He must be a good man if he appeared to me with the White Bear and the Turtle. And he must be important to me.

"Sit here, White Bear," said Owl Carver, and White Bear walked slowly toward him. Owl Carver gestured that he was to sit beside the pale eyes. White Bear felt his heart fluttering as he sat down. Owl Carver pointed to a place beside himself for Sun Woman. The four formed a semicircle, backs to the medicine lodge, faces toward the crowd of curious people.

As was the way of the Sauk, the four sat for a long time with no one speaking. White Bear's body grew colder and colder, and he had to fight to keep from trembling.

After a time, White Bear turned to the stranger and saw in the gaunt face a mixture of pain and joy. The man's pupils were a strange, almost frightening gray-blue color. From such eyes, White Bear knew, the Sauk took their name for this man's people.

As the man looked at White Bear and then over at Sun Woman, it seemed that his heart was glowing with happiness. But it was a happiness tinged by regret, the glow of a setting sun.

White Bear's inner sense told him that something was hurting more than the pale eye's spirit, was draining his life way. White Bear wished at once that he could work a healing of this good man's body.

But why was Sun Woman so unhappy? And why was Redbird frightened?

Owl Carver whispered to a small boy who stood beside him. The boy ran off.

Now the shaman sat nodding his head slowly. White Bear could see that Owl Carver stood at the branching of several paths and was trying to decide which one to take. White Bear's fear grew.

Owl Carver turned to White Bear. "This man is your father."
Yes!
Taught by Owl Carver that rather than puzzle over a vision it is

best to let it reveal its meaning in its own time, White Bear had chosen months ago not to ponder who the pale eyes in the Turtle's lodge might be. Owl Carver must have known when White Bear described the vision to him, but thought it better not to tell him.

White Bear turned and looked again at the man seated beside him, who raised his arms tentatively, as if he wanted to reach out to him. White Bear kept his hands in his lap, and the man lowered his arms again.

White Bear felt a strangeness, such as he had never known before. This man looked at him with love. He was certain, now, that because this man had come today, everything was going to be changed.

"Your father is called Star Arrow," said Owl Carver. He turned to Star Arrow and said, "Your son is called White Bear."

"I greet you, White Bear," Star Arrow said. White Bear was glad to hear this man speaking the Sauk language.

"I greet you, Star Arrow, my father," White Bear said. The word *father* felt strange on his tongue.

Star Arrow. He liked that name and wondered what it meant. *Father.* A shiver of joy went through him.

He spoke in the English Père Isaac had taught him. "Good day to you, Father."

"My son," said Star Arrow in the same tongue. White Bear saw now that tears were running down his father's face, just as they had in the vision.

He heard a commotion at the back of the crowd. People were stepping aside.

A thrill went through White Bear as he saw that Black Hawk was coming toward them. The leader's careworn face glowed as if he were seeing a long-lost brother. He shifted his feather-adorned war club to his left hand and raised his empty right hand in greeting to Star Arrow. White Bear was amazed. He could not remember seeing Black Hawk smile so happily.

Star Arrow raised his hand in reply. White Bear felt himself surrounded by giants—Black Hawk, Star Arrow, Owl Carver. He remembered the circle of trees he had been standing in when Sun Woman called to him.

"Star Arrow has come back to us," Black Hawk declared. "It is well."

Wolf Paw, Black Hawk's oldest son, now strode down the line of people. His presence, as always, made White Bear uneasy.

Sun Woman made room for Black Hawk to sit beside Owl Carver. The chief handed his feathered war club to Wolf Paw, who sat down behind him and rested the club across his knees.

Three more men pushed their way through the crowd. When they came to the front, White Bear saw that they were three chiefs, members of the council that ruled the day-to-day affairs of the Sauk and Fox in peacetime. One, Jumping Fish, was older than Black Hawk. Another, Broth, was a deep-chested man and a well-known orator. The third, Little Stabbing Chief, was a prominent member of the Fox tribe.

With a courteous gesture Black Hawk invited the three chiefs to join the sitting circle.

The nine sat quietly for a time before their people while a breeze whistled over the bark rooftops of Saukenuk.

Black Hawk broke the silence. "Our fathers and our grandfathers have known many kinds of pale eyes. The French pale eyes traded with us. The British pale eyes made us their allies in war. But the American pale eyes drive us from our land and kill us when we resist. American pale eyes are not our friends. But this man, Star Arrow, we call friend. We trust Star Arrow.

"Thirteen summers ago the British long knives made war on the American long knives. The great Shawnee chief, Shooting Star, led braves and warriors of many tribes to fight on the side of the British against the Americans. We among the Sauk and Foxes who followed Shooting Star have been known ever since as the British Band. This man was living among us then, seeking to trade with us and to know us better. When the war began there were some who said, 'He is an enemy. Kill him.' And I might have said so, too, but I did not, because already I knew that he was a good man. We could not send him back to the Americans, but we let him live among us. We even let him share the bed of Sun Woman.

"After the war, when Star Arrow went back to his own people, he left with us this boy, White Bear." Black Hawk turned to White Bear, and when their eyes met, White Bear trembled under Black Hawk's gaze. The chief's eyes were infinitely black, like a night without stars.

"He left us another gift," Black Hawk said.

He reached into a beaded bag hanging at his belt. He took out a shining metal disk on a thin silvery chain and held it up so that the people could see it.

"Inside this disk of metal there is an arrow that points always to the north. Even on a day when I cannot see the sun, on a night when I cannot see the stars, I know where the sun should be and I know where the Council Fire Star is, the star that does not move all night long. He gave us this magical gift. And so we give him his name among the Sauk—Star Arrow. His heart is as constant as the Council Fire Star and as true as the arrow."

There was a murmur of assent among the people.

Black Hawk raised his hand. "Let Star Arrow now tell us why he comes back." Black Hawk folded his arms.

White Bear, his heart beating as hard as a drum in a dance, turned to the pale eyes. Star Arrow turned his own head to look long and gravely at Sun Woman, then at White Bear.

Star Arrow said, "Chief Black Hawk, I lived with Sun Woman as her husband, and then I left her with a son, this young man, White Bear. I wronged Sun Woman and White Bear. He should have had a father as well as a mother. I went back to my people and married a pale eyes woman. Earthmaker has punished me by giving me no children by my second wife and at last taking her from me. Because of this my heart is like the ashes of an old fire."

He held out his arms toward Sun Woman. "Now I want to make it right."

Owl Carver leaned forward into the circle of speakers. "You want to come and live with us again, Star Arrow?"

At the thought of Star Arrow returning to the band, White Bear's heart leaped with happiness. All his life he had been hoping to meet his father, waiting for his father's return, but never believing it possible. So that his father, returning, might be pleased with him, he had even let Père Isaac teach him things he could never use.

To have this strange new man who was so respected by the Sauk living with him and Sun Woman—this was almost as thrilling a prospect as his dream of becoming a great shaman.

Star Arrow said, "No, I cannot stay among you. Nothing, I think, would make me happier, but I have many things to do among my own people. I own much land."

Owl Carver said, "If your land keeps you from doing what you want, then it owns *you*."

Star Arrow smiled ruefully. "Owl Carver speaks truly, but I cannot change this. I must care for my land myself, because there is no one who can do it for me."

Star Arrow turned to look at White Bear, who sensed a question: *Could you be one who helps me care for my land?*

Again White Bear felt the presence of a death-with-claws that had its grip on Star Arrow's body. He must speak to Owl Carver. Perhaps Owl Carver could tell him how to help his father.

Owl Carver said, "We know about your land, Star Arrow. You traded honorably with us, and gave us many valuable goods, so that you and your family could live on that land to the north and farm it and graze your animals on it."

"That is so," said Chief Jumping Fish. "Star Arrow gave me a fine rifle, and he made our tribe rich with what he paid us."

White Bear felt a chill of fear when he heard that Star Arrow lived to the north. There was danger, it seemed, in the north. Three Fox men, including Sun Fish, a youth his own age who had been a playmate of his, had gone north two moons ago to work a lead mine and had not been heard from.

Star Arrow said, "I have come to ask Sun Woman and White Bear to live with me in my home."

White Bear heard an amazed murmur from the crowd, and he himself felt his heart drop as if he plummeted unaware into a deep pit.

Leave the tribe? He could not picture it. It made no sense. Being without the tribe would be like trying to live without his arms or legs.

White Bear's eyes met Redbird's. Her slanting eyes were big with fear, and he tried to tell her with a look that he did not want this. Now he understood why she looked so unhappy. She must have guessed what Star Arrow would ask.

To leave Redbird. No longer to learn from Owl Carver. Give up hope of being a shaman. Leave the forest. Leave Saukenuk. He had heard that no spirits lived among the pale eyes. In the land of the pale eyes the tall prairie grass was burned away and the trees were cut down.

Black Hawk and Owl Carver looked at each other. In the glances that passed between them White Bear saw surprise, questioning, but no disapproval. He felt his hopes sink. Would he have to fight this fight alone?

No—his mother would say no to Star Arrow.

She stood up to speak, tall and stately. She turned to Star Arrow, and White Bear saw love mingle with the pain in her dark brown eyes.

"I am happy to call Star Arrow husband. He has not wronged me. It is right that a man should live among his people."

White Bear thought, *Now she will say that we must stay with our people and cannot go with him.*

"I am glad that Star Arrow remembers me and White Bear, that he comes to ask us to live with him. But I cannot go. I have my work, the gathering of medicines, the healing, the teaching of what I know." She turned to Redbird, who smiled uncertainly.

Sun Woman spoke on. "I could not look into pale eyes faces all day long. My heart would dry up."

In the long silence that followed, White Bear waited uneasily. Why had his mother not spoken of him?

Star Arrow unfolded his long, thin limbs, went over and stood before Sun Woman. He put his hands on her shoulders. A sudden breeze rattled the bark walls of Saukenuk.

"I understand what Sun Woman says."

Sun Woman and Star Arrow both looked at White Bear. He felt as if the ground were trembling under him. He wished it would open up and swallow him.

"This young man," said Sun Woman. "Your son, White Bear. Half of him is you. It is right that he should see the pale eyes who are also his people."

The earth was tilting. White Bear was falling.

His own mother—betraying him. Sending him away.

"I have always believed that Earthmaker meant some special destiny for White Bear," Sun Woman said.

The shout burst from White Bear. "No!" He did not even remember getting to his feet, but he was standing.

Heads turned toward him. Eyes opened wide. He saw Black Hawk lift a hand to silence him, then lower it again. The three chiefs stared angrily.

Words tumbled out of him. He spoke to his mother, who had turned against him.

"Earthmaker meant me to be a shaman. How can I learn to be a shaman if I live among pale eyes? If I spend many summers and winters away from the tribe I will no longer be a Sauk."

White Bear could see the pain-taut lines in Sun Woman's face.

This was hurting her, he knew that. But his anger at her burned in his chest. She was trading his life for hers. She would stay here in Saukenuk, but she would give Star Arrow part of what he wanted—his son. Why should he be sacrificed to make Star Arrow happy? It was she who had chosen to take this pale eyes into her lodge.

Sun Woman turned to Owl Carver. "We need to learn much more about the pale eyes if we are to protect ourselves from them. Some of us must live with them and come to understand them from within their tribe. Such a one must be young enough to learn new ways. And he should be specially gifted, a favorite of the spirits."

Then Owl Carver stood up to speak, facing White Bear.

"White Bear, listen to the words of your teacher. There is more than one way to become a shaman. Here in Saukenuk live many people of the Fox and some of the Winnebago, Piankeshaw and Kickapoo tribes. Who says their lives are over because they live among the Sauk? If you live with the tribe of pale eyes, it will make you a man of greater knowledge. To go among them will take the courage of a warrior and more. Of knowledge, of courage, is a shaman made."

Owl Carver turned to Black Hawk. "Sun Woman is right. Let the boy go with Star Arrow. I know Earthmaker has blazed this trail for White Bear." He crossed his arms before his chest and sat down again.

White Bear cast about desperately for words that would answer Owl Carver. He felt helpless to fight the current that was sweeping him away.

"If Earthmaker wants this for me, how is it that *I* do not know it?" he cried. He went cold inside, realizing that in his desperation he was defying Owl Carver before all the people. He was questioning Owl Carver's powers.

He wanted to say that he hoped to be the great prophet of the Sauk after Owl Carver had departed to the land of the spirits. But he did not dare say such a thing. Earthmaker himself might punish him for such presumption.

"Did I not come back to you from the sacred cave with the very words of the Turtle?" he said, holding his hands out in appeal. "Surely I will bring you other great visions if I stay with you. Among the Sauk I have grown to manhood. Why does this man come now to tear me away from the only tribe I have known?"

He was surprised to see Star Arrow smile warmly at him.

"This man is your father," Owl Carver declared. "You are a Sauk. A Sauk never shirks the demands of honor. A Sauk is loyal and respectful and obedient toward his father."

"I am proud of my son," said Star Arrow. "He speaks with power before the people."

At that, a hopeless feeling swept over White Bear. Star Arrow was not fighting him, any more than water fights a drowning man. Star Arrow was a current dragging him away from his people, his village.

And the village was not trying to hold him. Sun Woman, Owl Carver, Black Hawk, were pushing him out, as they would a man who was so wicked he could not be allowed to live with the people. He felt utterly alone.

What did he know of the pale eyes? Only the little that Père Isaac had taught him. And that they were great land thieves. Always they were scheming to take land away from the people who had held it since the Great River first began to flow from the Turtle's breast. Why must he live among his people's enemies?

Owl Carver sprang from his seat. He leaped at White Bear and crouched before him. His eyes opened wide as those of his totem bird. White Bear felt himself pulled toward their black centers, as if they were whirlpools in the Great River. Owl Carver's long white hair fanned out like wings on either side of his head.

"You will listen!" Owl Carver said in a soft voice of terrible intensity. *"You will hear!"*

Silently White Bear stood looking at the shaman.

"You are the son of my spirit as much as you are the son of Star Arrow's body. I tell you to live with this man as I told you to go to the sacred cave in the Moon of Ice. This is a far greater test for you. Going to live with the pale eyes will be like journeying to another sacred cave. And you will bring back other visions."

White Bear saw in the blackness of Owl Carver's eyes that if he defied this decision he would lose his place in the tribe. There was no way to break free from the current that was sweeping him away from Saukenuk.

White Bear felt as if something in him had broken. He held his face expressionless. He did not want to show his hurt before the tribe. But he knew he would soon be unable to stop himself from weeping.

Among the witnessing people he saw anguish and determination struggling in Sun Woman's face. Others looked at him only with curiosity, not sympathy. In all the people around him, the only face that shared his unrelieved wretchedness was Redbird's. His gaze met hers, and the pain they felt together deepened his despair.

Black Hawk spoke in a low voice over his shoulder to Wolf Paw, who stood up. As he left the circle before Owl Carver's medicine lodge, Wolf Paw glanced at White Bear, and White Bear saw the light of triumph in his eyes.

Black Hawk held a hand out to Star Arrow. "If we let you take White Bear, you must one day let him return to us, bringing his new knowledge to help the Sauk."

Owl Carver moved from his crouching position before White Bear and sat down again, facing Star Arrow. "This young man is most precious to us. The mysteries have been told to him, and he has seen visions of the past and future."

At this White Bear's heart was eased a bit. The tribe did want him to return.

I am both red and white.

And both his tribe and the pale eyes wanted him.

To go among the pale eyes will make you a man of knowledge, Owl Carver had said, and Black Hawk had agreed. Perhaps he could become a star arrow, pointing the way for his people in the troubled days the Turtle had foretold.

"I promise to keep him with me only for a time," said Star Arrow.

He has not long to live. That is why he can promise.

And that meant that White Bear's time of exile from the Sauk would be short. But knowing that brought White Bear no relief. He did not want his father, whom he had just met, to die so soon.

"I ask one more thing," said Star Arrow. "It will be harder for the boy to learn the ways of the pale eyes if he always feels the pull of his Sauk people. For the first few summers and winters that he is with us, I ask that he not return to you even for a visit, and that you send no messages to him and he send none to you."

"That is much to ask," said Owl Carver. "That is hard. The boy may die of longing for his people."

Star Arrow shook his head. "I would never let that happen. If I see that it is unbearable for him, I will send him back to you. But I will do everything I can to make him happy, and if he does not see the British Band or hear from them, the pain of parting will go away sooner."

"I understand what Star Arrow says," said Black Hawk. "It is granted."

White Bear sat down slowly, feeling as if he had been mortally wounded. Never to have a word from his mother or from Redbird—how could he bear it?

Star Arrow continued, "He will go to a fine school in the East. And when he has learned all he can learn, I will send him back to you."

"Let it be done," Black Hawk said.

Wolf Paw came through the crowd, holding up in both hands a calumet, a sacred pipe. Its hickory stem was as long as a man's arm, wrapped in blue and yellow bands, and its high, slender bowl was of dark red pipestone, quarried in a valley far to the west.

Black Hawk took the pipe from Wolf Paw and filled the bowl with tobacco from a beaded pouch at his waist. Owl Carver went into his lodge, and brought back a burning twig that Black Hawk used to light the pipe.

Black Hawk said, "By the smoking of the sacred tobacco let all these promises be sealed."

White Bear went cold as he saw the light gray smoke curl up from Black Hawk's pipe and smelled its sweet scent. Once he put the pipe to his lips and drew the smoke into his mouth, he would be bound to go with Star Arrow as firmly as he was bound to the Sauk tribe.

Holding the pipestem with one hand in the middle and the other at the end, Black Hawk ceremoniously drew on the pipe and let a cloud of smoke out of his mouth. He handed the pipe to Star Arrow, who fixed his gaze on White Bear and did the same. Next the pipe went to Owl Carver, who took the single puff that bound him to the agreement. Owl Carver took the pipe in turn to Jumping Fish, Broth and Little Stabbing Chief. Each puffed on it, bearing witness.

Then Owl Carver walked over to White Bear and handed him the pipe.

Trembling with fear that what he was about to do might be the ruin of him, White Bear took the pipe in his hands. His fingers felt the ridged wrappings and the smooth, warm stone of the bowl. He had never smoked a sacred pipe before.

He could hand the pipe back to Owl Carver and refuse. But he knew that this had gone so far that if he did that, not only would he never be accepted as a shaman, he might not even be accepted as a Sauk.

He wanted to look at Redbird, but he dared not. He looked instead at Sun Woman and saw her eyes warm with the wish that he would smoke the pipe.

He put the calumet to his lips and pulled the hot smoke into his mouth. It burned his tongue and the insides of his cheeks. He took the pipe away and held the smoke for a moment, then puffed it out. As he did so, a sigh went up from the watchers.

Black Hawk was standing before him. White Bear handed the pipe up to him.

"May you walk this path on which we send you with courage and honor," Black Hawk said.

He turned to the people. "This council is at an end."

White Bear knew he could not hold back his tears any longer. He sprang to his feet and blindly hurled himself into the crowd that was already beginning to disperse. He felt a hand on his arm, but he pulled away from it.

He began to run. He ran through Saukenuk, through the meadow, into the trees by the river's edge. He ran past the graves. He ran with the hard, steady stride of one carrying a message.

But a messenger did not run sobbing, with tears streaming down his face.

6

In the Ancient Grove

Redbird watched, an aching, empty place in her chest, as White Bear disappeared into the woods at the edge of the Rock River.

"What a fool!" Water Flows Fast, standing nearby, had spoken. "The pale eyes have steel knives and blankets and big sturdy lodges that are always warm and never leak. They always have enough food. I would be happy to go live with a pale eyes if he asked me."

"Is your prattling tongue never still, woman?" said her husband, Three Horses.

"It was my prattling tongue that agreed to marry you."

Redbird had no heart to listen to them bicker.

"Let me through!" she cried, and the crowd parted before her.

"Where are you going?" cried her mother. "It is shameful to run after him." She grabbed Redbird's sleeve. "All the people will laugh at you."

"Let me go!"

As Wind Bends Grass pulled at her, Redbird's eyes met those of Wolf Paw, standing beside his father, the war chief. He glared at her. She knew he, too, wanted to tell her not to run after White Bear. But if he showed that he cared that much, the people would make fun of *him*.

She turned her back on all of them—Wind Bends Grass, Wolf Paw, Black Hawk, Owl Carver—and began to run.

When she reached the riverbank she saw no sign of him. For one panic-stricken moment she thought, *Did he throw himself into the river?*

Then, downriver, she saw a canoe gliding over the glistening water. He was paddling hard and was almost out of sight around a bend.

Her own small bark canoe, on which she had painted a bird's wing in red, lay a short distance down the riverbank. She pushed it into the water, jumped into the rear and seated herself in the middle. The canoe's bottom scraped over the riverbank as she pushed off with her paddle.

She stayed a distance behind White Bear, just close enough to keep him in sight. He might not want her to follow him. She could not guess what was in his mind right now.

What would she do when she caught up with him? She had hoped to marry him, if not this summer, then the next. Ever since she was a small child she had found him endlessly fascinating. More so than ever since his return from his spirit journey. Nothing, she thought, would make her happier than living with him. Sun Woman had told her all about what happens when a man and a woman lie down together—knowledge that Wind Bends Grass had insisted that she did not yet need. It sounded painful, pleasurable, frightening and exciting. She had looked forward to lying down with White Bear.

But now she was going to lose him. How could Sun Woman send her own son away from the tribe?

And send him away from me. Redbird felt more hurt than if her own mother had turned against her.

And did White Bear truly mean to go with the pale eyes? He had smoked the calumet. He must.

The current carried her canoe through the water, brown with silt caught up in spring flooding, almost faster than she could paddle. Ahead the river divided, flowing around an island near the right bank, thick with trees. White Bear turned into the narrow channel that ran between island and shore, and she backpaddled to slow herself and watch.

His canoe rounded a huge fallen tree, whose exposed roots clutched at the island's shore like the fingers of a drowning man, and disappeared behind the trunk.

She let her paddle drag in the water, first on one side then on the other, holding her canoe back until he had time to land. Then she glided into the narrow channel and around the dead tree.

He had drawn his canoe up in a small sandy cove, and was gone. She landed on the patch of sand beside his canoe and pulled her canoe partway out of the water.

She listened, and for a moment heard nothing but the wind in the trees. A redbird, her namesake, trilled long and loud, and another answered from a more distant tree.

Then she heard a human voice. No words, just an outcry. A cry of pain.

She plunged into the forest that covered the island, pushing her way through the shrubbery toward the sound of his voice.

He was sobbing so loudly that she was sure he could not hear her coming. She had heard a man sob like that once before, a dying hunter whose leg had been torn to shreds by a bear.

She moved through some trees and saw him. He was sitting with his back against the big black trunk of an oak. He was in a grove of trees so big and so old that little grew in their heavy shade, and there was an open place to sit. The season was so young that their branches were still almost bare, and she could see White Bear clearly in the afternoon sunlight. He held a severed tree branch in his lap. His eyes were squeezed shut and his lips were drawn back from his teeth, and his cries of pain came one after another.

She stepped out of the bushes into the grove. He looked up, and the face he showed her was so twisted that she could not tell whether he saw her. He went on sobbing hoarsely.

Her heart hurt to see him suffer so. She sat down beside him.

For a long time she listened to him weep, waiting for a chance to speak to him.

She looked at the branch he was holding. It was almost as long as her arm, and, surprisingly, it had leaves at its tip, even though this was only the Moon of Buds. He clutched it as a child clutches a doll for comfort.

Gradually his weeping subsided. She reached out very carefully and patted his shoulder lightly. When he did not pull away, she rested her hand on him. She eased herself closer until they were pressed together side by side, and she slid her arm around his shoulders and held him tightly.

At first she felt no answering movement. He seemed only half alive. She wondered if he knew she was here. Then his head dropped to her shoulder. She felt the weight of his body yielding to her.

She put her other arm around him. She held him as if he were her child. In spite of his sorrow and her own, it was a great happiness to hold him like this.

He sighed and wiped his face with his hand. She stroked his cheek, brushing away the tears.

She wanted to talk to him, but waited for him to speak first.

"There is nothing I can do," he said. "I must go with Star Arrow, my father."

She studied his face as he stared off into the forest. She could see now the features of his father in him. There had always been something odd about his eyes, but she had never been quite able to decide what it was. Now she saw that they were rounder than most people's. They were shaped like his father's. His nose was thin and bony, with a high arch, and sharp at the end, like the beak of a bird. His eyebrows were thick, black and straight across. His chin was pointed. She loved the strangeness of his face.

She said, "When it gets dark we could go back to the village and fill our canoes with food and blankets and tools and weapons. There will be feasting tonight for Star Arrow. Everyone will sleep soundly after that. We could cross the Great River tonight, and tomorrow we could be far away."

He stared at her. "But I do not *want* to leave my people."

She had not thought that far ahead, about what it would be like to be away from Owl Carver, Iron Knife, Sun Woman, her sisters, her mother, all the others. Yes, it would be a great loss. But she could stand the pain, she thought, if she were beside White Bear.

"But we would have each other. Would it not hurt you less if you had me with you?"

He did not answer at once, and that made her feel as if a rough hand had squeezed her heart. But then he smiled at her, and she felt better.

"Yes, if I could share my life with you, the pain of leaving Saukenuk would be less." Then his face darkened. "But we could not live on our own. A man or a woman cut off from their tribe can no more be happy than a flower after it is picked can continue to grow. And I would have dishonored the promise I made with the sacred tobacco. The spirits would turn their backs on me. My mother and Owl Carver say that if I go with Star Arrow, I may learn things that would help our people."

She was thunderstruck to realize that he actually wanted to go with Star Arrow. Then what was all this weeping for?

He did not care for her as much as she did for him. That made her angry. She pushed herself a little apart from him.

"I see that I have been a fool to chase after you, just as my mother said. It means more to you to go and live with the pale eyes than it does to have Redbird as your woman."

His eyes widened. "We have never before today spoken of this, you and I."

"Did we have to speak?" She felt herself getting angrier and angrier. "Why do you think I went looking for you when you went on your vision quest? Why do you think I followed you from the village today? And why did I say I would go with you across the Great River? Yes, I did want to be your woman. But you do not want me. You want to go away with this pale eyes father of yours, and maybe you want to take a pale eyes woman for yourself."

His mouth as well as his eyes opened up in amazement. "I have never even seen a pale eyes woman. How could I want one? I do want Redbird to be my woman. And I weep at leaving Saukenuk because I must leave you."

Again she reached out to him, putting her hands on his arms. "I would rather be cast out of our tribe than lose you."

He shook his head. "We do not have to lose our people or each other. It was part of the promise sealed with sacred tobacco that I am to come back. If we ran away now, Earthmaker would be angry with us."

She moved closer to him. She had seen Earthmaker in dreams. He was taller than the tallest tree, and he carried a great war club with a ball-shaped rock at the end of it and looked much like Black Hawk, with a long black lock of hair coiling down from the top of a shaved head.

"I wish I could meet and talk with the spirits, as you have," she said. "Sometimes I think I do meet them, in dreams."

"It can be dangerous to meet with the spirits," he said. His eyes seemed to be looking into the distance. He had seen so many things she had not. It was unfair, she thought sadly.

She had gone out to him in the bitter cold when the world was an endless white waste. She might have frozen to death. She might have been punished by drowning in the icy river. She had risked almost as much as he had.

"I do not say that I am as strong as White Bear, or as worthy to speak with the spirits," she said. "I only wish I had a chance to."

He took her hands in his and looked deep into her eyes.

"The real danger of a shaman's vision is not to the body."

"What is the real danger?"

"I did not want to come back."

She felt a cold wind blowing across her neck, as if spirits had quietly entered this grove with them and were standing about them, listening to them, judging them.

"It is so wondrous," he said in a voice so low she had to strain to hear it over the wind whispering in the tree branches. "You are there with them. The White Bear, the Turtle. You see them, talk to them. You see the Tree of Life, the crystal lodge of the Turtle and the spirits of all living things. Why would anyone want to return?"

Redbird shivered. But she still envied him.

"Your hands are cold," White Bear said, and he put his arm around her and drew her close to nestle on his chest. She slid her hands under the leather vest he wore and felt the smooth warmth of his skin and the firmness of his muscles. How powerful his arms were around her. She thanked Earthmaker that White Bear had found the inner strength to return from that other land.

A new thought occurred to her. "What if you find that the land of the pale eyes holds you fast? Then you will never come back to me, and to the Sauk you will be dead."

He smiled gently and patted her shoulder. She pulled herself closer to him.

"Can the land of the pale eyes, altogether without spirits, hold me, when the spirits themselves could not?"

"I do not think so."

"Can the land of the pale eyes hold me, when Redbird is not in it? *I* do not think so."

Her body seemed to be melting. She wanted to flow together with White Bear as the Rock River flowed into the Great River.

His arms tightened around her. Then he raised his hand to brush the fringe of hair that fell over her forehead.

She moved against him until her cheek touched his. Slowly she slid one side of her face against his, then the other side. A hunger filled her. It was almost as if she wanted to devour White Bear, but all she could do was touch his smooth cheek with her fingertips.

His nostrils flared and his lips parted and she could hear his breathing. His hands were roaming over her body, awakening powerful feelings wherever he touched her, making her want more.

How did they come to be lying down? They must have moved without realizing it. She could see, feel and think only of White Bear. Her head was pillowed on his arm and her face was pressed against his. With his free hand he caressed her, seeking her flesh under her jacket and skirt. His hand became bolder, plucking at the laces that held her clothing together, baring places that only a husband should look at as he was looking now. And touching those places, sending ripples of delight all through her.

And she wanted him to do that. She felt no shame or fear, only happiness. She let him do whatever he wanted. She helped him. She moved her hands also, to touch more of him. Her hand found the oak branch that he had been holding just before she sat down with him. She put the branch aside and let her fingers feel the hardness pushing against his loincloth; he was ready to come into her in the way that Sun Woman had explained.

She could still stop him if she wanted to. She knew him and trusted that he would not do anything she did not want.

But she wanted this. She wanted his hand to go on skillfully preparing the way for him. She wanted this golden glow inside her to fill her more and more. This was happiness, and she was climbing toward a greater and greater happiness. She felt him move, and all at once her hand was not on his loincloth, but on his hot flesh. She wanted to open herself up to the part of him she held so tightly.

Then he was upon her, and she felt a sudden stabbing pain. She cried out. Almost at once his cry of pleasure followed on hers and his hips thrust forward violently and she felt him filling her. He let out a long sigh and relaxed, lying on top of her, resting all of his weight on her.

I am like the Turtle holding up the earth, she thought.

There had been mounting pleasure until her moment of pain. Now there was an ache and a faint memory of the good feelings. She wanted more pleasure. Sun Woman had told her it would hurt only the first time. And that from then on it would be better and better.

Slowly he withdrew from her and they lay on their sides looking at each other. His eyes were huge right before her face.

"For a moment," he said softly, "I felt as I did when I walked on the bridge of stars."

She thought of asking him whether it made him so happy that he would stay with her now instead of going to the country of the pale eyes with his father. But she knew what his answer would be, and that his saying it would only hurt him and her.

She said, "It was Sun Woman, your mother, who told me about this—about what men and women do together."

He laughed. "It was also she who told me." His face reddened. "I feel as if my mother were here watching us."

It was Redbird's turn to laugh. "What would she see that she did not know about already?"

He shook his head. "I would not want anybody to see us doing that."

"The spirits watch us."

"That is not the same. They watch everything, so it is not special to them."

"Is it special to you?" she asked.

"Oh, yes. Something has passed between us. I have given a part of myself to you. And I have a part of you too. Now, even if I must leave you, we will still be with each other."

She did not want to hear him speak of leaving. She wanted to stay here with him in this grove of ancient trees forever. When she had spoken to him of going off and being alone together, this was what she imagined it would be like. But then a dark thought crossed her mind.

"White Bear, they might send people looking for us. They might catch us together like this." Anxiously she started to pull her clothing together.

He sat up beside her and put his hand over hers. "I do not think anyone is coming." He sounded so sure that she thought he must be speaking as a shaman.

"They know I will come back to the village," he added. "They saw me smoke the calumet. And in a few days I will leave with Star Arrow."

He said it with such finality that the sun seemed to go out.

"And so there is time," he said, "If you want . . ." and guided her hand to touch him. To her joy she felt him strong in his readiness to be within her again. This time, she was sure, it would not hurt. She would know the full delight that Sun Woman had told her of. The afternoon sunlight slanting through the budding branches was warm again, bathing her and making her feel joyful and free.

Their flowing together lasted longer this time, and gave her all the happiness she had hoped for.

And it came to her, as they lay peacefully side by side afterward, that this might have happened someday, but it would not have happened today if Star Arrow had not come to claim his son.

7

Raoul's Mark

On the morning of the fourth day of their journey north from Saukenuk along the Great River, when the sun was halfway up the sky, White Bear and Star Arrow emerged from a forest into a prairie. To their right were gentle hills covered with new green buffalo grass and prairie flowers of every color. To their left the hills stood taller, then dropped suddenly to the Great River. White Bear saw a large boat with great white wings above it to carry it along.

Star Arrow brought his tall black stallion to a sudden halt and climbed down, gesturing to White Bear to dismount from his brown and white pony.

"Look at this stone," Star Arrow said, pointing to a large gray rock that stood upright on the edge of a bluff overlooking the river.

White Bear saw carving on the rock and, remembering Père Isaac's lessons, recognized it as the pale eyes' letter M.

"M for de Marion," said Star Arrow. "We are now on land belonging to the de Marion family. You see no fences here because we could not cut enough wood to fence off all our land. There is so much of it."

He reached out and rested his hand on White Bear's shoulder, his fingers squeezing through the buckskin shirt. "But before we come to the place where I live, and where you will live, we must speak of names. Among the pale eyes I am called Pierre de Marion. My full name is Pierre Louis Auguste de Marion."

He made White Bear say "Pierre de Marion" after him.

"According to our custom you should call me Father," Star Arrow said, saying the word in English. White Bear already knew it.

"Now I will tell you what your name will be among the pale eyes."

White Bear pulled free of Star Arrow's hand and took a step backward.

"I already have a name. I was born Gray Cloud because I am neither white nor red." He could hear reproach in his voice, though he had not meant to sound that way. "But now I am White Bear. That is the name given me by the shaman Owl Carver after my spirit journey. I must keep that name."

"And you will keep that name, son. You will always be White Bear. But, just as I am happy to have the British Band call me Star Arrow, so you can have a pale eyes' name. One that tells pale eyes when you go among them who you are—that you are a member of the de Marion family—that you are my son."

He is proud that I am his son. White Bear's anger faded and he felt a warmth toward this man who wanted to give him a name. He decided that if Star Arrow could have two names, so could he.

"What is my pale eyes' name to be, Father?"

Star Arrow put his hand on White Bear's shoulder. "I wish you to be called Auguste de Marion. Auguste is a very old name. It means 'consecrated,' a sacred person, and that is a good name for one who has seen a vision and wishes to be a shaman. Say it after me. Auguste."

"O-goose."

As they rode on through the de Marion lands, people called out from cabins. Mounted men, who saluted Pierre with a wave of their hands, rode among herds of cattle and horses.

Dozens of horses! Auguste thought, realizing he was seeing wealth that would amaze any man of the British Band.

Farther along they passed fields fenced off with logs split in two and piled one on top of the other. Sheep roamed over low hills and cropped the prairie grass to its very roots. Inside a smaller plot huge gray and pink pigs rolled in mud beside a pond.

They passed fields planted with crops. The whole village of Saukenuk with all the farmland around it would fit into one of those fields. He recognized one crop, corn. Corn as far as he could see. How much corn could the de Marions eat? They must be a huge tribe.

As they rode along, Pierre said, "One more thing for you to know, Auguste. You will meet the rest of your family today—your grandfather and your aunt, my sister." He stopped his horse. Auguste reined up his pony and waited. Unhappiness dragged down the lines in Pierre's face.

"I must tell you that I also have a brother, your uncle, who—" He hesitated. "Who may not be friendly to you."

"Why?" Auguste asked.

"Thirteen summers ago another sister of mine and he were captured by the Potawatomi during the war between the British and the Americans. My sister was murdered by them. Raoul, my brother, suffered greatly until we found him and ransomed him. He hates not just the Potawatomi, but all red men. He did not wish me to bring you back here to our home."

"I do not understand," said Auguste. How could a man hate all tribes because of what the men of one tribe had done to him? Again he realized what a mystery the pale eyes were, and he felt fear.

Pierre said, "He probably will not be there when we arrive. I had to tell you about Raoul, but I do not want you to be afraid of him."

But he *was* afraid, he told himself as they rode on. His belly felt hollow, and his heart beat faster than his pony's trotting hooves. He was afraid of the pale eyes and their strange ways. He felt more fear now than he had when he walked on the bridge of stars with the White Bear.

"There!" Pierre suddenly held out his hand. Auguste's eyes followed the gesture, and his mouth dropped open.

What at first he thought he saw was a forest of trees covered with snow. In their midst something rose like a great gray hill. Snow in the Moon of Buds? Perhaps the pale eyes did have a magic of their own.

As they rode closer, the snow on the trees turned into flowers. He had seen wild apple trees in bloom and knew that many trees flowered around this time. But these trees were all planted in straight rows, and each one was a mass of white blossoms.

What he had thought was a gray hill was the biggest lodge he had ever seen. He jerked the reins of his horse to stop, so that he could sit and wonder at what he was seeing. He felt Pierre stop beside him.

The great lodge seemed to be made of three or four lodges all joined together with one central building higher than all the rest. Its high peaked roof was of logs split in half with the flat sides turned outward. The lower part of the lodge was made of stones, the upper part of logs.

Dread filled him, seeing that these people could do so much. They could hold so much land that a rider needed half a day to cross from edge to center. They could make the land obey their wishes, fence it, fill it with animals, plant huge fields with crops, enjoy a forest of flowering trees. And in the very center of all this they could make a lodge gigantic enough to hold a hundred families.

The pale eyes could do anything. They were magicians so mighty as to make a shaman like Owl Carver look childish. How could he ever hope to know all that they knew?

Despair crushed him. He wanted to see no more.

Pierre patted Auguste's pony on the neck, and the little horse started forward again. Numbly, Auguste felt himself being led toward the great lodge, his pony's hooves falling softly on white petals.

Pierre pointed proudly. "We call our house Victoire."

Closer and closer they came until the house blocked out part of the sky. It was gray, the logs it was built of having weathered. Auguste saw that there were many smaller buildings scattered around the giant lodge—smaller only compared to the huge one in the center. Some of the smaller houses were connected to the great one by sheltered walkways. The smallest was much bigger than the biggest lodge in Saukenuk.

In a moment they would emerge from among the flowering trees. Auguste saw a log fence ahead. The fence surrounded a low hill covered with close-cropped grass, leading up to the house. One large old maple tree shaded the south side. He checked his pony. He could go no farther.

"What is it?" Pierre asked him.

"I cannot," Auguste said. "I cannot go there." He felt a quaver in his voice and his lips trembling, and he held himself rigid.

"Why not, Auguste?" Pierre said softly.

"I do not know what to do here. I have never seen such a place as this. I will do foolish things. All those people will laugh at me. You will not want me for a son."

"Let us wait," said Pierre. "Get down from your horse."

Biting his lip, Auguste dismounted.

"We shall sit here," said Pierre. They sat, facing each other. Auguste saw people approaching through the straight rows of trees. Pierre saw them, too, and waved them away.

They sat for a long time in silence while their horses grazed nearby. Auguste held his misery in until he felt calmer.

He looked at Pierre and nodded to say that he was in control of himself. Pierre nodded back. Auguste looked at the petal-covered ground, feeling crushed.

"All this is strange to you," Pierre said.

"Yes," said Auguste.

"And it is not foolish to fear. There are some people here who will hate you just because you are a red man. There are people who will be afraid of you. But there are dangers in the life you come from—fire and flood, sickness, bears and wolves, the Sioux and Osage, enemies of your people. You fear those things, but you have been taught how to live with those dangers. There are other people here, people like myself, who will care for you and protect you and teach you how to live with the dangers of the pale eyes' world. You must come to know these people who will help you. I want you to be glad you came from Saukenuk to Victoire."

Auguste did not answer. They sat in silence for a while. Then Pierre spoke again.

"The pale eyes are here, Auguste, and you must learn to live with us."

Auguste sighed and settled down again. He listened to the buzzing of locusts rise and fall.

If my vision of this man meant something, then come to me now, White Bear, and tell me what I must do.

He carried a handful of bits of magic mushroom in a saddlebag, but several times since his spirit journey the White Bear had spoken to him without the help of the mushroom and without his mind leaving his body. All he needed to do, sometimes, was sit quietly and listen. He waited now, sometimes looking at Pierre, sometimes looking at the twigs and moss and grass on the ground.

Perhaps no spirit can reach me here in the land of the pale eyes.

He was about to give up and get to his feet. He would beg Pierre to let him go back to the Sauk.

Then a voice spoke deep and clear in his mind, and it was not his voice.

Go and meet your grandfather.

A warmth spread from the center of his body to hands and feet that a moment ago had been icy with fear. Knowing that he had not left his spirit helper behind when he left Saukenuk gave him new confidence.

He held out his hands, palms up. "Let us go to meet my grandfather."

The smile on Pierre's long face mirrored the glow Auguste felt inside himself.

They remounted and rode around to a gateway in the west side of the fence surrounding the house. Auguste, with his newfound strength, endured the curious stares of the men and women gathered at the gate to greet Pierre.

"Look, your grandfather is waiting for you," said Pierre, his voice ringing with joy.

Before a doorway sheltered by its own wooden roof, an old man, a very stout young woman and a plump young man awaited them.

The old man's eyes were blue like Pierre's but they seemed to glitter and to see deeply into Auguste. He was tall and thin and slightly stooped with age. His clothes were simple—a black jacket over a white shirt, and black trousers that tightened below his knees and ended in straps that ran under shiny black shoes. He leaned on a black stick with a silver head.

His heart fluttering with excitement, Auguste got down from his horse and took a tentative step forward. The old man approached him, his expression as fierce as a hawk's. He looked hard into Auguste's face.

The old man spoke to him in a language of the pale eyes, so rapidly that Auguste could not hope to understand him.

Pierre said, "Your grandfather says he sees at once that you are a member of our family. He sees it in the shape of your eyes. He sees it in your nose, in your chin. He sees that like all de Marion men you are very tall."

"What is my grandfather's name?" Auguste asked.

"He is the Chevalier Elysée de Marion."

"El-izay," Auguste said, and his grandfather clapped his hands and grinned.

"But you should call him Grandpapa," Pierre concluded.

"Grandpapa." That was another word Père Isaac had taught him.

Grandpapa gave a cackling old man's laugh, threw his arms wide and hugged Auguste. Auguste hugged him back, rather gingerly, fearing his bones might crack. A thought came to Auguste, and he let go of his grandfather. He hurried back to his horse and took out of the saddlebag the tobacco pouch he had packed along with his small medicine bundle.

He went back to Elysée and held the pouch out with both hands.

In his best English he said, "Please, I give Grandpapa tobacco."

Elysée took the pouch and opened it, sniffed and grinned appreciatively. He and Pierre exchanged words.

Pierre said, "I have told him that among the Sauk, tobacco is offered to honored friends, to men of high rank and to great spirits. This pleases him."

"Thank you, Auguste," Grandpapa said. "I will smoke it in my pipe after we eat together." This time he spoke slowly enough for Auguste to understand him.

Grandpapa now took the stout woman by the arm and pulled her forward.

"This is your aunt, my sister, Nicole Hopkins," said Pierre.

Never among the Sauk had he seen a woman with such broad hips and such a vast bosom. She stepped forward and placed her lips, to Auguste's surprise, on his cheek, making a little smacking sound. Not sure what to do, Auguste put his arms around the woman as he had around his grandfather. She felt soft and comfortable and not at all fragile, and he hugged her hard. He felt powerful muscles under her ample flesh. His aunt returned the embrace with strong arms. She smelled of flowers.

All at once, Auguste sensed that there was a baby growing inside the woman holding him. Not because she was so big; it had nothing to do with the way she looked. It was a sensing, and he was pleased to know that, along with the White Bear, he had not left his powers behind at Saukenuk.

Pierre said, "Now meet Frank Hopkins, your uncle by marriage."

At Pierre's gesture the sandy-haired man approached Auguste. Auguste opened his arms to hug him, but the man stuck his right hand out. The man's fingers were black. That was odd; he had never seen painted fingers before. Was this another pale eyes custom?

Auguste decided he was expected to hold out his own right hand. Frank seized his hand in a strong grip and shook it up and down.

"Frank makes the talking papers from which people may read and learn things," said Pierre. "He also builds things of wood. He built some of the newer buildings here on our land. Frank and Nicole and their children live over by the river in a town called Victor. He built many of the houses there, too."

The people had been so friendly that Auguste had gotten over much of his fear, but when he saw Pierre wave him toward the door, which yawned above him like an enormous cave mouth, he felt cold once again.

But he followed Pierre through the door, and his breath left his body in amazement.

It was like being in a forest clearing where the trees towered over you and their branches met high up, blocking out the sky. In a Sauk lodge he could reach up and touch the roof without straightening his arm. Here the ceiling was hidden in shadows, and huge square-cut timbers crossed the open space above his head.

Hung by ropes from those timbers were big circles of wood that Père Isaac had said were called wheels. These wheels were turned on their sides, and set on them were dozens of the little white sticks of wax that pale eyes used to make light. A few of the more prosperous Sauk families sometimes used such wax sticks to light their lodges.

Auguste looked around in wonder. The huge room was full of objects whose purpose he could not guess. Doorways led to other parts of this house or to attached houses. Cooking smells of many kinds of good food filled the air.

Pale eyes men and women stood about in the hall and watched Auguste and his father and grandfather enter.

Two small boys and a girl running through the hall stopped to stare at him. Frank Hopkins called to them and they approached slowly.

"These are Thomas, Benjamin and Abigail, Nicole and Frank's children," said Pierre.

Their other children, thought Auguste, wondering whether Nicole herself knew what he knew about her.

Abigail stood close to her father, her mouth and eyes wide open.

Thomas, the biggest of the three, said, "Gosh almighty, I got a real Injun for a cousin!"

Benjamin walked slowly over to Auguste, suddenly reached out and gripped the deerhorn handle of the knife at his belt. Auguste tensed.

But Benjamin grinned up at Auguste and let go of the knife without trying to pull it out of its scabbard. Then he ran back to his father.

Grandpapa Elysée beckoned, and as Auguste walked toward him he noticed that the soles of his moccasins were striking a hard surface. He looked down to see that the floor of the lodge was covered with flat stones. Auguste and the others followed Grandpapa across the length of the floor to a stone hearth so big a man could stand inside it.

They passed three long, cloth-covered platforms raised as high above the floor as the sleeping platforms in Sauk and Fox summer lodges.

"Those are tables," Pierre said. Auguste remembered the word from a book of words and pictures Père Isaac had shown him. On the tables lay a confusion of shiny objects.

A man standing by the hearth, who appeared as old as Elysée, stepped forward and bowed. He had a round, bright red nose and white whiskers that stood out on either side of his face.

"This is Guichard, our majordomo," said Pierre.

"Ma-ja domo," repeated Auguste.

"Guichard came over from France with us thirty years ago."

Guichard said, "I greet you, Auguste." Auguste was amazed to hear him speak in the Sauk language. He spoke with a lisp, though, and Auguste noticed when he opened his mouth that he had no front teeth.

Pierre clapped Guichard on the shoulder. "I do not know how he does these things, but he always surprises us with what he has learned. And by his care for us in so many ways."

Guichard stepped back with another bow, and Pierre turned to a short man and a plump woman also standing before the hearth. The woman's full lips curved in a smile of greeting for Pierre; then she plucked at her skirts, lifting them a bit, and bent her knees and ducked her head.

"This is Marchette Perrault," Pierre said, and Auguste noticed that his normally pale face was flushed. "She reigns over our kitchen." Auguste did not need to rely on his special sense to see that there was a loving secret between Marchette and his father.

The man standing beside Marchette, short and powerful-looking, with a bristling brown beard, was staring at Pierre with hatred in his face, his eyes narrowed. His mouth was invisible in his beard, but Auguste knew that his lips were pressed together, his teeth clenched. He also knew that this short man was as strong as a bull buffalo.

The look the brown-bearded man gave Pierre frightened Auguste, and he wondered if he was the only one who could see it.

"Armand Perrault, here, is the overseer of our estate," Pierre said, apparently oblivious of the man's expression. "He makes the crops flourish, the trees bear fruit and the cattle grow fat. He and Marchette come from French families who settled here many generations ago."

Armand bowed, a quick jerk of his head and shoulders, to Pierre. Somewhat to Auguste's relief, the angry man did not even look at him. Abruptly he turned his back and strode across the hall to a side door.

Pierre said, "Most of those who live and work here at Victoire are Illinois people of French descent. The town, Victor, grew up after we built our home here. Most of the people there are Americans from Missouri, Kentucky or back East. Everyone you meet in America is from somewhere else."

Not my people, Auguste thought.

Marchette made another bow to Pierre and left, too, to go into another connected house in which Auguste saw a fire burning under a huge metal pot in another hearth. There was much smoke and steam in that lodge, and he could not see everything, but the good smells were coming from there, and he remembered that he had eaten nothing today but a little dried venison.

Pierre took Auguste by the arm and led him to a place at the table near Grandpapa. Guichard pushed a wooden seat made of sticks toward him. A "chair," Auguste remembered, from Père Isaac's picture book.

Why do they sit up high and raise their food up so high? Auguste wondered. Perhaps pale eyes did not keep their floors clean enough to sit on and eat from. But these appeared very clean.

"This is a special meal in your honor," said Pierre. "Most of the people who work on our land will be eating here with us." Men and women were seating themselves at the other tables.

A feast! thought Auguste. Perhaps there would be dancing afterward.

"How many people live on your land, Father?" he asked in Sauk.

"About a hundred men, women and children live and work here," Pierre answered. "Beyond the hills to the west, by the river, is the settlement called Victor, where another hundred people live. Many of them work for us too. Nicole and Frank live in Victor."

Two hundred, thought Auguste. That was not so many, after all. There were nearly two thousand people in the British Band.

Nicole sat beside him, Pierre across the table from him. Nicole went through the names of the objects on the table—"plate," "glass," "knife," "fork," "spoon." Guichard was going around the table behind the people sitting there, filling each glass with a red liquid from a pitcher.

Auguste had seen beads and other small objects made of glass at Saukenuk, but here glass was everywhere. What was glass, and how did the pale eyes make things from it?

Even as he was wondering about glass he saw his father take out of his coat pocket an oval silver case hanging from a purple cord around his neck. Pierre opened the case and took out yet two more small, round pieces of glass in a metal frame. To Auguste's bewilderment, he put these over his eyes, like a transparent mask. He smiled when he saw Auguste staring.

"Spectacles. I have trouble seeing things that are near to me, and these help. I like to see what I'm eating."

Last night, as Auguste lay beside the sleeping Star Arrow in the tall prairie grass, he had thought of quietly climbing on his pony and fleeing back to Saukenuk, in spite of the tobacco-sealed promise. Now he was glad he had not run away. The people all looked kindly at him, except for that man Armand, and there were so many wonders to see. He could feel his heart beating hard and his hands trembling with excitement.

When Guichard filled his glass with the red liquid, Auguste drank from it. The liquid was cool and burned at the same time. It was bitter and puckered his lips, but was sweet in his throat. He was thirsty, so he drank more of it.

"Wine," said Pierre. "You've had it before?"

This must be like that burning water the pale eyes call whiskey that I tasted at the council last Moon of Falling Leaves on the other side of the Great River. The chiefs and braves and warriors had drunk much of the burning water from a barrel, he remembered, and they had grown merrier and merrier. The women and boys were each allowed one small sip and the young girls none at all.

"I have tasted it," he said. Pierre frowned and seemed about to speak, but he said nothing when Auguste held his empty glass out for more wine to Guichard, who was going around again with the pitcher.

Men and women brought food to the table on big plates and in bowls. There was turkey, duck, fresh venison, flat bread and round bread, dark bread, white bread and yellow corn bread, cooked fruit and raw fruit, loaves of maple sugar, fruit baked inside crusts, heaps of mashed-up vegetables. There were slices of fish burned almost black and piles of boiled crawfish. The food, Auguste saw, was coming from the connected lodge Marchette had gone into, where the big pot was with all the smoke and steam.

Auguste watched the way the people at the table with him were eating. He tried to use his knife and fork as they did and saw Pierre smile approvingly. The sight and smell of the food made water fill his mouth and his stomach growl. But when he put a slice of meat in his mouth it was unexpectedly very hot to the taste. Not just hot from being cooked, but hot because of something cooked into it.

Peppers, he thought. His mother kept some, traded up from the south, in her collection of medicine plants, and he had tasted their fire.

Pierre himself, Auguste noticed, put very small portions of food on his plate and ate little of what was there. Auguste was saddened. If only there was something he could do for his father. He had consulted Owl Carver before leaving Saukenuk, but the old shaman had only said gloomily that in his experience such an evil spirit in the belly was usually fatal.

The hot food made Auguste thirsty, and he drank more wine. Each time he held his glass out, Guichard, smiling toothlessly, seemed to be there with the pitcher.

Still hungry, he grew impatient with knife and fork and began picking the food up with his hands. He tried to take small pieces with his fingers and eat quickly so that people would not notice, but then he caught the two boys and the girl, at the other end of the table, watching him and giggling and whispering to each other. His face went hot.

Nicole, sitting on his right, asked him short, simple questions about how the Sauk and Fox lived, and he answered with the little English he had. She smiled and nodded at him many times as he told her the Sauk names for things, and she repeated them after him. She seemed to find pronouncing them easy.

The other people mostly talked among themselves in their own language. The pale eyes never stopped talking, it seemed. Would there never be a moment of thoughtful silence? The voices, all speaking so fast, gabbling like a flock of turkeys, made him dizzy.

A strange feeling was coming over him. He heard a buzzing in his ears, like locusts on the prairie. His face felt numb. He reached up and touched his cheeks with his fingertips, and it was as if he felt his face through a thin, invisible cloth.

His stomach started to churn. He felt with a sudden panic that he could not hold all the food he had eaten. The peppers and the wine were burning together in his stomach. He lurched to his feet, swaying from side to side. The vast room seemed to be spinning like a canoe in a whirlpool, and the voices around him faded away.

He felt Nicole quickly stand up with him, her hand firmly on his arm, steadying him.

He shut his eyes and held his hand tightly over his mouth, wanting to die of shame and embarrassment. His belly bucked like a wild pony. Hot liquid spurted through his fingers.

"Here, son, here," a voice said. He opened his eyes to look into the face of his father, full of pain for him. Pierre held a large wooden bucket under his chin. On the other side of him Nicole had a strong grip on his shoulder.

Auguste took his hand away from his mouth and let his belly give up what it had held. Stained red by the wine, the food he had just eaten poured into the bucket. The smell of vomit filled his nostrils, making him feel even sicker.

He fell to his knees, coughing, choking, tears streaming from his eyes. Pierre knelt beside him, still holding the bucket for him. Auguste's stomach heaved again and again, forcing the remnants of his meal through his throat and past his slack lips.

As he recovered a bit, he heard someone laugh softly in a distant part of the room, and someone else speak in the pale eyes' language. The tone of contempt was unmistakable.

He was overwhelmed with shame. He had made a fool of himself before his entire de Marion family and their whole tribe. He had disgraced the Sauk. He had embarrassed his father.

It was as he had feared. He could not stay here. It was too painful.

Tonight, he promised himself, holding his aching belly. *Tonight I leave the land of the pale eyes forever.*

Reproaching himself, Pierre knelt beside Auguste, trying through the pressure of his hand on the boy's back to tell Auguste that he loved him.

He said he had tasted wine, but I should have known he could not drink so much. The poor boy must be dying of shame, and it is all the fault of stupid Pierre.

Auguste coughed and wiped the back of his hand over his face. Pierre patted him gently on the back.

Nicole, kneeling on Auguste's other side, suddenly turned her head toward the door and drew in a frightened breath. Pierre looked up to see what it was.

A figure filled the doorway, silhouetted in the yellow rectangle of afternoon sunlight.

Pierre at once recognized the truculent set of Raoul's broad shoulders, the forward thrust of his head under the wide-brimmed hat.

Pierre had time for one more anguished thought of self-reproach as his younger brother strode toward them.

For this, too, I should have better prepared Auguste.

Raoul's boots sounded on the flagstone floor.

Pierre tugged on Auguste's arm, helping him to his feet. He heard Nicole whisk away the bucket.

"So, this is the little mongrel?" Raoul's deep voice boomed in the cavernous log hall.

"Raoul," Pierre said, "this is your nephew, Auguste."

Pierre turned to Auguste and in Sauk said, "This is your uncle Raoul. He lives here with me and your grandfather. He speaks with a rough tongue, but do not fear him."

How could the boy not fear a man like Raoul?

"Auguste, is it? A fine French name for a redskin." Raoul set his fists on his hips, throwing back his blue jacket to show his gilt-handled pistol and a huge knife in its scabbard. At the sight of the weapons Pierre's heart pounded.

Raoul went up to Auguste and stared into his face as Pierre stood tensely.

Raoul said, "Well, brother, you actually did it. You made yourself a son."

"I'm glad you admit that," said Pierre.

"Oh, I admit that. He's got de Marion written all over his dirty face. But don't call him my 'nephew.' I reserve that title for legitimate kin."

Pierre hoped Auguste's knowledge of English was not enough to let him understand how he was being insulted. The boy looked from Pierre to Raoul as they spoke, his large, dark eyes watchful, his face expressionless.

"Raoul, stop this." It was Nicole, back from getting rid of the bucket. "I'm Auguste's aunt and you're his uncle, and you might as well get used to it."

"And you are spoiling our dinner, Raoul," Elysée said. "Either sit and eat with us like a civilized man or leave us alone."

"Spoiling your dinner?" Raoul gave a bellow of laughter. "Mean to tell me it doesn't spoil your dinner to see that savage puking in our great hall? Mean to tell me *he's* civilized?"

Pierre glanced across the table at his father and Frank Hopkins, who had both risen to their feet. Elysée's eyes burned with anger. Frank held his little girl's hand and looked sombrely at Raoul. The two Hopkins boys stared at their uncle.

I pray God they don't admire him. Boys have a way of looking up to men who behave like brutes.

Raoul turned to Nicole, his teeth flashing white under his thick black mustache. "You really want an Indian nephew? Have you forgot what Indians did to your sister?"

"No, I'll never forget what happened to Helene," Nicole said. "None of us will. But Auguste had nothing to do with that."

"You didn't watch your sister die," Raoul said. "So that just the sight of an Indian makes you want to kill."

Pierre saw that Raoul was working himself up into a rage. He would talk and talk, and every word he said would make him angrier, until at last, the explosion. A spasm of pain shot across Pierre's stomach.

Not now, he prayed. *God, let the illness leave me alone until I can be alone with it.*

Nicole's cheeks were an even brighter red than was usual for her, but she spoke gently. "Raoul, you do have a living sister. If it had been me at Fort Dearborn instead of Helene—if I had been raped and murdered—I would be looking down from Heaven, and I would be hoping your wound would heal. I would pray that you would welcome Pierre's son, your nephew, into your home."

"Stop saying that this filthy savage is my nephew," said Raoul. "Look at him standing there, staring at me. You know what the word mongrel means, redskin?"

Pierre felt a surge of pride as he saw Auguste standing straight and slender, gazing levelly at Raoul. Savage? Even though he had been sick only a moment ago, Auguste held himself as regally as a young prince.

"As for you, Nicole," Raoul went on, "don't ever think you can speak for Helene. She may be in Heaven now, but she got there by way of Hell. No decent woman could imagine what she suffered."

Pierre almost screamed aloud as the pain in his belly stabbed him again. He clutched at his stomach. Just when he needed all his strength!

Auguste looked into his eyes, then down at his hand.

"You hurt, Father," Auguste said in English. "Must sit down."

"Oh? He's already got a few words of English?" said Raoul. "You're training him to talk, eh? Like a parrot? Going to put him in a medicine show?"

Elysée suddenly spoke in a loud voice, "My friends—those who were invited to dine with us here today—will you please excuse us and give us privacy? We have family matters to discuss."

Silently, eyes cast down, the thirty or so servants and field workers who had been invited to celebrate the coming of Pierre's son filed out of the hall.

Pierre thought, *In so many things I have failed today.*

"Raoul," Elysée said, "I have not forgiven Helene's killers. But I am not stupid enough to hate all Indians, and neither should you be. Do you think whites have never tortured and killed Indian women?"

Raoul bared his teeth again. "If you can't hate the Indians for what they did to your daughter and to me, then you never loved either one of us."

Pierre felt a sudden surge of anger. "Raoul, I forbid you to speak that way to our father. You are cruel and unjust."

"You owe *me* justice, Pierre, you and Papa. Where was he when you abandoned me to the Indians? Where were you?"

Pierre's legs shook. He could feel the rage radiating from Raoul; it was like standing too close to a red-hot stove.

Auguste said, "Father."

Pierre turned and looked into the dark young eyes.

Auguste spoke in Sauk. "Father, I am the cause of this man's anger."

"There is much to explain, son," said Pierre. "Be patient and quiet, and all will be well."

Pierre saw fear struggling with resolution in his son's face. A pallor in the fine olive skin showed that Auguste had not yet gotten over being sick. Auguste squared his shoulders and took a step toward Raoul. He raised his right hand in greeting.

"I greet uncle," he said solemnly in English.

"Keep this mongrel away from me, Pierre," Raoul said.

"Frank," said Nicole, "take the children out of here."

Frank picked Abigail up and carried her, with Tom and Benjamin trailing. He walked off toward the kitchen, looking back over his shoulder at Nicole.

Elysée said, "Remember, Raoul, this is my grandson."

"Your grandson!" Raoul spat.

Auguste held out his right hand to Raoul. "I sorry you angry. Want be friend."

In a moment, Pierre thought, he would have to get between them. But his stomach hurt so badly that he could hardly move.

"If you want to be my friend, you mongrel bastard, get as far away from this house and from me as you can," Raoul said.

Auguste took another step toward Raoul, still holding out his hand. He'd learned about shaking hands from Frank Hopkins just a little while ago, Pierre remembered.

"Auguste, no!" Pierre cried.

"Don't you try to touch me, redskin."

Raoul thrust out his own hand and struck at Auguste's. He grabbed Auguste's shirt, twisting the buckskin in his big hand.

Raoul had lost all control. The fury was upon him. Pierre forgot about his own pain and tried to throw himself between Raoul and Auguste. His chest hit Raoul's arm, hard as an iron bar.

"Let go of him, Raoul," Pierre said.

"Raoul, stop it!" Elysée shouted.

"All right." Raoul punched his fist into Auguste's chest and released him, sending the boy staggering backward to fall to the floor.

Rage blazed up inside Pierre. The sight of his son knocked to the floor swept away all constraint. To the Devil with trying to reason with Raoul. He rushed at Raoul and swung his arm with all his strength, bringing his palm against Raoul's mouth.

Though open-handed, it was a blow that would have knocked many a man down. Raoul only staggered back half a step.

But a trickle of blood appeared at the corner of his mouth.

"You still fight like a Frenchman, Pierre," said Raoul with a grin, wiping his mouth. "Slapping a man. Think you're still a count or something? Fight like an American."

He lunged at Pierre. Pierre barely saw, out of the corner of his eye, the fist coming at him. A cannon went off at the side of his head.

He was on the floor, flat on his back.

Nicole screamed, "No! No, Auguste!"

Pierre rolled his aching head to one side to see Auguste standing over him, his hand on the deerhorn hilt of the knife that hung at his belt, the knife Pierre had left for him when he was a baby. Nicole held his arm with both hands.

"Want to fight with knives?" Raoul said. He slid his own huge hunting knife out and held it upright, the point glittering in the candlelight.

"Come on, redskin!" Raoul shouted, but even as he spoke he charged at Auguste, as Auguste struggled to break free from Nicole. Raoul's knife flashed and Pierre heard a cry of pain, and Nicole was between Auguste and Raoul, and Auguste had his hand to his face and blood was running through his fingers.

Raoul stepped away from Auguste and wiped his knife on a white tablecloth.

"What have you done?" Pierre shouted.

"I was kind," Raoul said with a white-toothed grin.

Pierre rushed to Auguste. Blood flowed from a long cut that ran straight down Auguste's cheek from just below his eye to the corner of his mouth. The front of Auguste's tan buckskin shirt was stained red.

"If he'd pulled that knife, I would have taken his eye," Raoul said softly. "I just left a mark on him. So he won't forget me."

"Let go of me, Father," Auguste said in Sauk, in a level, terrible voice. "I have to kill him."

"No!" said Pierre, holding Auguste tighter.

You're a brave boy, but I'm afraid it's you that would be killed, my son.

Blood pounded in Pierre's head. He wanted to take Auguste's knife—the knife he'd given Auguste long ago—and drive it into Raoul's chest.

If I were like Raoul, I would do just that. Or try to.

"Raoul, for this I will never forgive you."

"Forgive me?" Raoul shouted. "Can I forgive you for bringing this savage here to cheat me?"

Nicole took Auguste from Pierre's arms. She pressed a white napkin to his bleeding face and took him to a chair to sit down. As he sat, Auguste turned to shoot Raoul a look of pure hate.

"Cheat you? What are you talking about?"

"Just remember, when you die—and I hope God makes it soon— I *will* have this estate."

Pierre felt Raoul's words as if that blade had plunged into his heart. That his own brother should wish him dead . . .

Pierre went to stand by Auguste, seated in a chair with Nicole wiping his slashed face.

Pierre said, "In the will I wrote years ago I named you as my heir. I never thought to change that will. Until today."

Raoul, still wiping his knife, snorted. "No court in Illinois would let a man disinherit a legitimate white brother in favor of a half-Indian bastard."

Pierre let his hand rest on Auguste's shoulder. The boy's eyes burned up at him. Pierre looked down at the blood-soaked napkin that Nicole pressed to Auguste's cheek.

Auguste, speaking in the Sauk tongue, broke the silence that had followed Raoul's words. "Even if he is your brother and my uncle, this man is our enemy, Father. I will stand side by side with you against him." Auguste put his hand over the hand that lay on his shoulder.

Raoul slammed his knife into its sheath. "You've driven me out of my home, Pierre. I'm not living under the same roof with an Indian. I won't be back till I can come back as master of this house."

He strode to the door and turned again. "And then I'll bring my own family with me."

"What do you mean—your own family?" Elysée called across the long hall.

"I'm marrying Eli Greenglove's daughter," Raoul said with a grin. "And that mongrel had better not try to touch my children's birthright."

He was gone, leaving the door hanging open behind him, sunlight pouring in.

Pierre looked miserably down at Auguste and thought, *I hope your shaman's skills make you better at predicting the future than I have been, my son.*

BOOK 2

1831

Moon of Ripe Cherries

July

8

Homecoming

Rejoicing at the sight of Victor, Auguste stepped up to the gangplank of the paddle wheeler *Virginia* and paused there a moment to look around. He couldn't help himself: he smiled broadly. The settlement hugging the bluff was not home, but it was closer to home than he had been in a long time.

And this summer, he had decided, he would go back to his true home. He would end the sorrow of being cut off from his people.

This was the sixth spring since Pierre de Marion had come and taken him to Victoire, and, as with every spring before it, he missed Saukenuk terribly. He longed for his mother, for the teachings of Owl Carver, for the arms of Redbird, whom he had lost almost as soon as he made her his.

For six years—he had learned to count years as white people did—he had obeyed his father and the promise made with the calumet and had not tried even to send a message to the British Band. He even felt it was a wise rule. To communicate with his loved ones would have torn him in two. But more than a month ago in New York City, strolling in the warm evening air on the busy cobblestone streets, past dooryards where lilacs were blooming, he made up his mind that when he returned to Illinois he would visit Victoire only briefly and then would go back to Saukenuk. He was twenty-one years old now, and among white people that meant he was master of his own life.

He gazed up at the bluff. There were more houses up there than when he had last come out here, two years ago. Some were built on the bottomland itself, in spite of the danger of flooding.

He saw the palisade and flags and towers of Raoul de Marion's trading post at the top of the bluff, and felt his joy fading. He would have to face Raoul's insults and threats, as he had every other time he came back to Victor. His belly tightened as he remembered, as if it had just happened, that first encounter six years ago, the burning-ice feel of the knifepoint slicing into his cheek, his hand gripping his own knife, Aunt Nicole and Father holding him back.

Seemingly with a will of its own his hand went to the scar and his finger traced the ridge that ran from eye to mouth.

He brought his gaze down from the top of the bluff and saw a more welcome sight—Grandpapa, Aunt Nicole and Guichard in a black open carriage from the estate, waiting to take him up to Victoire. He ran down the gangplank and strode over to them.

"Auguste! My God, you're beautiful!" Aunt Nicole exclaimed, and then her face reddened and she looked downward.

He felt that he looked good, though "beautiful," as he understood English, was not the right word for a woman to use about a man. But he supposed she admired his new clothes, the fawn-colored cutaway coat and vest, the ruffled silk shirt, the tight, bottle-green trousers. He wished he were not already holding his tall beaver hat in his hand, so that he could tip it to her with the graceful motion he'd learned watching the dandies on Broad Way.

Grandpapa leaned out of the carriage and hugged Auguste. His embrace felt strong, and his eyes were bright. Auguste was happy to see him in good health.

But where is Father?

Auguste shook hands with Guichard, who had climbed down stiffly from the driver's seat.

"Your trunk, Monsieur Auguste?"

Auguste pointed out the big wooden chest with brass fittings that had been unloaded at the Victor pier along with bales and barrels from the hold of the *Virginia*.

Guichard approached two buckskin-clad men lounging by a piling. He pointed out the trunk as Auguste had done.

"For *him*?" said one of the men, glowering at Auguste from under his coonskin cap. "White men don't wait on goddamn Injuns." He spat tobacco juice at Guichard's feet and turned away, as did the other man.

Auguste wanted to throw the man who had spat at Guichard

into the river. He had no doubt that he could do it, though like most men who lived in Victor, the man was armed with knife and pistol. Auguste had been taught to fight as a Sauk, and he had been a champion boxer, wrestler and fencer at St. George's School. But he was not going to get into a brawl in his first minutes ashore. Time enough for that if he met Raoul.

"Come on, Guichard. The trunk's light enough. We don't need any help." The old servant taking one end and Auguste the other, they loaded it into the back of the carriage.

"Good to see you again, Grandpapa," Auguste said as he dropped into the seat facing Elysée and Nicole, his back to the driver. "Aunt Nicole, it's you who are beautiful. But where's Father?"

Grandpapa patted him on the knee. "Not feeling well, I'm afraid. He sends his apologies. We will go to him now, at once."

Grandpapa was trying to make his voice sound unconcerned. But Auguste heard an undertone of sorrow, the anguish of a father who had lost one of his children years ago and would soon lose another.

With understanding, grief sank into Auguste's marrow. Father— Star Arrow—had hung on these past six years, growing sicker and sicker, the evil in his belly swelling up like a poisonous toad. Now the end was near.

Auguste found himself looking deep into Aunt Nicole's eyes, full of shared sorrow.

Guichard flicked the reins, and the carriage started off, turning away from the dock, passing the warehouses and rattling down the long dusty-white road that led across the bottomland fields to the bluff. It must have been a good spring out here; though this was only the beginning of July, the corn was already up to a man's waist.

Auguste felt he would look better wearing his beaver hat as they rode along. He put it on his head, pulling the rolled-up brim down with both hands, and set it in place with a pat on the crown.

"So, you are now a finished graduate of St. George's School?" said Elysée with a smile. "Monsieur Charles Winans has sent long letters full of good reports about you."

Aunt Nicole reached over and squeezed his hand. "We're proud of you, Auguste." Her soft, fleshy hand was warm, and her eyes sparkled at him. He sensed a feeling in her that was more than the affection of an aunt for a nephew. She now had eight children, he knew, and every time he had seen her and Frank together, they had seemed very much in love. But Aunt Nicole was a big woman. She had room in her big heart, perhaps, for more than one love.

Embarrassed by what he felt radiating from her, Auguste turned to Elysée.

"If I learned anything at St. George's, I owe it all to the way you prepared me, Grandpapa. Anyone who could take a boy who could barely speak English, and in two years cram enough knowledge into his head for him to go to secondary school in New York City—such a man is no ordinary teacher."

"You were no ordinary pupil, my boy," said Elysée, leaning back in the carriage, his hands resting one on top of the other on his silver-headed cane. "And Père Isaac laid down a solid foundation in that head of yours. Those Jesuits are good for that, at least, black-hearted rogues though they may be in most other respects."

"Papa!" Nicole gave Elysée a reproving frown.

Elysée quickly patted her knee. "Forgive me, my child. Let me not shake the faith that sustains you."

"It would take more than your wicked tongue to disturb my faith, Papa," Nicole said with a wry smile.

It was amusing to hear Grandpapa and Aunt Nicole bicker about what the whites called "faith." As the carriage rolled along, Auguste recalled the many lectures he had listened to on Jesus and the Trinity at St. George's, which was affiliated with the Episcopal Church. But Auguste had walked with the White Bear and talked with the Turtle. He *knew* them as he had never known the white people's God, and what went on in their dimly lit, waxy-smelling churches had no attraction for him.

He knew that Christians, for the most part, saw his beliefs about the spirit world as rubbish sprung out of ignorance—or, worse, inspired by the Evil One. Père Isaac's efforts to persuade him to walk in the way of Jesus had prepared him for that. At school he did not speak of things sacred to him, so as not to expose them to white scorn. When teachers and fellow students tried to persuade him to take instruction in Christianity, he was polite and evasive.

And when he felt he was smothering in the noise and crowding and dirt of the huge city of New York, he would borrow a pony from the lady he called Aunt Emilie—his father's cousin, actually—and ride out of New York along a trail that led to the north end of the island of Manhattan. There in a forest cave he had found, he would chew a bit of the sacred mushroom Owl Carver had given him and restore his link with the spirit world by journeying with the White Bear. All through these six years, *his* faith had remained strong.

Nicole broke in on his thoughts. "You're still studying medicine?"

"Just a beginning. I've read some books, attended some lectures. I assisted a surgeon—Dr. Martin Bernard—at New York Hospital. I bought myself a surgeon's box of instruments—got it in the trunk, there. But if anybody came down with anything worse than an ingrown toenail, I'd be scared to do anything about it."

Elysée said, "You can pull teeth, I hope, like any proper surgeon?"

Auguste shrugged. "I do have a turnkey for that. But I've never actually used it."

"The only person in town who knows anything about treating the sick is Gram Medill, the midwife," Nicole said. "Tom Slattery, the blacksmith, pulls teeth. We need a real doctor."

Auguste felt a fluttering in his stomach as he wondered when he should tell this white family of his that he wanted to leave them. Nicole was thinking, he realized, that he would stay here at Victoire.

The steel-reinforced wooden wheels of the carriage bumped mercilessly over the rutted road, and Auguste hoped Nicole wasn't pregnant at the moment. The fact that his shaman's sense did not tell him reminded him that he had been too long away from the Sauk. As they began to climb the road that ran up the bluff, Nicole pointed out to Auguste that the newer houses were made of boards rather than logs, because Frank had set up a sawmill and workshop on the Peach River. Frank was now a master carpenter, with four workers to help him when there was a house to be built.

"But he'd sell the mill in a minute if printing alone would provide him with a living," she said. "That's where his heart is."

Elysée said, "Pierre and I offered Frank a regular income, so that he could give all his time to his newspaper and to printing, but he wouldn't hear of it. He got a bit haughty when I pressed him, and informed me that the system of feudal patronage is dead. I assured him that I was well aware of that, and that is why I am here and not in France."

"Frank is proud, Papa," said Nicole.

Elysée nodded. "I fear he is too often a proud papa."

Auguste roared, and Nicole, though she blushed, could not help laughing.

"The town grows bigger every year," Auguste said. Nicole nodded sympathetically; she seemed to have guessed what he was thinking: How numerous the whites were, as he had seen for himself in the East, and how inexorably they were filling up this part of the country, like a river in flood. Last year the New York papers had reported the results of the 1830 census; the United States was over twelve million, Auguste had read, a number he could not even imagine. And 150,000 of those were here in the state of Illinois, balanced against the six thousand Sauk and Fox. Black Hawk's people, the British Band, numbered only two thousand. Hopeless.

"Victor had a hundred or so people the year you came here," said Elysée. "Now there are over four hundred. As you see, the bluff is completely covered with houses. And we have many new industries and crafts. A preacher, a Reverend Hale, has put up a church on the prairie to the east of us. I am not sure whether his work counts as an industry or a craft. There is Frank's sawmill, as Nicole said. There are also a flour mill and a brewery, and a mason works at a limestone quarry nearby. And your father is planning to set up a kiln on the estate, so we can build a new Victoire of brick."

"How sick is my father?" Auguste asked abruptly, dreading the answer he would get.

"Ah, Nicole, there are your children waiting to greet us," Grandpapa cried, as if he had not heard Auguste's question.

Where the road made a sharp turn and started upward on a higher level, stood a two-story frame building painted white. A sign over the door read, THE VICTOR VISITOR, F. HOPKINS, PUBr, PRINTING AND ENGRAVING. CARPENTRY.

Auguste could hear the press clanking away inside the house as they approached. The three younger children, John, Rachel and Betsy, were lined up by the door, Rachel holding in her arms a baby that must be Nicole and Frank's newest. Three of the older ones, Benjamin, Abigail and Martha, leaned out a window to wave to Auguste from the second story. Auguste felt proud of himself, being able to remember all their names and which was which.

As Guichard reined up the horse and pushed the brake lever on the carriage, the sound of the press stopped and Frank came out through the open door wiping his ink-stained hands on his leather apron. His forehead was shiny with sweat. The oldest son, Thomas, followed him, pushing his hands down his own apron with the same gesture.

Auguste climbed down from the carriage and took Frank's hand, then shook with Thomas and the three little girls. The baby was Patrick, he learned. He lightly rubbed Patrick's fine hair.

"No wonder the town's population grows so fast, Aunt Nicole," Auguste said with a smile. "How many more do you think there will be for you and Frank?"

But as he spoke, his pleasure at his aunt's handsome family was dimmed by the thought that if all white families were as fertile as this, there was no hope at all for the red people.

"None, I hope," said Frank firmly. "We've got too big a tribe as it is."

Aunt Nicole's face reddened again, and Auguste reminded himself that white women were generally reluctant to talk about pregnancy and childbirth. Auguste recalled his mother, Sun Woman, speaking of a kind of tea that would keep a woman from getting pregnant. When he went back to Saukenuk he could find out more about it. He would surely come back here to visit, and then he could tell Aunt Nicole about it. If white women knew about that tea, maybe there would be fewer whites in years to come, and they would not have such a hunger for land.

As they drove on up the road to the top of the bluff, Auguste saw Nicole's face brighten, and he turned to see what she was looking at. A black buggy drawn by an old gray horse was coming toward them, having just rounded the bend in the road at the trading post palisade. Auguste caught a glimpse of blond braids under a red and white checkered bonnet.

Nicole said, "Auguste, here's a newcomer to our county. I think you'll enjoy meeting her."

"Ah yes," said Elysée. "Reverend Hale and his daughter, Mademoiselle Nancy. He came here over a year ago, Auguste, declared the town too corrupt for his church and started holding services for the farmers out on the prairie. They built him a church about five miles from town. Painted white, with a steeple one can see for miles. Its very simplicity makes it beautiful."

Nicole said, "As much could be said for Nancy."

Curious, Auguste tried to see the face under the red and white bonnet. Every day, and many times a day, he thought of Redbird and the joy they so briefly shared, but many of the young white women he had seen in the past six years had made his heart beat faster. Just last winter he'd gone with a group of his classmates to an elegant old house on Nassau Street where he discovered that the body of a white woman, under her many-layered dress, was in all important respects as interesting as the body of a woman of his own people. Even though he planned to leave Victoire as soon as he could, he was eager to meet the new minister's daughter.

The two carriages pulled side by side, and the drivers, Guichard and the Reverend Hale, a slab-faced man dressed in black, reined up for the customary exchange of greeting.

"Reverend Hale, Miss Hale," Elysée said, "may I present my grandson, Auguste de Marion."

The reverend stared at Auguste for a moment from under bushy brows before grunting an acknowledgment. Auguste suspected he had heard about his parentage and was looking for traces of Indian blood.

Indian. Auguste had never heard that word before he went to live among white people. His people were the Sauk, the People of the Place of Fire. And their allies were the Fox. And besides these there were Winnebago, Potawatomi, Chippewa, Kickapoo, Osage, Piankeshaw, Sioux, Shawnee—each a separate people. And besides these, hundreds more, whose names he did not even know. But the whites had one name for all these peoples—Indians. And that name, Grandpapa had explained to him with gentle irony, was altogether a mistake. The explorer Columbus had thought he had landed in India.

They do not even respect us enough to call us by an honest name.

But the sight of Nancy Hale drove the bitterness from his mind. Her braids, emerging from her red and white bonnet and lying on either side of her white lace collar, were yellow as ripe corn, and her face, while too long for ideal beauty, was pink and clear. Her mouth was wide, and her teeth were white when she smiled at Nicole and Elysée. She looked straight at Auguste for an instant, then she looked down, but in that moment he saw eyes a vivid shade of blue, like the turquoise stone from the Southwest he carried in his medicine bag.

"Visiting the members of your flock, are you, Reverend?" Elysée asked. Auguste noticed that he put the tiniest humorous inflection on the word "flock."

Hale's thick gray brows drew together as he nodded sourly. "Trying to bring the Word to that wilderness you call a town."

Here was an unhappy man, thought Auguste, whose life was dedicated to persuading those around him to be equally unhappy.

"Ah, yes," said Elysée with a broad smile. "Quite a population of sheep gone astray in Victor."

"In all of Smith County," said Hale.

It must scandalize him to think that my mother is an Indian woman and that my father, by the lights of this man, isn't even married to her.

Auguste suddenly wanted to defy the disapproval he felt from the reverend. He jumped out of the carriage and in an instant was standing on the road beside the minister's buggy. He swept off his high-crowned hat with the flourish he'd seen in New York and bowed deeply.

"Miss Hale," he said. "Auguste de Marion. At your service."

The blood rose to Nancy Hale's cheeks.

"My pleasure, Mr. de Marion," she murmured. Her large blue eyes looked frightened and her flush deepened, but she did not take her eyes away, and his gaze was locked to hers. His heart beat as hard as it had the first time he saw the White Bear.

"The Lord's work awaits us in Victor," said the Reverend Hale loudly. "You really must excuse us." And without waiting for a reply he snapped the reins of his buggy, and the old horse ambled off.

Auguste stood in the road waiting to see if Nancy would glance back at him. She did. Even at a distance and through dust he could see the blue of her eyes.

Elysée said, "Well, Auguste, close your mouth, put your hat back on and get back up here."

I'm going to meet her again, Auguste thought.

He still wanted just as much to go back to his people. He had not forgotten Redbird. By now, though, she had probably forgotten him. And so, what harm could there be in getting to know this white young lady a little better?

Then their carriage was passing the log wall around the trading post. A shadow fell over his enjoyment at meeting Nancy Hale. He ran his finger down the scar on his cheek.

"Is *he* in there?" he said abruptly to Nicole.

Her face paled. "He's down— You know about what's going on in the Rock River country, don't you?"

Auguste stiffened. "Has something happened to my people?"

He saw Nicole close her eyes and sigh when he said "my people."

"There has been trouble," said Elysée. "Did no news reach you in New York?"

O Earthmaker, let them come to no harm.

Twisting his hands in his lap, Auguste said, "The New York papers only report what happens on the eastern seaboard." He remembered now overhearing remarks by some of his fellow passengers on the *Virginia* about "Injun trouble." But he'd kept to himself on the trip up from St. Louis.

We steamed right past the mouth of the Rock River, and I never guessed!

Elysée nodded. "Well, your father insisted that no one write you about it. He feared it would distract you from your studies."

Auguste felt a sudden flash of anger at Pierre de Marion. *He does want me to forget that I am a Sauk. Not even telling me when my people are in danger.*

He gripped Elysée's arm. "What happened?"

Nicole said, "Frank has a correspondent who writes him regularly from Fort Armstrong."

The American fort, Auguste remembered, was at the mouth of the Rock River, six miles downriver from Saukenuk.

Nicole went on, "Black Hawk's band once again crossed the Mississippi to Saukenuk in the spring, even though the Army has told them over and over that the land now belongs to the Federal government and they must not return to it. This time they found settlers actually living in some of their houses and farming their fields. Black Hawk drove them out. Black Hawk's warriors de-

stroyed settlers' cabins nearby, shot their horses and cows, told them
to move away or be killed. Now Governor Reynolds has called up
the militia to drive Black Hawk and his people out of Illinois. His
proclamation says, 'Dead or alive.' "

Auguste's heart suddenly felt as if ice had formed around it.

Elysée said, "And Raoul and most of his cronies have gone to
join the militia."

Auguste whispered, "O Earthmaker, keep my people safe." The
carriage had reached the top of the hill and was passing the front
gate of the trading post, shut and locked with a chain. He trembled
at the thought of Redbird—Sun Woman—Owl Carver—Black
Hawk—all the people he had known and loved all of his life, facing
the rifles of men like Raoul.

"I must go there now," he said in a low voice.

"You can't," Nicole said quickly. "You can't get through the
militia lines. You'd be shot."

Auguste, fists clenched in his lap, shook his head. "If they are in
such danger, how can I stay away? I *must* be with them."

Elysée seized his wrist in a grip so powerful it startled him. "Listen to me. You cannot help them. You simply can't get there before
matters are settled, one way or another. And I am sure that when
your chief Black Hawk sees the size of the militia force, he will go
peacefully back across the Mississippi. The Sauk and Fox have
many young men. You are your father's only son. *He* needs you
now."

Auguste's heart ached as he saw the plea in Grandpapa's eyes.
How could he deny the old man? And his father's need for the love
of his son in his last days.

But the thought of thousands of armed and angry whites going
to drive his people out of Saukenuk smote him like a war club.
Grandpapa didn't know Black Hawk; Black Hawk was not likely
to yield peaceably. And whether or not Auguste could be any use
at Saukenuk, he had to be there.

Nicole said, "At least see your father and talk to him before you
decide what to do."

Auguste nodded. "Of course." He saw more pain in her face than
he could bear to look at. He turned to stare out at the hills as the
carriage carried them to Victoire.

Now they could see Victoire, the great stone and log house rising out of the prairie on its low hill. Elysée and Pierre liked to call it a château, but Auguste had learned that it was nothing like the castles in the land they had come from. And, much as he had marveled at Victoire when he first saw it, he had seen still bigger and finer houses in New York. But it was still the grandest house north of the Rock River's mouth, and Auguste couldn't help feeling proud when he realized that the blood of the men who built it flowed in his own veins.

Their carriage rattled through the gateway in the split-log fence. Auguste saw with pleasure that the maple tree that shaded the south side of the house was bigger than ever.

Most of the servants and field hands were gathered before the front door to greet Auguste. He remembered how they had assembled this way six years ago, when Star Arrow first brought him here from Saukenuk.

Every time he thought of Saukenuk, of his beleaguered people surrounded by an enemy army, his breathing grew fast and shallow.

But he was frightened, too, by the silence of the house. It whispered of his father's dying. He must face Pierre's death and suffer with him now. Auguste wanted to rush upstairs to Pierre and hold him tight. And also he did not want to go into Pierre's room at all.

Auguste and Elysée climbed the stairway from the great hall of the château to Pierre's second-story bedroom, Nicole following. At the door Auguste hesitated, and Elysée stepped forward and firmly knocked. A woman's voice called them in.

As Grandpapa pushed the door open, Auguste closed his eyes. He dreaded what he was about to see. His heart fluttered anxiously. Would there be anything, he wondered, he could do for his father?

Now the door was fully open, and he saw the long, thin figure stretched out under a sheet on a canopied bed. Marchette was sitting with a basin of water on her knees. She had been wiping Pierre's face with a damp cloth.

A flash of bright red caught Auguste's eye. On the floor by the bed was a second basin, partly covered by a towel which, Auguste suspected, Marchette must have hastily thrown over it. But part of the towel had fallen into the basin, and blood was soaking into the white linen.

A knot of grief filled Auguste's throat, blocking it so he could not speak. He rushed to the bed.

Pierre lay on his back, his head propped up by pillows, his long nose pointing straight at Auguste, his eyes turned toward him. His bony hands looked very large, because his arms were so thin. Pierre's gray hair, what was left of it, spread out on the pillow.

Pierre lifted his head a little.

"Son. Oh, I am glad to see you."

He raised his hands, and Auguste, biting his lip, leaned over the bed and put his hands under his father's shoulders. He held Pierre close and felt Pierre's hands come to rest on his back, light as autumn leaves. They held each other that way for a moment.

His father felt so light, as if he was starving to death. Auguste released him and sat on the edge of the bed. He said the first thing that came into his mind.

"Did you eat today, Father?"

Pierre's voice was like the wind in dead branches. "Marchette keeps me alive with clear soups. They are all that I can keep down."

A half-empty bowl of broth, Auguste now saw, stood on a table beside the bed. Next to the soup lay a Bible bound in black leather, and Pierre's silver spectacle case with its velvet ribbon.

What would Sun Woman and Owl Carver do for a man this sick? What would they feed him?

"Maybe I can help you, Father," he said.

"I don't think anyone can help me, son," Pierre said. "It's all right. Just having you here makes me feel better."

Auguste had learned enough about cancer to be sure that Pierre's condition was hopeless. Dr. Bernard—any of the other white physicians at New York Hospital—would say that nothing more could be done except to make the patient comfortable, give him laudanum perhaps, and wait for the end.

But that was merely what white medicine had taught Auguste. White doctors had sharp lancets to draw blood, scalpels to cut into sick people's bodies, saws to cut off infected limbs. They had huge thick books listing hundreds of diseases and prescribing treatments for them. But after spending many hours treating the sick in New York, Auguste had seen that there were many things the white physicians did not know how to do, had never even thought of doing. Perhaps greater hope for Pierre lay in the way of the shaman.

At the very least, Auguste, as White Bear, could speak to Pierre's soul, could summon the aid of the spirits, especially his own spirit helper and that of the sick man, to cure him if possible; if not, then to ease his suffering, help him to accept what was to happen to him and prepare him to walk in the other world.

With a jolt, the thought hit him anew: *If I stay here with Father, what of Saukenuk?*

Pierre said, "God has kept me alive because I must talk to you about our land, Auguste."

Auguste did not like the sound of that. The thousands of acres the de Marions owned had nothing to do with him, and he wanted to keep it that way.

Marchette stood up, pushing her chair back. "Perhaps the rest of us should leave you and Monsieur Auguste alone."

Auguste saw in her face the anguish of a woman who was losing a man she loved. Auguste had long suspected, seeing the looks that passed between Pierre and Marchette, and the way her husband, the brown-bearded Armand, glared at both of them, that there was— or at least had once been—something between the master of Victoire and the cook.

Pierre raised a tremulous hand. "Au contraire. I want the three of you—Papa, Nicole, Marchette—to hear what I say. Besides, you are the three I trust most. I want you to know my wishes, my true wishes, because after I am gone there are those who will lie about me."

Auguste took Pierre's hand, so big and yet so weak, in his own strong, brown one.

"Father, you must believe that you will live."

Auguste heard the others move closer to the bed. Nicole went to stand at the foot. Elysée seated himself in an old spindly-legged armchair brought over from France, his cane across his knees.

Pierre pointed a skeletal finger above his head to a shelf mounted on the white-painted plaster wall, where an Indian pipe lay, its bowl carved of red pipestone, its stem polished hickory.

"Take down the calumet," Pierre said. "Let me hold it."

Auguste took the pipe reverently, with a hand at each end of its three-foot length. Two black feathers with white tips fluttered from the bowl as he put the pipe into Pierre's hands. From the moment he touched the pipe, Auguste's hands were shaking as much as Pierre's. Only he and Pierre understood how much power was in this pipe—power to bind men for life to whatever they promised when they smoked the sacred tobacco.

Pierre let the pipe lie on his chest, his fingers touching it lightly.

"This pipe was given me a few years after you were born, Auguste, by Jumping Fish, who even then was one of the civil chiefs of the Sauk and Fox. It is the sign of an agreement between our family and the Sauk and Fox, fully understood and freely entered into by both sides."

Auguste looked in wonderment from Pierre to Elysée, and Grandpapa nodded solemnly.

Elysée said, "We had spent years exploring the more unsettled parts of the Illinois Territory, and we had decided that here was the land we wanted as our family seat in the New World. In 1809 we bought this land for a dollar an acre at the Federal land office in Kaskaskia. Thirty thousand dollars. The Federal government claimed that the Sauk and Fox had signed a treaty a few years earlier with Governor William Henry Harrison, selling fifty-one million acres, including all of northern Illinois, to the United States for a little over two thousand dollars, a shockingly paltry sum."

Pierre said, "But we knew that the Sauk and Fox disputed that claim."

Auguste said, "Yes, Black Hawk says Harrison cheated the Sauk and Fox. He says the chiefs who signed the treaty were drunk and could not speak English or read or write it, and did not know what they were agreeing to when they made their marks. He says that anyway those chiefs had no permission from the tribe to sell any land."

"Exactly," said Elysée. "And we wanted to live in peace with the Sauk and Fox. And that was why your father went to Saukenuk. We hoped to make reasonable payments for the land we would live on to those from whom it had been taken."

Pierre said, "I was still there with your mother, by my own choice, when war broke out in 1812, and then they required me to stay with them. You were already two years old. After the war, and after I left them, I sent the Sauk and Fox chiefs what they asked for—thirty thousand dollars, partly in coin and partly in trade goods, knives, steel axes, tin pots and kettles, blankets and bolts of cloth, rifles and barrels of gunpowder, bags of bullets. So, we paid for this land twice over. Despite that, I think it is far more valuable

still than all the money we spent for it. The chiefs recognize our
right to live on the land and use it. And Jumping Fish gave me this
calumet, and I gave him a fine Kentucky long rifle with brass and
silver inlay on the barrel and stock."

Auguste nodded eagerly. "Yes, yes, I've seen it. Jumping Fish
uses it to shoot the first buffalo every winter to start the hunt."

"And I gave Black Hawk the compass your war chief still treasures, from which I received my Sauk name."

"Yes."

Auguste looked across Pierre's bed and out the windows, of
costly clear glass shipped from Philadelphia, that gave a view south
across grass-covered prairie. Once all that prairie belonged to my
people, he thought.

As if knowing his thoughts, Pierre said, "I did not say the Sauk
and Fox sold us the land. I said they recognized our right to use it.
Do you understand?"

Auguste nodded, repeating what he had so often heard Black
Hawk say in the tribal meetings. "Land is not something to be
bought and sold. So we believe."

Pierre closed his eyes wearily, his fingertips still resting on the
calumet that lay across his chest. Auguste grieved. The father who
had left him when he was a little boy and then come back for him
was leaving him again, slipping away. Marchette wiped Pierre's face
with a damp cloth.

Nicole's lower lip trembled as she said, "My big brother. You've
always been here for me."

Elysée's face was crumpled by an unbearable sadness. He wishes,
Auguste thought, that it was him lying there dying, instead of his
son.

Pierre opened his eyes and lifted his head to look at Auguste.
Auguste gently pressed his hand against his father's balding brow.

"Rest, Father, rest."

"Not till we are done. You know that your grandfather turned
the estate over to me when I was forty years of age. Now I must
pass it on. Until recent years I had thought that the land would go
to Raoul when I died.

"But the enmity between me and Raoul has grown deeper and
deeper. A few times he and I and Papa have met together, trying to
come to terms. Each time, the words that passed between us were

more cruel. Then, a year ago, he even boasted to me that he killed three Sauk Indians who were taking lead from that mine he has been working, which they believe to be theirs."

Auguste gasped.

Sun Fish and the others! That must have been what happened to them.

Pierre said, "What is it?"

"I think I know those three. One of them was my age, and a friend of mine." His hatred for Raoul burned fiercer than ever.

Pierre said, "For a long time now there have been no words at all between Raoul and me."

Auguste said, "It was my coming here that turned you against each other."

Nicole spoke up. "Not you. Raoul has had a grudge against Pierre for as long as I can remember."

Elysée said, "Yes, Raoul has many quarrels with me—over land and how it is to be used, our paying the Sauk and Fox for it, the Fort Dearborn massacre. Yes, you are part of it, Auguste, but there is much more besides."

Auguste shook his head. "But before I came, Father and Raoul were speaking to each other and the question of who would get the estate was settled. And it still can be. Father, after you are gone I will go back to my people. You can tell Raoul that, and there will be peace between you."

With pain that tore all through him like lightning burning through a tree, Auguste realized that he had committed himself to stay here as long as his father lived. His Sauk family and loved ones were in terrible danger four days' ride from here, and he wanted to be with them. But he couldn't leave Pierre now. His fear for Sun Woman and Redbird and the others in peril, his shame at not going to help them, would be a terrible torment, but he would have to endure it. He could not leave his father to take his first steps on the Trail of Souls alone.

Pierre reached out suddenly and seized him by the wrist.

"You must not leave, even after I am gone. You must stay here as my heir."

Auguste gasped as the enormity of what Pierre was saying hit him. Heir! He tried to stand up, but Pierre's grip held him fast. Just as this huge house and all the land around it would hold him captive, forever parted from his people.

"No!"

"Listen, please, Auguste. I cannot will the land to Raoul."

Auguste lifted his free hand pleadingly.

"You can't will it to *me*. I know nothing about managing farms and raising livestock. Nothing about business. Raoul has been trained from childhood to do all the work of this estate. I can't do it, and I don't want it."

He looked around the room, hoping the others would help him persuade Pierre that what he wanted was impossible. Nicole and Marchette were both wide-eyed and open-mouthed. Elysée leaned forward in his chair, his eyes intent on Auguste.

Pierre said, "Once the land is your responsibility, you will do what is right with it. I know you will. I want to turn the estate over to you now, as Papa did with me, while I am still alive. I would be here to help you, for a little while. Your grandfather will advise you, as he has advised me all these years. There will be others to help you. Nicole, her husband, Marchette, Guichard."

Auguste said, "Grandpapa, tell him I can't do it."

Elysée, who had been sitting slumped and miserable in his fragile-looking armchair, roused himself and said, "I knew your father was going to propose this to you today, Auguste. This is what he wants. It is no mere whim. He has been thinking about it for a long time. And it is not impossible. You have shown yourself capable of learning quickly. I can only promise you that if you take up the burden your father offers you, I will be at your side to help you every way that I can."

For a moment Elysée's words made Auguste's resolve waver. Thirty thousand acres, he thought. And the United States stole fifty million acres from my people. Should not one Sauk get some of it back?

But he had some idea of the crushing responsibility a huge estate would entail. It was absurd to think of himself occupying such a place.

"But Raoul is also your son, Grandpapa," he said. "Don't you want him to inherit your land?"

Elysée shook his head. "Raoul is a murderer many times over, who has escaped punishment only because Smith County is on the frontier, where there is no law. He hates Indians with a passion that is close to madness. He is a crude, violent, greedy man. He shames our family. He is far less worthy than you."

Auguste felt anger boiling up under his dismay. Father and Sun Woman and Owl Carver and Black Hawk had promised him he would live among whites only for a time and then go back to the Sauk. They had all smoked the calumet, making that agreement sacred. He had lived for that homecoming, through these six years. He freed his wrist from Pierre's grip and held out his hands, pleading for understanding.

"But I can't stay here with white people for the rest of my life."

Pierre said, "You are not the same person you were when I took you out of the forest. You have been educated. You may yet become a doctor."

"Yes, and I want to be a doctor for my people."

"You can do more for them if you stay here, my son. The Sauk will need friends among the whites who have knowledge and wealth and power."

Auguste shook his head violently, as if to drive out Pierre's words. "I will never be happy, living as a white man. I must go back to my people. I beg you to let me go."

But even as he spoke he realized with a sudden pang that these loved ones, Pierre, Grandpapa, Nicole, were his people too.

Pierre's sunken eyes blazed at Auguste. "I have already written my new will, Auguste. There is one copy with the town clerk, Burke Russell, and one copy in your grandfather's keeping. It names you my sole heir. To all that I possess, the entire de Marion estate. If you accept what I am offering you, you will have to fight Raoul. It will all be upon your shoulders. I can only beg you with these last breaths to take what I would give you. You must decide."

A voice inside Auguste screamed, *You must not do this to me, Father. You will destroy me.*

He stood looking down at his father with his arms hanging at his sides, his shoulders straight, his head bowed. He could not say no so finally, so bluntly, to his dying father. He needed time to work his way free of this trap.

"Father, you know we Sauk never decide quickly. When it is a very important decision, we think, we go on with our work, we walk the sunwise circle, we wait in silence for the answer to come. You must give me time."

Pierre closed his eyes and his head fell back to the white pillows. "You have as much time as I do," he whispered. "But only that much."

Auguste turned away from the bed. His eyes met Nicole's. He saw sympathy for him in her face, but only another shaman could know the pain he was feeling inside.

9

Bequest

White Bear crouched over the brown blanket he had brought down from his room and unrolled it. Bare-chested and barefoot in white sailcloth workman's trousers he had bought in New York, he took from the blanket roll his powerful necklace of megis shells and hung it around his neck. Next he opened his soft leather medicine bag.

Propped up against the big old maple tree on the south side of Victoire, Pierre lay on his mattress with his head and shoulders resting on pillows. His cotton blanket, all he needed on this warm September day, was tucked around his chest, leaving his arms free. He had begged to be taken outside; the weather was so fine. As soon as the servants had carried him out and left him and White Bear alone, he had fallen asleep. These days, Pierre slept most of the time, as a baby would. But a baby slept to build up its strength, Pierre because he was losing strength.

White Bear—he did not think of himself as Auguste now—laid out the objects from his medicine bag on the unrolled blanket and contemplated them. They represented the seven sacred directions. First, East. He picked up a sparkling white rock and placed it on the east side of the tree. The color of East was white and therefore was White Bear's own color. Next was South. He took up the green stone on which the mound builders had long ago carved the figure of a winged man. This he laid on the earth next to the mattress on Pierre's left side. The ground under the maple tree was bare, and an early morning rain had left it damp and soft.

Now West. The spirits of men and women went West when they died, and the color of West was red. He set the red stone, with dark honeycomb markings that looked as if they had been painted on its highly polished surface, on the ground at Pierre's feet. By the north side of the mattress he placed a black stone, itself from the North, that Owl Carver had engraved with an owl image. The fifth direction, Up, was blue, and he put a blue stone, the color of Nancy Hale's eyes, on the pillow beside Pierre's head. He set a piece of brown sandstone for the sixth direction, Down, beside Pierre's blanket-covered feet.

Now for the seventh sacred direction—Here. He picked up the last and largest item from his medicine bag—the claw of a grizzly bear that had been killed by Black Hawk himself many years ago. After White Bear had come back from his first spirit quest with the prediction that Black Hawk would do deeds of courage and that his name would never be forgotten, the war chief had made him a gift of the grizzly claw. White Bear laid the saber-shaped claw on Pierre's chest, over his heart, with the brown tip toward the cancerous lump in Pierre's belly that was killing him.

He went back to his blanket and took out a dried gourd painted black and white. Slapping the gourd against the palm of his hand to make it rattle, he danced in a circle around Pierre and the maple tree, sunwise from east to south to west to north and back to east again, keeping Pierre on his right, singing softly, almost to himself:

> "Earthmaker, you made this man,
> Now we ask your help for him.
> He is a chief whose people need him.
> He still has far to walk.
> Lift him up, Earthmaker.
> Give him back his life."

When White Bear had danced the circle nine times, he put down the gourd. He had brought out from the château a kettle of freshly brewed willow-bark tea and a porcelain cup. It would ease the pain in Pierre's stomach and give him strength. Whenever Pierre ate solid food, blood would come trickling out of every opening in his body and he would grow weaker and paler. He was slowly bleeding and starving to death.

Smelling the tea as he poured it into the cup, White Bear remembered how he'd met Nancy Hale when he was collecting the bark yesterday along the bank of Red Creek. She'd been blueberrying. It was the fourth or fifth time he'd encountered her over the summer on the prairie near Victoire. The meetings weren't accidents; not for either of them. But he felt so uncertain about what he would do when Pierre died that he could only talk with Nancy about things of no importance.

He looked up to see his father's eyes open. They had sunk so far back in the skull-like face that they seemed like embers glowing in caves.

White Bear blew on the steaming cup and held it to Pierre's lips. He drank the tea down in small sips.

Pierre smiled faintly as his eyes traveled over his land. The nearby ground, covered with grass cropped short by sheep and goats, sloped down to the split-rail fence that surrounded the château's inner yard. To the west White Bear could see the two flags flying over Raoul's trading post on the bluff overlooking the river, and beyond that part of the river and the dark west bank, the Ioway country. In the other directions were orchards, farmlands, pastures, and the prairie, yellowing with fall, rolling on to the edge of the sky.

When Pierre had drunk most of the tea, White Bear put down the cup. He gathered up his sacred stones and put them back in his medicine bag.

Pierre said, "You did a Sauk ritual for me just now, did you not?"

"Yes," said White Bear. "It was meant to heal you. Or, if not, to give you strength to bear the pain."

"I do feel better today," Pierre said. "But I must also have a certain rite of the Church if I am to pass over into God's love. I sent a week ago to Kaskaskia for your old teacher, Père Isaac. He should be here any day. I have been a great sinner, White Bear."

It gladdened White Bear's heart that his father called him by his Sauk name.

"You are a *good* man, my father," he said in the Sauk tongue.

Pierre raised his head, and White Bear saw that the effort pained him. The burning, sunken eyes turned on White Bear.

"Son, I must have my answer now. Earthmaker let me live all

summer, that you might have time to decide. Now you must tell me."

"Can you not let me go back to my people, Father? Why do you ask me to stay here and fight for something I do not want?"

"I see what Raoul has become, and I do not want him to be the master here. I am proud of you and ashamed of him. I want you to be the future of the de Marions, not him. And what of this land that we have loved together, the land that Sun Woman's people have cherished for generations? Shall it fall to Raoul?"

White Bear remembered what Owl Carver had said to Pierre at Saukenuk: *If your land keeps you from doing what you want, then it owns you.*

"Why couldn't you will the estate to Nicole? She's a de Marion."

"Nicole cannot do battle with Raoul when she has eight children to care for. Her husband is an excellent man, but not a fighter. White Bear, you are the only one."

"I still think as a Sauk, Father. Among the Sauk one man may not own land. And to claim so much would be a great crime."

"In you the heritage of the de Marions and the Sauk claim to this land are indissolubly united. You will be doing this for the Sauk as well as for me and for yourself. I believe that it was God's plan that I father you, that you spend the first fifteen years of your life among the Sauk and then these past six as a white. Now you have a chance to be rich and to have power. You can learn how to use your wealth to protect your people. You can do much for them if you stay here and fight for what I give you."

Standing over his father, White Bear lifted his head and gazed up at the great stone and log house on the hilltop. He wondered whether he was not being foolishly stubborn, refusing Victoire and the land the château governed.

Pierre looked sad and weak and very old. All summer long White Bear, heartbroken, had watched him suffer and diminish. He knew he could do nothing to cure his father, and that his refusal to give him the answer he wanted to hear was prolonging his pain. White Bear felt he would agree to anything, if only it would give peace.

Looking into his father's pleading face, he saw that Pierre was using up his last strength. White Bear could not let the final word Pierre might hear from him be no.

White Bear could no longer separate his own anguish from Pierre's.

He drew a deep breath in through his nostrils. "Yes, Father. I agree. I will take what you offer me."

The look on Pierre's face was like a sunrise. White Bear saw a warm, pink color flowing back into the pallid cheeks.

Pierre took White Bear's hand. His touch felt cool, but his grip was firm.

"Thank you, my son. I will walk the Trail of Souls with a happy heart."

Yes, you will go in peace, but I must stay to fight and suffer, White Bear thought. But he was glad that he could make his father happy. He leaned back against the tree and watched huge white clouds drift over the distant river.

"Let us make this a sacred agreement, son," Pierre said. "Bring the calumet and let us smoke together."

"Yes, Father." White Bear sighed and stood up. Slowly, as if he were dragging chains, he walked up the grassy slope to the front door of the house.

As he passed through the great hall he saw Armand Perrault, seeming almost as broad as he was tall, staring at him. Armand's eyes were as small and full of hatred as a cornered boar's. Feeling a chill, realizing this man was one of those he would have to fight when the time came, White Bear nodded to him as he went up the stairs to Pierre's room. Armand stood motionless.

A short time later White Bear was back at Pierre's side with the feather-bedecked calumet and a lit candle protected by a glass chimney. From his own room he had brought down the deerskin pouch holding his small supply of Turkish tobacco, purchased in New York. It would serve. All tobacco was a sacred gift of Earthmaker.

He dribbled the moist brown grains through his fingertips into the pipe's narrow bowl and packed the tobacco down gently. Pierre's faded blue eyes, the whites a sickly yellow color, watched him closely.

He held the candle flame to the tobacco and drew in a series of rapid puffs, feeling the smoke burning his mouth. When the pipe was well-lit, he turned it and held the mouthpiece to Pierre's lips.

Pierre took a long puff, held it in his mouth and let it out. White Bear's heart lurched with fear as Pierre began to cough. Holding his throat with one hand, Pierre gestured with his other hand for White Bear to draw on the pipe.

The sight of beads of blood on his father's lips horrified White Bear. He took a corner of Pierre's blanket and wiped away the bright red drops. Then he took the pipe from his father's hands.

Grieving for the freedom he was giving up, he pulled the hot smoke in till it filled his mouth. He let its bitterness sink into his tongue as bitterness sank into his heart—the realization that this promise would cut him off forever from Redbird, from Sun Woman, from Owl Carver, from the life he longed to return to. He let the smoke out with a long sigh and laid the pipe down. He felt as if his life was over.

But he felt some relief, too, because he was no longer torn by indecision. Now Pierre and he were content to talk of small things—how full the corn bins were this year, what White Bear had seen and heard in New York City, whether it would rain again tomorrow.

Pierre's voice grew softer and softer, and gradually he drifted off to sleep. His grip on White Bear's hand was still strong. White Bear let his head rest against the tree trunk and returned to a favorite childhood pastime, trying to see animal shapes in the clouds.

He was not surprised when the Bear appeared at his side. The huge head, covered with fur white as the clouds, pushed past him, poking its black nose into Pierre's shoulder. Somehow White Bear knew that Pierre would feel no fear when he awoke, even though he had never seen the Bear before.

Pierre's eyes opened, and he looked up at the Bear and, as White Bear had expected, only sighed and smiled.

"Eh bien, je suis content." And Pierre got to his feet as easily as if he had never been sick.

Pierre did not say good-bye, but White Bear had not expected him to. They had said their good-byes already. White Bear remained where he was, sitting with his back to the maple tree.

With his left hand lifted to rest on the high hump at the Bear's shoulder, Pierre walked down the slope. White Bear saw, rising from the rim of the hill, the arc of a rainbow.

Pierre walked the rainbow path with the long, vigorous stride of a young man. The Bear accompanied him with a rolling gait, looking like the biggest dog that ever lived walking beside a hunter. White Bear smiled to watch them.

They climbed the archway of color that leaped out over the Great River until at last they disappeared in the dazzling disk of the sun.

White Bear's head fell back against the bark of the tree, and he closed his eyes.

When he opened them again, his father was lying beside him, still holding his hand. But Pierre's grip was without strength. He lay with his head sunk in the pillow, his mouth fallen open, the whites of his eyes showing between half-closed lids. He was not breathing.

White Bear's tears came hot. He heard a voice—his own voice—rising in his chest.

"Hu-hu-huuuu . . . Whu-whu-whuuuu . . ." It was the sound mourners made at Sauk funerals.

He wrapped his arms around his knees and rocked back and forth, sobbing and keening in the way of his people. Soon he would have to get up and go into the château and tell people Pierre de Marion was dead. He must be the first to bring the news to poor Grandpapa. But for a while he would sit alone with his father and wail for him.

Sitting on the ground under the maple tree, he looked down and was not surprised to see marks in the bare, damp earth. The prints of wide pads twice the size of a man's feet. At the end of each print, deep holes left by five claws.

R aoul did not think he could put up with much more of this funeral. He had to wait till it was all over before he could make himself master of Victoire, and he wanted desperately to act now. He tried to calm himself by remembering the Indians he'd stalked and killed at Saukenuk last May and June.

Raoul and the fifty men he'd recruited to represent Smith County in the state militia had arrived at the Rock River in style, carried up the Mississippi from Victor to Fort Armstrong, at the mouth of the Rock River, on Raoul's new steamer *Victory*. Paid for with the profits of the lead mine, the *Victory* was propelled by two side paddlewheels, and it could make the St. Louis–Galena round trip in exactly a week.

They'd come to hunt Indians and Raoul had made sure they did, camping in the woods on the south side of the Rock River opposite the Indian village and shooting at redskins whenever they had a chance. It pleased Raoul to think they'd gotten half a dozen, maybe more.

Finally fed up with talking, General Gaines had ordered a general assault on Black Hawk's town at the end of June. The militia were eager to slaughter every Indian in Saukenuk, and they'd swept in.

And the damned, sneaking redskins were gone. Seeing themselves outnumbered, they'd slipped out of the village, down the Rock River and across the Mississippi the night before. The Smith County boys, along with the other militiamen, were in a fury of frustration. They had to be content with the poor-second satisfaction of burning the Indian town to the ground.

To Raoul's great annoyance, instead of pursuing Black Hawk, Gaines sent a message to the chief asking for yet another parley. Black Hawk and some of his braves came back across the river to talk peace. Just like he hadn't shown the whole world what a coward he really was, the stubborn old Indian had marched up to Gaines's tent walking like a peacock, with feathers in his hair.

Hang the redskinned son of a bitch, was what Raoul thought. Instead, Gaines just made him sign another fool treaty—as if the Indians ever honored any treaties—and even promised to send them corn because they hadn't had time to plant any.

The disgusted militiamen called it the Corn Treaty. Old Gaines must be almost as big a coward as Black Hawk.

Raoul and the Smith County boys hung around the Rock River, sniping at Indians in canoes till their provisions ran out; they flagged the *Victory* down on her next northbound trip and rode her home.

Home, where what was going on made Raoul madder than ever. Pierre was dying and the mongrel—from the same tribe Raoul had been fighting down on the Rock River—was strutting around as if he already owned Victoire.

That would end today. If Raoul could pull it off.

Raoul eyed Nancy Hale, standing only a few feet from him among the two hundred or so mourners in the great hall of Victoire. What would she think, Raoul wondered, when he played his hand today? He pictured what the tall blond woman would look like naked under him in bed.

Oh, he'd make her sweat and moan and thank him for it.

But first, of course, he had to succeed today. He had to drive the mongrel away before he could court Nancy. Whether her preacher father approved of him or not, he couldn't turn away one of the biggest landowners in Illinois.

And that's what he'd be, after today.

He didn't see how he could fail. Surely the servants and the townspeople wouldn't take the mongrel's part.

Still warming himself by staring at Nancy Hale's straight back, Raoul thanked God he'd never been quite able to bring himself to marry Clarissa.

He felt a twinge of unease as he recalled that taking up with Nancy would mean kicking Clarissa out of his bed, and *that* might mean trouble with Eli. To his relief, Eli had accepted Raoul's not marrying Clarissa, even after she bore him two kids. But that was only because Eli figured it would happen eventually, maybe after Raoul got control of the estate.

Well, once he had the estate, he comforted himself, he could see that Clarissa and their two out-of-wedlock boys were well taken care of.

It galled Raoul to be so dependent on a man like Eli, to be—he hated to admit it to himself—afraid of him. A heap depended on Eli's playing his part today in helping him get control of the estate. Today, Eli would be leading the Smith County boys, ones who'd been at the Rock River last June. Having been offered a good day's pay, they would do a little more Indian fighting.

Raoul felt as if he were going to burst. He couldn't stand this waiting, while the priest droned on in singsong Latin at the linen-covered table that had been set up as an altar before the fireplace. Let the fight begin, for God's sake.

Indians are all cowards at heart. When I take over here, Pierre's precious little red bastard will slink away, like Black Hawk did last summer.

A chill spread across Raoul's back as he asked himself: What if Auguste doesn't slink away? He might try to rally the servants and some of the townspeople to fight for him.

They wouldn't fight for a mongrel bastard. People hated Indians. Look how many men rushed down to the Rock River to fight Black Hawk.

But many people had loved Pierre. This hall was filled, and there were more people outside who couldn't get in because there wasn't room. All of them paying their last respects to Pierre. And they knew that Pierre wanted Auguste to take his place. Would any of them fight to see that Pierre's will was done?

He felt colder still as he considered the odds. Just about every man in Smith County had his own rifle or pistol. And Raoul and the men he'd recruited for today were far outnumbered. He wished he had hired more men. But too many and the secret would be out, and then Auguste would be ready for him.

Raoul tried to calm himself. Everyone in Smith County might be armed, he reasoned, but not everyone wanted to use their weapons. A lot of men wouldn't fight unless their backs were to the wall. It was the ones who were willing to fight who got to give orders to the rest. The men Raoul had picked, Eli and Hodge and the rest of them, were born fighters.

There'd be those who would condemn him, he thought, for seizing the land the very day of his brother's funeral. It was indecent, he admitted to himself. But he had no choice. He couldn't allow Auguste to get his feet planted firmly. He couldn't allow Pierre's will to be read aloud.

He felt even better when he remembered that with Pierre dead the servants would be taking their orders from Armand. He looked around the hall for the overseer. There he was, near the door, most of his face buried by his thick brown beard. Armand's wife, Marchette, was standing next to him. Sporting a black eye, Raoul noticed with amusement.

Armand Perrault was one who didn't love Pierre.

That sanctimonious hypocrite Pierre. First the squaw, the mongrel's mother. Then he marries Marie-Blanche, and as soon as she dies, he's putting it to the cook.

Raoul took a deep breath of relief when he saw that Père Isaac had finally finished with the funeral mass. The old Jesuit was again sprinkling holy water on the black-painted coffin, heaped with wreaths of roses and chrysanthemums that lay on trestles in the center of the hall. Frank Hopkins, Raoul knew, had built that coffin of oak planks.

Old red-nosed Guichard came up to Raoul. "Your father requests that you be one of those who carries your brother's coffin to the wagon."

Raoul felt a momentary jolt of fear. Help pick up Pierre's coffin and carry it, when he was about to dispossess Pierre's son? If he laid a hand on Pierre's coffin, God might strike him dead. Or Pierre's ghost would rise up against him.

He shook his head. Fool's thinking.

"I wouldn't have it any other way, Guichard."

He was angered to see Auguste standing opposite him when he went to the head of the coffin. It was infuriating to see Pierre's features in that brown-skinned face. The half-breed was wearing a green clawhammer jacket, with a black silk band around the left arm.

His arms and back strained as they took the weight of his corner of the coffin. A chorus of grunts arose from Raoul, Auguste, Armand, Frank Hopkins, Jacques Manette and Jean-Paul Kobell as they hoisted the coffin to their shoulders. They trudged out the door with it and slid it on the bed of a flower-bedecked farm wagon. Guichard helped Elysée climb up on the wagon. A snap of the old servant's whip started the two horses moving, as black ribbons tied to their harnesses fluttered.

Raoul walked alone, following the cart the half mile south along the bluffs to the burial ground. Some of the hands had cut a track through the shoulder-high prairie grass for the funeral procession to follow. The fiddler Registre Bosquet marched right behind the wagon playing hymns, and the servants sang in French.

Raoul cast his eye back over the long line of people following the coffin. His glance slid past Nicole and Frank and their passel of kids. With a feeling of satisfaction he saw two of his key men walking near the end of the procession, Justus Bennett, the county land commissioner, and Burke Russell, the county clerk. One copy of Pierre's will was in Russell's keeping, and Raoul had already told him what to do with that. Russell's wife, Pamela, was walking beside him, a handsome woman with chestnut hair that she didn't braid as most women did but allowed to fall in soft waves under her broad-brimmed hat. Strongly attracted to her himself, Raoul wondered how a bespectacled weakling like Burke Russell had ever been able to attract such a fine-looking woman. And what she'd do if she had a sporting proposition from an equally fine-looking man.

They were at the cemetery now. Raoul liked this hillside rising out of the bluffs, where Pierre's wife, Marie-Blanche, lay overlooking the bottomland and the river. The graves of about a dozen others who had worked and died at Victoire were surrounded by a low split-rail fence. Tall cedar trees shadowed the white gravestones. The flat markers with their rounded tops, names, dates and inscriptions were chiseled by Warren Wilgus, the mason who'd recently moved into the area. Auguste had already made arrangements to have Pierre's headstone carved.

The sight of a solid limestone cube in the center of the cemetery gave Raoul a twinge of guilt, as it always did. It was the first stone to have been placed in the cemetery, and was a memorial to his mother, Estelle de Marion, who was buried not here but in Kaskaskia, where she had died in 1802 giving birth to him.

It wasn't my fault!

Helene was also remembered, though not buried here. The Indians had thrown her poor, mutilated body into Lake Michigan. Her memorial marker stood next to Maman's stone. A carved angel spread his wings over Helene's name and dates, "HELENE DE MARION VAILLANCOURT, Beloved Daughter and Sister. 1794–1812. She sings before the throne of God." Below that were inscribed the name and dates of her husband, Henri Vaillancourt, whose body also had never been found.

Raoul carried inside himself his own inscription for Helene: *Murdered by Indians, August 15, 1812. She will be avenged.*

And one act of vengeance would take place today, when the half-Sauk mongrel, whose presence was an affront to Helene, was thrown off this land.

It gave Raoul an uneasy feeling to be working with Auguste, lifting Pierre's coffin off the wagon. It might be bad luck. But the time to strike had not yet come, so he had to walk beside Auguste carrying the coffin to the newly dug grave. There, crouching in unison, the six pallbearers laid the coffin on a cradle of two ropes, each end held by two servants, over the oblong pit. Bending to let his burden down hurt Raoul's back, and he glanced over at Auguste, hoping to see him having trouble. But the mongrel's dark face was impassive.

When Raoul saw Elysée shuffling through the gate, leaning on his silver-headed walking stick, he felt a new tingle of dread. How would his father greet the move he was going to make? Except for a few brief and bitter meetings at which he and Papa and Pierre had tried and failed to settle their differences, he had not spoken to his father in six years. Armand often brought infuriating news of the old man's growing fondness for the mongrel, making Raoul hate the redskinned bastard all the more. Elysée would hardly be happy with what he did today, of course. But would Papa try to fight his only surviving son? If he did, Raoul would have to fight back, and then he might be punished by God.

Nonsense. God doesn't side with Indians. What I am doing is right, because Pierre was seduced and deluded.

But it wouldn't hurt to try to get in good with the old man. Raoul walked quickly over to him.

"Take my arm, Papa."

Elysée looked up at him, his eyes bloodshot and red-rimmed, his face blank, his skin wrinkled parchment.

The old man's had his share of grief. Too bad he couldn't find reason to be happy with me. But that's his fault.

In a low, hoarse voice Elysée said, "Thank you, son. It was good of you to come today."

Raoul sensed an accusation.

"Why wouldn't I come to my own brother's funeral?"

"Because you hated him," Elysée said softly.

At least the old man didn't seem to suspect that he had another reason for being here today. Containing his anger, Raoul helped his father walk to the grave. There he left Elysée with Guichard and went around to stand facing north, where he could see the château.

His nagging fear eased a little. So far he had seen no sign that he would meet with any opposition. It was hard to believe that the mongrel and his supporters could be planning anything in secret. Still he knew his heart would not slow down till this was all over.

Père Isaac stood at the head of Pierre's grave, next to Marie-Blanche's tombstone. A faint breeze from the river didn't disturb his gray-black hair or his beard, but rustled the tassels of the purple stole around his neck, the winglike sleeves of his white surplice and his ankle-length black cassock.

Trying to hold still as his heart pounded and his hands trembled, Raoul watched Père Isaac shake holy water over the coffin, which now lay at the bottom of the grave. The priest gave his sprinkler to one of the boys assisting him, opened a prayerbook bound in black leather and began the graveside prayers.

Will this never end?

Raoul stood with his head bowed. He puzzled over what Elysée had said about hating Pierre.

Papa always loved Pierre more than me. Thought I was some kind of savage because I don't have all those French ways like him and Pierre. I'm the most American member of this family, and he should be proud of me.

I didn't hate Pierre. It was just this damn business of him caring more about redskins than about his own people.

And he wasn't there when I needed him.

Raoul found himself wishing he could talk to Pierre one last time, try to make him understand why he felt as he did and had to do the things he did. Looking down at the coffin in the grave, Raoul thought back to the last time he had seen Pierre. In early spring after the last of the snow melted on the ground, out riding Banner on the prairie, alone, he'd come upon Pierre, also riding alone. They had stared at each other and passed without a word.

I didn't know then that was my last chance to speak to him.

Raoul's eyes traveled over the people standing by the grave. Auguste stood between Elysée and Nicole, looking down into the pit. It pleased Raoul to see that apparently Auguste had no idea what was about to happen to him.

But how could he be *sure* Auguste was unprepared?

Raoul looked over the heads of the mourners, and his heart beat faster with anticipation. There, across the flat prairie land, he saw tiny figures surrounding the château.

Raoul's fingernails dug into his palms as he clenched his fists to hold himself together. What if the secret had gotten out? If Auguste knew what was about to happen, he would surely have prepared some kind of counterattack. Indians were damned sly.

Père Isaac closed his prayerbook and put it into his coat pocket.

"This man whom we consign to American soil was, like so many of us, born on the other side of the ocean," he said. "He came of one of the oldest and noblest families of France, fleeing the Godless revolution that tormented their homeland, which was also my homeland. The de Marions gave themselves soul and body to this new land where they had to make their own way. Here titles and ancient lineage meant nothing."

Get on with it, dammit!

"God saw fit to try them sorely after they came here to Illinois. The mother of the family died in childbirth. A daughter died a horrid death at the hands of Indians, and a son"—he gestured at Raoul, who stared back at him, keeping his face expressionless—"held captive, a slave, by Indians for two years."

It was good that Père Isaac mentioned that. It would prepare people to accept what was about to happen.

"Pierre de Marion was a good man, but he was also a sinner, like all of us. He fell into the sin of lust, and that sin bore fruit. But Pierre did not hide his sin as so many men have. He reached out to his son through me and helped him. Eventually he acknowledged his son and brought him out of the wilderness to be educated for civilization."

Raoul looked across the open pit at Auguste. The half-breed's red-brown face was flushed an even darker color, but still he stared fixedly down into the grave.

Time to start.

It was an immense relief to begin to move. First, he had to get back to the château ahead of the funeral procession and join his men there. Slowly, so as not to attract attention, Raoul drew back from the graveside.

Auguste's feet felt heavy and confined in his cowhide boots as they crunched over the short stubble. He walked alone on the newly cut track back toward the great stone and log house. He could hear the sound of spades biting into the mound of dirt beside Pierre's grave and clods of earth thudding onto his coffin.

Auguste led the procession of mourners. The others let him walk apart, to be alone with his grief. Behind Auguste, he was aware, were Nicole and Frank and Nancy Hale and Père Isaac, and then a long line of servants and farm hands and village people. Near the end of the procession Registre Bosquet played a sprightly tune, as was the custom among the Illinois French, a way of saying that life goes on. In the rear was the cart that had carried Pierre's coffin, with Elysée and Guichard.

As Auguste walked, he brooded about Père Isaac calling him the fruit of sin. Why did the priest have to dishonor his mother and father so? In the eyes of the Sauk people he was no "bastard," as he knew some pale eyes called him. Still, he was glad that the priest said Pierre had done the right thing in bringing him here. Perhaps people would remember that, when Raoul tried to take the estate away from him.

As he surely would.

Auguste knew, with a sinking feeling in his stomach, that it was only a matter of time before Raoul would strike at him.

He felt himself wishing for Black Hawk and Iron Knife and the other Sauk warriors, even Wolf Paw, to be here to stand by him. And Owl Carver and Sun Woman to advise him. Now he wished he had not agreed, at his father's insistence, to have no contact with the band. While he was being educated, being cut off from them had helped him become more quickly a part of the white world. But now that Pierre was gone he felt so terribly alone.

A chill fell over him like a cold downpour. Looking up, he saw men standing just outside the fence that surrounded the château, strung out in a line along the west side, where the gateway was. He had noticed them as he was leaving the graveyard, but had thought they must be hands, with field work of some sort important enough to keep them from the funeral. Now he was close enough to see that they were carrying rifles. Auguste recognized Raoul himself standing squarely in the gateway. How had he gotten over there? Auguste had thought he was with the funeral procession.

A cold hollow opened in his stomach as he grasped what was happening.

The moment my father is buried. What a fool I was to think Raoul would wait awhile.

He heard people murmuring behind him.

"Oh my God," Nicole said. "Not now."

"Auguste!" It was Nancy's voice, shrill with fear. He shook his head, trying to tell her that he would not turn back, and kept on walking.

In a moment, thought Auguste, he might be joining his father on the Trail of Souls. He heard footsteps behind him crunching on the dry grass. It was a comfort to know that there were others near him, although he knew no one could really help him.

He had no idea what he would do. He asked Earthmaker to show him how to walk this path with courage and honor.

Keeping his stride firm and steady, Auguste went around the fence to approach the gate, glancing up at the maple tree under which Pierre had died.

As Auguste got closer, Raoul threw open his jacket, showing his gilt-handled pistol holstered on one hip, his huge knife, the one that had scarred Auguste, sheathed on the other. His eyes were shadowed by his broad-brimmed black hat, and the black mustache hid his mouth. His face was a mask.

When they were about ten feet apart, Raoul spoke. "Now that my brother is in the ground I can speak plain to you. It's over for you here. You're Pierre's natural son, and this is his burying day, so I won't kill you unless you force me to it. I want you off de Marion land right now. I want you out of Smith County by sundown. Get back to the woods where you came from."

You cannot know how happy it would make me to do just that, Raoul. Auguste stood with his feet planted firmly on the stubble. He did not try to think. He would rely on the spirits for help. He waited for the knowledge of what to do to come to him.

He felt people coming to stand beside him. He heard the creaking of wagon wheels and the soft clip-clop of horses' hooves as the cart carrying Guichard and Elysée rolled past the funeral procession and drew up alongside him. He glanced at the people standing beside him, to his right Frank and Nicole, their children behind them, to his left Nancy Hale and Père Isaac.

Auguste went colder still as he saw Eli Greenglove, who had been standing by the gate in the fence around the château, walk across the open space, the tail of his coonskin cap bobbing. Greenglove carried a long Kentucky rifle. Auguste had heard many a tale about Greenglove's deadly accuracy. The Missourian took a position to one side, between Raoul and Auguste.

He won't even need to be a good shot to kill me from that distance.

Words came suddenly to Auguste's mind. He spoke loudly, so everyone could hear, and he felt good that his voice was strong. He looked Raoul in the eye as he spoke.

"I am proud to be a son of the Sauk people. But my father told me I was his heir. It is in his will. He gave me this house and all this land. You have no right to force me to leave."

Raoul laughed and slapped the pistol and the knife. "These give me the right." He waved a hand at the men standing in a line along the fence. "And them."

Frank Hopkins cleared his throat and spoke. "Raoul, maybe

there's no law around right here and now to make you honor Pierre's will, but there are courts in Illinois, there's a legislature, there's a governor."

Raoul made a sound halfway between a laugh and a grunt. "Take your half-breed friend to the governor. John Reynolds wants the Indians out of Illinois as bad as anybody does. He was there with the militia on Rock River last June. Hell, go to the President. I'd like to see what an old Indian killer like Andy Jackson would say to you."

All too true, Auguste thought sadly. He had learned in New York of Jackson's "removal" policy, aiming to drive all the red people to the west side of the Mississippi. The work of the white chiefs was to take land from Indians, not help them keep it.

Père Isaac said, "To rob the orphan is a sin that cries out to Heaven for vengeance. If you came to me in confession I could not give you absolution."

"My conscience is clear," Raoul said. "Victoire is my rightful heritage. Do you know that this Indian boy you feel so sorry for isn't even a Christian? I am, Father. A Catholic."

"A very bad one," said Père Isaac. "I have known Auguste since he was a small boy. He behaves more like a Christian than you do."

A woman's voice, Nancy Hale's, rang out over the field. "Raoul de Marion, if you won't listen to your own priest, you'll still have to face my father. When he hears what you've done he'll preach against you and he'll stir people to make you do the right thing."

Raoul's face changed. He looked pained.

"Now Miss Nancy. It isn't proper for a lady like you to concern herself with what happens to trash like this. You know well and good that your father may have a low opinion of me, but he has an even lower opinion of Indians. He won't side with this Indian bastard."

Suddenly Nicole rushed past Auguste.

"You're the one who's trash, Raoul!" she cried, and ran across the intervening space and swung her hand to slap her brother. Raoul grabbed her arm and pushed her away roughly. Frank rushed to her side to hold her, his ink-stained fingers digging into her sleeves.

"I wouldn't want to fight with you, Nicole," said Raoul with a cruel grin. "I believe you've got the weight advantage on me."

"You're a murderer and a thief, Raoul," she shot back. "And the day will come when people will have enough of you and drive you out of this county."

Waves of heat and cold ran through Auguste's body, and when he clenched his fists he felt the sweat on his palms. He had to speak out. He owed it to his father to fight, somehow, for this land. But how could he drive away some twenty armed men?

A sudden thought came to him. "Raoul, I challenge you to fight me for the land. With pistols or knives or barehanded. Any way you want it."

Raoul grinned, white teeth appearing suddenly under the black mustache. "You've gotten big in the last six years, but I'm a better shot than you are, and I'd slice you to bits with my knife. In a barehanded fight I'd bite your ears off and ram 'em down your throat. We don't need a fight to prove what anybody can plainly see."

"If you won't fight me you're a coward as well as a thief."

Raoul's eyes narrowed, and his shoulders hunched forward, as if he was about to attack.

"Dueling is also a grave sin," said Père Isaac. "And it is against the law of this state. I forbid you to fight."

Raoul laughed and lifted his empty hands. "Too bad, mongrel. The father won't let us fight."

Auguste turned to Père Isaac. "How can you take from me the only way I have of fighting for this land?"

"If God wants you to have it, He will see that you get it without doing wrong," said Père Isaac calmly.

The face of Black Hawk appeared in Auguste's mind, and suddenly he understood the wrath that had always seemed to smolder just below the war chief's skin. This must be how Black Hawk felt when the pale eyes told him he could no longer come to Saukenuk. That was why Black Hawk had been leading his people back to Saukenuk year after year. He would not give up.

And neither would Auguste.

I must fight. I promised my father I would fight for this land. I smoked the calumet with him.

He remembered Pierre's words: *Now you have a chance to own land, to be rich and to have power. You can learn how to use your wealth to protect your people.*

And he was losing that chance. As he saw these rich acres being torn away from him, more and more he felt himself wanting them.

But how to fight for the land? To charge Raoul's pistol and the rifles of his men would simply mean death. Surely that was not what Pierre wanted for him.

An unfamiliar voice said, "Is this really how you settle land disputes in Smith County?"

Auguste turned to see David Cooper, a lean, hard-eyed man he had met several weeks earlier when Cooper had visited Pierre to pay his respects.

Raoul said, "Don't you like the way we do things here, Cooper?"

Cooper's cold expression did not change. "Just requesting information, Mr. de Marion. That's all."

Cooper had brought his family to Victor from some place in Indiana three years ago, buying a choice piece of bottomland from Pierre. Auguste had learned that he was a veteran of the War of 1812.

Justus Bennett, the county land commissioner, who Auguste knew to be one of Raoul's creatures, said, "Mr. Cooper, I've been reading law most of my adult life, and I can assure you Mr. Raoul de Marion has as sound a case under common law and English precedent as I've ever seen."

Auguste doubted that anyone here knew what that meant, impressive as it might sound.

The whites know how to twist any law to their advantage.

Cooper said nothing further.

These people might feel sorry for him, Auguste thought, and resent what Raoul was doing. But he'd get no help from any of the men who were standing around behind him. Raoul and his men were armed and determined, and the rest of the people here were not ready to give up their lives to help a half-breed.

But Auguste had taken advantage of Raoul's distraction with Cooper and Bennett to cut the distance between himself and his uncle in half. If he could get close enough to Raoul he might have a chance to get at him with his knife. He'd worn the deerhorn-handled knife today only because his father had given it to him.

As he hesitated, he heard footsteps in the grass and turned to see his grandfather walking toward Raoul with slow but firm steps, thumping his walking stick on the ground.

"No, Grandpapa!" Auguste called out to him.

"This is my son, I very much regret to say," said Elysée. "And I must administer correction."

Auguste started to follow Elysée, but Raoul dropped his hand warningly to his pistol.

"Don't come any closer, half-breed."

"I was with Pierre when he wrote his final will," said Elysée. "And I have a copy of it. I know his mind was sound. He gave the whole estate—except for the fur company, which we have always agreed would be yours—to Auguste."

"You gave the fur company to me when you divided the estate between me and Pierre years ago," Raoul said. "So my own good brother left me nothing. Thirty thousand acres of the best land in western Illinois go to a mongrel Indian, and you say his mind was sound? The more fool you."

"You are un bète!" Elysée shouted. "You are proof that there is no just God. If there were He would have taken you and let Pierre live."

"Monsieur de Marion!" the priest cried. "Think what you are saying. On this day of all days."

Raoul said, "I've always known that you loved Pierre and not me, Papa."

"You make it impossible to love you!" Elysée answered. "Now listen to me. Victoire is my home. I built this place. Those I love are buried here. I command you, leave at once. Get off this land."

Raoul, a head taller than the old man, took a step toward his father. "If you wanted it to be yours, you shouldn't have given it to Pierre. You have nothing now, you old fool."

Elysée swung the stick at Raoul's head. The thump resounded over the field, and Raoul staggered back, his broad-brimmed hat falling to the ground.

Raoul bared his teeth, drew back his fist and smashed it into his father's face. The blow knocked Elysée hard against one of the upright logs of the gateway. He cried out and fell heavily to the ground. He lay moaning and jerking his head from side to side in agony. The priest rushed to him, dropping to his knees.

With a scream Nicole threw herself down beside her father.

A red curtain swept over Auguste's eyes, blinding him momentarily. When he could see again he saw only the face of one man, Raoul, looking down at Elysée with triumph and contempt.

Knife in hand, Auguste threw himself at Raoul.

Raoul's pistol was out. His dark eyes gleamed with triumph as he pointed the muzzle at Auguste's chest.

He was hoping I would attack him, Auguste realized, knowing he would never reach Raoul before the pistol went off.

A sudden movement to his side caught his eye. In a glance he saw Eli Greenglove swinging a rifle butt at his head.

10

Dispossessed

Auguste woke.

He was in a room he had never seen before. A plain black cross hung high on one white plaster wall. He lay on a bed with a straw-filled mattress, on top of the quilt. He wasn't wearing his coat. Or his pale eyes' boots.

Pain throbbed in his head, and with each pulse his vision momentarily blurred.

He rolled his pounding head on the pillow and saw Nancy Hale sitting beside him. Her long blond braids glistened in the pale light that came through the oiled paper window.

The way she was looking down at him startled him. The blue of her eyes burned like the blue center of a flame. Her lips seemed fuller and redder than he'd ever seen them, and they were slightly parted. This was the way she had been looking at him while he lay unconscious, he realized, and he had seen it only because he had awakened suddenly and taken her by surprise.

"What happened?" he asked.

"That man of your uncle's, Eli Greenglove, hit you with his rifle. Your uncle said he'd kill you next time he sees you awake. So we took you out here to my father's parsonage."

"How long have I been asleep?" he said.

"A long time. Hours. I'm awfully glad to see you wake up, Auguste. I didn't know if you ever would. Greenglove hit you hard enough to kill you."

He remembered Elysée lying on the ground, writhing. Rage

boiled up inside him again as he thought of Raoul striking Grand-papa down.

"How is my grandfather?" He tried to sit up, and the room started to rock and pitch. The pain pounded on his head like a spiked war club. Nancy put a hand on his shoulder, and he lay back against the pillow. He shut his eyes momentarily to get his equilibrium back.

"We don't know—he may have broken his hip. But try not to worry, Auguste. Nicole and Frank took him back to their house."

That searing gaze of a moment ago was gone, but there was still a warm light in her eyes.

He heard a footstep on the other side of the bed. He turned, bringing back the ache in his head full force, to see the tall figure of Reverend Philip Hale standing in the doorway of the small room. Hale, dressed in a black clawhammer coat and black trousers with a white silk stock wrapped around his throat, stood with his arms folded, gazing at Auguste with pursed lips and a deep crease between his bushy eyebrows.

"You can thank the Lord's mercy you're not hurt worse, young man. I suppose you'll want to be on your way soon."

"Father!" Nancy exclaimed. "He just came awake. He might have a fractured skull."

"I think I'm all right," Auguste said. He tried to sit up again. He managed it, but he felt suddenly dizzy and sick to his stomach. He put his hand over his mouth. Nancy picked up a china chamber pot from the bedside and held it for him, but after a moment the spasm of nausea passed and, gingerly, he shook his head at her. His first afternoon at Victoire, when he had thrown up his dinner before everyone in the great hall, flickered through his memory.

He looked up and saw Hale staring at him with even deeper distaste. Clear enough that the reverend didn't like to see Nancy's care for him.

Grandpapa's hurt, and I'm the only one around here with medical training.

Auguste lifted his head again, determined to get up in spite of the pain. "I must go to my grandfather. He may die if he isn't cared for properly."

A spear of horror shot through him. His medicine bundle, containing his precious stones and the bear's claw, was still at the château. All his spiritual power was collected in that bag. Whatever the risk, he must go back and get it. And he wanted the bag of surgical instruments he'd brought back from New York.

"I'll be out of here as soon as I can stand, sir," he said. "I have much to do."

"No!" Nancy cried. "Auguste, you're not well enough to go anywhere. And, Father, I told you what happened at the funeral. We've got to help Auguste. If you speak, people will listen."

"I don't know the rights and wrongs of it," said Hale, looking irritated, presented with a problem he did not want to try to solve.

Auguste said, "My father wanted me to inherit Victoire. There are witnesses. There are two copies of his will, if Raoul hasn't already destroyed them."

Reverend Hale glowered at Auguste. "What if Raoul de Marion's men come looking for you?"

Suddenly, as when facing Raoul at the gateway to Victoire, Auguste felt terribly alone. Nancy would do anything she could for him; after seeing her loving look when he awoke he was sure of that. But there was little enough she could do. Especially because of the way her father so obviously felt about him.

"I'll be gone as quick as I can, Reverend Hale."

"If they come here while Auguste is here you'll have to tell them he's not here and refuse to let them in," said Nancy firmly.

"Lie to them? I'm not a Jesuit."

"Father! Would you let Auguste be killed?"

The word "killed" set a storm of frightful thoughts whirling through Auguste's head. Raoul's pistol had been pointed right at his chest. And Greenglove had tried to brain him. They wouldn't stop until they had killed him. Only then would Raoul be secure in his possession of Victoire. Dazed and hurting though he was, Auguste had to get out of Smith County if he was to live another day.

Hale turned and went back to his own room, shaking his head.

"Your father is no friend to me," said Auguste.

Nancy's face was like a lake whose surface was troubled by a wind. "He's very strict. He didn't go to your father's funeral because it was a Catholic service. But if anything happens he'll do the right thing. You can count on him for that."

Auguste said nothing. But he didn't share her confidence.

Early that evening, Auguste, Nancy and Reverend Hale were

sitting in the front room of the Hales' one-story house. They had eaten a rabbit stew with potatoes, onions and beans from the Hales' garden and hominy grits on the side that Nancy had pounded from corn. They washed it down with fresh-squeezed apple cider.

"I allow no spiritous liquors in my home," said Reverend Hale.

Now that it was dark Auguste wanted desperately to be off to see Grandpapa at Nicole and Frank's house. The old man had been badly hurt. He might be dying.

By candlelight Hale read the Bible aloud to Nancy and Auguste. It was his nightly custom, Nancy explained.

Auguste heard the soft clip-clop of a horse's hooves and the creak of carriage wheels and raised a hand to alert the others.

Putting a finger to her lips, Nancy went to the door. She opened it a crack, then pulled it wider and went out.

"Who is it?" Hale called anxiously.

His heart pounding, Auguste was on his feet, looking for a weapon or for a place to hide.

No answer came from Nancy, but a moment later she came back, one arm around another woman's shoulders, supporting her. A blue kerchief covered the woman's head.

"Who is this?" Hale said again.

"Bon soir, Reverend Hale. Forgive me for disturbing you."

It was a moment before Auguste recognized the battered, swollen face of Marchette. One of her eyes had been blackened this morning, but now there were ugly bruises around both eyes, her whole face was swollen and her lips were cut and puffed.

Heartbroken at the sight of her, Auguste rushed to the cook and took her hands in his.

"Marchette! What happened to you?"

"I cried very much when you and Monsieur Elysée were hurt today, Monsieur Auguste. Armand did not like this, and he beat me. It *looks* very bad, but he did not beat me hard, Monsieur. Whoever Armand beats hard, dies. But I resolved to do something for you. Monsieur Raoul, he had barrels of Kaintuck whiskey carted up to the château. Many guests and servants got very drunk. After a while Armand was lying on the floor beside the table, so then I went to fetch your things. Your trunk was unlocked, and I gathered up your clothes and books and put them in it and locked it. I had Bernadette Bosquet, the fiddler's wife, she is my friend, help carry your trunk down to the carriage."

Auguste felt as if a sudden bright light had flooded his room. His medicine bundle had been in the trunk. And his surgical instruments. They were safe.

He jumped up from the table. A throb of pain went through his head, and he felt dizzy and had to cling to the table for support. Marchette's eyes widened in alarm, and she put her hands out to him.

Recovered after a moment—and feeling much better now than he had a few hours ago—he took Marchette's hands in his.

"I can't tell you how much this means to me, Marchette. There were things in my trunk—sacred things—very important to me. Very precious. I thank you a thousand times."

Her swollen lips parted in a half smile. She reached into a pocket in her apron and brought out a large pocket watch gleaming a dull gold. Then she took out a familiar oval silver case with a velvet ribbon.

"These were your father's, monsieur. I believe he would wish that you have them."

Auguste opened the case and saw the round lenses for only a moment as his eyes blurred. He put his hand over his face and held it there until he no longer felt like weeping. Then he looked at the engraving on the watch—"Pierre Louis Auguste de Marion, A.D. 1800"—and his eyes filled up with tears. This, he thought, should go into his medicine bundle with the other sacred objects.

"Where were Raoul and Greenglove when you took my trunk and things in the carriage?"

"Before Armand got drunk, Monsieur Raoul made him look through Monsieur Elysée's room for the paper that says you are to inherit the estate. Armand found it and gave it to your uncle, and he threw it into the fire while Armand and Eli Greenglove watched and laughed. Then Monsieur Raoul, he got into a most furious argument with Eli Greenglove about Greenglove's daughter. They nearly fight, but I think they are afraid of each other. They are both great killers. So finally they went down to town. Monsieur Raoul agreed to bring his woman, Greenglove's daughter, and the two boys to the château."

"Disgraceful!" snorted Reverend Hale. "Publicly living in sin."

"I wonder why he didn't bring them to the funeral?" Nancy said.

Auguste thought he knew why. Clarissa Greenglove had been a pretty, full-bosomed girl when he first arrived at Victoire. But in the years during which she had borne two boys to Raoul, she had turned into a lank-haired, snuff-sniffing slattern. Years ago Raoul had said he was going to marry Clarissa, but he never had. And Auguste had seen Raoul bending a hungry look on Nancy throughout the funeral mass this morning. The thought of Raoul laying even a hand on Nancy angered him. It would anger Eli Greenglove, too, for a different reason.

Eli Greenglove, it was said, could shoot the wings off a fly one at a time at fifty yards and was wanted in Missouri for over a dozen murders. He might take orders from Raoul, but it would not do for Raoul to offend such a man. So if Eli persisted, Raoul probably would take Clarissa into the château.

Auguste felt a sinking in his stomach as he touched his fingers lightly to his throbbing head. He was alive now only because Greenglove had chosen to hit him instead of shooting him down—or instead of letting Raoul have that pleasure.

"Will you stay the night, Marchette?" Nancy asked.

"No, I must go back to the château before Armand wakes up. Otherwise he will beat me worse."

"I'm going with you," said Auguste.

"No," said Nancy. "They'll kill you."

Auguste looked across the table at Nancy, staring at him with round blue eyes full of the yearning, now mixed with fear, that he'd seen in them earlier. "Pale eyes," the Sauk term for her people, did no justice to her eyes, the color of the turquoise stone he kept in his medicine bag. Her blond hair made his blood race. His fingertips tingled with the desire to touch the white skin of her cheek.

Though Nancy's very differentness made him desire her, he knew that he and she could never belong to each other as completely as he and Redbird did. He could have a deep and lasting union with Redbird, a union that would make him feel whole.

But it had been six years since he had seen Redbird, and no woman of the Sauk would go without a man for that long.

My mother did, he reminded himself.

But Redbird had probably given in to Wolf Paw and married him. After all, she hadn't had a word from White Bear in all that time.

Marchette's urgent tone refocused his thoughts. "Monsieur Raoul, he stood up on the table and held up a bag full of Spanish dollars—he said there were fifty—and said he would give it to the man who shoots you. And there were many men who cheered at that and boasted they would be the one to win the silver."

Auguste pictured men scattering out all over Smith County, hunting for him. He could almost feel the rifle ball shattering his skull.

"I can't hide in your house forever, Nancy. Sooner or later they'll come looking for me, and I don't want to bring that down on your heads."

Reverend Hale said nothing, but Auguste saw relief in his square face—and grudging respect. But Hale's respect, he thought, would do him little good when he lay dead on the prairie.

Nancy's full lips quivered as she said, "You'll go to the château and let them shoot you?"

Auguste realized that his hands were cold with fear, and he rubbed them together to warm them. Hale's house was about ten miles across the prairie from the Mississippi. Could he cover all that distance without being seen and shot?

"I'm not going to the château. I'll just see that Marchette gets there safely. Traveling at night, she should have someone go back with her. Then I'll go on to town. To Nicole and Frank's house. To Grandpapa. I must see him." He turned toward the cook and felt a stabbing in his gut at the sight of her bruised face. She'd suffered that out of love for his father, he thought, and for his sake too.

"If you're seen you'll be shot," said Hale.

Don't you think I know that? he wanted to scream at the minister. What choice did he have? He was like a rabbit surrounded by wolves. He forced calm on himself and spoke with sarcasm.

"Surely you know, Reverend, that Indians are good at getting about unnoticed."

He felt his fear turning to a rising excitement as he recalled the lessons of stealth and cunning he'd learned as a child of the Sauk.

"But what will you do then?" Nancy asked. "How will you get back here?"

Auguste hesitated. Remembering that he was a Sauk had moved his thoughts in a new direction.

I have been dispossessed. Just as my people have been dispossessed.

Nancy was waiting for him to speak.

"Raoul told me to go back to the woods with the other Indians. Even though the advice came from him, I think that is just what I should do."

Nancy gasped as if he had struck her. There was silence in the cottage for a moment.

"How will you get back to your people?" she said. "How will you find them?"

He smiled, trying to get her to smile back at him. "I know exactly where they are. They've crossed the Mississippi to their hunting grounds in the Ioway Territory. I spent the first fifteen winters of my life there with the British Band."

Auguste remembered his dream of becoming a shaman. It had come back to life a bit with his effort to heal Pierre. Among the pale eyes there was no room for magic. But now he felt he could go back to his own people and find magic again.

Hale said, "An unwise decision, it seems to me. You've been educated. You've had an opportunity to learn about white Christian civilization. Your uncle can't take that away from you, and you should not throw it away."

Auguste said, "Reverend, you know what I'm leaving behind. But you don't know what I'm going back to."

Nancy started speaking rapidly, as if she was trying to hold back tears. "Well, what about these things of yours that Marchette brought here? There's no way you can carry a trunk on foot even as far as Nicole and Frank's house. Would you like us to keep your things here for you? Perhaps someday, after you've settled with your tribe"—she swallowed hard—"you could send for them."

Auguste heard the anguish in her voice but decided to take her words at only face value. "Yes, I'd be truly grateful if you'd keep them for me. The only thing I want to take now is my medicine bundle."

Reverend Hale pursed his lips and snorted, but Auguste ignored him.

Auguste thought a moment. "And I can use the surgical instruments. And at least one book."

"Let it be a Bible," said Hale. Auguste made no answer to that.

As Eli Greenglove struck him down, Auguste remembered, he had been charging at Raoul with his knife in his hand.

"What happened to my knife?"

"I picked it up," said Nancy in a clipped tone. She stood up and went over to an elaborately carved oak sideboard, a handsome piece of furniture that seemed out of place in this simple cabin, and took Auguste's knife out of a drawer. She handed it to him and he slipped it into the leather sheath at his belt.

"Thank you, Nancy. My father gave that to me a long time ago." Their eyes met, and he felt a warmth spread through him. It was going to be hard to leave her.

Nancy remained standing. "Let's go out to the wagon and see what Marchette has brought. I can help you carry your trunk in."

Marchette and Reverend Hale both said at the same time, "I can do that!" The coincidence made everyone laugh nervously.

"No," said Nancy firmly. "Marchette, you're hurt and tired. Father, why don't you see what consolation you can offer this poor, mistreated woman. Auguste's trunk can't be that heavy. Come on, Auguste."

Before either Hale or Marchette could answer, Nancy had Auguste out the door. He glanced back into the room just before the door closed and saw Hale's fists clenched on either side of his open Bible.

Auguste stood for a moment, letting his eyes adjust from the lamplight inside to the darkness out here. A fat moon hung overhead; he judged it would be full in two nights. With this much light he'd be in even more danger tonight. The white-painted steeple of Reverend Hale's little church, next to the cottage where he and Nancy lived, gleamed in the moonlight.

Beside him in the dark Nancy whispered fiercely, "I don't *want* you to go."

Sadly he said, "I know." He took her hand and squeezed it. Perhaps it was a mistake to do that, but he could not stop himself.

"Come away from the house," she said.

Now he could see the wagon Marchette had come in, the horse tied to a fence post beside the Hales' garden on the south side of the house. The horse shifted from foot to foot and burbled its breath out through its lips.

Holding tight to his hand, Nancy led him around to the rear of the house, beyond which rows of corn stood, their tassles silvery in the moonlight.

"You and your father grow all this corn?" Auguste asked.

"It's our land, but a neighbor does the work. He sells it in Victor and we share the proceeds." She led him into the corn, brushing past the crackling leaves. The concealment of the leaves and stalks made him feel closer to her than ever. He wanted to reach out to her.

But the corn evoked another feeling, as well.

She can't know it, but this field reminds me of the corn bottoms around Saukenuk. It makes me want to go back all the more.

When there were leafy stalks all around them, hiding them from the house, she turned to him again and said, "Please, Auguste, I don't want you to go away for good." Her eyes were bright in the moonlight.

Her nearness was thrilling. He wanted to forget the worries that made him hesitate, and take her in his arms.

"You don't want me to stay here and risk getting killed," he said.

"You could go to Vandalia," she said. "Tell Governor Reynolds what happened. If he can't do anything for you himself, maybe he can help you find a lawyer who will fight Raoul for you in the courts."

How innocent she was, he thought bitterly. "It was Governor Reynolds who called out the militia to drive my people from Saukenuk. It's just as Raoul said, he would be the last man to want to help an Indian fight for land with a white man."

"Your father sent you to school in the East because he wanted a different future for you than just spending your life hunting and living in a wigwam. You'll be throwing all that away."

He felt a flash of anger at her. She did not understand the Sauk way of life at all. She was just repeating what her father had said.

He remembered the way Nancy's eyes had shone each time they met on the prairie last summer. He had known then that if he spoke to Nancy of marriage, she would want it no matter how much it enraged her father. But marriage with Nancy would be a coming together of two strangers, of people whose worlds were utterly different. In the past six years he had learned much about her world, but that did not mean he belonged in it. And she knew next to nothing of his.

It hurt to hold himself back; he felt powerfully drawn to her. But what he was feeling was impossible. Impossible to fulfill.

"I can use my schooling to help my people make a better life for themselves. The gift my father gave me is a gift I will give to the Sauk. And it may be worth more than the land Raoul has stolen from me."

"I don't want to lose you," she sobbed. She threw herself against him and wrapped her arms around him. Her tear-wet cheek pressed against his. Her face was hot, as though she had a fever. She wanted him; he felt it now, just as he had seen it hours ago in her unguarded eyes.

"I've never cared for a man as I care for you, Auguste," she said. "Everything you say may be true, but if you go back to your tribe I'll never see you again."

It hurt Auguste to admit it, but it was almost certain that they would never meet again.

"If you want to—you could come with me." Even as he spoke, he was sure it would never work. Did she not dismiss the way of the Sauk as "hunting and living in a wigwam"?

And suppose Redbird *had* waited for him? What would he do with Nancy then?

"No," she said. "If I went with you my father would hunt us down and Raoul would help him. And besides—" She hesitated.

"What else?"

She shook her head. "I'm too afraid. Indians frighten me. Not you. Real Indians."

Real Indians?

Anger pulsed in his head. He wanted to pull away from her then, but she wouldn't let him go. Her arms tightened around him, and her body moved against him.

"Auguste, do you know where it says in the Bible, 'Adam knew Eve, his wife'? I want to know you—that way."

Her soft words thrilled him, and he forgot his anger. He felt exalted, and he held her tightly. He had wanted Nancy ever since he met her last June. All summer long, desiring her, he had fought his desire.

He pressed his mouth on hers, crushing her soft, full lips. She was pulling at him now, pulling him down. Pulling him to lie with her between the rows of corn.

I must not do this.

Abruptly he steadied his feet and drew his face away from hers. The vague shape of a future different from the one he planned shimmered in his mind. They could have each other here and now, and he could give up his decision to return to the Sauk. He might flee temporarily to some nearby county, find work, study until he could begin practicing medicine, marry Nancy, perhaps even try to win back the estate in the pale eyes' courts.

He would become, more or less, a pale eyes. It would be the end of him as a Sauk.

And the White Bear arose in his mind, as clearly as if he had suddenly stood up here among the corn stalks.

The White Bear said, *Your people need you.*

"Auguste, please, *please,*" Nancy whispered. "It isn't wrong. It's right for us. There's no other man but you who's right for me. I don't want to end up a dried-up old spinster who never knew the man she truly loved."

She slid down the length of him, falling to her knees in the furrow. She pressed her cheek against the hard bulge in his trousers, sending a thrill through his whole body.

"Please."

He wanted to let himself sink to the ground with her. He shut his eyes and saw the White Bear more vividly in his mind. It seemed to glow.

He held himself rigid, fighting the pressure inside him that made him want to give in to her. He told himself he could give Nancy this moment of love she wanted and still go back to the Sauk. If he did not take her now as she wanted to be taken, he would regret it bitterly later.

But if he did this with her it would tie them in a bond that would be wrong to break. If he gave her what she wanted and then left, it would hurt her, might even kill her.

He took a step backward, then another. His legs felt as if they were made of wood; he could barely move them.

Nancy let him go, put her hands to her face and sobbed, kneeling between the rows of corn.

He stood there a moment, feeling helpless. Then he went to her, took her arms and helped her to stand up.

"I do love you, Nancy," he said. "But if I knew you as Adam knew Eve, I would still have to leave you. And it would hurt both of us much more."

Sobs still shook her body. He did not even know if she heard him. But she let him lead her out of the cornfield, around the locked and silent church, and back to the wagon where his trunk lay. As they walked she pulled a handkerchief out of her sleeve, wiped her face and blew her nose.

His heart felt heavy as lead. Sure as he was that this was the right thing to do, he was almost as sure it was wrong.

When they got to the wagon, he was still holding her arm. Gently she pulled free of him.

"You're a good man, Auguste. I'm afraid I'll always love you. Whether you want me to or not."

"Are you all right?" he asked. He wanted to make her happy, and he felt terribly helpless.

"I will be," she said.

As he rode in the wagon back to the château with Marchette, the back of Auguste's neck tingled. He pictured silent hunters crouched out in the prairie, their Kentucky long rifles ready, their thoughts fixed on fifty pieces of silver. His eyes moved restlessly over the low hills around them. The nearly full moon was sinking before them in the west, a lantern at the end of their trail. In some places the prairie grass closed in around the horse and wagon, high as the horse's rump and the wagon's wheels, and it looked to Auguste as if they were pushing their way through a moonlit lake.

The loudest sound he heard was the steady singing of choruses of crickets more numerous than all the tribes of man. Somehow it seemed they always sang louder this time of year, as if they knew that frost and snow were coming soon to silence their song.

The château's peaked roof rose black against the stars. Before they reached the orchards, Auguste put his arm around Marchette and gave her a kiss on the cheek. Jumping down from the wagon, he tied to his shoulders with rawhide thongs the pack that held his medicine bundle, his instruments and his book.

"Good-bye and thank you, Marchette," he whispered, and darted off into the tall grass.

"God keep His eye upon you," she called softly after him.

Watching for Raoul's lurking hunters, he was soon past the château and slipping along the edge of the road that led through the hills to town.

He froze. He saw a light ahead of him, a swinging lantern moving away from him. Loud voices carried to him on the still night air.

Those must be some of Raoul's men. He was frightened, but he needed to know what Raoul was doing. Staying well in the shadows of the trees that grew along the edge of the road, he moved quickly and silently until he was close enough to make out words.

They staggered along, praising Raoul's generosity with Old Kaintuck. Auguste saw three of them in the lantern's yellow glow, each carrying a rifle.

He bit his lower lip, and fear formed a cold hollow in his chest. If these men saw him they would shoot him on the spot.

Or try to. He doubted they could hit anything, drunk as they looked. With that thought, his tense muscles eased a little.

The men crossed a narrow ridge that connected a hill with the bluff on which the trading post stood. Auguste flinched, startled by a whoop and a wail, followed by the crash of a body falling through shrubbery and a heavy clattering—probably a rifle—against rocks.

From the ridge came a burst of drunken laughter. Two of the men mocked their comrade who had rolled to the bottom of the hill. They wouldn't help him climb back up. Sleep it off down there, they told him. Curses floated faintly from below, then there was silence.

"What if that Indian is lurking around here?" said the man carrying the lantern. "He might come upon Hodge in the dark and scalp him or something."

Auguste thought, *How I would love to.* He recognized the Prussian accent of the man speaking. It was Otto Wegner, one of the men who worked at Raoul's trading post.

The other man said, "Hell, if the Injun ain't dead from the way Eli conked him with that rifle butt, he's halfway to Canada. He knows he'll get his red hide full of holes if he stays around Smith County."

"As for me, I do not shoot unarmed Indians," said Wegner. "Fifty Spanish dollars or not. I have my pride. I served under von Blücher at Waterloo."

"Waterloo, hah? Well, ain't you a hell of a fella! Raoul'd skin you alive and wear you for a hat if he heard you talking like that."

"He would not. I am his best rifleman—after Eli Greenglove. He knows my value. And my honor as a soldier is worth more to me than fifty pieces of eight."

Crouching in the shrubbery, Auguste shook his head in wonder. There was some sense of right and wrong even among Raoul's rogues.

But that hadn't stopped Wegner from being one of the men who backed Raoul with his rifle this morning.

He waited for the men to cross the ridge. He heard no sound from the one who had fallen; he had probably taken his comrades' advice and gone to sleep.

When the lantern swung out of sight around a corner of the trading post palisade, Auguste darted forward. Keeping low, he made a wide circle through the wooded slope above Victor. He scrambled down to the road where the Hopkins house stood. A long-eared black dog barked and ran at him when he passed one of the houses along the road. His heart stopped as he waited for doors to fly open and rifles to fire at him. But he kept walking, and the dog stopped barking when he was beyond the house it was guarding.

Hoping none of the neighbors would hear him, he knocked loudly at the Hopkins door to wake them up.

Frank Hopkins, holding a candle in his hand, stood in the doorway in a long nightshirt. "What the devil is it? We've got a sick man in here—" He peered closer. "My God, Auguste! Get inside, quick."

He reached out, dragged Auguste through the door and shut it quickly behind him.

"I thought you were out at the Hales'." They stood in Frank's ground-floor workshop. The iron printing press towered shadowy in the candle's glow.

"I came to see Grandpapa. And—Frank, I'm going back to my people. I need your help."

"Come upstairs." Frank helped Auguste untie his backpack.

The stairs led to a second-floor corridor, and Frank drew Auguste into a room where an oil lamp with a tall glass chimney burned next to a large bed. Nicole sat there. The lamplight revealed Elysée's sharp profile against the white of the pillow.

Nicole jumped to her feet. "Oh, Auguste! Are you all right?"

"I'm getting better. How is Grandpapa?"

"He's only been awake half the time. Gram Medill looked in on him. She said he wrenched his hip when he fell and had bad bruises, but he hadn't broken any bones. I've been sitting up with him. What about you—how is your head?"

Auguste felt as if chains had fallen away from his chest at the news that Grandpapa was not dying. Then his head started to hurt. In the excitement of slipping past his enemies, Auguste had forgotten his pain. Now he rubbed the spot above his right ear where Greenglove's rifle had hit him. He felt a lump that was sore to the touch. But he was able to smile reassuringly at Nicole.

He spoke in a low voice so as not to disturb Elysée. "I won't be able to put my fine beaver hat on over this bump. But I won't be taking my fine beaver hat where I'm going."

"I'll get some more chairs," Frank said. "We can talk in here. The old gentleman is sound asleep now. Could you use a drop of brandy, Auguste?"

Auguste nodded. "That might ease the pain." He thought not only of the pain from the rifle blow, but of the pain in his heart from having lost Victoire despite his promise to his father. And the pain of tearing himself away from Nancy.

He and Frank quietly removed chairs from the other upstairs rooms where the Hopkins children were sleeping. Frank went down to the kitchen and came back with a tray bearing three small bowl-shaped crystal glasses and a cut-glass decanter that twinkled in the lamplight.

"Handsome glassware," Auguste said, seating himself and carefully setting his backpack between his feet.

"From the time of Louis the Fifteenth," Nicole said. "One of the things Papa brought over from the old château in France. And he gave it to Frank and me as a wedding present. At least Raoul won't get his hands on this."

Auguste said, "But Raoul has everything else, because father left it all to me. I told him he should will it to you; I should have insisted." His face burned with shame.

Frank said, "I doubt we'd have held onto the estate any longer than you did. And, frankly, I don't want it any more than you do. I don't know how Nicole feels."

Now that the land was irrevocably lost to him, Auguste was no longer so sure that he did not want it. He twisted in his chair, angry at himself for his uncertainty.

Nicole shook her head. "I'm a wife and mother. I'm not prepared to be a châtelaine. Especially when I'd have to fight that—that beast."

As Frank poured an inch of the warm amber liquid into each of their glasses, Auguste noticed that his fingers were, as always, blackened. He must never get the stains of his trade off his hands.

Frank said, "I'm going to write in the *Visitor* about what happened today, tell what I saw, so the whole county will know what happened."

Auguste looked at Nicole. He saw fear in her eyes, but she said nothing.

"Why write about it?" Auguste said. "Raoul would do some harm to you. And it would change nothing. I won't even be here to read it." The last thing he wanted was these people, whom he cared about, getting into trouble because of him.

Frank smiled faintly. "You know that unlike just about every other man in Smith County, I don't carry a gun." He pointed downward, in the direction of the press on the floor below them. "That's my way of fighting."

For a moment Auguste felt ashamed that he was running away from that same fight.

"Because you stood by me today my heart will always sing your praises. Do you think my father's spirit will be sad if I do not stay and fight for the land until I die?"

"You almost did die, Auguste," Nicole said.

And I might yet, before I get away from here.

He sipped the brandy. It burned his tongue and his throat and lit a fire in his belly. It made him feel stronger.

Frank said, "Nobody's saying you should stay. I don't want to see you killed."

Nicole said, "Neither would your father. Pierre wanted you to have the estate, but he didn't want you dead on account of it."

"Amen to that," said Frank.

Yes, Auguste thought, despising himself, *but I think he expected me to keep the land for more than a day.*

Frank went on, "But if you go back to your people, you've got to tell them—they can no more fight the United States for their land than you could fight Raoul."

A fierce heat rose in Auguste as he took another sip of brandy.

"At St. George's School I read that the Indian does not make good use of the land. The whites need the land. Therefore the Indian must yield." He clenched his fist around the glass in his hand. "We were living on this land! Doesn't that mean anything?"

Frank said, "Auguste, you know better than any of your people how much power the United States have. You've got to tell them."

Auguste was silent for a moment.

The long knives, he thought. That was what his people called the American soldiers. But the British Band had no idea how very many long knives there were. He must make Black Hawk understand.

He sipped a little more of the brandy, and its fire flowed through his blood.

He sighed and nodded. "I will tell them. Frank, I need a boat."

Nicole said, "Your eyelids are drooping, Auguste. You're tired and you're still hurt. You can't go tonight."

True. And he wanted to stay long enough to see Grandpapa when he was awake.

Auguste's last memory that night was of letting Frank lead him across the corridor into a darkened bedroom, where he fell face down on an empty bed.

When he came to himself again, he was lying on the same bed, still fully clothed except for his boots. The room was not as dark as he remembered; it was in a sort of twilight. The one window was shuttered. A curtain covered the doorway. He looked around the room, saw boys' clothing hanging on pegs and piled on the floor, another bed, covered with rumpled sheets, empty. His own boots and his pack were set neatly at the foot of his bed.

An urgent pressure inside told him he had been sleeping a long time. He saw a chamber pot in one corner. Smart of them to leave the pot here, he thought as he filled it. He didn't dare to go to their outhouse during daylight.

He went to the window and cautiously looked through the shutter. The window looked south, and he could not see the sun, only the black shadows it painted in the ruts of the road that slanted up the hill past the Hopkins house. It must be late afternoon.

He wondered, were Raoul and his men out there somewhere, looking for him? Would he live to see another nightfall?

His head ached less than it had last night—until he touched it. Then the pain was like someone pounding a nail into his brain. The bump felt as big as a hen's egg.

Opening his backpack, he took out his leather medicine bag and drew out the stones one by one, rubbing his fingers over each. He opened his shirt and touched the tip of the bear's claw to the five scars on his chest.

Then, on impulse, he touched it to the old scar on his cheek.

A black leather bag contained his surgical instruments—two saws, a big one for legs and a smaller one for arms; four scalpels; lancets for bleeding; a turnkey for pulling teeth; a probe and tongs for removing bullets; a small jar of opium. Any of those things might be needed, where he was going.

Last, he took out a book, chosen almost at random from his small collection. On the spine of its brown leather cover was stamped in gold: "J. Milton. *Paradise Lost.*"

Reverend Hale had recommended that he take a Bible. This long poem giving the Christian account of creation was the next thing to a Bible. But he had read it at St. George's and enjoyed it. And its title and its story of Adam and Eve being driven out of the Garden of Eden made him think of how he was dispossessed. Perhaps he would find some wisdom or guidance in the book.

Today he thought, *Paradise lost? It may be that I'm returning to paradise.*

But then he remembered how Nancy had wanted to "know" him as Adam knew Eve. He *was* leaving behind what might have been a great happiness.

He opened the book and read the first verse his eye fell upon:

> High on a Throne of Royal State, which far
> Outshone the wealth of *Ormus* and of *Ind*,
> Or where the gorgeous East with richest hand
> Show'rs on her Kings *Barbaric* Pearl and Gold,
> Satan exalted sat . . .

Sounded like Raoul, with his fifty Spanish dollars and his steamboat and lead mine and trading post. Raoul was better fitted to be Satan than to be the angel at the gates of Eden keeping sinners away.

He heard voices nearby. One, faint but unmistakable, was Grandpapa's. His heart leaped. He quickly repacked his treasures.

He pushed the curtain aside and hurried across the hall. It was a joy to see Elysée's eyes looking at him, open and bright.

"I do not as a rule believe in miracles," Elysée said, smiling at Auguste, "but it's certainly a miracle that you could charge a man pointing a pistol at your chest and come out with nothing but a bump on your head."

"It's a bad enough bump, Grandpapa," said Auguste, dragging over the chair he had sat in last night and pulling it close to the side of the bed. "I wish I could stay and doctor you."

"Our local midwife says I too will heal," said Elysée. "I can move all my arms and legs without extreme pain. I think the worst injury was to my hip." He touched his right side gently. "I bruised it when I fell. There's swelling there, but I can move my leg. The hip is not broken." He closed his eyes, and Auguste knew that the old man was feeling a sharper pain in his heart than in his bones. "You must not think of staying here. I am afraid Raoul is perfectly capable of murdering you."

One son dead, the other an enemy. And now I must leave him. How much more can he stand?

Nicole was sitting beside Elysée's bed, just as she had been last night when Auguste arrived. He wondered whether she had slept.

Nicole smiled at him. "I sent the children down to play by the river. Having two injured adults to care for has been very restful for me."

Elysée sat up a little straighter, Nicole quickly plumping the pillows behind him, and turned a sharp, blue-eyed stare at Auguste.

"Nicole and Frank told me about your plan to go back to the Sauk. I can understand why you would wish to do so, but that is not the only choice open to you. You might consider going where people are much more civilized than they are around here—back East, where you were educated. Emilie and Charles would be happy, I am sure, to take you in again for a time. And I could help you. I have money banked with Irving and Sons on Wall Street. You could continue your education and follow the medical profession in New York."

Wishing he did not have to refuse the old man, Auguste said, "Grandpapa, I must go to the only other people I love in the world as much as I love you and Aunt Nicole."

Elysée uttered a little sigh. "I understand. Loyalty pulls you back to your mother's people. It is a family trait. I suppose your father must have told you about the mystery around the origin of our family name."

"Yes, Grandpapa." Wanting him to know his French forebears, Pierre had spent hours with Auguste recounting their names and deeds. And he had told him that, strangely, the de Marion records extended back only to the late thirteenth century, though the family was wealthy and powerful even then. According to a murky legend, one ancestor had committed treason against the King, and that one's son had deserted his wife and children, simply disappeared. Feeling the original name, whatever it had been, irreparably tarnished, the first recorded Count de Marion had destroyed all record of it— apparently with the approval and help of the royal authorities—and had taken his mother's family's name instead. The story had left Auguste wishing he could use his shaman's powers to learn more, but he doubted that the Sauk spirits could see clear across the ocean.

Elysée said, "We de Marions sometimes display an overabundance of loyalty, as if we were still trying to expiate that ancient guilt."

Puzzled, Auguste said, "There's nothing wrong with loyalty, is there?"

"Certainly not. But remember this—if I had let loyalty keep me in France, we would not be here in this primeval paradise."

He sees this land as a paradise too. But it has not been kind to him.

"Looking back, Grandpapa, do you think you would have done better to have stayed in France?"

Elysée laughed, a short, humorless bark. "Not at all. I would almost certainly have lost my head to Dr. Guillotine's wonderful invention. Our lands would have been confiscated, and that would have been the end of the family."

"But now, with most of the wealth in Raoul's hands—"

Elysée raised a hand and shook his head. "This is not the end. I do not believe in divine intervention, but I do believe there is a law of nature that says a bad man will do badly in the end."

Auguste was about to reply when he heard footsteps coming down the road toward the house, reminding him of how quiet it had been ever since he awakened. A good part of the town was sleeping off Raoul's Old Kaintuck, he suspected.

He heard the door open and close below. A moment later Frank

came into the room carrying a long rifle, with an ammunition bag
and a powder horn slung over his shoulder.

"Well, I bought you a little bateau that will get you across the
Mississippi," he said, "for five dollars, from an old trapper who
doesn't feel up to going out this winter. And for another twenty
dollars I got him to throw in his second best rifle and a good supply
of ammunition." He smiled grimly at Auguste. "I expect you'll find
this useful over in Ioway."

Auguste nodded. "I'll eat better. But—twenty-five dollars. Frank,
that's too much for you to spend on me." He felt a warm gratitude
toward the plump, sandy-haired man who was risking so much to
help him. Frank's newspaper, his printing business and his carpentry
all together could hardly bring in twenty-five dollars in a month,
little enough to feed a family of ten.

Elysée said, "I told you I had some money salted away, Auguste.
Let the boat and the rifle be my gift to you."

Auguste reached out and squeezed his grandfather's bony hand.

Frank said, "I've moved the boat about half a mile below town
and hidden it. We should be able to get down there unseen after
dark."

Nicole said, "If Auguste is leaving as Raoul wants him to, why
wouldn't Raoul just let him go?"

Frank said, "We can't take that chance. I believe Raoul won't be
content unless he kills Auguste."

Auguste shuddered inwardly at the thought that there was in the
world a man who would not be satisfied until he was dead. He could
not live with that kind of fear. He asked the White Bear, his spirit
guide, to give him courage.

He tried to push the fear out of his mind. He stood up to go
back to the room where he had slept. He would clean and repack
the things he was taking, he decided. He would get busy getting
ready and not give himself time to think about being afraid.

But nightfall seemed a long way off.

At nine o'clock in the evening by the Seth Thomas clock in
Frank's printing shop, which he reset every day at sunset, it was
dark enough and the town was quiet enough for Auguste to leave.
He held Nicole's ample body tight and kissed her, shook hands with
the boys and kissed the girls. His grandfather had drifted off to sleep
again, but the old man had kissed him on both cheeks, and they
had said their good-byes in the afternoon.

The road down the bluff from the town to the bottomland was empty. Most people in Victor went to bed soon after sunset, and those who didn't would be up in the taproom of the trading post inn.

Auguste did see candlelight flickering in a one-room log cabin they passed. A silhouette appeared in the window just as he looked in. A man reached out and slammed the shutters closed.

"Bad luck we should pass that house just as he came to the window," Frank said. "One of Raoul's men. But he's more than likely still half drunk."

Frank and Auguste followed the road past fields of corn ready for harvesting, their way lighted by the nearly full moon.

Up ahead the wooded sides of the bluff came down to the water's edge. Frank led Auguste out on a shrub-covered spit.

Not until he was nearly on top of the bateau did Auguste see it. Frank had pulled it up out of the water, covered it with branches, and tied it to the roots of a tree that had toppled into the water, undercut by the river.

With sinking heart Auguste saw that though the riverboat was small, it would be heavier and harder to row than a canoe. Well, Frank had done his best, and now he would have to do *his* best.

His heart leaped with fear as he heard hoofbeats.

Horsemen, coming down the road from Victor.

Frank stopped working on the boat and lifted his head. "Damn! That skunk must have seen you after all."

The pounding was coming rapidly closer. Auguste's heart was beating as fast as the oncoming hooves. He saw the horsemen by moonlight—*five* of them, racing through the high corn.

Frank and Auguste pushed the little boat into the water bow first, pointed stern resting on the shore. Auguste put his pack in the stern and the rifle and ammunition in the bow, where they were more likely to stay dry. The current pulled the bow downstream, the flat bottom grinding in the mud.

Auguste saw a flash and heard a loud boom. Something whistled through the bare branches of a bush beside him.

He leaped into the boat.

"Here. Beef and biscuit." Frank tossed a bag to Auguste, who set it on the seat beside him. Frank pushed the bateau's stern free.

"Now row for your life!"

Pulling as hard and fast as he could, Auguste steered diagonally into the Mississippi, trying to get beyond pistol range without spending all his strength fighting the current.

"Hopkins, goddamn it, I'll kill *you* if he gets away!"

Raoul's voice. Auguste wished he had time to load his rifle and shoot back, but if he stopped rowing they were sure to get him.

Five bright red flashes and five shots roared out one after the other from shore.

If one of those men is Eli Greenglove I'm dead for sure.

Auguste heard a sharp rap on the side of the boat and splashes in the water on his left. He felt naked sitting up in the boat pulling frantically on the oars. He could stop rowing and lie down using the side of the boat as a shield, but then he would remain within range, drifting south along the riverbank, and Raoul and his men could follow him and shoot at him at their leisure. He gritted his teeth and kept rowing, his shoulder muscles feeling as if they were about to tear loose from his bones.

He heard a ball whiz past his head. They must have stopped riding to reload and take better aim.

Another ball smashed into the boat just ahead of the wooden oarlock.

His body was coated with the cold sweat of fear. There was nothing he could do but sit here, a target in the moonlight, and pull on the oars with all his strength. If he missed one stroke it might be his death.

Earthmaker, do not let Raoul take revenge on Frank.

Pistol balls splashed water into the boat.

11

Redbird's Wickiup

White Bear rowed upstream on the Ioway River past stands of weeping willow whose yellowing fronds drooped into the dark green water. Even though the current was at its weakest now, his arms and shoulders felt as if they'd been beaten with clubs. If only Frank had been able to find a canoe for him instead of this heavy bateau that he'd had to push across the Great River and now up the Ioway.

His heart fluttered in his chest like a trapped bird as he sensed himself coming closer to the British Band's winter hunting camp. He had thought he would be happy at this homecoming, but he was terrified.

How would they receive him? After six years they must think he had forgotten all about them. Would they despise him? Maybe they would just make fun of him.

And in what state would he find the British Band? They'd had to get through the summer without the crops they always raised. Had any friends been shot by white snipers during the siege of Sauk-enuk? How many, weakened by hunger, might be ill or dead? Would his mother be alive?

And what of Redbird?

He had already met, just by chance, one member of the band, Three Horses, who had been fishing in the shallows on the Ioway shore of the Great River. And Three Horses had certainly been happy to see him. He'd jumped on his pony and had said he would ride back to the camp with the news that White Bear was back. He was so excited that he did not wait for White Bear to ask any questions about how his people had fared.

So they would all be waiting for him by the time he got there. The thought frightened him all the more.

Ahead, a row of bark and dugout canoes lay bottoms up on a dirt embankment.

He saw a flash of red in the trees near the canoes. For a moment he thought, with a joyous leap of his heart, that it might be Redbird. Then a man wearing a deep red blanket stepped out of the woods. He stood over the beached canoes with his arms folded.

Wolf Paw.

His eyes were like splinters of coal, and the black circles he had painted around them gave him a terrifying aspect. The crest of red-dyed deer hair that sprouted from his shaven skull seemed strange and savage to White Bear after six years away from the Sauk.

White Bear rowed in close to the riverbank, uncertain how to greet Wolf Paw. The brave said nothing, did nothing. A maple branch swayed in the wind. Red leaves fell, and sunlight flashed from a steel-headed tomahawk that Wolf Paw was holding.

White Bear's belly knotted.

He skidded the boat to a halt on the bank a short distance downriver from Wolf Paw. He climbed out the front end, pulled the boat up on the bank, unloaded it and turned it over.

Wolf Paw watched in silence as White Bear slung his pack and bags on his back, picked up his rifle and rested it on his shoulder. Looking at Wolf Paw's red crest and blanket and buckskin trousers, White Bear realized how strange he himself must seem to Wolf Paw in the green clawhammer jacket he had worn to his father's funeral.

Now they were face to face.

I will wait for him to move, if I have to stand here till sunset and all through the night. He chose this strange way of meeting me. Let him show me what is in his mind.

He heard the boughs creaking in the wind around him. River water rippled over the stones along the bank. He heard a redbird whistling in the distance.

Wolf Paw drew a deep breath, opened his mouth and let out a war whoop.

"Whoowhoowhoowhoo!"

White Bear's heart gave a great thump, and he fell back a step. He heard rage in the whoop, and the frustration. Wolf Paw was angry at him. Why? Maybe just for coming back.

Wolf Paw held the tomahawk high. Corded muscles and dark veins stood out in his rigid arm. Two feathers dyed red danced just under the steel head. He repeated his war whoop, and then his lips drew back from clenched white teeth.

He whirled and plunged into the woods, leaving White Bear shaken and open-mouthed. He stood still, listening to Wolf Paw crashing through the trees and shrubs, kicking piles of leaves, until the noise died away in the distance. No Sauk ran noisily through the woods like that, unless driven by some madness.

White Bear sighed. Oddly, he felt less frightened than he had before he met Wolf Paw. Before, he had not known what to expect. Now he felt ready for anything.

He strode into the woods following Three Horses' directions. As he walked he began to hear the sounds of people's voices and dogs barking. Gradually they drew nearer, until at last he broke through the trees into a clearing.

The sight made his eyes brim with tears.

A hundred or more women in brown, fringed skirts were facing him, and as he came forward they rushed to form a ring around him. His vision blurred as he recognized faces he had not seen in six years.

Beyond the women he could see the camp of the British Band. In his joy it seemed to him that the wickiups were bathed in a golden light. Rings of gray domes began near the trees where he stood and spread into the tall yellow prairie grass. Before the wickiups he could see what the women had been working at, tasks abandoned for the moment, clothing being mended, skins stretched, meat and fish cleaned and set on frames to dry.

"White Bear is here!" cried one woman, and he recognized Water Flows Fast, plump wife of Three Horses.

Three Horses, a short man with broad shoulders, stood beside his wife. His nose was flat and spread out. White Bear did not remember it that way. Something must have happened to Three Horses while he was gone.

Much has happened to them while I was gone.

"I told you White Bear had come back," Three Horses said over and over again.

White Bear breathed in the familiar smells of campfire smoke and roasting meat, of leather and freshly cut wood and tobacco smoke. His delighted eyes took in quillwork and beadwork and paint, blankets and ribbons, bodies clad in fringed buckskin, warm brown faces, dark, friendly eyes.

Murmuring greetings, he searched the crowd for specially loved faces.

"Where is Owl Carver?" he asked. After such a long time the Sauk language came awkwardly to his lips.

Three Horses said, "Owl Carver visits the camps of the Fox and the Kickapoo, to invite them to Black Hawk's council."

What is Black Hawk planning now?

White Bear did not like the sound of the news, but there would be time to think about it later.

"Where is Sun Woman, my mother?"

Water Flows Fast spoke up. "She has gone to gather medicine plants." She looked as cheerful as, he remembered, she always had, but her eyes penetrated him.

"Will no one find her and tell her that I am here?"

Water Flows Fast said, "Redbird should go and tell Sun Woman. Redbird lives with Sun Woman now."

Redbird!

He felt almost dizzy at the sound of her name, a name he had not heard spoken aloud in six years.

As soon as Water Flows Fast spoke, she started to giggle, putting her hands over her mouth. Many of the other women in the group giggled too. White Bear wanted to hide his burning face. He had forgotten how painful it could be to be made fun of by those who knew him so well.

But joy blazed up in his chest. Redbird living with Sun Woman? He wanted to whoop with happiness, even as Wolf Paw had whooped with rage. That could only mean that she had not taken a husband.

Then he took a deep breath and stiffened his body to hide his feelings. He looked at the laughing faces all around him, especially the bright, curious eyes of Water Flows Fast. If they saw how excited he was, they would laugh at him all the more.

Trying to keep his voice steady, he asked, "Where is my mother's wickiup?"

With a knowing smile—but what was it that she knew?—Water Flows Fast beckoned to the wickiup of Sun Woman—and Redbird. "Come. I will take you."

She turned, her fringed skirt swinging. The women parted to make way for her. Shouldering his rifle, White Bear followed. Three Horses walked beside him. White Bear heard the whisper of many moccasins and the murmur of many voices behind him.

Water Flows Fast marched up to a wickiup near the center of the camp. The dark, rounded shelter of sheets of elm bark and tree limbs was small, just big enough for two people, three at the most.

White Bear's heart was beating like a dance drum. The buffalo-hide flap was pulled down over the door, showing that if anyone was within they wanted privacy.

"The wickiup of Sun Woman," said Water Flows Fast. "And of Redbird." She looked at him expectantly.

"There is no one here," said White Bear.

This brought shouts of laughter from the women around him. He wished they would all go away.

"I saw Redbird go in there," said Water Flows Fast, "and I did not see her come out."

White Bear's discomfort increased as he watched her face redden and her cheeks puff out. It seemed that mirth would make her burst.

Every beat of his heart seemed to shake his whole body. He looked around slowly, trying to calm himself. Even if Redbird had waited for him, his sudden return must have shocked her. She needed time to prepare herself to meet him. And, like him, she did not want all these women watching their meeting and laughing. He would simply have to wait until Redbird was ready to greet him.

A rack of crisscrossed wooden sticks for drying skins stood by the closed doorway. Slowly, deliberately, he walked over to the rack, leaned his rifle against it, and laid down his pack and bags.

Then, turning his back on the wickiup, he sat down cross-legged on the ground.

Water Flows Fast looked at him, open-mouthed.

"Thank you for showing me the way," he said. Hiding his embarrassment, he made himself smile at the hundred or more women gathered to watch him.

"What are you going to do?" Water Flows Fast asked.

"I am going to rest and thank Earthmaker for seeing me here safely."

"White Bear is a man of sense," said Three Horses, smiling his approval.

"Is that all?" Water Flows Fast asked.

"I am going to wait for Sun Woman, my mother."

"Is *that* all?"

"That *is* all," said White Bear.

Three Horses, who was no taller than his wife, gripped her plump upper arm firmly. "Let White Bear alone."

"But—" Water Flows Fast started to protest, and her husband jerked her arm.

"We will leave this man in peace," he said.

Her lower lip jutting out, Water Flows Fast let Three Horses pull her away through the crowd.

White Bear sat with his eyes downcast to discourage people from talking to him. Gradually the rest of the crowd dispersed.

The back of his neck bristled. He knew Redbird was in the wick-iup behind him. Sooner or later she must come out.

To have her so close after all this time, to know she was there and to hear nothing but that terrible silence, and yet to sit with his back to that buffalo-hide curtain, all this was a torment for him. The urge to jump up and tear the curtain away pressed against his resolve to hold himself still. He thought he might explode like a barrel of gunpowder.

He forced himself to breathe slowly and pretend that he was hidden in shrubbery with a bow and arrow, watching for a deer.

After a time—he could not tell how much time—a face was peering into his. Dark and square. The brown eyes brimmed with tears.

His eyes opened wider. Sun Woman was kneeling before him.

"My son." She reached out to him, and he scrambled to embrace her. When her strong arms held him he felt like a little boy again.

He sat back to look at her dear face, wet with tears. Resting beside her on the ground was the familiar basket with blue cloth cover that she used to gather herbs.

He looked around for the sun. It was low and red on the western horizon. It had been high when he sat down here. He must have gone on a spirit walk.

"I knew it would be like this," Sun Woman said. "It would come one day when I least expected it—my son would be back again."

He sighed deeply. "To see my mother makes my heart as big as the prairie."

They sat facing each other and she gripped his shoulders. "You are a man now, a very handsome man." She ran her hand along his cheek, and his whole face felt warm. He kept his gaze fixed on her eyes.

She said, "You have learned much. You have been hurt. Your face is scarred." She followed the line of the scar with her thumb, leaning forward to peer still more closely at him. "I see sadness in you. Your father is dead. That is why you have come back."

She sat back and closed her eyes for a silent moment. Then she began a song for the dead.

> "Earthmaker, show him the way.
> Lead him over the bridge of stars and sunbeams,
> Along the westward Trail of Souls.
> Take his soul into your heart."

After she had finished the song, Sun Woman wiped the tears from her face with her blunt fingers. She reached out and stroked his cheeks as well. He had not realized that he was crying.

But grieving for Pierre reminded him to reach into his medicine bag.

"I have a gift for you, Mother." He took out the flat silver case with its velvet neck cord, opened it and showed her the pair of spectacles Marchette had brought to him from Victoire. "Do you know these?"

"Your father wore circles of glass like these. To see the marks on the talking paper."

"Yes. These are the same ones." He closed the case and pressed it into her hand. "Now you have something that was close to Star Arrow."

She said, "He was with me for five summers only, but in spirit, ever since. Now I will feel even closer to him." She slipped the ribbon over her head and dropped the case down the front of her doeskin dress.

He saw the tracks of more tears on her smooth brown cheeks in the fading light. This time she did not wipe them away.

"Tell me all that has happened to you," she said.

As White Bear talked, he deliberately made his voice loud enough to carry, so that Redbird, in the wickiup, might hear.

When he was through telling his story, he felt weighed down by guilt.

"I fled, Mother, even though I promised my father I would care for the land. And smoked tobacco with him to seal the promise. Should I have stayed?"

She put her hand on his shoulder and squeezed. "You kept your promise as far as you were able. That is all the calumet requires. Your father would not want you to die fighting for that land. It is better that you come back here and be a Sauk again."

White Bear looked down, unable to meet Sun Woman's eyes. Feeling an ache deep in the center of his body, remembering the great stone and log house, the blizzard of blossoms in the orchards, the fields of green corn and golden wheat, the herds that darkened the hillsides, he wanted to clutch his chest where it felt as if it had been torn open. He could not so easily forget Victoire.

When I was at Victoire I yearned to go back to my people. Now I am with my people and I miss Victoire. Will my heart never be at peace?

Nancy had wanted him so desperately before they parted; Redbird would not even let him see her.

White Bear saw that once again women had started to gather nearby, among them the round-faced Water Flows Fast. And now White Bear saw another familiar face he had not seen earlier, Redbird's mother, Wind Bends Grass. She glowered at him as she always had, her fists on her broad hips.

O Earthmaker! Why would Redbird not come out and speak to him?

A dozen cawing crows flew over the camp. Laughing at him.

He heard a movement behind him, a rustling of the buffalo-hide curtain. He dared not look around.

A voice at his back said, "Go away, White Bear!"

A cool, sweet flow poured from his heart like a mountain spring at the sound of Redbird's voice. He unfolded his legs, stiff from hours of sitting, and pushed himself to his feet. He turned.

Weakness washed over him; he thought he might fall to the ground. Redbird stood before him, her cheeks flushed, her slanting eyes sparkling with anger. Her face was thinner than he remembered, her lips fuller. She still wore a fringe of her hair over her forehead.

Standing silent and open-mouthed, he felt he must look utterly foolish.

"Go away," Redbird said again. "We do not want you here."

"To see you is a sunrise in my heart, Redbird."

"To see you is a foul day in my stomach!"

Reeling back from her anger, White Bear saw a little boy standing in the doorway behind her.

He was bare-chested, brown-skinned. He wore a loincloth of red flannel and fringed buckskin leggings. He was shifting uncomfortably from one moccasined foot to the other and clutching at himself under the loincloth.

Now White Bear understood why Redbird had finally come out. She and the boy must have been inside the wickiup all the time he was sitting out here, and the boy was about to burst.

It would have been funny, except that a much more important discovery struck White Bear.

He looked closer at the boy's urgent eyes. Blue eyes.

White Bear's own eyes were brown, but Pierre's were blue. Could eye color be passed in the blood from grandfather to grandson? Around his eyes, in the narrow shape of his head, his long chin coming to a sharp point, White Bear could see that this boy was a de Marion.

This is our son! Redbird's and mine!

Joy blazed up in his body like a fire that warms but does not hurt.

He asked, "What is his name, Redbird?"

She glanced over her shoulder at the boy. "What are you standing there for? You have to go. Go!" The boy ran off toward the woods. White Bear watched him. He ran well, even though he was very young and most uncomfortable.

White Bear wanted to reach out and take Redbird into his arms.

She turned back to him, her fists clenched at her sides, her nostrils flaring in fury.

"*Now* you want to know what his name is. Now, five winters after he was born."

He turned to Sun Woman. "Does she have a husband?"

Sun Woman raised her eyebrows. "There were many braves who wished to marry her. Wolf Paw was most insistent. He offered Owl Carver ten horses. Little Stabbing Chief of the Fox sought her. There were others, besides."

Wolf Paw had wanted to marry her. That must have been the

meaning of that strange encounter outside the camp. Wolf Paw probably wanted to kill him.

"Please, Sun Woman, do not talk to this man about me," Redbird said. "You are his mother, and a mother to me. But you cannot make peace between us."

"True," said Sun Woman, picking up her basket of herbs and bark. "Only you can do that, daughter."

She turned to White Bear. "If Redbird does not welcome you into this wickiup I share with her and Eagle Feather, I cannot invite you inside."

With that Sun Woman turned abruptly and trudged off toward the river.

Eagle Feather!

Redbird threw an exasperated look after Sun Woman.

Redbird's anger made White Bear feel as if one of the long knives' cannonballs had crushed his chest. Perhaps if he could put his arms around her she would remember how she had loved him. He took a step toward her, reaching for her.

She stepped back quickly, bent down and picked up a rock. "Go away. Now!"

How graceful all her movements are.

The rock was gray and somewhat larger than her fist. It had sharp, irregular edges and looked as if it had been used to chip arrowheads.

He said, "You would not be this angry at me if you did not want me back. Why did you refuse every man who asked for you?"

Her face twisted with rage, she threw the rock.

For an instant he was blinded as it hit his cheek, stunning him, and his head snapped back.

He felt a pounding pain in the back of his skull as his vision cleared. The ache from being hit with a rifle butt had come back.

He heard gasps of dismay from some of the watching women, laughter from others.

Wind Bends Grass called out scornfully, "I am ashamed to call this fool my daughter. I cast her out of my lodge because she would accept no suitors. At last comes the one who ruined her for all the others, and she drives him away with a rock. I think we should throw rocks at her."

The crowd's laughter was louder, although White Bear saw that Wind Bends Grass did not mean to be funny.

His left cheekbone throbbed, the cheek Raoul's knife had scarred, and he felt a trickle of blood. But he would not let himself lift his hand to wipe it away.

Redbird's hand went up to her own face, as if the rock had hit her. Her slanting eyes widened with a look of horror.

She whirled and ducked through her dark doorway.

"Go in there after her, White Bear!" one of the women called.

He would not do that. He would not go into her wickiup until she invited him. And in spite of the heaviness in his heart, in spite of the ache in his cheekbone and the pounding in his head, he believed that sooner or later invite him she would.

He turned his back on the empty doorway and sat down again.

The blue-eyed, brown-skinned boy was standing before him. A golden glow filled White Bear's chest.

"You are hurt," said the boy.

"It is nothing, Eagle Feather. A man must endure pain without complaint."

"Did my mother do that to you?"

"She wanted to punish me for staying away from you and her for so long. My name is White Bear."

"I know what your name is."

When he heard that, he was sure that he would win her back.

The boy darted around him.

Resting his hands on his knees, White Bear closed his eyes and let his mind dwell on a vast white-furred shape. Owl Carver had said that when a man wished to send his spirit on a journey in the other world, he need only think of his other self.

He saw the huge golden eyes, the massive, long-muzzled head, the towering body.

Soon he and the Bear spirit were walking together toward the sun.

Redbird did not understand herself. She hated White Bear, but when she saw blood running down his face, she had hated herself. She sat in darkness, biting her lips to keep from screaming.

She crept to the doorway and pushed the curtain open a crack. She could see him sitting again with his back to her, his shoulders broad in his green pale eyes' coat.

She drew back into the wickiup and saw the small steel knife she used to cut up food gleaming near the embers of her fire. She picked it up and held its edge against her feverish cheek.

The last light of day fell on her as the doorway curtain rose. Startled, she almost cut herself. She whirled to see Eagle Feather staring at her. She threw the knife down on the straw-covered floor.

Eagle Feather gave her a questioning look but said nothing.

She drew him down beside her and started telling him the story of why the leaves change colors and fall to the ground in autumn.

It was dark outside when Sun Woman came back from the river, where she had been washing the plants she had gathered. Redbird was afraid Sun Woman would ask her to forgive White Bear, but the older woman said nothing.

They passed what seemed like an ordinary evening, talking and telling stories and singing. But Redbird could not forget that figure sitting like a tree stump just beyond the buffalo-hide curtain.

Much later she went out, and by the light from tonight's full Moon of Falling Leaves, looked into White Bear's face. It was motionless, as if carved from wood.

He did not seem to see her. He must be on a spirit journey. Hot with rage, she kicked at his knee. What right had he to go on a spirit journey leaving his body to haunt her wickiup?

The impact of her moccasined foot shook him slightly, but it was like kicking a bundle of pelts.

Redbird's breath came out in a cloud, lit by the full moon. She gathered up some twigs, brought them into the wickiup and added them to the fire. Sun Woman went out carrying a blanket. Redbird saw her draping it over her son's shoulders.

He does not need that, Redbird thought, remembering how White Bear had come back, seemingly frozen, from his vision quest in the Moon of Ice.

Tightly wrapped in her own blankets with Eagle Feather curled up in the shelter of her body, Redbird lay awake, thinking that she had never in her life slept with a man. That was White Bear's fault, and she ground her teeth in the dark as she thought of the wrongs he had done her.

He left me in the Moon of First Buds, and he returns in the Moon of Falling Leaves—six summers later.

One afternoon they had been lovers. And then he had gone to live with the pale eyes. For nine moons she had carried his son and then given birth to him. He had not been here to give the baby a birth name. Owl Carver, the baby's grandfather, had to do that, embarrassed at the necessity, complaining that the people were laughing at their family. She knew Star Arrow had required that no messages pass between White Bear and the tribe. But if White Bear really loved her, could he not have broken that rule—even if he had smoked the calumet with Star Arrow—at least once? For six summers White Bear had been as silent, as absent, as if he were dead.

Even the dead sometimes send a sign.

The next day the sky was cloudy, and the air warmer than last night. All morning long women walked past Redbird's wickiup, looking curiously at the man who sat there motionless. Like Redbird herself, they had never before seen a man while his spirit had gone to walk the bridge of stars. When men went on spirit journeys they always retired to the forest or to caves.

In the afternoon He Who Sits in Grease, a Fox brave, came to Redbird as she and Sun Woman sat before their doorway plaiting baskets, a short distance from White Bear. The brave was carrying a stout bustard with feathers striped brown, black and white. He hunkered down facing her and laid the bird before her.

His thick lips worked nervously. "This is for White Bear," he said. "When he wakes up. It is the fattest of the three that I killed this morning. Tell him that He Who Sits in Grease gives him this gift. I want him to ask Earthmaker to make the animals come to me more willingly when I hunt them."

Before Redbird could protest, the brave stood up and backed away, his eyes timidly averted from the figure outside the doorway.

He thinks White Bear is holy! The thought made her more angry at White Bear than ever. She wanted to kick him again, but women were watching from a distance, and she knew they would make fun of her.

"Get *up*," she said softly to White Bear. "Go *away*," she said, grinding her teeth.

She wished Owl Carver would come back from visiting the other camps to put a stop to White Bear's torturing her like this.

But he might force me to accept White Bear as my man.

Amazingly, she felt a lift in her heart at this thought. She herself could never forgive White Bear, but if Owl Carver, her father and the shaman of the British Band, ordered her to, the decision would be made for her.

Then, at least, this torment would end.

Sun Woman silently picked up the bustard, sat down and began plucking the feathers, piling them in a basket to use for adornments and bedding.

To escape from being rubbed raw by White Bear's presence, Redbird went out into the woods along the Ioway River, as Sun Woman had done yesterday, to gather herbs. The medicine plants were at their most powerful now, because they had been gaining strength all summer long.

Late in the day the sky darkened rapidly. The purple-gray clouds seemed to hang so low that she could reach up and touch them. She heard the first drops pattering on the branches above her. As the rain started to fall faster, it drummed on her head and shoulders. Sighing at having to give up this comforting work, she put a lid on her basket, stood up and started back for the camp.

Her doeskin shirt and skirt kept the rain off her body, but her hair was soaked and her face was streaming by the time she got back to the wickiup. She would build up the fire and dry herself off. Its heat would feel so good. She hoped Eagle Feather and Sun Woman were already inside.

She stopped before the silent, sitting figure outside the wickiup. The brown blanket was pulled up over his head. Sun Woman must have done that. The blanket was sodden with rain, and he looked like a rock growing out of the ground.

The beating of rain filled her ears.

She squatted down and looked into his face. Water ran in rivulets down from the blanket into his half-closed eyes. He did not even blink.

She shivered. The cold rain was coming down so hard she could not see most of the camp. A lump blocked her throat.

"Come inside," she said. She had to raise her voice to hear it over the drumming of the rain.

White Bear neither spoke nor moved.

"Come in. It is raining. It is cold. You will die out here." She realized she was screaming at him.

"Oh!" she cried helplessly.

She sat on the ground, looking into the rain-slick, light-complexioned face with the strong nose and the long jaw that she had loved long ago, the face she had thought about so many times and had seen so often in dreams. A black crust of blood had dried over the place where her rock had gashed his cheek. On the same cheek a raised white line ran from just under his eye to the corner of his mouth.

To try to wake a man on a spirit journey could be dangerous for him.

But her hands seemed to have a will of their own. She had to touch him. She reached out, clutching his shoulders through the sopping blanket, heedless of the rain pouring down her own face, running under the collar of her doeskin shirt down her back and chest. She shook him.

"Get up! Come in out of the rain!"

His body felt lifeless when she shook him. But did she see a flicker in his eyes?

"Please, White Bear, please!"

He blinked.

She threw her arms around him.

"Oh, White Bear! I do want you back."

She crawled closer to him, pushing her body against his rigid form.

She felt pressure against her back, pulling her closer to him. His hand.

Then his other hand.

She felt his chest rising and falling against hers.

Strong arms were holding her.

She looked up into his face, and color had come into the pale cheeks. The brown eyes were looking down at her, warm with love. She forgot the rain and the cold, and nestled in his arms.

She saw tears spill out of his eyes, mingling with the rain on his face. She, too, was crying. She had been crying ever since she sat down with him. She held him tight.

Looking past him, she saw in the doorway of the wickiup the small form of Eagle Feather, staring at them.

12

The War Whoop

Owl Carver held the watch up by its chain; his smile of approval showed he'd lost a tooth in front since White Bear left with Star Arrow.

"A handsome gift. I thank you for it. But what do you mean by saying it tells us the time? Do we not *know* the time?"

White Bear scoured his brain for a way to explain.

Sitting close to the old shaman, White Bear saw that age had bent him a bit more and carved deeper lines in his brown face. Besides the megis-shell necklace White Bear remembered, Owl Carver wore a new necklace made of tiny beads forming a red, yellow, blue and white floral design, from which hung a sunburst pendant.

They sat facing each other in front of the shaman's wickiup in the center of the British Band's winter camp. In the fenced-off corral dozens of horses stamped their hooves and blew steamy breath into the gray sky. The hunters had returned with braces of pheasant and geese, with deer slung from poles, with buffalo and elk carcasses mounted on travois dragging behind their horses. White Bear felt his nostrils expand to take in the smells of meats being roasted and stewed. In a few days all the chiefs of the Sauk and Fox, along with representatives of the Winnebago, Potawatomi and Kickapoo, would be gathering here at Black Hawk's invitation.

Even sooner, though, a ceremony would take place that meant much more to White Bear. Tomorrow night he and Redbird would at last be married. And he had come to Redbird's father today to give him the only present he had to offer.

White Bear pointed to the dial of the watch. "Father of my bride, if you want to know when the sun will rise tomorrow, you look at where these two arrows are at sunrise today. When they are in the same place again, it will be half the time till the next sunrise. When they are in the same place after that, it will be sunrise the next day." He faltered. To himself, his explanation sounded at once useless and ridiculously complicated. ". . . Almost. In truth, the sun does not rise at the same time every day," he finished weakly.

Owl Carver stared at him as if he had uttered nonsense. "The sun rises at sunrise."

He remembered how Frank Hopkins always reset his clock at sunset. "Yes, but in summer the days are long and in winter the days are short. But the arrows on this watch cannot keep pace with the sun."

Owl Carver shook his head. "Many things the pale eyes make are useful, but I do not understand the use of this thing."

What a struggle!

White Bear had a sudden inspiration. "It is true, this watch cannot tell you as much as the sun does, but it can tell you one thing."

"What is that?" Owl Carver frowned, weighing the watch in his hand.

"It can tell you when a pale eyes will do something."

Owl Carver grunted. "Well, it is pretty to look at. And it moves and makes sounds."

White Bear snapped open the back of the case, where the key was kept, and showed Owl Carver how to wind the watch, impressing on him the need to handle it very gently. Then the shaman went into his wickiup to put the watch in his medicine bundle.

White Bear sighed. He missed talking with Elysée, missed the library at Victoire, from which he'd managed to take only one book.

Well, this world of sky and trees and rivers and animals is a library too. Owl Carver knows how to read in it, and he has taught me.

The old shaman came out with a long-stemmed pipe. He filled and lit it with a twig from the fire in his wickiup and smoked thoughtfully for a while before speaking. White Bear, sensing that Owl Carver had something important to say to him, waited quietly.

"We need to know more about the pale eyes than we can learn from that time-teller," Owl Carver said. "We need to know what they will do if we cross the Great River to Saukenuk next spring."

White Bear felt his heartbeat quicken.

"Is that what Black Hawk plans?"

"If he can get enough Sauk and Fox warriors and their families to follow him. At the council all the chiefs will hear Black Hawk. The Winnebago Prophet, Flying Cloud, is coming to the council from his town up the Rock River. He will add his voice to Black Hawk's. But the chiefs will also hear the snake's voice of He Who Moves Alertly." He spat contemptuously.

White Bear knew well why Owl Carver despised He Who Moves Alertly. During what the pale eyes called the War of 1812, while Black Hawk and his warriors were away fighting on the British side, the civil chiefs had appointed He Who Moves Alertly a war chief in case the Americans should attack the Sauk towns on the Great River. Not only had the new war chief never fought, he spoke much of the need to make peace with the Americans. He had about as many followers among the Sauk and Fox as Black Hawk did, people who believed that the tribes would fare best if they did whatever the pale eyes demanded. After the war He Who Moves Alertly was quick to make himself known to the Americans as a friend. In turn the long knives' chiefs showered him with gifts and honors, even taking him and his wives to Washington City to visit the Great Father, James Monroe. He had, in fact, been in the East when Star Arrow had come to Saukenuk to take White Bear to Victoire.

"Why does He Who Moves Alertly say we should not go back to Saukenuk?" White Bear asked cautiously. He did not want to anger Owl Carver by saying so, but he himself was sure that crossing the Great River could only lead to calamity.

Owl Carver said, "He Who Moves Alertly has always been a friend to the long knives, and they treat him as if he was a great chief and give presents to him. Last summer, when we went to plant corn at Saukenuk, he went among Black Hawk's followers and persuaded many of them to flee back across the river." The old shaman smiled at White Bear. "But now we have you, who have also been East and know the ways of the pale eyes. You will be able to answer him."

But all I can say is that he speaks the truth.

The words trembled on his lips: *The long knives are more powerful than you can imagine. We cannot stand against them.*

And yet he did not want to speak. He feared that Owl Carver would think him a traitor, as he did He Who Moves Alertly. And, in a way, he felt as Owl Carver and Black Hawk did. He became angry every time he thought about how the tribe had been driven from its homeland.

Owl Carver puffed on his pipe. "You will answer He Who Moves Alertly not just as one who has been among the pale eyes. The day after tomorrow, you must go to the cave of the ancestors and seek another vision."

White Bear's heart sank. "But I am to marry Redbird tomorrow night. Would you have me leave her the next day to seek a vision?"

Owl Carver spread his hands. "The council starts in three days." He grinned, showing the space where the tooth had been. "And it is not as if you and Redbird have never known the joy of the marriage bed."

White Bear felt his face grow hot, and he lowered his eyes. Since his return they had tried to crowd into a few nights all the pleasures they had missed over the last six years.

"You will not be gone from her for long," Owl Carver said.

"But why do you not prophesy?" White Bear asked. "You have been the shaman since long before I was born."

Owl Carver nodded sadly. "I have tried. It seems the spirits have nothing to say to me."

Maybe because you do not want to hear what they say.

As he thought about seeking a vision, White Bear began to feel more hopeful. He might not have to displease Owl Carver and Black Hawk by speaking of the strength of the long knives and sounding like He Who Moves Alertly. Instead, the Turtle, in that sacred cave looking over the river, would tell him what he should say. It was sure to be wiser counsel than anything he could think of himself.

He remembered his boyhood dream of being a prophet for the Sauk. Now he would be able to tell them where their future lay.

But then he remembered words Owl Carver himself had once spoken to him. They had stayed in his memory because they had made him so uneasy.

Many times the people do not want to listen to the shaman. The truer his words, the less they hear him.

The next night White Bear and Redbird sat facing each other on opposite sides of the wedding fire before Owl Carver's wickiup. White Bear's fringed shirt and trousers of soft doeskin, worked until it was nearly white, were a gift from a brave whose wife Sun Woman had helped with a difficult childbirth.

Redbird's dress was of white doeskin as well. Around her neck hung the necklace of the small, striped megis shells that had belonged to Sun Woman.

White Bear looked beyond the fire. Hundreds of men and women were standing in the shadows watching the ceremony, those of Redbird's Eagle Clan on her side of the fire, the Thunder Clan, kin of Sun Woman and himself, on this side. The daughter of the shaman was marrying the son of a pale eyes father and a medicine woman, and White Bear had returned from a long journey among the pale eyes and was a shaman himself. It was a wedding that people wanted to see.

Wind Bends Grass, standing behind Redbird, spoke of her daughter's character. Even though she had spent all of her life scolding her, tonight she extolled her to the skies. She was beautiful, loving, skilled, obedient. Then Wind Bends Grass instructed Redbird in her wifely duties, making one small change from the usual speech. Instead of telling her to give White Bear sons, she told her to give White Bear *more* sons.

Strangely, at this moment, White Bear found himself thinking of Nancy Hale. Was she still longing for him somewhere across the Great River?

If Raoul had not driven him out of Victoire, his promise to Pierre might have kept him there. He might never have come back here, not found out till much later that he had a son, never have been united with Redbird as he was tonight. Truly this was coming home. He felt so at peace, he could almost be grateful to Raoul.

White Bear was especially honored to have as his wedding sponsor the Thunder Clan's most prominent member—Black Hawk himself.

Black Hawk addressed Redbird and her relatives in his harsh, sombre voice. "I have known this young man since he was born. His father, Star Arrow, was a pale eyes, but he was a French pale eyes, and the French were always the best friends of the Sauk and Fox, even better than the British. White Bear has been trained in the way of the shaman, and he has lived among the pale eyes and learned their secrets as well."

What have I learned that my people can really use? White Bear wondered ruefully. *All I can tell them is that they cannot win a war with the long knives.*

"You must cherish Redbird and protect her," Black Hawk said

to White Bear. "You must give her the benefit of your wisdom. Because you yourself are a shaman, your responsibility to her is all the greater."

Then Owl Carver stood before the fire, between the bride and the groom, and raised his arms. "O Earthmaker, bless this man and this woman. May they walk with honor on the path they follow as one."

Redbird sang a wedding song to White Bear. Her voice rose clear and pure into the night air, and it seemed to White Bear that even the crackling fire quieted itself to listen.

> "I will build a lodge for you,
> I will grind the corn for you.
> I have no home but where you are;
> The trail you walk is also mine."

Then White Bear got up and went around the fire to Redbird. He handed Redbird a bouquet of pink roses that Sun Woman had carefully collected, dried and preserved. The orange glow of the fire danced in her black eyes, and White Bear felt an answering love blaze up within himself.

He was so much taller than Redbird that he had to bend his knees deeply so that Redbird could throw her braids over his shoulders, and he heard some chuckles and giggles from the watching people. But as her braids fell lightly on him he thought that he had never in his life been happier than at this moment.

Together they walked sunwise around the marriage fire, keeping it on their right: and on the east, south, west and north sides White Bear said loudly, "Redbird is now my wife!"

Eyes gleamed at him out of the darkness when he came back to the east side. Standing to the side and just a little behind Black Hawk was Wolf Paw. White Bear could not resist feeling a little thrill of triumph at the realization that he had won Redbird despite the best efforts of this mighty warrior, this chief's son, this man who owned many horses.

Not because I deserve it, he reminded himself. *Only because Redbird would have it so.*

And now, because she would have it so, we will be together forever.

Owl Carver bade them depart with the good wishes of the tribe,

and White Bear and Redbird walked to the new wickiup they had
built on the edge of the camp. Eagle Feather would live there with
them, but tonight Eagle Feather would stay with his grandmother,
Sun Woman.

Tonight they would have it to themselves.

Next day, in mid-afternoon, White Bear stood again in the center
of the camp wearing the same black bearskin he had worn six years
ago. Owl Carver did a shuffling sunwise dance around him, shaking
a gourd rattle and chanting:

> "Go forth and dance with the spirits,
> Become a spirit yourself.
> Bring back a gift for the people,
> Bring back the words of the spirits."

Black Hawk, standing in the circle that had gathered to watch,
stared at him with an intensity that frightened him. Sun Woman
and Redbird stood with smiles of quiet pride. This time Redbird
need not fear that he would freeze to death on his spirit journey.

It would be painful to be away from Redbird, he thought, as he
looked into her eyes, saying a silent good-bye. Now, after a brief
feast of love, they must go hungry again. But only for a night or two.

White Bear turned his back on the declining sun. The ceremonial
bearskin swung heavily on his head and shoulders as he trotted out
of the camp toward the trail that ran along the river's edge. As he
entered the woods, another pair of eyes, hostile, suspicious, caught
his. Wolf Paw again, standing with folded arms.

Wolf Paw still loves Redbird. And hates me.

He felt much stronger than he had when he arrived at the camp.
Alternately walking and running, he moved quickly and surely down
the Ioway River, and he remembered the way to the bluff of the
sacred cave. Several times along the way he met Sauk and Fox warriors. They recognized the sacred bearskin, with the bear's skull
covering his own as a partial mask, and stepped aside with eyes
averted as he passed them.

The sun had sunk behind him by the time he had come to the
end of the almost-imperceptible trail to the top of the bluff. He

stood there a moment, looking out across the clear blue sheet of water that was the Great River. He stared at the Illinois shore, the rich, flat bottomland at the river's edge, the wooded bluffs, much like the one he was standing on, forming a wall, beyond which rolled the autumn-tan, endless prairie.

A beautiful and fertile land, from which his people—and he himself—had been exiled. Would his vision show them a way back?

He scrambled down the face of the bluff to the cave and swung into the entrance.

In the shadows he could barely make out Owl Carver's wooden owl standing over the row of skulls with their stone necklaces; or the white bear statue guarding the unknown depths of the cave.

He settled himself facing the entrance and chewed some scraps of sacred mushroom Owl Carver had given him. Nothing to do now but sit and wait. Surely no watch made by pale eyes could measure the passage of this kind of time.

He heard a scraping and a grumbling from deep in the cave. He felt no fear now, only a warmth, as at the approach of an old friend. The White Bear, he now understood, was himself in a spirit form.

The huge snuffling Bear was at his side, and confidently he rose to step out of the cave, the Bear accompanying him with its rolling walk. He stepped on clouds, violet and gold and white and soft as snow under his feet.

The pathway through the sky turned northward. Through breaks in the clouds he looked down and caught glimpses of the river, a glistening blue snake. Ahead he could see clouds piling up on clouds, shot through with pale, blended rainbow colors, like the ornaments carved from shells gathered along the eastern sea.

Then he was inside the cloud tower, peering beyond the Tree of Life at the Turtle on his crystal perch. Drop by drop from the Turtle's heart flowed the waters of the Great River.

"What would you ask me, White Bear?" said the ancient voice like distant thunder.

"Is my father with you?"

"Your father walks the Trail of Souls far in the West," said the Turtle. "He will come back to earth soon, and he will be a great teacher of the people."

"Owl Carver and Black Hawk have sent me to ask, should the British Band go back to Saukenuk?"

The wrinkled voice said, "Behold."

The clouds changed to the walls of a room big enough to hold a Sauk camp, where curtained windows alternated with mirrors in gilded frames. Under each mirror was a fireplace. Three glittering chandeliers hung from the high ceiling. In the center of a vast flower-patterned carpet stood Black Hawk.

To White Bear's astonishment, Black Hawk was wearing the blue uniform of a long knife, with ropes of gold on his arms and fringes of gold on his sleeves and shoulders. But he carried no weapons. His face as usual was gloomy.

There were other men in the room, but White Bear could only clearly see one. A pale eyes.

He was exceedingly tall and thin; his hair was white, and his bright blue eyes stared piercingly at Black Hawk. He wore a black cutaway jacket and tight black trousers with shiny black leather shoes; and a white stock, a strip of silk, wound around his throat.

White Bear had seen this man before and recognized him at once.

He was known to red men as Sharp Knife—Andrew Jackson, President of the United States.

The man Raoul had called "a good old Indian killer."

Black Hawk was talking, and Sharp Knife was listening. But White Bear could not hear what Black Hawk was saying.

The room seemed to change. Black Hawk and Sharp Knife disappeared, and where Sharp Knife had been standing there was now another tall, thin man. He also wore black, but he had a black ribbon at his neck. A black beard covered his chin, and the expression on his sun-browned face was one of inconsolable grief. His sadness reminded White Bear of Black Hawk's.

All at once White Bear was on a broad field covered with short grass, divided by stone walls and wooden fences, with clumps of trees growing here and there. Terror clutched his belly as he saw coming at him thousands of long knives in blue uniforms with rifles and bayonets. He looked about frantically for a place to hide, but there was none. He was caught in the open.

But before the men could reach him they began to die.

Blood spurted from their blue tunics. They stopped running, staggered and fell to the ground, dropping their rifles. Faces vanished in bursts of red vapor. Arms and legs and heads flew through the air. Flashes of flame and smoke and flying shards of iron tore bodies to bits.

But no matter how many of them died, more and more of the white men in their blue jackets and trousers came marching over the horizon holding their bayonets before them. There was no end to them.

White Bear felt as if his heart might stop. He put his hands over his eyes.

And when he looked again he was back in the cloudy hall of the Turtle.

"What have you shown me?" he asked.

"I have shown you the future of both the red people and the white people on this island between two oceans," the Turtle rumbled. "It is given to you to know two futures because two streams of blood flow in you. You belong to both, and to neither."

It was painful to hear this. The Turtle was uttering thoughts that had occurred to White Bear many times; he had always tried to put them out of his mind. Could he not forget his years among the pale eyes and become entirely a Sauk?

Wisps of cloud drifted around the Turtle's scaly body. White Bear heard the drip-drip of water from the Turtle's heart into the blue-black, fish-crowded pool that fed the Great River. The sound was like the ringing of a hammer on an anvil, reverberating through the vast space in which they stood.

The Turtle spoke again. "Earthmaker has willed that the pale eyes shall fill this world of ours from the eastern sea to the western sea."

"Why?" cried White Bear in anguish.

"Earthmaker bestows evil as well as good on his children. Sickness and hunger and death come from Earthmaker, just as strong bodies, and good things to eat, and love."

"Will all Earthmaker's red children die?"

"Great numbers will die, and those who remain will be driven to unkind lands."

"What of the Sauk?" White Bear asked, trembling.

"The many who follow Black Hawk across the Great River will be few when they cross back."

Oh, no!

This was what he had come here to learn, but hearing it was like being cast down from this lodge in the clouds to crash to the earth.

"Then the British Band should not go back to Saukenuk?"

"You cannot stop them. For you as for all of my people, this is to be a time of testing and pain. I charge you to see that those who hurt my children do not gain from it. You will be the guardian of the land that has been placed in your keeping."

"But I have already lost that land," White Bear cried.

As if he had not heard White Bear, the Turtle said, "Know that long after all who live now have walked the Trail of Souls, my children will be many again, and let the knowing lift up your heart." The Turtle touched his own claws to the deep crevice in his under-shell from which the water perpetually dripped.

White Bear knew it was time to go.

When he awoke in his body he would grieve. He saw nothing but heavy, unending sorrow ahead for him and for those he loved.

Black Hawk slowly stood up. A mantle of buffalo fur draped over his shoulders and a crown of red and black feathers woven into his scalplock made him look even bigger and taller than he was.

White Bear sat close to the fire for its heat. The day was cold and overcast, and the damp air around him and the chill ground under him made him shiver in the white doeskin shirt he had worn for his wedding. Because Owl Carver had asked him, on the band's behalf, to seek a vision, he could now consider himself fully a shaman. He had costumed himself accordingly—three red streaks painted across his forehead, three more on each cheekbone, silver disks hanging from his ears, a three-strand necklace of megis shells around his neck. Silver clasps on his arms and silver bracelets around his wrists. All these things had been supplied by Owl Carver or traded for by Sun Woman. If he had to speak he might at least hope his words would be greeted with respect.

Redbird pressed against him, and her nearness warmed him. Flames danced over the pile of blackened logs in the center of the British Band's winter camp. Light gray smoke rose from the fire, the same color as the blanket of cloud that hid the afternoon sun.

Fear twisted its knife in White Bear's stomach. He did not want to tell this assembly what he knew. Most of them would hate him. The chiefs and braves and warriors of the British Band, Black Hawk and all the rest, would never forgive him. Owl Carver would feel betrayed.

Let them settle this without me.

But he knew it was a forlorn hope. When Owl Carver had asked him what he learned in his vision, he had answered evasively. And now Owl Carver was counting on him.

Around the fire sat the council of seven chiefs who governed the Sauk and Fox tribes, including Jumping Fish, Broth and Little Stabbing Chief. Beside them sat He Who Moves Alertly, the friend of the long knives, the war chief who had never made war. Prominent braves like Wolf Paw sat with them. The older and the younger shamans of the British Band sat there, Owl Carver and White Bear.

And there was another shaman at the fire as well, Flying Cloud, better known as the Winnebago Prophet. He was a broad man with a wolfskin thrown over his shoulders. Unlike nearly all the men of the tribes that lived along the Great River, he had a thick black mustache that drooped over the corners of his mouth. A silver nose ring rested on the mustache. He was head man of a Winnebago village called Prophet's Town, a day's journey up the Rock River from Saukenuk.

In the quiet that greeted Black Hawk, White Bear heard, over the crackle of the fire, the rattle of the war chief's bone bracelets as he held out his hand.

"I only want to go back to the land that belongs to me and dwell there and raise corn there. I will not be cheated. I will not be driven out."

Black Hawk did not have a pleasing speaking voice; it was hoarse and grating. But the assembly listened intently, because for over twenty summers there had been no greater warrior among the Sauk and Fox.

"With this hand I have killed seventy and three of the long knives. Every Sauk and Fox brave, every Winnebago and Potawatomi and Kickapoo, can do as much. Yes, we know the long knives outnumber us. But we can show them that if they want to steal Saukenuk from us, they will have to trade too many of their young men's lives for it.

"Last summer the long knives surrounded us and drove us out of Saukenuk. But that was because we were not ready to fight, and some of us were not *willing* to fight."

Black Hawk looked pointedly at He Who Moves Alertly, who sat expressionless, as if unaware of Black Hawk's disapproving gaze. His face was round and ruddy, like the full moon when it first appears above the horizon. He wore his glossy black hair long under an impressive buffalo headdress with gleaming horns, and had wrapped himself in a buffalo-hide robe painted with sunbursts.

Black Hawk said, "Next summer, it will be different. I have had messages from the Winnebago and the Potawatomi promising to help us if the long knives attack us. The Chippewa, up in the north, say they want to help us."

A burning log split in two with a noise like a gunshot, and the halves fell deeper into the fire with a shower of sparks.

Looking over the heads of those seated near him, White Bear saw columns of smoke from a dozen or more other campfires rising into the late afternoon sky. Around those campfires, feasting and gossiping, sat most of the people of the British Band and their guests from other Sauk and Fox bands, as well as some Winnebago, Potawatomi and Kickapoo braves. What was being decided here now would mean life or death to all who chose to follow these leaders.

Black Hawk said, "The pale eyes say we sold our land. I say that land cannot be sold. Earthmaker gives land to those who need it to live on, to grow food on, to hunt on, as he gives us air and water.

"The land has been good to us. It has given us game and fish, fruit and berries. It has let us grow our squash, beans, pumpkins and corn on it, and bury our mothers and fathers in it. The pale eyes are destroying the land, cutting down the trees, fencing off the prairie and plowing it up. The land is the mother of us all. When a man's mother is dishonored, he must fight. Earthmaker will give us this victory, because he is our father and he loves us."

With a chill that did not come from the air, White Bear remembered the words of the Turtle: *Earthmaker bestows evil as well as good on his children.*

White Bear prayed his own prayer to Earthmaker: that he not be asked to speak to this gathering.

Black Hawk lifted his rasping voice in a shout. "I, Black Hawk, raise the war whoop!"

He threw out his chest, lifted his head, and let loose an ululating cry that seemed to pierce the very clouds that hung over the camp. Wolf Paw, Iron Knife, Little Crow, Three Horses and a dozen other Sauk and Fox braves leaped up, waving rifles, tomahawks, bows and arrows, scalping knives, screaming their battle cries. Owl Carver beat furiously on a drum painted with a picture of the Hawk spirit.

The Winnebago Prophet lunged to his feet and joined the outcry, his gestures so wild and his shouts so loud that he almost seemed to be competing with Black Hawk.

Redbird spoke softly, close by White Bear's ear. "They are drunk on war."

The outcry died down. Black Hawk crossed his arms over his chest to show that he had finished speaking. The Winnebago Prophet remained standing and raised his arms.

"I have come to promise Black Hawk and his braves that if he goes to Saukenuk and the long knives attack him, the warriors of Prophet's Town will help them to fight back."

The chiefs and braves seated around the fire greeted this with much stamping and clapping. White Bear glanced at He Who Moves Alertly, who sat a quarter of the way around the circle from him. The face under the buffalo headdress was as still as if carved from wood.

Flying Cloud said, "I have sent messages to all the tribes that live near the Great River—Winnebago, Potawatomi, Kickapoo, Piankeshaw, Chippewa. When Black Hawk raises the tomahawk, they will raise the tomahawk too. And I have had a message from our allies of old, the British in Canada, who say the Americans have done us a great wrong, and we should not give up any more land to them. If American long knives attack us, the British long knives will come to our aid. With ships, with big guns, with rifles, powder and shot and food for us, with hundreds of red-coat soldiers. Now is the best of times to tell the long knives they cannot push us any further. Let all who are truly men take to the trail of war with Black Hawk!"

White Bear sensed deadly falsehood in the words of the Winnebago Prophet. When White Bear was in New York City he had heard many times that the enmity between Americans and British was a thing of the past. White Bear did not believe that the British up there in Canada had any intention of getting into a war between whites and Indians in Illinois. But how could he prove that what Flying Cloud said was untrue?

With a cry of "Ei! Ei!" Wolf Paw shook his rifle over his head. He snapped it to his shoulder and fired it with a deafening boom and a red flash and a big cloud of white smoke.

Someday he may wish he had not wasted that powder.

As White Bear and Redbird sat silently, braves all around them were up and shrieking, waving rifles and tomahawks, thrusting out arms and legs in the movements of a war dance. Owl Carver and some of the chiefs slapped the palms of their hands against the taut, painted deerskin of their drumheads.

A few other men did not join the shouts of approval, among them the round-faced He Who Moves Alertly.

White Bear sat with his fists clenched in his lap, wondering whether anyone would notice that the youngest of the three shamans among them was not shouting for war. He felt Redbird's hand grip his arm tightly, helping him to feel stronger.

Only to Redbird had White Bear told all of his vision. She shared his fear that if the British Band followed Black Hawk to war they would be destroyed, and she had insisted on sitting with him at the council fire. White Bear knew it was not the custom for a wife to sit with her husband at a council, but she had argued and pleaded until he had given in and brought her with him.

Her presence beside him both comforted him and made him uneasy. Owl Carver, when he came to the fire, had stared at his daughter, frowned and looked away. Wolf Paw had eyed them and smiled scornfully.

As the tumult inspired by the Winnebago Prophet quieted down, He Who Moves Alertly looked around the circle of chiefs and braves, his eyes pausing at anyone who had not joined the outcry for war. His gaze met White Bear's for an instant, and he nodded almost imperceptibly. White Bear had an eerie feeling that He Who Moves Alertly knew what was in his mind.

The chief who favored the long knives stood up.

A sullen muttering spread through the men around the council fire. Most of those who agreed with He Who Moves Alertly had stayed away from this council. White Bear felt admiration for anyone who could look so confident, standing before a crowd in which so many were against him.

"War is loud, and peace is quiet," He Who Moves Alertly began. "But peace keeps us alive. The real way to defeat the long knives is to stay alive."

His voice was deep and pleasant, and he smiled as if every man there were his friend.

"When is it right for a brave to go to war? When he must avenge himself on those who have done wrong to him. Black Hawk says

we should fight the pale eyes because they have stolen land from us.
But I have seen the papers with the marks of our chiefs on them.
Seven different times Sauk and Fox chiefs have made their marks on
papers agreeing to give up all claim to the land east of the Great
River. The long knives say our chiefs were paid in gold for the
land."

As his benign gaze swept the assembly, he said, "It is right for a
brave to go to war when he is strong enough to make war. He does
not go because he wants to be killed, because he wants to leave his
women and children unprotected. He knows he may die, but he
does not look for death."

He Who Moves Alertly was no longer smiling. He touched his
fingertips to his eyes, then raised his arms to the sky. "May Earthmaker strike me blind if I do not speak the truth.

"We are not strong enough to make war on the long knives. I
have traveled in the lands of the Americans, all the way to the eastern sea. I have seen so many long knives that I could not count them
all."

White Bear felt more and more uneasy as he listened. Black
Hawk and all the other braves of the British Band looked on He
Who Moves Alertly as an enemy. But White Bear knew that the
chief in the buffalo headdress was speaking the truth. Perhaps not
about the treaties, but surely about the vast numbers of long knives.

White Bear saw again the thousands of blue-uniformed soldiers
he had seen marching in New York on the Fourth of July a year
ago, and the other thousands he had seen in his vision, fighting and
dying but still advancing on some strange battlefield.

He Who Moves Alertly said, "Owl Carver and Black Hawk say
the Potawatomi and Winnebago will aid the British Band, and other
tribes from farther away. I say none of them will help. This quarrel
over Saukenuk is not their quarrel, and they have made their own
peace with the long knives.

"The Winnebago Prophet says the British will send us guns and
ammunition, even men. I say this is foolish talk. You call yourselves
the British Band, and think the British are your great friends. Many
summers ago, yes, the British were at war with the Americans and
got Sauk and Fox and many other tribes to help them. But when
that war was over, our people gained nothing and lost much. Many
tribes had to give up land to pay for fighting on the British side.

Now the British do not care about us. The British pale eyes and the American pale eyes are at peace.

"I say to those who will listen to me—come with me. I will lead you deep into this Ioway country, where there will be no pale eyes farmers to bother us. Their Great Father will show his gratitude to those who do not fight them. He will give us money and food and help us find good land. We will live!

"For those who follow Black Hawk, I grieve. They will not live."

He Who Moves Alertly's closing words rang. He crossed his hands over his chest and sat down amidst a silence touched by the crackling of the fire.

White Bear heard in his mind the rumbling voice: *The many who follow Black Hawk across the Great River will be few when they cross back.* He trembled inwardly.

The clouds overhead had broken up, and the rays of the sun, about to set, fell upon many faces full of anger and contempt. But White Bear also saw lips pursed in thought, eyes lowered.

White Bear could find little wrong with what He Who Moves Alertly said, but he did not like the way it pointed. To admit that the long knives could do whatever they wanted to the Sauk, to hope like little children that if they obeyed the Great Father in Washington City he would be kind to the Sauk and give gifts of food, clothing and shelter—was that not merely a slower kind of death?

He Who Moves Alertly did not seem to see that if the Sauk let the whites push them westward, there would be no end to it. Eventually the pale eyes would take all the land there was.

To drive a people from their home is to make them prey to hunger, disease, enemy tribes. It is to destroy them, even if not a single shot is fired.

If we must die, would it not be better to avenge ourselves on the pale eyes for their cruelty to us? Is it not better to die with pride than to just give up our good hunting and farming lands and go meekly into the desert?

He felt Redbird press against him. He had a sudden, strong feeling that they should follow He Who Moves Alertly farther into the Ioway country. That way they would surely live. How could he, White Bear, demand or permit that his wife and son endure the sufferings and the danger those who followed Black Hawk would face?

But at the thought of deserting the British Band he felt an unbearable anguish. One winter long ago he had found a trap that had been sprung. In the trap was the rear paw and part of the leg of a raccoon, ending in a bloody mass. The animal had chewed its own leg off to escape. He had seen a trail of blood leading into the woods. The raccoon had limped off to die, but to die free.

What He Who Moves Alertly offered was a trap. What Black Hawk offered was freedom, but with it the prospect of death.

He and Redbird could pack their belongings and leave after this council was over. White Bear was sure other families would be doing that.

But could he turn his back on Black Hawk, who had just spoken for him at his marriage, on Owl Carver, the father of his wife? On Sun Woman, who he was sure would stay with the British Band? On the people who had been part of his life as far back as he could remember?

Staying meant facing the long knives' guns. It meant starvation. It meant pain. Those who whooped for Black Hawk tonight did not see that. Or maybe they did see it but still embraced it. To see it clearly and accept it, not only for himself but for Redbird and Eagle Feather, hurt like biting off one of his own limbs. But he would not abandon his people. He had run away from his last fight over land. He would not run away from this one.

Owl Carver, holding up his owl-headed medicine stick with its red feathers, stood before the council fire. "He Who Moves Alertly thinks he is the only one who knows the Americans. But one of our own British Band has been to the big towns in the East. And he is a shaman to whom the Turtle has given special visions. I ask White Bear to tell us what he has seen."

At the sound of his name, White Bear felt a coldness spread upward from the base of his spine. He saw the look of earnest invitation on Owl Carver's face, he saw Black Hawk's expectancy. He would as soon spit at these two men he respected so much as disappoint them deeply. But now he must.

Redbird's fingers dug into his arm. Her slanting eyes were wide. "Speak truly," she whispered.

Slowly he stood up. It hurt to pull his arm from Redbird's grip, as if he was stripping his own skin from his arm. His eyes momentarily met those of He Who Moves Alertly, who stared at him intently.

As Owl Carver had, he raised the medicine stick he had cut for himself after his first vision, decorated with a single string of red and white beads. He held it up uncertainly. He hoped his shaman's adornments, the paint, the earrings, necklaces and bracelets, would impress them.

He was prepared in another way, as well. He had never spoken before the leaders of his band; but at St. George's School each boy was required to give a short speech to the members of his class once a week and a longer one before the whole school twice a year. Those speeches had to be written and memorized, and now White Bear must speak as the spirit moved him. But he knew how to stand, how to project his voice, how to measure his words. In his heart he thanked Mr. Winans for teaching him all that.

"The big American towns in the East are bigger than the biggest towns ever built by any red men," he began. "In those villages the pale eyes swarm like bees in a honey tree.

"Every summer the Americans have a great feast to celebrate the day they told the Great Father of the British that they would no longer be his children. One summer in a big town called New York I saw long knives walk in long lines to honor this big day. Each man had a new rifle. Eight at a time walked side by side, and it would take half a day to go from one end of their line to the other. Then came more long knives on horseback, as many as a herd of buffalo. And after them horses pulled big thunder guns on wheels that shoot iron balls the size of a man's head.

"The long knives were led by their Great Father, Sharp Knife, who was visiting New York. He is very thin, with a cruel face and white hair. He sits straight on his horse and wears a long knife at his belt.

"After all those long knives had walked through the town they came to an open field, where they fired off all their thunder guns. The noise made the earth tremble."

Allowing his legs and hands to shake also, as they demanded to do, White Bear paused and let his gaze travel over the faces in the big circle around the fire.

The red glow of the setting sun fell on the faintly smiling He Who Moves Alertly. Black Hawk's back was to the sun, his face in shadow. Redbird looked up at White Bear, eyes bright and full of love. Others might hate what he said, but he was glad that Redbird heard how well and truly he spoke.

Angry words hissed and sputtered like the burning logs. White Bear saw Wolf Paw poke Little Crow, one of the leading braves, who was seated beside him, and speak to him with muted voice but urgent gestures. The brave got up and left the fire.

Owl Carver, seated beside Black Hawk, lifted his head. White Bear saw bewilderment on his teacher's face, and shrank within himself at the sight.

Owl Carver said, "White Bear is both pale eyes and Sauk. So far he speaks to us only with the pale eyes half of his head. Let White Bear tell us what vision the Turtle has given him."

White Bear felt a small surge of hope. What he had seen as a traveler among the pale eyes might not discourage the British Band from making war, but his vision might move them more.

"The Turtle showed me Black Hawk talking to Sharp Knife," he said, pointing to the war chief, who lifted his feather-crowned head at the sound of his name. "They were in the house of the Great Father of the Americans in the village called Washington City."

He heard amazed murmurings all around him. Encouraged, he went on.

"Then I saw great numbers of long knives running toward me over a field. They were shooting and being shot at. I saw many of them hit, and they fell and died, but they kept coming on. I saw a tall, thin man with a beard, a sad man whom I have never seen before, mourning over the fallen long knives."

The sun had gone down. Now he could see the dark listening faces only by the yellow glow of the fire.

Owl Carver said, "White Bear's vision brings us hope. He sees our own Black Hawk meeting with Sharp Knife in Sharp Knife's house. Black Hawk will go to Sharp Knife's very house to lay down peace terms to the Americans."

That is not what it means! White Bear thought, shocked.

Owl Carver went on. "White Bear saw long knives dying. White Bear's vision foretells victory for the British Band."

From all around the campfire he heard grunts of approval at Owl Carver's words. White Bear's heart felt lost and sinking, like a stone thrown into the Great River.

"Listen!" he cried. "Owl Carver is my father in spirit, but he did not see this vision or feel its sadness. I did. I stood there before the Turtle, and I know that what he showed me was a warning. If the

British Band takes to the path of war, Black Hawk will be Sharp Knife's prisoner."

Shouts of protest erupted around him. He saw Little Crow come back to the fire with a bundle of bright red and blue cloth in his hands.

White Bear spoke on over the outcry. "Listen! When I saw the long knives dying, more and more of them came forward, and their numbers were endless. They were not fighting our warriors. They were fighting other long knives. The vision said that there would be many, many long knives in summers and winters to come, so many that they would fight each other."

Owl Carver said in a voice just loud enough for White Bear to hear, "Say no more. You do great harm."

"I must say more. You have asked me to speak. Now I must tell what I know. You must listen. The Turtle also spoke to me. He said, 'The many who follow Black Hawk across the Great River will be few when they cross back.' "

After a moment's hesitation Owl Carver lifted his hands. "They will be few because we will win back our land on the other side and stay there."

Before White Bear could answer, Black Hawk stood up, his face in the firelight a mask of wrath. White Bear trembled.

"Black Hawk will never be Sharp Knife's prisoner!" the war chief roared. "Black Hawk will die first."

Someone else was standing up before the fire. A woman.

Redbird.

White Bear felt himself trapped in a nightmare. Had his wife gone mad? She could not speak to a council of chiefs and braves. His heart beating furiously, he reached out to silence her. But she was already speaking.

"You are fools if you do not listen to White Bear," she cried. "He is gifted with the power of prophecy." She turned to Owl Carver. "My father, you know that the whole tribe crosses the river from east to west every year for the winter hunt. If the Turtle says few will cross back over the Great River, he means the rest of us will be dead."

Her words were greeted not with anger but with shouts of scornful laughter. White Bear knew that the chiefs and braves did not care what she said; they were merely amused that a woman dared try to speak to them at all. He burned with shame for himself and Redbird.

Beyond the circle of firelight he saw the shadows of men and women standing in the twilight. Word of the dispute at the council fire must be spreading through the camp and drawing more people to hear, perhaps to speak their own minds, as was their right. He glimpsed Sun Woman hurrying toward him, picking her way through the seated men.

Wolf Paw strode toward White Bear, holding in his hands the bundle of red and blue cloth Little Crow had brought him. He glared at Redbird.

"It is bad medicine for women to speak to the council."

Redbird stepped in front of White Bear to face Wolf Paw. "A medicine woman tells you: the words of White Bear are *good* medicine."

"How can White Bear tell the British Band what to do when he cannot make his wife behave as a woman should?" Wolf Paw said. "Sit down, Redbird." And he pushed her aside.

Rage shot White Bear forward like an arrow from a bow, arms outstretched to grapple with Wolf Paw. He lifted his medicine stick as if to strike at the red-crested brave.

Hands gripped his arms. He struggled, blind with fury, flailing his arms and kicking. Wolf Paw, his teeth bared, wrenched the medicine stick from White Bear's hand.

"Do not harm the medicine stick!" shouted Owl Carver.

Without looking at the old shaman, Wolf Paw handed him White Bear's medicine stick. Two big warriors held White Bear as Wolf Paw approached him, stretching his lips in a grin.

"A woman speaks for peace with the pale eyes," Wolf Paw said, "because peace is women's way. I once saw Redbird going to White Bear when he was on his vision quest. Maybe he gets his visions from her."

More and more men were on their feet, and they roared with laughter at Wolf Paw's gibe.

Sun Woman had made her way into the inner ring around the fire and now held Redbird.

"Come away, daughter," she said in a strong but soothing voice. "This does not help White Bear."

"Look!" shouted Wolf Paw. "Now he has both his wife and his mother at the council fire."

He shook out the red and blue cloth. It was a woman's dress.

"He speaks like a woman," Wolf Paw said. "He says what women tell him to say. Women speak for him. Let him dress like a woman. A pale eyes woman."

Wolf Paw flung the dress over White Bear's head, and the two men who held him pulled it down around him. White Bear felt wrapped in hopelessness as the cloth covered his head.

And he had wanted to be a prophet for the Sauk.

The truer his words, the less they hear him.

He struggled halfheartedly. He no longer cared what they did to him. His own failure and the sure destruction of his people chained him so that he could barely move. The warriors pulled the dress straight down over his arms, pinioning them to his sides. As his head emerged through the collar, laughter battered at him. Teeth gleamed in the firelight.

He saw Sun Woman holding Redbird. Tears squeezed through his wife's tightly shut eyelids. The face of his mother was heavy with woe.

Too despairing to resist, he let Wolf Paw and his men push and drag him away from the council fire and run him through the camp. He was blind to the laughing faces around him, deaf to the mocking cries.

But he saw one sight that all but killed him—looking up at him from somewhere in the crowd, the hurt, bewildered eyes of his son, Eagle Feather.

13

The Volunteers

Nicole and Frank had walked halfway across the main room of the trading post blockhouse when Nicole heard Raoul's voice thundering from the stone-walled counting office in the far corner.

"You and the boys will stay at Victoire!"

Nicole touched Frank's arm, and they stopped and drew back a little, standing beside the long black barrel of the six-pounder naval cannon Raoul had set up in the blockhouse. It would be best not to intrude on Raoul when he was in the midst of a quarrel.

"But none of them French people there like me," a woman answered, high, nasal, with a Missouri twang. "It's downright lonesome." Nicole recognized Clarissa Greenglove's voice.

"I'm going to be gone and your father's coming with me. Where the hell else would you stay?"

"With my Aunt Melinda in St. Louis. That'd be a perfect place. You could send me down on the *Victory*."

"Of course I could." Raoul's voice was creamy with sarcasm. "And then do you know what would happen? Half those men who are out in the courtyard now volunteering for my militia company would quit. Because if I send you and Phil and Andy away, it means *their* families aren't safe. And so they'd insist on staying home to protect them."

His voice rose to a shout. "Do you understand now, goddamn it? Then get the hell out of here."

A moment later Clarissa scurried out past the iron-reinforced

223

door of Raoul's counting room. The two small boys she'd borne to Raoul ran beside her floor-length calico skirt. She'd gotten to be round-shouldered, Nicole saw.

Clarissa nodded. "Mister, Miz Hopkins."

"Morning, Clarissa," said Nicole. To call her by her first name felt not quite respectful, but to call her "Miss Greenglove," especially with her two sons right there with her, seemed cruel.

Clarissa gave Nicole a woebegone look that seemed to be asking for something—Nicole wasn't quite sure what. Then she ducked her head, and her bonnet hid her eyes.

Phil, the five-year-old, looked up at Nicole. He had very light blond hair, almost silver, and large eyes that seemed set deep in his pale, thin face. A little ghost.

"My dad's gonna fight Injuns."

"That's fine." Nicole didn't know what else to say. Clarissa, who had taken a few steps ahead, reached back and jerked Phil's arm so hard that he hollered.

Raoul, when they entered his office, seemed unperturbed by his argument with Clarissa. But his eyes widened and flashed with momentary anger when he saw Nicole. Then he grinned, teeth white under his black mustache.

"Well, Nicole and Frank. Come to lay your hatchets to rest? Now that the Indians are waving theirs around?"

"That's why we're here, Raoul," said Frank.

"Yeah, I've read your paragraphs in the *Visitor*," said Raoul, one side of his mouth twisted up in a contemptuous smile. "Seems you'd just love to give Illinois back to the Indians."

"Nothing of the kind," Frank said gruffly.

How unfair, Nicole thought. Frank had written only that if the 1804 land agreement had been obtained through fraud, it would be better to negotiate a new treaty with the Sauk and Fox rather than meet them with armed force.

Raoul's tanned face reddened and his nostrils flared. "Give back Illinois," he persisted, "just like you wanted to give Victoire to Pierre's mongrel bastard."

Nicole saw not a trace of guilt on that broad, hard face over what he had done to Auguste. She clenched her fists. She must try to contain her anger.

Frank spoke. "Don't bring up Auguste now, Raoul. He's what

divides us, and we oughtn't to be divided now. We want to talk to you about protecting Victor."

Heat lightning flickered in Raoul's eyes, shifting quickly to a derisive gleam. "Well, that should be easy, Frank, with your attitude. You can make a white flag out of any bedsheet."

Nicole thought, *He's just using our coming here as an opportunity to rub our faces in the dirt.*

"Don't make this so hard for us, Raoul," she said. "We need each other."

"Really? What do I need you for?" His eyes were cold.

Many answers crowded Nicole's mind, but she thought for a moment before speaking.

"You need the people of this town to make a success of the estate, now you've taken it over, your orchards and farms, your shipping line, your trading ventures. Most of the people who live in Victor work for you, directly or indirectly. And you're leaving them unprotected."

Before Raoul could answer, Frank joined in. "From what I've seen, you plan to march every man who knows how to shoot a rifle away from here to fight the Indians down by the Rock River. If you take all the fighting men away, who's going to defend Victor and Victoire?"

Raoul threw back his head and roared with laughter. "God, I can't believe I'm hearing you right. Ever since last fall you've wished I would disappear from the face of the earth. Now you come to me begging for protection."

"It's not for ourselves that we're asking," said Nicole. "We just want you to leave enough men behind to defend the women and children and noncombatants who stay here."

Raoul's eyes narrowed and fixed on Frank. "Noncombatants like you, Frank? You won't pick up a rifle yourself, but you want some of my men to stay and guard you."

Frank looked back steadily. "I'm learning to shoot. Your father is teaching me." Nicole felt a rush of love for Frank, and pride in his willingness to learn to do something he hated, because he had to.

Raoul spread his hands. "Good for you, and good for Papa." He looked down, and his face reddened slightly. When he looked up, his dark eyes met Nicole's.

"How is Papa?"

Nicole checked the urge to remind him that he had nearly killed their father, and said, "He's tolerably well. The little house Frank has been building for him is finished. And he's able to walk. Guichard takes care of him."

Raoul clapped his hands together. "Good, good! Then that's two riflemen you've got right there. And I'll bet old Guichard could even shoot if it came to that. And you'll have David Cooper, he's a veteran of 'Twelve. He's going to keep an eye on the trading post for me, along with Burke Russell. I'm sure there'll be a few others. As for the rest of the men, if I didn't lead them down to the Rock River, they'd go anyway. They're raring to hunt redskins."

Nicole recalled the line of men she had seen just now in the trading post courtyard signing up for the Smith County volunteer militia. There must have been over a hundred of them, some wearing coonskin caps and fringed buckskins, others with straw hats, calico shirts and tow-linen pantaloons, two dozen or so sporting the head kerchiefs favored by men of French descent. They'd been in high spirits, laughing and talking about bringing back scalps.

Frank said, "Of course you don't *want* to think there'll be an Indian attack on Victor while you're gone. What you want is to go down to the Rock River country with the militia and win a great victory over the Indians. Or something you can call a great victory."

Raoul held out his hands. "Frank, you printed Reynolds's proclamation in your damned paper."

He pointed over his shoulder, where a copy of the Illinois governor's call to arms, cut from the *Victor Visitor* for April 17, 1832, was nailed to the wall. Nicole's eyes traveled over the opening lines.

FELLOW CITIZENS

Your country requires your services. The Indians have assumed a hostile attitude and have invaded the State in violation of the treaty of last summer.

The British Band of Sauks and other hostile Indians, headed by Black Hawk, are in possession of the Rock River country, to the great terror of the frontier inhabitants. I consider the settlers on the frontiers to be in imminent danger . . .

Raoul said, "He doesn't say stay home and defend your town. He says rendezvous at Beardstown. That is a lot closer to Black Hawk than it is to Victor."

Frank said, "That proclamation is for towns that are in safe territory. We're the settlers *on* the frontier, the ones Reynolds says are in danger. I was talking yesterday to a man from Galena, Raoul. Up there, the volunteers have formed a militia company, but they're going to stay right where they are, in case of Indian attack. We aren't *expected* to supply troops to chase Black Hawk."

Raoul shook his head. "We've got to hit Black Hawk hard and fast with all the men we can muster. Once we do, there'll be no danger to Victor."

Frank said, "If something like what happened at Fort Dearborn happens here at Victor, innocent people will pay for your decision. You want that on your conscience?"

At the mention of Fort Dearborn, Raoul's face had gone expressionless. He sat there and stared at Frank for a moment, then stood up abruptly.

"My conscience is clear," he said.

You have no conscience, Nicole thought. She stared sadly into the bright blue eyes that looked so blankly at her now, and wondered where her smiling little brother had gone, so many years ago. The smile still came readily to his face; but now it only mocked and taunted. Did those years of captivity with the Indians fully explain Raoul, or was he a throwback to some robber-baron ancestor whose only law was the sword?

"When a man goes off to war, Miss Nancy, it means the world to him to know he has someone to come home to."

Raoul smiled down from his chestnut stallion, Banner, at Nancy Hale in the driver's seat of her black buggy. At nineteen, she was a woman in full bloom. She'd probably have married a long time ago if she'd stayed back East. There were a lot of men out here on the frontier, but few good enough to court a woman like her.

She'd be a fool not to take my offer seriously. It's the best one she'll ever get.

Nancy looked first at the dusty road over the grass-covered hills between Victoire and Victor, the morning sun beating down on it, then up at him. The deep blue of her eyes was a marvel.

"You already have someone to come home to, Mr. de Marion. And children."

Children, yes, but the mingling of his de Marion blood with the nondescript Greenglove line could hardly produce the children he wanted. Nancy, on the other hand, from an old New England family that probably went back to even better English stock, was just the sort of woman he wanted to breed with.

"Clarissa and I have never stood up before a priest or a minister, Miss Hale. I've just been passing my time with her until the right lady came along."

Her gaze was cool and level. "As far as I'm concerned you're as good as married, and you have no right to be talking to me this way."

"Necessity makes your bedfellows out here on the frontier."

"Not mine." She shook her head, blond braids swinging. He could picture all that honey-gold hair spread out on a pillow, and he felt a pulse beat in his throat.

Nancy went on, "You must know how wrong it is for you to speak to me this way. Otherwise you wouldn't have ambushed me out here."

"I've waited days for a chance to speak to you in private."

Josiah Hode, Hodge Hode's boy, had ridden fast to the trading post this morning to tell Raoul that Miss Hale was driving her buggy into town and was traveling, for once, without her father. It was the news Raoul had been hoping for ever since the governor's proclamation had arrived in Victor. Knowing Miss Nancy was indignant over his treatment of the mongrel, Raoul had delayed approaching her. Now he could delay no longer.

"I leave with the militia next Monday," he said. "That gives you three days to think it over. I hope to carry your favorable answer with me when I ride off to defend you from the savages."

She smiled, but the smile was without humor or warmth. "Carry this answer with you if you wish: No." She flicked the reins, and her dappled gray horse speeded up to a trot.

Raoul spurred his own horse to keep pace with her. "Take time to consider."

"The answer will always be no."

White-hot anger exploded within him. His fists clenched on Banner's reins.

"You'll end up an old maid schoolmarm!" he shouted. "You'll never know what it is to have a man between your legs."

Her face went white. He had hurt her, and that made him feel better.

He kicked his heels hard into Banner's sides and the stallion uttered an angry whicker and broke into a gallop, leaving Nancy Hale and her buggy enveloped in dust.

He wished the country around here weren't so damned open. If he could have dragged her out of that buggy and into the woods, given her a taste of the real thing, she'd have changed her mind about him.

Is she still pining for the mongrel?

Well, he thought, as the gray log walls of the trading post came into sight around a bend in the ridge road, he *would* carry her answer to the war. And the Indians would suffer the more for it.

Prophet's Town was deserted. Black Hawk and his allies had fled.

Raoul reined up Banner in the very center of the rings of dark, silent Indian houses. Armand Perrault, Levi Pope, Hodge Hode and Otto Wegner stopped beside him. He did not know whether he was relieved or disappointed. His cap-and-ball pistol drawn, the hammer pulled back, he drew angry breaths and glared about him. He felt exposed, realizing that at any time an arrow aimed at his heart could come winging out of one of those long loaf-shaped bark and frame Winnebago lodges.

Because of Raoul's experience in the skirmishing around Saukenuk last year, General Henry Atkinson had commissioned him a colonel and put him in command of the advance guard, known as the spy battalion. He enjoyed the prestige of leading the spies, but he felt a constant tightness in his belly.

He reached down for the canteen in the Indian blanketwork bag strapped to his saddle, uncorked it and took a quick swallow of Old Kaintuck. It went down hot and spread warmth from his stomach through his whole body. He cooled his throat with water from a second canteen.

For three weeks now, slowed by heavy spring rains that swelled creeks to nearly impassable torrents, the militia had followed Black Hawk's trail up the Rock River. To the whites' disappointment, the Indians had bypassed Saukenuk, doubtless aware that the militia had come out against them. Instead, Black Hawk's band had trekked twenty-five miles upriver, reportedly stopping at Prophet's Town. Now, they were not here either.

Raoul hated the Indian village on sight. Built on land that sloped

gently down to the south bank of the Rock River, it surrounded
him, threatened him, lay dark, sullen and sinister under a gray sky
heavy with rain. It reminded him too vividly of the redskin villages
where he'd spent those two worst years of his life.

He saw no cooking fires, no drying meat or stacks of vegetables
by the dark doorways, no poles flaunting feathers, ribbons and enemy scalps. That characteristic odor of Indian towns, a mixture of
tobacco smoke and cooking hominy, hung in the air but was very
faint. He figured the Indians had left here days ago.

"Otto," Raoul said, "ride back to General Atkinson and report
the enemy has abandoned Prophet's Town."

Wegner gave Raoul a strenuous Prussian salute, pulled his spotted gray horse's head around and rode off.

The two hundred men of the spy battalion were trickling in
behind Raoul, hoofs pattering on the bare earth. In their coonskin
caps and dusty gray shirts and buckskin jackets, the men didn't
look like soldiers, but they had taken the oath and were under
military discipline till their term of enlistment was up at the end
of May.

The men called to one another and laughed as they gazed around
at the empty lodges. They were enjoying themselves immensely,
Raoul thought. This time of year most of them would be breaking
their backs doing spring plowing and planting. Now they could earn
twenty-one cents a day while going on something like an extended
hunting trip.

Most men would rather fight than work any day.

Eli Greenglove, on a brown and white pony, trotted up beside
Raoul. His silver lace captain's stripes glittered on the upper arms
of the blue tunic Raoul had bought for him. A long cavalry saber
hung from his white leather belt.

Eli grinned, and Raoul had to look away. It seemed that every
other tooth in Eli's head was missing, and the ones that were left
were stained brown from years of chewing tobacco.

And now Clarissa had taken up pipe smoking, making it even
harder for Raoul to enjoy bedding down with her.

If only Nancy—

But Nancy had made it plain that she despised him.

Damn shame. Of course, old Eli here would slit his throat if he
had any idea what Raoul was thinking.

Eli said, "You figger the Prophet's Town Injuns have joined up with Black Hawk's bunch?"

"Of course," said Raoul. "And that means Black Hawk now has about a thousand warriors behind him."

A movement on the south edge of the village in the surrounding woods caught Raoul's eyes. He swung around in that direction, pointing his pistol.

"Eli, get your rifle ready," he said.

"Loaded 'n' primed," said Greenglove, pulling his bright new Cramer percussion lock rifle—another present from Raoul—from its saddle sling, controlling his pony easily with his knees alone.

Indians walked out of the woods, four men. They held their empty hands high over their heads and shuffled forward slowly.

"Watch 'em," said Eli. "They may just be trying to get close enough to jump us."

Raoul studied the four advancing men. Two had their heads wrapped in turbans, one red, one blue. All four wore fringed buckskin leggings and gray flannel shirts. He saw no weapons.

Then he caught sight of more shadowy figures in the trees beyond the Indians. Instantly, he straighted his arm in that direction and pulled the trigger. His pistol went off with a boom, puffing out a cloud of gray smoke. He handed it to Armand to reload it while he reached for his own new rifle, a breech-loading Hall.

The Indian with the red turban was shouting something. Raoul recognized the language—Potawatomi. The sound of it made the blood pound in his temples.

"Those are only squaws and papooses," the Indian called in Potawatomi. "Please do not shoot them."

Raoul felt like shooting them all, just for being Potawatomi, but he held the impulse in check. He had to find out whatever they could tell him.

He addressed the Indians in their language, indelibly engraved in his mind by the acids of fear and hatred. "Tell them all to come out. We will kill anyone who hides from us."

The red-turbaned Indian called over his shoulder, and slowly a group of women and small children came out of the woods.

Raoul took his reloaded pistol back from Armand and walked Banner over to the little group. They started to lower their hands.

"Keep them up." He gestured with the pistol. Slowly the copper-skinned men straightened their raised arms again, looking at one another unhappily.

Probably thought we'd welcome them with kind words and gifts. The muscles in his neck and shoulders were so rigid they ached, and his stomach was boiling. In his mind he saw again the scarred face of Black Salmon, the brown fist raised, holding a horsewhip to beat him. The sounds of Potawatomi speech brought it all back.

He handed his horse's reins to Armand, who tied Banner to an upright post in front of a nearby lodge.

"Who are you?" Raoul demanded.

"I am Little Foot," said the Indian wearing the red turban. "I am head of the Deer Clan. We live here in the town of the Winnebago Prophet."

Little Foot's skin was dark, and he had a wide, flat nose. He wore no feathers on his head, probably not wanting to look warlike. Black hair streaked here and there with white hung down from under his turban in two braids to his shoulders. Raoul judged him to be in his fifties.

He could have been at Fort Dearborn twenty years ago.

One thing was certain. Little Foot was Potawatomi. Raoul felt his fingers tightening on his pistol as he held it at waist level.

Raoul turned to Levi Pope and some of his other Smith County boys who were seated on horses nearby. "Tie them up."

Levi, who wore six pistols at his belt, all primed and loaded, got down from his horse and unhooked a coiled rope from his saddle. "The squaws and little ones too?"

"Put their families in one of the lodges and keep a guard on them." Another thought occurred to him. "Eli, take some men and search these huts. Make sure there aren't any more Indians hiding out somewhere in this town."

Levi went to the red-turbaned Indian and pulled his arms down roughly to his sides. In a moment he had Little Foot's hands securely tied behind his back, while other grinning Smith County boys had done the same to the other three Indian men.

"Ankles too," said Raoul, and Levi and his men cut lengths of rope and knelt to hobble the Indians.

With his free hand Raoul took another long drink from the whiskey canteen hanging from his saddle.

He walked close to Little Foot and looked him in the eye. He did not like the way the Indian looked back at him. He saw no fear.

With a sudden movement he hooked his boot behind the Indian's hobbled ankles and pushed him hard. Little Foot fell heavily to the ground on his back, wincing with the unexpected pain.

As he pushed himself awkwardly into a sitting position, there was no mistaking the hatred in the way he looked up at Raoul.

"Why did you stay here?" Raoul asked.

"We do not think Black Hawk can win. We hope the long knives will treat kindly those who do not make war on them."

Raoul said, "Where has Black Hawk gone? What is he planning? Where are the people who were living in this town?"

"I promised the Winnebago Prophet I would say nothing about where they went. I will be accursed if I break my promise."

"The Winnebago Prophet's curse is nothing. You should be more afraid of me."

Little Foot remained stone-faced and silent.

What a pleasure to have a bunch of Potawatomi right where he could do anything he wanted to them.

A light rain started to patter down on the bark roofs and the hard-packed earth.

While Raoul had been talking with the Indians, more militiamen had reached Prophet's Town. Columns of men on horseback, four abreast, came to a halt in the grassland to the south of the village and fell out at their officers' commands. They climbed off their horses and walked them.

Otto Wegner rode up and dismounted.

"General Atkinson is going to encamp the rest of the army outside Prophet's Town, sir," he said, giving Raoul his usual vigorous salute, nearly dislodging the big hunting knife sheathed in a pocket of his leather shirt.

Raoul returned the salute carelessly, went back to Banner and took another swallow from the whiskey canteen.

Surprising that Atkinson should decide to set up camp here, when the day was only half over. Well, Henry Atkinson had a reputation for going slowly. Raoul had heard from friends among the regular officers that Atkinson had already received a sharply worded letter from the Secretary of War in Washington City reprimanding him for not moving fast enough to crush the Indians.

If I get a chance to take a crack at them I sure as hell won't be slow.

The early arrivals already had their tents up. Officers' tents were of white canvas, six feet from the ground to their peaked tops. Enlisted men set up pup tents just large enough to cover two men lying down. Most men didn't bother to carry tents and slept out in the open, rolled up in the coarse blankets they all carried.

Men were wandering through Prophet's Town peering into the lodges. They walked with slow caution, rifles ready.

Raoul watched Justus Bennett, in civilian life Smith County's land commissioner, ordering two privates in buckskins and coonskin caps to put up a tent for him. Bennett was always trying to make himself as comfortable as possible. His packhorse carried his tenting, a big bag full of fancy clothes, and a couple of heavy law books. Why on earth a man would think he needed such things in the wilderness, Raoul had no idea.

"Bennett!" Raoul called. "Take charge of the guard on those Indians."

Bennett looked annoyed, but gave some final instructions to the men putting up his tent and slouched over to the four Indians. A round-shouldered man of slight build, he looked decidedly unmilitary, but he'd explained to Raoul that for anyone who wanted to get ahead in politics, a war record would be a godsend.

Raoul called out, "Levi, you leave off guarding the Indians and get my tent up."

A crowd of men had gathered in a circle around the Indians. Maybe they wanted to give the redskins a few licks of their own.

"Afternoon, Colonel."

Raoul was used to looking down at other men, but he had to look up, a little, at the man who addressed him. His skinniness was like Pierre's in a way, but this man was a heap uglier than Raoul's brother had been. He looked like a half-starved nag.

I'll bet he trips all over himself when he walks, and when he rides he drags his feet on the ground.

Raoul gestured to the seated Potawatomi. "You boys ever see Indians up close before?"

"The way you've got them trussed up and guarded, Colonel," said the tall man, "I'd say they must be pretty desperate characters."

Raoul heard the smile in the drawling voice and felt heat rising up the back of his neck. He took a closer look at the man. He couldn't be much over twenty, but he looked a well-worn twenty.

A farmer's face, darkened by the sun. The gray eyes, set in deep hollows under heavy black brows, crinkled humorously. But Raoul saw cold judgment deeper in those eyes.

Like most of the volunteers, the tall man wore civilian clothes. His were gray trousers tucked into farmer's boots and a gray jacket over a blue calico shirt printed with white flowers. An officer's saber hung from a belt around his waist.

Raoul said, "Well, I reckon you signed up with the militia to fight Indians, so take a good look at your enemy."

The tall man walked around to stand in front of Little Foot, hunkered down and said, "Howdy."

Little Foot did not look back but gazed ahead with a blank face.

The lean man straightened up. "A mighty mean customer, sir."

Some of the other men in the ring around the Indians chuckled at this. Even Justus Bennett snickered.

Raoul was feeling angrier and angrier. He had looked forward to questioning Little Foot and the other Potawatomi, looked forward to having them resist and to breaking their resistance down with fear and pain. He'd even hoped they might give him reason to shoot them. These strange militiamen were becoming a nuisance.

"You seem to think this is pretty funny. Who the hell are you?" Raoul put a threat into his voice.

"I'm Captain Lincoln of the Sangamon County company, sir. We're with the Second Battalion."

Raoul let his gaze travel over the other Sangamon County men. "Any of the rest of you able to talk?"

One man laughed. "When Abe's around we mostly let him do the talking."

"That so? If you let somebody else do your talking for you, he may talk you into a spot you won't like."

Abe said, "Oh, I always make sure I say what the men want said, sir." That brought another laugh.

Raoul's anger at the Potawatomi found a new target in this bony volunteer. The heat of the whiskey raced through his bloodstream.

There was one simple way to show this upstart who was master here, and at the same time have his way with the redskins.

Raoul drew his pistol and hefted it in his hand.

The tall captain eyed Raoul warily and said nothing.

Raoul said, "I'm going to give this Potawatomi one more chance

to tell me now where Black Hawk went, and if he disobeys me again
I'm going to shoot him dead."

He stood before Little Foot and pointed the pistol at his head.

In Potawatomi he said, "Tell me what Black Hawk plans to do.
Is he lying in ambush farther up the trail? Does he have a secret
camp for his squaws and papooses? Tell me, or I will shoot you."
Swinging the muzzle of the pistol to the man in the blue turban
beside Little Foot, he said, "And then I will ask this man, and if he
does not tell me, I will kill him too."

The bony young man said, "With all due respect to your rank
and experience, sir, I must say that what you propose to do is
wrong."

Raoul's rage threatened to boil over. Tension jerked his right
arm. So as not to risk wasting a shot, he took his finger off the
trigger.

In a mild but somehow penetrating voice the Sangamon man
said, "I'll tell you why this is wrong, sir, if you'll allow me."

The man's politeness was infuriating. Raoul turned to him, letting the pistol fall to his side.

"Go on, Captain. Preach to me."

"If you had a white prisoner at your mercy, you would not shoot
him because he refused to betray his comrades. You would think it
honorable in him to answer your questions with silence. But this
red man is a human being with the same God-given right to his life
that you and I have."

Raoul realized all at once that the lean captain's backwoods
manner of speaking had fallen away like an unneeded cloak. He
sounded like a lawyer or a minister.

"I was a prisoner of the Potawatomi for two years. I can tell you
from experience they're not human at all."

How angry Pierre had been when Raoul had said Indians were
animals. But it was true.

"They treated you badly? Made a slave of you?"

"Damned right."

The young captain looked calmly at Raoul. "If to hold slaves
and treat them badly marks a man as less than human, then you
must so brand every wealthy white man in the Southern states."

A few of the men standing around laughed. "That Abe! Got an
answer for everything."

Again Raoul's hand tightened convulsively on the pistol grip. He'd wasted enough words on this walking skeleton from Sangamon County. He was quivering with rage.

There was one quick way to put an end to the arguing.

He swung around and stepped close to Little Foot, holding his pistol less than a foot from the red-turbaned head. With his left hand he pulled the hammer back to half-cock, then full. The double click sounded loud in a sudden, astonished silence.

And Little Foot's arms, unbound, shot up. Both his hands gripped the barrel of the pistol and yanked it to one side. About to pull the trigger, Raoul froze his finger as the muzzle was pulled aside from its target.

—And knew with a sudden sinking of his heart what a deadly mistake he had made in that instant.

The Potawatomi's powerful two-handed grip tore the pistol from his fingers.

I should have fired. Now I am a dead man.

Raoul saw a coil of rope lying on the ground beside Little Foot. The Indian must have been working his wrists loose while everyone's attention was on the argument.

Little Foot had already turned the loaded and cocked pistol around in his hands and pointed it at Raoul's heart. Raoul stared into black eyes that had no mercy for him.

A blurred figure seemed to fly across Raoul's vision.

The pistol went off with a boom.

Coughing, blinded, Raoul saw dimly through the gunsmoke that the skinny captain had thrown himself at Little Foot and thrust the pistol aside. Now Lincoln and Little Foot were wrestling, thrashing about like two wild animals.

By the time the smoke had cleared, the lean man had full control. Little Foot's ankles, Raoul saw, were still tied, and Lincoln's arms had snaked up under the Indian's. The Sangamon County man's big hands were behind Little Foot's head, pushing his chin down into his chest. His long legs were wrapped around Little Foot's middle, holding him in a crushing scissors grip.

Raoul stood shaking, his eyes watering from the faceful of powder smoke he'd taken. His heart was pounding frantically against his breastbone.

"Nicely done, sir!" Justus Bennett said to Lincoln.

And what the hell were you doing? Raoul thought, furious at Bennett.

With a trembling hand Raoul seized Bennett's pistol.

The four guards had their rifles pointed at Little Foot. Any one of them could have saved Raoul's life by shooting, but none of them had reacted quickly enough.

Only Lincoln had moved in time.

The lanky captain's comrades were cheering him. "Old Abe's the best wrassler in this army, Colonel, and now you've seen it for yourself."

Raoul wiped his eyes and shouted, "Stand aside, Lincoln. Now I'm going to blow this redskin's brains out." The quaver he heard in his own voice made him even angrier.

From behind Little Foot came a calm response. "I'm going to ask you not to do that, sir."

"He tried to kill me. Get up and stand aside, God damn you!"

"No, sir."

Lincoln did unwrap his arms from Little Foot's head and shoulders, but still held him with his legs. The Indian sat motionless, as if his effort to kill Raoul had taken the last of his strength. He muttered under his breath. Probably his death song, Raoul thought.

Lincoln quickly retied the Indian, then stood up, placing himself between Raoul and Little Foot. He held Raoul's empty pistol out to him, butt first.

"Colonel, I believe you're a fair man, and you'll agree that I just saved your life."

Raoul took his pistol and handed it to Armand, realizing that the tall man was maneuvering him into a difficult position. Too many men had seen what happened.

"Yes, you did save my life." The words hurt his throat, same as if that pistol ball had hit him and lodged there. "And I thank you. You have my most profound gratitude."

"That being so, and since I have done you what you might think a favor, will you grant me a life for a life?"

For a moment Raoul could not think of anything to say or do.

All he had to do was shove this Lincoln aside, put the muzzle of his pistol to Little Foot's head and pull the trigger.

He realized, too, that the longer he hesitated the more a fool he looked.

What right did the skinny captain have to demand that he spare Little Foot?

Raoul became aware that the crowd around them had grown to perhaps a couple of hundred men. The ones he could see wore little half smiles. Whoever came out the winner, they were having a fine old time watching.

Raoul was broader and maybe stronger than Lincoln. But how ridiculous he would look if he had to fight the man to get past him to shoot Little Foot.

And what if this bag of bones beat him?

Old Abe's the best wrassler in this army, Colonel.

The truth was bitter as vinegar, but the only course that would preserve his dignity would be to let Lincoln have his way.

"Ah, hell," he said loudly, and was pleased to hear that while he'd stood silently thinking, his voice had regained its strength. "Sure, I'll let the Indian live. He's nothing to me."

He noticed that his hand still shook a little as he gave Bennett's pistol back to him. He took his own, reloaded, from Armand and holstered it, hoping no one could see his tremor.

"My hand on it," he said, holding out his right hand, willing it to be steady.

The grip that met his was crushing. Even though he'd seen the bony young man immobilize Little Foot, Raoul was surprised.

He felt the men would expect him to do more to show his gratitude.

"Come and have a drink with me, Abe."

"My pleasure, sir."

Armand had finished putting Raoul's tent up. In the tent Armand uncorked a jug and handed it to Raoul, who offered it to Lincoln. The young man hooked his finger in the ring at the neck of the jug and raised it to his mouth. Raoul watched the prominent Adam's apple rise and fall as he took a long swallow.

"I normally don't touch whiskey, sir," Lincoln said, handing the jug back to Raoul. "I've seen it ruin too many good men. But I do appreciate this. It's not every day I grab a pistol as it goes off, wrestle an Indian and disobey a colonel."

"Well, that's the best whiskey there is. Old Kaintuck—O.K."

"Three things Kentucky makes better than anyplace else," said Lincoln. "Quilts, rifles and whiskey. I should know. That's where I hail from."

It was because of men like this, Raoul thought with some disdain, that Illinoisians got their nickname, "Suckers." The weak shoots of the tobacco plant that had to be stripped off and thrown away were called suckers, and Illinois was said to be largely populated by ne'er-do-well emigrants from tobacco-growing states like Kentucky.

"Then here's to Kentucky," said Raoul, loathing the tall, ugly man for spoiling his revenge.

He lifted the jug to his lips and let the burning liquid roll over his tongue and slide down his throat, grateful to it for the warmth that would melt away the chill of death he still felt around his heart.

A few more swigs and Raoul found himself wanting to bring Lincoln around to his way of thinking. The man, after all, *had* saved his life.

"You know, you went to a whole lot of bother over that Indian now," he said. "It's a waste of time. We're only going to have to kill them all later anyway."

Lincoln winced, as if Raoul's words had hurt him. "Why do you say that, sir?"

"I've got a big estate in Smith County, beside the Mississippi, miles and miles of wonderful fertile land just begging for the plow. And too much of it is growing nothing but prairie flowers, because I can't get enough people to come and work it for me. They're afraid of Indians!"

"Treat the Indians fairly and there would be nothing to fear," said Lincoln.

"Treat them fairly and they'll just continue to attack our settlements."

"I'd like to think you're wrong, Mr. de Marion."

"Why the hell did you volunteer for the militia, if you don't like killing Indians?"

Lincoln smiled faintly. "Well, a war record won't hurt when I make a run for the legislature."

Just another slimy politician. Same as Bennett.

A bluebelly, a blue-uniformed officer of the Federal army, pushed through the tent flap. He doffed his tall, cylindrical shako.

"General Atkinson's compliments, Colonel de Marion. We're breaking camp and moving on up the Rock River in pursuit of Black Hawk and his band. And he asks you to once again take up the lead position."

"How does the general know where the Sauk are?" he asked irritably.

"A couple of Winnebago known to the general came into camp and offered to guide us, sir. They say Black Hawk and the Winnebago Prophet are leading their people upriver to try to persuade the Potawatomi to join them. Black Hawk's whole band, except for the warriors, are on foot. The general thinks that if we ride hard we can catch them."

Lincoln held out his hand and shook again with Raoul.

"Thank you for the whiskey, sir."

"Thank you for turning that pistol aside."

Lincoln grinned. "Colonel, thank *you* for sparing that red man. I'll be going now, or by the time we finish thanking each other, Black Hawk will be in Checagou."

When Raoul emerged from his tent he saw that the Potawatomi prisoners were gone. He felt a surge of fury that someone had turned them loose without his permission. He still longed to put a ball into the skull of that sneaking Little Foot.

The next Indian who falls into my hands won't be so lucky.

By the time the men of his spy battalion had struck their tents and mounted up, he had decided on half a loaf of revenge. Seated on Banner, he held up a burning stick.

"All right, men, the Winnebago who lived here have joined up with Black Hawk. They're running ahead of us. Let's not leave them anything to come back to."

He drew his arm back and snapped it forward. The torch flew end over end and landed on the bark roof of the nearest Winnebago lodge. A circle of orange flame spread out quickly. It was still raining, but not enough to slow the fire down much.

Raoul's men whooped. Eli and Armand led the way in hurling flaming sticks into the dark brown Indian huts.

Armand, grinning, handed Raoul a long pole he'd pulled loose from the wall of a lodge, afire at one end. Waving his broadbrimmed hat, Raoul rode through the town touching the burning pole to the flimsy wall of each lodge he passed. The men of the battalion scattered, setting fires everywhere. Beyond the town the remaining militiamen stopped breaking camp to watch.

Soon, the roar of the burning lodges thundered in Raoul's ears like a big waterfall.

If they could catch Black Hawk, he thought, what glory that would be. No matter how many fighting men Black Hawk had, Raoul felt sure his battalion could crush them. The burning lodges, the whiskey in his blood, the hatred in his heart, all ran together so that Raoul felt like a prairie fire racing after the British Band.

14

First Blood

White Bear tried to think only about guiding his brown-spotted white pony over the grasslands and watching his two companions. He tried to put fear out of his mind.

I did not even have a chance to say good-bye to Redbird.

Redbird was a day's ride up the Rock River from here, at the camp the Potawatomi had allowed Black Hawk's people to set up. White Bear's body went cold with the thought that he might be killed today, and she be left alone and pursued by enemies.

I should have asked Wolf Paw to be her protector if I die. He hates me, but he cares for Redbird.

It was for Redbird and Eagle Feather, and for the baby growing inside Redbird, that he was risking his life today. His family was going hungry. It had been over six weeks, by pale eyes reckoning, since Black Hawk had led them across the Great River into Illinois. White Bear and Redbird, like other British Band families, could carry little food with them, and most of that was gone. With the long knives pressing behind them, White Bear had no time to hunt or fish, nor Redbird to gather food from the woodlands.

She must not go without food, especially not while carrying their child. The children of the British Band walked about hollow-eyed; the crying of hungry babies rose from every part of the camp. Old people, looking nearly dead, lay on the ground trying to husband their strength.

At a secret meeting last night the Potawatomi chiefs, despite Flying Cloud's prophecy, had refused to join Black Hawk in fighting the long knives or even to give his people supplies or let them remain long in Potawatomi territory. Black Hawk himself had been forced to admit that the only way to spare the band further hardship would be to go quietly back across the Great River.

To do that, he had to make peace with the long knives. Frightened though he was, White Bear, as the only member of the tribe who spoke fluent English, felt he must go with Black Hawk's emissaries.

White Bear's shoulders slumped in discouragement as he thought how Black Hawk and the rest of the band had been led astray. *No* other tribes were willing to ally themselves with the British Band. There had been *no* truth at all to the Winnebago Prophet's talk of aid from the British in Canada.

A delegation headed by Broth, the tribe's best speaker, had gone to the British fort at Malden, near Detroit, to ask for help. They had been sent back with the advice that the Sauk had better learn to live in peace with the Americans.

The people of Prophet's Town had left their homes with Black Hawk's band more out of fear of the oncoming long knives than out of a desire to help Black Hawk fight for Saukenuk. As Black Hawk's prospects worsened, most of them drifted away, even though the Prophet himself remained at Black Hawk's side.

Black Hawk had believed the Prophet because his promises gave the British Band the courage to defy the long knives. To White Bear's disgust, even now, when it was clear that Flying Cloud had simply made it all up, Black Hawk had forgiven the Prophet.

White Bear burned with resentment.

They mocked me when I told them the truth. That fat, posturing toad lied to them and they still honor him. Surely a false shaman is the worst kind of liar.

White Bear rode on Little Crow's right. As the oldest of the three men, Little Crow carried the white flag. Torn from a sheet the braves had found in a settler's hastily abandoned cabin, the flag was tied to a spear shaft from which the head had been removed. On Little Crow's left rode Three Horses.

Since they were not riding into battle, they had not taken any of the saddles with stirrups from the band's supply but were mounted with only blankets between themselves and the horses' backs. The three of them had painted their faces black, because they might be going to their deaths. But it was hard to believe that men might be killed on this beautiful afternoon in the middle of the Moon of Buds. A warm breeze blew over White Bear's bare chest and arms. Red, blue and yellow prairie flowers scattered over the land, as uncountable as the stars, delighted his eye in spite of his fear. All around him he heard red-winged blackbirds singing their spring challenges.

White Bear had left with Owl Carver everything he valued: his medicine stick, his Sauk medicine bag and his other bag of pale eyes' medical instruments, his megis-shell necklace, his brass and silver ornaments, his *Paradise Lost*, the deerhorn-handled knife his father had long ago given him. He had nothing with him but the clothing he wore, fringed buckskin leggings and a buckskin vest decorated with blue and green quillwork in diamond patterns.

He looked back and saw five mounted braves an arrow flight behind him on the prairie. Even from this distance he could tell that the tall one in the middle was Iron Knife. They would watch from hiding and would report back to Black Hawk how the long knives treated his peace messengers. Black Hawk himself, with Owl Carver, the Winnebago Prophet, Wolf Paw and about forty braves, waited a few miles farther up the Rock River at the place where he had met with the Potawatomi chiefs.

White Bear saw a small stand of woods ahead. Scouts had reported that beyond those woods, across Old Man's Creek, the long knives had set up camp. Glowing from behind young green leaves, set aflutter by the breeze, the setting sun dropped flecks of gold onto the blackened faces of White Bear's two companions. It would be almost nightfall by the time they encountered the long knives.

Three Horses said, "A man must be more brave, I think, to do this than to ride up to an enemy in battle and strike the first blow at him." His nose curved inward where the bridge should have been. White Bear had learned that a Sioux war club had done that to him while Auguste was studying Latin and geometry at St. George's School.

"I would much rather be fighting the long knives than trying to make peace with them," said Little Crow. "I do not trust them."

White Bear tried to reassure them and himself. "We must do

this. It is the only way we can get our people safely back across the Great River."

Little Crow said, "It seems you were right and we who wanted to take up the tomahawk were wrong."

In spite of his fear, White Bear felt a satisfied glow at Little Crow's words. Little Crow had been the one who brought the woman's dress that Wolf Paw had put on him that wretched night of the council.

They did not listen to me that night. The Turtle told me I would not be able to persuade the people not to cross the Great River, but I tried my best.

They entered the wood by way of a narrow trail, riding single file. Little Crow lowered the white flag to keep it from getting caught in the branches.

As they rode among the trees, the tightness of fear in White Bear's chest and stomach grew worse, until he had to struggle for breath. His palms sweat so much, the reins were slippery in his hands.

He turned and waved farewell to Iron Knife and the four other braves following them, who had halted their ponies at the edge of the woods and dismounted. They waved back. A moment more and White Bear looked back and could see them no more.

At least if I die today Iron Knife can tell Redbird how it came about.

He tried to guess how the long knives would greet them. They might shoot them down in spite of the white flag. He hoped they would be glad to learn that Black Hawk wanted to surrender and return in peace to Ioway. After all, that was what they were trying to force him to do, was it not? But some of the long knives, undoubtedly, wanted to kill "Injuns." Men like Raoul.

When they came out of the south edge of the woods, they found themselves on a grassy rise sloping down to a winding stream called Old Man's Creek. The sun was lower now and directly in White Bear's eyes. Across the creek was a sight that made him want to jerk his pony's head around and ride back into the trees as fast as he could go.

On high ground he saw the silhouettes of peaked tents and many men, some on horseback and some on foot, rifles in hand. The smoke of campfires drifted like gray feathers into the pale blue sky.

He heard voices calling to one another in English. One man shouted and pointed in their direction.

White Bear said, "Don't wait here at the edge of the trees, or they will think we are attackers. Ride forward slowly, waving the flag."

The men across the creek were yelling excitedly now. Rifle fire crackled and smoke billowed. A ball whizzed past White Bear and cracked a tree limb behind him. He held himself rigid.

Long knives rode toward them, urging their horses down the far side of the creekbank. White Bear and his companions rode into the creek to meet them.

In a moment bearded white faces, angry eyes, coonskin caps and straw hats were whirling about the three emissaries in the middle of the creek. Rifles and pistols were pointing at them from every side. Little Crow, his face tight, held the white flag high with both hands.

"We surrender!" White Bear shouted. "We are not armed. We have come to talk to General Atkinson."

"Listen to that, he's talking English," a blond boy exclaimed.

Another man yelled, "Shoot 'em. Then let 'em surrender."

White Bear's knees trembled against his horse's flanks. These were not regular U.S. government soldiers, but the volunteers, the armed settlers who had come out in answer to their governor's call. They would not wait for orders from their commanders. They would do whatever they felt like doing.

A red-bearded man stuck his face in White Bear's. "Get down off that horse, Injun! Now!" His shout blew a stink of whiskey into White Bear's face.

Others joined the outcry. "Get off them horses!"

"Ought to put a bullet in them right here in the creek."

"Look at them black faces. I thought they was niggers at first."

"Not even useful like niggers, damn redskins."

The man with the red beard grabbed White Bear's arm and jerked him half out of his saddle. White Bear slid down from his horse.

He stood up to his knees in the cold, rushing water of Old Man's Creek.

"We want to surrender," he said again. "We want to talk to your officers."

"Just shut up!" the red-bearded man roared, eyes rolling drunkenly.

White Bear felt a man grab him from behind. A rope scratched his wrists and tightened around them till the bones were crushed together.

He turned to see whether Little Crow and Three Horses were all right. The militiamen had bound them too. Both braves' black-painted faces were expressionless, but White Bear read fear in their eyes and in the set of their mouths—the same fear he felt, and tried not to show.

The red-bearded man leaned down from his saddle and grabbed a handful of White Bear's long hair. He jerked on it, dragging White Bear toward the bank. White Bear stumbled on the stony creekbed, bruising his feet through his moccasins.

"You wanna see our officers? Then step along!"

What had happened to the white flag? Without it, what did they have to show that they had come in peace?

"Will you bring our white flag?" he called desperately to a clean-shaven man wearing spectacles, who looked a little calmer than the others.

The man's face twisted into a snarl, and White Bear's heart fell.

"You'll get your white flag up your ass, redskin!"

"You sound just like a white man," said another militiaman. "You sure you ain't a white man in paint?"

"Listen to me," White Bear said hopelessly. He wanted to say, *If we don't fight it will save your lives as well as ours.* But how could he talk to these men, maddened by whiskey and war? His eyes met those of Little Crow and Three Horses. Again the red-bearded man jerked his hair, so hard White Bear thought he would pull it out of his scalp. He had to bite his lip to keep from crying out. Worse than the pain was the indignity.

Horses splashing water, mud and pebbles on them, long knives shouting curses and threats, the three Sauk stumbled out of the creek and through shoulder-high prairie grass into the militia camp.

The sun's last rays fell on flushed, sweating white faces, on glistening rifle barrels. To White Bear, most of the men looked younger than he.

"Somebody get the colonel," said the man with the red beard. "Tell him they claim they want to surrender. Might be we could catch old Black Hawk himself."

The three Sauks' only hope, White Bear thought, was that the commanding officer might be more willing to listen to them than his men were.

The Sauk and their captors stood in a circle where the grass had been trampled flat. A short distance away stood supply wagons and tents. The prairie surrounded them.

Some militiamen went to one wagon on which five kegs with spouts stood, filled tin cups from the kegs and drank from them. Whiskey, White Bear thought, seemed to be as important to these men as food.

The sun was down now, and the three stood in twilight, in the midst of the shouting mob.

"Look alive, you men! It's the colonel!"

The crowd opened up, and two men came through.

One of them, short, skinny, wearing a coonskin cap and a blue officer's coat, came up to White Bear and peered at him.

"I know you!"

Half his teeth were rotten and the rest were missing. White Bear knew him too. Eli Greenglove.

"By God, Raoul! I'll be a son of a bitch if it ain't that half-breed nephew of yours."

And there stood Raoul de Marion, gold epaulets glittering on his broad shoulders.

At the sight of that broad face with the black mustache, last seen looking at him over a pistol barrel, White Bear knew his life was about to end.

Could my luck be any worse?

All hope vanished as light faded from the sky.

Raoul stood before White Bear with his thumbs hooked into the white leather belt that cinched his blue uniform coat. His huge knife—the one that had cut White Bear's face years ago—hung at his left side, a pistol at his right. He grinned at White Bear.

"Well. I was hoping to meet you. I'd have liked it better on the field of battle, but here you are, in my camp. What were you doing, spying on us?"

White Bear sighed. Something crumbled inside him.

"Do you know this long knife?" Little Crow said in Sauk.

"Yes, he is my father's brother." A glimmer of hope appeared in Little Crow's eyes, but vanished when White Bear added, "And he is my worst enemy."

"Talk English around me!" Raoul shouted. "No Indian jabber."

"Black Hawk sent us," White Bear said. "He doesn't want to fight. We've come to make peace."

"The hell with that!" one of Raoul's men yelled. "We come out to fight Injuns."

"Well, hold on now!" cried another. "If they come peaceable, that means we can all go home and nobody hurt."

Raoul turned on the man. "I'll be the one to decide why they're here."

White Bear realized that the men with Raoul were barely under his control. There was no hope of talking to Raoul, but there might be others in this crowd, like the man who had just spoken, who would listen. He must keep trying.

Raising his voice White Bear said, "Chief Black Hawk knows you militiamen outnumber his warriors. He doesn't want to fight you. All he wants is to be allowed to go back down the Rock River and cross the Mississippi. He will never come back."

"Where'd that black-faced redskin learn to speak English so good?" one of the militiamen said.

"He's a renegade," said Raoul. "A part-white mongrel. He ought to be hanged as a traitor. Don't believe a word he says."

"They did come with a white flag," one of the men said.

"White flag, hell!" Raoul shouted. "They're trying to put us off guard." He swept a pointing finger across a group of men that included brown-bearded Armand Perrault. Among them White Bear recognized Levi Pope and Otto Wegner, the thick-mustached Prussian who worked at the trading post. He remembered Wegner had not wanted to kill him when Raoul offered a reward for his death, and he felt a little tremor of hope.

"Get on your horses," Raoul told his men. "Go out across the creek and look. If you don't find Indians skulking about in those woods, I'll be mighty surprised."

As Raoul's men rode off, White Bear was torn by indecision. Should he tell Raoul that other braves had followed them here, to see how they were treated? Or would that just endanger the lives of Iron Knife and the others?

He'll use everything I tell him against me.

Raoul's eyes stared death at White Bear. "Black Hawk's a damn liar. He's broken every treaty we ever made with you people. There's only one way to deal with your kind. If you can't be trusted to keep treaties, you have to be exterminated." He drew his pistol.

"Starting here."

Bear spirit, walk with me on the Trail of Souls.

Little Crow said, "What do they say, White Bear? Are they going to kill us?"

"It is our fate to have fallen into the hands of a bad man," said White Bear. Having to tell them hurt him all the more. It grieved him that these two good men must die along with him, their lives thrown away because of a bit of bad luck.

"We were fools to come here," said Three Horses.

"Not fools—braves," White Bear reassured him. "A man who gives his life to protect his people is never a fool. Whether or not he succeeds."

"You *are* a prophet, White Bear," said Little Crow.

Raoul was staring at White Bear's chest. White Bear wondered if his heart was beating so hard that Raoul could see it hammering.

"Look at those scars. Looks like a bear tried to get you a long time ago. Too bad he didn't finish you, would have saved me the trouble."

White Bear would not talk about anything sacred with Raoul. He looked back at him silently.

"Guess you don't know all there is to know about your nephew." Eli Greenglove laughed.

"Don't call him my nephew!" Raoul shouted.

White Bear saw some of Raoul's men exchange befuddled glances.

"Well, whatever he is, I kind of think we ought to send him and these others back down the line. Let them palaver with the general. It ain't for us to decide."

"What the hell do you mean?" Raoul thundered.

The popping of rifle fire on the other side of Old Man's Creek cut short the argument. White Bear turned to look.

A moment later Perrault, his horse's legs dripping creek water, came pounding up.

"You were right, mon colonel," he panted. "Those woods are full of Indians. They were sneaking up on the camp."

"These three were supposed to distract us with peace talk while the others snuck up on us," Raoul shouted to his men. "First we'll shoot these Indians. Then we'll hunt down the rest of them."

"It wasn't an ambush!" White Bear cried. "There were only five of them, and they were just there to see what happened to us."

"Well, why didn't you tell us they were out there?" Raoul said, smiling. "We'd have invited them in for a whiskey."

The coonskin-capped men standing near him guffawed.

Raoul's lips stretched in a grimace. "Eli, Armand, let's shoot these three redskins."

Greenglove said, "Raoul—Colonel—I still say you ought to think this over."

"Shut up and do what I say!" Raoul growled. "I want to get this done and ride after those other Indians."

Men were running for their horses and leaping into the saddle brandishing rifles. Without leaders or orders, they rode off across the creek with drunken whoops in the direction Armand had pointed out.

White Bear felt sick as he saw that many of the men who remained were grinning avidly. How, he wondered, could their deaths give such pleasure to these men?

Desperate to find help, he searched the ring of men surrounding him for a face to appeal to. It was already too dark to see expressions clearly. Hopelessness turned his heart to lead as he saw Otto Wegner turn and walk away from the crowd. Even though Wegner had always been Raoul's man and never a friend of his, he felt betrayed.

"All right," said Raoul, staring into White Bear's eyes. "I'll shoot the mongrel. Eli, you shoot the short one with the flat nose. Armand, you take the other one."

" 'Vec plaisir," said Armand, his teeth showing white in his brown beard as he brought his rifle up to his shoulder.

White Bear felt the clench of nausea in his middle. Only pride kept him from doubling up and vomiting in his terror.

"Don't do this, please," he cried. "We came to you to make peace."

"They mean to kill us," said Little Crow. "Talk no more to them, White Bear. Do not plead. It is unbecoming a Sauk." White Bear felt a rush of admiration for the strength and calm in Little Crow's voice. Here, truly, was a brave.

Little Crow raised his voice in song.

"In your brown blanket, O Earthmaker,
Wrap your son and carry him away.
Fold him again in your body.
Let his bones turn to rocks,
Let his flesh turn to grass.
Give his eyes to the birds,
Give his ears to the deer.
Grow flowers from his heart."

White Bear and Three Horses joined in. There was nothing else to do. White Bear wanted to die singing, not weeping.

What a miserable death this was, even so! And still, he found that the song made his heart feel strong and his terror give way to a stern anger. Murdered because of the simple, stupid bad luck that Raoul's band of militiamen happened to be the advance guard of the long knives. Surrounded by drunken savages—yes, they were the savages, not himself and Three Horses and Little Crow.

Infuriating to think of the love and education his father had lavished on him, all wasted now. All the years of following the shaman's path, ended by a lead ball. Before he had accomplished anything.

And Redbird and Eagle Feather and the baby to come— If not for them he might accept the inevitable. Step onto the Trail of Souls with grace and dignity. But, even more for their sake than for his own, he did not want to die.

Frantic with fear and anger, he looked for a way of escape. The camp was in the midst of prairie grass almost as high as a man's head. The sun had gone down, and twilight was deepening. But Raoul was walking toward him, holding his pistol high. And beyond him, between White Bear and the grass, was a ring of men with rifles.

All that was left for him was to die with honor.

He raised his voice to sing louder.

I must put all my strength into this. It is the last song I will sing on earth.

"Stop that goddamned caterwauling!" Raoul shouted.

White Bear watched numbly as Armand Perrault brought his rifle to his shoulder, stepped up to Little Crow, put the muzzle of the rifle to the brave's head and pulled the trigger. The flint clicked down and sparked, and powder sizzled in the pan. The rifle went off with a roar, enveloping the brave's head in a pink cloud of smoke, blood, bits of flesh and bone.

White Bear staggered backward, dizzy with shock and terror.

Three Horses shouted, "I will not die so!" He jerked free from the men who were holding him and plunged into the grass, hands still bound behind him. He ran toward the Rock River.

Rifles boomed.

In his panic, White Bear felt as if all the breath had been knocked out of him. Three Horses might have a chance. He was a short man, and the grass was tall. And light was fading moment by moment.

If White Bear stood where he was an instant longer he would be dead. This was his only chance. No one was holding him. No one was even pointing a gun at him. All of them, even Raoul, were staring after Three Horses. Many of the men had fired and would need time to reload.

Every muscle in his body quivered. He jerked his hands. The rope was still tight around his wrists. Running would be awkward. But Three Horses had shown that it could be done.

Run!

White Bear heard the voice in his mind. His own voice or the Bear spirit's? It did not matter.

He ran.

He threw all the strength in his legs into a sudden spring, away from the distracted long knives. He dove into the grass, running away from the river; opposite the way Three Horses had gone. With his arms behind him, he ran with his head and shoulders thrust forward. The grasses and tall plants slapped his face. His feet pounded the earth. His legs pumped furiously. His breath roared in his chest. His heart thundered.

"Hey, the other Injun's gettin' away!"

"Goddamn it, *get* him!" Raoul's voice, shrill with wild rage.

White Bear's moccasined feet seemed to be flying over the ground. He felt the Bear spirit giving him strength. A curtain of prairie grass fell away ahead of him and swished shut behind him. Even the grass was helping. It was almost high enough to hide him as he ran in a crouch, as his bound wrists forced him to do.

He was already deep into the prairie when he heard the calm voice of Eli Greenglove cutting through the cool, clear air.

"Hold your fire, everybody. He's mine. Got a bead on him."

A moment later lightning struck the side of White Bear's head, sudden and stunning. He heard the rifle's roar just an instant after the bullet hit him. It struck so hard, it left him no strength to scream. His right ear felt as if it had been torn away from his skull. A blaze of agony blinded him. He staggered.

But he was alive.

Play dead!

It was the same voice in his mind that had told him to run. Now he was sure it was the Bear spirit.

He shut his eyes, threw himself at once to the ground. The earth came up and hit him in the face as hard as a fist in the jaw. Stunned for a moment, he sucked air into his chest and let it out slowly. He lay perfectly still. His ear felt as if someone had laid a burning torch on it.

"Got the sonofabitch," came Eli Greenglove's flat voice from only a short distance away.

But he was still alive. And no one was shooting at him. His body went limp with relief.

He could not believe that he was still alive and conscious.

Maybe I am dead. Maybe my spirit will stand up in a moment and start walking west.

Greenglove was supposed to be the best shot in Smith County. Could he really mistakenly think he hit White Bear square in the head? His eyes were better than that.

White Bear heard distant shots.

Earthmaker, let Three Horses live!

If Three Horses had not run when he did, White Bear would not be alive now. But White Bear remembered with anguish that he had seen Little Crow die.

Oh, my brother! Even though half dead with pain and terror himself, he mourned the brave who had died before his eyes.

Blood pounded in White Bear's head. Night was growing steadily deeper. By not moving and by taking only the tiniest breaths he might appear to be dead. He lay with his mutilated right ear uppermost. He felt streams of blood running like lines of ants over his scalp and his cheek. They tickled his neck. To lie perfectly still was agony.

White Bear heard Raoul's voice say, "Make sure of him, Eli."

"Damn hellfire nation!" Eli came back. "Don't I know when I've put a man under?"

"It's dark and you've had a lot of whiskey. Make sure of him."

"Pure waste of time," said Greenglove.

White Bear heard footsteps rustling through the grass toward him. The effort of keeping himself from moving threatened to tear his muscles from his bones. His heart beat harder as the steps came closer. Surely Greenglove could hear its thudding. But he froze himself and held his breath as the feet stopped beside him. In stillness was his only hope. The pain throbbed in his ear.

He'll see that he just hit my ear, and that will be the end.

Should he jump up and run for it? No, Greenglove would not miss a second time. Let the Bear spirit dim Greenglove's sharp eyes. Let him be deceived into thinking White Bear dead. There was no other way he could escape.

He waited for the shot that would smash into his brain.

"Right through the skull," Greenglove called out. "Ain't even enough left to scalp him."

Amazement flooded through White Bear. That couldn't be what Greenglove saw. Unless he was blind drunk. Or blinded by the Bear.

Or he doesn't want to kill me.

Hadn't he tried to talk Raoul out of shooting the three of them?

White Bear remembered Greenglove swinging the rifle at him the day of his father's funeral. If Greenglove hadn't knocked him out, Raoul would have shot him.

He was too frightened to try to understand it. He was alive, that was all he could be sure of. Alive for a little while longer.

"He's in the happy hunting ground." Greenglove's voice faded a little as he walked away. "Want us to dig a hole for him?"

"We don't bury dead Indians," said Raoul. "Let them rot. Let the buzzards get fat on them." He raised his voice. "Every man mount up and chase the ones there in the woods across the creek. This may be our chance to finish Black Hawk."

"What happened to that other Injun that ran away?" Greenglove asked.

"We got him," a militiaman said. "He made it almost to the river. But he's got enough lead in him now to start his own mine."

Grief filled White Bear's motionless body. Little Crow and Three Horses, both killed. Three Horses' death had given him back his life. Three Horses, the first Sauk to greet him on his return to the tribe. His two comrades surely deserved to escape death as much as he did. Why had he alone been spared? He wanted to cry out, as sorrow for his fallen comrades tore into him, but he drew in his lower lip. He bit down on it hard, clenching his teeth in his flesh until he felt no pain anywhere else, in mind or body.

Good-bye, Three Horses. Good-bye, Little Crow. I will burn tobacco to the spirits for you.

Boots clumped through the prairie grass all around him. Hoof-beats pounded past him. He feared he would be trampled, and it took back-breaking effort to hold still. But the horses avoided his body.

Gradually the thundering passage of Raoul's men died away to the north.

For a long time White Bear heard nothing but the creek rippling over its bed of stones, the wind in the trees, crickets buzzing on the prairie. Tiny creatures tickled his flesh as they hurried over his face and body. To them he had already become part of the earth.

The burning in his ear settled down to a numb ache.

He heard the crack of rifle shots a long way off. Raoul's men, pursuing Black Hawk's scouts. Must more of his brothers die to-night?

He opened his eyes. It was now very dark; full night had fallen. He was lying on his left side in tall grass. He took a chance and raised his head a little way. Raoul had said he wanted no men to stay behind, but there might be someone about.

He dropped his head and tensed his hands and arms. The rope around his wrists had loosened. He could twist his wrists till the fingers of his right hand reached the knot. Pale eyes knew little about tying secure knots. After working patiently for a long time he freed his hands.

He still felt sick with grief, and did not have the strength to move away from this place where his comrades had died. Why not just lie here and wait for the long knives to come back and kill him?

But he thought of Redbird and Eagle Feather. And the fullness that had appeared in Redbird's belly before they crossed the Great

River from Ioway to Illinois. Using his knees and elbows to push himself through the grass, he began to crawl.

Slithering like a snake, his body and limbs flat to the ground, he wriggled along the edge of the creek till he felt sure any men that might be nearby could not see him; then he slid down the embankment. The side of his head throbbed with every movement.

He crossed the creek on all fours, the rocks biting into his palms and knees. Where the swift, cold water was deepest he lowered his head into the water to wash it. Agony exploded in his brain and he came close to fainting. But he forced the muscles of his neck to raise his head, and his arms and legs to push him along, out of the creek.

Soon he was in the shelter of the woods. He stood up and staggered through the shrubbery. Now that he was safer, the pain in his torn right ear pounded harder than ever.

He remembered that Raoul and his hundreds of mounted long knives had ridden toward the place where Black Hawk, with only forty braves, was waiting to learn how his peace emissaries fared.

He had stayed alive so far by luck, but he had no real hope of escaping to his people. Probably some of the long knives who had ridden out with Raoul would come across him, and that would be the end. As he neared the farther edge of the woods, a newly risen half-moon, like a white wickiup in a black field, shone at him through the trees ahead.

He was about to step out on the prairie when he heard the rumble of hooves coming toward him. He stopped in the shelter of the trees. He heard shots, screams of pain and terror.

Against the lighter prairie grass, men on horseback were dark shapes rushing at him from the horizon.

Their voices were high-pitched, fearful. They were crying out in English.

"Make a stand in the woods!"

"No! There's too many of them!"

"Just keep a-running. Follow the river."

White Bear looked about for a hiding place. The moon showed him that he was standing beside a big old oak, with branches low enough for him to jump to.

Grandfather Oak, will you shelter me?

Just before he jumped for a branch he noticed that a hollow had rotted out in the base of the tree. It was big enough for him to hide in, but then he would be on the same level as the militiamen. Safer up high.

He forced his tired legs to spring, managed to grip the lowest limb, one hand on each side of it, bark scratching his palms. He pressed the soles of his moccasins flat against the trunk and walked his body up, panting, until he was able to pull himself up over the limb and reach for the next one. The branches were stout and close together, and soon he was high above the floor of the wood.

You made a ladder for me. Thank you, Grandfather Oak.

Dozens of mounted militiamen were streaming past his tree, galloping right under him. The hoofbeats of the horses and the shouts of the men to one another, pitched high with terror, shattered the night air.

He saw the black shapes of more horses and riders swimming through the prairie grass. Their elated cries were Sauk war whoops.

The braves of his tribe, racing toward him as if to rescue him. A sun rose in his breast.

Rifles boomed and arrows whistled through the air after the fleeing militiamen, and he was thankful that he was up this high. He heard screams. Somewhere nearby a body crashed into shrubbery.

Some long knives, he saw, were trying to go around the woods, but the greater distance they had to travel gave the Sauk riders time to catch up with them. Rifle shots flashed like lightning in the darkness.

Two shadowy figures on foot, so close together they seemed one, stumbled out of the tall grass and pushed their way into the woods, careless of the noise they were making. White Bear held his breath, hoping they would not discover him above them.

A voice below him said, "You got to keep going. They'll catch you and tomahawk you sure."

Now the two men were standing by the tree in which he had taken shelter. He strained his ears to listen.

"Save yourself," said another voice, rasping with pain. "I cannot run. The arrow is under my kneecap. I will stay here and try to hold them off."

I know that voice, that accent. It is the Prussian, Otto Wegner.

White Bear remembered how Wegner had disappointed him back at Raoul's camp. Now his life was in danger; he deserved that.

"Hold them off? There's hunnerds of them." He'd heard the other man's voice before, but he sounded like so many long knives, White Bear could not be sure that he knew him.

"Well, maybe if I shoot a few of them, you can get away."

At that White Bear felt anger heating up in his chest. So Wegner would like to shoot a few Indians, would he? Being willing to stay and fight while his comrade got away, though—that was worthy of respect.

"Damn! I don't like leaving you, Otto."

"You have a wife and children."

"So do you."

"But you have a chance to get away. I don't. What good is it, two of us dead? Go!"

White Bear heard a sigh. "All right. Here's all my powder and shot. I ain't planning to stop to use them. Remember, keep your head low so you can see them above the horizon. If they ain't wearing hats, you can figger they're Injuns."

"Please, Levi, my wife and my children, tell how I died."

That was who the other man was—Levi Pope, another of Raoul's men.

"I'll tell them you was brave. Make sure they don't catch you alive, Otto. You know what Injuns do to white people. Use your last bullet on yourself."

White Bear felt his cheeks burn with shame. For himself, the idea of torturing a prisoner was unthinkable, and he did not believe Black Hawk would allow it. But he could not be sure. Many men and women of the British Band, he supposed, would enjoy making one of the dreaded long knives suffer.

White Bear heard Pope scurry off through the brush while Wegner, gasping with pain, settled himself in position at the base of the tree.

The boom of Wegner's rifle below him so startled White Bear that he almost fell from his perch. He heard an agonized cry from out on the prairie, saw a brave fall from a horse.

He killed one of my brothers. I can't let this happen.

He heard quick, metallic sounds of clicking and scraping below him, the sounds of a man loading his rifle.

In a moment another Sauk warrior will fall.

The racking grief White Bear had felt since the deaths of Little Crow and Three Horses changed all at once into a whirlwind of rage. He remembered Little Crow, bound and helpless, his head blown apart. He pictured Three Horses' body, torn by bullets. In his whole life up to now he had never killed a man, but surely now, after what he had suffered and seen, he had to kill.

Kill him how? He is armed and I am not.

But Wegner was in dire pain. White Bear could jump out of the tree on the Prussian's back and bring his foot down hard on the knee with the arrow in it. That should hurt Wegner enough to loosen his grip on his rifle, so that White Bear could get it away from him and shoot him with it or smash his skull.

More Sauk braves were riding closer, and Wegner must be taking aim in the darkness down there. White Bear scrambled down the ladder of tree limbs he had climbed.

As he reached the lowest limb, moonlight showed Wegner rolling over, his eyes gleaming. The rifle barrel swung toward him.

He heard me.

White Bear leaped.

The flash blinded him for an instant. In a suffocating cloud of powder smoke he hit Wegner's chest with knees and hands, an impact that knocked the breath from him. Wegner screamed in pain, a high, womanish sound that made White Bear's ears ring more than the shot had.

The Prussian, under him, battered him with the rifle, trying to turn it so that he could hit him with the butt. White Bear had both hands on the stock, and tried to kick Wegner's knee as their bodies bucked and thrashed at the base of the oak.

White Bear remembered that militiamen often carried hunting knives in shirt pockets. Gripping Wegner's rifle with one hand, he reached down the front of the Prussian's leather jacket. Wegner's eyes widened in fear, and he thrust frantically with his rifle. White Bear felt the handle of a knife and pulled it free. The broad steel blade twinkled, reflecting moon and stars.

Now. One thrust into his enemy's throat.

White Bear slid the point under the bandanna around Wegner's neck and pressed it into the soft place just above the collarbone. The man's eyes seemed about to pop out of his head. His thick, dark mustache was drawn back from his clenched teeth.

Trying to make himself kill the man, White Bear felt as sick in his stomach as he had when he was waiting for Raoul's bullet.

And he remembered again, the night after Raoul had driven him out of Victoire and offered fifty pieces of eight for his death, what he had heard Otto Wegner say.

He did not push the knife any farther. But he realized that Wegner would still kill him, given any chance. He held himself ready to strike.

"Drop your rifle," he whispered. "Slide it away from you. Make a sudden move and I'll cut your throat."

Wegner did as White Bear told him.

He said, "You are keeping me alive to torture me."

If he brought Wegner back to the Sauk, White Bear thought, the warriors would want to kill him slowly. Again he felt that hot shame.

"Do you know who I am?" he asked.

"You are Raoul de Marion's nephew, Auguste. How can you be still alive? I saw Greenglove shoot you."

White Bear ignored the question. "Three of us came to you under a white flag to talk peace, and you shot us."

"It was wrong."

"You say that now, when I hold a knife on you. Why didn't you speak up then?"

"Colonel de Marion is my commanding officer. Kill me, damn you. Is it not your duty?"

"A warrior does as he pleases with his captives."

White Bear heard all around him, on the prairie and in the woods, the war cries and whistle signals of the Sauk braves. It would not be long before someone discovered White Bear crouched on top of this man, holding a knife point to his throat.

Wegner said, "If I could, I would kill you."

"Yet if you had caught me the night my uncle offered fifty Spanish dollars for my death, you would have let me go."

"How do you know that?"

It amused him to answer Wegner's question by saying, "I am a shaman—a medicine man. We know things."

"Dummes Zeug," Wegner muttered. "Rubbish," he said louder, but his eyes wavered.

White Bear said, "I am a healer. That is my work. I will not kill you unless I have to. Give me your word you will not attack me, and I will take the knife from your throat."

Wegner closed his eyes and sighed. "You are civilized. Maybe I can trust you."

White Bear could not help laughing. "You saw today what civilized men do to their prisoners. You can trust me because I am a Sauk."

"And why do you trust me?"

"Because I think you are a man of honor."

"All right. You have my word."

White Bear slowly drew back and stood over Wegner. The Prussian sat up, then groaned. In the moonlight White Bear saw tears streaming uncontrollably from his eyes. White Bear had him sit with his back to the hollow tree. He brought his face close to the knee. With his eyes adjusted to the darkness, the half-moon's rays were enough to show him that Wegner had broken off the end of the arrow, and the rest of it protruded from his kneecap. The arrow had gone into the joint. It hurt White Bear just to look at it.

"I can try to pull this out," White Bear said.

"Go ahead."

"Give me that cloth around your neck."

With Wegner's bandanna White Bear wiped the blood off the arrow to make it less slippery. It would have been easier if Wegner had not broken the arrow. The protruding end was only long enough to let White Bear grip it with one hand. He wrapped his left hand around his right to give him a tighter grip, and pulled with all his strength.

Wegner fell over on his side in a faint.

Thank Earthmaker he didn't scream.

The arrow had not moved at all.

When Wegner came around, White Bear said, "There is nothing I can do for you. You need to get back to your own people."

Wegner's eyes widened. "You would let me go?"

"I have to. Or else kill you. If our warriors got you I couldn't stop them from killing you. Climb into this hollow in the tree and stay there till morning. By then, I think, our braves will be far from here."

He helped Wegner to stand and boosted him up into his hiding place. Wegner let out a groan as he drew his wounded leg inside the opening.

Take care of this pale eyes, Grandfather Oak.

"I will never forget this," said Wegner.

"Then remember my people."

He took Wegner's knife and rifle. He might have left the Prussian a weapon to defend himself, but he thought that would be going beyond kindness into foolishness.

He heard Sauk victory shouts coming from the other side of Old Man's Creek, where Raoul's camp had been. Little though he wanted to go back there, it seemed the surest way to safety. Carrying the rifle with one hand, the knife in his belt, he made his way through the woods to the creek.

Soon he was back in the center of what had been the long knives' camp, at the place where he had nearly been killed. A small fire burned here. Near it lay two bodies stretched out. The head of one was covered with a cloth. That, White Bear thought, must be Little Crow. Beside him lay Three Horses, a blanket draped over his short body, his face with its flattened nose uncovered. Standing around the bodies were half a dozen warriors.

By all rights he ought to be lying there too. He put a hand up to his ear, forgotten in the excitement of the encounter with Otto Wegner. The pain had settled to a dull pulsing. Gingerly, he felt the wound. The middle part of the ear was gone. The intact upper and lower parts were covered with crusted blood. He had washed the wound once in the creek. He must wash it again and bandage it.

Greenglove did that so blood would flow and it would seem to anyone who looked at me in the twilight that I'd been shot in the head. He was trying to save my life. Why?

One day, White Bear hoped, he would meet Greenglove and find out why he had spared him.

And that other time—when he hit me with his rifle just as Raoul was about to shoot me—did he do that, too, to save my life?

A solitary warrior sat before the fire, a long scalplock adorned with feathers hanging down the side of his head. The firelight gleamed on his shaven head and glittered on the beads around the rims of his ears. The bowl of the pipe he smoked was part of a steel tomahawk blade; the stem of the pipe was the tomahawk handle. He looked up, and his eyes widened when White Bear stepped into the firelight.

"White Bear!" came Black Hawk's gravelly voice. "Are you truly alive or do you come back from the Trail of Souls?"

White Bear felt an immense warmth as the firelight showed him Black Hawk's teeth flashing in one of his rare smiles.

"I am alive," said White Bear.

"I am happy! I am surprised!" Black Hawk cried, waving his pipe. "I thought all three of you were dead."

Sudden elation dizzied White Bear, and the flesh of his back prickled as he realized what it meant to see Black Hawk sitting quietly smoking his pipe in the center of Raoul's camp. Victory! The long knives routed. How had it happened? Black Hawk might have made a terrible mistake leading the Sauk across the Great River, but at that moment White Bear loved him.

Owl Carver stepped out of the shadows carrying a bundle of goods he had been gathering from the tents of the long knives. He dropped his bundle to throw his arms around White Bear.

"My son is restored to me."

White Bear sat down at the fire.

"How did you escape?" Black Hawk asked.

White Bear explained how he had played dead when Eli Greenglove claimed to have hit him. He said nothing about meeting Otto Wegner. He felt good about having spared Wegner's life, but he was not sure Black Hawk would understand. In fact, White Bear was not sure he himself understood.

Owl Carver made White Bear hold his head close to the firelight while he examined the wound, muttering.

"Truly, the things the long knives do pass all understanding," he said. "It was dark. You were in grass. Maybe he missed."

"He missed on purpose. He has great fame as a marksman; he sees very well. He came and stood over me, and must have known I was alive."

Owl Carver searched through his bundle of loot and found a Frenchman's kerchief and tied it around White Bear's head to protect the wounded ear.

Chills of exultation rippled up White Bear's spine as he looked around and saw Black Hawk's braves plundering the very camp where Raoul's men had swarmed and had killed his two companions at sunset.

"Earthmaker has given us a mighty victory," he said.

"We never expected it," said Owl Carver. "We were camped on the Rock River north of here when Iron Knife rode in after sunset to say that you three had been killed, and also two of the braves who had gone with him. He told us that a whole army of long knives was riding toward us."

Black Hawk said, "I was angry. They had killed my messengers of peace. I did not care that there were hundreds of them and only forty of us. I wanted vengeance for the blood they had shed."

White Bear laughed. "I heard them crying out as they fled your attack. They thought there were hundreds of *you*."

"The Hawk spirit flew with us, blinding them and striking fear into their hearts," said Black Hawk.

Owl Carver said, "And the spirits in their whiskey befuddled them too."

Black Hawk said, "I was surprised to see them turn tail and run. I thought Americans were better shooters and fiercer fighters than that. They outnumbered us many times over, but they showed no fight at all."

The Winnebago Prophet lumbered out of the darkness and sat down at the fireside opposite Black Hawk. The silver nose-ring lying against his mustache glittered red.

"It is well that you are here, Flying Cloud," said Black Hawk. "We must look along the trails that lie ahead of us."

White Bear turned away in disgust. After the Winnebago Prophet had misled Black Hawk so badly, how could he still rely on him?

A gruff voice said, "See, Father, I have lifted more hair from our enemies." White Bear looked up. Wolf Paw was standing over them, holding up two hanks of hair, each with a bloody, circular patch of flesh attached to it. White Bear hoped that one of those scalps did not belong to Otto Wegner.

Black Hawk stood up and seized Wolf Paw's shoulders. "My heart is big when I see my son is so mighty a warrior."

Sitting down beside his father, Wolf Paw stared at White Bear, and White Bear had to explain all over again how he came to be still alive.

After a moment of silence Black Hawk spoke. "Until tonight, there was no blood spilled between the long knives and us. But when we tried to surrender, they shot our messengers." He gestured to the bodies near the fire and to White Bear. "And now we have killed many of them."

White Bear felt himself trembling with rage. He remembered Raoul coming toward him, grinning, pistol raised—right on this spot—and he prayed that now his uncle might be lying dead somewhere on the prairie. An arrow in his back, killing him as he fled Black Hawk's warriors. A hole in his scalp, and his hair dangling from some brave's belt.

O Bear spirit, O Turtle, O Earthmaker, let it be so!

Then his fury faded away and became fear as he realized that he had just done, in his mind, a thing more terrible than murder. A man might call on the spirits for the strength and skill to fight an enemy—but to direct the power of the spirits against another man, no matter how wicked, was forbidden. He prayed no harm would come to him because of it.

Black Hawk said, "We have no choice now. The long knives have forced war upon me."

White Bear spoke up quickly, before Wolf Paw or Flying Cloud could call for war, as they were certain to do.

"It was my uncle, the brother of Star Arrow, who ordered us three to be killed. He has hated our people all of his life. He especially hates me. A different long-knife war chief might have opened his arms to us. Now that Black Hawk has shown the long knives that they will be hurt if they come against us, let us offer peace again. I am ready to go again with a white flag to talk of surrender with other long-knife war chiefs."

Black Hawk made a flat, rejecting hand gesture. "You have seen what happened. Pale eyes warriors would not let you get close enough to talk to their chiefs."

A warrior came over to the fire, holding a tin cup. He offered it to Black Hawk.

"The long knives left five barrels of whiskey, but they are almost empty."

Black Hawk turned the cup over, letting the whiskey soak into the dirt.

"Pour that poison on the ground," he said. "Whiskey made the long knives so foolish that when they looked at one of our braves they saw ten."

Wolf Paw said, "They abandoned wagonloads of food and ammunition. Even some rifles."

"We will need them," said Black Hawk. "Without more provisions we cannot go on."

After the warrior went away, Black Hawk gave his pipe toma-hawk to Wolf Paw to smoke. Owl Carver and the Winnebago Prophet brought out pipes of their own. Owl Carver offered his to White Bear, who declined it. Given what he had been through this day, and troubled by the fear that Black Hawk was determined to plunge his people into worse calamities, White Bear felt his stomach could not stand tobacco smoke.

Flying Cloud broke the thoughtful silence. "If forty Sauk war-riors could chase away two hundred long knives, then all the Sauk warriors can chase away the long knives' whole army. I say call out the six hundred warriors who wait at our main camp. We will drive the long knives all the way back to the Great River."

White Bear wanted to answer the Winnebago Prophet with an-gry words, but he felt light-headed and nauseated. He decided to wait and see what the others would say.

"The Prophet of the Winnebago speaks well," said Wolf Paw. "My blade is hungry for more long knives' scalps."

Of course, thought White Bear.

Owl Carver said drily, "We routed some drunk pale eyes who hardly deserve to be called long knives. Let us not waste any more of our young men's lives. Let us follow the northward curve of the Rock River to its very headwaters, far beyond any pale eyes' settle-ments, then travel westward toward the Great River. If we can cross the Great River safely, I do not think the long knives will chase us farther."

The five men sat in silence. A sudden thought struck White Bear. *This* was why Earthmaker had ordained that he be educated among the pale eyes—so that he could help his band understand how pale eyes thought. If they kept going north along the Rock River they would soon cross the northern border of the state of Illinois. That might seem to them to mean very little, but it could mean much to their pursuers. The country where they were headed did not belong to any state; it was part of a large land of many waters that was called the Michigan Territory.

Eagerly he said, "We may be able to escape the long knives by going north. Most of the long knives who are pursuing us were called out by the Great Father of the Illinois country. Once we are out of Illinois, maybe they will not follow."

Wolf Paw grunted, clearly insulted at the thought of their not being pursued.

The Prophet bestirred himself. "Many of my Winnebago brothers dwell in that country to the north. They will join us in fighting the long knives."

Like your people from Prophet's Town, who've been deserting us? White Bear thought.

A warrior set a long knives' saddlebag before Black Hawk, who opened it. The war chief pulled out an expensive-looking black wool suit and some white silk shirts with ruffles. Finally he took out two books bound in red and white leather. White Bear leaned over for a closer look.

"Bundles of the pale eyes' talking paper," said Black Hawk.

Wolf Paw said, "They are worthless, Father. Keep the clothing and put the talking paper on the fire."

But Black Hawk handed one of the books to White Bear. "What do the talking papers say to you, White Bear?"

White Bear picked up a book and read on the spine, *Chitty's Pleadings, Vol. I.* He opened and saw close-packed type, his eyes skimming over many legal terms in Latin. White Bear wondered whether the lawyer who owned these books was still alive. At the sight of books his heart gave an unexpected lurch. He felt a longing to be not in a plundered enemy camp on the prairie, but in a library, with books, pen and paper. The feeling took him by surprise. It had been many months since he had missed the pale eyes' world. A few pages of *Paradise Lost* now and then had satisfied any hankering for what they called "civilization."

"These papers tell about the pale eyes' laws," he said. "It is sometimes said that they have no magic. But there is powerful magic in their books and in their laws. It is the magic that binds them together."

The Prophet said, "The pale eyes' paper is bad medicine."

Black Hawk held out his hand, and White Bear gave him the book. It pained White Bear to think Black Hawk might throw it into the fire.

White Bear had seen many white leaders—mayors, congressmen, military officers, once even Sharp Knife himself, Andrew Jackson, the President of the United States. He had learned about them in school and read about them in newspapers. He felt Black Hawk was a match for any of them. More than a match in some ways; he was stronger and healthier than any white man his age that White Bear had known. What pale eyes of nearly seventy years could personally lead a cavalry charge against an enemy outnumbering him by ten to one and rout them? Black Hawk's great weakness was one that he shared with most people, whatever their race or their position in life: if he wanted a thing to be true, he believed it. That was why last winter he had listened to the Winnebago Prophet and not to White Bear.

Now White Bear hoped Black Hawk would show his intelligence by respecting the value of the book. Black Hawk frowned at the leather-bound volume, weighing it in his hand. He picked the other book up with his other hand.

"They are heavy. But since there is magic in them, I will keep these talking-paper bundles by me. And I will bring them with me when I speak in council."

White Bear breathed a small sigh of satisfaction.

Black Hawk laid the books down, one on each side of him, and put one hand on each book. He sat like that for a time, staring into the fire.

"I have done with trying to surrender to the long knives," he said, and it seemed to White Bear that his face became a fearsome mask in the firelight. "They have left me no choice. Yes, we will retreat from them. But we will not run like hunted deer. We will send out war parties, big and small, in every direction. We will lie in ambush on every trail. We will fall upon every settlement. We will attack every traveling party of long knives. No pale eyes north of the Rock River will be safe from us. Until we have crossed the Great River, we will give the pale eyes no peace."

At Black Hawk's words White Bear felt that an ice-cold hand had laid itself flat on his back, between his shoulder blades. With those words Black Hawk was condemning to cruel death hundreds of people—pale eyes and his own.

And one of the largest settlements north of the Rock River was Victor.

"What is the use of more killing?" he said. "It will only madden the long knives. They will come after us till they have destroyed us."

"I have decided," Black Hawk said. "We must fight back. We must be avenged. They stole our land. They burned Saukenuk. They burned Prophet's Town. We asked them for peace, and they killed us. Black Hawk will show them that they cannot do this and go unpunished."

"So it shall be!" the Winnebago Prophet growled.

And after that the long knives in their turn will have to be avenged.

Hopelessness lay like a heavy sodden blanket on White Bear. He saw the old warrior's determination, and said no more.

He could only pray that Earthmaker spare those he loved. On both sides.

Black Hawk stood up. "Let us go back to our camp."

Wolf Paw said, "Father, I want to stay here till tomorrow with a party of warriors. There are dead long knives scattered all over the prairie, but we cannot find them in the dark. In the morning we can take their scalps and their weapons."

His words stopped White Bear as he was about to turn away from the fire. Otto Wegner might still be hiding in that hollow tree, waiting for dawn.

Hurriedly, White Bear said, "I, too, will stay. I will help Wolf Paw search for the dead."

What could he do if Wolf Paw and his men captured Wegner? Perhaps not save the Prussian's life, but at least persuade the warriors to kill him cleanly and not torture him.

Haven't I done enough for Wegner? I want to go back to Redbird.

But his impulses were a shaman's impulses, and the harder to explain they were, the more he trusted them. It was important, for some reason, that he stay at Old Man's Creek a while longer.

Owl Carver looked surprised. "After all you have suffered, do you not want to return to your family?"

White Bear thought quickly. "There is a chance that murdering uncle of mine is one of those lying on the ground somewhere around here. It would be good to see him dead."

Owl Carver grunted. "I will tell Redbird that you are safe."

Fear and exertion had exhausted White Bear beyond ordinary fatigue, and he had barely enough energy now to roll himself in a blanket by the small fire. Unconsciousness hit him instantly.

In the morning he watched, sickened, as Wolf Paw not only scalped a long knife who lay dead in the tall grass, but slashed open the man's woollen trousers and sliced off his manly parts. Blood spattered over innocent prairie flowers of violet and yellow, and a swarm of flies buzzed around Wolf Paw, waiting to settle on the dead man when he moved away.

"Why do you do that?" White Bear demanded. "The Sauk have never done such things to a dead enemy before."

"The Winnebago Prophet says that the long knives are planning to kill all Sauk men, and then bring up black men from the country to the south to mate with our women. That way they hope to breed a race of slaves. This is our answer to that."

The story sounded absurd to White Bear. The pale eyes in Illinois didn't even keep black slaves. Just more of the Winnebago Prophet's babblings. But Wolf Paw firmly believed it.

At a sudden drumming of hooves, Wolf Paw and White Bear both looked south at Old Man's Creek. A Sauk warrior splashed through, waving his arm.

"Long knives coming!" he shouted.

Wolf Paw picked up two rifles, his own and the dead man's. They had found eleven bodies scattered along the edge of the Rock River, none of them Raoul's.

White Bear was disappointed, but not surprised, that Raoul had managed to escape. Surely he deserved killing more than any of his followers who did die. But White Bear had not stayed behind just to see Raoul dead.

In fact, it was a relief that the spirits had not answered White Bear's forbidden prayer.

He kept looking for movement out of the corner of his eye, trying to see whether Otto Wegner was anywhere about. But he saw no sign of him.

"How many long knives?" Wolf Paw said to the scout as he rode up. "Can we fight them?"

The scout's hand slashed a no. "Too many. Fifty at least. All on horseback. And they have a wagon with them."

"Coming to collect their dead," said Wolf Paw. "They will not like what they find." He grinned down at the corpse he had just carved.

"Better mount up and ride away from here," said the scout. "If they see us, they will chase us."

"They will not chase us," said Wolf Paw. "They will be afraid of an ambush." His smile broadened. "Maybe we will give them one."

At Wolf Paw's shouted command the six warriors who had remained with him moved into the trees north of Old Man's Creek, the same trees where White Bear had taken refuge last night. White

Bear tried to see the tree where he had hidden Wegner, but the woods looked different in daylight.

Wolf Paw ordered his party to mount their horses, tied up amidst the trees, and ride north to Black Hawk's camp. But though he swung into the saddle, he did not ride off with them. He sat on his white-spotted gray pony facing the direction the long knives would be coming from. A screen of low-hanging maple branches and wild grape vines concealed him. White Bear, on a brown mare captured in Raoul's camp last night, drew up beside him.

"Why are you staying?" White Bear asked.

"I counted only eleven dead long knives," said Wolf Paw. "I want to make it twelve." He put the hammer of his flintlock on half-cock, poured fine-grained priming powder on the pan from a small flask, and closed the fizzen over it.

White Bear sensed that something very important was about to happen and that he must wait with Wolf Paw.

"Why do *you* wait?" Wolf Paw demanded. "You have never killed anyone."

"Here they come," said White Bear, choosing not to answer him.

The two horses pulling the wagon, a flatbed with railed sides, halted at the creek. Most of the long knives dismounted and began to search through the remains of Raoul's camp. A few others rode across the creek. Wolf Paw raised his rifle.

The long knives cried out to one another and cursed as they found the mutilated bodies of their comrades.

Now they hate us more.

The long knives had rolled-up blankets tied across their horses' backs. They opened the blankets and used them to pick up the dead. One pair of men on foot was already carrying a blanket-wrapped body across the creek to the wagon.

One long knife rode slowly toward them. He was so tall that his legs dangled down from his horse almost to the ground. He came to the body Wolf Paw had just been stripping, and climbed down. He took off his broad-brimmed gray hat and stood holding it in both hands as he looked down at the body.

White Bear heard the click of a flintlock hammer being drawn back to full-cock. Wolf Paw sighted along the barrel.

The militiaman raised his head, and White Bear saw tears glistening in the morning sun as they ran down his cheeks.

White Bear knew this man.

A gaunt brown face with strong bones, deep-set gray eyes, a young face aged by grief. In White Bear's vision of last winter this man had a black beard; now he was clean-shaven. But this was the man the Turtle had shown him.

A sudden shout from the woods made both White Bear and Wolf Paw jump with surprise.

"Help! Help me, please!"

White Bear saw Otto Wegner stagger from the trees about a hundred feet to his right. He was trying to run toward the tall man.

He limped badly and let out an "Oh!" of pain with every step.

The tall man set his hat back on his head and ran toward the Prussian, who fell forward on his face in the grass a short distance from the edge of the woods.

Wolf Paw swung the rifle toward Otto, but before he could fire, Otto fell and was almost obscured by the tall grass. The blue-black rifle barrel lifted toward the man going to his aid. White Bear heard Wolf Paw draw a deep breath through his nostrils and saw his finger tighten on the trigger.

Even as the hammer fell and the spark set the powder sizzling in the pan, White Bear thrust his hand out. In the instant between the pulling of the trigger and the firing of the rifle White Bear pushed the barrel off target.

The rifle went off with a boom and a flash and a puff of blue smoke.

The lanky man jerked his head around and stared into the trees where Wolf Paw and White Bear sat hidden on their horses. He shouted and pointed. The long knives spread out between the creek and the woods brought their rifles to their shoulders. Some of them jumped on their horses.

"*Why did you do that?*" Wolf Paw shouted. It no longer mattered that the long knives could hear him.

He raised his rifle as if to hit White Bear with the butt end, as Eli Greenglove had done many moons ago.

"Come on," said White Bear, ignoring the threat and kicking his horse's sides to start him galloping through the woods. Wolf Paw, who had no time to reload, thundered behind him, uttering shouts of inarticulate rage.

White Bear was certain Wolf Paw would strike at him with rifle butt or tomahawk or knife before they cleared the woods, but Wolf Paw was wholly bent now on escape.

Now I understand!

The realization hit White Bear so suddenly and surprisingly that he sat up in his saddle. A tree limb flying toward him nearly hit him in the face. He ducked under it at the last moment.

This was why he had wanted to stay behind with Wolf Paw, even at the cost of delaying his reunion with Redbird, even at the risk of his life. It was not just to protect Otto Wegner. The Turtle—or perhaps even Earthmaker himself—had ordained it. If he had not been there Wolf Paw would have killed that tall, thin man who came to bury his fallen comrades.

White Bear remembered the rest of his vision—hundreds of blue-coated long knives charging and dying. Would this man send those long knives or their enemy into battle?

It was impossible to puzzle out. He might never know the answer.

They rode over the prairie on the other side of the woods, heading for Black Hawk's camp. The long knives following them had dropped away, doubtless afraid, as Wolf Paw had predicted, of an ambush.

Still expecting to feel a tomahawk blade split his spine, White Bear slowed down.

"So!" Wolf Paw shouted. "You are still a pale eyes!"

"No," White Bear tried to explain. "It was a vision I had. I had to save that man."

"A vision," Wolf Paw sneered. "I should kill you. If you were not a shaman— A warrior needs all his luck. But, since your pale eyes people are so precious to you, I will kill *them*. You heard what my father said. I will lead the war party that goes to your pale eyes' home. And this time you will not be along to save anyone."

They spoke no more. Though the morning sky was bright, a cloud of dread settled over White Bear. What would become of Nicole, Grandpapa, Frank and all the people of Victoire and Victor who had been his friends? At the prompting of some spirit, he had saved the tall, thin man, a stranger to him. And he had saved Otto Wegner, one of Raoul's hired men.

Was there *nothing* he could do for his own loved ones?

15

The Blockhouse

The devil's reek of gunpowder seared Nicole's nostrils. Arrows flew over the trading post palisade to fall in the courtyard, some quivering upright in the ground. She heard the piercing shrieks of the Indians above the steady crackling of rifle fire.

She stood in the open doorway of the blockhouse, her body tense with fear as she watched Frank, up on the catwalk above the main gate. He crouched behind the pointed logs of the palisade. Frowning with concentration, he was slowly reloading his rifle.

"Look at Frank up there," Nicole said to Pamela Russell, who stood beside her. "Oh, God, I hate to see him out in the open. Frank," she said, though she knew he couldn't hear her, "get into one of the towers!"

"Burke too," Pamela said. "Why do they do it?" She pointed to the east side of the palisade where her husband, a stocky man wearing spectacles, stood on the catwalk. With the Indians attacking the front gate, he was left alone to guard the east parapet. The rest of the men, ten of them, were at the front part of the palisades, banging away.

Twelve men. Twelve men who know how to use rifles. That's all we've got.

And four were Nicole's husband, two of her sons and her father. She gasped.

She saw a loop of rope fly through the air above the eastern wall and catch on one of the sharpened logs. A moment later a dark head crowned with feathers appeared above the palisade. And Burke Russell was looking the other way.

276

"Burke, look out!" Pamela screamed.

Burke heard that. He swung around, raising his rifle to his shoulder.

"Please, God!" Nicole cried.

The Indian leaped over the parapet. He seemed twice as tall as Burke, with bulging muscles that gleamed with oil. He wore only a loincloth, and his walnut-brown body was painted with red, yellow and black stripes. His scalplock flew out behind him as he rushed Burke, swinging a war club with a glittering metal spike protruding from its thick end.

Burke's rifle went off with an orange flash, a boom, a cloud of smoke.

The Indian wasn't stopped. The war club came down on Burke's head. Nicole heard the hollow thud and heard herself cry out.

Pamela screamed. "Oh, no, oh God, no! Burke! Burke!"

Burke's glasses flew from his face, hit the catwalk and caromed off to the ground. With his free hand the Indian giant seized the rifle as Burke crumpled. He raised both arms over his head, rifle in one hand, bloodstained club in the other, and shouted his triumph.

Nicole's stomach heaved.

Pamela fell against her, fainting. She threw an arm around Pamela and eased her to the ground, and she saw half a dozen more Indians waving rifles and tomahawks leap over the eastern parapet and land on the catwalk near Burke Russell's body.

"Frank! Behind you!" she screamed.

Frank turned, took aim and fired at the Indians. He ran for the nearest corner tower.

Nicole didn't see whether he hit any of the Indians. She dragged Pamela out of the doorway with the help of Ellen Slattery, the blacksmith's wife. They got Pamela sitting on a bench by the wall. Her thick chestnut hair tumbled forward as Nicole pushed her head down to revive her.

I don't know why I'm doing this. It's a mercy she's unconscious. Frank!

Her heart in her throat, Nicole pushed herself to her feet and ran back to the door. An arrow whizzed through the open doorway. It clanged off the iron muzzle of the cannon that stood in the center of the blockhouse hall.

I'd make a mighty big target for those Indians, she thought, the wry little joke helping to keep her from crying in her terror.

She peered around the edge of the doorway to see a fury of brown bodies on the southern catwalk where Frank had been standing. In the center of the catwalk, one brave with a rooster's comb of red-dyed hair shouted and brandished a steel-headed tomahawk, sending parties to hammer at the doors of the corner towers with clubs, tomahawks and rifle butts. Black rings painted around his eyes and yellow slashes on his cheekbones gave him a terrifying look.

Even in the midst of her fear and hatred she could see that his body was magnificent. The most beautiful man's body she'd ever seen.

To her relief Nicole saw no dead white men anywhere—except for Burke Russell, who lay still, his head a bright red mess, one arm hanging down over the edge of the eastern catwalk. She looked at him quickly and then looked away, feeling sick again.

What made it even more of a shame that Burke had died on the palisade was that the men never planned to hold it. They just wanted to delay the Indians a bit. Here in the blockhouse was where they hoped to be able to hold out.

With God's help.

"Oh, Burke! Oh my Burke!" Pamela Russell was awake and screaming. Ellen Slattery looked helplessly at Nicole.

Nicole felt heartbroken for Pamela, but she had to let her be. There was too much to do. She ran through the people crowded into the main room on the ground floor of the blockhouse. There must be four hundred people here, mostly women and children, she thought.

And Raoul's got over a hundred men from Victor with him. God knows where.

Here they had more rifles than men. Two dozen rifles leaned against the stone wall. Many families owned two or three rifles, and people had grabbed them as they fled to the trading post.

Well, a woman can ram a ball down a muzzle and pull a trigger too.

And miss, she thought, her heart a ball of ice. She hadn't seen one Indian hit yet.

Nicole spoke loudly to the women around her. "The Indians will be shooting down from the catwalk at our men when they try to get back here to us." She started to load a rifle. "We've got to shoot at the Indians and drive them to cover."

She had not held a rifle in her hands since marrying Frank, who would not have a firearm in the house. But Elysée de Marion had taught his daughter how to shoot, and she had not forgotten.

Piled by the rifles were flannel bags, powder horns and five small barrels, all full of gunpowder. In that frantic dawn, after fleeing here, the men and women had formed a relay line to rush the bags and barrels of gunpowder from Raoul's stone magazine to the blockhouse.

Feeling a bit more hopeful, Nicole noticed lead ingots lying beside the ammunition—probably from the lead mine that Raoul had shut down just before leaving Victor. And she saw scissor-shaped bullet molds. They had some of the things they needed.

If only they knew how to use these things.

"Who knows how to mold bullets?" she asked the group of women who'd been standing silently, watching her.

"I know," Elfrida Wegner said. Of course, thought Nicole. Her husband had been a soldier, over in Europe.

"Take some others and show them how to do it," Nicole said. "We're going to need all the bullets we can make."

Elfrida and two other women carried the lead bars and the molds to the huge fireplace at the rear of the hall.

From the hundred and more women crowded into the hall Nicole collected ten volunteers who knew something about rifles, five to shoot and five to load.

She called two of the bigger boys to carry baskets of shot upstairs. But carrying powder—that was dangerous. She couldn't make herself ask anyone else to do that.

She filled a bushel basket with sacks of cartridges, added a powder horn on top, swung it up to her shoulder and charged up the stairs, terrified all the way.

"Judas Priest, you're *strong*, Missuz Hopkins," said one of the boys carrying shot. It gave her a warm feeling to hear that; she figured most people thought of her as just plain fat.

She still couldn't believe she was going to do this. Going to try to kill people. She picked out a slot in the log wall and pushed her rifle barrel through it. She could see a bit of the courtyard below. White men were falling back from the towers. Indians were coming at them. All of them were moving slowly. White men backing up a step at a time. Indians matching them step for step. A dance. The brave with the red crest was still standing on the catwalk above the front gate, waving his tomahawk and shouting orders. The caller.

Nicole pulled open the drawstring of a bag of cartridges, bit off the end of a paper cartridge and poured the black powder down the muzzle of her rifle. She detached the ramrod from the stock of the rifle and wrapped a bullet in greased cloth, ramming it into place down the tight, rifled barrel. She thanked Heaven she hadn't forgotten how to do this.

She dropped the fine grains of priming powder from the horn into the powder pan, pointed her rifle at the red-crested brave and sighted down the black barrel at the center of his chest.

Her finger quivered on the trigger. She couldn't kill a man. Her eyes blurred.

If she didn't kill him, he might kill Frank. Or Tom or Ben. Or Papa. She remembered Burke Russell's smashed, bloody skull.

She had to do it. Her vision cleared.

She took deep breaths, steadying herself.

She heard the click of the hammer as she pulled back the trigger. The hammer snapped forward, the flint hit the fizzen, the spark struck the powder pan. The rifle went off with a thunderclap that made her ears ring, and her target was obscured by cream-colored smoke in front of the rifle port.

When the smoke cleared, the brave was still standing on the catwalk.

She clenched her fist and whispered, "Damn!"

The red-crested Indian glanced down to his right, as if he had heard a bullet strike the palisade wall there, then looked straight at her. She knew he couldn't really see her. She was hidden behind a log wall, and a hundred feet or more separated them. Even so, it seemed to her that his malevolent stare met her eyes.

She handed her rifle back to Bernadette Bosquet, a cook from the château, who gave her a loaded one.

Down in the yard, the Indians were charging the fur shop and the inn. The white men, retreating, were converging on the front door of the blockhouse.

She saw Elysée and Guichard emerge from behind the inn. The two old men moved slowly, Elysée limping heavily, both walking backward. Guichard fired a shot at the six or more crouching Indians coming at them. Elysée, his walking stick in his left hand, raised his pistol. Guichard worked quickly with powder horn and ramrod to load his rifle. Elysée fired, bringing down one of the Indians. Both men took a few steps backward as powder smoke enveloped their attackers. The Indians darted forward, and Guichard raised his rifle. The Indians hesitated. Elysée stepped behind Guichard and tucked his stick under one arm to reload his pistol. At a word from Elysée, Guichard fired, and a red man with a rifle crumpled. Guichard, reaching for his powder horn, stepped backward behind Elysée, who now kept the Indians covered.

Nicole felt her legs tremble and a lump form in her throat as she watched the fearless precision with which her father and his lifelong servant carried out their retreat. Those two old men shouldn't have to fight at all, but today every man was needed.

She saw Frank and her two oldest sons, Tom and Ben, running across the yard to the front door. They vanished under the overhang of the blockhouse's second story, made of logs. Thank God they'd made it to safety! She felt faint and took a deep breath.

She handed her rifle to Bernadette. "Here, you shoot. I've got to see my husband and sons."

"Merci, madame. I thought you'd never give me a turn."

By the time Nicole got downstairs, Frank and the other men had crowded into the hall. The heavy front door of the blockhouse was shut and barred, throwing the stone-walled lower floor into near-darkness. Two men were shooting through the rifle ports on either side of the door. Women were lighting oil lamps and candles and setting them on shelves around the edges of the room.

Women whose men were here were holding them tight. Nicole threw her arms around Frank, then opened them wider to take in Tom and Ben as they ran to join their mother and father.

She eyed the boys. Their faces were rosy and their eyes bright with excitement. They'd be men in another year or two. And after today, she thought, Frank would have a hard time keeping them away from rifles.

If we live through this day.

As she felt Frank strong and alive against her, a sudden intense desire to make love to him came over her. She was shocked at herself.

But she'd seen one man struck down already and knew that before sundown she or Frank might be dead. The realization of how precious Frank was to her had brought her body to passionate life.

She heard the shrieks and yips of the Indians in the yard of the trading post.

Hard-eyed David Cooper said, "We can't hold 'em off just shooting from the ground floor. We need shooters at every rifle port upstairs."

He nodded approvingly when he saw Elfrida Wegner and three other women molding bullets by the fire they had just kindled.

He called, "All right, four men and four of you women take rifle ports down here. The rest of you come up to the second story."

Gathering up extra rifles, five men and thirty or more women followed Cooper upstairs, where he organized them to shoot, each shooter to have someone to reload and carry ammunition.

Nicole might herself have volunteered to shoot through one of the upstairs rifle ports, but she chose to load for Frank. She felt it might be important to Frank that he be the one to shoot and she stand by, helping him. She would rather be at his side, anyway, than across the room somewhere shooting.

Frank pushed his octagonal rifle barrel out through his port. The port was only about six inches wide and three inches high, and the log wall was a foot thick or more, but Nicole still trembled at the thought that an Indian might manage to hit Frank with an arrow or a bullet. Working to load his second rifle, she tried not to think about that.

Thank God they had David Cooper here, someone who seemed to know what to do. She remembered how Cooper had spoken up the day Raoul had forced Auguste out of the château— *Is this how you do things in Smith County?* It was Cooper who had thrown open the trading post to the first refugees from the Indian raid, people from Victoire, shortly after dawn. He and Burke Russell. Burke. Her heart sank.

Nicole's fears turned to Victoire and to the outlying farms. The Indians had attacked so suddenly, whooping on horseback across the prairie, that there was just time for the people in Victor and some from the château to crowd into the trading post. Many of the children and some of the women gathered into the main room were still in their nightgowns. But missing from the crowd downstairs were people Nicole knew. Reverend Philip Hale and Nancy Hale,

Clarissa Greenglove and her two sons by Raoul, Marchette Perrault, many others. Fear twisted her belly as she thought of what the Indians might have done to them.

Cooper had assigned himself to a gunport in the east wall of the blockhouse. Nicole went to him.

"Mr. Cooper, could I have a look out there?"

"Certainly, ma'am." He sighed. "That used to be your home, that mansion on the hill, didn't it?"

Poor Burke Russell, she saw, was still lying on the eastern catwalk. Three dead Indians were sprawled there now to keep him company, though. She was a bit more hardened to such sights than she had been just a short time ago. But what she saw in the cheerful June sky beyond the palisade made her body go clammy-cold with horror.

A rope of thick, black smoke coiled upward, twisting this way and that, spreading till it seemed to stain the entire eastern quarter of the sky. The palisade was too high for her to see the fire itself, though red tongues of flame shot up now and again in the midst of the smoke. But she had no doubt at all about where the fire was.

"They're burning Victoire!" She started to cry.

She felt Frank's hand patting her shoulder, and turned.

"I was hoping the people of Victoire might be able to hold out," she said.

Frank put his arm around her. "Nicole, I'm sorry, it's pretty likely the only people left alive from Victoire are already here. Lucky most of them could outrun the Indians and get here."

"But, Frank, what's happened to the rest of them—Marchette, Clarissa—are they all dead?"

Frank didn't answer. He just stood there holding her.

Grief weighed on her like a cloak of iron. If she hadn't had Frank to lean against, she would surely have fallen to the floor. She looked out again and saw other, more distant columns of smoke. The Indians must have come from the east and struck every farmhouse they came across. They had surely destroyed Philip Hale's church. Poor Nancy!

David Cooper said, "Sometimes people manage to hide. The Indians can't look everywhere."

The weight on her back and shoulders seemed to lighten with that thought.

"Yes, the lead mine, for instance," Frank said. "A perfect place."

"Oh, they can't have killed all those people," Nicole said.

Please, let Marchette and Clarissa and Nancy and Reverend Hale be alive.

She desperately wanted to pray. She wanted to believe that a loving God was looking down on Victoire and Victor, protecting her friends and the people she had grown up with.

For the next hour or more Nicole thought of nothing and did nothing but bite cartridges and dump powder, ram home bullets, put one rifle into Frank's ink-stained hands, take the other rifle and load it. Her mouth was sore from biting the heavy paper. Her arms and hands ached from making the same movements over and over. The incessant shooting all around her deafened her, the stink—and, worse, the taste—of gunpowder turned her stomach, and her hands were blacker with the stuff than Frank's ever were from his printing press.

Frank was firing less and less often. He leaned against the log wall, wiping his arm across his forehead.

"We've kept pouring lead into the courtyard. That's driven them under cover. But they broke holes in the corner tower walls, and they're shooting back at us from there." An Indian yelp caught his attention, and he peered out again.

"Now, would you look at that!" he said. Nicole put her head next to his at the rifle port.

A blizzard in the trading post courtyard. Flecks of white filled the air between the inn and the blockhouse. She saw brown arms shaking slashed mattresses and pillows out the windows. Feathers floated up to the gunport. More feathers slowly drifted down to dot the fresh June grass with white. She heard yells and laughter from the inn.

They'd cut me open as soon as they'd cut open a pillow, and think that was just as funny.

"They're getting drunk," Frank said. "On all the liquor in Raoul's tavern. Must be looting the town too."

They'll burn our home. Everything will be gone, the beds and the dishes, the mirrors, the bureaus, the spinning wheel, the clock, the plates and silverware, our clothes, our books and old letters, children's toys, the spices, the cradle I rocked all our babies in. The machines and carpentry tools, and, oh, please, God, not Frank's printing press!

Stop it, Nicole. You're blessed! Blessed that they attacked at dawn when all the children were in the house and not scattered all over the countryside, and now they're safely in here. Blessed that your husband is standing here beside you and not dead on the palisade parapet like Burke Russell.

But even as she thought of things to be thankful for, she remembered what might happen to them in the next few hours.

An Indian charged out of the front door of the inn. He was waving a curving Navy cutlass. He ran at the blockhouse, screaming. His steps wavered, though, and Nicole guessed he must be full of whiskey.

Still she was terrified. What if everyone missed him and he somehow got in and others followed?

"Look out," Frank said, and gently nudged her away from the port. He pushed his rifle out and fired.

"I hit him, but he isn't falling."

Getting back into the routine, Nicole took Frank's rifle and loaded it. Rifles were booming all along the front of the blockhouse as men tried to stop the Indian with the cutlass. Frank's second rifle went off.

"He doesn't want to die," said Frank. "He's full of bullets." She heard pain in his voice, and as she handed him his freshly loaded rifle, Nicole saw that his upper lip was beaded with sweat. She hurt for him. He hated killing, and now he was forced to try again and again to kill this man.

Frank aimed and fired again. "There. I got him. He's down."

Frank pulled his rifle in and handed it to Nicole. As she started to reload it, he leaned against the wall. Slowly his knees bent and he slid down till he was sitting on the floor. She put the rifle down and crouched beside him, stroking his arm, her heart aching.

He covered his mouth with his hand. His body jerked, but he managed to hold in the vomit. After a moment, breathing heavily, he took his hand away from his mouth.

"Oh, Jesus! What am I doing?"

Nicole put her arms around him, and his head fell against her breast.

"Excuse me, Miz Hopkins," said a voice above her. She let go of Frank as David Cooper squatted down beside them and laid his hand on Frank's knee.

"Hopkins, you're all right. I was with Harrison at Tippecanoe

Village, and when the Indians came at us out of the woods, I don't believe more than half the men fired their rifles. There's really few men find it easy to kill. There's times we got to."

Frank wiped his eyes and laid a hand on top of Cooper's. "Thanks."

Cooper said, "If you still feel bad, just think about what they'd do to your wife and kids if they got in here."

Frank put a hand on the floor and pushed himself to his feet. "Yes, as long as I think about my family I'll be able to shoot." There was a bitterness in his voice, and Nicole felt she knew what he was thinking. How cruel the irony, that love for his family could make him into a killer.

"Here they come again!" a woman down the line shouted.

Again and again Nicole heard the rapping of bullets into the log wall near Frank's head as he fired steadily at Indians charging from the trading post buildings they had captured.

Frank turned from the rifle port to hand Nicole an empty rifle and take a loaded one. An arrow flashed through the narrow opening, missing his head by inches.

Thank you, God!

The defenders kept up a steady fire until the Indians withdrew again into the captured buildings. Nicole and Frank took turns watching through the rifle port. What was happening to their home at this moment?

The lull stretched on. Nicole went downstairs to look for her children, began picking her way through the crowd sitting on the floor of the blockhouse hall.

Stretched out on a bench was a woman whose name she didn't know, a newcomer to the settlement. The right side of her checkered dress was soaked with blood from shoulder to waist. Moaning faintly, the woman seemed half conscious.

"Arrow," said Ellen Slattery, who was pressing a folded cloth against the woman's shoulder.

Nicole shuddered and patted Ellen's back and went on. She saw Tom and Ben manning ground-floor gunports. Abigail, Martha and John were playing around the cannon, pretending to shoot it at the Indians. The three youngest, Rachel, Betsy and Patrick, were with a group gathered in the stone-walled rear room Raoul used as his office. They were singing hymns. Pamela Russell, she saw, was also with the hymn singers, tears running down her face. As Nicole went over to the fireplace to join the women molding bullets, she heard:

> "My God, how many are my fears,
> How fast my foes increase!
> Their number how it multiplies!
> How fatal to my peace."

That must be the first time those *walls have ever heard a hymn.*

Nicole took a turn at bullet making, ladling the silvery molten lead from a kettle over the fire into the tiny hole in the hollowed-out mold, opening the mold with its scissor handles and dropping the still-warm ball into a big basket. Another woman took each ball and filed away the bit of waste metal formed in the hole through which the lead was poured.

"Injuns!" a man yelled. The women and children crouched down on the floor, and Nicole hurried upstairs to help Frank.

After rifle fire from both levels drove back the latest assault, Frank said, "We get a few each time they attack, but it's not enough. I'm sure I saw over a hundred of them when I was on the parapet."

"We've no food and very little water," said Nicole. "They could just wait us out and we wouldn't last very long." The only water they had was in buckets the townspeople had brought into the blockhouse with them.

David Cooper said, "We've got to be ready for them to make one big rush for the blockhouse. They'll try to set the place on fire, so we better save as much water as we can. Ration it out."

Nicole's body broke out in a cold sweat at the thought of fire; she remembered all the gunpowder they'd relayed into the blockhouse.

Enough to blow us all up.

And then she remembered too, what had happened to Helene twenty years ago at Fort Dearborn.

Maybe being blown to bits would be a better way to go.

"And here's just the man to take charge of rationing the water," said Cooper.

Nicole turned to see her father climbing up the stairs, pulling himself along on the banister and leaning on his walking stick. As he reached the top of the stairs Frank took his arm and helped him over to sit on a wooden box near the rifle port.

Elysée said, "One of the women, Mrs. Russell, insisted on taking my rifle and standing guard in my place. I will be just as happy not to have to fire at any red men for a while. I keep thinking I might shoot Auguste."

Nicole gasped. "Auguste! Papa, he would never be out there."

"Perhaps not. Have you spoken to anyone who had news of my grandchildren?" Elysée asked her.

Nicole was about to say "They're all here" when she realized whom he meant.

"Raoul and Clarissa's children?" She shook her head sadly. "No, Papa. Anyone from Victoire who isn't here—we don't know what happened to them."

Elysée sighed. "Poor little things. In all the years since they were born, I got to speak to them only once or twice."

The cry of "Here the Injuns come!" broke in on them again.

David Cooper gave Elysée brief instructions on rationing water, and the old man limped downstairs as the firing began again.

Nicole, loading and reloading Frank's rifles with numb arms and mind, heard firing from all around her. The Indians were coming from every direction. Arrows and an occasional bullet whistled in through the ports, but no one was hit. Smoke drifted through the second story of the blockhouse, making her eyes water.

The Indians withdrew again. As the firing died down, Nicole was thankful to see that the powder smoke that had filled the second floor blew up toward the roof and vanished. Looking up, she saw that there was a space nearly a foot high between the top of the log wall and the roof. The roof rested on big vertical timbers, its over-hang covering the opening. Men could climb up there, she sup-posed, and shoot down; the attackers would have to be standing directly below them to shoot back.

There was a heap she didn't know about this fort. In the years since Raoul had built it she'd hardly ever had reason to set foot inside—the last time was when she and Frank had appealed to him to leave men behind to protect the town. Now her life depended on how well Raoul had built it, and it was bitter medicine to swallow.

David Cooper left his rifle port to talk to Frank.

"It's only a few hours till sunset," Cooper said in a low voice, "and I have a hunch they'll try one big attack to take this place before dark. If they come all at once, we don't have enough rifles to stop them."

His tone was matter-of-fact, but his words struck terror into Nicole's heart. She took Frank's hand and squeezed it. It felt cold as a dead man's.

Cooper went on. "I keep thinking about that cannon downstairs. You know, whatever we might say about Raoul de Marion, he did set this place up to be defended. I figure that cannon must be in working order."

"Do you know how to fire a cannon?" Frank asked.

Cooper shrugged. "I've stood near the artillerymen a time or two and watched them, but never thought to memorize what I saw. I couldn't even say how much gunpowder to use. If we put in too little, we'll waste our chance. If we put in too much, we could blow ourselves all to hell."

Nicole said, "I'd rather that than face whatever hell the Indians have in store for us."

Cooper looked at her with his hard eyes and nodded. "Indians won't get you, Miz Hopkins. I promise you that. Let's go take a look at that thing."

Frank, Cooper and Nicole, chilled but grimly reassured by Cooper's remark, cleared away the children who were straddling the cannon's four-foot-long black barrel, and the women who were sitting against its wooden carriage. Cooper stood frowning at the gun.

He sighed, and it sounded to Nicole like the sigh of a man about to step off a high cliff.

"Well, let's load 'er up."

He went over to the side of the room where the flannel bags of gunpowder were piled up, and he picked one up, holding it at arm's length as if it were a rattlesnake. He carried it back to the cannon and slid it into the muzzle. From the carriage he unstrapped the ramrod, a pole with a wad of cloth wrapped around its end, and used that to push the gunpowder down.

"Let's add another bag of powder," he said to Frank.

Women and children formed a circle to watch. Nicole pictured what the cannon would do to all the people in this room if it blew up, and shut her eyes.

After pushing a second bag of gunpowder down the muzzle, Cooper said, "What we need now is canister shot that'd spread all over the place and puncture a lot of Indians. I remember there was canister shot in the powder magazine, but it didn't seem all that important this morning, and we didn't have time to move it over here. Now we'll have to make do with what we've got. Give me a load of rifle bullets."

Someone handed him a basket full of lead balls, and he poured them into the cannon's throat and pushed them down with the ramrod.

"I don't want to use up all our rifle shot, but seems to me there's room inside this thing for a lot more." He turned to the onlookers. "Everybody spread out and bring me anything made of metal that'll fit in here."

Into the cannon's maw went two chains, a padlock, a handful of knives and forks. And a dozen lead soldiers, sent to war by the small boys who owned them.

"Here, Mr. Cooper, use these." Pamela Russell pushed her way through the crowd holding out a canvas bag. Her eyes were bloodshot, the lids swollen and red.

Cooper frowned. "What's that?"

"A bag of pieces of eight from Raoul de Marion's safe. When Burke knew he was going to be in the fighting, he gave me the trading post keys to hold for him." She stopped, red-faced and choking, then continued. "Burke didn't know anything about fighting Indians. My husband is dead because de Marion left us almost defenseless. He doesn't deserve to have this silver."

Feeling Pamela's agony, Nicole went over to her and put an arm around her back and hugged her. Pamela's body was stiff, unresponsive.

Cooper's gaze traveled over the people gathered around the cannon. "Any of you folks see anything wrong with us doing this?"

"We always use Spanish dollars out here on the frontier," said Elysée with a smile. "The U.S. Government simply didn't mint enough coins. I'm sure the Indians will accept them."

"Well, that defense will do for now," said Cooper, grinning as he slit the bag with his hunting knife and poured the glittering silver disks into the cannon. "Going to make some Indians rich today," he said. "Now, we need something to touch it off with. I don't see any linstock around here."

"A candle?" Frank found a long white candle that would burn for about an hour and lit it from another one mounted on a wall.

"Should work," said Cooper. "Keep a lighted candle by the cannon at all times. We have no way of knowing when they'll decide to make their big attack."

Pamela Russell pulled free of Nicole and gripped Cooper's arm.

"Let me touch off the cannon," she said.

There was something frightening, Nicole thought, in the avid light in her eyes.

Is that how I'd be if Frank were killed? Nicole wondered. *So utterly vengeful?*

Cooper said, "Sure you can do it?"

Pamela whispered through tight lips, "Oh, yes. Yes I am!"

"All right," said Cooper. "You can touch it off. But look out the Indians don't shoot you when we swing the door open."

Frank, Cooper and two more men kicked the chocks out from under the cannon's four wooden wheels. The men strained against the gun, and for a moment Nicole was afraid they wouldn't be able to move it. Then, grudgingly, it rumbled over the puncheon floor until Cooper set the four chocks back under the wheels. The cannon rested just a few feet back from the front door.

Looking through a port on the west side of the hall, Nicole saw the sun still high in the west. This was the month when days were longest.

And this has been the longest day of my life, she thought.

As the afternoon passed with agonizing slowness, Pamela Russell had to light yet a second candle, and then a third. She sat rigid in a chair beside the cannon, holding her candle upright, saying nothing, staring fixedly at the blockhouse door.

Nicole noticed a beam of sunlight from a west-facing rifle port lighting up the smoke and dust that drifted through the main hall of the blockhouse. The shaft of light looked like a solid bar of gold. She looked through the rifle port and was almost blinded by the sun just above the humped silhouettes of hills across the Mississippi.

She heard the Indians screaming, and her stomach turned over.

"Fire arrows!" someone yelled.

Nicole's heart stopped. If the Indians managed to set fire to the blockhouse, the hundreds of people who had taken shelter here would be driven out to be slaughtered.

She ran to the slot in the stone wall where Tom was standing with his rifle ready. Looking past her son's head, she saw an arrow with a cloth-wrapped, burning tip arc up from the courtyard. It disappeared, and she thought it must have hit the second-story log wall somewhere above her.

"Upstairs!" Cooper shouted. "Fill your buckets from the water barrels and come on." His sweeping finger included a bunch of excited smaller boys, who followed him up the stairs. Nicole hurried after them.

Cooper and the other men boosted boys with buckets to the top of the log walls. The boys pulled themselves up to the open space Nicole had noticed before under the overhang of the roof. Leaning out, sheltered, the boys were able to see where the fire arrows had stuck, and dumped water on them.

Cooper grinned. "De Marion built well. The ground floor's stone and the roof is covered with sheet lead. Injuns'll soon tire of this game."

The fire arrows became fewer. They stopped coming, and there was a breathless silence in which time did not seem to pass. Then Cooper led the way back down to the ground floor.

High-pitched Indians whoops sent a new chill through Nicole.

A rifle went off—Tom, at the gunport to the left of the front door.

"Hold your fire, boy!" Cooper called, watching from the other side of the doorway. "Let them come."

Nicole went to stand beside her oldest son again and look out. The front gate of the palisade was open and Indians were streaming in. Brown bodies painted with yellow and red and black slashes, arms waving knives, clubs, tomahawks, bows and arrows, rifles. More were tumbling out the front door of the inn. A flicker of red light caught her eye. Flames shot out the open front door of the fur shop. They were burning all those valuable pelts. Raoul would lose a lot today.

And not just money, she thought, recalling burning Victoire. Money would be the least of Raoul's loss. To her surprise she felt a moment's sorrow for the brother she had come to despise.

Twenty or more Indians came through the gate carrying a huge black log, its front end afire. The rest of the Indians gathered around them. All together they ran at the blockhouse door, the glowing, smoking tip of the log in the forefront.

"Everybody get as far away from this damned cannon as you can!" Frank shouted. People scrambled away, leaving an empty space around the six-pounder in the center of the floor. Some ran into the strong room and some scurried upstairs. Only Cooper, Frank and Pamela Russell stood by the cannon. Nicole stayed where she was, moving her body so that she was between Tom and the cannon.

Whatever happens will be what God wants to happen.

"Open the door!" Cooper ordered.

Tom Slattery, the blacksmith, swung the door open, and Nicole saw some of the Indians hesitate, then rush forward. She wondered if they could see the cannon in the shadowy interior of the blockhouse.

"Shoot!" yelled Cooper.

Carefully, deliberately, Pamela Russell lowered her candle to the cannon's touchhole.

"Fire in the hole!" Cooper called out.

Nicole heard the sizzle of gunpowder from where she stood.

The boom of the cannon hit Nicole's skull like a mallet. A huge white cloud belched out through the open door, and the sharp reek of burnt powder filled the air. The gun jumped right over the chocks set behind its wheels and flew back about six feet.

In the aftermath of the cannon's roar came whoops of delight from nearly a hundred small boys in the blockhouse.

Then Nicole heard the Indians screaming again, but now they were screams of agony, not war cries. A fierce joy rose in her as she stood in the open doorway and saw the yard of the trading post transformed into a vision of Hell. Through the haze she saw dark bodies sprawling on the ground. Some of the Indians writhed in the dust of the yard, some were motionless. Others were frantically pulling the fallen back, dragging them by the arms or legs. The log they were going to use to batter down the door lay smouldering, abandoned in the yard of the trading post.

As she took in more of the sight of blood and torn bodies and severed limbs, Nicole felt ashamed that she had rejoiced at first. Sickened, she turned away.

"Fire your rifles!" David Cooper yelled. "Shoot, shoot, shoot! Keep them on the run. And shut that damned door."

"Let me at the port, Maw," Tom demanded.

The rifles banged away, sounding puny in Nicole's ears after the roar of the cannon. Finally Cooper ordered an end to the shooting.

"If we let 'em drag their dead out of here, they may be in a mood to leave."

Nicole waited in dread, wondering whether the Indians would come again. The sunset rays pouring through the ports on the west side of the blockhouse slowly faded, leaving the main room dark. People lit more candles. David Cooper directed the reloading of the cannon.

The group in Raoul's office were singing hymns again, and many people sitting around the hall joined them. Nicole sat beside Pamela Russell on a bench and took her hand, and soon Pamela began to talk quietly. She told Nicole things about Burke, the books he enjoyed reading, his favorite dishes, jokes he used to tell her.

"I always envied you, Nicole, with so many children. We wanted children so much, and we never got any. And now we'll never—"

Nicole tried to think of something to say, but everything that came to her sounded foolish to her mind's ear. Looking at Frank standing by a port, she thought, *I have been blessed, and Pamela hasn't been. But why?* That had to mean something. She couldn't think what.

"It helps me, when life is hard, to believe that God has a plan," she said, patting Pamela's hand. "His plan is like a painting that's so big we can only see dark spots or bright spots without knowing what it all means. But I think one day he'll take us up with him, where we can see the whole picture and understand it."

"Nicole," Frank called. She gave Pamela's hand a squeeze and went to see what Frank was looking at through the rifle port.

Even at this distance she could hear the roaring of the flames. Sparks shot up past the palisade, and a red glow filled the sky.

"They're burning the town," he said. "Our home is gone. Our shop."

She turned back to see Pamela, sitting on the bench, a lost look on her pale face. She thought of the people who had not managed to reach the shelter of the trading post. She put her arm around Frank's waist and pressed herself against him.

"You and I are alive and all of our children are alive," she said. "God has blessed us."

16

Yellow Hair

"Wolf Paw has come back!"

White Bear felt a hollow in his stomach as the cry ran through the camp. Wolf Paw had vowed to bring death and destruction to the pale eyes such as they had never known before.

Before he left, Wolf Paw had held a ritual dog feast to insure success. He had hung one of his own dogs from a painted pole by its hind legs and disemboweled it alive, asking Earthmaker's blessing on the war party. Then his wives, Running Deer and Burning Pine, had cooked the dog and served bits of the meat to the braves and warriors who would follow Wolf Paw on this raid. If he would choose one of his cherished dogs to be sacrificed, what would he do to the people of Victor?

For days White Bear had held himself rigid, hardly able to eat, lying awake at night, waiting for Wolf Paw's war party to come back. What horrors would he have to face now?

Women and children ran to surround the returning braves and warriors. White Bear saw Iron Knife on horseback towering above the crowd, his huge arms lifted triumphantly. From each fist dangled a scalp. Beside him was Wolf Paw, a blue cloth, stained red with blood, wrapped around his left shoulder. Wolf Paw's right hand was raised high, gripping three long hanks of hair with disks of white flesh hanging from them. More braves rode behind them, also holding up scalps. Scalps, scalps, scalps.

White Bear staggered. He could not take his eyes from them. The hair was of many different colors—light brown, gray, dark brown, black. Some of the locks were very long, and must have been taken from women's heads.

Could Wolf Paw be holding Nicole's hair, or Frank's? Could it be Grandpapa's?

Heart pounding, White Bear forced himself to push through the crowd. He heard cattle lowing and horses neighing in the distance. Questioning shouts and cries of greeting.

A scream of agony froze him. A woman's voice. And then another, from another part of the crowd, piercing his eardrums. And still more screams. He realized what was happening. Women were learning that their men had not come back.

Scalps and screams. Wolf Paw's gifts to the British Band. White Bear worked his way past women calling out anxious questions.

He suddenly came upon his mother leading a wailing pregnant woman out of the crowd.

"She heard that her husband was killed, and she has gone into labor," Sun Woman said, her face hollow with her own pain. White Bear squeezed her arm briefly as she passed him.

When he got close to Wolf Paw he saw a bound woman's body draped face down across the back of the brave's gray pony.

She wore a ragged blue dress. Her feet were bare, dirty and covered with scratches. She did not stir. From this side of the pony White Bear could not see her face. A sickening suspicion gripped him, and he hesitated, not wanting his fear confirmed.

Wolf Paw, frowning down at him angrily, was still wearing his yellow and red war paint, faded by the ride of several days.

"I raided the town where you lived, White Bear. I took forty head of cattle and twenty horses from your pale eyes relatives."

"I am glad to hear of the cattle," said White Bear. "Our people are starving."

Wanting, and not wanting, to know who Wolf Paw's captive was, he walked around the brave's horse for a better look at the bound woman.

"We killed many pale eyes," Wolf Paw said. "They will never forget Wolf Paw's raid. Tonight we will have a scalp dance for the warriors who have become braves."

White Bear stopped walking. People he knew and loved on both sides had died; he had to learn which ones.

After a moment he collected himself. "And will you dance for the braves and warriors you did not bring back?" It was a cruel thing to say, but Wolf Paw deserved it. Wolf Paw did not answer.

White Bear had to fight himself to keep from crying aloud in anguish. He no longer had any doubt who the captive woman was who hung head down over the spotted pony.

One yellow braid was still tied with a blue bow. The other had come undone, and loose locks of blond hair hung down, almost brushing the ground.

He bent to see Nancy's unconscious face.

Coming up beside him Redbird asked quietly, "Do you know this woman?"

"Yes," he said. It all came back to him—last summer at Victoire, the meetings on the prairie, that night in the cornfield beside her father's house when she had begged him to "know" her. Had he missed her? Yes; he had to admit that. Did he love her? He was not sure, but, happy as he had been with Redbird, he often thought of Nancy and wondered if she still longed for him as she had when he left her.

How, without hurting Redbird, who stood next to him watching as he stared down at Nancy, could he explain what this white woman meant to him?

He reached out to untie the rope looped around Nancy's back that held her to Wolf Paw's horse.

"Do not touch her," Wolf Paw growled. "She is for me, and only for me."

No, White Bear thought, he could not let Nancy be kidnapped and raped by this man. Whatever bloody things had been done at Victor, this he must prevent. He readied himself to fight Wolf Paw if he had to.

And how would he explain *that* to Redbird?

Wolf Paw slid down from his horse and, one-handed, untied Nancy. Fresh blood was soaking through the cloth around his shoulder—a strip of blue gingham torn from Nancy's dress, White Bear now saw.

Weak from his wound, Wolf Paw could not lift Nancy and carry her. Regardless of Wolf Paw's warning, White Bear would not let her fall. He took her from Wolf Paw and eased her to the ground. Her eyelids were fluttering. Redbird, bending awkwardly with her swollen belly, helped him. Their eyes met, and she looked searchingly into his.

A woman's voice cried, "The pale eyes squaw is *not* for you, Wolf Paw. I will not have her in my wickiup." Running Deer, the older of Wolf Paw's two wives, strode up to Wolf Paw, thrusting her face into his. Behind her came Burning Pine, the younger wife, a papoose strapped to her back, looking equally determined.

"My wives will do as I say," Wolf Paw grumbled, but there was no strength in his voice.

Burning Pine said, "Your wives and children are hungry. We are eating roots and bark. We have no food for any pale eyes."

For now, Black Hawk's band was hidden away on an island of dry ground in the heart of a great marsh north of the headwaters of the Rock River, well into the Michigan Territory. But there was scarcely any game or fish here, and they could not stay in this place much longer.

Wolf Paw said, "I have brought cattle."

"Then the people will eat well because of my husband," Running Deer said. "But the pale eyes woman will not need to eat." Running Deer turned to the crowd. "Many women lost their husbands in Wolf Paw's raid. It is right that the women avenge themselves on this pale eyes."

White Bear's back crawled with gooseflesh. Running Deer meant for the women of the band to torture Nancy to death.

For as long as they could make her pain last, it would take their minds off their hunger and sickness and sorrow. And their own fear of death.

It must not happen. But how could he prevent it?

Feeling like a drowning man being swept away on rapids, White Bear watched Running Deer and Burning Pine lift Nancy from the ground and carry her off, with her feet dragging. Wolf Paw and most of the braves who had returned with him followed.

Wolf Paw's wives pulled Nancy through the band's collection of hastily built wickiups and lean-tos. They brought her to a tall elm tree growing up in the center of the camp. The tree was dying. Its bark had been stripped to cover a wickiup.

By the time White Bear caught up with the crowd around Nancy, her eyes were wide open, but unfocused. Running Deer pushed her against the trunk of the elm tree and drew a knife. With swift, angry slashes, Wolf Paw's senior wife stripped away Nancy's dress and the chemise under it. Nancy stood naked before the tribe. Her eyes were still open and unseeing. She made no attempt to cover herself. She did not seem to know what was happening to her. White Bear's skin crawled with shame at the sight of her degradation.

Women laughed. "Her skin is like a frog's belly!"

Men stared greedily.

Running Deer took a coil of rawhide rope and lashed Nancy to the tree, and White Bear felt the muscles of his neck and shoulders knotting till they ached. He could scarcely bear to look at Nancy, who hung in her bonds, her eyes closed again.

He did not care if they killed him. He would not let them do this. He would not allow it to go on a moment longer.

He put his hand over the five claw scars on his chest and spoke to his spirit self. O *Bear spirit, give me the power to move the people to mercy.*

He felt strength surge into his chest and arms, and raising his medicine stick, he strode forward.

When he was only a foot away from Nancy, her eyes opened suddenly, huge and turquoise, staring into his.

"Auguste!" Her voice and face were full of terror.

It came to him with a shock that he must look frightful to her. The man she had loved was transformed into a vision of savagery—painted face, a shoulder-length mane of hair, silver earrings, shell necklace, his scarred chest bare, holding high a painted stick adorned with feathers and beads. And what would she make of his right ear, torn in two by Eli Greenglove's rifle ball? After what she had already gone through, the sight of him must be yet another impossible shock.

"I'm going to help you," he said in English. "Try not to show that you're frightened." Useless advice, he thought. Still, it would be better for them both if the people respected her. There was nothing a Sauk despised more than a show of fear.

He pointed his medicine stick at Running Deer and said sternly, "Stand aside." She glowered at him but stepped back.

Last winter Wolf Paw had snatched this stick from his hand. But that was before White Bear had nearly been killed carrying Black Hawk's message of peace to the pale eyes. That was before they had begun to see for themselves that White Bear had spoken truly when he warned that Black Hawk's hope of a great alliance to defeat the long knives was an illusion. And that was before many of the people had felt his healing touch. He knew how to do things, because of his training with pale eyes doctors, that Owl Carver and Sun Woman did not.

Now White Bear's medicine stick had much more power than a few moons ago. Even at this moment when anxiety for Nancy gnawed at him, he felt pride in his power.

He turned to face the crowd, standing protectively in front of Nancy.

The braves and warriors stared at him, puzzled and angry.

"Is this how you show your strength and courage, by torturing a helpless woman?" he demanded.

Wolf Paw said, "She is a trophy honorably taken in battle."

White Bear pointed to Running Deer. "Wolf Paw meant to take the pale eyes woman into his wickiup for his pleasure. But his wife will not let him. So he pretends that it is his pleasure to let the women torture her."

Feeling stronger than ever, White Bear watched Wolf Paw's face darken. He might be able to outfight any man in the tribe bare-handed or with weapons, but not with words. This moment, thought White Bear, began to repay Wolf Paw for shaming him last winter before the council.

And he will have to let me tend his wound. That, too, will repay him.

Wolf Paw stood glowering at White Bear, his eyes glazing, his breath coming in gasps. He must be on the verge of fainting from the pain, White Bear thought.

"I captured the pale eyes woman," Wolf Paw said. "I give her to the tribe."

"Are we fighting the pale eyes so we can steal their women?" White Bear demanded. "As long as we torture and kill their people, the long knives will think of us as wild animals that must be destroyed. I have lived among the pale eyes, and I tell you that we must show them that we are worthy of their respect."

Wolf Paw grumbled, "We will win their respect by killing them. I have killed many."

Many at Victor, no doubt, White Bear thought, feeling as sick as Wolf Paw looked, hating him for his ignorance.

He addressed the whole gathering. "Since Wolf Paw has given this woman to the tribe, let the tribe treat her honorably," White

Bear said. "The day will come when we will have to sit down with the long knives and talk."

"Not if we win!" cried Wolf Paw.

"Win?" White Bear laughed scornfully. "Does Wolf Paw still imagine that thousands of long knives are going to surrender to our few hundred Sauk and Fox warriors? We can win only if they decide to stop fighting us. If we make them hate us, they will never stop fighting until all of us are dead."

It is probably already too late for talking with the long knives, but if I hold out the hope of peace, it may save Nancy's life.

He let his gaze travel over the people who stood in a ring around him. The dark eyes looking at him were mostly sullen and suspicious, because their shaman was telling them what they did not want to hear. No one seemed ready to challenge him, but he knew that if three or four braves were to overpower him and kill Nancy, the crowd would let it happen. His belly muscles knotted with tension.

But, as Wolf Paw had said, they needed all their luck, and it would be best not to tempt the wrath of the spirits by defying their shaman.

Redbird, you must not fail me. He gave his wife a look of appeal before he spoke further. Behind Redbird Iron Knife stood like a great oak tree. At least there was no threat to him in Iron Knife's face.

White Bear took a deep breath and his heart fluttered. His life and Nancy's depended on what happened next.

"I take the pale eyes woman under my protection," he said. "Redbird, untie her."

Redbird hesitated for just a moment, her eyes wide, and White Bear held his breath. If, moved by jealousy, she refused to obey him and sided with Running Deer, there was no hope for Nancy.

At that thought a resolve arose in him, dark and powerful as a storm on the Great River, and he filled his lungs and squared his shoulders.

If they try to kill her, they will have to kill me first. If she is doomed, so am I.

If he stood by and let the people torture Nancy to death, he would hate himself forever.

Redbird lowered her eyes and began to undo the rope around

Nancy. Iron Knife helped his sister. Relief brightened in White Bear, like sunlight on the river after a storm. Relief, and a surge of love for his wife. With Iron Knife siding with him and Wolf Paw weakened by his wound, no brave would dare to challenge him.

Eagle Feather was standing in front of the crowd, and White Bear felt proud that his son was seeing the people treat him with respect. That might balance out the memory of that shameful night of the woman's dress.

"Eagle Feather, run and get one of our blankets."

Nancy looked at White Bear with huge, frightened eyes, saying nothing. Terror must have struck her dumb. But he was relieved to see she was able to stand on her own. Redbird put a hand on her shoulder to steady her.

"You're going to be all right," White Bear said in English. "We will take you to my wickiup."

He turned to Wolf Paw. "Come with me. I will see to your wound." Wolf Paw's brown skin looked clammy and bloodless. He had ridden for four days with a bullet in his shoulder. It must come out at once, or it would kill him. But White Bear took pleasure in giving orders to Wolf Paw.

Eagle Feather came with a blanket, and Redbird wrapped it around Nancy.

Most of the people scattered, many to mourn their dead, others to hear the stories of the braves and warriors who had come back with the war party, still others to see the horses and to butcher some of the cattle they had brought back. A small crowd followed White Bear, the yellow-haired prisoner and Wolf Paw.

As Redbird and Iron Knife helped Nancy, now softly sobbing, into the low structure of branches and bark, Owl Carver came up to White Bear.

"I was ready to terrify the people if they turned against you, but you did not need my help. You spoke to them, and against their will they heeded you."

Owl Carver's praise delighted White Bear. But as he saw once again how the old shaman had declined, it took some of the edge from his pleasure.

Owl Carver's eyes were watery and his cheeks were sunken. His arms and legs were thin as spear shafts. The trek up the Rock River had not been good for him. White Bear and Sun Woman had taken over most of the work of caring for the wounded and sick, though Owl Carver did as much as he could.

"You are a Great Shaman, as I predicted you would be," Owl Carver said. "You foretold exactly what would happen if Black Hawk led the British Band across the Great River. But I am sad that your greatness must be proved by the suffering of our people."

White Bear felt his chest expand and a warmth spread through his limbs at these words of his teacher.

"I may need your help yet," he said. "The people do not like me protecting this pale eyes woman."

Owl Carver nodded. "But they respect you. And they will respect you more when you show them you have magical powers."

"I have no magical powers."

"You do. It was not I who put the mark of the Bear on your chest."

"What do you mean?"

"I mean that the White Bear is your spirit self. And he can act in this world. The mark of his claws is the mark of his favor."

As White Bear let this sink in, Wolf Paw approached with a stumbling walk. Running Deer and Burning Pine followed him.

Out of their wickiup Redbird brought a blanket, White Bear's Sauk medicine bag and his black bag of surgical instruments.

"Sit in the wickiup with the pale eyes woman," White Bear told Redbird. "She is very frightened."

"I am frightened too," said Redbird as she left him.

White Bear bit his lip. The tone of her voice said, *Who is this woman?*

As White Bear set out the markers for the seven directions, positioning four stones around Wolf Paw, he said, "This will hurt very much and Wolf Paw must not move."

Keeping in place the two stones and the bear's claw White Bear laid on Wolf Paw's chest would force the brave to lie still.

"You cannot hurt me," said Wolf Paw, just as if he were a captive and White Bear was about to torture him.

White Bear turned to the people standing around them.

"All of you join hands and ask Earthmaker to heal Wolf Paw's wound."

Running Deer's face, which had been hard with anger, now melted into tears. Burning Pine looked hopefully at White Bear.

White Bear gestured to Iron Knife to lift Wolf Paw's shoulder slightly. Carefully, gently, he untied and unwrapped the blood-soaked blue rag torn from Nancy's dress. Recent bleeding had softened the scab, so that the cloth came away easily from the wound, which was between Wolf Paw's left armpit and his collarbone. Its shape surprised White Bear: not a round bullet hole, but a long, narrow gash, surrounded by bruised and swollen flesh.

"How did this happen to you?" he asked. He was going to have to hurt Wolf Paw all the more because the wound had gone untreated for four days.

"When the braves attacked the blockhouse all together at the end of the day, the pale eyes opened the door and fired a big gun."

White Bear desperately wanted to make Wolf Paw tell him everything that had happened, but there was no time for that now. And after he heard Wolf Paw's tale, he might want to hurt him even more than he had to.

Raoul kept a naval six-pounder at the trading post; White Bear had heard about it. Probably this was a piece of what the long knives called canister shot or grapeshot in Wolf Paw's shoulder. But then why not a round hole?

White Bear slid the steel rod he would use to explore Wolf Paw's wound through a loop in the end of the tongs. To see how the brave was taking it, he looked up at his face. Wolf Paw stared back at him with hard black eyes as he pushed the probe into the wound with one hand, the other holding the handles of the tongs. When the rounded tip of the probe had gone in about half a finger's length, it touched something hard. Not a bone, White Bear was sure. He moved the probe up and down and from side to side. The only sign of pain Wolf Paw gave was deeper, heavier breathing.

How odd! The object was definitely flat and must have hit Wolf Paw edge on. It lay buried in a muscle. An inch higher and whatever it was would have broken Wolf Paw's shoulder. White Bear moved the tongs into position within the torn flesh, one end on each side of the flat object. His hand ached as he tightened his grip on the tongs. He had learned how to get a good grip on bullets, but the blood would make this flat missile slippery.

Wolf Paw was not breathing now. White Bear did not dare to look into his face. For both of them, White Bear understood, this was a moment of testing.

Holding his own breath, praying to Earthmaker to strengthen his grip on the tongs, White Bear began to pull.

Wolf Paw gave the faintest groan. Another man would probably be screaming.

The flat piece of metal came almost to the surface of Wolf Paw's blackened flesh, but slid out of the tongs' grip just as White Bear was about to draw it out. He gritted his teeth in anger.

Wolf Paw sighed. White Bear looked at his face and saw that only the whites of his eyes were showing under the half-closed lids. Mercifully—for both of them—he had fainted.

White Bear looked again at the object he was trying to pull out of Wolf Paw's shoulder. He could just see a corrugated edge covered with blood. With a bit of cloth he wiped the blood away and saw a bright silver gleam.

He gave a little gasp of amazement.

A silver coin. The last thing anyone would expect to find loaded into a cannon. Or embedded in a man's body. Those people at Victor must have been desperate.

That gave White Bear an inspiration. No one else was close enough to see what he had seen in the wound. He remembered what Owl Carver had said about showing the people magical powers.

He waited until he saw Wolf Paw's eyelids flutter and then said, "Wolf Paw, because you have allowed the pale eyes woman to live, the spirits will reward you."

Wolf Paw, his lips compressed, frowned at him.

"The spirits will allow me to change the lead ball the pale eyes shot into you to one of their silver coins." He spoke loudly so that the people watching could all hear him.

Wolf Paw stared, as White Bear passed his medicine stick three times in a sunwise circle over the bleeding shoulder.

Once again White Bear pushed the tongs into the wound. He pushed the ends in past the coin, to get a good purchase on it. Wolf Paw groaned. White Bear pulled.

Joy sprang up in him as he felt the silver coin coming free. He had it this time. The spirits might not have changed lead to silver, but they had made him skillful. The tongs came out holding an eight-real silver piece dripping with blood. White Bear held it up for all to see.

Wolf Paw's eyes grew round. The people cried out in amazement. Even Owl Carver looked astonished.

Delighted with the effect, White Bear wiped the blood from the Spanish dollar carefully with the rag from Nancy's dress. It shone in the afternoon sunlight, the head of the King of Spain on one side along with a Latin inscription and the date 1823. On the other side, a coat of arms.

Perfect! Now, he thought with pleasure, the braves and warriors and their wives would be more reluctant than ever to challenge him. And that meant Nancy would be safer.

He held the coin before Wolf Paw's face. "The form is the form of a pale eyes coin, but this is a gift from the spirits."

Wolf Paw, slowly sitting up, took the coin and said, "I will wear it around my neck. Maybe it will be a charm against more wounds."

"Let it remind you that it is honorable to treat prisoners kindly," said White Bear. He kept his face grave, but within he was bubbling over with triumph.

After stuffing the wound with buzzard's down and giving Wolf Paw herb tea to drink, White Bear sent him on his way. The brave stumbled off, leaning on Running Deer. White Bear stood up, stretched his tired arms and legs and turned to the doorway of his wickiup.

A painful moment of doubt assailed him. Was this what the way of the shaman came to, then? Trickery? Perhaps his visions, too, were only dreams. No, the White Bear spirit was real. He had seen the paw print beside his father's body. He bore the claw marks on his chest.

He had to force himself to stoop down, to step through the low doorway and face Nancy. He felt tremulous within. Whatever horrors Nancy had seen and endured, she would surely blame them on him. In all his paint and ornaments he was too obviously a Sauk.

And how would his efforts to protect Nancy and win her trust make Redbird feel? How could he make her truly understand what was between him and Nancy—and what was not?

He was not sure that he himself understood it.

In the light from the open doorway he saw Nancy, crouched on the opposite side of the round hut, trembling, still wrapped in the blanket Redbird had put on her. Redbird and Eagle Feather were sitting silently against the curving wall.

He sat down facing Nancy and she drew away, shuddering.

He said, "Don't be afraid of me, Nancy. I know I look strange to you. I'm the shaman, the medicine man, for my people."

"Your people!" she burst out. "Your people murdered my father!"

He had been afraid of that. He bowed his head and closed his eyes.

"Oh, Nancy. I'm sorry."

What a ridiculous, futile thing to say.

I must know what happened at Victor. Nancy's father was killed. Who else?

White Bear said, "Nancy, I don't ask you to forgive me for what my people did to you. But I did try to stop all this from happening. I pray you'll let me tell you how I tried to make peace. And you are safe now as long as you stay with me."

"Safe with you? Here?" She shuddered. "If I mean anything at all to you, you've got to help me to get away."

His heart sank. The one thing he was sure he could not do was have her set free.

"That will be hard."

"I heard you talking to them. You were ordering them to leave me alone, and they did. Tell them to let me go. Auguste, I'll go mad. I'm so frightened!"

She clutched at his arm. He could feel her fear pouring into his arm up to his heart. He put his hand on top of hers and held it firmly. He wanted to take her in his arms to comfort her, but Redbird's eyes were on him, and she would not understand. So he just patted Nancy's hand and released it.

He told Redbird what he had been saying to Nancy.

"Does she not see that the braves would kill you if you tried to set her free?" Redbird asked.

"She is too frightened to see anything," he said, and turned back to Nancy.

"The only man who can free you is Black Hawk. I'll try to convince him that he should, but he is away with a war party now."

"Killing more innocent men and women and children?" Her teeth and eyes gleamed in the faint light within the wickiup.

Her words left a hollow ache in his chest, but he went on speaking doggedly.

"When he comes back, I'll go to him. Meanwhile, ask your God to help you be brave."

She let go of his arm abruptly. "What do you know about my God, with your paint and your feathers and your magic wand?"

Her words hurt, and he was about to answer angrily, but he told himself she was half mad with terror and grief.

"Because I have these things I can help you," he said gently. "But I want so much to know what happened at Victor. Can you bear to tell me?"

She took his arm again. "I'd just gotten dressed to go out and feed the animals—when I saw the Indians riding toward our house. So many of them! I knew right away. I ran into the house and woke Father. By the time they got to the house he was standing in the doorway. He never even got his rifle loaded, Auguste. Before he could move there was an arrow in his chest."

White Bear knew that Reverend Hale had never liked him; but he was Nancy's father, and to see her father killed—how that must hurt her!

"He was a good man," he said. "He never did harm to our people. It is wrong that he died."

Nancy went on, sobbing softly. "I must have fainted. I remember a ride, I was thrown over the back of a horse, then we were at Victoire. Auguste, they—they just overran Victoire."

"Did anyone get away?"

"I think the people at Victoire must have seen our church and the farms burning, so they had some warning. I couldn't see much. I was left tied on the horse while they attacked. I did see them chase one woman and run a spear through her. It was over very quickly. They set fire to Victoire."

White Bear swallowed hard.

He saw the château with its magnificent hall and its great sweeping roof. There he had lived and learned so much from Grandpapa and Father. Their hopes, their lives, had gone into that great house. And the men and women of Victoire, kindly, cheerful hard-working people—Marchette Perrault, Registre and Bernadette Bosquet. They may not have tried to stop Raoul from seizing the estate, but they had, most of them, loved Elysée and Pierre and Auguste de Marion.

The pain in his chest spread till it seemed to fill his whole world, hammering at him inside and out.

Nancy said, "Then they rode on to Victor, taking me with them."

He choked as he asked, "Did they burn Victor down too?"

"Yes, as they left."

A voice seemed to echo inside him like a scream in a huge, empty hall.

Nicole! Frank! Grandpapa!

"Can you tell me—my family—were any of them hurt?"

Nancy said, "I think the people at Victor got into the trading post before the Indians got there. There were men on the palisade shooting at the Indians. The leader, the one with the red crest on his head, tied me to a tree. I had to watch it all."

"He is called Wolf Paw. He is Black Hawk's son."

"I hope the Army gets him and hangs him from the highest gallows in Illinois. He left me tied to that tree all day while they tried to take the trading post."

The words tumbled out faster and faster. When she had first regained consciousness she could hardly speak at all. Now her eyes glittered and she moved her hands violently. Hysteria had broken through her former numbness.

"I could see them using ropes to climb the palisade and charging in through the front gate. Every so often they would pull out some dead or wounded. Just before sunset the one you call Wolf Paw made a speech to them. Then they set fire to arrows and shot them at the blockhouse, and they all rushed in through the front gate. I thought that would be the end, but then I heard a tremendous explosion. I thought maybe somebody blew up the blockhouse. A big puff of smoke rose up over the palisade. Wolf Paw came out wounded. That very big man helped him put me on his horse and tie me there. And then we rode for four days till we got here."

Auguste began to breathe easier. He felt some relief, some hope, despite his pain for the loss of Victoire and for the people who had died there. It sounded as if many of the people of Victor, perhaps Nicole and her family, perhaps Grandpapa, might have come through unharmed.

But another fear took a grip on him. "On the way here, did Wolf Paw . . . hurt you, Nancy?"

"No. I think he was too tired and too badly hurt to want to do anything like that. We rode hard, and he kept me tied on his horse all the time. We stopped to sleep long after dark and started riding again before sunup. There was always at least one man awake to guard me."

All the while she had been talking, Nancy had kept a tight grasp on his arm. Now he gently pulled away from her and stood up.

"Nancy, I must leave you for a while."

"No!" Her voice was shrill with fear.

"I must. There are many wounded who need me."

Fearful of how she would react to what he was going to say next, he hesitated. Then he spoke quickly to get it over with, as he did when he had to hurt a patient. "This is my wife, Redbird. She will care for you."

"Your wife?" Even in the semidarkness of the wickiup White Bear could see pain in her eyes.

"Yes." He had no time now to ease her suffering on that score.

He turned to Redbird and said in Sauk, "Do what you can for her. She saw her father and many others of her people killed."

"I must know who she is," said Redbird, fixing him with her slanting eyes.

He laid a reassuring hand on her shoulder. "Have no fear. I will tell you everything, tonight. See that she eats. Give her maple sugar. Help her to rest."

White Bear spent the rest of the day moving through the wickiups under the trees with his Sauk medicine bag and his bag of pale eyes surgical instruments. Wolf Paw had brought back many wounded braves. Together with Sun Woman and Owl Carver, White Bear treated those he could and made the dying more comfortable. He went to the families of the braves and warriors who had been killed and tried to comfort them, performing rituals that helped them let their loved ones go, to walk west on the Trail of Souls.

By late afternoon White Bear was sick with disgust at the suffering and death this war had brought, and wanted nothing more than to go off by himself and weep for his people. Wolf Paw's raid had brought back cattle and horses, but nearly two dozen men had died and an equal number were badly hurt.

And all for what? To make the long knives hate us more.

At sunset another war party thundered in, this one led by Black Hawk himself, with the Winnebago Prophet riding beside him. And more wounded men to treat.

In the cool of the evening a delicious scent crept into White Bear's nostrils, one that neither he nor any of the British Band had smelled for far too long—roasting beef. Now that it was dark and smoke from fires could no longer be seen, people were roasting the cattle Wolf Paw had brought from Victoire. There were so many empty bellies to feed, they had probably butchered all the steers.

By rights those are my steers, White Bear thought wryly. *Raoul stole them from me, and Wolf Paw stole them from Raoul.*

White Bear saw many small fires throughout the camp. In time of peace a feast like this would call for one big fire, but that would send up a glow that could be seen from a distance.

He felt a surge of resentment when he saw how calm and contented Black Hawk looked, sitting at a fire before his wickiup, chewing on strips of beef his wife had laid before him on a mat.

Until today the people had been on the verge of starvation. And scouts had reported that an army of over two thousand long knives was working its way up the Rock River toward them. How could Black Hawk bear the responsibility for bringing so much anguish down on his people?

To White Bear's disappointment, the Winnebago Prophet sat next to Black Hawk. At the sight of Flying Cloud, with his long, greasy hair and the mustache that looked something like Raoul's, White Bear's shoulders slumped. He felt an impulse to turn away, and seek Black Hawk out another time.

The Prophet's Winnebago followers were long since gone, but the Prophet himself was still predicting mighty victories over the long knives. White Bear remembered a scripture reading he'd heard at St. George's, that false prophets would arise at the end of the world. This might well be the end of the world for the Sauk; they certainly had their false prophet.

But a talk with Black Hawk about Nancy was too important to put off. White Bear sat down, silently facing Black Hawk. He waited for the war leader to speak to him.

He felt ravenously hungry watching the two men chew their beef. He himself had not had time to eat.

Black Hawk's strong hand stroked the leather cover of one of the law books he had captured at Old Man's Creek.

"You healed my son and drew spirit silver from his body," Black Hawk said. "Accept my thanks."

"I am happy to have made Black Hawk happy."

Black Hawk gestured toward the beef. "Share my food."

White Bear picked up a strip of meat, still hot. Saliva seemed to flood his mouth. He chewed ferociously, closing his eyes for an instant in pleasure. Black Hawk smiled slightly, while Flying Cloud, paying no attention to White Bear, gnawed on a rib.

After a time during which White Bear could think of nothing but the hot, juicy meat, Black Hawk called him back to his reason for coming here.

"I am told you have a pale eyes woman prisoner."

"I came to speak to you about her," White Bear said, and silently asked his spirit self to help him persuade Black Hawk to let her go.

He told Black Hawk how he had convinced the people not to kill her.

"You did well," said Black Hawk. "We must make the long knives respect us, not just fear us. Warriors should not torture and kill prisoners. The great Shooting Star would never let his men torture prisoners."

White Bear felt a glow of pleasure at Black Hawk's approval. He felt more hopeful that Black Hawk might listen to him. He decided to plunge ahead with his request.

"If we give this woman back to the pale eyes, maybe they will talk peace with us."

The Winnebago Prophet stopped eating long enough to say, "Better to keep her. If the long knives attack us we can threaten to kill her."

Aware that Flying Cloud's argument made a kind of brutal sense, White Bear felt a sinking in his chest.

Black Hawk pursed his wide mouth thoughtfully. "The Prophet speaks wisely. It is foolish to give the woman to the long knives as a gift. We should hold her until we are ready to trade her for something." He turned his sombre gaze on White Bear. "You must keep her. You must not let her escape."

White Bear now had to go back to tell Nancy that the Sauk would not let her go. The thought of her terror and misery made him sick with sorrow for her.

And afraid for her too. Every day that the Sauk suffered hunger and illness, every time more men were killed, the women would want all the more to hurt the one pale eyes who was in their power. And the men would hunger to take pleasure with her fair-haired beauty. He could not guard her at every moment. How, then, could he keep her safe?

They sat in silence again. The Winnebago Prophet looked pleased with himself. Black Hawk was grim, probably brooding over how badly the war was progressing.

Desperate to protect Nancy, White Bear could think of only one way.

He said, "I want to make the pale eyes woman my wife."

Black Hawk's eyebrows rose. "Why should White Bear do that?"

"The people will not kill the wife of a shaman."

The Winnebago Prophet burst out, "This is wrong! The spirits have told me that our people must not mate with the pale eyes."

Black Hawk said, "White Bear's father was a pale eyes."

"The offspring of an impure mating should not be a shaman," Flying Cloud grumbled.

White Bear felt his cheeks burn; the Winnebago Prophet might as well have slapped him.

He remembered, so long ago it now seemed, though it was really only nine months, when Père Isaac, speaking at Pierre's funeral, had called White Bear "the fruit of sin." He had thought then that no red man would speak so demeaningly of his parentage, and here now was a shaman of the red men who did.

Black Hawk said, "White Bear has always been one of us. He has seen visions. He has saved many lives. The mark of the Bear, one of the most powerful spirits, is on him. Let him do as he thinks best."

The Prophet said, "The spirits have told me a man should not have more than one wife."

Black Hawk glared at him. "That is foolish talk. I have been content to have one wife, Singing Bird. But my son, Wolf Paw, has two wives, and many of our chiefs and braves have two or three wives. And when many men die in battle, many women need to be cared for."

Flying Cloud grunted and fell silent.

White Bear took his leave of Black Hawk and threaded his way among the shelters and past the small campfires where beef was still roasting on spits.

Redbird must agree to his plan before he could tell it to Nancy. He was afraid; afraid that she would say no, and afraid that his request would hurt her.

When he reached his wickiup he called Redbird out, and they walked through the camp together.

"Sun Woman is with the yellow-haired woman in the wickiup," Redbird said. "Sun Woman speaks to her in the pale eyes' language that she learned from your father. I think the yellow-hair is not so frightened anymore."

"That is good," said White Bear gloomily, "because Black Hawk says she must remain a prisoner."

Redbird sighed. "I feared he would say that."

They climbed a low hill north of the camp and sat on a huge half-buried boulder overlooking a small lake. A newly risen crescent moon was reflected in the still black water.

White Bear put his hand on Redbird's belly and felt the movement of the child within her.

Redbird said, "What is this woman to you?"

White Bear stiffened. Would she understand? Would she believe him?

White Bear searched his mind for a way to explain. "She was a friend to me when I lived at Victor."

"Was she your woman?" Redbird asked.

"No. She wanted to be, but I would not let it happen, because I knew that one day I must leave her."

And I feared that if I let myself love Nancy I would never return to my people, and to you.

"You did not even lie with her?"

"No."

"I would be foolish to believe that."

"I would tell you if I had done that. I did want to, and she wanted to, but I would not. Does it make you hate her to know she wanted that of me?"

Redbird's head was bowed so that he could not see her face. "You are a man many women would want. I cannot hate them all."

"When I asked you to untie Nancy today and take her to our wickiup, you could have refused me, as Running Deer did to Wolf Paw. Then the women would have cut her to pieces. I could not have stopped them. I thank you for honoring my wishes."

Redbird said, "You would have tried to stop them, and you would have been hurt. I did not want that to happen." She looked up at him suddenly, smiling. "And I knew that people would say, 'See, White Bear's wife does as he asks, but Wolf Paw's wife makes him look foolish.' It felt good to make Wolf Paw look foolish, after what he did to us."

It warmed him to hear her say "us."

"Now I want to do something more for her," he said. "But I can only do it if you will say yes to it." He held his breath.

Redbird said, "If you made her your wife, then no one in the band would dare to hurt her."

White Bear let out a deep sigh. He should have known her

thoughts would move as swiftly as his own. He had wondered how to say it to her, and she had said it for him.

"Only to protect her. Not to be truly my wife. Will you consent?"

She stroked the back of his hand. "I think it would be a good thing if we keep her safe. You and I did not want our people to fight and kill the pale eyes." She pressed her warm hand against his. "At least we can keep them from killing this one."

The ripples on the lake reflected fragments of moonlight. White Bear felt he could see his love for Redbird, and it looked like what lay before him—a lake of silver. He leaned against her, and her back rested against his arm.

"I promise you I will not bed with her."

She smiled at him again. "Why promise that?"

The question surprised him. "You are my true wife and the only wife I want." He recalled Black Hawk's loyalty to Singing Bird. That was the right way to live.

Redbird said, "If you do go to her in the night, I will understand. Especially now when I am so big and we cannot get together easily. I believe you when you say you love me more than her. But she is tall and has hair like gold and very white skin, and I am small and have brown skin. Perhaps the pale eyes in you would prefer her."

"I think the pale eyes in me and the Sauk in me are one. And that one prefers you."

She took his hand and moved it down her body till he felt the warm, soft place whence, in little more than a moon, their baby would emerge.

"I want to do this with you now," she whispered. "I think we can, if you go into me only a little way."

When Redbird and White Bear returned to their wickiup, the crescent moon had reached the high point of its trail across the sky. Within the simple shelter he and Redbird had built, it was too dark to see anyone.

His mother's voice whispered, "Eagle Feather and Yellow Hair are sleeping. She is terribly frightened, but she has been through so much she is exhausted."

"I thank you for helping her," White Bear whispered. "In the morning I must tell her that Black Hawk will not let her go."

"That makes me sad for her," said Sun Woman. "She is in such misery. I sense a strength in her, but this is a very bad time for her. You must not stop being kind to her, not even for a moment."

Sun Woman ducked out through the doorway of the wickiup.

Nancy was sleeping in Redbird's bed. Redbird and White Bear lay down together on his pallet of reeds and blankets, her back against his chest, and slept.

When White Bear's eyes opened, the faint light filtering through the layer of bark overhead let him see a figure sitting up across from him. Outside, he heard the sounds of the camp stirring, men and women calling to one another, horses stamping.

He felt a rush of pity as he recognized Nancy. What she must be feeling at this moment!

"Oh my God," he heard her say. "Lord Jesus, help me." It must have taken her a moment to realize where she was.

"Nancy," he said, trying to keep his voice calm and pleasant, "come with me and let us talk."

They left the wickiup and she walked through the camp with her eyes on the ground, too frightened, he supposed, to look about her. People stared, but White Bear wore a forbidding look, and they kept their distance.

She had on a doeskin dress that Sun Woman had given her, and she had done up her two blond braids the way she always had. He felt a little catch in his throat as he looked at her and remembered those not-accidental meetings on the prairie near Victoire.

Every so often as they walked along she twisted her shoulders inside the soft leather and rubbed her arms uncomfortably. They passed a group of warriors who had felled a big oak tree and were burning and scraping its inside to make a dugout. The men stopped work to watch her go by.

Seeing the way they looked at her, White Bear thought, *Yes, she must marry me.* He hoped he could persuade her that it would be the only way for her to be safe.

He led her to the western edge of the high ground on which the band had made their camp. They stopped when the earth underfoot turned soft and wet. Before them lay an expanse of reeds that vanished into morning mist.

"Did you talk to Black Hawk?" she asked, her voice trembling. "Can I get away from here?"

White Bear remembered Sun Woman's admonition to be kind to Nancy at every moment. He tried to think how best to tell her the bad news, how to add only the smallest possible amount of fear to her burden.

"Black Hawk is pleased that I stopped the people from hurting you yesterday," he began tentatively. "He said the white men despise Indians when they kill their prisoners."

Her lips trembled. "He's not going to let me go, is he?" she said, and sobs began to shake her body. When she was able, she turned pleadingly toward him. "Couldn't you do anything for me?"

White Bear spread his hands helplessly. "I talked to him as best I could." He tried to tell her something encouraging. "He just wants to keep you until he can talk to the soldiers and make some kind of a truce."

She drew away from him, her red-rimmed eyes wide. "A truce? Does Black Hawk really think he can make a truce? Don't you realize what *your people*, your brave Indians, have been doing all over the frontier? Burnings and massacres everywhere. I told you what they did at Victor. Do you think the soldiers would ever be willing to talk peace with Black Hawk now?"

White Bear had listened to the returning warriors' tales of victories over the long knives at Kellogg's Grove, at Indian Creek, along the Checagou-Galena road. In despair he had realized that what the Sauk saw as battles in a war to defend their homeland were, to the white people of Illinois, bloody and abominable crimes. Who, after all, had Black Hawk's war parties been killing? Some soldiers, but mostly farmers and their wives and children.

It tormented him now, as it did day and night, that no one could see the bloodshed as he did, with the eyes of both a white man and a Sauk. To him, what the Sauk were doing was horrible, but it was done out of a desperate need to cling to the land that meant life to them.

And Nancy's capture showed him how much his years among the pale eyes had changed him. Even if Wolf Paw had brought back a captive woman who was a stranger to him, he would have tried to save her. Nor could he feel that a people willing to torture any woman to death were fully *his* people.

Nancy shook her head. "There will be no truce, Auguste. They're coming to destroy you."

"We asked for peace," he began, "before all this killing started. I went with a white flag myself—"

Her chest heaved, and her face was a mottled red and white.

"They don't *want* peace with you. Your braves will kill me when they realize that. Or the soldiers will kill me when they kill all of your people."

"No!" he cried, knowing the truth in her words and fighting the agony within.

"Let me go!" she screamed.

She suddenly whirled away from him and threw herself into the reeds. She tried to run, and in a moment was in water up to her hips. Frantically battering at the tall water grasses, she struggled to keep going. The mist was beginning to swallow her up.

Too surprised to move, White Bear stood watching her for a moment. She would surely die out there in the marsh, and she didn't realize it. He plunged into the marsh after her. He drove his legs through the cold water. The mud sucked at his moccasins. By the time he caught up with her, he was barefoot.

He threw his arms around her. She thrashed about, turned and struck at his face with her fists. Her eyes were wild, like a trapped fox's, her cheeks bright red, her mouth twisted and quivering.

"I've got to get away!"

"Nancy, you can't." They were waist deep in water, and he felt his feet sinking into the mud.

He grabbed her shoulders and shook her as hard as he could. "Listen to me!"

She went limp in his arms, and he had to hold her up.

"I can't stay here. I won't let them kill me!"

He pulled her toward dry ground, the cold water swirling around them, slimy mud tugging at their feet.

When they were out of the water, dripping, he said, "If there were any way you could escape from here, I'd help you. If you try to get away, you'll die. There are miles of swamp in every direction. Only Black Hawk and a few braves know the way out. You'd drown or be buried alive in quicksand. Or the warriors would catch you, and they would kill you no matter what I did. And they'll kill me if I help you try to escape."

"I'll die if I stay here." Her eyes were dull with hopelessness.

"No you won't. I'll take care of you. My family will protect you—Redbird, Sun Woman, Owl Carver, Iron Knife. You'll be safe with me."

She leaned against him. "Auguste, I can't bear being so frightened. My heart is so full of fear it will burst."

"The band will not free you, but they will not hurt you. They respect me. I talk to the spirits for them and heal them."

She took a long look at him and spoke more calmly. "You look so strange, dressed like a—like a—"

"Like a real Indian?" He tried giving her a little smile. For an instant a little life came back into her face.

I can heal her fear, too, if she will let me.

He felt an inward glow as she managed to return a tremulous smile.

She said, "But you're still that fine young gentleman who charmed me so, back at Victor, aren't you?"

"Yes, I'm that man too." He looked down at her bare feet. "You've lost your moccasins. We must get you another pair." And she was lucky not to have a leech or two clinging to her feet; so was he. His moccasins were lost too. Clothing would be hard to come by, with the band on the run in strange country, but he need not make her feel worse by telling her that.

"I have to resign myself to staying with your people, don't I?" she asked. "Thank God you're here, Auguste. Maybe it was Providence that your uncle stole your estate from you."

Yes, Earthmaker's way is surprising, he thought.

"One thing I must ask of you, Nancy. For your protection, you and I must go through a wedding ceremony. Then no one will be allowed to bother you."

"A wedding!" She let go of him and stepped away quickly.

His heartbeat quickened with anxiety over her apparent shock.

"Nothing to be afraid of. A simple ceremony." He recalled his wedding to Redbird last fall. He might be a shaman, but he'd not had the slightest premonition that he would go through the same ceremony with a different woman less than a year later.

"But you already have a wife. That pretty little woman who is . . . expecting." She reddened. "You told me she was your wife." Soaking wet, she turned forlornly away from him.

"In our tribe men may have more than one wife."

He expected to see contempt in her eyes, her pale eyes' morality outraged.

Instead she said sadly, "Is she the reason you would not do what I wanted the night you left Victor? Were you married to her even then?"

He had to force the words out. "No, but I did love her even then. And she— That blue-eyed boy you've seen in our wickiup—he is our son. He was born after my father took me to Victoire."

She shook her head, the blond braids swinging. "You were honest with me. You didn't tell me about Redbird, but you didn't make a fool of me, as another man might have. A man like your uncle. But how does your wife feel about me?"

What did she mean, *A man like your uncle?* Had Raoul approached her? He put that question aside while he framed an answer to her question.

"Redbird agrees to this wedding. She, too, wants to help you. If you are part of our family you will be protected. She wants that."

She stared at him. "But I'm a Christian! I can't go through a pagan wedding ceremony to be your *second wife.* How could I do that to my father, a minister?"

He tried to sound reassuring. "We will all know, you and I and Redbird, that it is not a real marriage. I've no doubt your Christian God will see and understand. And your father, if he sees you, surely he wants you to live."

No, Philip Hale, as I remember him, might well expect her to die for her faith. He might well want his daughter to join him in the other world. But never mind.

He went on quickly, "Of course, you will not have to—know me, as your Bible says. In the sight of the tribe you will be my wife, that is all. In our wickiup your virtue will be respected."

She laughed ruefully, but tears were running down her cheeks. "Oh, Auguste, remember how I begged you to marry me? I even prayed for it, would you have imagined that? And now my prayer has been answered. Only it didn't turn out exactly the way I hoped, did it?"

White Bear's heart filled up with a dark foreboding. Nothing had turned out as any of them hoped, but much had happened as they feared.

17

Uncle Sam's Men

Tears filled Raoul's eyes, blurring the newspaper and the letter on his candlelit camp table. His hands were cold as a corpse's as he pressed them against the sides of his head.

Oh, God! A drink! I need a drink!

He reached for the jug beside the letter. A hand lifted the tent flap and Eli Greenglove slouched in.

The sight of him frightened Raoul. Did he know yet?

Not much chance there'd be a letter for Eli in the sack of two-week-old mail that had just caught up with Raoul's battalion. No one in Victor likely to write to Eli. Not now.

Eli's mouth was drawn hard. It was a hot night, and he wore no jacket, only a plain brown calico work shirt, with a pistol and a knife at his wide brown belt.

"Levi Pope got a letter from his missuz. There was an Injun raid on Victor. You hear anything?" Eli's voice was as flat as the prairie. He sat on Raoul's camp trunk.

"Yes," Raoul said, choking on the single word. "A war party attacked Victoire."

He took a swallow from the jug. A cold, aching space was growing in the pit of his stomach. The whiskey settled in the middle of the ache like a tiny campfire in the middle of a blizzard.

He handed the jug to Eli, and Eli sipped and put the jug back on the table.

"Goddammit, don't just sit there staring at me." Eli displayed his ruined teeth as his lip curled back in a snarl. *"What 'n hell happened?"*

321

Raoul picked up the letter in a shaking hand and read aloud—
horrible words, written in a flowing black script.

" 'It is my sad duty as your sister to send you the news that
Clarissa Greenglove and your two sons have perished at the hands
of Indians.' "

"Oh, Lord God an' Savior," Eli groaned. His head fell back on
his neck, his mouth open. His Adam's apple stuck out.

" 'Also that our beloved Victoire has burned to the ground.' "
Raoul went on:

"Clarissa and Andrew and Philip, along with other people who
lived at Victoire and in Victor, were murdered on the morning
of June seventeenth.

"In your sorrow, may it comfort you to know that your
fortified trading post, where we took shelter and defended ourselves, saved the lives of most of us. The cannon that you set in
the blockhouse was employed to good effect, even though we
hesitated at first to use it, since no one here knew how to fire
such a weapon. Nevertheless, fire it we did, and broke the Indians' last charge and drove them off.

"Mr. Burke Russell, whom you placed in charge of the trading post, was killed whilst fighting on the parapet. Mr. David
Cooper, whom you also appointed as caretaker, gave us the
leadership and strength we badly needed to see us through. He
was the only experienced fighting man among us.

"I cannot bear to write more. The sights we saw when we
came out of the blockhouse will haunt my dreams forever.

"Though the Indians could not lay hands on our bodies, they
destroyed our property. Our house was burned down and our
printing press and woodworking machines ruined.

"When it was all over, Frank rode to Galena, though I
begged him not to, for fear there were Indians yet lurking about.
But he must needs publish his paper. He arranged to have an
edition of the *Visitor* printed on the press of the Galena *Miners
Gazette*, and brought the copies back here on a wagon. I am
sending you a copy of the paper under this cover. Frank's account will tell you everything there is to know about the raid,
and more perhaps than you would wish to know.

"Our father is well. He and Guichard fought bravely in our
defense.

"I do not reproach you. My heart goes out to you, Brother, for I know you must be suffering. Remember that all happens as God ordains. May He grant you peace."

What the hell does she mean, "All happens as God ordains?" God wanted my woman and my kids murdered by Indians?

"Oh, Christ Jesus," Eli said. He shook his head, then resting his elbows on his knees, pressed his hands to the top of his head.

Even Papa had to fight.

Raoul's heart felt bruised, as if beaten with a hammer.

I do not reproach you. That was reproach enough. He had taken every man who would sign up for the militia. He had promised them their wives and children would be safe. He'd led them away in pursuit of Black Hawk, vengeance and glory.

Eli looked up. "What does it say in the newspaper?"

Raoul started to hand it to him.

"You read it to me."

Raoul had forgotten that Eli couldn't read. Clarissa couldn't either. Now she'd never learn. Nor would the boys.

He shook his head and brushed his hand across his forehead. "I *can't* read this out loud."

Greenglove's eyes were hard as bullets. "You wipe your damned eyes and read that damned newspaper."

Raoul rubbed his eyes and took another pull from the jug. Greenglove held out his hand and Raoul passed him the jug.

Raoul picked up the newspaper, hating the sight of it, and began to read the column headed with the single word, MASSACRE!

Frank's story told how the people in the trading post held the Indians off all day and finally drove them away by firing the cannon. Then came the grievous task of finding and burying those who had not had time to reach safety.

Then, for Raoul, the most dreadful lines of all:

In the ashes of Victoire, it appeared from examination of the charred remains that the skulls of the men and women had been cloven by tomahawk blows. Parts of the children's bodies were scattered about the ruins, as if they had been chopped to bits before the Indians set fire to the great house.

Why hadn't Clarissa gotten away? She'd taken to drinking heavily in the last year, so much so that he'd had to hit her more than once for letting the boys run loose without keeping an eye on them. She had probably been lying abed in a drunken stupor while everyone was fleeing the château, the boys sleeping in the room with her. Hadn't anyone tried to wake them?

Those faithful French servants who loved Elysée and Pierre so much, they didn't give a damn about Raoul's whore and his bastard sons. After all, he had thwarted Pierre's dying wishes. And he had struck his aged father with his fist in front of all those Victoire people.

Still, they'd have been human enough to try to do *something*. If they'd had time. They'd holler and bang on the door. Try to wake them up. But there wouldn't have been time. A hundred or more Indians galloping down on the château. The servants who saw them coming would barely have time to get away. Some of them hadn't made it. Some of them had died with Clarissa and the boys; maybe the ones who'd stayed behind to try to warn them.

That was how it must have been.

Frank's article in the *Visitor* said that some of the people in the distant farms had saved themselves by hiding in root cellars or in nearby woods. The Indians were in too much of a hurry to get to Victor to bother searching carefully. One family, the Flemings, had ridden to the shut-down lead mine. Some Indians pursued them to the mine but didn't follow them in. The Flemings hid so deep in the mine they had trouble finding their way out again, but they did survive.

But one person had neither hidden nor been killed:

While the body of the Reverend Philip Hale, D.D., was found in the burnt wreckage of his house, his daughter, Miss Nancy Hale, has not been found. It is feared Miss Hale may have been kidnapped by the Indians. Both the church and the house Reverend Hale built on the prairie were burned down.

As Raoul read aloud the list of the dead, he thought of Nancy and then of his sister Helene. Did they do *that* to Nancy? The red devils! Probably did. Horrible!

He saw the naked, slashed, violated body lying on the prairie. Nancy Hale's body. Just like Helene's.

But it could be, too, she was alive. And if he kept after Black Hawk, he might be the one to rescue her. There was comfort in that.

A little comfort.

And then a black bile of hatred for himself trickled up into his throat.

Great God in Heaven, this man he was sitting with—he'd had this man's daughter in his bed for six years. And now she was murdered. And already he was figuring how to replace her.

Maybe I am as bad a man as Papa said I was.

That's what Nicole meant by "All happens as God ordains." This was to punish me.

He took a drink to wash that thought away.

He winced when he came to the name Marchette Perrault on the list of dead. Maybe she had died trying to help Clarissa. Did Armand know yet?

Eli stood up. "Well, poor Clarissa. Poor little boys. It was a black day in our lives when Clarissa and me met up with you, Raoul de Marion."

The words tore at a wound that was fresh and bleeding.

"Look here, now, Eli. Don't you know that I feel as bad as you do?"

"No, I don't know that. Clarissa was all I had in the world. I kept hoping you'd find it in your heart to marry her, but you never treated her decent. Never cared enough for them kids to give them your name. Your brother, he did more for that half-Injun son of his than you did for your two that was all white."

All white they were, but half Puke, Raoul thought, feeling his disdain for the man who stood slumped before him.

Puke, a good nickname for Greenglove's breed. Missouri puked up the worst of its people, and they landed in Illinois. Clarissa's breasts flattening and sagging, her shoulders round, her teeth stained by pipe smoke. So slatternly she'd gotten to be, he hardly cared to take her to bed. And Phil and Andy growing up with that same washed-out, weak-boned Greenglove look.

How could I think that way about my own kids? What kind of a man am I? And now they've been murdered, and I'm still despising them.

He had to quit this. He was torturing himself. Wasn't it bad enough? It was the goddamned Indians he should be hating.

"We'll have our revenge, Eli. We'll kill a hundred Indians for each of ours who died."

"Like you murdered them three at Old Man's Creek. I warned you not to do that. That was what got Clarissa and her kids killed. I won't be helping you get your vengeance, Colonel Raoul de Marion. Because if I did stay around you, sooner or later I'd want blood for blood of mine that's been spilled."

Raoul felt a chill, facing Greenglove's implacable, dull-eyed hatred. But he was damned if he'd back down before this human weed.

"You'll leave this company when your term of enlistment is up and not one damned day sooner. You're captain of the Smith County company."

Greenglove's mouth curled in a cold smile.

"By tomorrow there won't be any company. The Smith County boys heard about what happened at Victor. Most of them'll be quitting."

Raoul felt the heat rising in his neck and head.

"The hell they will! My Smith County boys will want Indian blood just like I do. And just like you would if you hadn't taken a notion to blame Clarissa's death on me."

Auguste. The half-breed. Raoul felt his blood boiling as he saw the olive-skinned face mingling Pierre's features with Indian looks. The face he'd never stopped hating from the moment he first saw it. Auguste was dead. Eli, here, had shot him. His body was rotting away somewhere on the prairie behind them.

But the Indians of the British Band were alive—Auguste's people. They snuck up on Victoire, Raoul's home. Burned it to the ground. Tomahawked his woman. Chopped his children, his two boys, Andy and Phil, to pieces.

To pieces.

He saw that, for a moment, too vividly, and almost screamed. He grabbed the jug and burned the bloody picture out of his mind with a swallow.

Auguste's band, skulking around up the river somewhere.

Why, Auguste might have given them the idea. Told them all about Victoire and Victor. Lots of helpless women and children there. A rich trading post. A big white man's house to burn down.

My uncle kicked me off the land, Auguste might have said. *Avenge me. Go kill his woman and his children and burn his house down. And while you're at it, kill every one of those white dogs in Smith County.*

Sure, he probably put the idea in those devils' heads before he got shot.

It hadn't been enough to kill Auguste. Wasn't enough.

He had to kill off every last one of Black Hawk's Indians. Exterminate the whole band—bucks, squaws and papooses.

And he would shoot any shirker who refused to go with him.

Greenglove shrugged. "Go chase Injuns, then, if that's your heart's desire." Then he smiled in a knowing way Raoul found strangely disturbing. "But you'll maybe find a surprise waiting for you up there in Michigan Territory. Almost makes me want to stay with you, just so's I could see the look on your face."

Raoul felt a chill. Why the hell was Greenglove grinning like that?

"Damn you, you can't just walk off, Eli! You took an oath. You signed up for another thirty days when your enlistment was up in May. I can have you shot for desertion."

"Go ahead. Shoot me yourself."

Eli slowly raised the tent flap and stood there a moment, turning to give Raoul one last, strange, unmirthful smile. Raoul eyed the pistol at Eli's belt. Most likely all primed and loaded. His own pistol, unloaded, was hanging from a tent pole behind him.

If I went for my pistol, that'd give him an excuse to put a ball in me. And he'd do it before I could even get a damned cap in place.

Eli gave Raoul one final nod, as if he knew what Raoul had been thinking, and let the tent flap fall behind him.

Raoul reached for the jug. It felt light in his hand, and he shook it. Empty.

Everything. Empty, empty, empty!

He got up, weaving slightly, and walked to the opening of the tent.

"Armand!" he shouted.

Oh my God, now I'll have to give Armand the news about Marchette.

Raoul awakened, sweating. One side of his tent was glowing white, the sun beating down on it; he had been sleeping in an oven. He sat up, and his vision went black and his head spun. He swung his feet, still in dirty gray stockings, over the side of his cot. He nearly stepped on Armand, who was lying flat on his back on the straw-covered floor, his beard fluttering as he snored through his open mouth.

Standing, Raoul saw Nicole's letter and the *Victor Visitor* lying on his camp table beside a burned-down candle and four empty jugs. He remembered what had happened at Victor. He fell back onto his cot and pounded his fist on his chest, trying to numb the pain in his heart.

God damn the Sauk! Damn them! Damn them!

Armand, when he learned what happened at Victoire, had not blamed Raoul as Eli had. He'd wept over Marchette—whom he'd beaten almost daily when she was alive—and had sworn vengeance on her murderers, the British Band. And he had sat with Raoul till both of them were drunk enough to sleep.

Raoul's head and body felt as if they were on fire. His fingers curled, grasping at empty air.

He buckled on his belt with his pistol and his Bowie knife, stumbled out of his tent and stood beside it, pissing in the tall grass.

He was facing the Rock River, less than a quarter-mile wide here, a sheet of sparkling blue water bordered by forest. Lined up along the bank before him were a dozen big box-shaped flatboats. The tents of his own militia battalion and of two others were spread over the grassland around him.

He suddenly sensed that something was wrong. He hadn't heard the bugler blow the dozen notes signaling the start of the day. He saw now that the men weren't assembled but were wandering aimlessly about the camp.

What the hell was it Greenglove had said?

By tomorrow there won't be any company.

Down near the flatboats a big crowd was gathered. One man, standing on a barrel, was addressing them. His voice, shrill and insistent, carried to Raoul on the warm June air, but he couldn't make out what the man was saying.

Raoul didn't like this. He didn't like this at all.

He started walking toward the river and found Levi Pope and Hodge Hode squatting in front of a fire, making coffee simply by boiling water with coffee grounds in it.

"Sorry for your loss, Colonel," said Pope.

Hearing Pope speak of what happened at Victoire was like being kicked in a spot that was already bruised. Raoul had to pause a moment before he could speak.

"Thank you. Your family come through all right?" He dreaded what he might hear in answer.

"Your sister wrote a letter for my missuz," Pope said. "They came through tolerably. Thanks to the way you fortified the trading post. That was mighty foresighted, Colonel."

Raoul's chest expanded and he felt a little better. This was how he'd hoped the men would react, not blaming him for the tragedy as that bastard Greenglove had.

"Levi's letter told as how my boy Josiah made it to the trading post too," Hodge said. "Mr. Cooper even let him do some shootin' at the redskins."

Mr. Cooper? Since when did David Cooper get to be so high and mighty?

"I need some of that coffee," Raoul said. Hodge strained the grounds out of the coffee by pouring it through a kerchief into a tin cup and handed the cup to Raoul.

The black liquid scalded Raoul's lips and tongue, and didn't treat him any better when it bit into his whiskey-burned stomach.

"Anything to eat?"

With a bitter grunt, Levi Pope took a square biscuit out of a paper wrapper and held it out. "These worm cakes is pretty lively, but dip 'em in the coffee a couple of times and you'll boil the little buggers to death."

Raoul shut his eyes and waved the weevil-riddled hardtack away.

"What the hell is that bunch doing down by the river?"

Hodge Hode grinned. "They call it a 'pub-lic in-dig-nation' meeting." He drawled out the words, amused. "Say they won't go across the river into Michigan Territory. Say they want to go home."

"Any of our men talking that way?"

"Oh, a heap of them, Colonel," said Levi.

"I'll see about that."

"Hodge and me ain't quittin'. We won't go home till we've killed us some Injun trash." Levi lovingly stroked the handles of his six holstered pistols, three on each side of his belt.

But Levi and Hodge made no move to get up and join Raoul.

They would go with him across the river, he saw, but they were not about to help him discipline the other men. He thought of ordering them to come with him, but decided not to test their loyalty that far. Eli had walked out on him. He didn't know who he could trust.

Hell, he could do it without these two, anyway.

For reassurance Raoul took a grip on the handle of his Bowie knife as he approached the crowd. Could he cow dozens of men if they were determined not to obey him?

Sure. Might have to carve a few bellies, but the rest will fall into line.

That was how he ran Smith County.

The man standing on the barrel was saying, "You know what the Injuns call that country up there? The Trembling Lands. It's all swamp, water and quicksand. You take a horse out on what looks like solid ground, before you can blink, he sinks belly deep."

That kind of talk made Raoul want to use his knife. But that would probably only rile these rebellious bastards all the more.

Got to put a stop to this. Line them all up by the boats. Tell the first man to get in. If he won't, shoot him. Then go on to the next. That'll change their minds in a hurry.

He told himself disgustedly to quit dreaming. Not even in Smith County could he get away with shooting white men just because they wouldn't obey him. Not in broad daylight, anyway.

The man standing on the barrel said, "If Black Hawk has holed up in that country, that means he's finished. Hell, his people will starve to death up there. What do we got to follow him for?"

Pushing his way through the crowd, Raoul heard a man near him call out, "Volunteers is what we are. That means we serve at our own pleasure. Well, I'm not volunteering for any more."

A chorus—"Right!" "Yeah!" "Me neither!" "That's telling 'em!"— rose all around Raoul, maddening him as a swarm of biting flies would madden a horse.

He saw a familiar stoop-shouldered back in the crowd—Justus Bennett. Ever since Old Man's Creek, Bennett had been whining about the fine suit of clothes and the two expensive law books he'd lost, demanding that the state of Illinois pay for them. Now he was standing here, encouraging would-be deserters just by listening to them.

Raoul grabbed his shoulder and pulled him around. "You're a

lawyer. You know damned well this meeting is illegal. Get over there with Pope and Hode, or you're no more a lieutenant in my battalion."

Bennett stared back at him with beady eyes. "That's immaterial, seeing as we're all going home."

"No one's going home," said Raoul, loud enough to make the men around him turn to look. "Get the hell back to your outfit."

He gave Bennett a shove. The lawyer glowered at him, but slunk away.

Raoul pushed his way to the front of the crowd. The men fell back, making way for his blue jacket with its officer's gold stripes. But the sun beat down on his head. He realized that he had forgotten to put on his hat, and he wasn't shaved and his jacket was unbuttoned.

And, nothing. Hell, he could handle men. He didn't have to dress up for that. He drew his knife and faced the man on the barrel.

"Get down off there."

"Now listen, Colonel, this is a public meeting."

Raoul waved the knife. "You've had your say. Jump."

The man stared defiantly at Raoul. Raoul thought he might have to cut him up a little, and wondered if he was up to it. The man's eyes wavered from Raoul's down to the thirteen-inch blade. And he jumped.

But he wasn't quite done talking. "It's a free country, Colonel. Man's got a right to speak his mind."

Raoul said, "Tell that to Black Hawk."

He wasn't quite sure what he meant by that, but he heard several chuckles and was encouraged.

He scrambled up on the three-foot-high barrel. It rocked under him, and the dregs of whiskey sloshing around in his body made him feel dizzy. He decided, after he got his feet set near the rim of the barrel, that he would be safer if he sheathed his knife.

"You men's term of enlistment is not up. Any man who won't cross that river is a coward and a deserter, and I'll see you're dealt with."

"Go to hell!" one man shouted.

"You talk about cowards," another man called. "Didn't your whole battalion run all the way from Old Man's Creek to Dixon's Ferry, from forty Injun bucks?"

"They don't call it Old Man's Creek no more," a raucous voice cried. "Now it's de Marion's Run."

Raoul pulled his knife again.

"The man who said that about de Marion's Run—come up here and say it again." He shook the knife.

"Quit wavin' that pig sticker around and get down off that barrel, de Marion. We heard enough from you." Raoul saw a rifle pointed at him. The blood pumping through his body suddenly went from hot to cold.

A new voice broke in.

"Lower that rifle!"

The tone was deep, easy and confident in command. It offered no alternative. The rifle came down as quickly as if in response to a drill sergeant's order.

A short, plump officer with thick black eyebrows came up to stand beside Raoul's barrel. He wore a stained, broad-brimmed wool hat and a blue Army jacket over fringed buckskin trousers. The gold stripes on his upper arm identified him as a colonel. The saber at his side nearly dragged on the ground. He might have been comical looking, but somehow he wasn't. Raoul had seen the officer at command meetings and knew that despite his mixed dress, he was Regular Army. This morning, though, he couldn't remember his name.

Movement in the distance caught Raoul's eye. A long line of blue-uniformed troops was marching across the prairie about a hundred yards away, their shakoes bobbing. They came to a halt, turned and faced the militiamen. They came to parade rest, each man with a rifle at his side. The morning sun glittered on bayonets.

Some militiamen glanced over their shoulders at the line of Federal soldiers, and a nervous muttering of "Bluebellies!" spread through the crowd.

"You can get down from there now, Colonel de Marion," said the short officer. "I'd appreciate it if you'd let me handle this."

Raoul hated to admit it to himself, but he was relieved. Crouching slowly and carefully, so as not to make an ass of himself by falling, he climbed down from the barrel.

"That's Zachary Taylor," Raoul heard someone in the crowd say as he moved, now unnoticed, to stand apart on the riverbank. Raoul felt foolish that he had forgotten Taylor's name, especially when Taylor knew his.

Instead of standing on the barrel, Taylor hitched himself up and sat on it, gesturing in a friendly way to the men to gather around him.

He spoke with an easy southern drawl, but he made his voice carry.

"Now, men, I don't set myself up as your superior, even though I am a Federal officer. We're all equal Americans here." He nodded as if thinking something over. "In fact, many of you are important men in civilian life, and I have no doubt some of you will hold public office and be giving orders to *me* some day."

Raoul's eyes traveled over the crowd, and he noticed one figure taller than most, eyes grave as he listened intently to Taylor. That Lincoln fellow, who had been such a nuisance at Prophet's Town. Raoul wondered if the young man was for or against crossing the Rock River today.

Taylor said, "The best assurance you have that I'll obey your orders when it comes your turn is that I'm obeying the orders I've got now. I will tell you in a moment what those orders are. But let me refresh your memory about what Black Hawk and his savages have done to the people you and I are sworn to defend."

He pulled a folded paper from the side pocket of his blue jacket and read from it.

"One man killed at Bureau Creek. One man at Buffalo Grove, another at the Fox River. Two on the Checagou Road. A woman and two men killed on the outskirts of Galena. Apple River Fort besieged, four dead. Seven men massacred at Kellogg's Grove. Three whole families, fifteen people, wiped out at Indian Creek. Victor besieged, and seventeen men, women and children massacred."

Raoul saw the shamefaced glances of men who knew him shift his way. He looked down at the ground angrily. He didn't want these men pitying him.

But an image of burned and scattered flesh and bones reared up suddenly in his mind. It struck at him like a rattlesnake. He almost threw up. He clenched his fists and held himself rigid.

One man called out, "Colonel Taylor, that's why we don't want to cross the state line. The Indians are attacking all over the place, and we want to be back home to protect our people."

Taylor nodded. "That's understandable. But I've been fighting Indians for a long time. I came up against old Black Hawk nearly twenty years ago in the war against the British. I've got a score to settle with him, because he whipped me then, and I promise you he will not whip *us* this time. Yes, that's wild country up there, no doubt about it. But we'll have a band of Potawatomi scouts led by one of their chiefs, Billy Caldwell, to guide us. And General Winfield Scott is coming across the Great Lakes with five hundred more Federal troops. With all that help, we'll finish Black Hawk.

"And we must finish him. The murders and massacres will not stop as long as Black Hawk and his tribe are on the loose. If you go back to your farms and settlements, there'll be a dozen of you in one place and twenty in another. And one morning or night you'll find yourself facing a war party of a hundred, hundred fifty braves, like the people at Apple River and Victor did. Our strength is in our numbers, and while we are three thousand and more together, we've got to seek out the British Band of the Sauk and Fox and destroy them."

Raoul heard a murmur of assent. His heart lifted. The little colonel was winning them over, and the war would go on.

"In plain English, gentlemen and fellow citizens, my orders from Washington City are to pursue Black Hawk wherever he goes, and to take the Illinois militia with me. I mean to do both. Now, there are the flatboats drawn up on the shore." He paused, then slid down from his perch on the barrel and, standing very straight, pointed over their heads. "And here are Uncle Sam's men, drawn up behind you on the prairie."

Taylor was so short that only the men near him could see where he was pointing. They turned first, and then in an ever-widening ring the men in the farther reaches of the crowd turned to look at the long, blue-clad line stretched behind them like a chain.

Raoul heard resignation in the militiamen's voices.

"Boys, I'm for the flatboats."

"Me too. I signed up to fight Injuns, not Americans."

A man called out, "Hell, Colonel, we're *all* Uncle Sam's men."

Taylor smiled, reached up to settle his mottled hat on his head, and said, "Then I will be proud to lead you."

He strode through the assembly.

At the edge of the crowd he turned and raised his voice. "Officers, assemble your men. We'll take the troops over first, then the horses. I want everyone on the other side by noon."

Taylor walked over to Raoul, squinted at him and sniffed audibly.

"You look like the backside of hell, sir. You been drinking this early in the day?"

"I haven't touched whiskey this morning," Raoul said, not adding that it was only because when he woke up all the jugs in his tent were empty.

"Well, then you were drinking damned late last night. Appearing in front of these unruly men looking like a sot is no way to get them to obey you."

Raoul eyed the short colonel's mismatched uniform parts and wondered where he got the gall to criticize. But he wanted to be on this man's good side.

"My wife and two sons were murdered by the redskins. At Victor. They've been dead for two weeks, and I just found out about it last night."

Taylor reached out and gripped his arm. "Damn! I am sorry, Colonel de Marion. I should have realized you might have lost loved ones there. I'll see that *you* get leave to go home."

Back to Victor? Raoul trembled at the thought of having to see the ruins of Victoire and the town—the graves of Clarissa and Phil and Andy. Having to face people who, like Eli, might believe that he put them in harm's way. Besides, he had a mission to carry out. Kill Indians. And there were no Indians to kill in Victor now.

"No, Colonel, no," he stammered. "I want to go after Black Hawk's people. We can't let them get away."

"Nor will we. General Atkinson and I were talking about that just yesterday—and about you, as it happens. You own a Mississippi steamboat, don't you?"

Puzzled, Raoul answered, "Yes, the *Victory*. It makes a regular run from St. Louis to Galena."

"We're certain that if we don't catch up with Black Hawk, wherever he's hiding up in the Michigan Territory, that he'll try to take his band west, to the Mississippi. If he gets across it, we'll have a hell of a time catching him." Taylor's eyes glinted hard as glass marbles. "We are determined, Colonel, not to allow him to make a successful retreat. We have to show all the tribes that they can't murder white people and then light out for Indian country and get off scot-free."

Taylor's words, now that the near-mutiny was over, lifted Raoul's heart. He had left Victor in April hoping for revenge for Helene and for his own sufferings of years ago. But now there were more slaughtered innocents to avenge—and now he had the army of the United States to help him do it.

"I'll do anything to get those redskins."

"With your ship patrolling the stretch of river where they're likely to cross, we could be sure that Black Hawk won't escape us."

"You want me to go back and get the *Victory* ready?" He felt himself trembling again.

"For now you'll go along with us into the Michigan Territory," Taylor said. "But if it looks as if Black Hawk is making a run for the Mississippi, you'll see that we cut them off. The *Victory*, eh? Aptly named."

Raoul's grieving, vengeful heart rejoiced. When the time came, he'd have the cannon from the trading post mounted in the bow of the *Victory*. Then let any damned Indians try to cross the Mississippi. He'd pay them back for what they did to Victoire.

But he remembered Nicole and Frank coming to him, telling him the militia was needed to guard Victor. He'd laughed at their fears. If he'd listened to them, Clarissa and Andy and Phil and those other people might still be alive. Victoire and Victor would still be standing. Hadn't he had some hand in bringing death and destruction upon his home?

No, it was all the Indians' doing.

I'll get you, Black Hawk. If I have to follow you all the way to Hudson's Bay. There won't be a one of your damned British Band left alive when I'm done.

He would make them suffer. From this moment on, he had only one thing to think of and only one thing to do: kill Indians.

BOOK 3

1832

Moon of Strawberries

June

18

The Trembling Lands

Redbird thought, *Our land by the Rock River was so good to us, and now see what we have come to.*

Only starving people tried to make food from cattail seeds and the inner bark of slippery elm and willow trees.

With a small steel knife Redbird cut cattails, dropping them into a basket she carried over her arm. It would take thousands of the tiny seeds, painstakingly picked from the white fuzz and then ground into meal, to make a little bread that must be shared among five people.

Redbird moved slowly, pushing her swollen belly before her. As much as her back and her feet hurt, she was determined to spend every day out foraging until the baby was born. For the baby's sake she had to eat as much as she could, but she did not want to take that extra portion from the rest of her family without contributing as much as she could to the common supply.

She sang as she walked along, asking the Trembling Lands to yield fruits and berries. She found no fruits or berries, but singing kept her spirits up, and she thought it helped the others too. Yellow Hair smiled and nodded to her to show that she liked the song.

Sweat trickled down her back and inside her doeskin dress. Gray clouds lay heavily over the Trembling Lands, and the air was warm and wet. Even though the water of the lake was dark and muddy, Redbird was looking forward to bathing in it.

And she was looking forward to a private talk with Yellow Hair. Yellow Hair had been with them for many days and nights. It was time she went to bed with White Bear.

Yellow Hair walked beside her around the edge of the lake. Ahead of them ran Eagle Feather with a captive pale eyes boy named Woodrow. Iron Knife had brought Woodrow back from a raid, and White Bear had taken him under his protection too.

Woodrow, a few years older than Eagle Feather, was darting this way and that, uprooting plants and throwing them down, tasting berries and spitting them out. Redbird watched him with amusement. She had already grown fond of him.

Woodrow said something to Yellow Hair, who smiled and turned to Redbird.

Speaking the pale eyes' tongue slowly, adding the few Sauk words she knew and using gestures, Yellow Hair managed to explain to Redbird that Woodrow was unhappy because he did not know what to pick.

"If look good, pick," Redbird said, using the little English White Bear had taught her. "Not eat. If I say good, then eat."

Woodrow grinned and nodded to Redbird to show he understood. He ran off after Eagle Feather, who was looking for birds and squirrels to shoot with his small bow and arrow. Woodrow had been a captive only half as long as Yellow Hair, but unlike her, he seemed happy with his lot.

Redbird doubted that Eagle Feather and Woodrow would find any squirrels or birds. Very little that was edible, plant or animal, lived in this marsh, and over a thousand people had been foraging in the area for more than a moon. The last time the British Band had eaten well was when Wolf Paw brought the cattle. And among so many people, those cattle had not lasted long. Many people were digging in the ground for worms and grubs, roasting them and eating them in handfuls. Some people were even secretly killing and eating horses, though Black Hawk had decreed death for anyone caught doing that.

As for Redbird herself, she felt an emptiness in her belly from the time she woke till the time she went to sleep, and she found herself wanting to sleep longer and longer as her strength ebbed away. She worried constantly that the baby inside her was not getting enough nourishment and would die or be stunted. The people around her were starting to look like walking skeletons.

They came to a point of land covered with pale green shrubs thrusting out into the lake. Redbird called Eagle Feather.

"Go for a swim around the other side of this point and take the pale eyes boy with you."

Eagle Feather's blue eyes glowed. "Maybe I can shoot a frog."

Once the boys were gone, she said to Yellow Hair, "We take bath." Yellow Hair smiled gratefully.

As they waded naked into the greenish, murky water, Redbird eyed Yellow Hair's body, so different from a Sauk woman's. She remembered how hungrily the braves had stared at Yellow Hair when Wolf Paw's wife stripped her before the tribe.

Yet it was easy to imagine that such pale skin was a sign of sickness. Yellow Hair's face and hands were somewhat tan, but every other part of her was white as milk. Her ribs were showing, a sign of the hunger they were all suffering. Still, her breasts were round, with pretty pink nipples. Her legs were long, and her buttocks curved out sharply; those of Sauk women were flatter. Even though the hair under her arms and between her legs was light in color, she had an abundance of it, much more than the fine tufts of black hair Redbird had in those places. She had undone her braids, and her hair fell like a golden curtain down her back halfway to her waist.

What a beautiful creature she is!

What an evil, stupid thing it would have been if Running Deer and the others had been allowed to cut her to bits and burn her.

A man might find Yellow Hair's differences from Sauk women attractive. A man such as White Bear.

She felt no fear that the pale eyes woman would take White Bear away from her. He showed many times every day, with his looks, with his movements, with his words, that Redbird, and not Yellow Hair, was first in his heart.

Redbird waded into the lake until the water was up to her breasts and her feet were sinking in the ooze. Then she pushed herself forward and dog-paddled through the reeds. It was wonderful to let the water take the weight of her belly off her hips and legs, a welcome relief to feel so cool.

In the night in the wickiup she often heard Yellow Hair moving or weeping softly. And that meant that Yellow Hair must have heard White Bear and Redbird loving each other in bed. This was only to be expected. When families slept all together in lodges and wickiups, the children early came to know how their parents took pleasure together during the night, and were unembarrassed when they grew up and their turn came. But how did the sounds of White Bear and Redbird together make Yellow Hair feel?

White Bear had said that Yellow Hair had wanted him when he lived among the pale eyes. And lately Redbird and White Bear had been sleeping apart on their separate pallets more often, because Redbird, in the discomfort of the final moon of carrying this baby, rarely wanted White Bear inside her.

And so Redbird had searched her heart and knew that she was willing to share her husband with Yellow Hair.

White Bear and Yellow Hair could go to bed with each other.

And should.

It would be good for Yellow Hair if her yearning for White Bear could be satisfied, at least for a time. The pleasure of mating was a healing thing. It restored the ill to health, and it made the well strong and happy.

Redbird could see in Yellow Hair's eyes—such a bright blue— how much she longed for White Bear. Being close to him, Redbird thought, helped Yellow Hair forget she was a captive.

Some days ago, not long after White Bear had taken in Wood-row, Redbird had told White Bear she would not mind if he took Yellow Hair into his bed. He had laughed and patted her belly and insisted he could wait until she wanted him again.

Why should he *have* to wait, when a woman who desired him was right there in his wickiup?

It was good that she had spoken to him, even though he claimed he did not want Yellow Hair. At least he knew that if Yellow Hair did come to him in the night, they both had Redbird's blessing. But she doubted that Yellow Hair would ever approach White Bear that way. Not without encouragement.

She stopped swimming, and let her feet down into the mud so that she stood beside Yellow Hair. Here the water of the lake almost came up to Redbird's shoulders, but Yellow Hair's breasts were well above it. They smiled at each other.

Yellow Hair crouched down in the water till it was up to her neck. She dipped her hair into the water, then lifted her head and squeezed the water out of her hair with her hands.

The water was good and cool, she said, but she wished she had some soap.

White Bear had explained what soap was, and Redbird smiled

and shook her head. If water would not wash dirt away, a Sauk scrubbed with sand. As for hair, Redbird left hers braided. Once at the beginning of summer and once at the end, she felt, was often enough to let water touch her unbound hair.

Now that she had decided to talk to Yellow Hair, Redbird felt a tightness in her throat. What if the idea of sharing White Bear made Yellow Hair angry? Sharing a mate was not, Redbird knew, according to pale eyes custom.

There was only one way: to begin in spite of her fear.

She said, "You know about woman and man? What they do?" She signed with her fingers to make her meaning plain, and saw that she had succeeded when the pale eyes woman's face turned a deep red. Redbird wished Yellow Hair were standing up in the water, so she could see whether the rest of her body turned red too.

Yellow Hair said she knew a little about what men and women did, but her mother had died a long time ago and her father never spoke of such things.

"You want me teach?" Redbird asked.

Yellow Hair turned red again, looked down at the water and nodded.

So, as they waded back to the shore of the lake, Redbird tried with many gestures and a few words to teach Yellow Hair, as Sun Woman many summers ago had taught her. When they were out of the water, Redbird picked up a stick and drew a little picture on the mudbank. When she was finished, she giggled. Yellow Hair took a good look and turned red again, all the way down to her waist, Redbird noticed. She turned away, but Redbird saw to her relief that she was laughing. Redbird scratched out the picture.

They sat on the bank where they had left their clothing, letting the air dry their bodies. From a pouch she had brought with her Redbird took a wood-stoppered gourd containing musk oil. She and Yellow Hair rubbed the oil on their bodies to keep mosquitoes off.

Yellow Hair wanted to know if the first time with a man hurt very much.

"Some women hurt much. Other women little."

She patted Yellow Hair's wrist to reassure her. "I think you hurt little. After that, feel very, very good." She patted herself between her legs to make plain what she was talking about, and Yellow Hair blushed again.

"*Best* feeling," Redbird added, smiling. It was surprising, Redbird thought, that Yellow Hair could become a fully grown woman and yet still have her first time with a man to look forward to.

They sat in silence for a time, Redbird afraid again because now she had to take the next step.

But before she could speak, tears began to trickle down Yellow Hair's cheeks. She spoke brokenly, and it was hard for Redbird to follow her. She seemed to be saying that she expected to die before she ever knew those good feelings Redbird talked about with a man she loved. She had already lived for twenty summers, and now it seemed she might not live much longer. And never have a man.

It was true. There was big danger to Yellow Hair. If anything happened to White Bear, she would have no protector. Many Sauk hated pale eyes. One might get at her. Or her own people might even kill her by mistake.

Yellow Hair had missed so much. So tall and beautiful, but she had nothing to show for her life—no man, no children. Redbird felt sorry for her.

"You love White Bear?" she asked, hugging herself as she said the word "love" to show what she meant.

Now Yellow Hair turned pale—even paler than usual—and drew away from Redbird. She shook her head violently, her bright golden hair swinging all wild and loose, and said, "No, no, no!"

But she stared at Redbird too fixedly, and Redbird could see that she did not mean what she said.

White Bear wanted Yellow Hair, but said he did not want her. Yellow Hair loved White Bear, but said she did not love him.

White Bear and Yellow Hair were both being foolish. It came of Yellow Hair being pale eyes and White Bear being part pale eyes.

And so now Redbird took a deep breath and said, "When we sleep tonight, you go to bed of White Bear. He make you happy."

Yellow Hair's eyes grew huge and her face glowed with a joyous wonder. She stammered and gasped as she asked Redbird if she really meant it, if she would really let such a thing happen.

"I happy when you happy, White Bear happy," Redbird said.

Redbird had come to see Yellow Hair as a younger sister who needed her help and guidance. She liked Yellow Hair much more, in fact, than she liked either Wild Grape or Robin's Nest. Her sisters had always sneered at White Bear, and Yellow Hair saw what a fine man he was.

Yellow Hair suddenly looked frightened. She stood up abruptly, picked up her fringed doeskin dress and struggled into it. When her head appeared through the neck of the dress and she shook her hair free, she was crying again.

No, she insisted, she couldn't do that. It would be wrong.

Redbird thought she understood. This hungry, dangerous time was a terrible time for a woman to be carrying a baby.

"You not want baby? Sun Woman makes tea keeps woman from getting baby."

Yellow Hair talked for a long time. Redbird tried hard to follow what she said, asking questions and making her repeat herself. It had to do with Jesus, the pale eyes spirit Père Isaac always talked about. Jesus would not like it if Yellow Hair went to bed with White Bear.

Redbird remembered White Bear telling her that Yellow Hair was the daughter of a pale eyes shaman. The Jesus spirit might be a special spirit for her, then.

But I am also the daughter of a shaman. I can teach her what we believe.

"Jesus not here," Redbird pointed out. "We children of Earthmaker."

But also, Yellow Hair explained, by pale eyes custom a woman who slept with another woman's husband was a bad woman.

"White Bear *is* your husband," Redbird said. "My father shaman. He marry you and White Bear." Surely that was more important than what a lot of pale eyes who were not even here to see might think. Among the Sauk, many would call Yellow Hair a bad woman for *not* sleeping with White Bear.

"We Sauk people. What you do with my Sauk man is good."

Yellow Hair sighed and wiped her tears with her fingers. Maybe she would go to White Bear in the night, and maybe not. She spread her hands helplessly. She did not know what to do.

Redbird saw that she could tell Yellow Hair no more. The pale eyes would have to make up her own mind.

Yellow Hair gave Redbird a sad smile and thanked her for her kindness. And after Redbird had put on her dress and her moccasins, Yellow Hair gave her a little kiss on the cheek.

With a wooden comb Redbird had given her, Yellow Hair combed out her long blond locks and began to braid them again.

They rejoined Eagle Feather and Woodrow and spent the rest of the afternoon searching for food, returning to camp when the clouds overhead turned purple and the sun made a brief appearance, blazing like a prairie fire on the flat horizon of the marshland.

Redbird bit her lip anxiously as they walked back to the camp. If Yellow Hair decided not to go to bed with White Bear, she might think, according to her pale eyes custom, that Redbird was a bad woman for saying she should. But what if Yellow Hair went to bed with White Bear and he came to love Yellow Hair more than he did Redbird? She had thought that could not happen, but now that she had spoken out, she was not so sure.

That night Redbird curled up on her solitary pallet of blankets laid over a mat of reeds on one side of the wickiup. Yellow Hair lay in her sleeping place, and the boys were in the one they shared. White Bear was still visiting and treating ill people. Many people, especially the very old and the very young, were falling ill in the Trembling Lands. There had been many deaths since they crossed the Great River. Bit by bit the band was losing the wisdom of the old and the promise of the young.

White Bear came in long after the two women and the boys had settled down for the night. He went to his own pallet on the east side of the wickiup.

Now that Redbird was ready for sleep, the baby within her woke up, and its kicking, along with burning feelings that rose from her stomach to her throat, kept her awake.

The stillness was disturbed only by the chirping of countless frogs.

Where were those frogs today when we were looking for food? We must ask the Frog spirit to let us catch some of them.

Then she heard another movement. Someone was crawling across the reed-covered floor of the wickiup. She caught her breath. Yellow Hair's sleeping place was on the side opposite White Bear's, and the movement was unmistakably from her bed to his.

A little later she heard other sounds that were also easy to recognize—the crackling of a bed's reed matting, whispers, little gasps and groans, loud, fast breathing.

Yellow Hair's cry of pain sounded as if it had come through clenched teeth. She still did not want anyone to know. Redbird smiled to herself.

As she listened to White Bear's heavy panting, Redbird remembered the sharp pain inside her when she first received him on the island near Saukenuk.

White Bear sighed loudly, and then everything was still for a time, and Redbird heard the frogs once more. They were probably mating too. How wise of Earthmaker to make his creatures into woman and man, so they could give each other such wonderful pleasure. Earthmaker knew everything, but it was hard to see how he could have invented man and woman without having seen something that gave him the idea.

Him? Redbird had always pictured Earthmaker as a man, a giant warrior, but now she wondered whether the spirit that gave life to the world and all things in it might be a she. Or, better yet, maybe there were two Earthmakers, a he and a she.

As she had so many times before, she wished now that the tribe's custom would permit her to become a shaman, so that she might see into these mysteries with her own eyes, as White Bear and Owl Carver had.

The sounds started up again from White Bear's bed, the movements, the whisperings. Redbird thought about how good it was to have her man filling her solidly, giving her delicious feelings as he moved in and out. And she felt herself warm with desire.

She smiled ruefully in the dark.

Now I want him and I cannot have him, because I sent Yellow Hair to his bed.

I hope this baby will be born soon, so I can lie with White Bear again. Of course, even then I will still let Yellow Hair have him, sometimes.

When Redbird awoke at sunrise and got up to begin the day's foraging, Yellow Hair was back sleeping in her own place. In the faint light that filtered through the wickiup's elm-bark skin, her pink mouth looked soft and childlike.

White Bear was seated cross-legged on his bed, loading the rifle he had brought with him when he came back to the tribe. With food so short, even the shaman had to go out and try to hunt to supply his family; the people he treated had no gifts to give him. She stood looking at him, waiting for him to speak to her, but he kept his eyes on his rifle with foolish shyness.

Did he think she was angry at him, or that she was going to tease him, the way Water Flows Fast might?

Poor Water Flows Fast—she made few jokes since her husband, Three Horses, was killed at Old Man's Creek.

Redbird said, "I know what happened last night. I am glad that it happened. It was good for her and for you."

Now White Bear's dark eyes met hers, troubled. "Yes, it is good for me and Nancy—Yellow Hair—but only for now."

"What troubles you?" she asked him.

"One day, when Yellow Hair must leave us and go back to her own people, I think she will be very sad. That is why I did not lie with her when she wanted me to at Victor. I knew we would have to part."

"Now she has what she wants, at least for as long as she stays with us. Now she will have something to think about besides how afraid she is."

He smiled at her. "And you made it happen. I know that you sent her to me. You are a great troublemaker."

He stood up and stroked her cheek with his fingertips, and she felt a glow inside, certain now that speaking to Yellow Hair had been right.

The afternoon sun heated the interior of the birthing wickiup till it felt like a sweat lodge.

Redbird screamed. It was not a baby; it was a wild horse down there, kicking its way out. She felt about to faint.

The pain died away. Groaning, Redbird went limp between Wind Bends Grass and Yellow Hair, who held her arms. Sun Woman crouched before Redbird, observing the progress of the birth by the light of a single candle.

Her skin slick with sweat, Redbird was squatting naked over a pile of blankets in the center of the wickiup. Her back and legs ached unbearably.

"You don't have to scream so loud," Wind Bends Grass said abruptly. "It doesn't hurt that much."

Redbird wished her mother could feel this pain and know how much it hurt. She felt like telling Wind Bends Grass to leave the birthing wickiup.

Sun Woman said gently, "No one knows how much another person hurts."

I don't remember this much pain when Eagle Feather was born. Maybe I am going to die.

Sun Woman stood up and wiped Redbird's forehead with a cool, wet kerchief, then cleaned her bottom for her, where a little blood was dripping.

"I can see the top of the baby's head," Sun Woman said. "It will be a good birth. You are almost done now."

Redbird looked up at the mare's tail, dyed red, that hung over the wickiup doorway, medicine to make the birth go easier.

Let it be over soon, she prayed. Her pains had started at dawn, and now it was past midday. Sun Woman had used up four candles, and in the whole band there were hardly any candles left. It had not taken this long with Eagle Feather.

Yellow Hair rubbed the arm she was holding, and Redbird managed to look at her and smile. Though Redbird had meant to honor Yellow Hair by asking her to help here, she was not sure now that she had done the right thing. The pale eyes woman's face was icy white, and she kept biting her lips as if trying to keep from being sick. She had probably never seen anything like this before.

Wind Bends Grass had insisted that it was bad luck to have Yellow Hair present, but Redbird had ignored her.

The next pain came, and Redbird, to show her mother how much it hurt, screamed even louder and longer than she had to. This time the pain gave her hardly any rest before it came again. And another came stepping on its heels. And another.

Her screams were continuous now, and she was hoarse and coughing and did not have to pretend. Her eyes were blind with tears. She dug her nails into the arms of Wind Bends Grass and Yellow Hair and bent forward, pushing as hard as she could.

She felt the enormous mass breaking out of her, and found her voice again in a scream that could split the very sky open even as the baby was tearing her in two.

Her ears rang. She felt broken and useless, like an empty eggshell. She hurt terribly, but a great weight was gone from inside her.

Wind Bends Grass said, "You have done well, my daughter."

Redbird started to cry, from pain, from relief, and because she had finally pleased her mother.

From the floor she heard a tiny cough, and then a drawn-out wail. She looked down and saw the little bright red figure in Sun

Woman's arms, its eyes screwed shut, its mouth wide open, at the joining of its legs the life-giving crevice. A glistening blue cord coiling up from the baby's belly joined her still to Redbird's body.

She felt another pain now, and pushed out the afterbirth with a groan. Wind Bends Grass and Yellow Hair helped her to stumble to the bed against the wall of the wickiup. They wrapped her in a light blanket, while Sun Woman cut the cord and set it aside to be dried and put in the baby's medicine bag. Then Wind Bends Grass bathed the tiny body first with water, then with oil. She put her granddaughter in her daughter's arms.

"What will you call her?" she asked.

Redbird had thought of a name in the lake where she and Yellow Hair had been bathing several days ago. "I will call her Floating Lily."

"A good name," Sun Woman said.

Floating Lily's voice was strong. Hungry already, and she had only been in the world a few moments. Redbird pressed the little mouth against her breast. She prayed that she would have milk. She had eaten as much as she could; now she must give nourishment.

She felt the rhythmic pull on her breast. The baby's mouth was full of milk; no more crying. A warm feeling spread through Redbird's body.

After Redbird had fed Floating Lily, they both slept. It was near sundown when the three women attending her helped her limp with the baby back to her own wickiup. Each time she took a step it felt as if a club hit her between her legs, but her heart rejoiced that the ordeal was over.

Yellow Hair said that she would go and look for Woodrow and Eagle Feather. She was crying. Redbird was not sure why.

In the wickiup, White Bear was waiting for her. As she lay on her bed with Floating Lily, his eyes lit up with joy at the sight of his daughter. He picked the baby up, which made her cry, and he laughed and handed her back to Redbird.

"I was not with you to see our son born," he said. "I have never been happier in my life than I am at this moment."

The hide curtain over the wickiup doorway was pulled aside and Owl Carver entered, holding his owl's head medicine stick in one hand and a bowl of smoking aromatic herbs and wood shavings in another. His white hair was getting thinner and thinner, Redbird noticed, and he walked with a permanent stoop. He blew the smoke over Redbird and Floating Lily to bless them.

"May she walk her path with honor," he said, laying his hand on Floating Lily's head. He left, the scented smoke lingering behind him.

When Redbird bared her breast, White Bear leaned over and kissed her nipple, his lips catching a droplet of milk that had formed there. She put Floating Lily to her breast and lay in contented silence with her husband sitting beside her.

He took up his book and read aloud:

> "Whence Hail to thee,
> Eve, rightly called Mother of all Mankind,
> Mother of all things living, since by thee
> Man is to live, and all things live for Man."

"What does that mean?" she asked.

He translated the words into Sauk, and said, "It means that all life comes from woman."

Iron Knife's head suddenly appeared in the doorway, his eyes wide, his mouth drawn down.

"White Bear! Long knives coming this way, thousands of them."

Redbird's body went cold, and she clutched the baby to her. How could she keep this tender new life safe in the midst of flight and fighting?

"Maybe they will not be able to find us," White Bear said.

"No, the scouts say they have Potawatomi guides riding with them, who know where to look for us. Potawatomi dogs! To side with the long knives against us."

"The Potawatomi must have been forced to help," said White Bear quietly.

Iron Knife said, "Black Hawk says we must break camp right now. We will head west as quickly as we can toward the Great River."

Redbird tightened her arms around Floating Lily until the baby cried out in pain. Instantly she relaxed her grip, but in her mind she saw the long knives coming, with their cruel, hairy faces, murdering them all with their guns and their swords. She saw the people she loved sprawled dead in the mud of the Trembling Lands. White Bear had told her that Black Hawk's war parties had killed many pale eyes, even women and children. Now the long knives would take terrible vengeance. Even as she stroked the baby and whispered to soothe her, her heart pounded in her chest.

There would be hard traveling ahead and even less food, thought Redbird. Trying to walk after just giving birth, the pain would kill her.

For an instant she hated Black Hawk for having led them into this suffering. If only the British Band had listened last winter to White Bear. And to her. Then hatred gave way to sick despair. She would die before they ever reached the Great River. And Floating Lily, who had just come into the world, would die too.

Iron Knife left them. White Bear turned to Redbird, and she saw in his eyes the same hopelessness she felt. But if he gave up, too, they were truly lost. Why, then, go through the agony of a flight from the long knives? They might as well stay here and let the long knives come and kill them.

White Bear said, "The Turtle told me, 'The many who follow Black Hawk across the Great River will be few when they cross back.' " A chill went through her as she saw how those prophetic words were coming true.

The little bundle in Redbird's arms stirred. Anger rose in her. Despite Black Hawk's blundering, despite the deadly hatred of the long knives, she and her husband and her son and her baby daughter would not let themselves be killed.

"Then if we do not cross the Great River we will escape in some other direction," she said firmly. "Go and find Eagle Feather and Woodrow. I will start to pack our belongings."

He smiled gratefully at her, reached for her and held her. She felt herself gaining strength from his strong arms around her.

"For a few days I will not be able to walk or ride. You will have to tie me to a travois and pull me along, as we do with old people."

"If I have to carry you in my arms," said White Bear, "I will do that."

Now that she was determined to fight to stay alive, she smiled up at White Bear and pressed herself against him. She *was* love. The power of a great spirit, perhaps that she-Earthmaker she had once thought of, filled her.

The Turtle, she thought, had said that many would die. But he had also said that a few would live.

She and her husband and her children, they would live.

19

The Band Divided

The setting sun, warming the flat land at the foot of a hill beside the Great River, cast deep shadows in the hollows of Redbird's and Nancy's faces. How thin they were getting to be. Fear for them wriggled snakelike through White Bear's own empty stomach.

Has Earthmaker abandoned his people? No—worse—this is the fate he has chosen *for us. He bestows evil as well as good on his children.*

Redbird said wearily, "What did the council decide?" She unfastened the sling in which she carried Floating Lily on her back and cradled the baby in her arms, frowning into the tiny brown face. White Bear knew what she was thinking. Floating Lily was too quiet.

White Bear said, "Black Hawk wants to go north and seek refuge with the Chippewa. He took the compass my father gave him out of his medicine bag and showed it to the chiefs and braves. He said we must follow its arrow north. But Iron Knife disagreed with him."

Redbird's eyes widened. "My brother never disagrees with Black Hawk. Black Hawk has lived three times as long as he has."

"Iron Knife spoke for many of the younger braves," White Bear said. "They want to cross the Great River here, now, and bring the war to an end. Black Hawk reminded them that we have only three canoes. Each canoe can hold only six people, and two of those six must paddle back and forth. They would have to ferry nearly a thousand people. He said the long knives would reach us long before we all got across. Iron Knife said they would make rafts and more canoes. In the end the three chiefs and most of the braves said

353

they would cross the river. Only a few have agreed to go north with Black Hawk."

It had taken a whole moon to cross from east to west, from their camp in the Trembling Lands to this place where the Bad Axe River emptied into the Great River. The land through which they passed, following an old Winnebago trail, was rolling prairie at first. Then they plunged into country that was ever wilder and more mountainous as they struggled westward. At the last they had to cut their own trail. They marked their passage with kettles, blankets, tent poles and other possessions too heavy to carry—and their dying old people who could walk no more, and their dead children. The only good thing about this rugged land was that it slowed down the long knives even more than it did Black Hawk's people, who knew by the time they reached the Great River that their pursuers were two days behind them.

White Bear told Nancy in English what he had just told Redbird about the council.

"If the band is dividing, where will *we* go?" Nancy asked.

"I asked Black Hawk—I begged him—to let you and Woodrow go." Anger crept into White Bear's voice as he recalled Black Hawk's stubbornness. "He still refuses. He wants to take the two of you north with him."

Redbird said, "But pale eyes prisoners are no good to Black Hawk now." White Bear was pleased to see that she had learned to get the drift of English conversations between him and Nancy. He did not like to feel that he was leaving Redbird out of anything, especially since he *knew* Nancy now.

"True," White Bear said to Redbird in Sauk. "And if we meet up with long knives again they will shoot first and not think to look for pale eyes among us. I want to get Yellow Hair and Woodrow away from the tribe before there is another battle."

There had been one great battle with the long knives halfway through their trek, on the south shore of the Ouisconsin River. Many had died on both sides, but Black Hawk had managed to get most of his people away after nightfall. Right now White Bear could almost hear the huge army of long knives crashing through the forests behind them.

But Nancy shook her head violently. "I feel safer with you." Her eyes glistened with tears.

Ever since Redbird had encouraged Nancy to seek his bed, White Bear had feared that when the time came for their parting, it would hurt her badly.

And him as well. In the moon just past he and Nancy had joined bodies and hearts many times. Now it seared his throat to speak aloud his decision that Nancy must leave the British Band.

He sat down on a fallen tree trunk and reached out to her. Nancy came over and took his hands and sat beside him.

"With the band going in two different directions, this is your best chance to get away. You and I have loved each other, but you are still a white woman, and my people murdered your father. Why should you share our fate? And what about Woodrow? If you and he go together, you have a better chance of reaching safety."

She bent over, her shoulders shaking with sobs. "If you're going to die, I want to die with you."

A moon ago, he thought, she had desperately wanted to escape from the British Band. Now her own heart was holding her captive.

Eve's words to Adam as they left Paradise rose unbidden in his mind: *With thee to go, is to stay here; without thee here to stay, is to go hence unwilling.*

"But no one wants to die," he said gently. "For you to stay now when you can escape would be madness."

It was a madness he felt himself. There was a part of him that wanted to keep her with him, to let her stay, however all this might end. He had to force himself to keep to his plan to help her get away.

Eagle Feather and Woodrow came from the woods along the south bank of the Bad Axe River, arms loaded with boughs for the wickiup that now they would not bother to build.

White Bear squatted down before Woodrow and grasped his shoulders.

"Tonight I am going to help you and Miss Nancy to get away from our band and back to the white people." He would be sorry to lose the boy.

Eagle Feather, standing nearby, said nothing. But his face, full of woe, told White Bear that he understood.

"I guess Miss Nancy and me could find our way to white folks if we follow the river," Woodrow said uncertainly. With the beaded headband Iron Knife had given him wrapped around his high forehead, and his face browned by the summer sun, he looked like a Sauk boy, except for his light brown hair. He seemed not much happier about leaving the band than Nancy.

"I'm not going to send you to find your way alone," White Bear said. "I'll go with you until I see you in safe hands. Prairie du Chien and Fort Crawford are south of here on the river. If we go in that direction we're bound to meet some of your people."

"I got no people but you," said Woodrow. "You treated me better than my folks ever did."

White Bear felt a catch in his throat. He remembered how, seven years ago, he had fought against being sent from the tribe when Star Arrow came looking for him.

Eagle Feather's blue eyes rested gravely on White Bear. "What about Mother and Floating Lily and me? Are we going to cross the Great River now?"

White Bear remembered again what the Turtle had said in his vision. He looked out at the river, tinged with red by the sunset, and felt a chill. Calamity, his shaman's sense told him, awaited those who tried to escape by crossing the river again.

"No." White Bear looked over at Redbird, who held Floating Lily to her breast. "Day after tomorrow at the latest, the long knives will be here. I want you to go with Black Hawk. Though I think Black Hawk had led us unwisely, still, to go north is safer. Three lodges, about fifty people, are going with Black Hawk. Owl Carver, Flying Cloud, Wolf Paw—they will follow him."

He shook his head sadly.

"What is it?" Redbird asked.

"Even Wolf Paw disagrees with Black Hawk about going north. He himself will remain at his father's side, but he is sending his two wives and his children across the river. He thinks they will be safer. I think he is wrong."

He gazed out at the reddened river and shook his head again.

"Wolf Paw made the right choice for his family," said a deep voice behind him. White Bear turned to see Iron Knife's huge figure, silhouetted by the setting sun. Behind him trudged a much smaller shadow whom White Bear recognized at once—Sun Woman.

White Bear hurried to his mother, put his arm around her shoulders and led her to the fallen tree to sit down. He could feel her bones under her doeskin dress.

"How is my mother?"

She patted his hand. "Very tired. But alive."

"Are you hungry?"

"One good thing about getting old is that I do not want as much food."

White Bear felt immediate relief that they did not have to share their few boiled roots and their bits of meal cake, and then he hated himself for begrudging food to his own mother.

Getting old, she had said. She was not an old woman. From what she had told him, he guessed her age was less than fifty summers. But the woman before him was terribly gaunt and stooped. The privations of the moons just past had aged her beyond her years.

He felt a stone block his throat as he realized that his mother might not have much longer to live.

Iron Knife bent down and hugged Redbird, then patted Woodrow's head with a big hand while the boy looked up at him with shining eyes. It was Iron Knife, leading the war party that had captured Woodrow, who had insisted the boy be allowed to live.

Like everyone else in the band, Iron Knife was mostly brown skin stretched over a skeleton, but his was a very big skeleton, a head taller than White Bear's. Studying Iron Knife, White Bear wondered whether he could ask his help in getting Woodrow and Nancy safely away.

Iron Knife said, "There is no safety in following Black Hawk. He said the British and the Potawatomi and Winnebago would join forces with us, and they did not. Now he says the Chippewa will help us. He is sure to be wrong again. And before he gets to the Chippewa he must travel through Winnebago country for many days, and now most of the Winnebago are helping the long knives hunt us."

Sun Woman said, "Black Hawk knows that if we join the rest of the tribe in Ioway, he will no longer be leader. No doubt those who accepted He Who Moves Alertly as their chief have prospered as much as we have suffered. Black Hawk will have to take second place to He Who Moves Alertly. That sticks in his throat like a fishbone. He would rather lead us on and on until we all die."

White Bear had to force his voice from a chest tight with urgency. "You will not have time to build enough canoes and rafts before the long knives are upon you."

And the heads of the long knives would be full of names like

Kellogg's Grove, Old Man's Creek, Apple River Fort, Indian Creek and Victor, and their hearts would be ravenous for revenge.

Iron Knife sat down on the tree trunk beside Sun Woman and pointed at the river. "If they attack us before we can cross, we can defend ourselves on that island."

White Bear followed Iron Knife's gesture. The sun had just set behind the western hills, and the Great River now reflected a pale blue back at the sky. A long, low island covered with spruce and hemlock trees bulked darkly an arrow's flight from shore. White Bear shivered. His shaman's senses told him that this was a place of grief and horror, an isle of death. He did not like the name of this river at whose mouth they were camped—the Bad Axe.

Trying to ignore the rapid thudding of his heart, White Bear readied himself to talk to Iron Knife about Woodrow and Nancy. He hated having to reveal his plan. If Iron Knife was against letting the two pale eyes escape, all would be lost. He opened his mouth, hesitating.

But he needed Iron Knife's help getting horses and avoiding the warriors guarding the camp. He reminded himself that Redbird's brother had always given him help when he needed it. He decided to go ahead and talk to him.

He said, "It would not be good for Yellow Hair and the boy to cross the river or to go with Black Hawk. I have taken them into my care, and now I am afraid for them. If there is a battle, the long knives may kill them by mistake."

Iron Knife grunted. "I would be sorry to see that happen."

White Bear's heartbeat steadied. He felt more sure of himself now.

He took a deep breath and said, "I have been thinking of helping them to get away."

Iron Knife smiled at White Bear, reached across Sun Woman and patted his knee. "That is well."

"It honors you, my son," said Sun Woman.

White Bear felt knots released in his chest and shoulders. "I was hoping you would see this as I see it."

"I will offer to watch the horses tonight," Iron Knife said. "Come when you are ready, and I will have three picked for you."

Sun Woman said, "If the long knives see you with Yellow Hair and the boy, they will try to shoot you."

White Bear put an arm around her bony shoulders and pulled her to him. "There is danger all around us, Mother. I think those who follow Black Hawk to the north will be safest. Redbird and the children will go that way. I think you should too. Do not try to cross the Great River."

"I have walked enough," said Sun Woman. "My legs ache and my feet are bruised. If I follow Black Hawk, I will end like the old people who sit down by the trail and wait for death."

"I speak as a shaman," White Bear said. "I have a bad feeling about this river crossing."

Sun Woman stood up. "And I speak as a medicine woman. I have seen many kinds of death, and I would rather drown or be shot than die little by little of hunger and weariness."

White Bear hugged his mother again. "I know we will meet again in the West," he said. That, as they both knew, could mean across the river or at the other end of the Trail of Souls.

Sun Woman said, "My son, you have made my heart glad. Every day of your life you have walked your path with courage and honor. May you walk the same way always."

Redbird held Sun Woman and Iron Knife, each in turn, for a long time. And after they had gone, White Bear and Redbird went together into the thick woods along the edge of the Great River.

Away from the others, White Bear became aware of the shrill chirping of choirs of crickets filling the night air. Mosquitoes shrilled around his ears and stung his hands and face. He and Redbird had long since used up the oil that kept them off. But the scratches and bruises of the trail of hardship they had walked these past moons had toughened their skins and their spirits so that mosquito stings meant little.

White Bear found a clear spot in the midst of a stand of young maples, and they lay down side by side. He put his hand on her breast, fuller than he had ever felt it, swollen with milk for Floating Lily. She slipped her dress down off her shoulders and let him touch her bare flesh. Very gently, knowing it was tender from nursing, he caressed her nipple with his fingertips.

"Before I leave tonight I will give you the deerhorn-handled dagger my father gave me," he said softly. "I must go unarmed, so that the long knives will not kill me if they catch me. Keep it for me till I come back."

"I am afraid," she whispered. "When you and Yellow Hair and Woodrow are gone, Black Hawk will know you helped them escape. What will he do to you when you come back?"

"By the time I return to you, he will not be angry. He will realize he did not really need them."

And then, too, White Bear might be captured or killed. The last time he had gone to the long knives they had nearly killed him. The sight of Little Crow's head bursting, blood flying everywhere as Armand Perrault's bullet smashed it, would never leave his memory.

If that happened to him, Black Hawk's anger would not matter.

Redbird wriggled closer to him, her hand stroking his chest as his stroked hers. "I do not think any Sauk warrior would be willing to steal prisoners away from his chief. I think you do this because you have lived so long with pale eyes."

White Bear felt desire for her swelling in him. They had coupled twice only since Floating Lily was born. He pulled her skirt up so he could stroke her belly and the smooth insides of her thighs.

"From what I saw among the pale eyes," he said, knowing a bitterness even as he sought the joy of Redbird, "they are more obedient to their chiefs than we are. And though it makes our hearts weep, if our people are not to disappear, we must learn to obey our leaders as the pale eyes do. But this night I must disobey our war chief."

"We must change," said Redbird. "But if we become like the pale eyes it will be the same as disappearing." Then she whispered, "Oh!" as his touch in a warm, moist place pleased her.

She loosened his loincloth, and his breathing quickened as her fingertips played awhile with him; then she grasped his hard flesh firmly. He sighed as he felt her fingers squeezing him. He should save his strength, he thought, because he would be awake and traveling all night, and probably all day tomorrow, with Nancy and Woodrow. But he and Redbird might never be together like this again. He rolled over on top of her and let her small, gentle hand guide him into her as he groaned aloud with the pleasure of it.

A tiny sliver of a new moon had risen just above the hills on this side of the river. White Bear, Nancy and Woodrow made their way south of the band's camp to a meadow in a hollow between hills.

Here the band had turned out their few remaining horses to graze and sleep. From the north end of the camp, beside the Bad Axe River, came the sound of men's voices and the light of fires. Men were stripping the bark from elm trees to make simple canoes and tying driftwood logs together to make rafts.

White Bear, Nancy and Woodrow worked their way around the edge of the meadow. The horses were dark shapes standing quietly. White Bear could hear Nancy stifle a sob every now and then. She had been crying all evening.

He wanted to take her in his arms and hold her close and tell her she did not have to leave him. He was the cause of her pain and could do nothing about it. He could, possibly, save her life, but he could not make her happy.

A tall shadow suddenly stood in his path.

"I have three horses ready for you," said Iron Knife. "I even found saddles, to make it easier for you to ride. They belonged to men who died at the Ouisconsin River battle."

White Bear had been carrying the rifle and powder horn Frank had given him. He thrust them at Iron Knife.

"I want you to have this rifle. A pale eyes uncle of mine—a good uncle—gave it to me. If I meet the long knives now, a rifle will not help me."

Iron Knife took the rifle and slung the horn over his shoulder. "May the spirit of the Great River watch over you."

His heart aching, White Bear opened his mouth, wanting to tell Iron Knife again to go with Black Hawk, not to stay here at the mouth of the Bad Axe. But he knew Iron Knife's mind was made up. Redbird's brother was strong, not only in body, but in doing what he had decided.

Instead of speaking, White Bear reached up and grasped Iron Knife's broad shoulders and squeezed hard.

White Bear, Nancy and Woodrow led their horses quietly along the riverbank, finding places where the shrubbery was thin enough to allow passage. White Bear kept glancing over his shoulder, and when he could no longer see the band's fires to the north he whispered to Nancy and Woodrow to mount.

He let his horse find its own path beside the rippling water.

Many times as they rode southward he caught himself dozing off, fatigued not only by exertion and lack of sleep but by hunger. He watched the thumbnail-shaped moon slide across the sky over the river. As it sank in the west he called a halt and told Nancy and Woodrow they could rest till sunup.

They tied their horses to saplings and crawled in under the boughs of a big spruce tree. Woodrow fell asleep at once, but Nancy crept into White Bear's arms.

By her movements she told him that she wanted him.

"Forgive me," he said. "I am so tired." She stroked his cheek reassuringly. But her face against his was tear-wet.

She fell asleep with her head on his chest.

Daylight and a loud chorus of birdsong woke them. Soon after they started riding, they passed through an empty village of bark-covered lodges, Winnebago he was sure, beside the river. Winnebago friends of Black Hawk had said that the long knives had ordered all Winnebago to camp within sight of the forts to show that they were not helping Black Hawk.

A clear trail led south from the village along the riverbank, and White Bear, Nancy and Woodrow rode along it. By the end of the day they should be near the settlement of Prairie du Chien and the long knives' Fort Crawford.

When the sun was high over the river, White Bear heard a sound that sent fear rustling down his back—the drawn-out shouts of long knife leaders calling orders. The cries came from somewhere to the south.

With horror, he saw it at once in his mind: One long knife army coming from the east. Now another marching up from the south. Both heading for the mouth of the Bad Axe where the people were trying desperately to get across the river.

A little later he heard the rumble of many hooves.

He wanted to turn and gallop back to warn the band. They had no notion that this second army, much closer to them, was coming.

Nancy said, "You'd better leave us here. They'll shoot at you."

Fear for himself and for his people tempted him to agree, but he firmly shook his head.

"I must stay with you until I'm sure you're safe. It is a matter only of minutes."

Soon White Bear glimpsed the Stars and Stripes fluttering among distant trees and the noon sun glittering on brass buttons. Federal troops. At a clear spot on the trail, where Nancy and Woodrow would be visible from a distance, he called a halt.

"You two stay on the trail. Nancy, pull your braids around to the front so they can see your blond hair. Woodrow, take that headband off. You want to make sure they see that you're white. Just hold your horses still, and when you see the first soldiers, raise your hands above your heads. And call out to them in English."

Oh, Earthmaker, keep them safe. This was the best he could do for them.

Nancy kissed him hard on the mouth.

"I love you so much," she said, her voice breaking. "And I know I'll never see you again. Go on, get away from here!"

White Bear led his horse back into the woods between the river and the bluffs. He tied the horse and then crept back through the shrubbery to watch Nancy and Woodrow.

Terrified by the thought that he might see them shot down before his eyes by careless soldiers, he held his breath.

He heard hoofbeats approaching at the gallop.

He heard Nancy cry, "Help us, please! We're white people!"

Good.

Two men wearing tall, cylindrical black shakoes and blue jackets with white crossbelts rode up to Nancy and Woodrow, who lowered their hands. After a brief conversation, all four rode off down the trail.

In a burst of relief, White Bear let his breath out. For a moment he could not move, so limp had his fear for Nancy and Woodrow left him. He whispered a prayer of thanks to Earthmaker.

He crept back to his horse and walked it till he found a deer track the horse could follow, then mounted and trotted northward.

He was back riding on the trail when an arrow, thrumming, buried its head in the dirt just in front of him. It startled him so that he nearly fell out of the saddle. He reined in his horse.

Men on horseback emerged from the trees ahead of him. They rode toward him silently, five of them. Two pointed rifles at him, the other three bows and arrows. They were red men, but wore pale eyes' shirts and trousers. Their hair was long, bound by brightly colored sashcloth bands, and they grew it full, not shaving part of their heads as most Sauk men did.

He sighed and held his hands out from his sides to show that they were empty. The Winnebago could have shot him off his horse without warning, so he supposed they meant to let him live.

The man on the right side of the trail, who held a bow with an arrow aimed at White Bear's heart said, in Sauk, "I am called Wave. We are looking for Black Hawk. Where can we find him?"

White Bear decided to make a joke of that. "Do you want to help him fight the long knives?"

Wave laughed, and translated it for his companions, who laughed also. He wore a brave's red and white feathers dangling from earrings, with two more standing upright in his hair.

He said, "The long knives have offered horses and gold to who- ever captures Black Hawk. We are not enemies of the Sauk, but we want the long knives' friendship." The man spoke Sauk fluently and without an accent.

"It is a shame that the Winnebago fight on the side of the long knives," White Bear said. "One day they will take your land from you, as they have taken ours from us."

Wave shrugged. "Look what has happened to you, who fought against them."

Red man betrays red man, and only the whites gain. It is as I told Redbird. If we want to live in this land, we ourselves must become like the whites.

"Come," said Wave. "We must take you to the long knives' war chief."

White Bear slumped in despair, realizing that he was no longer a free man. He looked about him. The trees, the birds, the Great River, they were all free, but he was in the power of his enemies. The world was a darker place. Black Hawk's war, for him, was over. He wished he could have warned his people about the ap- proaching army of long knives. And also, his heart ached for the Sauk he was unable to warn of the second long knife army. A yearn- ing for Redbird and Eagle Feather and Floating Lily seemed almost to pull his heart from his body. He prayed that they had safely left the Bad Axe country by now and headed north with Black Hawk. Probably he would never see them again. Probably the long knives would kill him. With a sigh, he turned his horse's head in the direc- tion Wave had pointed.

While his regiment rode by, the long knife war chief, a stocky man with a long face, thick eyebrows and hard blue eyes, stood by the side of the trail facing White Bear. He was Colonel Zachary Taylor, he had told White Bear. A burly, red-faced soldier with a sergeant's three chevrons on his forearm stood beside Taylor staring at White Bear with open hatred.

"What are you, a renegade white man?" Taylor demanded. "How come you speak good English?"

"I am Sauk, Colonel. My name is White Bear. My father was white, and he took me to be educated among the whites for several years."

"Well, White Bear, what were you doing on this trail? Chasing the white woman and the boy we just picked up?"

"It was I who brought them to you."

Taylor snorted. "You expect me to believe that?"

"Miss Hale will tell you it is true."

"Well, we already sent her and the boy back to Fort Crawford with an escort, so that will have to wait. But you do have her name right. Where are the rest of the Sauk? Trying to cross the Mississippi?"

"I cannot help you, Colonel. Any more than you would give information to the Sauk, if we captured you."

Taylor's sergeant said, "Sir, let me and a couple of my men take this half-breed for a stroll in the woods. We'll find out what you want to know."

"No, Benson, no." Taylor brushed the suggestion aside with an irritated wave of his hand. "Showing how they can resist torture is a regular game with Indians. He'll just sing Indian songs till he dies, and listening to that would be worse agony for you than anything you could do to him."

"Well, then let's shoot the bastard, sir, and be done with him. The militia don't take no prisoners. Why should we?"

Taylor threw back his head, and even though he was shorter than the sergeant, managed to look down his nose at him. "We're professional soldiers, Sergeant. I trust we know how to conduct ourselves better than the state militia. No, we'll just take him along with us. An Indian who speaks both Sauk and English could be of use to us, alive. I see you have a full head of hair and you wear no feathers, White Bear. That mean you haven't killed anybody? Or just that you don't want the fact known?"

"I haven't killed anybody." White Bear thought of adding that

he had saved more than one white life. But he couldn't expect them
to believe that. He would not expose himself to their scorn.

He said, "I am a medicine man, a shaman."

Taylor looked at him gravely. "Educated as a white man and
educated in the way of the spirits, too, eh? And with all that learning you couldn't warn Black Hawk away from this disaster?"

White Bear shook his head. "He listened to other voices."

Taylor's eyes narrowed. "Well, whatever advice you gave him,
it's all over for your chief now. God pity your people."

White Bear said, "All they want now is to go back across the
Mississippi and live in peace. Those who are left."

Taylor fixed him with an angry stare. "It's too late for that.
Things have gone too far. You people are going to have to suffer
for what you've done."

White Bear felt his limbs go cold as he heard the steel in Taylor's
voice. This was not a bad man, White Bear sensed, not a man like
Raoul. But whatever mercy was in him had no doubt long since
been washed away by the blood shed by Black Hawk's war parties.

*No doubt while he talks about making my people suffer he thinks
of himself as quite a civilized man.*

"Revenge, Colonel?" White Bear said. "I thought you were professional soldiers."

The sergeant balled his fists. "Please, sir, let me teach him some
respect."

Taylor cocked his head, listening to a distant sound, then turned
to look downriver.

"He's got a much more bitter lesson to learn, Sergeant. As do
all his people."

White Bear heard it too. A chugging sound. It had been a while
since he had heard a noise like that. He followed Taylor's gaze
down the river. All he could see was a column of gray smoke in the
sky to the south. But he knew what it was.

A steamship.

Because he could not ride to warn his people, he wanted to cry
out in agony. He saw what would happen—those few frail canoes,
the steamship bearing down on them, two long knife armies marching inexorably toward the mouth of the Bad Axe.

*The many who follow Black Hawk across the Great River will
be few when they cross back.*

20

River of Blood

Raoul uncorked the jug standing on the chart table and held it out to Bill Helmer, captain of the steamship *Victory*. A portly man with muttonchop whiskers, his hands firmly gripping the polished oak steering wheel, Helmer silently shook his head.

Raoul lifted the jug in a mock toast. "May we have a merry day of Indian fighting." He took two long swallows, and decided he felt strong and happy.

Helmer shook his head. "Mr. de Marion, there's nothing merry about fighting Indians."

"If that's your opinion, Captain, I'll thank you to keep it to yourself," said Raoul. He wanted a little warmth right now besides what he was getting from the jug, and he despised this dour man for not giving it to him.

Helmer shrugged and bent his gaze on the river.

Raoul knotted his fingers behind his back, and found that the effort relieved the tightness in his belly. He went to stand at the pilot house window and stared out at the forested bank where the Bad Axe River emptied into the Mississippi.

Militiamen were wading across the Bad Axe from south to north, holding their rifles, bayonets fixed, over their heads. The Bad Axe was more a creek than a river, shallow now in August, winding through a channel thick with bright green reeds. As the men slogged up the north bank, they leveled their rifles and plunged into the trees.

A blue haze of powder smoke already drifted amidst the pine

and spruce north of the Bad Axe mouth. The popping of rifles carried to Raoul across the water over the wheeze and clank of the *Victory*'s steam engine, fueled with oak and split pine.

Raoul wondered what was happening in those woods. Were the Indians fighting back, defending their women and children? He hoped the militiamen would go on killing until they'd exterminated the whole band. After four months of chasing the Indians across Illinois and the Michigan Territory, after all the innocents murdered—*Clarissa, Phil, Andy*—surely the militiamen would not be soft.

He felt tears starting up, and he quickly took another pull at the jug. He wished he could be in at the kill instead of out here in the river.

I want their blood on my own hands.

Lieutenant Kingsbury, in command of the gunnery crew assigned to Raoul from Fort Crawford, came up the stairs from the foredeck to the hurricane deck and entered the pilot house. He mopped his brow as he set his cylindrical shako, sporting its red plume and gold crossed-cannons artillery badge, on the chart table.

"Gets damned sticky on the river in August."

Raoul offered his jug. "Help you forget the heat."

Kingsbury grinned, thanked Raoul and took a big drink. His cheeks reddened, and he dabbed at his thick brown mustache with his fingertips.

"I don't hear much shooting on shore," he said, handing the jug back to Raoul, who took a swallow before setting it down.

"Just what I was thinking," said Raoul. "Where the hell are all the redskins? I figure there's about a thousand left. They can't all have crossed the Mississippi before we got here unless they had a whole fleet of canoes."

The *Victory* had caught one canoe in midstream when she arrived on the scene. Raoul's militia sharpshooters had blanketed it with rifle fire, killing all six Indians aboard, and the overturned canoe had drifted downstream, out of sight.

Raoul picked up a brass telescope from the chart table and studied the riverbank, moving the circular field from point to point. He saw plenty of militiamen, but no sign of Indians.

"Look," said Kingsbury. "Militiamen coming back out of the woods."

Raoul swept his telescope back over the riverbank. Men in buckskins were dragging their rifle butts along the ground, sitting down on the river's edge and splashing water on their faces, shaking their heads angrily, raccoon tails on their caps wagging.

One man did emerge from the trees with a big grin, holding high three bloody scalps dangling from hanks of black hair. Another man led two Indian ponies. So, the Sauk still had a few horses with them.

Kingsbury said, "Looks like they only met a handful."

Raoul drummed his fingers on the polished oak sill. "A rear guard. The rest could have headed north. But I don't think they did. They were aiming to cross the Mississippi."

His telescope brought closer an island north of the Bad Axe mouth, about fifty yards out from the Mississippi's east bank, thickly covered with spruce and hemlock. He saw two bark canoes with stove-in bottoms beached at the island's southern tip. Between the island and the riverbank the water had a pale green look that said it was shallow.

"I've got a feeling most of the Indians are hiding out on that island." His pulse quickened and his breath came fast.

His first thought was to land on the island with his men and flush the Indians out. But there could still be a couple of hundred warriors left to the band. No, they'd have to use the six-pounder first.

"Captain Bill, sail along the west side of that island. I want to get a closer look at it."

The spokes flew under Helmer's hands, and the *Victory*'s side paddles churned up the water.

Raoul, followed by Kingsbury, hurried down the stairs to the foredeck, where his own dozen militiamen, all Smith County boys who had reenlisted, watched him stride the planks to stand beside the six-pounder. It had saved the townspeople at Victor; now, mounted on the *Victory*'s foredeck, it would finish the Sauk.

The late morning sun beat without mercy on the open deck, and sweat trickled down from Raoul's armpits. He wanted to throw his jacket off and wear just a shirt, but the military blue, the gold braid and the brass buttons gave him authority that he'd found he needed, not so much in dealing with his own men as with other officers.

Hodge Hode said, "We got 'em treed now, Colonel."

"But stay under cover," said Raoul. "These raccoons will be

shooting back." His eyes tried to tear holes in the thick greenery on the island.

The Smith County boys crouched down behind the bales of hay lined along the railings and cocked their flintlocks.

Raoul patted the gun's black muzzle affectionately, and the three artillerists in blue jackets grinned and nodded at him. They had put their shakoes aside and wrapped rags around their heads to keep the sweat out of their eyes. Beside the cannon were stacked canisters of grapeshot and flannel bags of powder. In a few minutes, Raoul thought with pleasure, that grape would be sending a heap of red devils to Hell.

As the *Victory* steamed around the tip of the island, Raoul searched the forest with his telescope. He guessed the island to be a quarter of a mile long. It was deeply forested enough to conceal hundreds of Indians.

Midway along, he saw a gleam of sun on brown skin in the shrubbery near the river's edge. He swung the telescope back to the spot. Nothing now. But the quarry was there, all right. His lips drew back from his teeth.

"Captain Bill," he called to the pilot house. "Turn our bow toward the island. Kingsbury, get ready to fire."

Kingsbury saluted and called orders to the gun crew. A gunner slid a bag of powder into the six-pounder's muzzle and rammed it home. Another pushed a canister of grapeshot in after it. The third held the burning linstock ready.

Raoul called to the bridge. "Captain, hold her position." The captain waved acknowledgment from behind the glass, and Raoul heard him ring a bell relaying his orders belowdecks. A moment later levers clanked and Raoul felt the deck tremble as the paddle wheels on the sides of the ship reversed themselves.

"Shoot when you're ready, Lieutenant," Raoul said.

God, how I love this!

Kingsbury shouted, "Fire!"

The gun thundered, deafening him, and leaped back in its cradle of tackle. Raoul watched the woods eagerly as a white smoke cloud spread over the water. On the island, branches flew in all directions. A big tree fell. He heard a scream followed by a series of wailing cries. He almost cried aloud with pleasure.

An Indian staggered out from behind the trunk of a tall pine.

He dragged one leg, a useless mass of bloody meat, and fell heavily to the ground. He held a rifle. He shook his fist at the *Victory*, then aimed the rifle from his prone position.

In sudden fear, Raoul was about to duck behind a hay bale when a dozen shots cracked out from the railings beside him. Bleeding from his chest and his head, the Indian collapsed and rolled into the Mississippi. Nodding happily, Raoul watched the current catch his body. It drifted slowly downstream, trailing blood.

"Keep firing!" Raoul roared. A cannoneer swabbed inside the gun barrel to cool it down for more powder. In a moment the gun boomed out again. More trees splintered, but no more Indians were flushed out.

"Raise elevation ten degrees," Kingsbury called to the gunners. "They're probably lurking farther back in the woods."

Raoul heard the clicks as the gunners used hand spikes to raise the cannon in its carriage.

After the cannon went off, dirt and broken tree limbs sprayed out of the forest, and Raoul heard shrieking sounds that he hoped were the screams of Indians.

The cannon boomed again and again. With hand signals to Captain Bill in the pilot house, Raoul had the *Victory*'s bow swung to starboard and then to port, so that the grapeshot struck the island in a wide arc. Trees slowly toppled over, and shrieks of pain and shouts of rage and defiance pierced the silence between the roars of the cannon.

He pictured the lead balls tearing into howling Indians, ripping their flesh apart. He remembered Helene's body in Lake Michigan. He remembered Black Salmon's lash on his back. He saw—as he had seen them two weeks ago—the heap of blackened, split logs that had been Victoire, his home, the place where Clarissa, Phil and Andy died. He saw the mound of earth in the family cemetery where they lay together. What little had been left of them.

The cannon's heat was his rage. The cannon's boom was his roar. The grapeshot was his vengeance. He hurled his hatred over the water and into the trees, blowing Indian bodies to shreds.

He heard something hum past his head and plunk into the pilot house behind him. He saw smoke puff from the shadowy base of a clump of spruces. Another puff, and another. The reports of rifles carried across the water.

"Sir!" Kingsbury's hand gripped his shoulder, the fingers digging in.

Raoul realized he had been momentarily out of his mind with fury. Breathing heavily, he got his eyes focused on the brown-mustached lieutenant.

"Get down, sir, before you get hit."

Reluctantly, because he wanted to see where the grapeshot was hitting, Raoul crouched down behind a hay bale. When he'd first come out on deck he'd been afraid of being shot at. Now he felt sure they couldn't hit him.

The six-pounder repeatedly tore into the area on shore where powder smoke had appeared. Raoul saw no sign of Indian bodies, but the firing from the trees stopped.

"Gawd, I'd hate to be on the angry side of this gun," said Levi Pope.

A dozen or more Indians burst from the trees and dove into the water. Some of them started swimming out toward the *Victory*; others turned south, following the current. Some just splashed helplessly.

"Shoot!" Raoul shouted.

Gleefully, he ran into the pilot's house and grabbed his breech-loading Hall rifle. He rushed back to stand by the rail. He took aim at the nearest Indian in the water. He heard his breath coming heavy, as it did when he was in bed with a woman.

Only the warrior's shaven head, scalplock flowing behind, was far enough out of the water to present a clear target. The Indian seemed to be trying to swim past the *Victory*, toward the distant shore opposite. Raoul took his time aiming at the shiny brown dome and pulled the trigger. He saw a splash of red, then the Indian's arms and legs stopped moving and the body drifted southward with the current.

Pushing cloth-wrapped bullets down the tight, rifled bores of their muzzle loaders with practiced speed, Raoul's men could easily get off three shots or more in a minute. The sky blue of the river soon turned red with blood from bodies that floated swiftly away.

"Yee-hah!" Hodge Hode yelled. "This is more fun than huntin' wild goose."

"The ones we do not get, they will drown," said Armand Perrault. "There is no place for them to swim to."

It was true; the opposite shore of the Mississippi was too far away, and this shore was lined with Federal troops and state militia, who would shoot any swimming redskin they saw. The Indians must have known they were doomed, but still they came on, little groups jumping into the water, each one probably hoping to be lucky enough to escape alive. Most of the heads Raoul saw in the water streamed black hair; must be women and children, not scalplocked warriors.

But it didn't really matter what they were.

They killed my woman and my kids.

He saw a head trailing long black hair and blood in the water not ten feet off the starboard bow. Close enough to see it was a boy. He was trying desperately to swim with one arm, his face distorted with agony. Raoul aimed his rifle between the wide, terrified eyes that stared into his own. He pulled the trigger. The brown face sank below the water.

That's for Phil and Andy.

Groups of Indians threw themselves into the river from the distant parts of the island, but the steamboat turned quickly upstream and downstream, back and forth again and again, to pursue them, Raoul's sharpshooters wiping out each party of swimmers in turn. Captain Bill might not enjoy this work, but he did it well.

Raoul heard himself laughing under his breath as he thought of all the Indians who were dying before his eyes, because of *his* ship and *his* cannon and *his* riflemen.

Then the *Victory* resumed steaming slowly along the length of the island, stopping at intervals for the cannoneers to blast the forest. Kingsbury changed elevation with each shot, so that showers of grapeshot blanketed the island from side to side.

Finally Raoul decided that they had done all they could from the ship. All that blood in the water made a fine sight, made him yearn all the more to wet his hands with blood.

Climbing back up to the pilot house, he said, "Take her to the south end of the island, Captain Bill. As close as you can. We're going to land."

Helmer stared at him, but said nothing.

He'd better say nothing.

Raoul took his pistol out of its holster and checked to see that it was primed and loaded. He unsheathed his replica of Bowie's knife. He hefted it, heavy as a meat cleaver, in his hand and tested the edge with his thumb. It would cut. By God, it would cut. He slid it back into its sheath.

He opened his mouth, gulping air in his excitement. His hands tingled and his whole body felt as if it were growing bigger. He wanted to kill Indians. He wanted to wade in their blood. Maybe find Black Hawk himself and take his scalp with the big Bowie knife. He hoped there would be hundreds of redskins still alive, cowering on that island. He needed to kill them by the hundreds.

The ship's progress down the length of the island seemed to take forever.

He tried to calm himself. After that bombardment with grapeshot, after so many Indians had been shot trying to swim away, there probably wouldn't be many left alive on the island. It wouldn't really be a fight; they'd be close to helpless.

"After we're ashore," he said to Helmer, "take the ship over to the troops on the Mississippi bank and tell General Atkinson we've found the main body of the Sauk. Tell him to send as many men as the *Victory* will carry."

The steamboat's shallow draft allowed her to move in close, so Raoul and his dozen Smith County boys could jump down into knee-deep water, holding rifles, bayonets screwed in place, and pistols and cases of cartridges and shot over their heads. The water was cold and clammy through Raoul's flannel trousers, and his feet squelched in his boots.

The *Victory* drew away with a thumping of her engine and puffs of thick, black smoke from her two smokestacks. Just the sight of that steamship should have been enough to scare hell out of the Indians, Raoul thought.

He and his men clambered up sloping rocks to stand in a clear area of level ground. Just where the woods started, the upper half of an Indian lay on his back, trailing long, bloody ribbons of gut. The eyes were open, staring.

Now, that's what I wanted to see.

"Remember that we take no prisoners," he said.

Hodge Hode said, "Well, come on, let's knock them 'coons out of the trees."

An arrow punched through Hodge's neck from front to back.

Raoul's heart stopped, then thumped so hard with fear that he thought it might split his chest open.

Hodge dropped his rifle and fell to the ground, gagging.

Raoul went down on his knees beside Hodge, seized the arrow just under its knife-sharp flint head and pulled it through. As the feathered end went through his neck Hodge made a retching sound. His tongue stuck out of his mouth.

Raoul cursed under his breath as he bent over Hodge. This couldn't be happening.

More arrows were flying past them. Raoul's men fired a ragged volley into the woods, and the arrows stopped.

The arrow had cut through an artery and pierced Hodge's windpipe. His breath whistled in and out through the hole in his throat, his blood pumping out of him and soaking into his red beard.

"He is going," said Armand, kneeling beside Raoul.

"Aw no," Hodge managed to murmur.

Raoul felt sick as he watched blood fill Hodge's mouth and pour out of it. Then the big man went limp and his eyes rolled up in his head.

"Let's get the bastards!" Raoul growled. He was left scared as hell by Hodge's death, but he was damned if he'd show it.

They climbed over big branches knocked down by the *Victory*'s cannon and ran in among the trees, Raoul taking the lead. Spruce branches whipped his face.

I must be crazy, charging into the woods like this. We could all get what Hodge got.

High-pitched war whoops shrilled out of the forest shadows ahead, and more arrows whistled at them.

Knowing it was only luck that none of them hit him, Raoul wanted desperately to fire his rifle into the forest. But he forced himself not to shoot until he could see a target.

Brown figures rushed toward him, darting from tree to tree. He fired at a warrior leaping between the thick trunks of two pines. The Indian disappeared, but Raoul was sure he'd missed. He jerked the breech of his rifle open and slapped in another ball-and-powder cartridge with frantic speed.

The same Indian reappeared from behind another tree only six feet away. Raoul brought the rifle up and fired. The Indian fell over backward.

Another brave leaped at him from the side, swinging a tomahawk. Raoul shifted his rifle to his left hand and pulled out his Bowie knife. The Indian's eyes were huge and white and wild. His upraised arms left his chest wide open, ribs showing so sharp you could count them. Raoul lunged, thrusting the knife. The Indian's rush drove him onto the blade. His tomahawk came down on Raoul's forearm. It hurt, but it didn't even hit hard enough to cut through Raoul's sleeve. Raoul planted his foot in the already-dead Indian's belly and jerked the knife out of his body.

As the warrior collapsed, Raoul noticed that his face was bare brown skin devoid of paint. They'd even run out of war paint, he thought. In the middle of this battle, that gave him a moment of pleasure.

Rifles were going off on both sides of him. Levi Pope fired into the upper branches of an elm tree and whooped as a warrior's body came crashing down. The air was full of blinding, bitter smoke.

Then silence. Motionless Indians lay on the forest floor.

But so did two more of Raoul's own men. One lay face down, perfectly still. The other was on his back, head propped against a tree trunk. An arrow, feathers black and white, stuck out of his chest. His eyes were open but saw nothing. His arms and empty hands jerked, the movements less like a human being's than like a dying insect's. Raoul felt bile rising in his throat and bit his lips hard to stop himself from puking.

That could just as easily have been me.

Another man had an arrow in his arm. Armand pulled it out of him with a mighty jerk. The man screamed, and Armand clapped a big hand over his mouth.

Raoul's nine remaining men looked from the two dead men— the second man's arms had stopped jerking—to Raoul. Were they just waiting for orders, or were they accusing him?

"Injuns're gettin' ready for another charge," Levi Pope said. "I can see them skulkin' out there."

"Pull back!" Raoul ordered. "Pick up those dead men's rifles." His voice rang out strangely in the still forest.

Reloading and walking backward, rifles pointed up, Raoul and his men retreated to the tip of the island. Armand carried the extra rifles. They piled up fallen trees to make a hasty barricade.

Raoul lay behind tree trunks long enough for the sweat to cool on his body. Mosquitoes and little black flies stung him incessantly.

He wondered if the Indians would ever attack. He'd gotten himself into a very bad spot.

Rifles went off, and bullets plunked into the tree barricade. Brown bodies came leaping out of the forest. Raoul suddenly remembered how the Indians had rushed out from behind the Lake Michigan dunes twenty years ago, and for a moment he was a terrified little boy. His hands shook so violently he almost dropped his rifle.

With shrill yips and yells Indians came at them. Arrows and bullets whizzed over the heads of Raoul's men as they ducked down behind their shelter. Raoul forced himself to concentrate on shooting. He poked his rifle through an opening between broken tree limbs, aimed at a running Indian and fired.

His two remaining close companions in this war, Levi and Armand, lay shooting on either side of him. Hodge was dead, his body sprawled a few feet behind them, and that by itself brought Raoul close to panic. He had always felt the big redheaded backwoodsman could never be hurt.

Arrows flew thick and fast. Raoul and his men, reloading from the cartridge and shot cases they had carried ashore, kept up a steady answering fire.

He felt shame smouldering in his spine and along his limbs. What a damned fool he'd been. He had been so sure that storm of grapeshot from the *Victory* would finish off the Indians. He had expected this to be nothing more than a stroll through the forest, counting the dead and killing off the helpless remnant. Instead it seemed there were plenty of Sauk warriors left, very much alive, fierce as wolverines. And he and his men were trapped at the tip of this damned island with no place to retreat but the river. In the river they'd be helpless under enemy arrows and bullets, just like the redskins who had tried earlier to swim away.

The Sauk war cries had fallen silent, and the shots and arrows had stopped. Raoul peered through a chink in the tree trunks piled before him. All he could see was dark green boughs with no sign of movement.

"What you figger they're doing now?" Levi said. He had his six pistols laid out on a log in front of him.

"Probably getting ready to charge us," said Raoul.

How long before the *Victory* got back? From here at the south end of the island he could see the white steamship anchored off the riverbank, her two black stacks giving off little white puffs, her side paddle wheels motionless. She looked very small and very far away. No chance Helmer or Kingsbury could see that Raoul and his men were fighting for their lives here.

What were the men, Levi and Armand and the others, thinking? Again and again, it seemed, his decisions cost lives. He remembered Old Man's Creek—de Marion's Run—and he felt his face get fiery hot at the shame of it.

And then there was Eli Greenglove's bitterness that night they parted, accusing him of putting Clarissa and the boys in harm's way. And something about a shock Raoul would get—what had Eli meant by that?

He heard a splash and turned to look behind him. His heart stopped. A near-naked Indian was rushing at him out of the water, scalping knife high.

Hands trembling, Raoul had barely time to roll over on his back and fire his rifle up at the screaming warrior. Sunlight glinted off the long steel blade. There was a moment of black terror after the rifle went off. Nothing seemed to happen. His hands had been shaking too hard, he thought, to aim well.

But then the Sauk dropped to his knees and fell over on his side. The knife dropped from his hand. Seeing he was safe for this instant, Raoul took another ball and powder cartridge out of his case and shoved it into the breech.

The Indian rolled over and pushed himself up on his hands and knees, a long string of blood and spittle dangling from his mouth. Calmer now, Raoul took careful aim and put a bullet in the shaven brown skull.

Two more dripping Indians were charging out of the water. Rifles went off beside Raoul. One Sauk fell, then the other, just as he was swinging his tomahawk at a man on the right end of Raoul's line.

The militiaman screamed. The steel head of the tomahawk was buried in his buckskin-clad leg.

"See to him, Armand," Raoul said.

Armand, crouching, ran over to the wounded man. But first he attended to the fallen Indian next to him. He grabbed the brave's head and twisted it around. Raoul heard the crack of bones.

"To make bien sure," Armand said, teeth flashing in his brown beard.

Three men dead, two wounded. Eight men left. Maybe a hundred Sauk warriors out there, maybe more.

What a stupid time to die, right when the war's almost over.

Raoul gnawed on the ends of his mustache and peered into the impenetrable forest. He and his men were all going to die. He was sure of it. He felt fear, but more painful than the fear was an ache in his heart for all that he was going to lose—all that was due him that life hadn't paid out to him like he deserved. He wanted so much to live.

A line of Indians came out of the trees, some with rifles, some with bows and arrows. There must be twenty or thirty of them. They weren't whooping, as they usually did. They were silent, their eyes big, their mouths set in lipless lines. They were like walking dead men, coming at him. That was what they were. They knew they were going to die, but they were going to take this little band of white men with them.

Raoul had all he could do to keep from curling up behind his tree barricade, head in his arms, whimpering with grief and fear. He made himself aim and fire. The Indian he'd picked out as a target kept on coming.

We're done for, he thought, over and over again. *We're done for.*

Slowly—he did not seem able to move quickly—he inserted another cartridge into the breech of his rifle. All around him rifles were going off with deafening booms.

And from behind him there was more booming.

He looked up. Indians were falling. One here, one there, then three, then two more. Their line was breaking up.

God, the men are shooting good!

He heard voices behind him and looked around.

At the same moment Levi Pope said, "Well, here be a sight to welcome."

Ten feet or so behind him a line of men in coonskin caps and gray shirts were methodically firing over his head. He'd been so lost in panic and despair he hadn't heard them coming.

He looked back at the Indians. Brown bodies lay tumbled on the ground, some only a few feet from his barricade. Those on their feet were backing up. They melted into the tattered forest.

For a moment Raoul could not move. He lay clutching his rifle
with a grip so hard it hurt his hands, panting heavily.

"It's safe now," Levi Pope said quietly, standing up.

Raoul pushed himself to his feet. His legs were shaking so hard
he could barely stand. He looked around and saw militiamen wading across to the island from the east bank of the Mississippi.

The men who had been skirmishing in the forest north of the
Bad Axe must have seen the fighting on the island.

Too dazed even to feel happy, Raoul stood taking long breaths
and watched the militiamen come.

He had never in his life needed a drink more than he did now,
and he had forgotten to bring any whiskey with him.

The southern tip of the island was soon crowded with riflemen.
Raoul's three dead were stretched out under blankets, and a burly
horse doctor from the mining country was bandaging the leg of the
man with the tomahawk wound.

"Colonel Henry Dodge," said a tall, whip-lean officer wearing
a bicorn hat. He shook hands with Raoul. "We're almost neighbors. I'm from Dodgeville settlement, just a little ways north of
Galena."

"I'm damned glad you came over, Colonel," said Raoul, feeling
like a fool to have gotten himself trapped. "The Sauk still seem to
have a power of fighting men left."

"Glad you saved a few for us. There were only about two dozen
redskins on the north side of the Bad Axe. They let us see them to
draw us away, I guess, from the main body hiding out here. But the
way you were blasting this island with grape, I was afraid we'd have
nothing to do but bury Indians. Or pieces of them."

Dodge ordered his men to spread out in two lines, one behind
the other, across the width of the island. Raoul positioned his little
party in the center of the foremost line.

"Advance, my brave Suckers!" Dodge called, and the men
laughed at the nickname for Illinoisians. Holding up a long cavalry
saber, Dodge led the militia line, bayonets leveled, into the broken
trees.

Raoul looked downriver for the *Victory*. She had dropped a
wooden ramp to the riverbank, and blue-uniformed regulars were

boarding. When they got here there would be enough soldiers on the island to wipe out the Indians ten times over.

That would be Zachary Taylor's outfit, from Fort Crawford. Raoul had heard that the five hundred Federal troops sent from the East had been decimated by cholera, though their commander, Winfield Scott, was still on the way here.

Raoul turned and pushed forward, stumbling over tree trunks, shoving branches out of the way with his rifle, muscles rigid against the arrow he feared would come whistling out of the gloomy shadows ahead. He saw no living Indians, but many mangled corpses. He tripped over a bare, brown severed leg. A moccasin, flaps decorated with undulating red, white and black beadwork, was still on the foot.

Three Indians, swinging tomahawks and war clubs, sprang out from behind a pile of grape-blasted birch trees. Raoul and the men flanking him started shooting. The Indians were riddled before they got within ten feet.

Raoul was sure he'd killed one of the warriors. He went to the body, drew his Bowie knife and gripped the long black scalplock. He carved a circle with the sharp point in the shaved skin around the scalplock. White bone showed through when he pulled the patch of skin loose, the round spot quickly filling with blood.

The scalplock was long enough to let him tie it around his belt. The hair felt coarser than a white man's.

They pressed on into the forest, again and again meeting desperate little bands of red men, who rushed them only to be felled by a hail of lead balls. Raoul heard the constant banging of many rifles going off in other parts of the forest.

And sometimes he heard the high screams of women and children. After the screams, silence.

Raoul smiled to himself. This was how he wanted it. No prisoners.

Killing no longer seemed dangerous. It no longer felt like sport. It became simply work through the day's heat. It was tiring work, but good. With some surprise Raoul realized that the line of troops had swept most of the island and were now approaching the north end. He could see Indians up ahead through the trees. This might well be the last of them. Eagerly, rifle ready, he rushed forward.

He burst into a clearing and found himself facing a half circle of nearly a dozen bucks, their shaved scalps and bare chests gleaming with sweat. Behind them cowered a pack of squaws and children.

The warriors shouted at Raoul and his men and beckoned to them. Right in the center was one man much taller than the rest, with the red and white feathers of a brave tied into his scalplock. Whatever insults or challenges he was uttering, he looked Raoul right in the eye and shouted directly at him.

Raoul felt a chill of fear. The Indian's flesh was wasted, but his skeleton was huge. He looked like he'd be as hard to stop as a tornado. And he was holding a rifle in arms and hands so big that they made it look small.

The other warriors didn't have rifles or even bows. They must have run out of powder and shot and arrows. They held clubs and knives and tomahawks.

They want us to fight hand to hand. That's what Indians do to show their courage.

The hell with that.

With a movement that seemed almost contemptuous, the big Indian dropped the rifle to the ground. He reached down and picked up a war club painted red and black, with a huge spike at its end.

"Let's pay 'em back, boys!" Raoul shouted. "For all of our people they killed."

"Oui! For Marchette," said Armand, raising his rifle. His first shot caught a warrior in the chest and knocked him down.

At that the Indians rushed Raoul and his men.

Raoul felt himself trembling uncontrollably as the bony giant in the center came straight at him. The big Indian held his war club in front of him, as if to deflect bullets.

Forcing his arms to hold steady, Raoul aimed his rifle at the Indian's head and fired.

And missed.

I should have aimed at his chest.

Raoul cursed his shaking hand as he dropped his rifle and pulled his pistol.

The brown giant gave a long, full-throated war cry.

Raoul pulled the trigger. He saw a spark, heard the bang of the percussion cap, but there was nothing more. He cried out in a fury. His sweat must have dampened the powder.

The club came down on the pistol, and Raoul to his horror felt

it knocked out of his hand. Again the big Indian screamed out his
blood-freezing war whoop and raised the club high.

Raoul's empty hand fumbled for his Bowie knife. He had it out,
a death grip on the hilt. He lunged at his enemy. A jolt ran through
Raoul's arm to his shoulder as the point of the knife sank deep
between two thick ribs.

The Indian gave a deep groan and staggered back. He swung his
club, but too late. Raoul felt a numbing blow just where his neck
met his shoulder, and fell to his knees.

He was looking right into the dark brown eyes of the Indian,
who had also fallen. The eyes were unblinking, dead. The massive
body collapsed against him.

Raoul shouted, a wordless cry of rage, and a red curtain swept
over his eyes. He jerked the knife out, releasing a cataract of blood.
With an effort that wrenched his arms he hurled the brown giant
away from him.

Taking a scalp wasn't enough, after a fight like that. Raoul
got a firm grip on the thick, stiff-standing hank of black hair in
the center of his enemy's head and brought the knife down on the
brown throat. Chopping and slicing and sawing, as if butchering
a steer, Raoul cut through the thick neck until at last the head
came free.

He lofted the head in his left hand, looking up at the still-open
dead eyes.

"There, you goddamned redskin son of a bitch! Thought you
could kill me, huh?"

A shrill woman's voice broke in on his triumph.

He turned to see a witchlike woman wrapped in a blanket. Her
finger was pointing at him. Her voice went on and on, screeching
at him.

She was tall, but starvation had stripped the flesh from her bones.
Her sunken eyes seemed to glow in her skull-like face. He felt as if
he was facing some horrid spectre.

He threw the warrior's head down. Curse him, would she? He
snarled like an angry wolf as he reached for the woman. She didn't
even try to get away. He seized the scrawny neck and pulled her to
him, bringing the Bowie knife's point up against her throat.

She started singing, a weird, high-pitched caterwauling. He'd
heard something like it before. Where?

When he'd been about to shoot Auguste and those two other
Indians at Old Man's Creek. They'd sung like that right at the end.

Her dark eyes held him. They were not clouded over with anger
or terror, but clear with full understanding that he was going to kill
her. She was not afraid. He wished he could frighten her, force
her to grovel, but someone might try to stop him from doing it. Her
voice went on and on, chanting, up and down.

He'd silence her now. Redskin bitch.

He drove the knife into her throat and jerked it sideways. Her
song ended in a sickening rasp.

Still the brown eyes were fixed on him. Her blood spurted out
of the gash he had cut open, splashed over his knife blade, poured
hot on his hand. It spread down over her dress and over the gold
lace on his sleeve. He looked down at his red hand and felt some
force within him stretch his lips and bare his teeth.

He thrust the woman away from him. Her eyes were still open,
but she looked at no one and nothing. She fell to the ground like a
bundle of sticks. She lay on her back, the deep wound in her throat
spread wide, her eyes staring up.

He stood over her and saw that something shiny had fallen out
of the front of her dress and lay beside her head. Tied around her
neck with a purple ribbon was an oval metal case splashed with
blood.

He had seen the case, or one like it. He reached down with the
knife and slashed the ribbon. He wiped his knife on his jacket and
slammed it into its sheath, then picked up the slippery case and
opened it.

A pair of spectacles. Round, gold frames, thick glass lenses.

They looked exactly like Pierre's old spectacles. Was that possible? How could this Indian woman have gotten them? Stolen from
Victoire, when the Sauk burned it?

Or had the mongrel somehow gotten his father's spectacles, taken
them with him when he fled from Victor? Pierre's watch had disappeared then; Raoul was sure Auguste had stolen it. And if this
woman had Pierre's glasses now, could she be the Sauk woman
Pierre had lived with, the mother of his bastard son?

Despite the August heat beating down on the clearing, the air
around Raoul suddenly felt winter cold. All day long while he fought
the Indians he'd struggled with his fear of being killed. Now a worse

fear had him in its grip, a fear of something worse than death, of having called down upon himself a vengeance that would follow him beyond the grave.

My God! I've just killed Pierre's squaw.

The spectacles stared up at him like accusing eyes. The flesh of his back prickled.

He shut the case and dropped it into his pocket. If it was Pierre's he couldn't just throw it away.

The few remaining Indians, a flock of women and children, huddled weeping with their backs to a big tree, arms around one another. Some were already wounded and screaming in pain.

Tiredly Raoul told himself he must reload rifle and pistol and get on with the killing. But his anger was spent. He felt empty, worn out.

From somewhere behind him came a shout of, "Cease fire!"

It was welcome. He'd done enough.

"Yonder come the bluebellies," said Levi.

"Ah, merde," muttered Armand, standing with red-dripping bayonet above a pile of bodies.

Raoul looked around. The order to stop the shooting had come from their rear, from a short, stout officer who, as Dodge had, was advancing with drawn saber. Colonel Zachary Taylor.

Taylor looked around the smoking glade at the dead, big bodies and little ones, brown flesh and tan deerskin splashed with bright red, eyes staring, limbs helter-skelter.

"Jesus Christ." He turned to Raoul, pain in his bright blue eyes.

Raoul felt his face grow hot. "Colonel," he said, "you understand why we had to—"

Taylor's expression changed from sadness to weariness. "I've been out on the frontier for over twenty years. I don't see anything here that I haven't seen before." He turned away before Raoul could answer and called, "Lieutenant Davis!"

A tall young officer with a handsome, angular face came up to him and saluted.

Taylor said, "Jeff, run ahead and make sure any Indians left on this island get a chance to surrender." He turned to Raoul again, shaking his head.

"Why let them surrender?" Raoul said.

"There's only a few left alive," said Taylor. "And we're not going to kill them. And if you need a reason, it's because I wouldn't feel right about it, and I know a lot of the men wouldn't feel right about it."

Taylor turned to one of his men, a red-faced trooper with a thick blond mustache. "Sergeant Benson, get me that Sauk man we captured. We'll be needing to talk to the Indians. We want to find out what's happened to Black Hawk."

Raoul was painfully aware that Taylor's eyes had shifted to his right hand, covered with blood. He wanted to hide it behind his back.

He looked Raoul up and down. "Good God, man. Do you know you've got blood all over you?"

"Enemy blood," said Raoul.

"I see you've got a scalp tied to your belt," Taylor said. "General Atkinson issued an order against mutilating enemy dead."

Raoul felt himself shaking again, not with fear, but with anger. "I saw one of my best friends shot dead with an arrow through the throat today."

"And this?" Taylor asked, pointing to the severed head of the big brave lying a few feet from Raoul's red-spotted boots. "Was this to avenge your friend too? You'd better get back to your steamship, Mr. de Marion. I don't think we have any more need of your services here."

It was not so much Taylor's words, but the mingled contempt and pity in his voice that enraged Raoul. His fist clenched on the handle of his knife.

Taylor wore a pistol and carried a saber, but he was a far smaller man than Raoul, and his stout body, dressed today in a blue jacket and knee-high fringed buckskin boots, seemed to invite attack.

Taylor's calm blue eyes went to Raoul's hand, then back to his face. He stood motionless, waiting.

God! What am I thinking? The regulars would shoot me down the minute I drew this knife.

Raoul silently beckoned to his men and started back through the broken trees the way they had come.

After walking a short distance, Raoul saw the sergeant Taylor had sent behind the lines coming toward him with an Indian walking beside him.

Raoul glanced at the Indian and stopped dead.

He felt as if the arrow he'd been expecting and fearing all day had finally struck him.

There are no ghosts.

But Auguste couldn't be alive. He'd been shot to death at Old Man's Creek.

Was this what killing Pierre's squaw had brought on him?

The man before him had gone hungry for a long time. His almost skull-like face was a chilling reminder of the woman whose throat Raoul had slashed. But his gauntness also made him look more like Pierre than ever before. His buckskin leggings, like those of the Indians Raoul had just killed, were dirty and full of rips and holes. But the pale scar line running down his cheek, and those five parallel scars on his bare chest, left Raoul in no doubt who this was. Auguste's dark eyes burned at Raoul, alight with a fierce hatred.

The sergeant pulled Auguste by the arm. As the mongrel turned, Raoul suddenly saw that the middle of his ear was missing, the empty space bordered by partly healed red flesh.

Stunned speechless, Raoul looked at Levi and Armand, who stared back at him. They couldn't speak either. They were just as shaken.

Still burning at Taylor's high-and-mighty dismissal of him, Raoul was staggered by the shock of this meeting. But he saw one thing clear. All right, Auguste was still alive. That meant Raoul's revenge on the Sauk was not complete. Auguste was a traitor. Auguste was a murderer. And Raoul was going to work day and night to get him hanged.

21

The Red Blanket

Longing to hear that White Bear was safe, Redbird could not stop thinking about him. She sat cross-legged on the ground with Floating Lily bundled in a blanket on her lap. She gazed out at the small lake where Black Hawk and his few remaining followers had set up camp. This was a peaceful place, but with White Bear gone and her dread of what might have happened to her loved ones at the Bad Axe, she could feel no peace.

"A lovely place, this lake," said Owl Carver, sitting beside her.

But it is far from White Bear.

The thought of White Bear's having to make his way through Winnebago country haunted her. She longed to look into the birch forest behind her lean-to and see him walking toward her through the white tree trunks.

She missed Yellow Hair and Woodrow too. They were to her another sister, another son. She hoped that by now they were out of danger.

She had left so many people behind at the Bad Axe, people who had always been part of her life—Sun Woman, Iron Knife, her two sisters. In the seven days since Black Hawk had led their little group north on the ridge trail leading to Chippewa country, there had been no word from the rest of the band.

Redbird's fear for the people she loved was like a ferret eating away at her insides.

From his medicine bag Owl Carver took the pale eyes time teller White Bear had given him and opened its gold outer shell. Redbird saw black markings on its inner surface and two black arrows.

Could it tell me when White Bear will come back?

The old shaman dangled the time teller by its gold chain over Floating Lily's tiny head. The gold disk gave off a regular, clicking sound, like the beating of a metal heart. Floating Lily's brown eyes opened wide and her flower-petal lips curved in a wide, toothless smile.

Eagle Feather, sitting beside Redbird, said, "Grandfather? Is it right to use a sacred thing just to make the baby smile?"

Owl Carver smiled. His face these days seemed to have caved in. All of his front teeth were gone, and his mouth was as sunken as Floating Lily's, while his chin and his nose jutted out.

"A baby's smile is also a sacred thing."

Redbird said, "Have you asked the spirits what has become of the rest of our people?"

From a cord around his waist Owl Carver untied a medicine bag decorated with a beadwork owl. He opened it, let little gray scraps sift through his fingers and sighed.

"Last night I chewed bits of sacred mushroom," Owl Carver said. "I saw pale eyes' things—lodges that travel over the ground on trails made of metal, smoking boats with bonfires in their bellies, villages as big as prairies. Crowds of pale eyes seemed to be cheering for me. It made no sense. It told me nothing about what happened at the Bad Axe. Maybe I took too much."

Redbird glanced down at Eagle Feather. His mouth was a circle, and his blue eyes as he stared up at Owl Carver were so wide that she could see the whites above and below them. He strained toward Owl Carver, his longing to follow his father and grandfather in the way of the shaman showing in every line of his body.

She had always felt that same longing.

"Let me try your sacred mushrooms," said Redbird. "Sun Woman says sometimes women can see into places where men cannot see."

Owl Carver set the medicine bag down between himself and Eagle Feather. He sliced his hand through the air, palm down, in refusal.

"The magic might get into your milk and be bad for the baby."

Resentment was a bitter taste in Redbird's mouth. But she had to admit there was no telling what the mushrooms might do to Floating Lily's unformed spirit. Still, she knew Owl Carver welcomed that excuse because he did not want to give the mushrooms to a woman.

Eagle Feather shouted, "Look!" He pointed up at the sky.

Owl Carver and Redbird both looked up. Scanning the cloudless midday sky for a moment, she saw two tiny black shapes high up, circling slowly.

"Eagles!" said the boy. "My guardian spirits."

Redbird squinted. Yes, those were the wide-spreading wings of eagles. The birds were searching for prey. Like the long knives and their Winnebago allies. Their remorseless circling frightened her.

Those bright blue eyes of Eagle Feather's saw farther than hers did, thought Redbird. She looked down at him proudly, as he wiped his hand across his mouth and smiled up at her. His pointed chin reminded her of White Bear.

"If the Winnebago find us here, will they kill us?" she asked her father.

Owl Carver waved his hands. "They are not our enemies, but they will do what the long knives demand."

In a strange voice Eagle Feather said, "Mother?"

Frightened by his flat tone, she reached for him. But with the baby in her lap she could not get to him before Eagle Feather fell over on his side with his eyes shut.

She screamed.

She laid Floating Lily on the ground and picked up Eagle Feather. He lay limp in her arms, his head lolling, his mouth hanging open.

After all they had been through, this was more than she could bear. She burst into tears, her heart thudding like a deerskin drum.

"What is it?" She turned to Owl Carver. "Help him."

The shaman crouched over his grandson, looking down into his face, bending low to sniff his breath.

"Redbird, be very quiet. We must not wake him."

"What happened to him?" she whispered, trembling.

"This." He gestured to the open medicine bag that lay where he and Eagle Feather had been sitting. "He must have taken some bits of mushroom while we were looking up at the eagles."

Terror cascaded over her. "What will it do to him?"

Owl Carver emptied the gray scraps into his hand and then poured them back into the bag. "What a foolish old man I am, leaving that bag open right next to him."

Eagle Feather had gone on a spirit journey. And her own sensitivity to the other world told her that he was *meant* to. She felt for him the fear she had felt for White Bear in that long-ago Moon of Ice.

"No," said Redbird sadly. "You were not foolish. It was Earth-maker's way. He sent those eagles to take our eyes away from the medicine bag."

With infinite care, so as not to disturb him, Redbird carried Eagle Feather into the lean-to, resting his head on the blanket roll that held everything she had been able to carry.

"I will stay with you until Eagle Feather comes back," said Owl Carver. Redbird picked up Floating Lily and held her tightly.

As the sun crossed above the lake, they sat watching the small, still body. Redbird could barely see Eagle Feather's narrow chest rise and fall in the shadowy lean-to. There were moments when she was sure he was dead.

Sunset had turned the small lake to a sheet of beaten gold when Eagle Feather sat up suddenly, his eyes wide.

"The Bad Axe!" he shrieked. It was the voice of a child struggling with a nightmare.

"Eagle Feather!" Redbird cried.

Owl Carver put his hand on her knee. "Be quiet."

"The Bad Axe!" Eagle Feather called out again, staring at something no one else could see. "The Great River runs red!" His eyes closed and he fell back.

Redbird felt as if she were shivering in a blizzard. Eagle Feather's words seemed to open a doorway of second sight in her own mind, disclosing a horrifying vision of bodies drifting in red-tinged water.

She heard a sound behind her. Suddenly terrified, she whirled. In the birch forest she saw a man riding toward them on a gray pony. The beat of hooves sounded hollow among the trees.

Feeling on the edge of madness, she let out a scream. She had wanted so much for White Bear to come to her that way, that she thought for a moment it was he. Like White Bear's, his head was unshaved, his hair long.

But as he came closer through the white tree trunks, a hand raised in greeting, she saw he was not White Bear. His full head of hair had a brave's feathers tied into it. A Winnebago. She saw a second rider behind him. An attack? But they were approaching slowly, their hands empty.

The Winnebago dismounted and led his pony till he was standing over them.

He wore four red and white feathers, one hanging from each silver earring, two tied into his hair. A leader of warriors. Heart pounding, she moved protectively closer to the lean-to where Eagle Feather lay. Owl Carver slowly got to his feet. She glanced at him, and when she saw how grim his face was, her own terror increased.

Another Winnebago rode out of the woods, dismounted and stood beside his companion.

The first man turned to take something from his saddle.

Scooping Floating Lily up in her arms, Redbird leaped up to give the alarm. The brave held out a restraining hand.

"Wait! We are two only, and we come to talk peace." The man spoke Sauk.

He faced her, smiling tentatively, and held up a beautiful calumet, its red pipestone bowl gleaming in the sunset, its polished hickory stem as long as a man's arm.

Owl Carver drew himself up in all his white-haired shaman's majesty. "Who are you?"

"I am called Wave," said the man holding the calumet. "This is He Who Lights the Water. He does not speak Sauk."

Redbird glanced down into the lean-to, to make sure Eagle Feather was all right.

"Who is in the lean-to?" Wave asked a little suspiciously as He Who Lights the Water stepped forward to look in.

"My grandson," said Owl Carver. "He is sick."

"Many of you must be sick. And hungry," said Wave. "Time your leaders took pity on the women and children and ended this war."

More Sauk men and women were coming over now to see the newcomers. The two Winnebago were men of courage, Redbird thought, coming alone as they had into a camp of fifty or more desperate people.

Redbird's mother came to stand beside Owl Carver. She asked what was wrong with Eagle Feather, and Owl Carver explained in a whisper.

"Children will eat anything they can get their hands on," Wind Bends Grass scolded. "Now he will probably grow up to be a madman." Redbird held back a shriek of rage.

Black Hawk and the Winnebago Prophet strode through the gathering crowd to face the newcomers. Black Hawk carried under one arm one of those heavy paper bundles captured at Old Man's Creek. He glanced at Redbird, and she thought she saw reproach in his eyes, even though he had said he forgave her for her part in Yellow Hair's and Woodrow's escape.

Flying Cloud addressed Wave in a strange tongue.

"This Winnebago brave is the son of my sister," said the Prophet pompously in Sauk.

Does he think that means we are saved? Redbird wondered, sick of the Winnebago Prophet forever claiming that victory awaited just a little farther along the trail, when it was so clear that the trail led only to death.

Wave said in Sauk, "My father is a Sauk who married into the Winnebago. So I come to you as one joined with you by blood. We were sent by the chief of our band, Falcon."

"How did you find us?" Black Hawk asked.

"One of our hunters was passing this way and saw your camp. He was afraid to come near you, but he told me. I have been looking for you for many days."

Wolf Paw, his face so deeply lined that he looked as old as his father, came to stand beside Black Hawk. "Do you have news of our people who were trying to cross the Great River?" he asked. He touched the silver coin that hung around his neck, as if for luck.

Dread flowed cold through Redbird's arms and legs.

Now we will know.

Wave and He Who Lights the Water looked at each other for a long, silent moment.

"What has happened?" Black Hawk pressed them.

"The long knives caught up with them," said Wave. "Most of the people were hiding on an island in the Great River. The long knives had a smoke boat that fired a thunder gun at the island and killed many people. Then the long knives landed on the island and killed nearly all that were left."

Redbird reeled, stunned.

Sun Woman! My second mother! Iron Knife! Oh, no! O Earth-maker, let it not be so.

Cold crept over her as she remembered Eagle Feather's cry: *The Bad Axe! The Great River runs red!*

Black Hawk gave a cry of anguish. His paper bundle dropped
to the ground with a thud. He sat down on the ground, picked up
a handful of ashes from Redbird's campfire and threw them on his
head. The people around him screamed and wept and held one another in their grief.

Wind Bends Grass fell against Owl Carver, and both of them
sank to the ground weeping. Redbird saw Wolf Paw standing
slumped and motionless, his arms hanging helpless at his sides, his
face gray. He had insisted that both his wives and his four children
try to cross the Great River at the Bad Axe, thinking they would be
safer.

Sobbing and clutching her baby, Redbird watched the orange
sun disappear behind the pointed treetops on the western shore of
the little lake. She thought, Iron Knife, so strong and always there
when she needed him, must be gone. Her two sisters and their new
husbands, probably dead.

The people mourned, some sitting on the ground, some walking
about distractedly, some standing, holding each other.

And now Eagle Feather was stricken. She could not get the chill
out of her body.

When it was dark she relit her fire. Floating Lily woke and cried,
and Redbird held her to her breast. Then she crawled under her
lean-to to look at Eagle Feather. His eyes were still shut. He had
not moved since his outcry, and his breathing was shallow.

*I cannot bear this. Eagle Feather lying as if dead, White Bear
vanished, most of my people dead.*

Why have I been spared to suffer so?

Black Hawk began to mourn aloud for his lost people:

"Hu-hu-hu-u-u-u . . . Whu-whu-whu-u-u-u . . ."

The rest of the people joined in the wailing. Redbird noticed
that Wave and He Who Lights the Water cried out, too, and tears
ran from their eyes. She liked them for joining the mourning.

Owl Carver was sitting beside her, holding the hands of weeping
Wind Bends Grass. His own features, as much of them as she could
see in the twilight, were still and drawn, shrunken by sorrow.

Redbird thought, the Sauk were known far and wide as a people
who never shirked the demands of honor. If even one man of Black
Hawk's party smoked the calumet with Wave, that would oblige
Black Hawk and his remaining braves to surrender to the Winnebago and make peace.

Redbird said, "Now, with so many dead, can we have peace? Will you smoke the pipe with these two men?"

Owl Carver said, "If I were alone, I would smoke the pipe with them. But I will not go against Black Hawk."

"We are all that is left of the band," she said. "Someone must take the calumet and smoke it."

And by that odious Sauk custom, she thought, clenching her jaw, it would have to be a man.

As darkness deepened, the wailing died down. Wave and He Who Lights the Water made a little fire at the edge of the lake near Redbird's lean-to.

One by one the last people of Black Hawk's band drifted close to Wave's fire.

The Winnebago brave stood before the fire holding the peace pipe. Twilight lingered in the sky behind him while the firelight before him illuminated his heavy features.

Sitting near Eagle Feather, Redbird looked around and saw silent figures standing in the shadows as the people waited to hear what Wave had to say. Gravely he took tobacco out of a pouch at his waist and filled the bowl of the calumet. Then he touched a dry stick to his fire and carried the flame to the pipe. It flared up bright yellow over the pipe bowl as he puffed on it.

Wave cleared his throat and spoke in a strong voice. "Earthmaker gave us the sacred tobacco as a means of making peace among us. No one may break a promise sealed with tobacco. Our chief, Falcon, asks me to say this to you:

"Black Hawk, you have frightened the long knives greatly, brought them much sorrow, and forced them to pursue you over rivers and swamps and mountains. Black Hawk, your honor has been satisfied. Falcon offers this tobacco to you and asks that you end this war, for the sake of your women who are hungry and sick and your children who are without fathers."

Yes, let it be done. Let this war be over before all of us are dead.

Redbird's heart leaped with hope as she saw Black Hawk reach toward the pipe that Wave held out to him. He was about to take it and smoke it! But his hand, instead of grasping, only pointed at the pipe.

"I will not smoke this pipe. I believe the Sauk should fight on until they cannot fight anymore."

Please, Earthmaker, let at least one man be moved to stand for peace.

Wave added more tobacco to the pipe and puffed on it again. He stood before the Winnebago Prophet.

"Show your wisdom, Uncle. Smoke the sacred tobacco."

Flying Cloud took a step backward and raised both arms. "It is wrong for the Winnebago to turn against us in our time of need. Go back and tell your Chief Falcon that if he does not join us in making war on the long knives, they will take his land from him as they have taken ours from us." He crossed his arms before his chest.

Despairing, Redbird realized that the Winnebago Prophet could not smoke the pipe because that would be admitting that all his advice up to now had been wrong.

"What will you do, Sauk shaman?" Wave said to Owl Carver. "Do not the spirits tell you to smoke the calumet?"

"Please do it, Father," Redbird whispered.

She wanted to shout it aloud. But she held her tongue. She remembered with pain the derision of Wolf Paw and the others when she spoke out at the war council.

She bit her lip. Maybe, by speaking out that time, she had turned people away from the path she wanted them to take. She would not make that mistake again.

Owl Carver said, "Black Hawk has always been my chief. I follow where he leads."

Redbird groaned. Now she wished she had spoken out.

Eagle Feather stirred beside her. Heart frozen, she looked down at him. But he was motionless again.

Wave turned next to Wolf Paw, who closed his eyes, bowed his head and made no move to accept the pipe. Redbird saw that the red crest on his head was faded and limp.

She could only watch as the two Winnebago went from man to man in the circle of firelight, holding out the pipe, each man refusing.

"Please," Wave pleaded, "is there not a man here wise and strong enough to smoke the calumet and save the lives of his people? Please—more pain and death is needless."

In a day or two a war band of Winnebago would come after Black Hawk's party. They would greatly outnumber these fifty people. They would have rifles with plenty of powder and shot, given to them by the long knives. They would slaughter the men and take the women and children into captivity.

Earthmaker, I beg you, do not let your children die.

She heard a rustling beside her. She gasped in fright and her hands went cold.

Eagle Feather was up on his hands and knees.

The boy crawled out from under the lean-to, climbed to his feet and stood straight.

A half-moon hung over the little lake, and she could see Eagle Feather's set face, one side red with firelight and the other pale white in moonlight. His bright blue eyes fixed on Wave, he strode forward, a small, determined figure.

Astonished, Redbird could only stand and watch. How could this be happening?

He stood before Wave and held up his hands. For a moment there was silence in the camp, disturbed only by the crackling of the fire and the rustling of the birch leaves around them.

"No!" Black Hawk cried, his rasping voice full of anguish. "Do not do it!"

"Stop!" The Winnebago Prophet reached for Eagle Feather. Owl Carver quickly blocked his way.

"You must not touch him. He returns from a spirit walk."

Solemnly Wave handed the pipe down to Eagle Feather.

Others took up the cry. "No! No!" But no one laid a hand on Eagle Feather.

And many were silent, and Redbird knew that she was not the only one in the camp who wanted Eagle Feather to smoke the pipe.

Awed, Redbird realized that the spirits hovered over Eagle Feather, guiding him. Her son had been chosen to save the remnant of the band, though only six summers had passed since his birth. She felt her mouth trembling.

Eagle Feather put the mouthpiece of the pipe to his lips and drew in. A deep puff. Though he was but six years old and had never smoked before, he showed no pain as the hot smoke filled his tender mouth, nor did he cough. Redbird's heart swelled with pride.

Eagle Feather blew the smoke out again. A single puff, according to custom.

Wave's thick features were breaking in tearful relief.

Eagle Feather had known just what to do. And there could be no doubt in anyone's mind that he meant to do what he had done. He held the pipe up to Wave.

A new cry of pain rose from Black Hawk, and the Winnebago Prophet joined him as loudly.

But Redbird's heart was happy. She hugged Floating Lily.

Their long agony was over at last.

Eagle Feather turned and walked back to her, straight and steady, as if he had not been lying all day long unconscious. She quickly handed Floating Lily to Wind Bends Grass, knelt down and held her arms out to her son. He ran into them, and they held each other tightly.

"It was good that you smoked the pipe. Very good."

Eagle Feather said, "When the eagles came over the lake, my spirit self whispered to me to eat from Grandfather's medicine bag. Then I went to many strange places and saw many very bad things. The long knives killed many people. At the end of it all, I lay in the lean-to and I heard a voice say that if someone would smoke the calumet there would be peace. And my father's spirit self, the White Bear, came to me and told me to smoke."

If White Bear had been here he would have smoked the calumet. I know he would.

Owl Carver put his hand on Eagle Feather's shoulder.

"The boy is the grandson of Owl Carver and of Sun Woman. He is the son of White Bear. He has had his first vision. It is fore-ordained that he should be a Great Shaman."

Redbird felt flames burning under the skin of her face.

"He is the son of Redbird as well," she said, her voice shaking.

Owl Carver put his other hand on Redbird's shoulder. "Yes, he is your son."

Suddenly his old face crumbled. "And all my other children are gone," he wept. "Redbird, you are the only one left."

Redbird trembled as she saw Fort Crawford, a great square formed by long stone lodges connected by log palisade walls. Hard-faced long knives in blue jackets surrounded the Sauk, pointing rifles at them. Redbird drew the sling in which she carried Floating Lily around from her back to hold her tight. With one hand she pulled Eagle Feather, who stumbled under a heavy blanket roll, close to her.

"You will all camp in the field beside the fort," said Wave. "If anyone tries to escape, those left behind will be punished."

Redbird heard a wordless cry from behind her. She turned and was astonished to see a group of gray shadows standing in a meadow outside the fort. She saw they were Sauk women, some holding babies, some with small children standing beside them.

Redbird swung Floating Lily around to her back and rushed to the silent women, praying that among them she would see Sun Woman or her sisters. She moved more slowly as she realized that the eyes of each silent face she peered into were lifeless and the mouths slack.

These few, she grasped with horror, were all that was left of the people who had tried to cross the Great River at the Bad Axe. Just as White Bear had predicted.

She came to Water Flows Fast, barely able to recognize her. She had changed terribly, a change that had begun when the long knives killed her husband, Three Horses, at Old Man's Creek. The older woman's face had lost its roundness. Her cheeks sagged and her head shook with a constant tremor.

"Is it really you, Redbird? In the flesh? I am not on the Trail of Souls?"

Redbird drew Water Flows Fast to her.

"Redbird, they killed everybody. They kept killing and killing. They would not stop. Even babies. I don't know why I'm still alive. My children are dead. They tried to swim away, and the long knives shot them in the water."

Wild Grape, Redbird's younger sister, rushed up to her. They fell into each other's arms, weeping. Redbird had never loved her sister as much as she did at this moment.

Wild Grape said, "I saw Robin's Nest die. She stood before a long knife. She was holding her baby son. She begged for her life. He just smiled and shot her. She dropped the baby, and the long knife shot him on the ground. They would have killed me, but a long knife chief came along and stopped it."

"And Iron Knife?" Redbird asked. "What about Iron Knife?"

Wild Grape drew back and looked at Redbird with huge eyes. "Redbird, one of them cut off Iron Knife's head."

Redbird screamed as Wild Grape babbled on.

"Yes, with a knife this big." She held her hands wide apart. "And Sun Woman called down the wrath of Earthmaker upon him, and with the same knife he cut her throat."

Redbird fell to her knees sobbing. "Oh, no more! No more!"

Water Flows Fast and Wild Grape knelt with her and held her, and they wept together.

Redbird cried until Floating Lily began to wail. Redbird gave her daughter the breast and a warmth spread from her baby's sucking lips, blunting the edge of grief and calming her a little.

Wild Grape said, "I have seen White Bear."

Redbird's body went rigid. Floating Lily pulled her mouth away from Redbird's breast and started to cry again.

"White Bear? Alive?"

Wild Grape nodded. "When the long knives were killing us at the Bad Axe, he came. He was the long knife war chief's prisoner. He spoke for the long knife chief, told us not to be afraid. But then he saw Sun Woman lying on the ground with her throat cut. He fell down beside her and screamed and tore at his face. The long knives had to hold him. I thought they might kill him, or he might kill himself. They dragged him away. I think he is a prisoner right there in that fort."

Or perhaps he is dead, Redbird thought bitterly. *Like everyone else.*

In miserable silence she made a little tent out of her blanket in the field by the fort, using sticks Eagle Feather found for her. She and her children huddled under the blanket, the sorrow in her belly like a wolf inside her trying to gnaw and claw its way out.

The thought that White Bear might be on the other side of those walls of white-painted limestone was more than she could stand. She could not move or speak. Long knives stood around the edges of the field, watching the remnant of the British Band with their cold pale eyes. Redbird almost wished one of them would shoot her and end her pain. But then what would her children do? She did not want Eagle Feather and Floating Lily to die.

Later that day Owl Carver hobbled over to her, followed by a thin-lipped long knife with a rifle.

"Good-bye, my daughter." He looked very old and tired. It was a miracle that he had lived through this war. She noticed that he held in his hand the owl-decorated medicine bag.

"Where are you going, Father?"

"The Winnebago Prophet, Black Hawk and I must go into the fort to meet the pale eyes war chiefs. I guess they will shoot us or hang us. I cannot see the future anymore. Wave tells me that the rest of you are to walk south to the Rock River. The long knives will keep you at their fort there till next spring. Then they will let you cross the river to join He Who Moves Alertly in Ioway country. Take care of your mother and your sister. You are the strongest and wisest of my children."

He thrust his medicine bag at her.

"If I bring this into the fort it may be lost to our people forever. You are my child. You must be the spirit walker for the British Band."

A golden glow spread through her body. She took the bag from him—it was very light in her hands—and held it against her chest. She tried to speak, but her throat closed up on her.

Owl Carver said, "Remember always, all people, even the pale eyes, are children of Earthmaker. Whatever power Earthmaker gives you, never use it against another person. If the long knives hurt you, you can ask for strength to fight them yourself, but never call on the spirits to attack them."

"Yes, Father."

Even if they have killed White Bear, I will not use the power of the spirits against them.

"Farewell, my child."

Redbird took Owl Carver's hand. "If you meet White Bear there in the fort, tell him I am alive and Eagle Feather and Floating Lily are alive, and one day we will all be together."

Wolf Paw stood beside her, watching Black Hawk, the Winnebago Prophet and Owl Carver walk into the square of buildings. They were followed by six blue-coated long knives pointing rifles at them and by a delegation of Winnebago chiefs and braves.

She clutched the medicine bag tightly.

Her eyes clouded over. She saw a crowd of pale eyes with distorted mouths, shouting. Terror seized her, and she tried to cry aloud, but she could not. The white faces dissolved, and she saw a mound of earth in a forest. Atop it was a willow wand with a small strip of red blanket tied to it. Darkness closed in around her.

She felt strong hands gripping her arms. Her sight cleared, and she realized that Wolf Paw was holding her.

"You were falling," he said.

"I am afraid," she said. "I have seen death on the trail before us."

Wolf Paw looked down at her with earnest eyes. He had aged so much! He had untied the red horsehair crest from his head, a wise thing to do, because there were pale eyes who might recognize him as a leading Sauk brave and want revenge. He now had only a short, irregular growth of black hair on the middle of his scalp and stubble growing around it, but he still wore the silver coin around his neck.

He said, "Whatever we must face, you have more courage than any of us. I have not forgotten many winters ago when the spirit Bear came to our camp. I turned and ran while you stood fast."

She waved a hand. "It was only White Bear."

"We did not know that then. From that day when I ran and you stood, I have always wished that a child of mine might possess your courage and wisdom."

She remembered how he had pushed her aside the night she stood beside White Bear and warned the tribe against going to war. She remembered the woman's dress he had forced on White Bear. But the man she saw before her was lost and grieving. He had lost his war. He had let his wives and children be killed. He had failed himself. He had nothing left to believe in.

So she only said, "Be as a father to the children I do have. Help me protect them."

The sun beat down on her bare head, and the dust of the trail choked her. This was the Moon of Dry Rivers, the hottest time of summer. Every step hurt her heart, because every step took her farther away from that fort where the long knives might be holding White Bear. Might be. She had never been able to find out.

By the third day of their trek southward along the Great River, the soles of Redbird's moccasins had worn through. She stumbled over ruts dug in the wide trail by pale eyes' wagon wheels. The sun had baked the packed dirt of the trail till it was hard as stone.

When the long knives let them stop to rest at midday, she took from her blanket roll White Bear's knife. With the knife she cut strips away from her doeskin dress and bound them around her feet. She cut up Eagle Feather's shirt and wrapped his moccasins so they would last longer.

A long knife with a thick blond mustache was standing over her with his hand out.

"Give me that. No knives."

He spoke the pale eyes' tongue, but she knew enough of it to understand. But she couldn't give up the knife. It was all she had left of White Bear. Her grip tightened on the deerhorn handle, and she thought she would stab the long knife—or herself—before she would let go of it.

She tried to tell him that this was precious, that it belonged to her husband who was a shaman. But she did not have the American words to say that.

He just kept saying "No knives," and his face turned a deep red. His hand rested on the butt of his pistol.

Wolf Paw came over. He took her wrist in a strong grip and took the knife from her hand and held it out, handle first, to the blue-coat.

She understood why Wolf Paw had forced her to give up the knife, but she was angry with him.

"That was White Bear's knife from his father," she said.

"The long knife would have killed you," Wolf Paw said. "We cannot fight them." She saw the hopelessness in his eyes, and she put her hand reassuringly on his arm. When the long knives ordered them to get up and start walking, he walked beside her.

She was hungry all day long. A food wagon followed the party. Three times a day the soldiers got meat and bread from it, but the Sauk got only corn mash on tin plates, which they washed out in the river and returned to the food wagon. Several times a day they were allowed to stop and drink from the river. Redbird prayed that her milk would hold out for Floating Lily.

She sang a walking song, to try to forget her pain and to help her put one aching foot in front of the other.

> "We walk this trail, following the deer.
> Sing as you walk, oh, braves and squaws!
> Last night I dreamed my moccasins
> Struck fire as they touched the ground."

When she raised her voice others joined in. After a while even Wolf Paw began to sing in a deep voice.

Five blue-coated long knives rode before the Sauk and another five behind them. Redbird looked around at her people, a hundred or so, mostly women and children. The men numbered about twenty. Tired, hungry, sick, broken in spirit. All of them on foot now, the last of their horses having been taken away at Fort Crawford.

She remembered Owl Carver's parting words to her. *You must be the spirit walker for the British Band.* And Wolf Paw had said that she had the courage and wisdom to face death on the trail.

Whatever this remnant of her people might have to meet now, she promised herself that she would use all her strength to help them through it.

They came to a smaller river, the Fever, that flowed into the Great River. A flatboat to take travelers across was drawn up on shore. The long knives had angry words with the men who would pole the flatboat. Redbird understood that the boatmen would not carry her people. Let them swim, their gestures said. But the river was too deep and its current too swift for these half-starved, exhausted people.

While the long knives argued with the boatmen, more pale eyes came to watch. They must have a town nearby. Redbird felt a chill of fear at the hatred she saw in their faces. How frightened of the British Band they must have been only a moon or two ago. Now they had what was left of the British Band at their mercy.

The long knife leader shouted and drew his pistol and waved it. Shaking his head, the chief of the boatmen made an angry gesture toward the flatboat. The long knife took coins from his saddlebag and handed them down to the boatman. The long knives began to herd Redbird's people on board.

It took three trips to carry all of the Sauk across the Fever River. By this time hundreds of pale eyes men, women and children had gathered at the riverbank.

Redbird and her children were in the last group to cross. She heard angry cries. The pale eyes were throwing rotten vegetables, clumps of dirt and small rocks. She pulled Floating Lily around from her back to hold her in her arms. A soft tomato hit Redbird in the ear. She heard laughter. She wanted to keep both hands on the baby, so she did not wipe away the pulp and seeds that dripped down her neck. She ran on board the boat.

When she stumbled off on the other side of the river she was panting, breathless with relief. She felt a hand wiping the tomato pulp from her neck—Wolf Paw. It was good to know he was nearby.

The next morning when they set out, Wolf Paw picked up Eagle Feather, whose ragged moccasins had fallen from his feet. He lifted him over his head and set him on his shoulders. Redbird smiled her thanks, and Wolf Paw returned a sad look, then sighed and lowered his gaze to the ground. All that day he trudged beside her with Eagle Feather on his back. That night he slept near Redbird and her children.

The following day the trail led past flat fields, mostly planted with corn, stretching to the edge of the Great River. For a moment, reminded of the cornfields around Saukenuk, Redbird's heart lifted. Then she recalled that from now on only pale eyes would plant corn in this country.

On her left bluffs rose up, overlooking the river like the statues of spirits. Ahead she could see many pale eyes lodges built on the side of a hill. At the top of the hill was a fort surrounded by a wall of upright logs. She saw a dark mass of people spread across the trail ahead.

They were not standing to one side, as those at the last town had. They were blocking the way.

She felt that she knew this place, though she had never been here before. After a moment she understood why. White Bear and Yellow Hair had both talked to her many times about the village where White Bear had lived with his father, Star Arrow. The great lodge they lived in must be somewhere beyond that hill. And the walled building at the top of the hill would be the trading post of White Bear's uncle, the one who had driven him away from here and who had tried to kill him at Old Man's Creek.

As she got closer she heard angry voices. Again she took her baby in her arms. She looked around for Wolf Paw and was grateful to see him at her side. He set Eagle Feather down, and the boy seized her skirt.

But if this was the town where White Bear had lived, this was where Wolf Paw's war party had killed many men, women and children. This was where the big gun had fired into Wolf Paw's body the silver coin that still hung around his neck. What if these people recognized him? She was glad again that he had taken off his red crest. The coin, she noticed, had disappeared, too, inside his buckskin shirt.

But whether they recognized Wolf Paw or not, these people would hate her people.

Terror seized her as she remembered her vision at Fort Crawford—death on the trail. She tried to stop walking, but the people behind her pushed her on. The mounted long knives behind them were driving everyone forward.

Closer to the pale eyes standing in the trail, she saw that most of those in front were men, and they were holding clubs and rocks. Her legs turned to water and she felt that she might fall down. She did not have the strength to go on, to walk toward the death she had foreseen days ago. Her own people jostled her. The long knives were calling orders, trying to make the Sauk move ahead, but nobody wanted to be the first to come near that angry crowd.

The long knife with the yellow mustache rode ahead and spoke to the crowd, waving his hand at them to clear the way. They shouted back at him.

The crowd surged forward.

And the blue-coats rode into the fields on either side of the trail.

She could not see the villagers, because Wolf Paw had stepped in front of her.

Eagle Feather's frantic grip was hurting her leg. She hugged Floating Lily tightly in her arms, hoping that if she were felled by a stone, her body would protect her baby.

They are going to kill all of us.

The shouts of the pale eyes battered at her ears. Rocks, many bigger than a man's fist, hurtled through the air. Redbird saw women and children falling around her.

She heard a thud that made her ears ring, and suddenly Wolf Paw was slumping to the rutted trail in front of her.

Men charged at the fallen Wolf Paw with rocks and clubs raised. Eagle Feather suddenly let go of Redbird and plunged into the crowd of Sauk behind her. She watched him disappear as he burrowed in among the legs of the women and men.

"Redbird!"

Squeezing Floating Lily against her chest, Redbird looked around frantically at the sound of her name.

At the edge of the crowd she saw yellow braids and blue eyes

and arms waving. Yellow Hair, her face twisted with anguish, was
trying to force her way through to her.

There were other people with Yellow Hair. A very stout woman
was pushing and pulling at the angry men and women around her,
shouting at them to stop what they were doing. And a man with
sandy hair was also fighting the other villagers.

White Bear had an aunt and uncle in this village.

But the crowd pushed forward, and she could no longer see
those few who were trying to help her people.

The men were beating Wolf Paw. One powerful-looking man
with broad shoulders and chest and a thick brown beard lifted a
club to bring it down on Wolf Paw's head.

In the pale eyes' tongue Redbird cried out, "No! Please!"

The man turned and stared at her, madness in his eyes.

"You kill my wife!" he roared. His spittle wet her face. He
reached for her.

She screamed and screamed. His hand grabbed at Floating Lily's
tiny body, and the baby shrieked with pain and terror. Redbird tried
to bite and kick him, to squirm away. He swung his club at her and
hit the side of her head. The blow stunned her, weakening her grip
on her baby.

The brown-bearded man wrenched Floating Lily from her arms.

Her screams tore her throat. The man whirled away from her,
lifted Floating Lily high over his head. The crowd enveloped him,
and the baby disappeared in their midst. Screaming, punching and
kicking, she fought to get at Floating Lily, but people pushed her
back and threw her to the ground.

Her voice was gone. She crawled through the stones and the dirt.
She saw the legs of pale eyes men and the skirts of pale eyes women,
and in their midst a small unmoving body, wrapped in a blanket
soaked with blood.

The people rushed off in a different direction, and she crawled
along the trail until she could reach out and take her daughter in
her arms. She pulled herself into a sitting position, holding the bundle in her lap. Her hands were wet with blood. She looked down at
the tiny crumpled face, blood running out of the baby mouth. No
movement. Arms and legs limp. No sound. No breath.

Her mind went blank. A mantle of blackness covered her eyes.

When she came awake, Yellow Hair was sitting beside her, hold-

ing her in her arms and sobbing. The fat pale eyes woman was
standing over both of them, tears streaking her face. She was holding a red blanket in her hands, offering it to Redbird.

At the sight of the strange white face Redbird screamed and
shrank away, pressing the baby in her arms to her breast. She pulled
away from Yellow Hair, who sat on the ground and buried her face
in her hands.

The fat woman put the blanket on the ground and stumbled
away from Redbird. She got a short distance and began to throw
up, coughing and sobbing. The sandy-haired man went to her and
held her.

Redbird watched the anguish of Yellow Hair and the fat
woman numbly. She hurt too much to have any feeling for anyone else. She understood that the woman had given her the blanket to wrap Floating Lily. She hitched herself over to the blanket
and picked it up and wrapped it around the bloody bundle without looking at it.

The bright red of the blanket, she thought, would keep Floating
Lily warm.

From some distance away the anguished cries of other people
reached Redbird's ears. Others must have been hurt by the pale eyes
villagers.

Yellow Hair, still crying so hard she was unable to speak, moved
beside Redbird and put her hand on the blanket.

The crowd that had attacked the Sauk were gathered in a field
beside the trail. The ten long knives on horseback had formed a line
and had pushed them back. Too late.

The fat woman seemed to have forgotten Redbird. She staggered
away from the Sauk, screaming at the people in the field. It was
impossible for Redbird to understand her words, but her voice was
full of rage. Some of the people answered back, but in sullen voices
Redbird could hardly hear.

Redbird could not stand up. She felt no strength at all in her
trembling legs.

"Eagle Feather!" she cried. She called her son again and again.

He came and stood before her. "Is Floating Lily dead? Did they
kill her?"

"Yes," said Redbird.

Eagle Feather began to cry. "Why did they kill my little sister?"

Redbird felt a touch on her shoulder. Wolf Paw's hand. His forehead was gashed and blood was running down into one eye that was swollen and shut.

"I thought they killed you," she said.

"It would have been good if they had."

"No," she said, "do not wish that."

Redbird sensed a silence and realized that Yellow Hair was no longer crying. She and Wolf Paw were staring at each other.

Now, thought Redbird, Yellow Hair could have her revenge for her father's death, for her own suffering. All she had to do was tell the villagers who Wolf Paw was, the leader of the war band that had attacked Victor. The brave who had kidnapped her. The long knives could not—would not—stop the people from killing him on the spot.

Yellow Hair sighed and put her arm around Redbird's shoulders. Perhaps she didn't want revenge. Redbird was too sick with grief to wonder much about it.

Wolf Paw said, "Four others are dead, and many more are hurt. We will carry our dead away from this place. I think the long knives will let us bury them farther along this trail."

Holding Floating Lily's body tightly, Redbird let Wolf Paw take her by the elbows and lift her to her feet. She felt Yellow Hair's arm still around her shoulders. She began to cry quietly.

Wolf Paw said, "Even though you grieve for your baby, the people who are wounded need your help. Sun Woman taught you, and you were White Bear's wife and Owl Carver's daughter. You are the only one who knows what to do."

"I have hardly any medicines left," she said.

"You can pray for those who are hurt," Wolf Paw said. "And when we bury the dead, you can speak to their spirits for us."

You must be the spirit walker for the British Band.

A long knife rode over and spoke to Yellow Hair. Redbird understood that he was telling her that she could not stay with the Sauk prisoners.

In the way they had learned to talk to each other Yellow Hair told Redbird that she would have gladly died to save Floating Lily. She promised to do what she could for the remaining people.

"You, me, sisters," Redbird said.

Yellow Hair put her arms around Redbird, pressing Floating Lily between them. She bent and kissed Redbird on the cheek, her tears wetting Redbird's face.

Redbird glanced up at the long knife who had spoken to Yellow Hair. His mouth under his yellow mustache twisted in scorn.

Yellow Hair began to sob again, and her arms tightened around Redbird. Redbird felt White Bear's aunt and uncle gently trying to pull Yellow Hair away from her.

The mounted long knife shouted angrily. Would they shoot Yellow Hair if she didn't leave?

Frightened for Yellow Hair, Redbird twisted her arms and shoulders and broke free from her.

The fat woman and the sandy-haired man drew Yellow Hair away. But her sobs became louder, turned to screams.

"My baby!"

Redbird knew those pale eyes' words. And it was true, she thought. Had not Yellow Hair been in the birthing wickiup with Redbird? Had she not been present for every instant of Floating Lily's early life? Was she not also White Bear's wife?

She feels the same pain I do.

Yellow Hair's screams died away as White Bear's aunt and uncle half carried her away from the trail. Her cries were drowned out by the shouts of the long knives, ordering the Sauk to get to their feet and start walking again.

As Redbird, holding Floating Lily, stumbled down the trail she looked at the crowd in the field. They were not shouting or throwing rocks now. They just stared. Perhaps they were satisfied.

Her eyes met those of the brown-bearded man who had torn Floating Lily from her arms. He saw her holding her dead daughter, and his face was still red and rigid with hatred.

She had understood enough of his tongue to understand what he had shouted at her: *You kill my wife.*

At the sight of him she felt heavy as a stone. There was nothing she could do that would bring Floating Lily back. Her baby's little feet were on the Trail of Souls. Only death would free Redbird from pain.

Wolf Paw, once again carrying Eagle Feather, walked beside her. She sensed someone walking on her other side and turned to look. She saw a shrunken, wizened woman with a sad face. It took her a moment to realize that it was her mother, Wind Bends Grass.

Many footsteps later, when their trail passed through woods, the long knives let them stop. They unstrapped small shovels from their saddles and gave them to some of the men. The Sauk men dug five deep graves and placed the bodies—three women, one man, and a baby—sitting upright in them.

Wolf Paw dug Floating Lily's grave, letting Eagle Feather do part of the work.

Before covering Floating Lily with earth, Redbird tore a small strip from the red blanket the fat woman had given her and set it beside the grave.

When the five were buried Redbird saw the eyes of all the people turned toward her, and she knew they expected her, in spite of the grief that was killing her, to complete the rite.

First, she sang.

> "In your brown blanket, O Earthmaker,
>   Wrap your children and carry them away,
>   Fold them again in your body . . ."

When she had finished the song, she spoke to the dead.

"You are innocent of wrongdoing," she said. "You have no debt to pay, no promise to keep. You have kept faith and walked with honor the path that led to these graves. Do not linger here in hope of avenging yourselves on those who killed you. Great happiness awaits you in the West. The Owl spirit will show you how to set your feet on the Trail of Souls. Go now, begin your journey."

After she had spoken, the people broke willow wands from trees growing by the water and set them upright on the mounds of earth. Redbird took the piece of red blanket and tied it to the end of the wand over Floating Lily's grave.

Your path on this earth was a short one, my daughter. But the earth is not a good place for our people just now. And many, many of your Sauk brothers and sisters will journey with you on the Trail of Souls. Go now into the West, and your father and brother and I will one day follow after, and we will all be together again.

As she stepped back from the grave she remembered how, two days ago, far to the north, she had seen this grave in her mind and had fainted. With a sinking heart she understood how terrible were the shaman's gifts she had longed for all her life.

The long knives had sat silently beside the trail, letting their horses graze while the people buried their dead. They did not seem worried that anyone might try to escape. After all, where could a Sauk go in this country? Once they might have walked freely anywhere this side of the Great River. Now all who lived in this land hated them.

Redbird could not tell whether the long knives were ashamed that they let these people in their care be killed. Maybe they were pleased, maybe it did not matter to them. When the people came out of the woods, the long knives stood up, silent and expressionless, and mounted their horses again for the journey south.

Wolf Paw walked beside Redbird and Eagle Feather. Redbird missed the familiar weight of the baby on her back, and started to weep again. Her breasts, filling with milk that would not be sucked, began to ache.

After they had walked a long time in silence, Wolf Paw said, "I failed you, Redbird. You asked me to protect your children. I sent my own wives and my children to their deaths, and now I did not save your daughter. I am not a man."

The pale eyes had not killed Wolf Paw, Redbird thought, but they had killed his spirit. She would try to heal him. Nothing would bring back Floating Lily, but perhaps she could give new life to this man.

When they stopped to sleep that night she lay on her back on the ground staring up at the sky, Eagle Feather snuggled close to her, Wolf Paw and Wind Bends Grass nearby.

A bird appeared on a tree limb overhead.

Even though it was night, she could somehow see that the bird's plumage was a red as bright as the strip of blanket she had left on Floating Lily's grave. Around his eyes was a black mask, and on his head a crest of red feathers.

The bird flew to a more distant tree limb, and she felt that he called her to follow him. She stood up, and none of the sleeping people noticed her. She walked past a long knife on guard with a rifle, and he looked right through her.

The bright bird darted into a black opening in the hillside above the river, and Redbird followed. In the cave all she could see was the glow of red wings far ahead of her. There were many twists and turns, and she went down very far.

She began to see light ahead. It appeared so gradually that her eyes adjusted to it easily, and when she came to a chamber that was brightly lit she was neither dazzled nor blinded.

The walls of the chamber rose high above her, hard and smooth and clear as ice, and they glistened with a light that seemed to be everywhere behind them. She heard a murmuring and a rustling, and saw in niches cut into the wall many kinds of creatures, plants and animals and birds. She looked down at fish swimming restlessly in the dark pool that formed most of the floor.

In the center of the pool was an island, and on the island a huge ancient Turtle squatted on four wrinkled, gray-green legs.

Welcome, daughter, said the Turtle.

22

Renegade

Raoul sat on the edge of his chair in Fort Crawford's assembly room, waiting for the guards to bring in Auguste. In a row beside him sat seven other militia officers, all of whom had been witnesses against the Indian leaders.

Raoul discovered all at once that he was trembling with anticipation.

Let today be the day—it was almost a prayer, but he did not know who would hear such a prayer—*let them string him up today.*

Let me see that damned mongrel die.

Today the commanders of the army that had defeated Black Hawk would tell the Sauk and Fox leaders their fate. The less important Indians were to be dealt with first, so Auguste would be coming in now.

Raoul watched avidly as Auguste walked in between two privates, his wrists handcuffed, carrying an iron ball at the end of a chain attached to his ankles. The sight of the mongrel in chains was more satisfying than a good swig of Old Kaintuck.

Raoul had not seen Auguste since the day they had faced each other too briefly on that bloody island off the mouth of the Bad Axe. Again Raoul saw that Auguste's right ear, partly covered by his long black locks, was split into upper and lower halves, with a red, partly healed gap between them.

Eli's bullet must have gone through his ear instead of his head. And, knowing Eli, that was no accident. That was why he said I'd find a surprise up in Michigan Territory.

Raoul's fingers worked in his lap. That gap-toothed old bastard had deliberately lied to him about killing Auguste. Why? What could he gain by keeping Auguste alive?

Auguste's dark eyes widened as they met Raoul's, and from across the room his hatred struck Raoul like a blow. Raoul remembered the woman whose throat he had cut.

His mother. But killing her was still not enough to pay me back for Clarissa and Phil and Andy. For the burning of Victoire.

Auguste turned his back to Raoul and faced the three commanders, who sat at a long table behind which a big American flag was nailed to the plaster wall.

In the center was Major General Winfield Scott, finally arrived from the East to take charge of what was left of the war. Raoul hoped Scott had come out here with President Jackson's orders to send this pack of savages to the gallows. The general had listened intently to everything Raoul had to say against the mongrel. Raoul distrusted Scott's fancy uniform, his heavy gold-braided epaulets and the white plume on the cocked hat that lay beside him. But Scott's features were severe, his brows straight and black, his nose sharp and his mouth tight. Raoul saw no pity in the look he bent on Auguste.

Flanking Scott were Colonel Zachary Taylor and white-bearded Brigadier General Henry Atkinson, who had commanded the militia and troops right up to the battle at the Bad Axe.

Winfield Scott glanced at a paper before him and said, "Auguste de Marion, by some also called White Bear, you are named in Colonel Taylor's report as one of the ringleaders of Black Hawk's uprising. We have heard testimony that you are a renegade and murderer."

Auguste glanced at Raoul and then said, "Have I the right to hear what has been said against me?"

Scott shook his head. "This is only a hearing, not a court-martial. What do you have to say for yourself?"

"I advised my people to keep the peace," Auguste said. "And the British Band did not take my advice. So I am not much of a ringleader. And I never killed anyone, so I am no murderer. As for being a renegade, I was born a Sauk. I'm no more a renegade than any other member of my tribe who followed Black Hawk."

Auguste's voice rang loud and clear. Raoul noticed that his

speech seemed more accented than he remembered it. Probably from living with Indians and talking only their talk for nearly a year.

Is it only a year since I drove him from Victoire? Seems a whole lifetime away.

Scott cast sideways glances at Taylor and Atkinson.

"We are told you are an American citizen," said Zachary Taylor.

Auguste said, "Sir, my father was Pierre de Marion, an American citizen, and because it was his wish, I lived as a white man for six years. But my mother was Sun Woman of the Sauk tribe, and I remained a Sauk in my heart."

Scott said, "Your heart doesn't matter to the law. What was your conduct during the war?"

Raoul listened, blood hammering in his skull, to Auguste's account of Old Man's Creek. Auguste named him, turned and pointed to him.

"Then he came toward me to shoot me. I ran into the tall grass. Eli Greenglove, one of his men, shot me." He touched his mangled ear. "It was dark and the men were drunk, and I was able to stay alive by pretending to be dead. When Black Hawk found out that his emissaries had been shot, he believed he had no choice but to go on fighting. It was only then that the British Band began to attack whites."

Anger drove Raoul to his feet. "Sir, I must answer that."

Scott turned hard blue eyes on Raoul. "That won't be necessary, Colonel. I've already had a complete report of what happened at Old Man's Creek." Raoul heard a faint disdain in Scott's elegant Virginia drawl and felt his face turn hot.

Scott consulted in a murmur with Taylor and Atkinson. Raoul sat down slowly and drummed his fingers on his knee. He looked up to see Auguste staring stonily at him, his manacled hands clenched into fists. Raoul made himself hold Auguste's gaze.

Shaman. I wonder if he does have any power to hurt me.
Nonsense.
But what is he thinking, what is he planning?

Scott said, "We've read depositions from Miss Hale and the boy Woodrow Prewitt stating that Auguste and his squaw protected them and cared for them while they were captives of the Sauk and that Auguste eventually led them to safety."

Raoul clenched his jaw and his breath steamed out of his nostrils. He wished he could give Nancy Hale the back of his hand across her stuck-up face. The redskins had murdered her father. They'd kidnapped her. Probably they'd raped her, though she'd never admit it. How in hell could she defend this mongrel?

Scott said, "It seems to me we have no evidence that this man did any harm to the United States or to any of our citizens. However, there are serious accusations against him, such as the charge that he instigated the Sauk raid on Victor. If he is not legally an Indian, which this board of inquiry is not competent to determine, then any acts of war he participated in were crimes against the people of Illinois. His guilt or innocence must then be a matter for a civilian court to decide. And the appropriate place would be the county where he lived with his father, where there would be records and witnesses."

Raoul could hardly hold himself back from jumping up and shouting in triumph. He forced himself to look anywhere but at Auguste, knowing that what he felt would be all too easy for the others to read.

"You may as well hang me yourself, General," Auguste said quietly, pointing at Raoul. "*He* runs that whole county. No witnesses will dare to come forward for me, and he's had all my records destroyed."

"Without records, nothing can be proved *against* you," said Scott.

Raoul felt a hollow open in his stomach. What the hell had Burke Russell done with Auguste's adoption records and Pierre's will? The damned Indians had killed Russell. And that pretty wife of his just refused to speak to Raoul.

Auguste said, "But, sir, I don't believe there's even a court in Smith County to try me."

Zachary Taylor shuffled some papers. "Yes there is. Smith County had a special election a month after that bad Indian raid. Elected county commissioners, and a man named Cooper is judge of the circuit court. I think we can guarantee White Bear, or Auguste de Marion, a proper trial.'

Raoul clenched his fists. Things had gone sour in Smith County while he was off fighting the Sauk.

General Atkinson said, "I don't know about that. Seventeen men, women and children were killed in that raid. Sending this man to stand trial there could be simply condemning him to death by Lynch's law."

I wish it could be that simple. Remembering the cool reception he'd gotten in Victor when he went there to outfit the *Victory* for the war, Raoul began to have second thoughts about whether things would go his way.

I'll have to get my Smith County boys together and make sure Cooper runs that trial right.

Raoul stole a glance at Auguste and saw that his face was set in that hard, expressionless mold Indians took on when they didn't want to show what they were feeling.

Scott said, "Send a good officer and a couple of men to Victor to escort this man and insure a fair trial."

"Right, sir," said Zachary Taylor, making a note. "Lieutenant Jefferson Davis and two enlisted men will go along with him."

Damn! Taylor had jumped at the chance to send Lieutenant Davis away from the fort, Raoul thought with annoyance. The gossip around Fort Crawford was that Davis was courting Taylor's pretty daughter, and Taylor didn't approve.

Scott turned his gaze on Raoul. "And you, Colonel de Marion. By all accounts you're a very prominent citizen in that community. It's obvious there's bad blood between you and your nephew. I'll hold you responsible if there's any violence against him."

"Understood, sir," said Raoul, calmly enough, but hating to hear the mongrel called his nephew. Scott's threat was empty; once the general was back East he wouldn't care about the fate of one half-breed out on the frontier.

Scott turned to Auguste with a small smile. "While you are on trial, I'll be negotiating a treaty with the Sauk. And after that, if they don't hang you, I think President Jackson would be most interested in meeting you."

A treaty? A meeting with Jackson? Raoul quivered with anger and could barely keep himself from letting out a shout. Did that mean Scott wasn't going to hang Black Hawk and the rest of them? Was he taking the Sauk leaders to meet the President?

Well, if he does, the mongrel won't be with them, Raoul thought, comforting himself with the picture of a hempen rope around Auguste's neck.

M*y baby!*

Auguste felt as heavy as if he had turned to stone. He sat hunched over on the plank bed covered with a corn-husk mattress, in his cell in Victor's village hall, clutching his stomach as tears ran from his eyes.

After what Frank Hopkins had just told him, he no longer cared what happened to him here in Victor. These people had killed Floating Lily. Let them kill him too. He did not want to live in a world that had killed his baby daughter.

He felt a comforting hand on his shoulder. He glanced at it and saw Frank's ink-blackened fingers pressing into the blue calico shirt his captors at Fort Crawford had given him.

He looked up to see lawyer Thomas Ford's sad eyes on him, but kindly gestures and looks meant nothing to him now. How could people tear a baby girl from her mother's arms and beat her to death?

But the Sauk war parties killed children too. All people are cruel, white and red.

"I would be better off on the Trail of Souls," he said in a low voice.

My mother and my daughter, Sun Woman and Floating Lily, both dead.

"Nancy and Nicole and I tried to stop them," Frank said, his eyes moist, "but the crowd was too big. We couldn't get through until it was too late. Nancy told us the baby was your daughter. Nicole and Nancy tried as best they could to comfort your wife."

For all he knew, Redbird might think him dead. He had asked his guards at Fort Crawford to pass word to her that he was alive, but he had no idea whether any of his messages had reached her.

Ford, the lawyer from Vandalia Frank had hired to defend Auguste, said, "What happened shows how angry the people of Victor still are against the Sauk. I still think we have to ask for a change of venue." Ford was a short, slender man with a round face and bright, intelligent eyes. Leaning against the rough-hewn log wall of Auguste's cell, he wore a dark brown frock coat with a high collar that came up to his ears.

Frank said, "Many people here feel terribly sorry for Auguste. And a lot of us decided, after we survived the siege, that we wouldn't put up anymore with the lawlessness that Raoul and his crew represent."

But Raoul is back now, Auguste thought. *He'll start to take control again.*

Ford said, "Well, Auguste ought to tell us what he thinks. It's his neck."

Auguste took a deep breath. The clean smell of fresh-cut wood filled his nostrils. A good smell, but it reminded him that this village hall was only recently rebuilt, that last June Wolf Paw's raiding party had burned down everything in Victor except Raoul's trading post. How could he possibly get a fair trial here?

Auguste said, "At least here I have some people who know me and care about me."

Ford sighed. "So be it. Frank, I want a list of every man who was in the mob that attacked the Sauk prisoners. We don't want any of them sitting on the jury."

As Frank and Ford discussed trial tactics, Auguste gazed around at this dark little chamber on the second floor of the village hall. It might be his last home on earth. The only window was a square barred hole high up on the south wall, too small to let much light in—or for a man to climb out through. This morning a light rain falling outside spattered through the window, and the cell felt damp and cool.

When Frank built this cell, he could never have thought his own nephew would be a prisoner in it.

"We have a power of work to do, Auguste," Ford interrupted his thoughts. "So far I can't find anyone who confirms your story of what happened at Old Man's Creek. This Otto Wegner fellow whose life you saved, he and his family have moved down to the Texas country in Mexico."

Frank said, "We do have two people who'll testify that you protected them and never went on any war parties while they were prisoners of the British Band—Miss Hale and the boy Woodrow."

At the mention of Nancy's name Auguste felt a wrench in his heart. He knew that she had stayed in Victor, teaching in a new schoolhouse Frank had built for her on the site of her father's church. Her absence in the week he had been here had hurt him deeply.

"Frank," he said, "why hasn't Nancy come to see me?"

Thomas Ford said, "Miss Hale is a very bright young lady, and instead of rushing down here to visit you when you arrived, she waited till I got here and then she asked me what she should do. I told her that there must not be even a breath of a suggestion that there was anything between you two. If people believed she had, ah, been intimate with you, they'd consider her a loose woman—doubly so because you're an Indian—and they wouldn't listen to a word she said."

"I understand," Auguste said, feeling bitter, but also feeling that the load of grief he'd borne since arriving at Victor had lightened a little. Nancy had not forgotten him, as he'd feared she might after she got back among whites. He felt shame that he had even imagined she might turn against him. And when the trial started, at least he would see her again.

The smell of fresh-cut wood pervaded the courtroom on the first floor of the village hall, as it did Auguste's cell. Frank must have worked seven days a week since last June, Auguste thought. Even though he'd hired half a dozen assistants, it was a wonder he'd found time to write and publish his newspaper.

Judge David Cooper, a man with a square, muscular face and piercing blue eyes, sat at a long table with the flags of the United States and the state of Illinois on stands behind him. A carpenter's mallet lay on the table. Probably borrowed from Frank, Auguste thought. He had a vague memory of Cooper's being present and saying something to Raoul the day he'd been driven from Victoire. Auguste stood as Cooper read out the charge of complicity in the murder of 223 citizens of the state of Illinois by the British Band of the Sauk and Fox Indian tribes.

Behind Auguste sat three blue-coats, Lieutenant Jefferson Davis and his two corporals. The prosecutor, Justus Bennett, and his assistant occupied a third table. The courtroom being not quite finished, the twelve jurymen sat on one side of the room in two pews carried over from the Presbyterian church.

Auguste knew only three of the jurors—Robert McAllister, a farmer whose family had survived Wolf Paw's raid by hiding in their root cellar; Tom Slattery, the blacksmith; and Jean-Paul Kobell, a stableman from Victoire. He had no reason to think any of those three bore him any special ill will, though they might have good reason to hate any Sauk. The others he knew not at all, which meant they must have moved to Victor since he left.

Behind the trial participants about fifty citizens of Smith County were crowded into the courtroom, sitting in chairs or on benches they had carried into the village hall themselves. More stood along the walls.

During the first hour of the trial Raoul de Marion, the first witness for the prosecution, testified. He lounged in a chair beside the judge's table.

Auguste sat in a cold fury as he heard, for the first time, an account of the war between the British Band and the people of Illinois as many pale eyes must have seen it. A murdering band of savages had invaded the state. The brave volunteers had pursued them, endured the loss of comrades, but eventually had triumphed, administering a righteous retaliation by exterminating most of the invaders.

Bennett, a lean man whose rounded shoulders gave him a serpentine look, turned to Thomas Ford. "Your witness, sir."

Ford, very erect in contrast to Bennett, stood up and walked toward Raoul. "Mr. de Marion, why on the night of September fifteenth, 1831, did you offer a reward of fifty pieces of eight to anyone who would kill your nephew, Auguste de Marion?"

"Objection," Bennett called from his seat. "This has nothing to do with the defendant's conduct in the Black Hawk War."

"On the contrary Your Honor," said Ford. "It explains how my client got involved in the war."

"I'll allow it," said David Cooper.

After Ford repeated his question, Raoul said, "I don't remember offering any reward."

"I can produce at least ten witnesses who heard you and saw you hold up a money bag."

"Well, he provoked me. He'd tried to cheat me out of my inheritance."

"Apparently you'd already got control of the estate. By force of arms. Was it necessary to go on and incite men to kill him?"

"I figured he might do just what he did—stir up the Sauk against us and try to use them to take the land away from me."

Ford turned to the jury, and the spectators could see the incredulous look on his face. Auguste felt a warmth for Ford. He seemed to know what he was doing. But it still made him uneasy to know that his life was in the hands of another man, no matter how competent.

"And why were you going to shoot Auguste, when he came to you with a white flag at Old Man's Creek?"

"He was trying to lead us into an ambush."

Ford sighed, clasped his hands behind his back and took a few paces away from Raoul. He threw an exasperated look at the jury, as if to say, *What can I do with this man?*

Then he turned suddenly and said, "Mr. de Marion, in 1812, when you were just a boy, were you not present at the incident known as the Fort Dearborn Massacre?"

"Objection," said Bennett. "This certainly has nothing to do with the man who's on trial."

"Goes to the character of the witness, Your Honor," said Ford.

"I'll let you ask the question," said Cooper. "Please answer, Mr. de Marion."

Raoul hunched over and his face grew darker. "God knows I was at Fort Dearborn."

"And did you not see your sister horribly murdered by Indians. Were you not subjected to two years of captivity and slavery?"

"I did. I was." The words came out in a hoarse whisper.

Ford said, "Mr. de Marion, after those terrible boyhood experiences, to have your brother attempt to bring an Indian into the family must have seemed the crowning insult. I put it to you that your accusations against Auguste stem, not from any misdeeds of his, but from your hatred for him because he is an Indian."

Justus Bennett was on his feet. "Objection. The honorable defense attorney isn't asking questions. He's making a speech defaming the witness."

Cooper nodded. "Sustained." He turned to the jury and said, "The jury will forget about everything they just heard the defense attorney say."

Auguste shook his head. How could any man forget something he had just so clearly heard? In all his years of living among the pale eyes, he had never attended a trial. Now, on trial for his own life, he saw that the ways of the pale eyes were even stranger than he had ever realized.

The next prosecution witness was Armand Perrault.

At the sight of Armand, Auguste broke out in a cold sweat of fury. This man, Frank had said, was the one who snatched Floating Lily from Redbird's arms. Walking up to the witness chair, Armand avoided Auguste's eyes. Always before he had shot Auguste looks of hatred. Today he was showing his guilt.

Aching knots spread through all Auguste's muscles. Were he alone with Armand, he would hurl himself at him and try to kill him, bare-handed. But in this crowded courtroom he was helpless. His hands tightened on the links of his chain till they hurt.

He felt a firm grip on his forearm; Ford, sitting beside him, letting him know that he sensed his pain.

Led by Bennett's questions, Armand repeated Raoul's claim that the three peace messengers were actually the vanguard of a Sauk attack.

"Why do they keep harping on this?" Auguste asked Ford in a whisper.

"Makes you out a murderer," Ford said out of the side of his mouth, "if you tried to lead the white militiamen into a trap at Old Man's Creek."

When it was Ford's turn to question Armand he said, "You pulled the trigger on one of Black Hawk's peace messengers, didn't you?"

"Yes," said Armand, his teeth gleaming in his brown beard. "And I did not miss."

"And you killed an Indian baby on the road going through town about three weeks ago, didn't you?"

"I don't remember."

Ford raised his hands toward the beamed ceiling. "Come now, Mr. Perrault. A hundred or more people saw you drag that child from its mother's arms."

"These were the same Indians who came here and murdered my wife, Monsieur Légiste."

"That baby probably wasn't even born when your wife was murdered, Mr. Perrault."

If I ever get free I'll kill you, Perrault. By the White Bear spirit I swear it.

A chill came over Auguste at his own thought. He recalled Owl Carver's warning against trying to turn the power of the spirits against any other human being. Terrible consequences lay in store for the shaman who did so.

I'm probably going to be hanged as it is. What else can happen to me?

Auguste heard Raoul's voice from somewhere behind him, among the spectators. "Hey, Bennett! Aren't you going to say anything? What's this got to do with the mongrel?"

"Order!" Cooper rapped on his table with a carpenter's mallet.

Bennett stood up a little uncertainly. "If it please your honor, I called Mr. Perrault to testify about what happened at Old Man's Creek. I don't see why counsel for the defense is bringing up this other incident."

"All right, Your Honor," said Ford. "I have no more questions for this baby killer." Auguste saw sudden pallor in the part of Armand's face not covered by his beard.

"Objection!" shouted Bennett.

Ford looked pained. "What in Heaven's name is wrong with calling a spade a spade?"

Cooper said, "Well, try to keep your language a little more elevated, Mr. Ford."

"Certainly, Your Honor. I have no more questions for this infanticide."

As Ford turned away to sit down, Auguste saw a quick little smile crease Judge Cooper's face, then disappear. He began to feel hope stirring in a heart that had been heavy ever since he came to Victor. This trial would not be conducted according to Lynch's law.

But he still burned with hatred for Armand Perrault. He turned to watch Perrault go back to his seat.

And his skin tingled. Just past the gaunt-faced Lieutenant Davis, Nancy was sitting, only two rows of chairs away. Her deep blue eyes widened as she looked at him. Her smile was, as Cooper's had been, just a brief shadow, but her face flushed, and she shook her head almost imperceptibly.

Auguste understood. As Ford had said, if Nancy were to testify in his behalf, people must never know what they had been to each other. All their hatred for red men would come boiling up, and they would hang him for having intercourse with a white woman, if for nothing else. He nodded ever so slightly, tore his eyes away from hers.

Woodrow was sitting beside Nancy, holding her hand. He had no need to hide his feelings, and gave Auguste a big grin. Auguste smiled back at him, but at the sight of Woodrow, longing for Eagle Feather was a knife in his heart.

I don't even know whether Eagle Feather is alive.

And grief for poor little Floating Lily crushed him.

There were Frank and Nicole sitting together, with one of their smaller children—Patrick, Auguste thought—squirming on Nicole's lap. The sight of the baby made him want to weep.

There were Elysée and Guichard, two old men sitting side by side. Grandpapa had a home of his own now, he'd told Auguste while visiting him, a small frame house on a hillside north of town, also built by Frank. And a young doctor named Surrey who had just moved into the county looked in on Elysée regularly.

Good that they have a new doctor here.

Too bad, though, Gram Medill had died. Of an infection, Auguste had heard, that she'd refused to let Dr. Surrey treat.

Auguste saw many more spectators whom he did not recognize, people who stared back at him with hostility or—at best—curiosity.

A handsome young woman wearing a black bonnet and a black dress caught his eye. There was a strange intensity in her look, but her mouth was drawn tight, and he could not tell whether she felt hatred or sympathy for him. Then he remembered who she was— Pamela Russell, widow of the town clerk whose brains had been dashed out by a Sauk war club during the attack on Victor. Nicole, on one of her visits to the village hall, had described Russell's death to him and told him how Pamela had insisted on touching off the cannon that broke the war party's attack.

She will probably want to be the one to put the rope around my neck.

The prosecutor called Levi Pope to the stand. The shambling backwoodsman held his coonskin cap in his hand as he approached the witness chair. This was the first time Auguste could remember seeing him without a rifle. Its absence made him look strange.

Bennett led Levi Pope through an account of Old Man's Creek. Then Thomas Ford rose to question him.

"All right, Levi. When the three Indians, including Auguste, came into your camp with the peace flag, how'd you know it was treachery?"

Levi frowned and shook his head. "Well, when we seen that the woods was full of Injuns."

"Now, we've heard many times during this trial that 'the woods was full of Injuns.' How many Indians did you see?"

" 'Twasn't me that saw them. It was the scouts Colonel Raoul sent out."

"So you didn't see any sign yourself that the Indians were trying to lead you into some kind of trap?"

"Well—no, sir."

"And when you rode into the forest on the north side of Old Man's Creek, did you see any Indians?"

"No, sir. They must of all run off by that time."

"When did you first meet up with Indians?"

"Oh, we rode maybe an hour up along the river. It was full dark then, and they come down off a hill in front of us, a-yelling and screaming."

"A frontal attack, then. If the Indians were planning to ambush you, what did they gain by sending three men into your camp claiming they wanted to talk surrender?"

Levi Pope's face seemed to elongate as he contemplated Ford's question. "I don't rightly know."

"Do you think the Indians are stupid, Mr. Pope?"

"Well, they was stupid to start this war." Levi grinned at Ford, looking pleased with himself. Auguste heard some appreciative chuckles from the spectators. He turned and saw Levi Pope's wife, a skinny, pale woman, frowning at her husband as if his testimony made her angry.

Ford nodded and held off on making his reply while he paced the open space before the judge's table and let his calm gaze travel over all the spectators and jurymen. He waited until the hall was quiet.

"Maybe the Indians thought it was a stupid war, too, Mr. Pope. Maybe that is the real reason Black Hawk sent those three braves to your camp."

"Objection," called Bennett. "Mr. Ford is just speculating."

Ford said, "Your Honor, the claim by Colonel de Marion and others that the Indian attempt to make peace, in which Auguste de Marion participated, was some kind of dastardly trick is, itself, merely speculation."

Judge Cooper grunted. "Well, let's stick to what people know, not what they think they know."

"Fine with me, Your Honor," said Ford, "as long as the prosecution is held to the same standard."

Auguste's belly tightened as he heard Ford speak sharply to the judge. He'd seen some hope in Cooper. He didn't want him antagonized. Then he slumped, letting his manacled hands dangle. What difference? He didn't have a chance anyway.

Ford went back to his seat, smiling grimly at Auguste, and Levi Pope, looking somewhat puzzled, slouched back to his place among the spectators. Judge Cooper declared that proceedings were over for the day and that the defense would call its witnesses tomorrow.

Hopelessly, Auguste stood up and bent over to pick up the iron ball chained to his leg. Perhaps, he thought, Lynch's law would be better. At least it would not prolong his suffering, make him relive moment by moment everything he and those he loved had suffered over the past year. And sooner or later he was bound to end up in the same place—a grave.

The following day Nicole was sitting in the witness chair, answering Ford's questions in a soft, melodious voice.

Ford asked, "Do you agree, Mrs. Hopkins, with your brother's charge that Auguste is a renegade and murderer?"

Nicole's full face reddened with anger. "My God, no! Auguste never turned against us. He left Smith County because Raoul would have had him murdered if he'd stayed. Auguste has never harmed anyone."

Ford's next witness was Mrs. Pamela Russell. Hearing the spectators murmuring questions to one another after Ford called her name, Auguste wondered anxiously what a woman whose husband had been killed by Wolf Paw's raid on Victor could possibly say that would help him. Her black dress and bonnet made her face look even paler. She clutched a black leather bag in her lap.

Ford said, "Mrs. Russell, did your late husband entrust any papers to you concerning Auguste de Marion?"

"Not exactly, but he kept such papers in our house and told me about them. I kept them safe after he died."

"What were they?"

"A certificate of adoption and a will."

"Why did he keep them in your home instead of in the village hall?"

Pamela Russell's dark eyes flashed as she searched the courtroom, looking, Auguste suspected, for Raoul.

"Raoul de Marion, who never let my husband forget that he owed his job to him, ordered Burke to destroy both papers."

"That's a lie!" came Raoul's shout from the back of the hall.

Justus Bennett looked toward Raoul and said, "Colonel de Marion, please. What this woman is saying might even help our case."

"All right," Raoul called. "But you watch what you're doing."

"Now, Mrs. Russell—" Ford began again.

"Burke knew that what he told him to do was wrong. So, instead of destroying the adoption certificate and the will, he brought them home and kept them in his strongbox in our cellar. When the Indians burned our house, the papers survived." She paused, gazing over Ford's head. "The papers survived."

"Do you have them now, Mrs. Russell?"

She unbuckled the strap that closed the leather bag in her lap and drew out two folded pieces of paper. She handed them to Ford, who unfolded them with a flourish and turned to the judge.

Ford asked, "Your Honor, may I read these documents to the court?"

"Go right ahead," said Judge Cooper.

"First, the certificate of adoption," said Ford.

Auguste felt a hard lump rise to block his throat as Ford read the statement that Pierre de Marion, on the sixteenth day of August, 1825, did declare his natural son, hereafter to be known as Auguste de Marion, to be his lawful son, granting him all rights and privileges to which that status might entitle him.

Auguste covered his burning eyes with his hand.

I meant so much to him.

"Now," said Ford, "the will: 'I, Pierre de Marion, residing on the estate called Victoire, in the County of Smith and State of Illinois, make this my will and revoke all prior wills and codicils.' "

It was the will Auguste had fought against until Pierre had finally persuaded him to smoke the calumet; the will giving the château and the land to Auguste. There were also monetary gifts to a number of servants, including one of two hundred dollars to Armand and Marchette Perrault. Auguste heard an angry-bee buzzing among the spectators. By seizing the estate, and concealing the will, Raoul had wiped out these gifts. He'd have to face some angry servants today, Auguste thought with satisfaction. Including that swine Perrault.

"The prosecution will want to see those papers," said Bennett when Ford had finished reading.

"Of course," said Cooper. "You may have a look any time. In my presence."

After Ford had given the jurors the two papers to look at and had returned them to Cooper's table, he turned to Bennett.

"Your witness."

Bennett slouched into the open area before the judge's table. "No questions. Mrs. Russell, widowed by those savages, has surely suffered enough."

Pamela Russell stayed sitting in the chair beside the judge's table, clutching her leather bag. Her bosom, Auguste saw, was rising and falling with some powerful emotion.

"That's all, Pamela," David Cooper said softly. "You can go now."

She stood up, looking like a woman in a trance, and moved slowly toward the door in the rear of the courtroom. Auguste turned in his seat to watch her. She stopped before Raoul, who was sitting near the back. He stared up at her as she pointed at him.

"How dare you call me a liar, Raoul de Marion! When it's you that lied about what you told my husband. My husband never fired a gun before in his life, and he had to stand up and be killed, because you took all the men who could shoot away with you. I hope those papers ruin you."

Spots of red stood out on her cheeks. She covered her face with her hand and rushed out of the courtroom.

"How come you didn't shut her up, Judge?" Raoul shouted after she was gone.

"I figured she deserved to have her say," said Cooper calmly.

Ford said, "The defense calls Miss Nancy Hale."

Auguste's heart started to beat harder as he watched Nancy, tall and straight in a pale violet dress, walk to the witness's chair. Just what he had feared a year ago, when Nancy first asked him to make love to her, had happened. He felt a love for her—an impossible love, now—that was as strong in its way as the love he felt for Redbird.

In answer to Ford's soft-spoken questions, Nancy told how she had been captured and how Auguste had intervened to protect her, and later to protect Woodrow. She told how he had risked his life to escort her and Woodrow to safety, and had ended up being captured.

Bennett got up to cross-question.

"Miss Hale, this may be a hard question for you to answer in open court. But it is important to this trial. It's well-known that Indians are no respecters of the virtue of white women. So, what I'm asking you is . . ." He paused and leaned over her. "Were you subjected to anything of a shameful nature while you were a prisoner of the Sauk?"

"Objection," called Ford. "The question itself is shameful. It has no possible bearing on this case."

Judge Cooper glared at Bennett. "What call do you have to ask her that?"

"Defense counsel has taken us down a lot of winding roads, Your Honor. I'm attempting to determine facts about the defendant's character."

"I'll allow it," said Cooper, his voice low and reluctant, and Bennett turned with a look of satisfaction to Nancy and repeated his question.

Nancy looked him coldly in the eye. "I've already said. Auguste de Marion protected me. I was never harmed."

Bennett narrowed his eyes. Raoul had chosen the man well for his purposes, Auguste thought, hating Bennett for tormenting Nancy.

"Well, but what about Auguste de Marion himself? Didn't you live in one of their huts with him? Did he ever approach you with lewd intent?"

"Certainly not!" said Nancy. "Yes, I did live in his—the word is wickiup, Mr. Bennett. But the situation was perfectly proper. His wife and child were with us all the time."

From the back of the hall Raoul brayed, "She probably enjoyed it. She always had an eye for the mongrel."

Auguste felt his neck grow hot. He wanted to kill. But someone would stop him before he reached Raoul; and even to try to attack him would only confirm the picture Bennett was trying to paint, of a murderous savage. He forced himself to sit still.

And yet, he thought, as he breathed deeply to calm himself, it was Nancy who was concealing the truth and Bennett and Raoul who sensed what had really happened. But their very words for it—"shameful," "lewd intent"—turned the truth into a lie.

He and Nancy had proclaimed their love in honor before the British Band. Now he felt as if he were tied down on a forest floor and weasels and crows were biting and pecking at him. Why must he and Nancy hide their love from these hate-filled people?

He heard indignant murmurs provoked by Raoul's outburst.

"Shocking!" someone said.

"No gentleman would talk that way."

Auguste heard Lieutenant Davis sitting behind him, say to one of his men, "If I weren't on duty, I'd teach that scoundrel a lesson."

Someone with the accent of Victoire called out, "Raoul, your father is right! Tu es un sauvage!"

Cooper pounded on his table with his wooden mallet until there was silence.

Thomas Ford called, "Master Woodrow Prewitt, will you take the stand, please?"

Woodrow walked past Auguste, who felt a warmth for him and, again, a pang of longing for Eagle Feather.

Under Ford's questions, Woodrow told how White Bear and Redbird had treated him like a foster son, and how White Bear had helped them escape.

When it was Bennett's turn, he stood threateningly over Woodrow. "Have you forgotten, young man, that you had a real, white, Christian father and mother? Have you forgotten what the Indians did to them?"

"No, sir," said Woodrow in a small voice.

"Well, then, how can you make it out that this half-Indian and his squaw were such fine people? They held you prisoner!"

"Sir, my pa used to whip me before breakfast and after supper. My ma laid in bed most days, drunk. White Bear—Mr. Auguste—he was kind to me. So was his missus. Living with them was shinin'."

"Shining!" Bennett looked disgusted.

Woodrow shrugged. "Well, would'a been, if the soldiers hadn't always been chasing us."

August heard the thump of boots. He turned to see Raoul storming up from the back of the room.

"That boy's lying!" Raoul roared. "Indians took me prisoner when I was his age—I know firsthand how kind they are, I got the scars to prove it. The half-breed's white squaw has made it worthwhile for the kid to lie. If I get my hands on him, I'll beat the truth out of him."

"Sit down, sir!" Lieutenant Davis jumped up from his seat behind Auguste and blocked Raoul's way. Auguste turned to see Raoul's big frame just a few feet from him, close enough for him to smell whiskey fumes.

"This is none of your business, Davis," Raoul growled.

"General Winfield Scott and Colonel Zachary Taylor commanded me to see that this man receives a proper trial," said Davis in a calm, steady voice.

Judge Cooper rapped his mallet. "De Marion, I won't allow you to disrupt this court."

Raoul shouted at Cooper over Davis's shoulder. "Don't you forget, Cooper, that when you're not wearing that black robe you're just a small farmer who bought his land from me and sells his crop to me."

Cooper was standing now, his jaw clenched. "That's enough, de Marion. Sit down."

Raoul's head turned slowly from side to side. For a moment he stared at Auguste, his eyes full of hate. Auguste felt an answering hatred boiling up in his chest.

Raoul and the lieutenant stood facing each other for a long, silent moment. Then Raoul turned abruptly and strode back to his seat. Auguste, whose attention had been fixed on Raoul and Davis, became aware of men sitting down all over the courtroom. He wondered whether they were Raoul's men.

Auguste felt his guts squirm as he realized what a thin barrier protected this trial from being abruptly ended. Raoul could call on his crew of rogues to drag him out and hang him at once. The judge and the three Federal soldiers might not be able to stop him.

Ford called Auguste to the witness chair. Auguste had sat rigid for so long that standing up made him stumble, and Ford put a steadying hand on his arm.

As he sat down he felt himself trembling at the sight of dozens of pale eyes faces, hard, solemn and expressionless, looking at him. Bearded men squirting tobacco juice into brass spittoons. Women eyeing him from under bonnets. He looked for the friendly faces in the room—Nancy, Woodrow, Elysée, Guichard, Nicole, Frank.

Ford said, "We've heard bits and pieces of your story from many different people, Auguste. If you were just another Sauk Indian you wouldn't be on trial here today. You'd be with your people, what's left of them. But because you've lived with whites and your father was white and you have a claim to a white man's property, you're accused of being a traitor and a murderer. I want you to tell us about your life. How come you're both Indian and white man?"

As Auguste talked he forgot the watching faces and saw again Sun Woman and Star Arrow, Black Hawk and Owl Carver, Redbird and Nancy, Saukenuk and Victoire, Old Man's Creek and the Bad Axe.

When he was done, Ford thanked him quietly and sat down. It was Bennett's turn.

He shuffled toward Auguste, fixing him with small eyes that glinted with malice.

"We have to take your word for it that you spoke for peace in the councils of the Sauk and Fox Indians, don't we? And we have to take your word that you went to the camp of Colonel de Marion's spy battalion on an errand of peace, don't we?"

"That's right," Auguste said bitterly. "Because all my witnesses are dead."

"Don't try to get us to feel sorry for you," Bennett rasped. "This courtroom is full of people who've seen loved ones stabbed, shot, scalped, cut to pieces, burnt to ashes. At the hands of your Indians." He raised his voice to a shout. "And while that was happening, you were behind the red fiends! Urging them on to kill and kill some more!" He turned away, face twisted in disgust. "I have no more questions for you."

Cooper said, "Does the defense have any more witnesses?"

"No, Your Honor," said Ford, and Auguste's heart sank as he walked back to his seat. Bennett, he felt, had finished him with those few sentences reminding people what the Sauk had done to them.

Auguste turned to Ford, whose round face was blank, unreadable. No hope there. Ford had done his best, Auguste was sure. But he had no more chance against the hatred here in Victor than the Black Hawk's band had against the armies of the United States.

I am going to be hanged.

"Hold it there!" called a voice from the doorway of the court-room. "He *has* got two more witnesses."

Auguste saw a tall, mustached man thumping up from the back of the court with the aid of a crutch and a peg leg. Beside him a skinny man with a small head and a gap-toothed grin shuffled over the plank floor. A rifle hung from one long arm.

It took him a moment to recognize Otto Wegner and Eli Green-glove.

Alert, wary, he watched them come up the aisle between the spectators' chairs.

Cooper raised a hand in warning, said, "Mr. Greenglove, you'll have to put that rifle down before you come any farther."

"So be it," said Greenglove, handing the rifle to one of Jefferson Davis's corporals who had risen to bar his way. "I just needed it to make sure I got this far alive."

Ford came over to Auguste and said in a low voice, "I take it these men are offering to testify in your defense. Do you want them?"

"I think Wegner must be here to help me," said Auguste. "But I don't know why Greenglove is here." He remembered his conviction that Greenglove had missed him on purpose, and shrugged. "I haven't got much to lose."

Ford began with Wegner, asking him how he came to be in Victor when word was he had emigrated to Texas.

"My family and I only got as far as New Orleans, where we are buying provisions to join the colony at San Felipe de Austin. Then this gentleman comes to me." Wegner pointed to Greenglove, now sitting in the front row of spectators. "He tells me Herr Auguste is to be tried at Victor. At once we take the steamboat. I pay for both his passage and mine, using money my family needs. I tell you this not to praise myself but to show how much that man means to me." Now Wegner pointed to Auguste, who looked down at the floor, his face hot and his throat choked.

Ford nodded gravely. "I understand you were at Old Man's Creek, Mr. Wegner. What happened to you?"

Wegner told the story just as Auguste remembered it, ending, "I lost my leg, but I still have my life, thanks to Auguste de Marion, for whom I never did a single thing good."

If I could have taken him back to the Sauk camp, I might even have saved his leg.

Ford said, "Mr. Wegner, we've heard that Auguste de Marion is a murderer and a traitor to his country."

"Lies!" said Otto Wegner firmly. "By the rules of war he had every right to kill me and he did not. He is the most Christian man I have ever known."

I wonder if Wegner knows I have never believed in any spirits but Earthmaker and the Turtle and the Bear.

Returning from the witness chair, Wegner stopped to take Auguste's hand in both of his. "I am so glad I could come and speak for you. You are a *great* man, Herr Auguste."

Auguste, struggling to hold back tears, murmured his thanks. Perhaps Elysée could replace the money Wegner had spent getting here, if the Prussian was not too proud to take it.

Ford began questioning Eli Greenglove about Old Man's Creek.

"Hell, there weren't no Injuns in ambush in the woods," Greenglove drawled. " 'Twas plain as day what was going on. They was a few scouts that come to watch what happened to the peace party. Most of our men were carrying a right powerful load of whiskey. Some of the men saw the scouts hiding in the woods and got excited. Colonel Raoul, he used that as an excuse to order us to finish off the Injuns with the white flag."

"And you shot Auguste?" Ford asked.

"I give him that ear." Greenglove pointed in the general direction of Auguste's right ear. "Hoped he'd be smart enough to play possum after he was hit."

"Why did you choose not to kill Auguste? Did you think it would be murder?"

Greenglove cackled scornfully. "Hell, that never stopped me before. No, it was real simple." He paused, and the courtroom was still. "I saved that boy's life because I wanted Colonel Raoul to marry my daughter, Clarissa."

And suddenly Eli Greenglove started to cry. Tears ran down his bony cheeks and sobs shook his lean frame.

Ford stood looking wide-eyed, turned to stare at Auguste, who himself was dumbfounded, having never seen a man like Eli Greenglove cry.

Bennett broke the embarrassed silence. "Your Honor, I don't see what this man's daughter has to do with the case."

Greenglove's moist eyes narrowed to angry slits. "Just shut up a minute, lawyer, and I'll tell you. My daughter lived with Raoul de Marion for seven years and bore him two kids, but he wouldn't marry her because she weren't good enough for him. No, he had to have the preacher's daughter. That lady, Miss Hale." He pointed toward the spectators. "But she was sweet on Mr. Pierre's boy, Auguste, and I could see he had an eye for her too. As long as Auguste was alive, I figured there'd be a chance that Miss Hale would run off with him. So I made sure to keep him alive."

Auguste's heart sank. If the jury believed what Greenglove was saying now, wouldn't that make them think that there must have been something between him and Nancy when she was kidnapped by the Sauk?

Greenglove's lips drew back from his stained teeth. "But then that sonofabitch Raoul had to go and kill Black Hawk's men that brought the white flag. There weren't no real war before that happened. If he'd sent them messengers on to General Atkinson, the whole thing would've been over in May. Every one of them white people, soldiers and farmers, men, women and children, was killed by that man there." He pointed a skinny finger in Raoul's direction. "Meanin' my daughter Clarissa and my two grandkids."

"Your daughter was a slut, Greenglove," Raoul shouted. "I'd've never married her if she lived to be a hundred." Auguste turned and saw him standing in the back of the courtroom, Perrault and a few more of his bully boys flanking him.

"Oh?" said Greenglove in a whisper that somehow was loud enough for the whole court to hear. "You are very lucky they took my rifle away from me, Colonel Raoul."

Ford said, "I think that's all. Mr. Bennett, do you wish to cross-examine?"

Raoul, from the back, cut in, "Judge, this man is a deserter from my militia battalion. He's been on the run for the past three months. What he's said here is worth nothing."

Cooper frowned at Greenglove, then at Raoul. "I don't see what difference that makes. They bring convicted criminals out of prison cells to testify."

Ford said, "In fact, if this man risked arrest to come here, that makes his testimony all the more believable. To say nothing of going all the way to New Orleans to bring Mr. Wegner back."

"No, it doesn't show him any more honest," Bennett spoke up. "It just means he wants revenge against Raoul de Marion."

Cooper rapped with his mallet. "The testimony can stand. The jury'll decide what it's worth. Lieutenant Davis, have your corporals see that Mr. Wegner and Mr. Greenglove reach the town limits safely. And then, Lieutenant, I'd like a word with you. Meanwhile, the lawyers for each side can sum up."

Flanked by the two blue-coated corporals, Greenglove and Otto Wegner started side by side toward the courtroom door, Wegner's peg leg thumping on the plank floor.

"You go to Hell, Eli!" Raoul snarled as Greenglove passed him.

Greenglove laughed. "I got a better idea from ol' Otto here. I'm a-going to Texas!"

The two men walked out the door as a silence fell over the courtroom.

Auguste wondered, had their testimony saved him? They had told the truth about what happened at Old Man's Creek, but since when had truth meant anything to the pale eyes? If those twelve men sitting in church pews on the right side of the courtroom decided they wanted to hang him, they would hang him even if their Jesus spirit himself came into the courtroom and told the truth about him.

And after seeing the slaughter at the Bad Axe, could Auguste doubt that killing all red people was what all pale eyes most wanted to do?

Cooper and the lieutenant talked quietly at the judge's table. When Cooper called on Bennett to sum up, the prosecutor rose and sidled over to the jury.

"About the supposed adoption papers and Pierre de Marion's alleged will, Mrs. Russell's claim that Mr. Raoul de Marion ordered these papers destroyed is hearsay. She has no direct knowledge that Mr. de Marion gave any such instructions to her husband. More important—if Pierre de Marion adopted Auguste, that makes Auguste a U.S. citizen, and his participating in acts of war by the Sauk nation against the United States is treason. Auguste made war on his own flag.

"Whether Raoul de Marion did right or wrong in running his nephew off Victoire, gentlemen, one thing is sure. Auguste went back to the British Band carrying a powerful grudge against this place and these people. So, I put it to you, he decided that if he could not be a white landowner, he would destroy the white land-owners.

"And he had the power to do it, because the Indians would listen to him. They knew him as a witch doctor, and they also knew that he had been educated among whites. And so he used his power to push Black Hawk toward war. He is an accomplice to the murder of every white man, woman and child killed by his fellow tribesmen.

"Auguste de Marion or White Bear or whatever he chooses to call himself"—Bennett pointed an accusing finger at Auguste—"should be hanged as a traitor and a butcher of his own people."

Auguste heard mutterings of approval from around the court-room and a loud "Damned right!" from Raoul. His feeling that this trial was hopeless grew deeper. Bennett had told the jury what they wanted to hear—the version of the truth that would let them do what they wanted to him.

Ford stood up, wiping his brow. The room was hot for late September. He crossed the front of the courtroom to stand before the two rows of jurymen in their borrowed church pews.

"Gentlemen of the jury, I took up arms against the Sauk and Fox Indians under General Edmund Gaines in 1831. I am not prej-udiced in favor of Indians. I only ask that you try to understand *this* man whose life is in your hands.

"You have to decide two questions: One, by traveling and living with the British Band of the Sauk and Fox from September 1831 to August 1832, did Auguste de Marion commit treason against the United States? Two, is Auguste de Marion guilty of the murder of any citizens of the United States or the state of Illinois?

"Is Auguste a traitor to his country? Well, it seems to me that if anything, Auguste holds dual citizenship in the United States and in the Sauk and Fox nation. And, far from being a traitor to either, he tried to make peace between them. The only thing he ever carried against the United States was a white flag.

"Has Auguste committed murder? All we know for a fact is that no one has seen him raise a violent hand against another human being. Otto Wegner told you how Auguste had a chance to kill him, and instead helped him escape. At great peril to himself.

"You've heard Pierre de Marion's will, which explains why Raoul de Marion, who illegally seized the great house known as Victoire, has been so eager to hound this young man to his death.

"This man has lost everything a man holds dear. His father and mother. His home here in Victor. His home among the Sauk.

"Almost all of his people, his loved ones and the friends of his youth, have been killed. Everyone who lives in Victor knows to their sorrow what happened to his infant daughter. His wife and son are captives, too, and he cannot be with them or provide for them. Which of you, having had so much taken from him so cruelly, would not go mad with grief?

"He has lost so much. All he has left is his life. Let us not, I beg of you, take that from him as well."

Ford sat down in the midst of a heavy silence. Auguste tried to send his shaman's sense forward into the future to tell him how the jury would decide, but his spirit met a blank wall.

He glanced out a nearby unshuttered window and saw a blue afternoon sky with a few white clouds. Within the wooden walls of this courtroom, sky and sun, prairie and river, seemed very far away.

Judge Cooper said, "Gentlemen of the jury, we have prepared a room upstairs for you. We'll send food and drink to you as you require. There are cots in case you can't make up your minds to-day."

As he watched the twelve men file up the stairs behind the judge's table, Auguste could not stop his mind from wandering to the worst. He thought about what it would be like to be hanged, the rough grip of the rope on his neck, the blood bursting in his head, the world going black, his body jerking in hopeless struggle, breath cut off, lungs aching, the final silencing of his heart.

He heard a harsh laugh in the back of the room. He turned and saw Raoul in the midst of a group of men standing near the doorway of the courtroom. Beside Raoul was Armand Perrault. Raoul looked at Auguste and smiled. Auguste knew what that smile meant.

Whatever the jury decided, for him there would be no escape from death.

23

Sharp Knife

Late that afternoon, Lieutenant Davis called Auguste from his cell and took him down to the courtroom.

"Judge said send for you. I think maybe the jury's reached a verdict."

Entering through the rear door of the courtroom, Auguste met Raoul's eyes and his longing for vengeance made his blood feel like molten metal in his veins.

The jurymen came in through a side door. Robert McAllister, foreman of the jury, glanced at Auguste, then handed David Cooper a folded piece of paper.

"He looked at you," Ford whispered. "It's an old tale among lawyers that if members of the jury have found the defendant guilty, they don't look at him."

Cooper read the note and sighed loudly, as if he found the message burdensome. Then he took goose quill and ink and wrote a note of his own. McAllister watched him write, looking over his shoulder, sighed as heavily as Cooper had, looked at Auguste again. After a moment he nodded and took the judge's note back upstairs.

"Well," said Judge Cooper to the courtroom at large, "it seems the jury's a pretty fair distance from a verdict. They can't agree on a lot of things. So, I've given orders that they stay upstairs and keep at it. It looks like we won't have a guilty or not guilty until tomorrow. The prisoner will go back upstairs to his cell. Court will open at nine o'clock in the morning."

Auguste heard the rear door of the courtroom slam and knew without looking around that Raoul had left.

That night Auguste lay on his corn-husk mattress wondering whether he should try to run away when they took him out. To be shot while trying to escape might be more honorable than hanging. He wished he could see Redbird and Eagle Feather one last time. He wished Nancy would come to visit him. Or at least Nicole, Grandpapa or Frank. But Lieutenant Davis said that for the prisoner's safety no one would be allowed into the village hall tonight.

He heard a key turning in his door lock. He climbed to his feet.

"Come on," said Davis quickly. "We're taking you out of here."

They've come to kill me, Auguste thought. It would not be the first time an inconvenient Indian was "shot while trying to escape." But his shaman's insight told him Davis was as trustworthy as any Sauk.

"Why? Before the verdict?"

"They did reach a verdict today. You are found not guilty."

Not guilty! Joy flooded through him as he stood, so amazed that he could not move, staring at the open cell door.

When he had recovered enough to move, Auguste followed Davis out of the village hall, to where the two corporals waited with horses in the silent street. The river rippled black and silver in the light of a three-quarter moon. The Ioway bluffs opposite were black bison shapes under a sky spangled with stars.

The moonlight helped Auguste guide his horse up the steep road out of the village. Davis led, followed by Auguste, the two corporals bringing up the rear. After weeks of imprisonment, Auguste reveled in the cool night air blowing in his face.

They passed the trading post. The road was wider here, and the three soldiers bunched around him. Raoul was surely in there getting drunk, laughing as he looked forward to seeing Auguste swinging at a rope's end.

They trotted along the ridge leading to Victoire. Auguste's heart started to beat harder as he approached the place that had been his home.

The remains of the mansion sprawled on its hilltop like the skeleton of some huge animal, blackened timbers rearing up in the moonlight. People had died bloody, horrible deaths there. Was the place haunted now? Accursed?

A longing came over him to climb that hill again, to sweep away that ruin and rebuild. Put up a fine new house like the ones he'd seen in the East.

I could do so much with this land, but I'm running away from it again. Leaving it to Raoul again.

Then they were past Victoire, but the yearning for it clung to him like a lover's scent.

"By morning you'll be far out of your uncle's reach," said Davis, riding beside him.

Auguste's heart swelled in his chest with the thought that he was more nearly a free man than he had been in weeks.

"If I'm not guilty, why must I run away?"

"Surely you realize that your uncle and his cronies were planning to take you straight from the courtroom to the nearest tall tree if the court didn't sentence you to death. The foreman brought Judge Cooper a note stating their verdict. The judge wrote back, telling them he would say they hadn't reached a verdict, and he wanted them to remain in seclusion overnight while we spirited you out of town. They were willing to put up with the inconvenience. After all, who'd want to find a man not guilty and then see him taken out and hanged?"

Auguste's heart felt like a cup that was overflowing. The jury had understood him; they had believed him.

"I never even got a chance to thank Mr. Ford."

"Main thanks he'd want is knowing that you got away safely."

As they rode on, Auguste's happiness faded. The town that had been his home for six years had exonerated him. But he still had to run away from it at night, for the second time in his life. He hated to do this.

This was something else Raoul had taken from him—his moment of vindication.

Pain throbbed in Auguste's chest with the jouncing of the horse under him. He remembered his mother's body, like a castaway doll, her eyes pathetically wide, the gash in her throat, the splash of blood on her doeskin dress. She must be avenged. How could he let the man who murdered her walk free? Silently he called on the Bear spirit to avenge Sun Woman.

Again he remembered it was wrong to ask a spirit to harm any person. Even so, if he could not hurt Raoul himself, he wanted him hurt, whatever price he himself might pay.

And once again he was fleeing from people he loved. Elysée. Nicole and Frank.

Nancy.

"Soon I must go back," he said.

Davis turned his head to stare at him. "Go back? In the name of the great Jehovah, what for?"

It was Auguste's turn to be surprised. It seemed so obvious that he had to return to Victor and face Raoul.

"I belong in Victor as much as I belong with the Sauk."

He could not, he decided, turn his back on Victor a second time.

"Why are we going east?" he asked.

"You've have been found not guilty in Victor, but you're still a prisoner of war, Auguste. Your future is in the hands of the President of the United States."

Auguste remembered now. General Winfield Scott at the hearing at Fort Crawford had said, *If the people of Smith County don't hang you, I think President Jackson would find a meeting with you most interesting.*

A chill spread across his back at the thought of meeting Andrew Jackson himself. What would he and Sharp Knife have to say to each other?

Auguste leaned into a small window cut in the thick stone wall of Fort Monroe. He stared through iron grillwork at a blue-gray expanse of rippling water. Eastward on the horizon lay low land, the other side of Chesapeake Bay. Pressing his forehead against the bars he could see the bay opening to the south into that vast open ocean the pale eyes had crossed in their relentless search for new land.

A faint breeze cooled Auguste's sweat-beaded brow. This was the Moon of Falling Leaves, but it was still hot as summer.

Black Hawk had said little since their arrival. No doubt, Auguste thought, the old war leader was comparing this huge stone fortress with the log forts of the long knives he had besieged in his own country. He must be absorbing the lesson it taught of the true magnitude of the long knives' power. But when he did speak he sounded as defiant as ever.

"Why must I wear the clothing of my enemies?" Black Hawk stood in his loincloth staring at the uniform that a soldier had laid out on his bed. Auguste admired Black Hawk's lean, muscular body. It was hard to believe that he had seen sixty-seven summers and winters. His wide mouth was drawn down with distaste as he eyed the tall, red-plumed shako, the dark blue jacket with its gold-trimmed collar, gold lace chevrons on the upper arms and brass buttons, the lighter blue trousers, the white leather belt.

"Sharp Knife wishes to show his respect for you by giving you the dress of one of his war chiefs," said Auguste.

It is also his way of reminding you that you are subject to him.

Owl Carver said, "It is a mark of hospitality. Just as Chief Falcon gave us new doeskin garments when we surrendered to the Winnebago."

Auguste felt a thrill of pride as he recalled the amazing tale Owl Carver had told him about Eagle Feather's part in that surrender. A boy not yet seven summers old whose vision moved him and showed him how to bring a war to an end was surely destined for great things.

Owl Carver looked strange, with his long white hair and megis-shell necklace, in a peacock-blue cutaway coat and tight gray trousers. Auguste was also wearing a pale eyes' suit with a dark brown jacket. The Winnebago Prophet was dressed similarly in shades of green and gray. Auguste had shown Owl Carver and Flying Cloud how to don the pale eyes' clothing, and now they stood stiff and uncomfortable in the room they shared, waiting for Black Hawk to put on his military garb.

Owl Carver said, "And the American pale eyes are not your enemies any more. You have made your mark on the treaty paper."

"This time for all time," said Auguste, putting his heart into his voice, remembering that Black Hawk had signed and broken treaties before.

Black Hawk sighed. "The spirits of hundreds dead at the Bad Axe cry out to me that the Americans are still our enemies."

That was ever Black Hawk's way, Auguste thought, brooding on old wrongs, regretting agreements made with the pale eyes. Irreconcilable.

He will never change. But we must change.

One hope had preoccupied Auguste throughout the month-long journey east, by steamboat to Cincinnati, where he caught up with Black Hawk's party, by horse-drawn coach and finally by that astonishing new pale eyes' invention, the railroad. Auguste must find a way for the Sauk to live in a world where the pale eyes ruled absolutely. He was the only one who understood both Sauk and pale eyes. It was up to him.

"Do you want to say again the words you will speak to Sharp Knife?" Auguste asked.

"Yes," said Black Hawk. "Will he be surprised to hear me speak to him in his own language?"

"Very surprised. He will know you are a very smart man."

Haltingly Black Hawk repeated his speech in English, which Auguste had, at the chief's request, been teaching him. Black Hawk had told Auguste what he wanted to say. Auguste had translated it, and the old leader had learned it word by word.

Smiling, Owl Carver said, "This is just what your vision foretold, White Bear, that Black Hawk would speak to Sharp Knife in Sharp Knife's own lodge."

Yes, and I told you then that it did not mean Black Hawk would conquer Sharp Knife.

But Auguste did not have the heart to remind Owl Carver of the unhappy reality. Silently he helped the reluctant Black Hawk dress.

He wished now that he might have another vision of the future beyond this moment.

It took Black Hawk and his companions two days to travel by steamboat from Fort Monroe to Washington City. As the meeting with Sharp Knife drew closer, Auguste grew more and more fearful. If Jackson and Black Hawk quarreled, the President might decide to throw all of them into prison for life. He might even have them quietly killed. He was the most powerful man between the two oceans.

They slept overnight in the ship's cabin. Auguste dreamed that he stood empty-handed and helpless while Raoul came at him with a huge dagger.

The next day, at about nine in the morning, Black Hawk and his three advisors were riding in an open carriage down Pennsylvania Avenue, with columns of long knives four abreast on horseback before and behind. Auguste felt bewildered listening to the rattle of hooves. Only a few moons ago the long knives were hunting Black Hawk and his band. Now they escorted Black Hawk with honor. The change was dizzying.

Auguste looked about him curiously at the capital of the United States. It was a sprawl of large brick and frame houses, and Pennsylvania Avenue was a muddy, deeply rutted thoroughfare as wide as a cornfield. Behind them on its hill was the Capitol Building, an immense square stone structure topped by three low domes. The air was thick and damp and hot, and moisture-laden gray clouds lay overhead. Auguste longed for the drier climate of Illinois.

Pale eyes and many of their black-skinned slaves stood under the poplar trees lining the sides of the avenue. They waved cheerfully to Black Hawk and clapped their hands. From time to time Black Hawk raised a hand in solemn greeting.

Auguste had expected that they would have to endure jeers and cries of hatred when they were paraded through Washington City. But, surprisingly, people were welcoming them as if they were heroes. It gave him a feeling of hope. His people might learn to live with these people.

Auguste was awed by the size of the President's House, three or four times bigger than Victoire. It stood behind an iron fence at the western end of Pennsylvania Avenue. All this for the Great Father, thought Auguste. It seemed all the more impressive because the entire building was painted white.

Among the Sauk, colors always meant something. Auguste asked Jefferson Davis, who had ridden with their mounted escort, what the white of the President's House meant.

Davis smiled wryly. "Why, that's to hide the scorch marks from where the redcoats burned it in 1814."

But how fitting it seemed that the Great Father of the white people should live in a white palace. Auguste felt a tingle of excitement as the blue-coated officers ushered his party up the front steps.

Owl Carver stuck his hand into a pocket of his jacket and pulled out the gold watch that had once been Pierre de Marion's. He smiled, toothless, at Auguste.

"You told me I could use this to tell when the pale eyes will do things. See now. One of the long knife chiefs told me this." He pointed to the face of the watch. "When the long arrow is here and the short arrow is here, we will meet with Sharp Knife." He had pointed to the numerals XII and XI—eleven o'clock in the morning.

They awaited Sharp Knife in the East Room of the President's House. An officer told the four Sauk to stand abreast, with Black

Hawk at the right end of their line and Auguste on the left. The arrangement told Auguste that the long knives considered him the least important member of the Sauk delegation, an estimate with which he agreed. A dozen long knife colonels, majors, captains, lieutenants, all in blue jackets and gold braid, stood in two groups flanking the Sauk.

Even though he had never had any reason to doubt his shaman's vision, Auguste was surprised at how exactly he had seen the room they were standing in—its rows of windows with blue and yellow drapes, its three glittering chandeliers and the four huge mirrors in gilded frames facing each other across an immense blue and yellow carpet with a red border. Under each mirror was a fireplace. Four fireplaces, to keep one room warm in winter.

The long arrow on Owl Carver's watch had moved from XII to VI, and the old man was uttering doubts of its power to tell him anything when a black servant opened a door at the far end of the room and all the long knives in the room drew themselves up stiffly, clicking their heels together. Sharp Knife came slowly into the room.

Andrew Jackson in person looked just as he had in Auguste's vision, only more terrifying. Whatever unknown red man had first called him Sharp Knife had chosen aptly. With his long, narrow face and his extraordinarily tall, thin body, he looked like a blade come to life. A shock of white hair stood up as stiff as Wolf Paw's crest on top of his head, and thick white eyebrows shadowed eyes as bright as splinters of steel.

Raoul's words of over a year ago came back to Auguste: *I'd like to see what an old Indian killer like Andy Jackson would say to you.*

Auguste felt he was face to face with the power that had destroyed the Sauk. This man, with his own hand, had slain Indians by the hundreds, had uprooted whole nations and driven them westward. This was the leader of those endless swarms of murderous, grasping pale eyes who, territory by territory, were driving the red people from their homes. This was the man who willed that white people should fill all the land from ocean to ocean.

But Sharp Knife was also frail as an icicle. He moved one step at a time, as if in great pain, and Auguste sensed that he was afflicted with many ailments and troubled by many old wounds. Auguste saw in him an immeasurably powerful spirit that kept him going in spite of so much sickness and pain.

"Which of you is the one that can speak English?" Jackson asked. Auguste had expected his voice to be like thunder, but it shrilled like a knife on a grindstone.

Feeling a painful hollow in his belly Auguste said, "I am, Mr. President." Only this morning Davis had told him that was the way Jackson was to be addressed. "I am White Bear, also called Auguste de Marion."

When Jackson turned his gaze on him, Auguste felt it with the force of an icy gale.

"Colonel Taylor wrote me a long letter about you. I want to have a talk with you later. Now, tell the chief I am happy to greet him as a friend. Tell him there will be peace between me and my red children as long as the grass shall grow and the rivers shall run."

A talk later? What did Jackson have in mind for him? Auguste wondered as he translated for Black Hawk.

"Now shall I speak to him in his tongue?" Black Hawk asked.

"This would be a good time," said Auguste.

Black Hawk took a step forward, leaving Owl Carver, Flying Cloud and Auguste standing behind him. Auguste saw that Black Hawk was shorter than Jackson, but broader in chest and shoulders. And, Auguste believed, stronger and healthier though they were about the same age.

Black Hawk raised his right hand in greeting and said in English, "I am a man. And you are a man like me."

Jackson looked startled, then stood very straight and stared intently at Black Hawk's bronze face as the war leader spoke the memorized words slowly, one at a time.

"We did not expect to conquer your people. I took up the tomahawk to avenge great wrongs that we could no longer bear. If I had not been willing to fight, the young men would have said Black Hawk is too old to be chief. They would have said Black Hawk is a woman. They would have said he is no Sauk. So I raised the war whoop. You are a war leader, and you understand me. I need say no more. I ask you to give me your hand in friendship and to let us return to our people."

"A very fine speech," said Jackson. "I was not told that you spoke English, Chief."

Auguste repeated the President's comment in Sauk.

Black Hawk said, "Tell him that you taught me how to say what I wanted to say in the pale eyes' tongue."

Jackson grunted. "I see. Yes, White Bear, you and I will have to talk. Well, tell him that we will send him back to his people when we are certain we'll have no more trouble from them."

Auguste wanted to say, *Almost all the people who caused you trouble are dead.* But he merely translated Jackson's words for Black Hawk.

Why does Jackson want to talk to me? Auguste did not like the sound of it. Did Sharp Knife have in mind some treachery against Black Hawk?

Black Hawk said, "Tell the Great Father that the Sauk will be quiet as long as the pale eyes do no more harm to them." Auguste had a sinking feeling, as he translated this, that he might well be reopening hostilities right here in the President's House.

Jackson answered, "We never have done any wrong to your tribe. When we buy land from people we expect them to honor their agreements."

Two stubborn men, thought Auguste. Black Hawk was right in saying that they were alike.

When he told Black Hawk what Jackson had said, the chief answered, "Say to him that I have thought much about this. I do not think land can be bought and sold. Earthmaker put it there for our use. If people leave their land, then someone else can take it and use it. But it is not something like a blanket or a pot, that can be carried away by its owner. It belongs to all Earthmaker's children."

Black Hawk's words worried Auguste, giving him the feeling that a storm was about to break. Jackson, he knew, was a hot-tempered man, a man who had killed others in duels. Black Hawk might be bringing further trouble on himself, on all of them, by speaking so candidly to Sharp Knife.

He considered changing Black Hawk's words to a speech more agreeable-sounding. But that would be a kind of treachery, he decided. Out of loyalty to Black Hawk, he must convey his meaning exactly to Sharp Knife. So, watching with inner trembling as Jackson frowned and shook his head, he faithfully translated.

Jackson looked directly at Auguste, not at Black Hawk, as he answered.

"You Indians just do not understand that land is the source of all the goods of civilization. That's why the white man is so much richer and more powerful than the red man. Among us, every piece of land is owned by a particular man, and that man makes good use of his land to produce wealth. Never mind, don't translate that," he ordered. "It's just as well the chief and I have no more words on this point right now."

Auguste felt deep relief that Black Hawk's words had not angered Jackson. Unsmiling, the President took a stiff step toward Black Hawk and thrust out his hand. Black Hawk reached out to him, and they clasped hands solemnly, staring into each other's eyes. Auguste felt a shiver run through him at the sight of that handclasp. Now Black Hawk's war with the pale eyes was truly at an end.

The white officers standing on either side of Jackson and Black Hawk clapped their hands, and after a moment of hesitation Auguste, Owl Carver and the Winnebago Prophet applauded too.

Jackson said, "Lieutenant Davis, take the chief and these two older medicine men on a tour of the President's House and the gardens." He turned his blue eyes on Auguste. "White Bear—Mr. de Marion—I'd like you to accompany me to my office for a private word."

Now Auguste's heart pounded as he followed Jackson, accompanied by two soldiers, up a flight of stairs. He sensed that Jackson must have demands in mind, and knew that because of what he had been—*old Indian killer*—the Sauk would not be helped by his yielding to those demands. But what might refusal mean? Imprisonment? Death?

Jackson's office was a large room, well lit by big glass windows, where the President's polished oak desk was piled high with papers. The two soldiers stationed themselves on either side of the door, and as Auguste entered behind Jackson he saw a guard with a bayonet-mounted rifle standing like a wooden statue in one corner of the room. Auguste wondered whether there was always a guard there, or only when Jackson had an Indian visitor. Jackson folded his tall body inch by painful inch into a large mahogany chair. With a gesture he invited Auguste to sit opposite him in a comfortable chair with curving wooden arms and legs.

"I want you to consider staying here in Washington City, Mr. de Marion," Jackson said abruptly. "I think you can be of great service to your Indian people and to the United States. I'm impressed by the way you prepared that speech for Black Hawk. Zack Taylor has written me that you're a remarkably learned fellow. There are plenty of men and women who straddle the border between the white and the red races, but most of them are trash—illiterates and drunks who hang around Army posts. You seem to be an important man both in the white world and among your fellow tribesmen."

Auguste's body went cold. Jackson did want him to work for him. He found himself resenting the President's apparent expectation that he could easily be won over. But he was afraid that if he refused outright Jackson might take it out on the Sauk.

He shook his head. "You overestimate me, Mr. President. I have no importance in the white world. I had a place, but it was taken from me. Among the Sauk—yes, I am what you would call a medicine man, but I begged them not to go to war against the whites and they did not listen to me."

Jackson waved that away with a long, bony hand. "I can see that you are capable of accomplishing much. I have a situation for you in my Bureau of Indian Affairs. If you do well in that post you might one day head the bureau as Commissioner, responsible for the welfare of all the Indian tribes under the protection of the United States."

Auguste felt overwhelmed. Jackson's proposal went far beyond anything he had imagined. Was he wrong in thinking that he must refuse?

No, he must reject Jackson's offer. The President meant to use him against his own people.

Auguste looked straight into Jackson's steel-splinter eyes. "You expect more trouble with the Indians, don't you, Mr. President?"

Jackson frowned. "Why do you say that?"

"Up to now you've been assuring the red men that they could live in peace on the west side of the Mississippi. But now you can't promise them that anymore."

"You *are* a medicine man, de Marion. How have you divined that?"

Auguste felt as if he were walking on bad ice and might at any moment break through and drown. He should not be so bold with this all-powerful man.

"I know that General Scott has signed a treaty with He Who Moves Alertly whereby the Sauk give up a strip of land fifty miles wide running down the *west* side of the Mississippi."

Jackson clenched his fist until the knuckles showed white. "You were not supposed to learn about that treaty till you returned to Sauk country."

"We traveled over a thousand miles, Mr. President. We talked to many people, and they talked to us."

"And with someone who speaks English as well as you do in the party, you were bound to learn. Does Black Hawk know about this?"

"No, sir."

Jackson's smile was knowing. *He thinks I'm willing to betray Black Hawk.*

Before Jackson could speak, Auguste said, "He would be angry if he knew. He would protest to you. And it would do no good. It would only mar the meeting between you and him."

Sharp Knife's smile broadened. "Exactly the sort of tactful decision I'd expect of you. Just why I want you to help me."

Auguste was frightened, but felt he must make it clear to Jackson where he stood.

"Mr. President, when you force the red people to give up land west of the Great River, how will they live? Soon there won't be enough land for them to hunt on."

Jackson spread his hands. "If their food supply runs short, our Indian agents can supply them until they find other means of livelihood."

To depend on government agents for the very food they put into their mouths? That would be a kind of prison.

His heart galloping, Auguste decided to speak even more boldly. "You are looking for someone to reconcile the red man to having his land stolen from him, Mr. President."

"Mr. de Marion, the United States is not a thief." A fierce glare lit Jackson's eyes.

I must try to be bold without being rude.

"I meant no insult, Mr. President. The red man *thinks* his land is being stolen from him."

Jackson frowned at Auguste as if he was not sure whether he was being sarcastic, and, indeed, hearing his own words, Auguste was not quite sure how he meant them.

"Exactly," Jackson said. "The red man doesn't understand what is happening. You can help to see that this *must* be."

Auguste hesitated. He had not had time to think. He was not ready to decide his whole future and perhaps bargain away the future of his people in a moment. Staying here in Washington City just might be the best thing he could do for the Sauk. Working for and with Jackson, he could protect his people, warn them of danger, avert attacks on them.

But his choosing to refuse Jackson was not the outcome of a momentary impulse. His whole life had taken him to this place on his path. The path might wind; its direction might sometimes be lost in shadows. But it did not lead to Sharp Knife. Jackson was a far better man than Raoul, but they were both on the same side, the side of the dispossessors.

"What the red men don't understand, Mr. President, is how much they are giving up."

"Black Hawk said land can't be bought and sold," Jackson said. "Then it belongs to whoever can make the best use of it."

Each man owning his own land and defending it against all comers, thought Auguste, that was the centerpost of the white way of life.

"I understand that you feel a responsibility to your people, to provide them with land," Auguste said. "But whether it is legal or illegal, just or unjust, I can't help you to move my people or any other red people off the land they are living on."

Jackson's face seemed to sharpen. "You could have done much for Indians by working for me. I'm surprised that a man of your intelligence and education would prefer running around in the woods wearing a loincloth."

Auguste was reminded of Nancy's words, *hunting and living in wigwams*.

Jackson reached into an inner pocket of his black jacket and took out a pair of spectacles. To Auguste they looked somewhat like Pierre's. Auguste thought with sorrow of Sun Woman and wondered what had happened to the spectacles he had given her. Jackson bent forward and picked up a sheet of paper from one of the piles on his desk.

"Ask one of the soldiers in the next room to help you find the rest of your party."

A few days later Jefferson Davis came to see Auguste in his new room, a small wedge-shaped chamber in one of the towers of Fort Monroe.

"I see they've moved you," said Davis with a smile.

Auguste nodded. "I believe President Jackson prefers that I no longer associate with Black Hawk and his party."

"Seems so," Davis said. "President Jackson plans to send Chief Black Hawk and Owl Carver and the Prophet on a tour of our big cities. Jackson's up for reelection next month. And, of course, he wants Black Hawk to see at first hand what he's up against. The President has made it clear that you are not to go along."

Auguste shrugged. "He offered me a position. I refused."

A smile warmed Davis's pale, gaunt face. "People don't ordinarily say no to the President of the United States. Well, you'll go home all the sooner. Black Hawk and the others won't get back to the Sauk reservation in Ioway till sometime next year. But I'm leaving tomorrow to rejoin Zachary Taylor's command at Fort Crawford, and I'm to take you with me, to return you to your people."

Auguste did not answer. He sat down heavily on his bed, which he had pulled next to the one small window in his room, overlooking the strait called Hampton Roads.

Did he want to go back to his people? He remembered a thought that had come to him while talking with Andrew Jackson. Each man owning his own land. That was the key to the white way of life.

But he longed to see Redbird and Eagle Feather again. Were they well or sick? He wanted to hold Redbird in his arms, mourn Floating Lily with her. That wonderful story he had heard from Owl Carver about Eagle Feather and the calumet—he wanted to tell Eagle Feather he had done well.

But, go back to the Sauk? He knew now, especially after talking to Jackson, what the future of the Sauk would be. Never to see the Great River again. To lose their land bit by bit. To be confined to a tract of land in Ioway far smaller than the territory they'd formerly ranged over. Not permitted to hunt where they wished. Might have to beg food from an Indian agent, as Jackson had said. They would not choose their own chiefs as they always had, but would have chiefs picked for them by the whites, men like He Who Moves Alertly, who knew how to use both the pale eyes and their own people to advance themselves. A miserable life, a prison life, a slave's life.

Memories crowded his mind. The words of the Turtle: *You will be guardian of that land that has been placed in your keeping.* Sun Woman's lifeless brown eyes staring up at him at the Bad Axe. The charred ribs of Victoire under a three-quarter moon.

He thought of the endless acres of farm and grazing land stretching around Victoire. He remembered the verdict Not Guilty. The eyes of David Cooper, hard but honest.

If he could take Victoire away from Raoul . . .

Then he would have something to offer Redbird and Eagle Feather. If he won his rightful place in the world the whites were building, he could bring his wife and son to share it with him.

"What's the matter?" said Davis, breaking in on his thoughts. "Doesn't the idea of going back to your people make you happy?"

Auguste shook his head. "No."

"What other choice do you have?"

"I could do more for my people by staying in the white world. Not as Jackson's Judas goat, but as master of Victoire."

Davis took a step backward, astonished. "Master of Victoire! Have you lost your senses, man? We barely got you out of Smith County alive."

"Will you take me back there instead of to the Sauk in Ioway?"

Davis shook his head. "I'm not authorized to do that."

"Am I still a prisoner?"

"You're a guest of Uncle Sam. But that doesn't mean I can spend Uncle Sam's money taking you anywhere you want to go." Davis frowned in thought. "But I could turn you loose in Galena instead of taking you all the way over to Ioway. That wouldn't make any difference, monetarily. Not that I'm ready to go along with this, but could you manage to make it to Victor from there?"

"I'll write to my grandfather and ask him to send a horse to Galena for me."

"If your grandfather has any sense he'll tell you to get the hell across the Mississippi to the Sauk reservation."

"My grandfather has a power of sense. But he also loves me and will want to see me again."

"If you show your face in Victor you'll be swinging from a tree limb before the sun sets."

"Not if I can take Raoul by surprise."

Davis shook his head. "This is wrong. I'm letting you go to your death."

Frightened, seeing his plan through Davis's eyes, Auguste was tempted to change his mind. Yes, go back to Ioway, live safely in the warm heart of the tribe. Why face a mob of rifle-toting bullies led by Raoul? It was hopeless. He would surely die.

But he saw again those rolling acres, the great house rebuilt, the wealth and what he could do with it. If he turned his back on that, he would stunt the rest of his life with regret and longing.

He said, "It's not suicide. I'm risking my life, yes. But if I don't try to right the wrong that has been done to me, life will not be worth living."

Davis sighed. "A man has to stand up for what he believes in, even if it looks like a lost cause. I guess that's what you and Black Hawk and all your people have been doing all along."

Now that Auguste was committed, fear came back. He'd have to face Raoul's men, dozens of them, alone. Even the Bear spirit could not give him the strength and skill to do that.

There must be a way to meet Raoul alone. Ambush him? But that way, even if he succeeded in killing Raoul, the town and Raoul's friends would never accept him as master of Victoire.

The man he'd just met, Andrew Jackson, was well known as a duelist. In his years at Victoire Auguste had heard more than once of Raoul meeting men in single combat. Pierre and Elysée had spoken with disgust of Raoul's dozen or more killings.

A duel. That would be the way to do it. If he succeeded in killing Raoul in a duel, no one would try to stop him from retaking Victoire. With Raoul gone, his men would be leaderless.

Of course, Raoul had killed many men and Auguste had killed none. But the Bear spirit would fight on Auguste's side. And if he failed, he would rather die fighting for what was rightfully his than spend his life drinking the bitter water of defeat.

A few days before he left Fort Monroe, Auguste persuaded Davis to let him be allowed to walk on the parade ground at the same time as Owl Carver. A sadness came over him at the sight of the old shaman, a gray army blanket thrown over his shoulders despite the warmth of the day, walking with stiff steps across the grass. The heavy-lidded eyes did not light up with recognition until Auguste came close to him.

Then Owl Carver took both Auguste's hands in his, and Auguste noticed something he had never seen before. The sudden realization awed him.

His eyes look so much like those of the Turtle!

Wondering how Owl Carver would think of what he was doing, he told him, "I am going back to the pale eyes' town. Back to Star Arrow's home. I mean to try to take back the land from my uncle."

Owl Carver closed those ancient eyes. He spoke after a moment's hesitation, and when he did his voice frightened Auguste. It was the eerie singsong voice he used when he was prophesying for the tribe.

"When a man or woman suffers an injury too great for them to bear, an evil spirit is born in them, a spirt of hate. The evil spirit ruins whoever harbors it. The evil spirit occupies a man and drives him onward until he does things to others that make them hate in their turn, and thus the spirit continues. I think your uncle has been carrying such an evil spirit."

August broke out in a cold sweat hearing the warning in Owl Carver's words. He remembered the hatred that rose in him whenever he thought of Raoul. Was the spirit of hatred kindled in Raoul at Fort Dearborn now passing to him?

"I pledged to my father, smoking the sacred tobacco, that I would hold the land he gave me," Auguste said, as much to hearten himself as to persuade Owl Carver. "Tobacco bound you and Black Hawk in honor to surrender when Eagle Feather smoked it. I must honor my promise."

But he still felt cold within, as Owl Carver, his eyes now clear-sighted and grave, gripped his wrist tightly. "Do not let your uncle's evil spirit cross over to you. See that it be your promise, and not greed, like the greed of the pale eyes, that takes you back to that land. And, above all, do not use your shaman's power to harm your enemy, or you will suffer for it."

"I will not," said Auguste, but he felt unsure of himself. After all the evil he had endured, how could he *know* that he would not unleash his greatest powers if that were the only way he could destroy Raoul?

The grip of the bony fingers on his wrist tightened. "Set your heart, White Bear, not upon getting back this land, but just upon walking your path."

The deep lines in Owl Carver's face were drawn downward with pain, and Auguste felt the crushing weight of grief as he realized they were both thinking the same thought—that they would never see each other again.

24

Challenge

Following the dimly seen figures of Guichard and his horse, Auguste breathlessly climbed a narrow, steep pathway that switched back and forth up the steep, wooded hillside. He led his horse by the reins. Halfway up the hill they came to a flat place, an open clearing. Auguste smelled wood smoke. The windows of a cottage glowed yellow, promising safety.

While Auguste waited in the dark, Guichard stabled the horses, then knocked on the cottage door.

"We have arrived, monsieur," he called, and pushed the door inward.

Auguste blinked in the light of a dozen candles set on a circular chandelier. Across the room by the fireplace a book fell to the rug, a Kentucky quilt was swept back and a pair of long, skinny legs draped in a nightshirt swung over the side of a chaise longue.

"Grandpapa, don't get up." But Elysée was already hobbling across the room to Auguste's outstretched arms.

Elysée buried his white head in his grandson's chest. Auguste held his grandfather tightly; the answering embrace was not as strong as it had been even a few months ago when the old man had visited him in his cell. The fragility and weakness saddened Auguste.

Bare feet peeping from under another nightshirt pattered down a ladder from the second-story loft. Before he reached the bottom, Woodrow jumped and rushed to hug Auguste.

"I been staying here ever since we found out you were coming. So I could tell Miss Nancy right away when you got here."

Nancy. His heart raced as he remembered her in the witness chair defending him and standing up to Raoul's abuse. He badly wanted to see her, to hold her in his arms.

But could he allow himself to feel so much for Nancy, when he hoped to bring Redbird here?

That is looking too far down the trail. I may not live to see Redbird again.

Out there in the dark the enemy might be gathering even now.

"You still live with Miss Nancy, Woodrow?"

"She's adopted me." The boy stared down at Elysée's small Chinese rug. "I guess that makes me your son too."

Auguste understood what Woodrow meant. Auguste had taken Nancy as his wife according to Sauk custom, and Woodrow knew it. He saw Elysée's puzzled look, and knew that he might have difficulty explaining later. But he must not hesitate now. He squeezed Woodrow's bony shoulder.

"I'm proud."

"I'm proud of you, White Bear. I'm glad you came back. I'm off to Miss Nancy's soon as I get my britches on." The boy scampered back up the ladder.

"Guichard, go get Nicole and Frank," said Elysée as he drew Auguste across the room and gently pushed him into a chair.

"They'll be sleeping, Grandpapa," Auguste protested.

"They would be furious if we did not wake them," said Elysée, his falcon's face severe. "And it is safest that we meet late at night."

Auguste wondered, was any time safe? Did not the enemy have eyes and ears for the night?

Auguste threw off the riding coat Guichard had given him in Galena and sat down in a straight wooden chair by the chaise longue, close to the welcome warmth of the fire. He noticed a pistol and a rifle mounted on brackets over the mantel, with two powder horns hanging beside them. Guichard filled three small glasses with an inch of brandy apiece, drained one quickly and left the other two and the decanter on a small table within easy reach.

"I felt ten years younger when I saw Raoul's face turn purple when he came into court with his rogues and heard that you had been spirited away." Elysée wiped his wet cheeks with a blue kerchief. "I cry so easily. I *am* getting old."

"I am crying, too, Grandpapa."

Elysée turned a stern but still moist eye on him. "Enough crying, then. Tell me everything you have seen and done since the trial."

Auguste described his journey to Washington City and the meeting with Andrew Jackson.

Woodrow, dressed now for riding, lingered to listen as Auguste repeated Black Hawk's speech to Jackson. Then he solemnly shook hands with Auguste and left.

"Be careful out there," Auguste called after him.

Elysée said, "President Jackson, what sort of man is he?"

"His nickname, Old Hickory, is apt. He's hard, very hard."

Auguste told about his refusal of Jackson's offer of a post and being cut out of Black Hawk's touring party.

Elysée shook his head doubtfully. "To take a position in the government might have opened up an excellent career for you."

Auguste shook his head. "I knew what Jackson wanted to use me for. The Bear spirit would tear my heart out if I ever consented."

Elysée raised an eyebrow. "You still believe in such things—bear spirits and all that?"

Auguste thought of his resolve to succeed as a white man. Even so, the Bear spirit was as real as his grandfather.

"I don't just believe, Grandpapa. I know."

Elysée's reply was cut off when a weeping Nicole pushed the door open, followed by Frank and Guichard. Auguste held his aunt in his arms, rejoicing in the strength he felt in her ample body. Guichard brought more chairs from a rear room and set them close to the fire. They sat in a circle, their backs to the dark outside.

"All this going from house to house isn't safe," said Nicole. "Raoul is probably having all of us watched. He won't feel he really owns Victoire as long as Auguste is alive."

Frank said, "He might know that President Jackson sent you back from Washington City. We've been getting regular reports from back East about Chief Black Hawk's tour, and your name wasn't mentioned."

"Do you have any news about the rest of my people?" Auguste asked.

Nicole said, "The Sauk prisoners who walked through here are being held at Rock Island."

Auguste said, "I must go there and find Redbird and Eagle Feather."

Hearing that she was still in Illinois, he wanted more than ever to rescue her from hunger and fear and captivity, to bring her and Eagle Feather here to Victoire.

If I live to do that.

"Will you join the other Sauk in Iowa after you find your family?" Frank asked.

Auguste shook his head. "No, I must take my rightful place here. I can no longer live as a Sauk. If we are to live and prosper, we must live as the whites do, each man holding and tending his own land. I want to show my people how it can be done. I want to take Victoire back."

A silence filled the room. A log on the fire broke in two with a loud crack, spattering sparks on the screen.

Auguste looked at each of them in turn. There was worry in Elysée's eyes. Nicole's full face was pale with fear, and Frank looked bewildered. Guichard, standing against the wall, sipped brandy.

Frank said, "But Raoul—he'll try to kill you."

"I mean to let him try. I mean to challenge him."

"You can't." Nicole's voice was shrill. "He's got dozens of men behind him."

"He will have to fight me man to man. Raoul can hold his place only as long as his followers think he is the strongest and bravest. They don't respect him the way they used to. He made too many mistakes. And some of those mistakes have cost lives among his own men. If he tries to kill me without fighting me, he'll slip further in their eyes. If he loses the respect of his men, he loses everything."

Nicole said, "But you're going up against someone who has killed many times."

True. And he killed Iron Knife, the biggest and strongest brave in the British Band.

"I must do this," said Auguste. "I have never killed, but I know how to use weapons. I must do it for my mother. For all the Sauk that he has killed. And so that my father's will may be done. I believe the Bear spirit will help me."

He hoped he sounded more confident than he felt. If he let these people persuade him, he might give up and run away.

Elysée groaned. "The Bear spirit again. Auguste, think how many men have gone into battle believing God and the saints and the angels would help them. And have died."

Auguste wished he could explain. Maybe for white men the spirits did not exist. But he knew that his visions were real. The Bear spirit was not just another part of his mind. It had a life of its own. It had left the marks of its claws on his body. It had left its paw print in the earth beside Pierre's body when it took his spirit away.

"If it was wrong for me to try to fight Raoul, Grandpapa, I would receive a warning."

Elysée shook his head sadly, disbelieving. Auguste was sad, too, thinking how much more there was to the world than Grandpapa would ever let himself know.

The Seth Thomas clock on the mantel over the fireplace chimed once, making them all jump. One o'clock in the morning. Auguste, at the end of a journey by railroad, steamboat, coach and horseback that had taken weeks, felt a bone-deep ache of exhaustion. But it was only bodily fatigue. Now that he was in Victor he was excited, and his mind was wide awake.

Frank put an ink-stained hand on Auguste's shoulder.

"Listen, Auguste. Even if you were to succeed in killing Raoul, you wouldn't get Victoire back."

"Why not?"

"Things have changed around here. People don't hold with the idea that every man should carry a gun and be a law unto himself. They've seen that only leads to a gang like Raoul and his rogues running things. They've decided they wanted the county run by those they've picked. And men like David Cooper and Tom Slattery came forward. Slattery is our new sheriff."

Elysée said, "The *Victor Visitor* has had much to do with this change."

Frank shrugged modestly and went on, "Right after your trial a group of men in Victor and on the farms hereabouts, mostly newcomers, formed an organization called the Regulators. They said it was a disgrace that the Army had to guard you during your trial and that you had to flee from the town when it was over. They're determined to keep order in Smith County, and Slattery has sworn them all in as deputies to make what they do legal. Things are tense now between the Regulators and Raoul's men, but the Regulators have more numbers and more spirit."

"Well then," said Auguste, exasperated, "why wouldn't these Regulators support me if I kill Raoul?"

"Because dueling is against the law. You'd stand trial again, for murder. And, by God, much as it might pain him, Cooper will hang you."

"And if you don't kill Raoul," said Nicole, "you'll die and he will still have Victoire."

Auguste felt as if he were struggling in a net of heavy ropes. His hands and heart ached for revenge on Raoul. Even if he did not get Victoire back.

But that was madness, to kill Raoul and be hanged for it.

"What can I do, then?" he asked in a low voice.

Nicole said, "David Cooper still has the papers that prove Pierre adopted you and left Victoire to you."

For just a moment Auguste felt his burden of fear grow lighter. He would fight Raoul in a courtroom. No one need die.

But no—he waved the idea away.

"They acquitted me of murder, but a jury of new settlers in Illinois is not likely to make an Indian the biggest landholder in the county."

Nicole said, "They would, because they would know that if they found for you and against Raoul, they would be finding for the whole family, not just you."

Auguste said, "Even if I could get a fair trial, I wouldn't live to hear the verdict."

"Yes you would," said Frank. "Fear of the Regulators would stop Raoul from murdering you."

Auguste felt the ropy net tightening. Three moons ago his life had been in the hands of twelve white men. Now Frank was asking him to trust unknown white men again. And again, it seemed, he had no choice.

"Is there nothing else I can do?" The words came out as a cry of pain.

"You said you want to live as whites do," said Frank. "Then you have to start to think and act like a civilized white man. Seek your remedy in the law."

More than once, Auguste thought, he'd seen that civilized white men were as quick to flout the law as to seek a remedy in it. But, resigned, he slumped in his chair, his hands hanging down between his knees.

"I will follow your advice."

Nicole came over to him and stroked his hair. "We'll be beside you every moment, Auguste."

The menace of rope or bullet or knife seemed driven off a bit, as Guichard put another log on the fire and they began to talk about going to Vandalia, finding a lawyer—perhaps Thomas Ford again—and filing suit against Raoul. There was still the possibility—the likelihood—of failure. But at least he might come through alive.

The clock struck two.

A sharp banging on the door startled Auguste. Everyone fell silent, dreading what might be out there.

Guichard went to the door, opened it a crack, then pulled it wide.

Auguste saw a flash of blond hair under a bonnet and eyes of deepest blue. The sudden leap of his heart lifted him out of his chair. He barely heard the little serving table beside him topple over, spilling his brandy.

He ran to Nancy, holding out his arms.

The lenses on the desk stared accusingly up at Raoul.

Why do I keep taking them out and looking at them?

It was like picking at a scab, making it bleed over and over again, so that the wound never healed.

With a gentle hand he closed the silver case. He had long since cleaned and polished it, but he still remembered it as he had first seen it, streaked with the blood of the Indian woman he had just killed. He put the case in his desk drawer.

Armand Perrault, sitting across the desk from Raoul, grunted with disgust.

Ignoring him, Raoul picked up his whiskey glass and sipped from it, running the tip of his tongue over the ends of his mustache.

"Why don't you get rid of those damned spectacles?" Armand said as he refilled his glass from Raoul's jug.

When Armand picked up his glass it left a wet ring that would stain the polished maple surface. There were already many rings on the desk, even though it had been shipped out from Philadelphia only two months ago. They looked like owl's eyes, staring as the spectacles stared.

But Raoul couldn't bring himself to care about how his desk

looked, just as he couldn't care enough to get started on rebuilding
Victoire. He preferred to live at the trading post. He hadn't felt like
doing anything, ever since Auguste's second escape from Victor.
Next spring, he told himself, he'd get the work going.

And so he sat up late every night in his counting room with
Armand and they drank and told each other the same stories about
the war with Black Hawk's band. There were men to drink with in
the trading post taproom, but he didn't care for most of them. Armand had been with him longer than anybody. Raoul might not like
him much, but he was used to him.

Armand had grudgingly accepted Raoul's explanation that he
hadn't read his copy of the will carefully before sticking it in the
fire. He thanked Raoul for the belated two hundred dollars and
dismissed Pierre's generosity as an attempted bribe from beyond the
grave.

Raoul stared at his stained desk. The drawer was still open, the
silver case still visible. "They were my brother's spectacles."

"I know that. Why do you keep them? You hated your brother."

Raoul brought the flat of his hand heavily down on the desk.
"Shut up! You know nothing about it."

*How do I feel about Pierre? Do I still love him in a way? Is that
why I keep his spectacles?*

Unwilling suddenly to consign the silver case to his desk, he
dropped it into his jacket pocket. Armand probably wanted him to
throw it away so he could retrieve the case and sell it for the silver.

Armand said, "Your brother put the horns on me. And his Injun
friends killed my wife. Mon Dieu, how I wanted to see that bastard
son of his hang for that!"

Raoul was tired of hearing Armand go on about dead Marchette, to whom he'd given nothing but blows and contempt when
she was alive. Going to bed with Pierre was the only good thing
that ever happened to that poor woman. But he said nothing; after
all, he himself had cared little enough for Clarissa when she was
alive.

"You'll get a chance to kill him yet," said Raoul. "He'll be back
this way."

It was now nearly a week since the sergeant at Fort Crawford in
Raoul's pay passed the word that Andrew Jackson had sent the
mongrel back West. To think, that vermin meeting the President!

If Auguste traveled as fast as the news, he must be nearly here. Raoul's informant said that Auguste was supposed to be sent with a military escort to the new Sauk reservation in Ioway. Raoul was sure Auguste would come to Victor instead.

When Auguste came back to Victor, he would go at once to Nancy Hale's cabin, or send for her. Surely she had lied in court about what she and Auguste were to each other. The boys Raoul had sent to watch her cabin would let him know of Auguste's arrival.

Armand nodded vigorously. "May le Bon Dieu grant me the chance to kill him. But what makes you so sure he will come here?"

"Because he knows that he can prove Pierre left Victoire to him. Cooper has those papers, and Cooper helped him escape, so he has Cooper on his side."

Armand said, "Two pieces of paper. Easy enough to make them disappear."

"How in hell am I going to get them away from Cooper? Him and his Regulators."

Glowering at Raoul, Armand leaned back in his chair, making it creak. He folded his hands across the big belly that stretched his homespun shirt.

"Kill Cooper and there will be no more Regulators."

How I wish I could.

Pouring himself another drink, Raoul said, "Armand, you're damn near as stupid as an Indian."

Armand's eyes narrowed and for a moment Raoul saw a flash of hatred that reminded him of the way the overseer used to look at Pierre.

"Have a care how you talk to me, mon colonel," Armand said in a voice that sounded like millstones grinding together, "I am your one friend. Otto Wegner and Eli Greenglove turned on you, Hodge Hode is dead, Levi Pope has joined the Regulators."

It's true. I have no other friends but Armand. I have no family. What's happened to me?

"Damn it, it *is* plain stupid to talk about fighting the Regulators, Armand. Kill Cooper and we'd have a countywide war on our hands."

"I believe we could frighten the Regulators into backing down, mon colonel—if *we* showed some courage."

That's a jab at me.

Whiskey and anger almost made Raoul lash out again at Armand, but he felt a sudden fear that Armand would turn on him and he would be all alone.

Raoul brooded for a time, then finally spoke.

"Wait till I get the lead mine opened up next spring. We'll go up to Galena, you and I, and we'll recruit the roughest, meanest miners we can find. And we'll make it plain to them that they'll have two jobs—to dig for lead and to fight Regulators. When we've got enough of them down here, we'll take on Cooper and his crowd in the next election. I'll spread whiskey and money around and our boys will beat up anybody who says he won't vote our way. Smith County will belong to us again, Armand."

He heard hurried footsteps echoing on the split-log floor of the fort's main room. Someone rapped on his office door. Like a swimmer coming up from the bottom of a lake after a dive, Raoul rose up out of his comfortable whiskey haze.

"Who's there?" he growled.

Josiah Hode, a skinny, red-haired youth in dark calico shirt and workman's trousers, a big hunting knife at his waist, pushed the door open. Hodge's orphaned son.

This is what my Andy and Phil would have grown to look like.
The thought hurt Raoul because Andy and Phil were dead and because he had never really loved them.

"What is it, Josiah?"

"Someone rode up to Miz Hale's door and banged on it. I snuck right up to the fence. When they came out I saw it was that Woodrow kid that lives with her. And she got out her own horse and rode toward town with him."

"Did you follow them?"

"Long enough to see that they went up to old Mr. de Marion's place."

"*He's* there!" Raoul said. He felt as if he were out hunting on a frosty morning and had just sighted a buck with spreading antlers. He clenched his fist and brought it down on his desk, hard. He opened the drawer again, took out a small bag of coins and slammed the drawer shut.

He counted out nine Spanish dollars. "Josiah, you divide these between the three of you for keeping good watch." He dropped a tenth piece of eight into the boy's cupped hands. "That's for you, for bringing me the good news."

Josiah grinned, all teeth. "Thanks a heap, Mr. de Marion."

"Armand, I want about twenty men. Go round them up. Have them meet me at the trading post gate."

"Très bon, mon colonel."

Raoul thought a moment. He had planned to hang Auguste, but they couldn't leave a body around for the Regulators to find.

"We'll take him out to the lead mine and finish him there. I know parts of that mine where nobody'll ever find anything."

"Can I come, Mr. de Marion?" Josiah asked. The glow of admiration in his eyes warmed Raoul.

Raoul gave the boy a grin. "Sure, Josiah. Bring your dad's rifle. I'll show you how Smith County takes care of its Indian problem."

"Do Nicole and Grandpapa know about us?" Auguste asked Nancy as they sat side by side on the split-rail fence Guichard had built around Elysée's garden.

"I told Nicole," she said. "I was afraid she'd condemn me, but I had to confide in someone. She was very sweet to me about it, not a hint of reproach."

"Nicole understands." His voice sounded choked. He didn't know how he knew Nicole that well—from glances, from hints in her voice perhaps—but he was sure that her own desires were as large as she was. And her generosity larger still. She would feel nothing but goodwill toward another woman's longing for a man.

Nancy put her hand on Auguste's, and his breath quickened. Her face seemed to pull his eyes, and he saw, in the light of the waxing moon, that she was more beautiful tonight than he had ever seen her. Her cheeks were rounder now: he hadn't fully realized how haggard she had been as a captive of the Sauk.

We all looked like buzzards' meals. But even then I loved to look at her.

Right now he felt the blood throbbing in his body. He wanted to pick her up and carry her into the woods beyond the house and be upon her. As any healthy Sauk husband and wife would greet each other after a long time apart. He was so aware of his hunger for Nancy and hers for him that he could hardly think of anything

else. Their need lit up the little garden with a glow brighter than
the moon's.

But what of Redbird? Even though she accepted Nancy as truly
his wife, as much as herself, somehow it did not seem right for him
to love Nancy now. It had been right when they were living with
the British Band; here in Victor it was not right.

"I knew you would come back," Nancy said, sensing his desire
but not his hesitancy, bringing her lips so close to his he could
almost taste them.

He inched away from her, so as not to be utterly overcome by
her nearness.

He decided to talk of other things. He told her of the plan he
had come here with, to challenge Raoul. He told her how Frank
had persuaded him to try to retake Victoire with the law's help.

"The Turtle has said that I must be guardian of the land and see
to it that no pale eyes prospers by stealing from the Sauk," he said.
"If I can take Victoire back from Raoul, my people will have a place
to come to in the land that was once theirs."

"You mean for the tribe to come back and live on the estate?"

"No, they could never come back to Illinois as a tribe. But families could come and live here for a while—they could send their
children here—they could learn our ways. And the wealth of the
estate could help them, wherever they might be."

"Will you bring Redbird and Eagle Feather here?" she asked,
squeezing his hand.

*Does she want me to say I won't? No, she cares for them too.
We were a family.*

He said, "Yes, if I can get Victoire away from Raoul, I will bring
them here."

He saw her eyes close and knew that he was hurting her, and
that deepened his own pain still more.

She let go his hand and twisted her fingers together in her lap.
"Of course Redbird is first in your heart. But how can she live here
with you? Where her baby was torn out of her arms and killed by
a mob of white people."

"I've asked myself that many times. I will have to hear what
Redbird says."

He remembered what Sun Woman had said when Pierre asked
her to come with him to Victoire. *I could not look into pale eyes*

faces all day long. My heart would dry up. And surely Redbird had more reason to hate the sight of white faces than Sun Woman had seven years ago.

Could he himself live here? He talked about retaking Victoire, about living as a white man, but he recalled the heaps of dead he had seen on that blood-soaked island off the Bad Axe River. Could he live among the people who had done that?

Nancy said, "Would you still want to live at Victoire if Redbird said she would not come with you?"

He saw Redbird's small face, her slanting eyes, the fringe of black hair that fell over her forehead. He felt her slender arms around him as they had held him so many nights in their wickiup. He saw the love and fear in Eagle Feather's eyes when they parted so that he could take Nancy and Woodrow to safety. The pain of being away from them almost made him want to weep.

"I don't know the answer to that. The trail I follow is dark. I must go one step at a time."

The chill night air carried a sound to his ears. Off in the distance, on the bluff south of this hill, a man's low voice spoke a few words, then another voice answered. He heard a boot crunch on gravel. A door slam.

The hair on the back of his neck lifted.

He raised his head, and his ears felt as if they were opening wider, to take in everything that came to him. The noises were all faint; no pale eyes would even have noticed them.

"What is it?" said Nancy.

The sounds seemed to come from the town. Who would be up so long after midnight?

"Some men talking, a long way off." He listened for the space of a few breaths. "I don't hear anything now."

Victor, he decided, was making him overly fearful.

Nancy said, "If Redbird does come to live with you, what will become of you and me?" She took his hand in both of hers, stroking his fingers. "I love you, Auguste. Now more than ever. Before, my life depended on you. Now I know that I love you of my own free will."

"And I love you, Nancy."

"But you love Redbird too. More than me."

"Not more than you. In another way. Sometimes I seem to be two people."

"Among the Sauk you could have both me and Redbird as wives. And when I was a captive, and I thought I might die at any time without ever having loved you, then I accepted your way. But if Redbird lived here, you and I would have to be together in secret. And I couldn't live my whole life that way."

He had known it would hurt like this. This was the very reason he had tried again and again to renounce Nancy's love.

"I understand," he said, and the words seared his throat.

But now I would never give up a moment I spent with her, even to escape this pain.

He ached to put his arms around Nancy and to feel her holding him. But he made himself sit rigid, fingers digging into his thighs.

Nancy spoke, and he could hear the iron of grief in her voice. "If Redbird comes here as your wife—I'll leave here. Maybe we'll go back East. Woodrow and I."

She stopped abruptly, too choked by tears to speak. The fence rail they were sitting on shook with her sobs.

Something broke inside Auguste, and he felt his eyes burn as the wetness trickled down his cheeks. He slid from the fence and held out his arms to her.

"To see you again and hear you say you'll leave me forever," he said. "It hurts too much."

She came into his arms, pressing her wet face against his. Her lips twisted against his, burning, devouring. Her arms slid around him, her hands stroking his neck. He could feel her pulling at him as he held her and her legs gave way.

He knew they were going to have each other and could not help themselves.

He pressed his hand on her breast, loving its softness, feeling her risen nipple push against his palm through silk and calico.

Footsteps crackled in the shrubbery at the bottom of the hill.

He froze, all his senses straining.

The hot blood in his veins turned in an instant to icy water.

"Auguste, for God's sake," she whispered.

"Someone's coming," he said. He felt her shiver against him.

He heard many men. They were trying to move quietly, filtering up the hill through the woods. But few pale eyes could walk unheard among shrubs and trees and piles of fallen leaves, especially at night.

Along with fear, he felt a sudden anger at himself that made him want to pound his fist on his head. He'd heard the voices before, farther off, in the village. He should have listened. He'd have known who and what they were.

His ears told him the approaching men had formed a semicircle, slowly closing as they climbed toward Elysée's cottage. His heart fluttered in his rib cage, skipping beats, then pounding hard.

Nancy seized his hand.

"God protect us, Auguste!" she whispered. "I hear them too. Your uncle must have found out that you're here. You've got to get away."

"Into the house. Hurry."

In the front room of Elysée's cottage Frank and Nicole were sitting by the embers of the fire. The others had gone to sleep. Nancy flew into Nicole's arms.

"We've got to get word to the Regulators," said Frank when Auguste told him about the men coming up the hill. He shook Woodrow, who had been napping on the chaise longue.

"Go by way of the ravine on the other side of this hill," Frank told the boy. "Tell Judge Cooper Raoul and his men are coming to kill Auguste." He turned worried eyes on Auguste. "Perhaps you'd better go with Woodrow. You'd be safe at Cooper's."

"No," said Auguste. "If I run for it and they catch me, they'll surely kill me. I'm going to do what I came to do. When Raoul gets here, I will challenge him." His heart pounded so hard that his voice shook.

"Oh, no, Auguste!" Nancy cried.

Woodrow stood hesitating by the door, listening.

"They're almost here."

"Go!" Frank snapped at him. Woodrow ran out.

"Go carefully, Woodrow," Nancy called after him.

"Challenging Raoul is just—just madness," said Frank. He went to the mantel and reached for Elysée's pistol.

"Frank, you can't!" Nicole cried.

"What choice do we have?" he said. He took one of the powder horns down and sat to load and prime the pistol.

Auguste said, "Frank, there are too many of them. If you try to fight them you'll only fire that pistol once, and then you'll be dead."

Frank said, "In a few minutes Cooper and the Regulators will be here. All we have to do is hold Raoul and his men off a bit."

"Please," Auguste said. "Let me go out and meet Raoul alone."

Elysée said, "Absolutely not." He stood in his long nightshirt in the doorway of his bedroom. He gestured to Guichard, who had followed him out.

"Load my rifle, Guichard."

"Grandpapa, no!" Auguste cried. He wanted to throw his arms around the old man and protect him.

Elysée shrugged. "Perhaps as Frank says, we can face them down without shooting. You stay out of sight, Auguste. They cannot know for certain that you are here."

"I will not let this happen," Auguste said. "I'll leave now. I'll follow Woodrow." He strode to the door.

They could be out there.

If they are, then I can face Raoul as I first planned.

He yanked the door open and saw Raoul grinning at him, his face yellow in the candlelight from the cottage.

And beyond Raoul, filling the clearing, a crowd of men with rifles.

Raoul couldn't see the mongrel's face. The light spilling out of Elysée's house left Auguste in shadow. But he did see the split right ear, partly hidden by Auguste's long black hair. He hefted the cap-and-ball pistol held loosely in his right hand. This time there would be no missing.

Now. Point the pistol and pull the trigger. He isn't even armed.

But behind Auguste, Raoul saw Frank Hopkins with a pistol and Papa with a rifle. If he shot Auguste, he'd have no time to reload. They'd have the drop on him. And even if they didn't shoot back, they'd be witnesses against him.

Looking past Frank he saw Nicole and Nancy Hale glaring at him, wide-eyed. At the sight of Nancy his jaw muscles clenched and his hand tightened on the pistol grip.

How could she turn away from me and take up again with that redskin bastard?

"Come on out, mongrel," he said to Auguste. "Maybe a jury found you not guilty, but we know you're guilty as hell. You sent that Sauk war party here." He raised his voice. "And you, Papa, Frank—you're fools to defend him. His Indians were trying to kill you too."

Auguste said, "Raoul, you were the cause of the Sauk coming to Victor. You are a liar and a fool and a coward. And a thief and a murderer."

Auguste stepped forward and slapped Raoul's face.

The blow came too suddenly for Raoul to react. It wasn't even hard enough to hurt much. It was purely a gesture of contempt.

Then Raoul's rage came. It flared up like a forest fire. He brought up the pistol. Auguste's unprotected chest was less than a foot away.

But Auguste spoke again before Raoul could fire. "Will you shoot an unarmed man now, Raoul? Go ahead, prove yourself a coward. When you took Victoire away from me, you wouldn't fight me. At Old Man's Creek—de Marion's Run—I stood before you with my hands empty, and then you tried to shoot me. You don't have the sand in you to face me fairly."

Raoul sensed that Auguste's words were aimed not at him, but at the men behind him. He felt angry, trapped.

Shoot, dammit! Shut him up.

No, it's too late. All these men heard what he said.

"You're afraid to fight me man to man. I challenged you the day you drove me away from Victoire, and you backed down. I challenge you again, Raoul."

An answer sprang into Raoul's mind. "I accept. Let the weapons be your neck and a rope."

But even as he spoke he had a sinking, uneasy feeling.

He did not hear any of his men laughing.

Armand said, "What the hell, Raoul. You've killed hundreds of Indians, some of them a lot bigger than this one. Give him his duel."

For a moment Raoul felt like turning his pistol on Armand. The overseer was paying him back, he realized, for the contempt he'd endured.

"I'm ready to meet you now or any time, mongrel. Let it be tonight. But where there will be no witnesses to charge the winner with murder."

Auguste said, "I would be a fool to trust you and your men."

"You have to," said Raoul. "I'm not giving you any choice. The men will see to it that it's a fair fight. That's what they want." He couldn't keep the bitterness out of his voice. "Come with us, or I'll shoot you down on this doorstep."

Frank Hopkins, pistol pointing at Raoul, crowded into the doorway beside Auguste.

The black O of the muzzle pointed at him chilled Raoul. He'd heard that Frank had fired on the Indians attacking the trading post. Seemed that day had changed him. Now he was a man like any other, taking up the gun like any other.

Frank said, "Auguste is not going with you. There will be no duel. Get away from this house now."

Seeing Frank's foolish defiance in the face of over twenty armed men, Raoul almost laughed.

But that pistol in Frank's hand could end his life. He couldn't shoot Auguste while Frank held it on him.

Raoul swung the barrel of his own pistol to cover Frank's chest.

"Get back inside, Frank," he said, putting a steel edge into it.

Instead, with a sudden movement that almost made Raoul squeeze the trigger, Frank came forward, stepping in front of Auguste.

Raoul saw another movement in the doorway, and then he was staring into his father's glittering eyes. Elysée's rifle, long barrel trembling only slightly, was leveled at him.

Raoul decided the best attack was to laugh at them. "Look at the mongrel's protectors. A weakling who would never carry a pistol and a lame old man in his nightshirt."

He heard a few snickers among the men behind him and felt encouraged.

But, he thought with fury, he was still trapped. His pistol was aimed at Frank, but Frank's pistol and his father's rifle were both pointed at him. If he shot Frank, would Elysée shoot him?

With the palm of his hand he pushed back the hammer of his cap-and-ball pistol, the muzzle still aimed square at Frank's chest.

"Papa, Frank, both of you get out of the way, or Frank is a dead man."

But Raoul felt as if the bottom was dropping out of his stomach as he looked at the two men. Neither Elysée nor Frank replied. Raoul saw resolution in Frank's light blue eyes. The man who had never wanted to kill was prepared to die.

I have to shoot first.

He heard Nicole scream as his finger tightened on the trigger.

Frank and Elysée were pushed apart. Raoul was looking into Auguste's eyes, blazing with a dark fire.

Kill the mongrel now, and you're done with him forever.

He squeezed the trigger hard. The hammer fell, and the pistol boomed and blossomed red fire and white smoke.

The pistol and the rifle pointed at Raoul both went off, hurling a blinding bitter cloud back into his face.

He stood unhurt.

Elysée and Frank had fired, but by pushing unexpectedly between them Auguste had spoiled their aim.

The smoke cleared. Raoul saw a black spot on the left side of Auguste's white shirt. In an instant it was a spreading scarlet stain.

Auguste's eyes were shut. He fell back against Nicole, his knees buckled and he sagged to the ground. Nicole, her skirts billowing, threw her arms around Auguste and eased him down.

Raoul felt a surge of triumph.

At last! I killed the sonofabitch!

But below the triumph, like chill black water under thin ice, lay fear of what might happen now. His knees trembled.

Raoul saw Nancy Hale staring at him, her eyes full of hate.

Well, if I couldn't have you, he won't either.

"It was you led me to him, Nancy," he said, grinning as he saw her mouth twist in anguish. "When you came here, we knew he was here."

"I pray that you burn in Hell for all eternity, Raoul de Marion!"

"Pretty talk for a minister's daughter," he laughed.

"Mon colonel!" Armand called. "We hear men running this way. Must be Regulators. Let us ambush them. We have time to find hiding places."

"No," said Raoul. "We'd have to silence this bunch."

He gestured at Frank, Elysée, Guichard and Nicole, who were lifting Auguste's body into the house.

Will I truly have to stand trial for murder? Me? I never have before.

He stared into the empty doorway. Had he really finished Auguste? He'd better go in there and see. But there were three armed men in there, and if he had killed Auguste, nothing could stop them from trying to kill him.

In fact, it might be a good idea to get away from here. With his family all fired up and the Regulators on the way, a very good idea.

He heard Nancy scream again and again. Nicole suddenly appeared in the doorway.

"You are not my brother anymore, Raoul. I'll bear witness against you and so will Papa and Frank." She broke down and sobbed, then caught herself. "You'll hang for this murder, and then, just like Nancy says, you'll burn in Hell."

She says it is murder. Then the mongrel must be dead for certain.

Raoul felt a vast relief. At last he had lifted from his shoulders the burden that had crushed them ever since Pierre brought the savage boy out of the forest.

But the relief lasted only for a moment. The fear came back. His legs were still shaking. He wanted to run for it at once, to get a horse and ride out of Smith County and keep going.

It wasn't just that he had killed a man. This killing was not like other killings. This was not some nameless Indian or some river rat knifed in a taproom brawl. This was his brother's son. The people in this house had loved Auguste.

He remembered, and it was like something breathing cold on his neck, the fear he'd felt looking into Auguste's eyes at Fort Crawford. Medicine man. Was there some way Auguste could hurt him? Could Auguste, even in death, get at him?

Raoul shook himself, shook off the haunting, frightening thoughts like a dog shaking off water.

He had never meant to shoot Auguste in front of witnesses. Now the Regulators were coming and they'd find the body in the house, and him with the smoke practically still twisting up from his pistol barrel. And he wasn't ready to fight them. The trial wouldn't last even as long as Auguste's had.

He had to go to ground somewhere until he could collect more men.

The lead mine.

Even if they came there looking for him, he knew the mine so much better than anyone in Smith County that they'd never find him. Only two or three men who had worked the mine before the Indian war still lived in Victor, and they would not help the Regulators. In fact, he was sure he was the only one who knew about some parts of the mine.

"Speak to us, mon colonel!" Armand demanded. "Do we fight?"

"No," said Raoul. "They outnumber us."

He pulled Armand to the edge of the clearing around Elysée's little house.

"I'm going to make a run. I can be out of the county by daybreak. I'll come back in a couple of weeks, maybe a month. By that time things will quiet down, and I'll bring with me the men we need to run these Regulators out."

Let them think he was going to ride straight out of the county. Let the Regulators chase him along the Checagou road, and the Galena road and the Fort Armstrong road. Meanwhile, he'd hide out in the mine till they quit looking for him. Then he'd leave the county. But it would be best if no one at all knew exactly what he had planned.

"What will *we* do, mon colonel?" There was accusation in Armand's eyes. He probably felt Raoul was deserting them. What the hell did Armand expect him to do? He was doing the best he could for them; if he led them into a fight he'd only get them killed.

Like he'd gotten men killed at de Marion's Run and at the Bad Axe.

"For now, scatter. Deny you had any part in this. Wait for me to come back."

"It will not go easy for us, mon colonel," Armand growled.

"I'll be back," Raoul said. "And when I am, it will be just like old times in Victor."

He plunged into the trees behind Elysée's house. While the Regulators charged up the hill, he'd have no trouble finding his way back to the trading post by moonlight.

Alone, moving quickly through woods he'd known since boyhood, he felt suddenly lighthearted. He might be on the run, but he'd done the most important thing. He'd killed Auguste. He had a winter to get through, maybe a hard winter. But by next spring things would be back the way they were in the days when he'd been happiest. Before he'd ever heard that Pierre had a son. When he'd ruled like a king in Smith County.

25

The Other World

To Nancy, young Dr. Surrey looked like a brainless clothier's mannequin in his black frock coat and ruffled white shirt. Though Woodrow had routed him out of bed at nearly three in the morning and he had spent over an hour working on Auguste, he didn't seem tired. If he wasn't tired, what in God's name had he been doing? Now he was leaving, and Auguste was still unconscious.

A helplessness in Surrey's face, round and blank as an unbaked pie crust, turned Nancy's grief and fear into fury. She wanted to grab his shoulders and shake him until he promised that he could and would save Auguste.

"The bullet pierced his left lung," Surrey said. "But it was a shoot-through, luckily, so I didn't have to dig in there and pull it out. Many a doctor has killed a pistol-shot man that way."

Nancy took a step toward the doctor. He was her only hope, and she would not let him escape.

"Aside from not killing him, Doctor, what have you done for him?"

"I packed the wound with cotton, front and back, to stop the bleeding. I put dressings on. I told Mrs. Hopkins how to change the cotton and dressings. And now he is in the hands of the Almighty."

Earthmaker, Auguste would say.

"I hope the Almighty guided *your* hand, Doctor."

"Knowing your father was a man of the Lord, I'm sure your prayers for Auguste will be heard. He's got to stay where he is, in his grandfather's bed, and fight for his life. I expect he'll take a fever, maybe pneumonia. The punctured lung is of no use to him. He'll draw breath with the other one. He'll be delirious, and you've got to get some food into him—soup's the best, because he'll probably be able to swallow that. His body will fight while his mind sleeps. I'll be back to see him every day."

Through tight lips she said, "Tell me the truth, Doctor. Do you think he'll get better?"

"One man in four survives such a wound, Miss Hale."

Nancy's shoulders slumped. This man could do nothing more.

"Good night, then, Dr. Surrey."

Back in the bedroom, Nancy could hear the crackling that was Auguste's breathing, as blood bubbled in his pierced lung. His face beeswax-yellow in the candlelight, he lay under the canopy of Elysée's four-poster, covered to his chest by a quilt. His arms lay stretched out on either side, his fingers slightly curled.

His breathing is so noisy, at least we'll know when he stops.

Nancy felt as if she herself were being swept away on a black tide of sorrow.

Elysée, sitting by the bed staring into his grandson's face, looked almost as near death as Auguste. Guichard stood behind him, a clawlike hand perched on his master's shoulder.

Nicole, her eyes round and dark with suffering, asked, "What can we do for him?"

Nancy said, "The doctor says it's up to Auguste and God."

Elysée grunted. "Where was God when this happened?"

If Auguste were conscious, Nancy thought, he would be asking Earthmaker for help. In the camps of the British Band Nancy had never seen Auguste give up on a sick or wounded person. He had applied his remedies, gone into his trance, danced and chanted to summon the aid of his spirit helpers, wrestled with the hurt till either the man's soul left his body or the healing was well begun. At first his practices had seemed foolish and savage to her. But Auguste had done his work with such devotion that she came, watching him, to love him all the more. And, out of love, to respect what he did.

But he's not the only one who practices that calling.

Maybe that was what he needed now. One of his own people to call on the spirits for him.

If only Auguste were awake, he could tell her what to do.

Redbird had helped Auguste with his work.

She remembered the last time she had seen Redbird, small, emaciated, holding the broken body of Floating Lily in her arms. Redbird was probably more in need of help than able to give it.

And yet, Nancy had seen that she had a marvelous knowledge of healing. Besides, she had told Nancy that she wanted to be a shaman herself, like White Bear and Owl Carver.

It would be better to go to Redbird than sit here and watch Auguste die.

"I'm going to his people," Nancy said. "To find someone I think can help him."

"No Sauk will be willing to come here," said Frank. "Not after what these people did to them."

"This one will," said Nancy.

A heavy, cold rain drummed on the leather top of Nancy's buggy. Driven by a sergeant, the little carriage splashed into the Sauk camp that huddled beside the wooden walls of Fort Armstrong. A dozen peaked army tents, their grayish-white canvas sagging under the rain in a muddy field, were all Nancy could see. There were no people in sight. "I don't know how you're going to find anybody here, ma'am," said the sergeant. Nancy judged him to be a few years older than she was. His name was Benson. He had tomato-red cheeks and a blond mustache so thick that it completely hid his mouth.

Dark faces started to appear at the tent flaps. She wanted to weep as she saw the misery of the women and children who slowly came out, some of them holding blankets over their heads, to stand in the mud and stare at her.

Shouldn't I be glad to see the Sauk brought so low?

Didn't she owe it to her father, Nancy asked herself, to rejoice in the fate of the people who had murdered him? And what about the horrid things they'd done to her? So proud they'd been, the yellow-and-red-streaked faces, the feathers in their hair, the day Wolf Paw led them to burn and kill at Victor. Now they huddled, what was left of them, in the rain in a muddy field in tattered army tents.

But she felt no pleasure seeing the Sauk in final defeat. Through Auguste, they had become her people.

She felt suddenly uncomfortable sitting in the shelter of the buggy's top, staring down at the sodden figures in the rain. If they could stand in the rain, she decided, she could too. She jumped down.

"Ma'am!" the sergeant called, sounding alarmed. But he made no move to follow.

In an instant her bonnet, her shawl, her dress, were all sopping. But she didn't care, because the people she was looking at were soaked too. She looked for familiar faces. The people standing before her seemed made of mud. From head to foot they were a dull brown color.

"It is Yellow Hair!" She understood the Sauk words and looked around to see who had spoken, but all she saw were black eyes wide with sudden fear. Of course they all remembered her as the pale eyes woman who had been kidnapped and nearly killed, and who had escaped. They must think she had come to accuse and punish.

Yes, now that they knew her, they were backing away, ducking into their tents.

"No—wait—" Nancy cried. She wanted to tell them not to be afraid, but didn't know how. Redbird was the only one she could talk to. And *fear* was not a word Redbird had taught her.

A man was standing in front of her. His eyes were empty, his face thin and dirty. He seemed familiar. He held out his hands. He seemed to be saying, "Here I am. Take me."

All at once Nancy recognized Wolf Paw.

His hair had grown out, hanging down in short black strands all around his head. But at last she recognized that noble face that— much though she'd hated him at first—had always reminded her of the engravings she'd seen of Roman statues.

She understood what he was trying to tell her. If she'd come to find the murderer of her father, the man who had kidnapped her, here he was. He was at her mercy.

He seemed to have lost everything else, she thought, but not his courage.

"Is that Injun threatening you, ma'am?" called the sergeant from the shelter of the buggy.

"Not at all," she said, and smiled at Wolf Paw. She felt heartsick to see how the splendid warrior had declined into a shabby spectre.

She tried to tell Wolf Paw, in the mixture of Sauk, English and gesture that she had used with Redbird, that she had not come here to avenge herself on him, that all she wanted was to find Redbird.

But then Redbird was standing before her.

Like Wolf Paw, she had changed so much that for a moment Nancy wasn't sure this *was* Redbird. She was as thin as a fence rail, and those colorful things Nancy remembered her wearing, the feathers and beads, the dyed quills, the painted figures on her dress, all were gone. She clutched a coarse brown blanket around her shoulders. Her head was bare. Water dripped from the fringe of hair across her forehead and poured from her braids. She wore, not the doeskin clothing Nancy remembered, but a torn gray cotton dress that was too big for her and dirty around the bottom edge. Looking down, Nancy saw that Redbird's feet were bare, her toes sinking into the mud.

Nancy felt warm tears mingling with the cold rain on her face as she saw Redbird smiling at her.

"Redbird, I am glad to see my sister," Nancy said in their special language. "Where is your wickiup?"

Redbird spoke to Wolf Paw in Sauk words too low and rapid for Nancy to follow. He grunted assent and trudged through the mud toward a distant tent. Watching him, Nancy felt pity at his rounded shoulders and old man's shuffle.

Redbird beckoned Nancy to follow her to the tent she'd come from.

"Where you going, ma'am?" the sergeant called.

"I'll be all right," Nancy called over her shoulder, raising her voice over the drumming of the rain. "This is the woman I came to find."

She could see the young soldier shaking his head. Why would a young white woman go into the filthy, disease-ridden tents of these Indians?

May the Lord open his eyes and heart.

At first the inside of the tent seemed black as a moonless night to Nancy, and the smell of damp, unwashed bodies made her stomach churn. She took Redbird's hand and held it for reassurance. Not too tightly; the bones felt delicate.

Redbird explained that they had no dry wood for a fire. The long knives had promised to bring them some, but they hadn't yet. The air was as chill in the tent as it was outside, and Nancy heard women and children coughing.

They sat in silence for a time, Sauk fashion. Nancy's eyes adjusted to the dim light filtering through the canvas till she could see Redbird's face. She saw Eagle Feather looking at her out of the shadows with huge blue eyes, a little skeleton whose covering of skin looked like stretched brown leather. Hurting inside, she greeted him with a pat on the arm. If only she could do for him what she had done for Woodrow. Now she could see four other women and two little girls huddled together near the rear.

Nancy broke the silence. "Redbird, White Bear needs you."

Wincing in pain, Redbird narrowed her slanting eyes. She asked what had happened to White Bear.

Redbird, Nancy learned, had heard no news of Auguste since the day he left Black Hawk's camp to take Woodrow and Nancy back to the whites. Auguste had told Nancy that he had tried to get word to Redbird; now she silently damned the soldiers for not bothering to pass the messages on. No doubt they thought it not worth the trouble.

When Nancy told Redbird that she had left White Bear four days ago, unconscious with a bullet wound in his chest, she saw the gleam of tears on Redbird's cheeks.

"The pale eyes doctor says he can do no more," Nancy finished. "You are the only one who can help him now. You know the Sauk way of healing. You told me you wanted to be a shaman."

No, Redbird said quietly, she *was* a shaman. The declaration startled Nancy.

"You told me the men wouldn't let you be one."

In their private language, Redbird said that for a long time she had not understood what it meant to be a shaman. She had thought that a shaman must be made by another shaman. But now she knew that if people came to a person for help, that person was a shaman. And people were coming to her.

"I have come to you," Nancy said. "You can help White Bear."

Redbird gave a helpless grunt that said she could not. The soldiers would not let her leave.

Nancy reached into her handbag and drew out a folded paper. "I have spoken with General Winfield Scott. This says that you may come with me."

Redbird sat in the damp straw looking down at her hands folded in her lap. Nancy waited anxiously for her to speak.

After a moment, her voice full of pain and uncertainty, Redbird asked, did White Bear *want* to see her?

The question shocked Nancy. It had not occurred to Nancy that Redbird might ever doubt Auguste's love for her.

Recovering from her surprise, Nancy said, "Before his uncle shot him, White Bear told me he was going to come here to find you and Eagle Feather. You are first in his heart, Redbird."

And, my God, how I wish it could be me!

Redbird looked sadly at Nancy. She was not first in White Bear's heart, she said. That land that had been stolen from him was.

Shocked, Nancy started to blurt out a denial. But she realized she could not. Auguste had gone to Victor before he went anywhere else.

But he is dying!

"Do you want to save his life?" Nancy asked.

Oh, yes, Redbird did, if Earthmaker would help her. In the shadows of the tent Nancy could see the glint of tears on Redbird's cheek.

"Then you will come with me?"

Redbird lowered her pain-twisted face. Must she go back to the place where they killed her baby?

At the memory, Nancy broke into sobs and threw her arms around Redbird, as she had done that terrible day.

"I will always remember Floating Lily," Nancy said. "I fought to save her. I thought she was my baby too."

They held each other in silence for a while, and then the thought came to Nancy that even a small delay might make the difference between Auguste's living and dying. Nancy felt a chill that ran deeper than the cold, damp air in the tent.

"Redbird, he will die if you do not come. You have to come."

Redbird sighed. It was true; she would go with Yellow Hair.

Nancy's heavy heart felt a little lighter. If there was any hope at all for Auguste, it lay with Redbird.

One thing they must take with them, Redbird told her. When they were marching to this place, a soldier had taken White Bear's deerhorn-handled knife from Redbird. It was the same soldier who had come with Yellow Hair today, the one with the red face and the yellow mustache. It would be well if Yellow Hair could get it from him so they could bring it back to White Bear. It would give him strength.

"I brought money with me," Nancy said. "I will buy it back from him if I have to."

I'll get it back from him if I have to kill him.

Redbird's eyes blurred as she stared at White Bear's face, as pale as the moon. She wanted to scream, to throw herself weeping on his form. Her longing to see him open his eyes, to hear his voice, was so strong it hurt her. She remembered the night of his vision quest, when she was sure he would freeze to death. She thought of the summers they had been apart, the nights they had lain together. She thought of poor, dead Floating Lily and of blue-eyed Eagle Feather, left in Wolf Paw's keeping.

O come back to me, White Bear!

She had never tried to heal anyone this close to death. When she and Yellow Hair arrived, the grandfather said that White Bear had sometimes opened his eyes and spoken. But each day he had been awake a shorter time.

Redbird saw that White Bear was already wandering in the other world. A thread no stronger than a strand of spider's silk linked his spirit with his body.

She let the love she felt for White Bear flow through her, giving her strength. She felt the eyes of Yellow Hair, the grandfather and the old servant upon her, but she ignored them. She squatted down on the floor beside White Bear's bed and unrolled the blanket in which she carried her medicines and supplies and the possessions White Bear had left with her at the Bad Axe.

Her eye fell on the bundle of talking papers White Bear had cherished so, that he said was called something like "The Lost Land of Happiness." There was power in that bundle of words. Gently she laid it on his left side, near the wound. On his right she placed the knife that Yellow Hair had been able to retrieve for her.

Arranging the three medicine bags on the floor, she took pieces of elm bark from the largest one and gave them to Yellow Hair.

"Make a tea for him from this. It will give him strength when he awakens."

She forced herself to turn her back on White Bear and go out of the house. With her she carried the blanket and the medicine bag adorned with the beadwork owl. She crossed the little clearing around the house and entered the woods. Here, where no one could see her, she opened the medicine bag and took out five tiny gray scraps of the magic mushroom. She put them into her mouth and chewed and swallowed slowly.

Then she got down on her hands and knees and spread her blanket. Oak, maple and elm leaves, brown, red and yellow, lay thick on the ground. She scooped leaves into the blanket. When she had gathered a big pile, she bundled them up and went back into the house.

Carefully she spread the leaves on the bed over White Bear's body. She heard the grandfather say something to Yellow Hair.

Yellow Hair spoke quietly to her, saying that the grandfather feared that the leaves were not clean and would make White Bear sicker.

How could the leaves not be clean, Redbird wondered, when they came from the woods, outside any dwelling?

But she answered, "Must do what I know. If seem wrong to him, must do anyway, or can do nothing."

She heard Yellow Hair talking quietly to the grandfather while she settled herself on the floor beside the east side of the bed. She could not understand the words, but she heard acceptance in the old man's sigh.

Grief and fear that White Bear would die trembled inside her. Breathing deeply, she let the strength of those feelings enter into her spirit, urging her on to begin the journey she must make.

She must go into the other world and find her guide. She began the medicine woman's chant Sun Woman had taught her:

> "Let me walk through the dark place
> To the light of the other world.
> Oh my red spirit Bird, fly to me,
> Sing to me from the other world.

> "Let me walk the sunwise circle
> Into the night that hides this man.
> Oh my red spirit Bird, sing to me
> And fly with me to the other world.

> "Sing and fly,
> Sing and fly,

In the sunwise circle
To the other world,
Into the night."

She allowed the chant to settle into a simple, repetitious humming that slowly, with the help of the magic mushroom, drew her soul out of her body.

She stood up. The three people gathered at the foot of the bed did not see her standing. They were looking at her seated body. She looked down at White Bear. She saw through the leaves she had spread over him and right through his skin.

Five glowing streaks ran from his collarbone to his belly. The claw marks of his guardian.

She saw the hole in his chest, how it ran between his ribs. In the eight days he had been lying here, the wound had closed up. If he lived long enough, it would heal slowly. But there was water pooling in his chest, and the longer he lay there unconscious, the more the water would fill up his chest until he drowned.

His spirit must be coaxed back from the other world.

She began to walk the sunwise circle around White Bear's bed, from the east to the south, White Bear on her right. She passed Yellow Hair, White Bear's grandfather and the old servant. They stood like carved statues, unseeing. She walked around the west side of the bed. The head of the bed was against the north wall of the room, but she simply walked through the wall on one side of the bed, took a few steps along the north side of the cottage, then entered the wall again and continued her circle.

When she had completed her ninth circuit of the bed, she saw a cave mouth in the eastern wall of the bedroom. Unhesitatingly she walked into the black, circular opening.

She could not see where the light in the cave was coming from, but its curving walls were clearly visible to her. Here and there she passed paintings. She had seen them when she made her first journey to the other world, after she buried Floating Lily. She saw the Wolf, the Coyote, the Elk and the Buffalo. Near the floor of the cave she passed paintings of the Trout, the Pike, the Salmon and other fish. She looked up and saw the Owl, her father's guardian spirit.

The passage slanted downward and grew narrower until her head brushed the cave roof and her shoulders touched the walls. Then she rounded a bend and bright blue light greeted her.

The cave opened out high on a hillside. She was looking down at tall yellow grass rolling in waves to distant hills.

A black cloud of crows flapped up out of the grass and flew over her head, laughing raucously.

Then she heard a marvelous singing.

She recognized it at once, the song of her guardian spirit, the Redbird. She saw a blood-colored flash, and then the Bird perched on a branch of blue spruce on the hillside. He had one bright eye cocked at her, ringed in black. His red crest stood up on his head as Wolf Paw's had in better days.

"White Bear is out there on the prairie," the Redbird spirit sang. "He is hunting his uncle."

"Can I heal him?" Redbird asked.

The dazzling Bird chirped a yes. "He is lost. He is wandering with his other self, the Bear spirit. He will not leave the spirit world until the Bear finds his uncle."

Redbird shivered. "What will White Bear's guardian do to his uncle?" She remembered both Owl Carver and Sun Woman saying that a shaman's power must never be used to harm any person.

"What must happen, must happen," the Bird sang. "If White Bear is to be free to go back to his body."

Redbird still felt uneasy. A shadow, like a sudden prairie storm, seemed to fall upon the landscape.

The streak of scarlet sailed out over the endless grass, and Redbird ran down the hill until the tassels were waving high over her head. She could see nothing on all sides of her but yellow spears of straw. Overhead was a patch of bright blue framed by tassels. In the center of the blue the Bird spirit hovered, wings a blur of red. She pushed her way through the stalks as the Bird led her.

On and on flew her spirit guide. Redbird did not tire either, as she would have in the ordinary world, trudging through the grass. She could not see the sun, but the light seemed never to change. And no matter how long she walked, the same bit of cloudless sky remained overhead.

Then White Bear stood before her.

He was wearing only a deerskin loincloth and moccasins. His long hair was bound with a beaded band. The scar on his cheek stood out white against his tan skin. She looked at his naked chest and saw the five shining claw marks, and the small navel-like opening of the bullet wound.

She looked deep into his dark eyes. His love flowed out to her, and she bathed in it, as in a warm river. She knew his thoughts, how happy and surprised he was to see her.

I was lost out here. You have come for me.

He held out his arms, and she rushed into them. She felt his arms around her even though he was a spirit and she was a spirit. She laid her head against his scarred chest and listened to his beating heart. Would she ever again, back in the world of flesh, hold him like this?

A huge white-furred head crashed through the wall of grass around them, and enormous golden eyes looked at her. White Bear had described his guardian spirit to her, but she had never realized the Bear was so big. She looked at black lips that bared yellow teeth longer than her fingers, she stared down at claws that crushed the grass and sank into the prairie sod. She shivered at the thought of what might happen to White Bear's uncle if this spirit found him.

Perched on the head of the Bear was the tiny red spirit Bird.

We are looking for my father's brother, came White Bear's thought. *He killed my mother and many brothers and sisters of yours and mine. He shot me.*

The Bird sang to Redbird, "I know where the uncle is, but I can only lead the Bear to him if you say I must do it."

"I say you must, then," she said, just above a whisper. Whatever was needed to save White Bear's life, she had to do it. Whatever she must give up in return.

The Bird leaped into the air, his crest a bloody spearpoint. The Bear lifted a black nose the size of Redbird's fist, and the white body turned to follow, passing before her like a mountain of snow.

Hand in hand White Bear and Redbird followed. The Bird flew far ahead, and they could not see him, but the Bear trampled down the grass and left a path that was easy to follow.

Loving thoughts passed between White Bear and Redbird. If they always met like this, Redbird thought, they could know what was in each other's heart and their love would be deeper.

Then she remembered Wolf Paw and the new life that she alone knew was growing in her belly. The life that fulfilled Wolf Paw's wish to have a child with her.

She felt like a statue carved in ice. And at that very moment

White Bear let go of her hand. Somehow she knew that he was withdrawing from her, not because he had sensed her thought about Wolf Paw, but because he was troubled by some thought of his own. But instantly there was a space between them, and she no longer knew his mind.

He was still walking beside her. He walked straight ahead, not looking at her. She turned her head to the front and did the same.

She felt as if she had been pushed away, hard, and it hurt.

It seemed to her that they walked for days through the unchanging grass, but the sun remained fixed somewhere beyond the tasseled curtain.

Yellow and blue, yellow and blue, the whole world had been reduced to those colors. And to one sound, whispering grass.

The Bear stopped walking. Redbird and White Bear went around the huge animal, Redbird to the right and White Bear to the left.

She found herself on the edge of a great crack in the ground, so deep that its bottom lay in shadow. It zigzagged from somewhere, appearing out of grass, and continued toward somewhere, vanishing back into the prairie. A stream of bright blue water wound through the dark bottom of the ravine; water had cut this wound in the prairie. The Bird spirit swooped and darted in the crack like a living fire arrow.

"White Bear's uncle hides there," the Bird trilled.

She heard a growl beside her deep as distant thunder, and the ground seemed to tremble.

The Bird flew up, swooped to hover over the Bear's head, then dove down into the canyon. Down to an entrance into the earth framed by two upright wooden posts and a beam laid across them.

Beside the square of darkness were abandoned wooden carts and a hill of gray gravel that partly blocked the stream. This was a mine, Redbird understood, where the pale eyes dug metal out of the ground.

The Bear spirit put one paw in front of the other and, with grace and balance astonishing in a creature so huge, walked down a narrow path Redbird had not noticed before to the shadowy bottom of the ravine. Then it lumbered up to the mine mouth.

She opened her mouth to cry out in fear, but the Bear was gone.

There is a man in there.

And her spirit helper, the Redbird, had led that giant Bear to him. She had commanded it. She had not wanted to use her shaman's powers to hurt anyone, not even one she hated as much as this uncle of White Bear's. White Bear had saved many lives and never killed anyone.

Even though she was a spirit and this great grassland was sunny, she felt cold, and her stomach knotted.

I will lose something because I did this. I only did it to bring White Bear back to his body. But I will suffer for it, even so.

And so will White Bear.

Only let White Bear live, she prayed to the powers that brought life into the world.

White Bear turned to her. *It is done,* said his spirit voice. *My other self has found Raoul de Marion.*

Now you can come with me, she answered him. *Back to your body.*

Back to my home, came his whisper, and she shuddered even as she turned, following the Bird spirit as he fluttered over her head. When he thought of his home, he meant the great lodge the pale eyes called Victoire.

Redbird opened her eyes in the room where White Bear lay, to find herself once again sitting on the floor beside the bed. The three people were looking at her, Yellow Hair with tears running down her cheeks, the grandfather's withered face paler than the fur of White Bear's guardian spirit, the old servant's bloodshot eyes wide.

She remembered that the sun had been low in the west when she came to this house. Sunlight still slanted through the paper-covered west window and fell on the layer of leaves that covered White Bear's bed.

But when she tried to move, pain struck her like knives driven into her knees and elbows, as if she had been sitting in the same position for days.

"His eyes!" Yellow Hair cried, pointing at White Bear. From the floor Redbird could not see what Yellow Hair was seeing. She forced her aching legs to lift her.

White Bear looked at Redbird, then at Yellow Hair. He smiled faintly.

She had done it. He was back in his body.

A spring of pure, sweet joy burst up inside her. A sob welled from her lips. She stumbled toward Yellow Hair and felt that she was going to fall. Yellow Hair's arms held her up.

She saw his mouth open, heard him whisper to her, "You brought me back. I will always love you."

"And I will always love you," Redbird said. Her voice was a croak, as if she had not spoken in days.

She turned to Yellow Hair. "Now he will live."

Laughing and crying at once, Yellow Hair thanked Redbird again and again in their common language, calling on her God to bless Redbird.

Bless me? But what of that man in the mine?

"Give White Bear the tea of elm bark now. Later, little food, only little," Redbird said. "Easy-eat food. Hominy good. Later, soup with meat."

Yellow Hair eagerly agreed.

"Must sleep," said Redbird. She slurred her words, too worn out to speak clearly.

She could lie down in another room, Yellow Hair said, leading her away from the canopied bed where the weeping grandfather bent over White Bear, holding him by his shoulders.

"I gone many days?" Redbird asked.

Yellow Hair's deep blue eyes widened. She shook her head at the word "days." She assured Redbird that she had been silent only for an instant. She had been singing, then she closed her eyes, and a moment later when she opened them again, White Bear had opened his. Yellow Hair hugged her so hard it hurt her.

Just an instant? Every time Redbird went on a shaman's journey she learned something new.

Yellow Hair, her arm around Redbird's shoulders, led her to a bed in another room. Redbird had never lain on a pale eyes' bed, but she sat down on the edge and fell back. If she was not so tired she would not have been able to sleep in this bed. It was too soft. Yellow Hair lifted her legs onto the bed for her.

That was the last thing Redbird remembered.

After a day and a night of sleep, Redbird woke refreshed. And hungry. A cure for that was quickly produced for her; and now she was sitting on a pale eyes' chair at a pale eyes' table, devouring slices of fried pig meat and fluffy cakes brought to her by the old servant.

Seated across from her was a fat, smiling woman she had met

once before. This woman had tried to comfort her the day Floating Lily was killed. This, she knew, was White Bear's aunt.

Yellow Hair, tears streaming from her turquoise eyes, appeared in the doorway of the room where White Bear lay.

White Bear, she said, wanted Redbird to come to him.

Redbird's hunger vanished. She went rigid.

Yellow Hair weeps now, but I will weep forever after.

She heard the suffering in Yellow Hair's voice and knew that her heart was hurting because she believed Redbird was going to take White Bear away from her.

Redbird knew better. She had defiled her powers by using them to destroy White Bear's uncle, and now she must pay for it.

The lance twisted in her heart as she stood up at the table.

The fat woman stood up when Redbird did, came around the table and hugged her. She smelled of fresh-baked bread.

Redbird walked past Yellow Hair to enter the bedroom. White Bear was reclining with pillows behind his head in the bed where he had lain for so many days. His chest was bare except for the white bindings that protected his wound. The wrappings made his olive skin look darker, and above the cloth Redbird could see the start of the five shining scars that ran down his chest.

The leaves had been cleared away from the quilt that covered him. His bundle of talking papers telling the story of the first man and woman and how they lost their land of happiness was on the table beside his bed. Next to it lay the knife Star Arrow had given him when he was a small boy.

When he saw her his face glowed and he held out his arms to her. She rushed to him, and heard a cry of pain behind her. The door of the bedroom shut softly.

She threw herself across the bed, longing to hold White Bear. His arms around her were not as strong as she remembered them, but his embrace was firm.

"You came to me while my spirit wandered on the prairie," he said.

"The Redbird guided me to you."

"Before you came I saw many things."

"What things?"

He said, "The pale eyes will spread across the Great River and even into the Great Desert. There will be no place left for our people."

"If we go far enough west—" she began.

"No," he said. "They will go as far as the western ocean. The Turtle warned me about this." He stroked her hair lightly, and she rested her head on his shoulder.

She had a heart-crushing feeling that she would never lie like this with him again.

"You are so much better today," she said.

"You, too, know the way of the shaman now. You healed me."

She lifted her head and looked into his eyes. This was the moment when they must decide.

"I am the only shaman our people have now," she forced herself to say. "The few who are left need me. I must go back to them."

His eyes shut tight suddenly, as if his wound was paining him.

"Stay here with me," he said.

His words struck her and tore through her, as his uncle's bullet had torn through him.

"I could never stay here. When you are well enough, will you not come back to your people?"

He shook his head. "We cannot fight the pale eyes and we cannot run from them. They will destroy us. Unless we learn to live as the pale eyes do."

"That destroys us too."

"That saves us!" His nostrils flared and his dark eyes glowed. "I can use the power this wealth and this land gives me to fight for our people. And you can do it with me. And Eagle Feather. I will show the people how to make use of pale eyes' ways. I will share my land with them."

Her heart felt as if it were being ground between stones. This, she understood, was what she must suffer because she had used her shaman's powers to hurt another. She was going to lose White Bear. She had saved him from death. He was going to live, but not with her.

The claws of that giant Bear that was his other self seemed to stab into her chest and tear her in two. She could not live with this pain. She must surrender to White Bear.

Yes, I must stay with him. I cannot leave him. Eagle Feather needs him. We will be safe here, and comfortable, and at peace.

She would send for Eagle Feather. The fat aunt and the grandfather would love them and care for them.

She tried to see herself living here with White Bear. For a moment the picture was clear in her mind. Then it dissolved in blackness as she realized that taking herself out of the Sauk tribe would be like pulling a medicine plant up by its roots without its consent.

She would die. It would be a slow death that would be worse than the pain she was suffering now.

And then another thought struck her.

Children!

Her heart felt heavy as a mountain.

She remembered how Owl Carver had said, after Eagle Feather smoked the peace pipe with the Winnebago, that he could be a greater shaman than any of them. But that would happen only if he was raised as a Sauk.

Floating Lily was dead. Redbird could not live with the people who had murdered her.

And—she touched her belly—this was not White Bear's child.

She began to cry aloud.

She sobbed till she thought her ribs would crack. Her throat burned; her voice rasped. She pressed her forehead against his chest. She heard him groan in pain, but he was hurting her more than she could ever hurt him.

"How can you ask me to stay where they killed Floating Lily? How can *you* stay here?"

"What would you have me do?"

A sudden thought occurred to her. "The pale eyes give gold for land. Take pale eyes gold for this land, and you can take the gold with you to the Ioway country and share it with our people."

"No, Redbird," he said sadly. "What could we do with gold, out there in Ioway? Sometimes the long knives have given our chiefs gold in return for land, yes. In no time the gold melted away. Gold by itself is like seed corn. Without the right ground to plant it in, it is soon used up and gone. The only way I can use the wealth my father Star Arrow left to me is to stay here and work with it."

She had stopped crying. This hurt too much for tears. Only when Floating Lily was killed had she felt more pain than this.

For a moment she could not bring herself to say the words she had to say.

From somewhere she summoned the strength to speak.

"Then I must leave you."

Each word, she felt, was an arrow fired into him.

His arms tightened around her. "I beg you to stay."

Spirit of the Redbird, help me to do what I must.

It would hurt less if she acted at once. She pushed herself away from him. She stood up and crossed the room to the closed door.

"May you walk always in honor, White Bear."

"No, Redbird, no!" *He* was crying bitterly now, and he rolled over and buried his head in his pillows, beating the bed with his clenched fists.

She could not bear to leave him weeping like this, like a child she was abandoning. She would rather see him angry.

Then the spirit Bird, whom she had called on for help, sent her a message. She saw Wolf Paw, as he had looked when he was proud and undefeated, with the red crest on his head, a red blanket wrapped around him and black paint around his eyes.

Why did I never see it before?

Wolf Paw wore the markings of the Bird she was named after, the Bird that was her spirit guide. Neither she nor he had been aware of it. But it must mean that they were destined for each other, and that what had already happened between herself and Wolf Paw *had* to happen.

To live out her life with Wolf Paw and never to see White Bear again was like being told she would never again see a day with sunlight.

But it was as the spirit Bird had sung to her—*What must happen, must happen.*

She breathed deeply. She hated having to tell White Bear about Wolf Paw. If he had been willing to come with her, she would not have had to say anything. Wolf Paw would not have tried to hold her. And if she gave birth a moon or two too soon, White Bear would have forgiven her. But now she had to use Wolf Paw to hurt White Bear.

To hurt him so as to heal him.

But when I am gone from here, who will heal me? Must the shaman suffer wounds that can never be healed?

Yes, if she has dealt such wounds.

"You would not want me anymore, White Bear," she said. "These past moons since you left us I have been Wolf Paw's woman."

He raised his tear-streaked face from the pillow and stared at her. "What are you saying?"

"Wolf Paw lost his wives and his children at the Bad Axe. He was like a dead man. I wanted to heal him, and I will heal him, by living with him."

His eyes widened. She could see anger darkening his cheeks.

He said, "After my father took me to live here, you waited six summers for me while Wolf Paw courted you. Could you not keep him off for a few moons?"

She held out her hands imploringly. "Before, when he was an honored warrior and had his family, he had no need of me. He wanted me as he wanted another feather to hang in his hair. But now he needs me. Without me he would be as good as dead. And he is the last brave in our band."

"I need you."

She put her hands over her belly. It was still flat, but she knew what was there.

"I am carrying Wolf Paw's child."

He pushed against the bed till he was sitting bolt upright, and he pounded his fist on his knee. He was still badly wounded. He could hurt himself. What if he tried to get out of bed, and tore the wound open?

But when he looked up at her his eyes were large and dark with sadness.

"I still love you, whatever you did with Wolf Paw. And I will love *any* baby you bear."

She felt his hands seize her heart, tearing it out of her chest, crushing it. She cried out with the pain and staggered backward.

She cried, "You offer me everything but the one thing I want—for you to come back to our people."

"What I do, I do for our people." His voice was so low that she could barely hear him. "One Sauk, at least, will take back land the pale eyes stole from us."

The world grew darker and darker for her. With every word he spoke she was losing him a little more.

She made the flat-handed "no" gesture. "The pale eyes here in this

land are too strong for the red people. And in you there is both pale
eyes and red man, and the pale eyes is stronger than the red."

His shoulders slumped. She saw a dullness in his eyes that made
her think of Wolf Paw as he had looked after the people of Victor
had killed Floating Lily.

Have I hurt White Bear so badly that he will get sick again?
Sudden fear rippled through her.

But then he lifted his head and looked at her, and there was
strength in his gaunt face.

"I will always love you. And as long as this place is mine, there
will be a home here for you, for Eagle Feather, for any child of
yours. For any Sauk. When you go back, tell them that."

Grief crushed her as she gazed at the man she loved, knowing
that they were parting forever.

He reached out to her, and she went back to lie beside him on
the bed. It felt so good to be held by him, and it hurt so much to
know that this was the last time they would ever lie heart against
heart, she thought she would scream at the agony of it.

*Good-bye, Floating Lily, my daughter. I may never be able to come
back here again. I hope you have begun your journey West. But if
your spirit lingers here, know that your father is close by.*

Redbird stood a moment looking down at the mound of earth,
now covered with leaves, the strip of red blanket tied to the willow
wand now faded. She rocked back and forth in the pale eyes shoes
made of heavy leather that Yellow Hair had given her. She wailed
softly in her sorrow for Floating Lily.

Then she turned to Yellow Hair, who stood under a nearby
maple.

"You take White Bear here and show him."

Yellow Hair nodded.

They went back to Yellow Hair's carriage. The buggy was laden
with food and blankets, and Redbird carried with her a heavy bag
of gold coins given her by White Bear's grandfather. Used wisely,
the gold would buy blankets and food, rifles and ammunition from
the traders to help the Sauk get through the winter. Now they would
not have to winter over at Fort Armstrong, but could cross over at
once to join the rest of the tribe in Ioway.

The wound in Redbird's heart ached constantly, and she sat bent forward on the buggy seat, her hands gripping her knees. As they rattled down the road to Fort Armstrong she felt some small relief at leaving the place where she had lost so much. She tried to tell herself that she was on the way to a new life.

Yellow Hair said she didn't understand why White Bear was not with them. She wanted to know if he would follow Redbird when he got better.

She understands, but she does not dare believe he is going to stay with her. She thinks it is too much to hope for.

Redbird said, "He still your husband, Yellow Hair. You want him?"

Yellow Hair's lips quivered as she asked, would Redbird not come back to be with White Bear?

Redbird gritted her teeth. It hurt to have to explain to Yellow Hair.

Redbird made the flat-hand motion. "He not follow me. I never come back here."

Now Yellow Hair's eyes were glowing like turquoise set in silver. But she put a comforting hand on Redbird's arm.

She wanted to know why. How could Redbird part from White Bear and he from her? Did it not hurt too much?

"Yes, hurt much," said Redbird softly, watching the rutted dirt road pass under the wheels of the buggy.

But Yellow Hair pressed her. How could White Bear tear himself away from the Sauk?

"Pale eyes family now his people."

But his son—how could he give up his son?

Redbird struggled to find words and gestures to explain this. "Maybe some day White Bear come for Eagle Feather, like Star Arrow once come for White Bear." She remembered how White Bear had wept when Sun Woman told him he must go to live with the pale eyes. "That day, I not say Eagle Feather must go or must not go. Eagle Feather do what he want."

Yellow Hair shook her head, her braids lashing. She repeated over and over again an English word Redbird understood, but it asked a question she could never answer.

"Why?"

Again Redbird wrestled with the English words. "Land of his father and grandfather holds him. He not want to leave."

But what about the uncle who nearly killed him?

"That uncle no more trouble," said Redbird.

And because of that, I must lose him.

Then when would Redbird see White Bear again? Yellow Hair's question buried itself in Redbird's heart like a steel arrowhead.

"Never!" she screamed.

Yellow Hair shrank back, her eyes wide with shock. Redbird sighed and let her body droop.

They drove on in silence. Redbird heard small sounds beside her that told her Yellow Hair was weeping.

Redbird reached over and took Yellow Hair's hand.

"Make him happy."

Yellow Hair uttered a sob and turned her head away.

But Redbird was no longer crying. Dry-eyed, she stared ahead at the road south. Her sorrow was too deep for tears.

26

Blood on the Land

Raoul François Philippe Charles de Marion woke trembling in damp blackness, wondering whether it was day or night outside. His heart was beating so hard that it ached. For a moment he couldn't think what had scared him so badly. Then he remembered the dream.

He struggled out of the old blanket he'd wrapped around himself and sat up, panting.

A white bear coming at him down here in the mine. Why in hell would he dream about a creature like that? There were white bears up in Canada, he'd heard, but he'd never even seen one.

White Bear—that was Auguste's Indian name. Was he dreaming about Auguste coming after him?

Well, Auguste is rotting in the ground now. I killed him.

He still hated Auguste even after his death. Because of Auguste he had to stay holed up here, blackness pressing on his eyeballs. His eyes were wide open and he stared till they hurt, but he could see nothing, nothing at all. It was like being blind.

He wished he had told just one of his men where to find him. He badly wanted news of what was going on back at Victor. But if he'd told anyone it would have been Armand, and he couldn't trust the bastard. Armand might stupidly let himself be followed here. Or give way to threats, or even sell him out, if Papa offered a big enough reward.

Armand would. Sure he would. I could see in his eyes how he resented me. He hated Pierre and he hated me too.

503

Raoul only had two candles left. Should he light one now? He could spare it, because he was going to get out of this mine today— or tonight. He'd waited long enough.

He wasn't sure anymore how long he'd been hiding down here in the dark. When he slept, he had no idea how long he slept. A watch was one of the many things he had forgotten to bring with him, leaving in such a hurry. And yet he'd stupidly brought the silver case with Pierre's spectacles in it. Stuck it in his pocket when he left the trading post to get the mongrel. He felt it now, a hard oval in his coat pocket.

How long?

The men pursuing him had searched the mine, as he figured they would. Days had passed, he was sure, since he'd heard their voices in the mine, footsteps echoing. He was certain he was the only man in Victor who knew about the tunnel he was hiding in, its entrance, just big enough to crawl through, covered by a pile of gravel that appeared to have nothing but wall behind it. He'd tried to disturb the gravel as little as possible while crawling in, and had carefully replaced what he'd pushed aside.

But he might have left some trace on the other side. He'd sat in the blackness, waiting to hear the sounds of digging, his back pressed against the damp rock wall, knees drawn up to his chin. His hands, cold as if they'd been plunged into a snowdrift, had rested on his loaded rifle and his pistol. And he'd drawn his Bowie knife and laid it beside him. They'd pay dearly to take him. If there were no more than four or five of them, he might manage to kill them all and get away.

But the sounds of the search party had faded away. He'd welcomed the black cotton silence that had followed. He would stay down here as long as he could. He'd found a place in his tunnel where underground water had seeped in, and was able to keep refilling his canteen from that. He found another small branch tunnel some distance from where he slept, where he could piss and shit. But he'd come into the mine with only six candles, and he was afraid to use them up, so he spent most of the time sitting in the dark feeling as if he was going mad with alternating worry and boredom.

He had brought his canteen of whiskey down here with him, and it had made time pass easier for a while. But now it was all gone. Seemed like a hell of a long time since he'd had a drink.

He made a flame with flint, steel and cotton wool, lit his next to last candle and set it in a pool of its own wax. The light hurt his eyes for a moment, and the sight of his own shadow moving on the dark gray rock walls frightened him.

His hollow belly kept squealing and grumbling, and visions of beef and turkey and duck and pork tormented him. Out of one of his saddlebags he took the bundle of corn biscuits and dried beef he'd thrown together at the trading post in his flight. He bit into a biscuit as hard and dry as a lump of wood and rolled it around in his mouth until his saliva softened it enough to chew and swallow.

Now he'd go up to the mine entrance, and if it was nighttime he'd leave. The Flemings had their cabin about a mile from here. Their men had joined the Regulators, so they deserved to have him take a horse from them. Then he'd ride north to Galena.

He hefted the other saddlebag, loaded with gold and silver coins and Bank of Illinois paper. He'd had to leave a lot behind in his office safe, and they'd probably steal it from him. But he'd get it all back.

Because this was enough to buy him an army.

Galena would be crowded with the roughest men in the Northwest Territory right now. Surely more men than could make a living in the mines around there, boom or no boom. Rough and hungry, just what he needed.

I'll yet see that high-and-mighty Cooper swinging from a tree. And I'll piss on Auguste's grave.

He bit into a slice of dried beef. It was tough as rawhide, but he forced it down.

When I'm running things in Smith County again, Nicole and Frank and that pack of squalling brats are leaving. I've put up with Frank and his damned newspaper long enough, just because he's married to my sister.

If Frank gave any trouble, his new press, the one Papa helped him buy, would end up at the bottom of the Mississippi. Or maybe he'd even be Cooper's dancing partner on that tree.

I've knocked my father down. I've killed my brother's squaw and his mongrel bastard son. Why put up with my sister and her husband? What have they ever done, except hate me?

And the old man would have to go, too, if he was still alive, and that brandy-pickled bag of bones, Guichard. Time to be rid of them all. De Marion would still be the foremost name in Smith County, but it would be a new de Marion family, not this old Injun-loving bunch that understood nothing.

Nancy. What about her?

The teacher needed to be taught a lesson or two. If she hadn't let Auguste service her when she was captured by the Injuns, then she'd probably never had a man's cock up inside her. Once she found out what pleasure he could give her, she'd forget about Auguste. She was still young enough for children, good-looking children, and smart.

That brat Woodrow that she had living with her. Imagine him saying in court that the redskins treated him better than his parents did. Send him packing, just like the Hopkinses.

With Smith County and with Nancy all his, it would be time to rebuild Victoire.

He'd put that off because he wanted to do it right. And he'd left the ruin till now to remind himself and everyone in Victor why the Sauk had to be driven out of Illinois.

No, that was a damned lie.

Alone here in the dark he could not keep the truth from pecking at his brain like a buzzard's beak: Every time he went near the ruin of the château, he thought of Clarissa and the boys, and guilt stabbed him without mercy. He'd looked down on Clarissa, and he had not felt for the boys as a father should.

He'd left them unprotected, let them die horribly, just as Helene had died.

I did to Andy and Phil just what Papa and Pierre did to me. When my boys needed me most, I wasn't there.

And the Sauk never would have attacked Victor if I hadn't shot Auguste and the other two redskins at Old Man's Creek.

He forced himself to stop thinking about the family he'd made without wanting to and then had lost. Their blood was spilled, and nothing would bring them back. He'd shed plenty of Indian blood to avenge them.

He remembered the Indian witch woman, Auguste's mother, the Bowie knife slicing open her throat, her blood warm on his hand. What curse had she laid on him before he killed her?

He put her out of his mind and thought of Victoire. When he rebuilt Victoire it would not be just another blockhouse, but a stone mansion that could be seen from the river. It would be the center of Raoul de Marion's new empire—steamships, railroads, cattle, farmlands, mines. Now that the Indians were gone for good, now that Pierre's bastard was dead, there was no limit to what Raoul could make of the family's wealth.

The dreams heartened him. Time to move. He stuffed the little bundle of beef and biscuit into one saddlebag. He slung the saddlebags over his shoulder, the light one with food hanging down his front, the heavy one with the money in it on his back. He loosened the Bowie knife in its sheath on his left hip. He checked the loads in his pistol and his rifle again.

As he pushed back his coat to holster his pistol, he felt Pierre's spectacle case in his pocket.

What the hell am I carrying that around for?

At times he'd suspected that he kept Pierre's spectacles because he really did love his older brother, in spite of everything Pierre had done to him.

The silver case, he told himself, was valuable. But the spectacles were worthless. The eyes that had needed them had stopped seeing a year ago.

Had they?

He opened the case. The lenses glinted in the candlelight as if there were eyes behind them.

"Goddamn it!" he shouted, and turned the case over, dropping the spectacles to the stone floor. They shattered with a crack that sounded loud as a pistol shot. He stamped on them for good measure, crushing the glass to glittering splinters and twisting the frames out of shape under the sole of his boot.

He threw the case into a pile of rock shards. Valuable or not, he didn't want the damned thing anymore.

"I hope you're in Hell, Pierre!"

He didn't love Pierre. He hated him. He'd never loved him. He'd always hated him, ever since Fort Dearborn.

Holding the bit of candle high in his left hand, his rifle in his right, he started up the sloping tunnel. It was a long climb; the sacks of coins in the saddlebag on his back weighed him down.

He stopped at the gravel pile that blocked entry to this tunnel. He listened, and heard nothing but his blood hissing in his ears. He scraped chunks of stone away from the pile until he could crawl through.

After more walking and climbing through tunnels and shafts, he no longer had any notion how long it had been since he left his hideout. He saw ahead a little square of gray, in the center of the black all around him. And then he could make out the walls and floor of the tunnel. Moonlight or starlight must be illuminating the mine entrance. Night, then. Good, he could leave at once.

About twenty feet from the entrance he saw up ahead an opening where another tunnel branched off from this one. He remembered it. This was the side tunnel where the Indian he'd killed seven years ago had hidden.

As he came close to that opening he heard a rumbling sound.

The growl of an animal.

He felt as if he'd been doused with ice-cold water.

He took a few steps back from the branch tunnel opening, curled his finger around the trigger of his rifle and raised it, one-handed. He didn't want to let go of the candle.

It hadn't just been a dream. There *was* something in this mine.

Maybe a wolf. Or a bear would like a deserted mine like this for a den.

He heard snuffling, grunting noises. Then a growl so deep it seemed to shake the stone under his feet. He felt his stomach clench, and he nearly lost his grip on his bowels.

Claws scraped on rock. With trembling fingers he set the candle in one of the wall niches the miners had carved for their lanterns and raised his rifle to his shoulder.

The bear came out of the branch tunnel. He saw the huge, pointed white head from the side at first, with a golden eye that glared at him. A perfectly white bear.

Like his dream.

The head swung toward him, a gaping mouth lined with teeth like ivory daggers.

The whole white body emerged, bigger than a bull bison.

It roared, deafening as a cannon blast. It reared up on its hind legs, filling the tunnel like a white avalanche. After the roar, it rumbled steadily, deep in its chest. Though it was more than ten feet away, he could smell its rotten-meat breath.

He squeezed the trigger. His rifle thundered, echoes slamming the sides of his head. Smoke obscured the vast white body. His ears jangled.

He felt a sudden terror that the shot might start a cave-in.

But it didn't.

It didn't stop the bear either. It came on, padded feet scraping on the tunnel floor, swinging claws like rows of sickles.

I couldn't have missed. Oh Jesus, oh God, I couldn't have.

He threw the rifle down, snatched his pistol out of his holster and fired again.

Blinding flash, deafening blast, stinking smoke.

And the bear kept coming.

It was so close, the lead balls *must* have gone into it. It must be just so damned big it would take more than two shots to kill it.

But there was no time to reload. The bear towered over him, white body filling the whole world, eyes, claws, teeth, all shining in the glow of that pitiful little candle that somehow had stayed lit.

He screamed and sobbed like a little boy in his terror, but he managed to get his Bowie knife out. He'd killed a big Indian with this knife.

A paw the size of his head knocked the knife from his hand.

"Oh, please don't kill me!" he wept. "For the love of Jesus!"

The other paw hit his chest like a sledgehammer. He felt his ribs cave in. He felt the claws stab into his lungs.

His breath flew from his body. His strength drained away. He couldn't scream anymore. He couldn't beg for his life. His voice was gone. Only blood came out of his throat. The last thing he saw was an enormous mouth gaping, full of yellow-white pointed teeth coming at him. He felt claws rip again through his chest and belly and knew that he was going.

The pale eyes' smoke boat was a frightening thing, shooting black clouds and sparks from two black-painted iron tubes that rose up from a big lodge in its middle. On each side of the boat was a wheel with wooden boards attached, and the wheels and boards pushed the boat through the water. Standing on the floor of wood planks at the front end of the boat, Redbird tried to understand how fire in the boat's belly could make wheels turn. She felt the monstrous thing tremble under her as it swam across the river.

About a hundred women and children with a few men were crowded at the front of the boat, watching the Ioway shore of the Great River come closer. By unspoken agreement they kept their

backs turned to the land that had once been so good to them, the
land they had forever lost.

The happy land that was lost, Redbird thought.

At the memory of White Bear, grief stabbed her, and she had to
rest against the railing of the boat. She felt an aching hollow as if
she had been gutted like a butchered deer.

In their midst rose a little mountain of boxes, barrels, sacks and
bales, the supplies they had bought with White Bear's grandfather's
gold. But they had no horses, and when they got to the Ioway shore
they would have to carry these goods on their backs, a journey of
probably four days across the strip of land by the river that He Who
Moves Alertly had surrendered to the long knives. Somewhere beyond that land they would find the Sauk and Fox who had been
wise enough not to follow Black Hawk. She hoped it would not
start to snow before they reached the camps of their people.

Wolf Paw said, "I have heard that this is the very boat that killed
so many of our people at the Bad Axe."

This boat had killed his wives and his children, then, thought
Redbird. She rested her hand on his arm.

"See there," he said, pointing to holes and black marks on the
wood at the very front end. "A thunder gun was set there. It fired
at our people and tore them to pieces. Like the one that killed so
many of our warriors at the pale eyes town." Through his worn
buckskin shirt he touched the silver coin that still hung around his
neck on a leather thong. Redbird remembered the day White Bear
had dug the coin out of Wolf Paw's body, claiming he had changed
a lead ball into a coin.

She put her hand on her aching heart. Would things ever stop
reminding her of White Bear?

She stared down at the gray-green water rushing by the side of
the boat, and it made her dizzy. A canoe could never travel this fast,
even a big one paddled by many men. And a canoe could never go
straight across the river, without being pushed downstream by the
current, as this smoke-belching boat was doing.

Had she been wrong not to stay with White Bear, as he had
begged her to? She missed him so much. Tears came to her eyes.
She hoped Wolf Paw and Eagle Feather would not see her crying,
and she wiped her eyes quickly.

She felt like jumping from this boat and swimming back to shore.

If she drowned in the Great River, even that would be better than being carried away from White Bear.

She told herself she had made up her mind. She was determined to be a Sauk for the rest of her days. And Eagle Feather would be a Sauk.

White Bear is wrong to stay behind, even for all that land.

Eagle Feather gripped her arm. "Do not be afraid, Mother. The pale eyes will not hurt us today." His blue eyes were sad. He must have noticed her misery.

Wolf Paw smiled faintly. "No, today they only want to be rid of us."

Eagle Feather said, "One day Earthmaker will give us a medicine so strong that the long knives' guns will not hurt us."

Redbird smiled at her son. "May it be you who finds that medicine."

We can hope for that. Now that we have lost so much, the spirits might grant us new powers that will help us to resist the pale eyes.

Of one thing she was sure, White Bear's way was not a trail that the people should travel. For a Sauk to become a pale eyes was a kind of death.

We are Sauk, or we are nothing. White Bear is no longer a Sauk. My husband is dead.

She turned back to Wolf Paw and Eagle Feather. She did not like to see Wolf Paw's hair hanging loose around his head, his slumped shoulders. He had always stood so straight. Before the people at Victor killed Floating Lily.

She put her hand on his back and stroked it with a circular motion, and he straightened his shoulders. As he looked at her a light dawned in his eyes.

She must get him to shave his head again, to put the red crest back in place. The people needed a new leader, a true leader. Black Hawk had been wrong too many times, and He Who Moves Alertly would do whatever the pale eyes told him to do. Wolf Paw would help her heal the people.

How I hated him the night he mocked White Bear, putting a woman's dress on him. But he has suffered much since then, and he is a wiser man now.

Eagle Feather was standing at the rail looking across the purple river at the winter-gray hills on the Ioway shore. Redbird moved to stand behind him and put her hands on his small, square shoulders. He held himself very straight.

Eagle Feather said suddenly, "I wish I could have seen my father one last time." She could barely hear him above the noise of the smoke boat and the rushing water.

She closed her eyes against the pain of that and bit her lower lip to keep it from trembling.

When she was able to speak she said, "I think that one day you will see him again."

But for now Eagle Feather and White Bear must be parted. Because Eagle Feather must grow up as a Sauk. The people would need him, too, in summers and winters to come.

But until Eagle Feather was grown, the people would turn to her. The men, like Wolf Paw, had lost heart. She would give them heart again.

In spite of the pale eyes, the Sauk would find a good trail.

The walk from Grandpapa's house to the ruins of Victoire seemed to Auguste to take all morning. By the time he stood facing the blackened chimney that towered over him like some ancient idol, his legs hurt. He was panting, but the crisp winter air infused vigor into his nostrils and lungs. He sat down to rest on a broken beam that had once held up the ceiling of the great hall.

He was still weak from having been so badly wounded and from lying in bed recovering. And even now his left lung was still not able to fill itself full with air, and probably never would be.

This was the farthest he had ever walked. Too far, really. But the bright December day invited him out of doors, and he wanted to see his land.

My land.

It was his now, without question. Now that Raoul's body had been found.

He was glad there had been no marks on the body. Glad that the Fleming children, who had found it day before yesterday while playing down in the gorge, hadn't had to see a human body torn to pieces, as he feared Raoul might be found.

Ginnie, the middle Fleming girl, had followed a cardinal into the mine entrance; once the child had seen the body, the little redbird had flown out again and disappeared.

Raoul's rifle and his pistol, both of which he apparently had fired just before he died, lay beside him. His Bowie knife had fallen a short distance away, as if he had thrown it.

When Auguste and Grandpapa had gone to see the body laid out in Dr. Surrey's examining room, Auguste had been shocked to see the grimace of terror frozen on Raoul's face—jaws wide apart, lips drawn back from his teeth, eyes bulging. A good thing the light in the mine had been dim and the Fleming girl hadn't gotten a good look at that face.

Auguste and Dr. Surrey had both carefully examined the body and could find no cause of death. Surrey opined that Raoul had gone mad hiding in the mine and had been frightened to death by his own hallucinations.

Auguste knew what had killed Raoul. He vividly remembered his wanderings in the other world, in that endless prairie, with Redbird.

Auguste could only imagine what the encounter between Raoul and the White Bear had been like. It had taken place in the other world. The White Bear spirit must have attacked and destroyed Raoul's soul—if a soul could be destroyed. Like the men on spirit journeys who died because their souls never returned to their bodies, Raoul's body had been deprived of life. The White Bear could leave its mark in this world when it chose, but usually it left tangible signs as a mark of favor. This time the only mark it had left was that look of terror on Raoul's dead face.

And Auguste had paid the price for having sent the White Bear against Raoul: he had lost Redbird.

For the rest of my life I will never see a cardinal without my heart breaking all over again.

They would bury Raoul, with a mass, in the little cemetery overlooking the river, just like any other member of the de Marion family. There would be no revenge after death. Père Isaac was coming up from Kaskaskia to officiate.

And I'm afraid it will not be long before Grandpapa lies down to rest not far from Raoul.

Even as Auguste had begun to get out of bed and walk about, Elysée seemed to be spending more and more time sleeping. One day, Auguste expected, he would simply not wake up at all. Though he mourned in expectation of the old man's passing, it was with a warm feeling that Elysée had done much, had walked a long trail with honor. It was now right that his spirit move on and his body return to the earth.

I am thinking like a Sauk.

And then it all swept over him in a wave of anguish. He saw the happiness he had lost. He saw the gardens and long houses of Sauk-enuk, cool and pleasant in the summer, the snow-covered, warm winter wickiups in Ioway. The hunting and fishing, the feasts, the dances. The beloved faces drew close before his eyes—Sun Woman, Floating Lily, Eagle Feather, Owl Carver, Black Hawk.

Redbird.

He gave an agonized shout that reverberated in the stone chimney that towered over him. He beat his chest with his fist again and again, until a bolt of pain shot through him where Raoul's bullet had pierced him. He did not want to stop hurting himself, but he could not hit his chest anymore. His head hung down and he sobbed brokenly.

He had sacrificed too much. He had given up everything he really loved to become a prisoner of this place. He was trapped on this land. The ancient wealth of the de Marions held him in golden chains.

I could ride away from all this, even now. I could take a horse and swim it across the Mississippi—the Great River—and I could find the Sauk and live with them again. I could be free.

Redbird had said she had become Wolf Paw's woman. Anger boiled him at the thought of that. But he knew it was the healer in her who had chosen that path. As she had said, Wolf Paw was one of the last braves of the British Band, and by healing him she healed the people.

And was he not lying to himself to think he could do anything for the Sauk here? How could he resist the immense power of men like Sharp Knife, who, he was sure, were bent on exterminating the Sauk, on exterminating all the red people on this continent?

To make the de Marion estate prosper he would have to learn to perform a thousand tasks about which he knew almost nothing. He must give all his heart and mind and strength to this domain if it was to flourish. That was the burden Star Arrow, Pierre de Marion, had laid on him. In taking up that burden, might he not forget his other tie, to the Sauk, so far away?

But it was his being a Sauk that chained him so irrevocably to Victoire—the afternoon he smoked the calumet with Star Arrow— the Turtle calling on him to be guardian of this land.

Somehow he must try both to be master of Victoire and to fulfill his destiny as a Sauk.

This land, right here, once belonged to my people. If I leave it, it will never belong to them again.

I will dedicate my possessions to them. I will send them what they need. I will use the influence my wealth gives me with the lawyers and politicians to protect them, so they will never be driven from their land gain, never be massacred again.

He stood up and walked away from the charred wreckage of Victoire into the fields that surrounded it. The farmhands had planted corn last spring, but the Sauk raiders had burned it, and some prairie grass had come back. It had only had time to grow chest high before the frost killed it, and as he pushed his way through it he could see fields beyond, where the yellow horizon met the sky.

Nancy would share this land with him. She would love him, and they would raise Woodrow together and have children of their own. He loved Nancy, though there were places in him that only Redbird could touch. Those places would be sealed off now. Hand in hand Nancy and he would walk their path together.

> The World was all before them, where to choose
> Their place of rest, and Providence their guide:
> They hand in hand with wand'ring steps and slow,
> Through Eden took their solitary way.

But he would never stop missing Redbird and Eagle Feather.

And he would never stop wishing he could live out his life as a Sauk. Inwardly he would always be a Sauk. The Bear spirit would always be with him to guide him.

I failed the Sauk when they needed me. I warned them not to go to war, but I could not make them listen. They need a shaman who will make them listen.

He thought of the many, more than a thousand, who had died

following Black Hawk, and a sudden, crushing grief struck him to his knees.

"Hu-hu-hu-u-u-u-u," he wailed, stretching his arms wide and lifting his face up to look at long, faint streaks of cloud that stretched across the sky. "Whu-whu-whu-u-u-u-u."

He tore open his coat and his shirt. Kneeling, he could see only a patch of blue directly overhead, framed by the tassels of the prairie grass that rose up all around him. Staring up into the blue he wailed for the dead for a long time.

He felt something wet running down his chest. He felt the cold grip of fear on his heart. When he had struck his breast before, had he reopened the hole Raoul's bullet made?

He looked down. Beads of dark red were pushing their way through the five claw scars. Further down his chest they ran together as rivulets. Five streams of blood trickled down his stomach.

The sight of flowing blood lifted his heart. It was a sign that the Bear spirit was still with him. He bent forward and put out his hands to grip the land at the roots of the prairie grass. His fingers dug into the ashes of corn stalks and the roots of grass. A bright red spot appeared on the ground between his hands and knees, and then another.

My blood drips into the soil. I give myself to this land.

"I hold this land for the Sauk nation," he said. First he said it in Sauk, then he repeated it again in English.

He pushed himself to his feet and drew from its sheath at his waist the knife Star Arrow had left him long ago.

Standing, he could see over the waving grass. He flourished the knife blade at the vast dome of sky covering the prairie. He faced toward the east, whence came those waves of pale eyes that had driven his people from their homes. Whence, too, had come his father and one of his grandfathers.

The last Sauk shaman this side of the Great River held up his knife so the sun glinted from it.

"I will defend this land!" he shouted.

As long as he lived, he would give his blood to this earth.

Afterword

The reader may suspect the author of a bit of frontier-style exaggeration, with one President and three future Presidents—two of the United States and one of the Confederacy—playing parts in this novel. But it's a historic fact that Colonel Zachary Taylor and Lieutenant Jefferson Davis were among the regular Army officers who pursued Black Hawk's people. The two ultimately drew even closer, when Davis married Taylor's daughter Sarah. Davis resigned from the military and took his new bride back to Mississippi, where they settled on a plantation. But the daughter of U.S. President Zachary Taylor was not to be First Lady of the Confederacy; she died of malaria a few months after the wedding. And after the Civil War Jefferson Davis saw the inside of Fort Monroe once again—as a prisoner.

The meeting of Andrew Jackson and Black Hawk in the President's House—as the White House was known in 1832—is also an actual historical incident. When Sharp Knife sent the Sauk leaders on a tour of major Eastern cities, including Baltimore, Philadelphia and New York, the crowds that came to see Black Hawk greeted him as if he was a conquering hero, somewhat to Jackson's chagrin. But "King Andrew," as his political opponents called him, handily won the election of 1832. During the second four years of his reign Congress enacted into law his policy of forcing all Native American tribes in the U.S. to move west of the Mississippi. Even though the Winnebago and the Potawatomi remained neutral or actively helped the Americans, they also had to give up their land in Illinois and Wisconsin and move westward.

Abraham Lincoln, aged twenty-three, joined the Illinois militia in April 1832, and was promptly elected captain of the Sangamon County company of volunteers. In May, Lincoln was one of those who helped bury the slain militiamen at Old Man's Creek. When his company was disbanded, the men having served their four weeks' enlistment, Lincoln signed up for two more short hitches. He served them as a private, and was finally mustered out in July. His horse was stolen, and he and a friend walked and canoed 250 miles southward to their home, in New Salem, Illinois. Though Black Hawk War veterans tended to make much of their exploits, Lincoln was content to say afterward that the only combat he saw was against flies and mosquitoes. Thomas Ford, Auguste's attorney, served as governor of Illinois from 1842 to 1846. His *History of Illinois*, written in 1847, is one of the sources for this novel.

Other than Black Hawk himself, the most historically prominent Sauk in these pages is He Who Moves Alertly. For the sake of consistency I've translated all the Native American names in the novel into English. Otherwise you'd have met He Who Moves Alertly under the name he's better known by—Keokuk. And I would have referred to Shooting Star, the Shawnee war chief mentioned in Chapters Five and Sixteen, as Tecumseh. But then I'd have had to call Black Hawk by his Sauk name, Makataimeshekiakiak. No wonder Emerson called consistency a hobgoblin.

Also an unfamiliar name today is Michigan Territory as a term for the land north of Illinois through which Black Hawk and his people made their final trek from the Trembling Lands to the mouth of the Bad Axe. That land would soon become the state of Wisconsin. After achieving statehood in 1848, Wisconsin promptly laid claim to the prosperous northern portion of Illinois, including Chicago; but Illinois politicians knew all about clout even then, and beat the Badgers back.

Large parts of Illinois and Wisconsin were lands previously occupied by the Sauk and Fox. In the seventeenth century the Sauk migrated from Canada, driven by wars with the Iroquois, down into what is today eastern Wisconsin. During the eighteenth century they formed a confederacy with the Fox and moved into the southwestern part of Wisconsin and northern Illinois. In Black Hawk's time there were about four thousand Sauk and sixteen hundred Fox, living in villages along the Wisconsin (earlier spelled Ouisconsin) and Mississippi rivers and at the mouth of the Rock River.

With the Louisiana Purchase of 1803, the U.S. took charge of the Sauk and Fox homeland. In 1804 white settlers attacked a party of Sauk men, women and children, and three whites were killed. As territorial Governor William Henry Harrison demanded, a delegation of five Sauk and Fox chiefs brought one of the accused killers to St. Louis. Harrison used the occasion to negotiate a treaty in which the Sauk and Fox ceded to the U.S. all their land east of the Mississippi, including what is today northwestern Illinois and southwestern Wisconsin, as well as a portion of Missouri. All together the Sauk gave up 51 million acres. For this they got $2234.50 and an annual payment of $1000 worth of goods. Later one of the chiefs who had signed the treaty said that the delegation had been drunk most of the time they were in St. Louis. The prisoner the chiefs had delivered to Harrison was "killed while trying to escape."

Black Hawk never recognized this treaty or later confirmations of it. In defiance, he led his people back to Saukenuk every spring.

There is a gaudy rural playground area in south-central Wisconsin known as the Wisconsin Dells, where local folks will show tourists a cave in which, they swear, Black Hawk was hiding when captured by two Winnebago warriors named Chaetar and One Eye Decorah. But Dr. Nancy O. Lurie of the Milwaukee Public Museum has unearthed a different account of Black Hawk's surrender, written by John Blackhawk, grandson of a Winnebago chief and no relation to the Sauk leader. I find the John Blackhawk version much more probable than the Wisconsin Dells story, and it's the one I've followed, adding, inevitably, my own fictional elaborations. Be it noted that the incident of the small boy who commits Black Hawk's party to surrendering by smoking Wave's peace pipe is not my invention, but is reported in the John Blackhawk manuscript. Tobacco was that sacred to the Native Americans of those times.

Another matter on which historians disagree is the origin of the expression "O.K.," which made its appearance in the American language in the 1830s. Here I propose an explanation (see page 239) that I haven't seen anywhere else, but that, like John Blackhawk's story, makes sense to me. People at that time attached the adjective "old" to anyone or anything they felt affectionate about—Old Glory, Old Ironsides, Old Hickory. By the time he got around to running for President, Zachary Taylor was "Old Rough and Ready." The most popular alcoholic beverage in early nineteenth-century America was whiskey, and the best whiskey was distilled in Kentucky and widely known as Old Kaintuck. It was a jug of Old Kaintuck that Raoul grudgingly shared with Abe Lincoln. It seems likely enough that the nickname Old Kaintuck would in time be shortened to "O.K."—easier to say after you've had a few—and come to mean the good stuff in any area of life.

About the Author

Robert Shea is the co-author of the epic fantasy *The Illuminatus! Trilogy* and author of the two-volume *Shike*, among other novels. For many years he worked for magazines, and he has been writing novels full-time since 1977. He lives in Glencoe, Illinois.